THAT CHILDHOOD COUNTRY

Following a career as one of Ireland's top journalists, Deirdre Purcell's six novels, *A Place of Stones*, *That Childhood Country*, *Falling for a Dancer*, *Francey*, *Sky* and *Love Like Hate Adore* have proven her to be an acclaimed and bestselling author. She lives in Dublin.

ALSO BY DEIRDRE PURCELL

A Place of Stones
Falling for a Dancer
Francey
Sky
Love Like Hate Adore

DEIRDRE PURCELL

THAT CHILDHOOD COUNTRY

Town House, Dublin

First published 1992 by Town and Country House, Dublin
First published in Great Britain 1992 by Macmillan

This edition published 1993 by Pan Books
an imprint of Pan Macmillan Ltd
Pan Macmillan, 20 New Wharf Road, London N1 9RR
Basingstoke and Oxford
Associated companies throughout the world
www.panmacmillan.com

ISBN 0 330 32965 0

The author and publisher are grateful to Faber and Faber Ltd
for permission to quote from 'The Love Song of J. Alfred Prufrock'
in *Collected Poems 1909–1969* by T. S. Eliot.

10

A CIP catalogue record for this book is available from
the British Library.

Printed and bound in Great Britain by
Mackays of Chatham plc, Chatham, Kent

For Kevin

ACKNOWLEDGEMENTS

Thanks to all who helped:
To Jim MacNeill of Prince Edward Island for books, history and advice, to Treasa Davison for travelling to the Island with me and for all her encouragement and moral support when I needed it.

To Captain Frank Forde who went to a great deal of trouble when I sought information on ships, also to his friend Tom Dolan from Liverpool who knows everything there is to know about the Empress liners and who lent me some of his valuable souvenirs. I should like to thank Malcolm and Margery Nash from Orpington in Kent, who also served on the Atlantic with Canadian Pacific and who expended so much energy in answering a long list of questions. Thanks, too, to Ludmilla Rickwood and David Plane from Plymouth Polytechnic South West, also to Tom Manson and to Roger Seymour of Denholm Coates.

Thanks to the Canadian Embassy in Dublin; to the Parks Department on PEI; to Charlie Byrne, the gamekeeper at Lough Fee, who gave me an afternoon; to Julie Lordan who discovered the answers to ten extraordinary queries, to Professor John Harbison who shared his forensic expertise, to Jacqueline Duffy, Frank Hession and Roger Cronin for crucial details; also to Dr Sean O'Loughlin and Eilish O'Leary of the Mater Hospital, Antoinette Francois of the Department of Health, and not least, to Martin Clancy for a seminal idea.

Thanks, too, to my editor, Jane Wood, to Treasa Coady and Charles Pick, to Felicity Rubinstein – and once again, love and gratitude to my patient family, Kevin, Adrian and Simon.

Deirdre Purcell
Dublin, February 1992.

PROLOGUE

Ten minutes later, Rose pulled up at the cemetery gates. His car was there all right, but the driver's door was swinging open and the interior light was burning. The boot lid, she saw, was also gaping. She scanned the immediate surroundings but there was no sign of him.

Closing the car door so the light went off, she passed through the semi-circular gate at the entrance and paused to get her bearings. Now her nerve almost failed her. The place was so still, the air so sharp and hostile under the white three-quarters moon that fear, tangible physical terror, constricted her throat. But she had driven too far and her purpose was too strong to turn back now. She pulled her coat collar tightly around the lower part of her face. Her breath warmed her nose and mouth and gave her courage.

The graveyard straggled across the knoll of a little hill; its stone walls were overgrown with blackberry and twisted hawthorn and, at the brow, a leafless thorn tree etched itself like a deformed hand against the sky brilliant with stars. The Catholic dead of the district had been buried here for centuries; many of the ancient stone slabs and Celtic crosses leaned at crazy angles or had been overrun by a tangled carpet of ivy, nettles and tough, woody undergrowth. All around was that sharp, sweet smell peculiar to cemeteries, a combination of turned earth, rotting vegetation – and something else Rose did not care to think about. She steeled herself and walked towards the newer section of the graveyard in which burials still took place, the area where so recently she herself had stood. Her footsteps made no sound on the grassy pathway.

This section of the cemetery, just ahead now, was neater, cleaner. Its graves were still tended, their marble tombstones gleaming cold and hard. But just where the old part of the graveyard ended and the new part began, a lichen-covered Jesus figure had tumbled backwards off its plinth and lay on a cushion of brambles, arms for ever helpless and upwardly supplicating, stony, sightless eyes fixed for ever on resurrection.

By some trick of the moonlight Rose, staring at them, felt the eyes of the Jesus were staring back at her. Everything in the cemetery seemed abruptly larger, more sinister. A statue of an angel, wings outspread, seemed suddenly to lunge towards her from the head of a grave just to the side of the pathway; at her feet, artificial flowers bleached of colour by the moon, pushed malevolent tentacles against their plastic domes as though to engulf and draw her down; the black earth and gravel on the graves all around seemed too insubstantial to keep its occupants safely beneath.

She couldn't face it. She would wait outside the gates beside his car. If indeed he was in here, he had to come out sooner or later.

Then she heard a sound, a single chink, as though someone had struck a china cup with a spoon.

She forced herself to stay still and listen. There it was again, unmistakable.

And again.

And again and again – a rhythmic, one-note clinking, coming from the other side of the hill.

Cautiously, a pulse in her throat beating like a trip-hammer, she walked up the hill until she was right at the summit beside the thorn tree and could see over the whole cemetery. She saw him immediately, squatting on a grave, his bright hair outlined against the grave's dark headstone. She tried to call out to him but her throat was too dry and no sound came. Hoping he would hear her and look up, she took a few steps towards him. But he was too absorbed in his task.

And then she saw what he was doing: he was chipping a name off the tombstone.

PART ONE

CHAPTER ONE

John Flynn always suffered when his twin was ill.

He sat miserably in a corner of the kitchen of the gate lodge while their mother flapped a dishtowel at the side of the range, directing the steam from two boiling kettles towards the chair on which Derek, phlegm rattling in his chest, sat bundled up in blankets and gasping for breath.

Mary Flynn's face was red from the exertion of working the dishtowel and the heat and steam around the stove. She reminded John of an exhausted sparrow as she drooped in her chair, her thin face seeming much older than her forty-nine years. He hated to see her like this; he knew it was nothing to do with him but as he watched her he could not help but feel responsible for her difficult life and early widowhood. 'Is there anything I can do, Mam?' he asked.

Using the dishtowel to wipe the sweat off her face, she raised herself heavily to her feet and walked the few paces to the back door, lifting the lid of the milk churn which stood beside it. 'We could do with a drop more water,' she said. The Flynns had two butts outside the back door to catch rainwater but had to carry their drinking water from the pump on the public road.

John was glad of the opportunity to escape from the kitchen. He knew that his brother's attacks of congestion looked more dangerous than they actually were but it had been over an hour since his mother had sent him down to the post office to ask the postmistress to telephone for the doctor. Why didn't the man come? He extracted two galvanised buckets from beneath the sink and went out into the yard at the back of the house; as soon as she heard him, the tame nanny goat they kept for her milk ran up to him, nuzzling at his hand.

It was fresh and quiet outside after the steamy kitchen; the leaves of the blackthorn hedge behind the house rustled in the

5

warm June breeze and only six yards from where he stood, a blackbird cocked its head and looked John straight in the eye before whizzing off to the safety of a tree. The goat nuzzled at John again so he opened the vegetable bin which stood against the gable wall of the house and fed a carrot to the animal which took it from his fingers as delicately as a society lady.

He had not gone fifty yards down the road when the doctor's black Prefect pulled abreast of him. The doctor let down the window. 'Hello, John,' he called, 'just coming to see your brother.'

'I know, doctor,' said John. 'It was me sent for you.'

'Ah well, we'll get him fixed up. See you later.'

John stood in the road watching the car negotiate the gates. It had been Dr Markey who had come to take Derek to the sanatorium in the predecessor of the Prefect, a big Morris Cowley. They had just passed their twelfth birthday and John had been allowed to stay home from school to say goodbye. When the time came, however, he was not able to say the words. Derek had not said goodbye either but had picked up his canvas bag and walked out of the back door into the yard, followed for a few steps by their weeping mother. Dry-eyed, John had hung back and watched as his brother, white and scared, followed the doctor out to the car. The sanatorium was somewhere near Dublin, an unreachable distance from Drumboola although in reality it was just a little over fifty miles.

That day was the first in his life that John had gone missing from the house. He had walked for miles across the fields until, late in the afternoon, he had discovered a stream which had carved a little clearing for itself in the depths of a forest, far from the familiar territory of the estate. The ground to each side of the stream was soft with ferns. Choosing a spot under a pine, he had built a nest of dead leaves and grasses and lay in it until after dark, letting the pine needles fall on him like soft rain. All the time he travelled in his heart with Derek to Dublin and could feel Derek's fear growing with every mile.

His mother had been frantic with worry when he got home and relief had made her brutal. Stoically, offering up the pain to God as a hostage to Derek's return, John endured the switching she gave him, one of the few she had ever inflicted on either of them, without uttering a sound. It was only in bed afterwards that he let the tears come. He had always shared a double bed with his twin and this was the first night he had slept in it alone. Use had carved a hollow for each of them in the horsehair mattress. John had moved into Derek's hollow that night and had slept in it each night of the eleven months it took until his twin came home.

He waited now until he heard the doctor's engine cut out and the car door slam before setting off again for the pump, set back a little from the road on a small concrete plinth and rising from a pillow of briars. John lifted the heavy iron handle and primed it, raising and lowering the handle a few times until the first gouts of water, brown with rust, spilled onto the concrete. He pumped until it ran clear, filled the buckets as the flow died to a trickle, then placed his hands under it, catching some and raising it to his mouth.

As he drank, the smaller sounds and silences of the countryside stole over him again like a quilt. The birds, so noisy only a month ago, were hushed and only the occasional cheep or chirp betrayed their presence in the hedges. The breeze had all but died; leaves hung motionless from trees, cattle ruminated in the fields and even the dogs of the neighbourhood were quiet. Wiping his wet mouth on his sleeve, John lifted the full buckets and set off for home. By now, he knew, Derek's breathing problems would have been eased. Yet although he worried about his twin, the closeness of their early relationship had not survived the separation.

The day Derek returned had been hot and sultry. Shirtless, John had been cutting the hedge around the vegetable garden in their yard when he had heard the distant hum of the doctor's car. He had thrown down the clippers and raced into the kitchen to alert his mother, who had torn off her apron and run to the mirror on the wall beside the back door to tidy her hair. By the time the two of them had got out of the back door and around the side of the house, the car was already pulling in through the gates.

John could see Derek behind the glass of the car window but had been overcome with a tide of shyness. He had looked forward so much to this moment but now that it was here, he did not know what to do or say and was afraid he might cry. He glanced across at his mother but she, too, seemed paralysed.

7

The doctor had opened the driver's door and got out of the car. 'Come on, young fella!' he had called. 'What are you waiting for?'

Their mother had run forward then and thrown her arms around Derek so John was able to run forward too and the three of them had got tangled up together in a hug. But that was the moment he had known something was wrong; Derek had had his arm up to his eyes, covering them with the crook of his elbow as if to ward off him and their mother, and even while hugging him John had felt his brother's resistance.

For the next hour or so, in the house, he had watched Derek closely. Although thin, his twin looked healthy, but he had become slightly misshapen, with a dropped shoulder. 'What's wrong with your shoulder?' The question had been out before he had had time to stop it.

Derek had coloured. 'What do you mean? There's nothing wrong with my shoulder. What's wrong with your own shoulder?'

Later, when Derek was out in the privy, it was their mother who had explained that his slight deformity was to be expected; that despite physiotherapy after the removal of a lung, it was not unusual that the shoulder on the empty side of the chest remained lower than its fellow.

All that evening, John tried to tell himself that the new strangeness between himself and Derek was temporary, that it was only to be expected and that the barriers would come down with time. And indeed, that night, he and Derek had gone to bed together as they used to, talking together in whispers. But long after his brother had gone to sleep, John stayed unhappily awake, staring at the shadows on the walls and ceiling of their room, trying to puzzle things out.

It was just not the same.

On the surface, however, life had returned to normal. The two of them were on their summer holidays from school and, after their chores were done, went rabbiting together in the fields or fishing in the streams. The only difference from other summers was that Derek was not allowed outside when it was raining or cold. On those days John stayed indoors too, but even that small sacrifice had seemed a cause of resentment to Derek.

The situation came to a head one drizzly afternoon, about

8

five weeks after Derek's return. They had run out of library books and there was absolutely nothing at all John could think of to suggest by way of diversion. Their mother was out visiting a neighbour and he had walked over to the window to scan the sky. 'Looks like it might clear up,' he said, but without much hope.

'Well, what are you staying in for? You don't have to stay in, you know – you can go out if you want to. Who needs you around here, anyway? I wish you *would* go out and leave me alone!' Derek's face was contorted and he was almost spitting. His fury was so sudden and violent that John was too shocked to react. He walked slowly out of the kitchen and into the little bedroom. Derek followed him. 'I'm sorry, John, I didn't mean it, I really didn't.'

But John knew with certainty that his brother had meant it. 'That's all right,' he said. 'Don't worry about it.' He turned away and straightened his already-straight pillow.

'Oh, for God's sake!' Derek went back out to the kitchen.

Over the next few years, John adapted to his new relationship with his twin. Cosseted by their mother, with egg-flips for his breakfast and a half tumbler of stout with his supper, Derek's respiratory attacks became fewer and less distressing. But each time Derek did become ill, like today, the feelings of loss were stirred up all over again in his brother.

The heavy buckets were dragging at John's arm muscles and he put them down. As he did so, he glanced over the hedge into the oak field.

The massive tree which gave the field its name had been split and killed by lightning before he and Derek were born but, for some reason, had never been cut down. Standing on a knoll in the centre of the pasture, its gnarled, child-friendly stump hosted a miniature universe of wildlife. Looking towards it now, John saw in his mind not the insects, birds and small mammals which scurried in and out of the thick, rotting wood, but himself and Derek, not more than three years old, sitting a few feet apart in two clefts in the trunk of the old tree and laughing so hard they were in danger of falling off.

Alive with midges, the oak field had hummed that particular summer evening as bees and butterflies foraged in the cowslips and clover, and flies swarmed on the cowpats. There was another figure in the picture, their father, standing in front of the tree, hands on hips, head thrown back. This memory was one of the few John still held of Matty Flynn. During the course of a walk, Matty had taken the twins into the field, lifted them simultaneously into their perches and then stood back to admire them and to laugh. 'Two bookends!' he had shouted. 'Me fine pair of bookends!'

Neither John nor Derek had known what a bookend was but, delighted at their father's good humour, they had laughed along. The more they laughed, the more their father laughed until at last, still roaring, he had reached up and plucked them off the tree, then, one on each shoulder, strode off towards the boundary of the field jouncing them around so much that, instinctively, John and Derek held hands behind his neck.

After their father died, he and Derek continued to come to the oak field to play in the tree and in the stream, which ran through a small gully at the field's far end. There were gudgeon in that stream, invisible unless the twins bent close and peered for a long time into the brown water. The two of them used to stand very, very still, spreading their toes in the oozy bottom, convinced that if they did not move a muscle, the fish would tickle their bare shins. Standing in the dusty road now, bathed in the smell of warm earth, John mourned the loss of that simplicity and joy.

He sighed and picked up his buckets again. Life had changed so much; it had been so simple when they were young and now they were about to go through the most dramatic change of all. They would be seventeen in August and since their mother could no longer afford to send them to school, they had to get jobs now. Any kind of job. In former years they might have been assured of work on the estate, but with the decline in the fortunes of the O'Beirne Moffats who owned it, that option was now closed.

The road curved along the boundary wall of the estate and, as he rounded a bend, John saw the roof of the gate lodge. If the worst came to the worst, one or other of them, perhaps both, would have to emigrate. He wondered if they would be separated permanently and, despite all their problems, the prospect filled him with despair. And what would happen to their mother?

*

10

At the last minute, Rose O'Beirne Moffat decided to go with her father to Carrick. 'Wait, Daddy, wait!' she called, hurtling down the front steps three at a time, scattering the weedy gravel of the forecourt.

'You changed your mind, then?' Gus O'Beirne Moffat, reins in hand, smiled down at his daughter as she skidded to a halt beside the trap. He had prominent teeth and the smile, like a candle, lit and softened his florid face.

'Yes, why not?' panted Rose, climbing into the seat opposite his and swinging the door of the trap after her. 'Nothing else to do.' She secured the door with a frayed piece of rope and sat back.

'Won't you be cold?' Gus wore a scarf under his jacket and had jammed a soft tweed hat well down on his head over his ears. He looked doubtfully at Rose's sleeveless linen dress but she waved her hand. 'Not at all, Daddy, I'll be fine. I'm boiling.' She looked up at the leaden sky. 'And it's not going to rain either. It never does when it's this humid.'

'Hmm,' said Gus. 'Don't know what kind of geography lessons they're giving you up there in that school. Are you sure you'll be all right?'

'Oh, Daddy, don't fuss!' She folded her hands in her lap.

'On your own head!' Gus flapped the reins over the pony's fat back and the animal broke immediately into a stiff-legged trot. Rose, jerked sideways on her seat, lost her balance. 'He does that *deliberately*, Daddy,' she accused, brushing down her dress. The driveway to the front gates, which even in summer rarely dried out completely, curved through a heavy green tunnel of entwined chestnuts. Rose shivered slightly but, having made a point about it earlier, tried to hide the shiver from her father. She leaned out of the trap to pluck a flower from a rhododendron tree but just as she did so one of the wheels of the trap bounced violently in a pothole and again she lost her balance. 'This is terrible, Daddy,' she shouted when she had righted herself for the second time. 'When are we going to get the bloody car fixed?'

'Rose!' exclaimed her father. 'Don't swear.'

'Sorry.' She sighed and looked back through the trees at Sundarbans, the house in which she was born and had lived for almost all of her sixteen years. Considering its location and squat

11

ugliness, the name was wholly inappropriate. It had been built in the middle of the eighteenth century by an ancestor who had been invalided out of the Indian army but whose heart remained for ever on the sub-continent. Subsequent generations of the O'Beirne Moffats had tried to keep the house going but, these days, its roof was gapped, its windows dull, its stone façade pocked with lichen and several of the tall chimneystacks supported colonies of buddleia. Frequently Rose longed to live, like most of her Dublin classmates, in a tidy warm suburban house with central heating and plumbing that worked. She saw that a down-pipe had come loose from its guttering and was leaning away from a corner of the house at an angle; briefly, she entertained the notion that it might fall one night and pull the whole building with it.

She looked covertly at her father. She had had quite a shock this time when she arrived home from school. Up to now, Gus had seemed to be robust and immutable; he had always looked quite old – he had been bald since she could remember – but this time, something was missing. He was more abstracted than usual and seemed, in the two and a half months since the Easter holidays, to have had the marrow sucked clean out of him, leaving him limp.

She was keenly aware of the losing battle he was waging in an effort to maintain some standard of living for his small family. And although he never complained, she knew well the dent her own school fees were making in the ever-shrinking budget. 'Tell you what, Daddy,' she said suddenly as they turned out of the gates and onto the main road, 'why don't I give up that convent and go to school locally? I could travel in every day. Someone'd give me a lift . . . '

'What brought this on?' Gus's fair eyebrows disappeared under the brim of his hat.

'Nothing. It's just that there's nothing I can learn up there that I couldn't learn just as well here. I've only a year to go now anyway. I'm well into the curriculum and I know exactly what I have to do for the Leaving—'

'Rose,' said Gus, 'you'll do no such thing. As you say, there's only one year to go and we'll manage perfectly well.'

He smiled his rabbit smile and flicked the reins but the

pony continued to clop doggedly along at the speed that suited him. 'That's Dr Markey's car,' he said as they passed the gate lodge which stood a little back from the ornate iron gates, drunkenly and permanently open on rusted hinges. 'Young Flynn must be bad again.'

'Really?' said Rose, without interest. She was regretting her decision not to fetch a cardigan. Although the air was warm, the passage of the trap created a draught and her arms were goosebumped. As they turned into the main road, she saw the second Flynn boy, who was carrying two buckets, step onto the grass verge.

'Hello there!' called Gus as they passed him. Rose registered that the boy had grown very tall since she had last seen him but not much else. The surface of the road was as bad as the driveway and she was intent on keeping her balance. 'Nice boy,' said Gus, when they had passed. 'Might call in on the way back. Make sure everything's all right . . . '

'All right,' said Rose without enthusiasm. Never knowing quite how to behave, she hated the awkward formal visits they made to the handful of workers or former tenants who still lived on the estate. She hated the obsequiousness, even the resentment she sometimes sensed. She had not been in the Flynns' gate lodge for years but knew that the family was on seriously hard times. As such she felt they were a reproach to her own lifestyle and she always felt guilty.

For several miles they did not meet another vehicle. Although it was 1953, this part of Ireland, always depressed, was recovering only slowly from the war years, and motor cars and the petrol to put in them were scarce luxuries. Many people, even the well-off, still used horses and ponies to get around but this time of the afternoon, just after the midday dinner, was always quiet. Rose concentrated on keeping her balance, spreading her arms on each side along the rim of the trap. Gazing around her at the fallow under-used land of small hills and hedged fields, she saw they were, except for a few bullocks, largely empty of stock.

At school in Dublin for most of the year, she loved her own county at any season, but particularly now, at the beginning of summer. After a warm wet May, the landscape was rampant with growth, the colours deepened today by the lack of direct sunlight.

13

Buttercups and silverweed spread across the fields and although the late primroses and hawthorn were withered and almost gone from the hedgerows, dogroses, bindweed and yarrow were beginning to bud and the foot-high grasses encroached unchecked on the roadway, bright green and glossy with health and moisture. The swampy low places were dotted with white and purple flag iris and the honeysuckle was beginning to show its pale, salmon-coloured heads between the rowans and the thorn bushes. Here and there, tiny lakes, little more than overfilled marshes, spread across the hollows and hosted squads of duck, moorhen and other wildfowl.

The low sky trapped all scents underneath it, distilling them so that dung and clay, water and grass, flowers and animals combined in one distinctive aroma which Rose, inhaling, always recognised as summer in Monaghan. 'Can I drive, Daddy?' she shouted, when they were about a mile from the town.

'Sure, go ahead,' said Gus, handing over the reins. 'Just be firm with him, that's all.'

They encountered only three motor cars before they got to the outskirts of the town. Rose wondered what it would be like to drive one and, on reflection, felt it could not possibly be as satisfying as this feeling of connection to a live creature through the skeins of warm leather in her hands. She slowed the pony to a walk as they turned the corner at the top of the town. Almost everyone in the road and on the footpath said 'hello' or tipped caps to them as they passed along the main street. Although they were landed, the O'Beirne Moffats were regarded in the district as being 'decent' people and, except for a few diehards, no one resented their gentry status. The Sundarbans estate, still large but now only one-fiftieth of its original size, had long since ceased to have tenants and the fact that the family was Catholic – through the conversion of a remote ancestor – was regarded locally as a big plus.

Gus had come to town to collect a number of parcels from Dublin but as Rose negotiated the wide street, walking the pony around the carelessly parked horse carts, lorries and bicycles, she saw that the bus had not yet arrived. She pulled up the pony and jumped down, passing the reins over its head and tying them to a lamp-post. Gus climbed down after her and consulted his watch.

14

'Ten minutes to three,' he said. 'We're a bit early. Tell you what, poppet, I'll just go into McCaig's for a newspaper. All right?'

'Right,' agreed Rose. 'I'll follow you in, Daddy.' She double-checked that the pony's reins were secure and strolled across the street to where a group of itinerant traders had set up two long trestle tables to display goods for sale. Rose moved along the tables, picking up and discarding various objects, bright kettles and cans, a wellington boot, china ornaments and tea sets; she examined the washboards, candles, and primus stoves, bicycle tubes, threads, horse and pony harness, thought briefly about buying a Sacred Heart statue but settled for three ancient horse brasses. Behind her, she watched with interest as two men haggled over a round object with jagged iron teeth which Rose did not recognise but guessed it had something to do with a tractor. Nothing else attracted her and she left the crowd and crossed the street towards the newsagents.

A bell jangled as she pushed open the door. Rose loved the smell of McCaig's. It was heavy with tobacco and a certain scent which always brought her back to her early childhood, the distinctive tang of hard sweets wrapped in Cellophane. The shop owner looked up from her knitting. 'Well, hello, Rose!' she said. 'Back for the summer?'

'Back again, Mrs McCaig,' answered Rose. 'Isn't it a lovely day? I thought Daddy was here?'

'Well, so long as the rain holds off,' said the woman. 'He was here a minute ago but he went out. To wait for the bus, he said.'

'Thanks,' said Rose. As she spoke, she saw the dark shape of the bus passing the shop window. 'Oh, here it is now.' She thanked the shopkeeper and went outside. Roof-rack bristling with bicycles, suitcases and parcels, the single-decker, a snub-nosed green hippopotamus, nosed to a halt at its stop, where the driver left it to thrum noisily to itself as he mounted the ladder to the roof and began handing down the parcels and luggage. Rose went to join Gus whose packages, large, heavy and mis-shapen, were among the last to be unloaded. 'What are they?' asked Rose as she helped him carry them to the trap.

'Car parts,' he answered. 'Hope to get the old thing going again now.'

'Well, thank God for that,' said Rose. 'Will you have it fixed in time for tomorrow?'

'What's tomorrow?' asked Gus, his pink face innocent as a baby's.

'Daddy!' said Rose, pausing in the act of pulling one of the parcels into the trap. 'You know perfectly well!'

'Oh yes, something about a birthday, wasn't it?'

'Well, will it?'

'Will what? Will it what?'

'Will the car be fixed?'

'We'll see.'

They were half-way home when they met the doctor's car and stopped for a chat. 'Hello there, Rose,' he said, 'nice to see you. This is the first time we've seen you this summer. Back for long?'

'Only been here a few days, doctor,' said Rose cheerfully.

'That's nice, that's nice. The whole summer to come.'

'Yes,' Rose agreed.

'You must come up to the house, the girls would love to see you.'

'I'd like that.'

He had a bevy of daughters, six of them, aged from fourteen to twenty-six, all still living at home. They were pleasant, unruly girls and Rose liked them although, accustomed to the glacial spaces inside Sundarbans, she was always a bit overawed by the clutter and cheerful noise in the doctor's home.

'Nothing urgent at the gate lodge, I hope?' asked Gus.

'Not too bad, not too bad,' said the doctor. 'Young Derek again. Just a cold. He'll be fine. In fact there's nothing to worry about there any more – that boy's in better shape now than most of the population!'

'That's good,' said Gus. The twins' father had been Gus's farm manager in the days before the estate had fallen into the sad state it was in now and, after his death, Gus had let the family stay on at the gate lodge. 'Must call in one of these days.'

'Do that, Colonel,' said the doctor, revving his engine a little, 'must be off now. Bye, Rose,' he called, as the car moved off.

'Bye,' said Rose automatically.

16

As they approached the entrance gates, she plucked at her father's sleeve. 'Daddy? Don't let's visit the Flynns today.'

'Why not?'

'It's just that I'm very cold. You were right. I want to get home and get a cardigan as quickly as possible.'

Gus shrugged. 'All right, Rose, whatever you say. Might pop down myself later . . . '

That evening, having finished supper, Rose sat in the window-well of her room, trying to summon up enough enthusiasm to make an entry in her diary. The low sky of the afternoon had lifted and the sun blazed on her face.

The only part of the gardens of Sundarbans which now received any attention at all was the sweep of grass in front of the house, too weedy and rough to be called a lawn, but from this distance, green and pretty; Rose watched dreamily as two of the dogs, a Dalmatian and a mongrel, a boxer/Labrador cross, chased each other across it and wrestled for possession of a deflated rubber ball. The vigour and action of the dogs served to counterpoint the stillness all around and, together with the warmth on her face, promoted a delicious feeling of languor.

The house had been built on the crest of a small hill and the lawn sloped away from it towards the forest and the lake, not actually visible except as a shimmering reflection of the sunlight in the spaces between distant greenery. Rose let her eyes and mind wander. On one of her Christmas treat visits to Dublin, she had seen a performance of *Giselle* and been greatly taken by its romance and pathos. Although it was so bright, she imagined now that she was a wili, floating out through her window and being carried by the soft air across the lawn and out over the trees until she could drift free and wraith-like above the lake. But there was something missing. A *him*. Who would be her Albrecht?

Being an only child had always been a drawback but, now that she was a teenager, listening to her school friends going on and on about their brothers' friends served only to emphasise Rose's isolation. She sighed. The summer holidays stretched ahead of her like a desert. The only hope was Horse Show week in Dublin but that was not until August.

She looked down at the diary on her lap. It was a five-year affair with a flimsy gilt lock and lay open at the last entry, 1 June,

17

the night before she had come home from school for the summer. Here it was, 9 June and she had not had the energy or discipline to make any entries at all since then. She had been given it as a present the previous Christmas but Rose seriously doubted if she would ever fill it; at the rate she was going, she would hardly make the end of the current year.

What had she done since she had come home? Nothing much – two trips to Carrick, a few hacks around the estate on her pony. As well as the old pony who pulled the trap, Gus kept two other horses, a hunter, which was almost as old as the pony, and a five-year old grey Connemara mare he had acquired for Rose the previous year at the Ballinasloe horse fair. Rose enjoyed riding and liked the mare but she wished with all her heart she had someone to ride out with.

She read the diary entry for 1 June:

Marmalade for breakfast, egg hard *again*. Well, at least the food will be better at home.
    What lies ahead this summer? I wonder. Maybe I'll meet HIM. I wonder who he'll be . . . Certainly no one in Drumboola. Nearly sweet sixteen and never been kissed properly. Maybe this year!!! Gemma T. *swears* she did IT in the back of a car last Christmas. Liar!
    Well, that's it, dear Diary, for another school year. Next year the dreaded Leaving! I wonder if I'll be a PREFECT????????!!
    Next entry will be from Sundarbans.

Rose had to admit that this was not inspiring stuff. She had taken to reading the Brontës and Jane Austen and felt she could identify romantically with their heroines. When she had started her diary, she had looked ahead and seen it as a possibility to create the bones of great literature. After all, her own home life was, in some ways, just as bulging with literary possibilities as those of the parsonage daughters. She leafed back to the beginning of the year. Having started well, the diary entries got shorter and less frequent. After the first month, there were huge gaps for up to a week at a time. She was annoyed with herself for her negligence.

18

Out on the grass, the dogs were playing tug-of-war with a tree branch. Rose made up her mind that her task this summer would be to improve her literary style. Every single night, no matter *what* else she had to do or *how* tired she might be, she would fill an entire page of the diary with real words, thoughts and feelings. She would concentrate on nature. God knows, there was plenty of that around Sundarbans. Then there were *boys* and important topics.

However, boys did not feature largely in her life. She would have to make the best of a bad job and concentrate on important topics. She decided to make a point of listening to the half-one news on the wireless every day. That way her diary, like Anne Frank's, would have historical context and some relevance for her future work. She should start right now: she picked up her pen and thought hard.

All that had happened that day was the trip into Carrick-macross.

She closed the diary, crossed the room and placed it four-square on her bedside table with the pen neatly beside it. She would start tomorrow in earnest. In the meantime, she would not waste this beautiful evening. She would go for a walk and gather important material about nature.

Full of purpose, she left the room. By avoiding the worn carpet which ran down the middle of the wide staircase, she deliberately made a stir in the huge, oak-vaulted hallway as her footsteps rang and echoed on the marble, creating eddies of sound.

No one came to investigate: the housekeeper, who no longer lived in, would have gone home; Gus would be out in the stables or walking with the gun-dogs, her grandmother was probably already in bed, book drooping from her hands, her two ancient Pekinese dogs snoozing on her coverlet.

Then there was her mother. Rose knew she would be doing something either pious or useful in the small sitting room off the main, shrouded drawing room. Daphne O'Beirne Moffat was an English convert who had zealously embraced everything about the Catholic Church, including its charitable institutions and altar societies. She spent a great deal of her time in voluntary work, her current project being the decoration of altar vestments for a mission diocese. Rose could imagine her now, work basket at her

19

feet, her chair adrift in a sea of stiff brocades and glowing embroidery silks. Tiptoeing through the flagged hall and down the passageway which led past the kitchens and towards the back door, she stopped to pat the hard, threadbare forehead of a deer-head, mounted at eye level on the panelled wall. In early childhood, she had named the creature Roger and, even at this advanced age, never passed him without acknowledging his presence. Roger sported antlers on only one side of his head, an affliction which gave him a certain rakish air. Secure there was no one to overhear her, Rose looked the animal straight in one of his glass eyes. ''Evening, Roger,' she whispered gaily, 'just going out for my evening constitutional . . . '

As she pushed open the back door, which had not seen a coat of paint for years, Rose hesitated. Although it was so warm and dry at present, she remembered that the ground around the lakeside where she intended to walk was probably muddy. She slipped off her shoes and selected two wellington boots from a jumbled heap in a corner behind the door. They were black and fitted her well enough, but were not quite a pair – one had a broken band of red around the sole. She stood and surveyed them on her feet, thinking that they were not exactly appropriate for wearing with a sleeveless linen dress. 'Ahh – who'll see me?' she said aloud and, pushing open the door again, went out into the bright evening.

She crossed the lawn, whistling at the two dogs which came rushing to meet her from the belt of trees to the south-east of the house. They frolicked in front of her as she walked down the slope past the overgrown, nettled enclosure which the family still referred to as the pleasure garden, a name given to it long ago when it was formally laid out with rose beds, herbaceous borders and tidy privet hedges. Rose had vague memories of being lifted up to look at the face of a sundial by two gardeners, an old man and a boy, but the sundial had long ago been sold, the roses had reverted to their wild, bushy state and the only statuary remaining was one cracked and armless stone figure covered with slimy green algae.

Except for the sound of the dogs snuffling through the undergrowth ahead of her, it was very quiet under the trees after she entered the wood. She stood stock still for a while, allowing the dogs to get even farther away, listening to the smaller sounds of the forest. True to her resolve about her diary, she listened selectively, trying to choose the words she imagined a real writer would use to describe what she saw, heard and smelled around her.

Dappled. Dappled evening sunlight. Filtering. Dappled evening sunlight filtering through the overhead greenery. Rustling, scurrying noises on the ground . . .

No, that wasn't good enough. *Furtive rustling scurrying on the ground.* That was better.

Self-consciously, she raised her head and took a deep breath. *Clean fresh smells. Pine-fresh.* No, that was too much like describing a lavatory. The Jeyes Fluid bottle in the bathroom. *Green-fresh.* Yes, that was better. *Green-fresh.*

She might even write a poem: *Green-fresh pines under the evening sun* . . .

Pleased with herself, she strolled on.

Rose felt as excited as she used to when she was a little girl and embarking on a new hobby. Each one was always the real one, trailing shining resolution: she would keep it up and it would afford her life-long pleasure. Whether it was collecting stamps, scraps, postcards or shells, or knitting or art, at each new beginning, Rose foresaw a picture of herself as a pleasant grey-haired old lady, sitting by a crackling fire in a flower-covered cottage, still collecting or knitting or drawing and telling her grandchildren what a life-long pleasure it had been.

Up to now, however, each new pastime had lasted a mere few weeks. Consequently, Rose went through life feeling guilty about her inconsistency or indiscipline, a fault in her character which was constantly being pointed out to her by the nuns at school.

Writing, thought Rose as she followed the dogs, would definitely be different. She was almost at the lake now, she could see a wedge of the water, absolutely flat, a few yards ahead of her. 'Here, Muffin, here, Charlie,' she called to the dogs but they did not come. She called them again and then she heard Muffin, the mongrel, give a faint bark. Surprised that they had not responded to her, she emerged onto the grassy foreshore of the lake and looked in the direction from which she had heard the

21

bark. Both dogs were a hundred yards to the west of her, on a rocky promontory which jutted into the water and which the family used as a secondary jetty; the real jetty, a hundred yards farther up the lake was made of wood and had rotted and collapsed. The dogs were wagging their tails and sniffing around the feet of a tall boy who was looking in her direction, a fishing rod in his hands.

The sun was in her eyes and she shaded them with her hand in an effort to recognise him. Whoever he was, he was trespassing. These lands were private.

Rose hesitated. It was against her nature to be belligerent but she had so often heard Gus complain about poachers that she decided it was her duty to do something. She walked towards the promontory but the boy did not move as she got nearer and she became conscious of the ridiculous combination of the floppy wellingtons and the linen dress. Although the sun was still in her eyes, she managed to stop squinting and to sound authoritarian as she came within speaking distance. 'Who are you? What are you doing here?' she asked, stopping about twenty yards from him and placing her hands on her hips in a fair imitation of her mother.

'Hello, Miss Rose,' the boy called out in reply.

'John!' Rose, again shading her eyes, was embarrassed not to have recognised him. 'I'm sorry,' she said when she reached him, 'I didn't know you. Of course, go ahead, do whatever it was you were doing.' Strictly speaking, Rose knew, the Flynns had no more right to trespass on the Sundarbans land than anyone else but she knew that Gus turned a blind eye to the occasional trout or pheasant taken for the pot by the Flynns who were having such a hard time.

'That's all right, Miss Rose,' said John, reeling in his line. 'I was nearly finished anyway, there's nothing rising here this evening.' He did not seem in any hurry and, feeling completely out of her depth, Rose did not know what to say next. Having stopped, she could hardly walk on now. The panting of the dogs, who sat, awaiting further instructions, between John Flynn and herself, sounded loud in her ears.

To hide her discomfiture, she bent and patted Charlie. She had never met the Flynns socially outside their kitchen. In the early years, while the twins' father was still alive, she and her parents always paid a visit to the gate lodge for the annual distribution of Christmas largesse – a pound of butter, a pound of tea, a pound of rashers and a half-crown. The well-scrubbed twins, who were then little more than babies as was Rose herself, would be presented for inspection and on prompting would bow and say 'Good afternoon, Miss Rose,' 'Good afternoon, Colonel,' 'Good afternoon, madam,' to each of them in turn. Since their father died, she had spoken to one or other of the twins only half a dozen times and never when she was alone. 'How've you been, John?' she asked now, hoping she did not sound as if she was playing lady of the manor and yet feeling that she was. 'Saw you on the road today, you looked well.'

'I've been well, thank you,' he replied, retrieving his hook and attaching it safely to one of the eyes of the rod.

'And your brother?' continued Rose, risking a look at him, the first proper look she had ever taken at him. His hair, she saw, was fair and curly and he had grey eyes.

'Derek's been fine too – well, not quite. He's had one of his attacks, and the doctor was with him this afternoon.'

'Oh, that's too bad. Actually we met the doctor.' Rose tried frantically to remember the name of what it was that John Flynn's brother suffered from and failed. 'I hope the attack wasn't too severe?'

He picked up the old canvas bag at his feet. 'No, Miss Rose, just a cold.' He stood politely in front of her as though waiting to be dismissed.

'Yes, well,' said Rose, 'please give him our good wishes – I mean *my* good wishes, for his complete recovery.'

'I will that,' he said.

Rose had recovered some of her poise. He was quite a handsome boy. It was out of the question that he could turn out to be *him* but, on the other hand, a person should remain open to all possibilities. He was really very nice-looking. His grey eyes were deep-set and far apart and slanted upwards at the outer corners and, unlike the vast majority of Irish boys Rose had encountered, his teeth were good. 'What's it like to be a twin?' she asked impulsively. 'Are people always mistaking you for one another?'

He laughed. 'Not really. We're alike all right, but we're not identical, you know. And anyway, there's Derek's shoulder.' Seeing her look of incomprehension, he explained, 'One of his shoulders is a little bit lower than the other because he has only one lung.'

'I see,' she said. Then, after a pause, 'Listen, I've nothing to do this summer, would you teach me to fish?'

The way he reacted, she might have asked him to take her to the moon. 'What?' he asked, alarm in his voice.

'Would you teach me to fish, John – please?' she added, cocking her head winsomely to one side and smiling her best smile at him.

He pushed one hand through his hair. She hoped then that he didn't consider he would *have* to teach her to fish because she had asked and she was from the Big House. 'Of course, if it's too much trouble, or if you're too busy—' She stopped. She realised she really did want him to teach her to fish. 'I – I'm going to write about fishing,' she said.

'In a book?' he asked. He lengthened the 'o' in the local way so it came out as 'bewk'.

'Maybe some day it will be in a book, but at present I'm just making notes,' she improvised.

He hesitated. 'Have you never fished before?' he asked at last.

She shook her head.

'Well, there's all different kinds of fishing, you know. I don't know what kind you want to learn.'

'Any kind,' said Rose. 'What would you suggest?' She realised she had grasped Charlie's collar. She let go of it and he immediately ran off the promontory. The two of them turned to watch as he lapped at the lake-water where it broke lazily on the shore. 'Do you like dogs?' she asked.

'They're all right, I like them well enough.' He paused. 'Actually I would like a dog.'

'Well, why don't you get one? It's not as if they're scarce.'

'We couldn't afford to feed a dog,' he said quietly.

'Give him leftovers,' answered Rose in astonishment but then she could have kicked herself as, belatedly, she realised that the Flynn family would not have leftovers. 'Maybe some day,' she said then, but the damage was done. She could see it in his face.

'About the fishing,' he said. 'There's trout in this lake and bream and a few small pike and you fish them all different. And I could show you where you might get a salmon.'

'Ugh!' Rose made a face. 'I hate the sight of pike.' She exaggerated. She had never seen a live one, but two massive specimens, with baleful glass eyes and gaping jaws, were displayed in glass cases in the front hall of Sundarbans. 'Could you show me how to try for trout?'

'That's the most difficult of all, Miss Rose—'

'If you're going to be my fishing teacher then you can't call me Miss Rose, now can you?'

He pushed his hand through his hair again. 'I suppose not. But it will seem very strange *not* calling you Miss Rose.'

'How about just plain Rose?'

'I don't think I could.'

'Try it once – go on!' After her gaffe, Rose was back in control of the situation.

'Maybe later, when we get to know each other.' He grinned. When he smiled, his incisors showed. They were very white and much more prominent than the four teeth in between, giving him a wolfish look. He was *very* good-looking, Rose decided, and thanked her lucky stars she was wearing the good linen dress. Then she remembered the wellies. 'Sorry about the footwear,' she said. The words shot out of her mouth before she could stop them and she was mortified.

He glanced down at her feet. 'Why are you sorry? Sure, what else would you wear around a lake?' His own feet, she saw, were bare. They were large and brown, with long toes. He smiled again. 'Do you want to start learning now?'

'But didn't you say there was nothing rising this evening?'

'So, when do you want to start?' He hefted the bag over one shoulder.

'I don't know really. Are you very busy these days?'

He laughed. 'No, I'm not busy at all.' Then he became serious. 'I'd like to be, though. I'm looking for a job. We've – I've left school.'

'And is your brother looking for a job too?'

'Yes,' he said. 'Although there's nothing around here, as far as I can see.'

They had begun to walk along the shoreline. Rose realised

25

that on the promontory he must have been standing in a depression of the rock because when they were side by side, he was at least six inches taller than she was. She felt all jumbled up inside. Her experience of boys was practically nil. Two years previously, on one of their Horse Show trips to Dublin, Gus had arranged that she should go to a 'mixed' party in the house of a family friend and, encountering boys socially for the first time, she had been paralysed with shyness. She had been kissed during a game of spin-the-bottle and the pleasure of that kiss, hurried and embarrassing though it had been, had shocked her. For weeks afterwards, long after she was safely back in the convent dormitory, she had lain awake, fervently pressing the backs of two fingers to her lips in an effort to re-create the sensation.

As they walked along, she found herself wondering what John Flynn's lips would feel like on her own and the thought sent splinters of electricity through her blood. So that he wouldn't see her agitation, she bent to examine a pebble. It was a perfectly ordinary pebble, smooth and grey, but she held it up to the sky as though she was an expert on pebbles and this the most valuable she had ever seen. She stucked it into the pocket of her dress and resumed her walk. 'I want to be a writer, you know.' She heard the reckless proclamation as though it came from someone else's mouth.

'Do you?' He seemed genuinely impressed. 'I never met anyone who's going to be a writer before.'

'Ahh.' She nodded in an effort to look wise and mature. 'I said I *want* to be a writer. There's a great difference, I'm afraid, in *wanting* something and actually *being* it.'

'Still . . . ' he said slowly, 'it's a great thing to know what it is you want.'

Rose, whose ambition was so newly minted, was scared that he might probe into it and find it lacking. 'What are you going to be, John?' she asked. 'Or rather, what would you like to be?'

'I have no idea,' he said. 'And anyway, there's no point in my wanting to be anything. I just have to get a job, that's all.'

He looked out over the lake and that seemed to Rose to be the end of the conversation. As they continued to walk along, he did not seem inclined to talk any further and she could not, for

26

the life of her, think of any other topic. 'It's my birthday tomorrow,' she said, for want of anything better.

'I see. Happy birthday,' and he smiled down at her again.

His mouth was long and curved back over the incisors. Rose got goose-pimples. At the same time she was slightly peeved. Surely he was the one who should have been uncomfortable? After all, it was he who was the trespasser. 'How's your mother?' she said, aping a certain tone of graciousness she had heard in her mother's voice when Daphne was interviewing tradesmen about their bills.

John Flynn, however, did not seem to notice that he was being patronised. 'Mam's finding it hard,' he said simply. 'And I don't know how she'll manage if we go away. In one way, it'll be better for her, cheaper, I mean. But I don't know who's going to chop the wood and get the water – that kind of thing,' he said. He mumbled the last few words and Rose got the impression he felt he had said more than he should.

'Are you going away?' she asked gently.

'I don't know,' he said. 'If we can't get jobs here, we'll have to.'

'Where would you go?' asked Rose. 'Couldn't your mother go with you?'

'No, I don't think so. She's lived here all her life. She has a sister and brother over by Carrickasedge, maybe she could go live with them.'

Money, or the lack of it, was almost the sole topic of conversation at Sundarbans nowadays, but no matter how poor she and her family became, Rose had long ago realised that their poverty would always be relative, that at least she would have some choices in her life. And if she had to earn her living, with her Leaving Cert under her belt, she could, as the nuns were always pointing out, sit the exams for the civil service or the banks. And, as it happened, she secretly fancied working as an air hostess with the new Irish airline, Aer Lingus. One of the pupils from the St Louis convent in Carrickmacross had achieved that height and her picture had been on the front page of the *Argus*.

They had come to a place on the lakeshore where the rhododendrons had massed into a dense, impassable thicket right down to the edge of the water. They had either to turn inland or back the way they had come. Rose called the dogs and listened, but they had turned for home. 'Let's sit down a while,' she suggested. Again she was surprised at her own daring.

John hesitated. 'I don't know . . . '

'Oh, come on! Who'll see us?' urged Rose. She walked a few steps to where the grass bank had collapsed, creating a little crescent which resembled a seat. After a few moments, he put down the rod he had been carrying over his shoulder and followed her. He did not sit beside her, but flopped down a short distance in front of her, facing the water. He picked up a handful of stones and started to throw them, one by one, into the lake.

They watched as the ripples he had created widened and widened until they travelled out of sight and the lake returned to its mirror-like calm. Fifty feet to their left, where the shoreline curved, a heron stood absolutely motionless in the reeds; a few midges hovered near the water's edge but, other than that, there was no sign of life on the shining expanse in front of them. The water lapping the stones a few feet away was barely audible and the only sound which travelled across it from the far side was of some sort of engine, so faint that Rose could not decide whether it was a tractor or a chain-saw.

The minutes passed. Ten yards offshore, a fish rose with a small plop and John turned round. 'Trout,' he said.

Rose nodded. 'You'll teach me?'

'Birthday present,' he said.

CHAPTER TWO

Derek Flynn had been watching out for his brother for more than an hour. Confined to bed on the doctor's orders 'for safety's sake' his bronchial spasm had long passed and he was not physically miserable any more, merely bored.

The blackthorn hedge outside the window of the bedroom blocked out a lot of the sky but, above it, Derek could see that the oblong which was visible had taken on the lighter blue colour it always did a short time before sunset. He could hear his mother working in the kitchen and, by the steady, rhythmic sound of her movements, knew she was kneading bread. 'What time is it, Mam?' he called.

He heard her crossing to the mantelpiece and picking up the tin clock which lay permanently on its face. 'It's just after half nine,' she called back. He heard her resume kneading.

'What time's John coming back?' he called again.

'I suppose it depends on the fishing,' she answered. 'He brought the rod with him and I expect he's gone up to Swan's Lake.'

'It's not fair,' complained Derek.

'What's not fair?'

'It's just not fair.'

His mother kept her peace. Derek was sweating a little, partly from the medication he had taken, partly because the evening was so warm. The rough cotton sheet was irritating the skin of his legs and he threw it off to lie uncovered on the lumpy bed. He surveyed the bedroom. The floral wallpaper was faded with age and, near the ceiling, stained with dark circles of damp. The room was just big enough to accommodate the iron double bed, two wooden chairs and a set of rickety handmade shelves, the bottom half of which was curtained and held the boys' shirts and underwear. The back of the bedroom door was fitted with wooden pegs to hold their jackets and trousers while the open part of the shelving displayed their meagre personal possessions and Derek's eclectic, well-read collection of books, many of which had come from the Big House. There were two framed pictures on the walls, a lurid print of Christ, the Good Shepherd, above the bedhead and on the long wall opposite the window a picture of Our Lady of Good Counsel, her gold crown faintly gleaming in the evening light. He was sick of the sight of both of them. He sat up. 'Can I get up now, Mam?' he called. 'I'm feeling fine, really.'

He listened for the reply but, instead, his mother came and stood in the doorway. 'Cover yourself up,' she commanded. 'You'll catch your death of cold.'

'For God's sake, Mam, it's summer. I'm not a baby.'

'Cover yourself up, Derek!'

She came alongside the bed and eased the pillow from behind his head to plump it but as she shook it, feathers flew in all directions. Derek sneezed when his breath sucked one of them towards his nose. 'You see?' said his mother. 'I told you you'd catch your death.' She handed him back the pillow. 'Give that to me in the morning and I'll mend it.' She left the room and a few seconds later he heard her riddling the ashes in the range. He closed his eyes and tried unsuccessfully to doze.

It was an hour later and the oblong of sky above the hedge had turned to light gold when at last he heard his twin come in through the outside door. He sat up again. 'John,' he called and, a second later, his brother came into the bedroom.

'Where were you?' Derek asked.

'Out.'

'Yes, but where?'

'I was up by the lake.'

'All this time?'

'What do you want?' asked John patiently.

'Nothing.'

John turned and went out into the kitchen and Derek flopped prone in the bed again. 'Mam,' he called, 'can I have something to eat?'

'I'll get you your supper now,' his mother called back, but ten minutes later it was John who brought in a mug of tea and a cut of bread spread thickly with lard. He handed the meal to Derek and sat on the side of the bed.

Derek saw that something had happened to his twin. 'Catch anything?' he inquired, his mouth full of the bread, but John shook his head.

'Not even a bite.'

'See anything interesting?' When they were younger, the two of them had spent patient hours hidden securely in the woods, watching for badgers and red squirrels.

John shook his head again and continued to gaze out of the window. Then, 'Hold on,' he said, 'and I'll get a cup of tea for myself and be in to you.' He left and Derek heard him clattering cups in the kitchen and saying goodnight to their mother. When he came back into the room, which was almost completely dark now, he closed the door after him, lit their candle and undressed. Then he eased himself into the bed. 'Guess what?' he said at last, settling himself, tea in hand.

'What?'

'Guess who I met today?'

'Who?'

'Guess!'

'I give up.'

'Rose O'Beirne Moffat.'

'Oh,' said Derek. 'Did you now? Miss Hoity-Toity herself.'

'No,' said John, 'she's not like that at all when you get to know her. We had a good chat.'

'What about?'

'Oh, things. You know . . . '

'No, I don't know.' Derek finished his tea and put the empty mug on the floor. Girls were a mystery to him. The twins' primary education had been in a small local national school, which catered for both boys and girls although intermingling was not the norm. In fact, being placed among the desks occupied by the opposite sex was an effective and humiliating punishment. For the past three years he and John had been attending a single-sex secondary school. The boys from the college did encounter girls from the convent on the streets of Carrickmacross, but communication was usually shouted across a distance from one group to another.

The two of them had a few cousins in various townlands around Drumboola, but none, they agreed, was anything to write home about. In any event, in the presence of the opposite sex, the girl cousins were as tongue-tied as they were themselves. John and Derek had long ago decided that not a single one of them was worth the waste of a fantasy.

Derek settled back in bed. 'Tell us about her,' he said. 'I haven't seen that one for ages. What's she like now? Is her accent still funny?' performing a bad imitation of Rose's 'posh' Anglo accent. He saw John smile.

'It's hard to describe her,' he said slowly. 'She's pretty grown-up, sort of soft and yet at the same time not soft.'

'Yes, but what does she *look* like now?'

The candle flickered and spilled a soft light around the bed, creating a halo of intimacy. John took a meditative sip of his tea. 'She's tall,' he said, 'well, sort of tall,' he amended, 'taller than most of the young ones around here. Her hair's long now and she had a kind of ribbon around it – like the picture of Alice in Wonderland in your book beyond,' he added. He finished the tea and put the mug on the floor. Then he slid down beneath the bedclothes, hands behind his head on the pillow.

'Go on,' said Derek. 'What did you talk about? How did you meet her? How did it happen?'

'At the lake. There was nothing rising and I was going to give it up for the night but I decided to have one more cast. Then two of the dogs came up to me and she came after them. I think she was surprised to see me. She didn't recognise me, actually.'

'What did she say?'

'Well, at first, she acted as if I had no right to be there. Then she did see who I was and I think she was sorry.'

'What happened then?'

'We went for a walk.'

'Straight away? You went for a walk straight away? Just like that? Did you say, "Let's go for a walk", or what?'

'No, it just sort of happened. First thing I knew, we were just walking along.'

'Where?'

'Along the shore of the lake, towards the black hole.' The black hole was a childhood name the twins had given to the place

32

where the lake shelved steeply. Local legend had it that the lake at that point was bottomless. It was where generations of kittens and unwanted pups had met their deaths, tied in flour sacks and weighted with stones.

'Did she know about the black hole?'

'I dunno. We didn't talk about it.'

'Well, then, what did you talk about, what did you do?'

'We sat down for a while.'

Derek could hear the closing-down in his brother's voice. 'Go on, John,' he said. 'Tell us.'

'Well, that's all there's to it, really. We just sat down and watched the water for a while.'

'Did you not talk any more?'

'Yes, but nothing important. She told me about her school in Dublin.'

'And what did you tell her?'

'I told her we were looking for jobs.'

'That *we* were looking for jobs?' He considered. 'Did Miss Rose ask anything about me?'

'Yes, as a matter of fact. She was asking about you.'

'Did she just say out of the blue, "How's Derek"?'

'Something like that.'

'Was that all she said about me?'

'I think so.' John leaned over and extinguished the candle. 'I'm going to be seeing her again,' he said casually.

Derek waited for his eyes to adjust to the sudden darkness. He kept them fixed on the faint glitter where the crown of Our Lady of Good Counsel caught the last feeble glow from the window and had to struggle to keep his jealousy from showing. 'Are you?' he asked.

'Yes,' said John, settling down to sleep. 'She wants me to teach her to fish.'

Rose's birthday dawned clear and fine. Her room was in a corner of the house with windows on two sides and when she woke, the sunlight was streaming through the one which faced east. Good weather on her birthday was only as she had expected. Although she was prepared to admit that her memory may have been selective, as long as she could remember, the morning of 10 June

33

had always been sunny. She checked her watch and saw it was just after a quarter to six.

She threw back the covers, got out of bed, and crossed to the south window to look out. The tops of the trees sparkled in the just-risen sun and shreds of mist rose from the grass.

To her delight, in the centre of the lawn between two monkey-puzzle trees, as if posing expressly for her eyes, three hares grazed a few feet apart from one another. Then, just outside the perimeter of the woods, she caught a tiny flicker of movement. She held her breath. Delicately, a deer, so well camouflaged that she did not know for sure it was a deer until it moved, stepped out from the trees. Nose high, it stood stock still for a minute or so, sniffing the early morning air. Rose settled in the windowseat to watch but as she did the deer saw or sensed the movement behind the window. It turned towards her, poised for flight. She kept as still as a mouse and after a few seconds it lowered its head and started to browse.

Rose hugged her knees. For nearly ten minutes, she sat watching the hares and the deer until the deer strolled back towards the trees and vanished. Then she got up from the windowseat and walked back to her warm bed, stepping across the heap of clothing in the middle of the floor. She was supposed to keep her room tidy but its ceiling was so high and the floor area so vast that a little ordinary mess made hardly any impact, at least in her opinion. The diary and pen, so precisely placed the night before on her bedside table, demanded her attention but she ignored them. It was her birthday. She was entitled to a bit of leeway on her birthday and, anyway, it was far too early to do any work or even to get up. Mrs McKenna, the housekeeper, did not arrive each day until eight o'clock and it was only after that that the household got going properly.

Rose had inherited a feather mattress. She stretched her legs in its warmth and, as she lay, luxuriated deliberately in the picture of John Flynn which floated near the surface of her brain as it had since she had met him last evening.

Who would have thought? John Flynn of all people! Up to yesterday, if anyone had asked Rose to describe John Flynn, she would have been hard pressed and would have remembered him and his brother only as two small boys, inevitably together, who always seemed to melt away from view whenever she encountered

34

them on the estate. They used to open and close the big iron gates beside their house whenever she passed through in the trap, on horseback or in the car but that practice had ceased soon after their father had died.

Although she was aware of her family's downhill financial slide, the workings of her father's estate and the farm were, to Rose, a mystery about which her father had always insisted that she need not worry herself. She did know, however, that apart from the distant two-storey house in which the present farm and forest manager lived, the Flynn cottage was the only one on the estate still inhabited by any of the people formerly connected to it. All the labourers' cottages had long been abandoned and were falling into disrepair, two of the gate lodges, although intact, were empty and the fourth was rented to an English artist.

She wiggled her toes, digging them deep into the feathers. What would her mother say? Rose squashed that niggle as soon as it arose. Where was the harm in John Flynn teaching her to fish on their own lake and in their own rivers?

In return for the fishing lessons, she had promised to teach John to ride. That, at any rate, should be no problem. Gus was always saying that his hunter was too fat and didn't get enough exercise. The elderly animal was wide-backed and calm as a rocking-chair, a perfect vehicle for teaching. Rose revelled in the thought of leading John Flynn around a field at the end of a lunge. She closed her eyes to picture his face; his lips were long and evenly matched in size. As she had twenty times since she met him, she imagined what they would feel like against her own. Firm yet soft. She shuddered with pleasure and then immediately giggled into her pillow, hearing in her imagination the school cautions against impure thoughts. She had news for the nuns. She was having thoughts of the most delicious impurity and she loved them.

She managed to doze during the next hour or so, drifting in and out of light dreamy sleep until she heard the tyres of Mrs McKenna's bicycle scrunching the gravel at the front of the house. She jumped out of bed and got dressed quickly, picking an outfit at random from the heap in the middle of the floor. She tidied the bed rudimentarily so that it looked neat, on the surface at least.

She met Gus on the first landing, just at the head of the

stairs. With some surprise, she saw he was dressed more smartly than usual, in a snowy white shirt and tweed tie and his best suit, the jacket of which he carried over his arm. His shoes were gleaming. 'Morning, Daddy,' she said happily. 'You look like you're going to church.'

'Happy birthday, poppet,' said Gus, giving her a hug and then, as they walked down the staircase together, 'Wish it was church. Have to go out immediately after breakfast. Appointment with the bank manager, I'm afraid.'

'Oh dear,' said Rose sympathetically. 'Well, maybe it won't be so bad.'

'Always is,' said Gus gloomily and then cheered up. 'I have a present for you, Rose.'

'Whoopee!' She linked her arm in his as they walked together towards the big kitchen from which the smell of frying bacon already emanated. It was constantly a source of wonder to Rose how quickly Mrs McKenna could cook. The family now ate all meals in the big kitchen except at Christmas and Easter and on the rare occasions when they had company. The draughty dining room was too big for them and too far from the kitchen for Mrs McKenna, who was getting on in years and a martyr to her bunions.

The housekeeper, still wearing her toque, was busy turning rashers in the frying pan and had her back to them as they entered the kitchen. 'Morning, Mrs McKenna,' called Gus.

'Morning, Colonel,' she answered, without turning away from the Aga. She broke half a dozen eggs into the pan and raised her voice above their sizzle, 'and a happy birthday to you, Miss Rose!'

'Thanks, Mrs McKenna,' said Rose. She saw then that her place at the table had not yet been laid but where her knife and fork should be, someone had placed a package. She ran across and picked it up.

'Sorry about the brown paper,' said Gus, watching her. 'Should have had my wits about me and remembered to get coloured stuff in Carrick yesterday but I forgot.'

'That's all right, Daddy,' said Rose, shaking the package a few inches from her ear. 'What is it?'

'Open it and see.'

Rose tore off the wrapping paper, revealing a flat jewellery case covered in worn red velvet. She held her breath and undid the gilt clasp. 'Oh, my God!' she said when she raised the lid.

Glimmering like drops of seawater on red velvet mounts were a necklace, bracelet and earrings of precious stones mounted in old reddish gold. She put the case on the table and drew out the necklace. It was heavy in her hands and as she held it up to the light of the kitchen window she saw the stones were faintly purple, like heather. 'They're amethysts,' said Gus, watching her face.

Rose ran to him and hugged him. 'Oh, Daddy, thank you! They must have cost a *fortune!*'

Gus disentangled himself. 'No, Rose,' he said quietly, 'they were Lizzie's. They've been in a safety deposit box since she died. I couldn't bring myself to sell them and I promised I'd give them to my daughter, if I had one, on her sixteenth birthday. She would have wanted you to have them, I know. They're a bit dim. I meant to get them polished up before I gave them to you but what with one thing and another . . . '

'Oh, Daddy,' said Rose again. 'They're perfect the way they are. I don't want you to have them *touched*.' Elizabeth O'Beirne Moffat had been her father's only sister. She had died from tuberculosis, when it was still called consumption, at the early age of twenty-eight and Rose knew her only from blurred snapshots in an old album. 'I'll take really good care of them, Daddy, I promise.'

'I have a present for you too, Miss Rose,' said Mrs McKenna shyly. She went to her handbag and took out a parcel.

'Oh, Mrs McKenna, you shouldn't have,' said Rose, when she unwrapped the present and found a gift-set of lily-of-the-valley soap and talcum powder. 'Thank you very, very much.'

'The eggs'll be hard,' said Mrs McKenna, pleased, turning back to the Aga.

The housekeeper had gone upstairs with the breakfast tray for Rose's grandmother and Rose and her father had just sat down at the table when her mother came in. Unlike her daughter, Daphne O'Beirne Moffat was fully and correctly dressed, in a sensible tweed skirt, twinset and pearls. 'Happy birthday, Rose,' she said, crossing the floor and bending down to touch Rose's

37

cheek with her own, which smelled of Pond's face powder. 'I have your present upstairs,' she continued. 'I'll give it to you later.'

'Did you see what Daddy gave me, Mother?' asked Rose, indicating the jewellery case.

'Yes, I did,' said Daphne. 'Now, Rose, you should put it straight back into the safety deposit box at the bank. It's the only place for it. You never know what could happen if you kept it here or wore it. It's much too valuable to have lying around.'

Rose was determined not to let go of her delight in her father's gift and did not enter into any argument. Instead she changed the subject. 'I think Muffin's pregnant again,' she announced, a statement which produced exactly the effect she knew it would.

Her mother grimaced. 'Rose! Not at the breakfast table, please.'

Rose cut energetically into the rasher on her plate while Daphne went to the Aga, helped herself to a rasher and an egg and sat in her place with it. Reverently, she bent her head and folded her hands in prayer, then made the Sign of the Cross and began to eat.

Rose finished as quickly as she could, gathering up her plate, cup and cutlery and rinsing them under the brass tap in the sink before leaving them for Mrs McKenna to wash. 'Good luck with the bank, Daddy,' she called as, picking up the jewellery case, she walked with it towards the door.

'Where are you going?' asked her mother.

'I've a million things to do today,' lied Rose.

'Like what?'

'Oh,' Rose waved her hand vaguely in the air, 'just things. I've to do a bit of writing, actually – for school,' she added. 'You know, holiday essays, that kind of thing.'

'That's good, Rose,' said her mother. 'I'm glad to see you're getting sense and not leaving your tasks until the last day as usual. Now, don't forget I've a present for you too.'

Rose knew only too well that her mother's present would be a 'sensible' one. 'Thanks, Mother,' she said, trying to sound enthusiastic, 'I won't. But I want to spread the treats out. I'll see you later.'

'Have a good birthday,' called Gus, as she escaped from

the kitchen. As she climbed the stairs, she took out the bracelet and fastened it on her wrist. The stones lay on her skin like liquid violets.

Five hours later, John Flynn's heart thumped with anticipation as he finished his dinner. He got up from the table and scraped his potato peels and the few pieces of cabbage left on his plate into the bucket kept inside the door for the goat. 'Is there anything else you want me to do, Mam?' he asked his mother, who had already finished her own meal and was standing by the range, pouring boiling water into the tea-pot.

'Is there enough water?' she asked.

John lifted the lid of the milk churn and saw that it was more than half full. 'Plenty,' he said, easing the lid back inside the neck of the vessel.

'What's your hurry?' demanded Derek, who was toying with a piece of salt bacon, pushing it around on his plate.

'No hurry,' said John.

'John's going fishing, Mam,' said Derek.

If their mother, who was waiting for the tea to draw, noticed the sarcastic undertone in his voice she did not react to it. 'That's nice,' she said.

'Why don't you ask him where he's going?'

She turned around in surprise. 'What do you mean? What does it matter?'

'Ask him.'

John cut in. 'I'm going up to the lake, Mam.'

Their mother looked from one to the other. 'John, what's this about?'

'Nothing, Mam,' replied John. Before his twin could say anything else, he snatched up the fishing rod and bag from where they were stored in a corner of the kitchen and went outside, scattering the hens which pecked around the threshold of the house.

John could have murdered Derek. Not that their mother would have forbidden him to go up to the lake, but he knew she would have been dead set against social association with anyone from the Big House. Mary Flynn, like everyone else in the district, held rigid views about class and keeping within your own.

Knowing he was far too early, he set off; his chores were finished and he certainly had no intention of going back indoors to endure more of his brother's carping. It took him fifteen minutes to get to the promontory where he had been fishing the evening before. But when he did reach it, there was still an hour or so to go before the appointment so he took off his shirt and stretched out fully on the warm rock to sunbathe. He was facing away from the lake and kept his eyes open, staring straight up into the cloudless sky. After a few moments, he had the oddest sensation. It was as though his whole body started to spin slowly and was being drawn right up into a deep blue bowl, into infinity. The sensation made him feel giddy and he closed his eyes to blot it out.

Rose was early for her fishing lesson and would have been even earlier had she not tried on and discarded six outfits before settling for a puff-sleeved button-through dress of white cotton, tightly belted with a wide white belt of imitation patent leather. She put on a pair of white strappy sandals more suitable for display than for walking on a stony lakeshore but, knowing that they set off her long legs and narrow feet, did not care.

She saw him on the promontory when she was still fifty yards away. Her sandals were quiet on the grass and as he did not stir as she approached, she had time to study him. He was stretched full-length on the rock, his head slightly to one side and one hand splayed across his stomach. Not sure whether he was actually asleep, she stopped for a moment, but after a few seconds, when he still did not move, she settled down on her heels about four feet away from him. She was close enough to see the gilding on the tips of the line of fine hairs which stretched from his breastbone to his belt.

She had to resist an urge to reach out a finger to stroke them.

After a minute or so, he opened his eyes. For a moment they were opaque and puzzled, then he saw her and sprang upright, reaching for his shirt. 'I'm early,' said Rose. 'I'm sorry I woke you, you looked so peaceful.'

'I wasn't asleep. How long have you been there?' He was clearly embarrassed.

'Oh, only a minute or two. I hope you don't get sunburned,' she added demurely. 'It's very hot today.'

He was concentrating on buttoning his shirt and it gave Rose some satisfaction to see that again she had the upper hand. 'I see you brought the rod,' she said.

'Yes.' He got to his feet, blotting out the sun as he stood over her. 'Are you ready to start?'

'Sure.' Rose, too, scrambled to her feet.

'Right-oh.' He picked up an old canvas bag which lay on the rock beside his rod and took out a little tin box, which he opened.

Rose was surprised and delighted: the flies, some tiny, some as big as bees, glowed in their slots like dolls' jewels. Although there was some ancient tackle in the gunroom, Gus did not have the patience to be a fisherman and she had never seen a fly-box before. 'They're really gorgeous, John,' she exclaimed, touching one of the delicate feathery things with a finger.

'Nice, aren't they?' he agreed, pleased that she was pleased. 'I got them from my uncle. He's dead now.'

'Oh, I'm sorry,' said Rose.

'That's all right, he's been dead for ages. He went a couple of years after my father.' Carefully, he picked up one of the flies, which he told her was called a Bibio, and while he showed her how to thread the line through the wire rings on the rod and to tie the fly to the end of it, he named some of the others. They squatted low on the rock, heads close together over the box and the work he was doing. Rose tried to concentrate as the unfamiliar words floated past her ear, Black Pennell, Hare's Ear, Silver Badger, Connemara Black, Kingsmill, Claret, Grey Duster, Green Drake, Sooty Olive. She could smell his hair, warm and slightly sweet; and even though she tried to keep her mind on the lesson, she could not keep her eyes off his long narrow fingers as they worked precisely with the fly and line. Their small deft movements induced in her a deep feeling of tranquillity. She did not want John to stop working on that fly ever. To prolong the feeling, she pointed to a particularly beautiful specimen in the box. 'What's that one called?'

'That's a Green Peter,' he said, glancing at it.

'But it's not green at all,' she protested. 'It's all different colours.'

'Well, that's what it's called.'

41

'I see,' said Rose humbly. 'And that Bibio, are we sure we'll catch something with it?'

He smiled. 'Listen,' he said, 'three o'clock on a hot June afternoon like this, with not a cloud in the sky, is not exactly the best time for anything off the bank. In fact it's probably the worst possible time.'

'Would it be better out in the middle in a boat?' asked Rose. She saw flecks of green in his eyes. 'We could use one of the boats.' Even as she suggested it she half regretted the offer. She had no idea in what condition the boats would be. The family kept two of them, open rowboats, in the dilapidated boathouse a little way up the shore. When she was younger, Gus used to amuse her by rowing about a bit, hugging the shoreline, but as far as she knew, none of the family had been near the boathouse for years.

John seemed to hesitate. He looked at the sky and out on the water and Rose, who had never before been in such close proximity to a boy for so long, saw that when he raised his head, his Adam's apple became very prominent. 'Would they mind?' he asked then and Rose knew instantly what he meant and that it had nothing to do with the boats. All doubts about their soundness were instantly dispelled.

'Of course they wouldn't,' she said firmly. 'It's my birthday, anyway, and I can do what I like on my birthday.'

'All right, we might have a better chance out there,' he said, 'but I can't promise anything.' He stood up. 'First you have to learn to cast.'

This proved easier said than done. When the line was at last organised to his satisfaction, he began the lesson. He did not immediately give the rod to her but broke a branch off a nearby tree, stripping it of leaves and branchlings until it was bare. Then, using this, he showed her how to cast: lift, tap, tap, *out*; lift, tap, tap, *out* . . . 'Now you try it.'

She took the branch. Feeling foolish, she waved the branch upwards and behind her head. 'No,' he said, picking up the rod itself. 'You've got to do it in a sort of rhythm. Like this: one . . . two, three and *four*!' Making a swishing noise, the fly sailed effortlessly out over the water, snaking the line after it.

Rose raised her branch again: 'One, two, three, *four* . . . '

'That's not bad,' said John, reeling in his line. 'Do it a few

more times and then I'll give you a go of the rod.' Rose delighted
in the meagre praise. Over and over again, she raised and tapped
and counted, raised and tapped and counted. When he gave it to
her, the rod was surprisingly light but it was very long and felt
unbalanced in her hand; the tip of it bounced and juddered with
every slight movement. 'Don't do anything with it for a while,'
John cautioned, 'just get the feel of it.' Rose now mourned her
choice of clothing. The tight, belted dress constricted her movements so that when she raised her arms, she felt her breasts strain
at the buttons. She shot a glance at him, wondering if he noticed
but his face was serious. To cover her confusion, she kept the rod
low, hefting it in her hand and pretending to be considering its
weight.

But then she could not resist showing off a little. 'I think I
have it, I think I'll just have a little cast.' She raised the rod as
she had the branch. But the rod was more than three times the
length of the branch and her impulse was too sharp; the tip curved
low behind her head and sprang the line so that the fly shot
backwards and sideways into one of the rhododendron trees where
it became entangled in the upper branches. Rose panicked and
dropped the rod on the ground as though it were red hot.

John laughed. 'Don't worry, it happens to everyone.' He
went to the base of the tree and tugged at the line, but nothing
happened, the fly was well stuck. He manipulated the line to the
left and right but could not shift it. 'I'll have to go up,' he said.
'I don't want to lose it.' He shinned up the tree.

As she watched him tug at the hook, Rose wondered if this
was love: this confusion, this wave of excitement crashing around
her whole body at the sight of John Flynn's long agile frame
spread against the bole of the glossy green tree. He too was
wearing white, a spotless white shirt over dark grey trousers. The
shirt was slightly too big for him and collarless. It ballooned away
from his neck and back as, guiding the fishhook through the dense
greenery, he leaned backwards. He had rolled up the sleeves of
the shirt, exposing long, sinewy forearms.

Rose's breath was constricted in her throat. She turned her
back and pretended to be gazing at something far out in the lake.
'I wonder why no one calls the lake by its real name,' she called
to him, over her shoulder.

'You mean Swan's Lake?'

'I think the real name is nicer, Allabawn.'

'Same thing. I don't call it that, nobody does.'

'I know, but Lough Allabawn is its real name.'

Behind her, she heard the thud as he dropped back to the ground. He came alongside her and picked up the rod from where she had dropped it. ' "Allabawn" means "white swan", ' he said, reeling in the trailing line, 'so what's the difference?'

She was sorry now that she had raised the subject of the lake's name at all. It sounded so schoolgirlish. 'I only asked,' she muttered. 'It doesn't matter. Are we going out in this boat?'

'You'll have to learn a bit more about casting, I'm afraid. I don't want you to drown or capsize us.'

Rose did quite well for the next ten minutes. Although her attention was only half focused on the finer points of fly-fishing, she managed to cast the fly into the lake several times without getting entangled in anything and finally John Flynn pronounced her safe to try her luck in a boat.

As they walked along the shoreline, she hoped fervently that, after the bravado of her offer, the boathouse would not be locked. She remembered that, several years previously, there had been talk in the district that the IRA was about to become active along the border with Northern Ireland which was only a few miles away from them. Gus had pooh-poohed the rumours but Daphne had insisted on ordering a new door for the gunroom and locks and bolts to be fixed to all the doors of the house and even the stables. Rose hoped now that her mother had overlooked the boathouse, so long unused.

As they got near it, her heart sank. It was a sorry sight, with faded, peeling paintwork, the remaining shards of the one window black with grime. A thick undergrowth of bramble scratched her bare legs as they pushed their way to the front of it and she had to pick her way around clumps of nettles which rampaged two feet high on either side of the mossed, concrete slipway leading to the double doors. She saw to her relief that a big iron padlock, open and brown with rust, lay partly concealed in the long grass in front of the doors. 'Must be from the last century,' she commented, pushing it out of the way with her foot and taking hold of the hasp to pull the doors open.

'Are you sure this is all right?' John was hanging back.

'Of course it is. I told you – everything's all right on my birthday.' He stepped forward then to lend his weight in getting the doors open, but when this was achieved they saw that the boathouse inside was even sorrier-looking than outside. The boats were there all right, but barely visible behind a grey veil of cobwebs, which stretched, as thick as cotton wool, from wall to wall. Inside, Rose heard skittering and rustling. She shuddered. She had no fear of mice but she detested rats. 'No one's been near this place for donkey's years,' she said. 'God knows what's in there.'

'There's boats anyhow,' said John cheerfully, plunging his hand into the centre of the cobweb curtain and tearing it down the middle. Rose jumped backwards instinctively and John himself ducked and brushed at his hair with his hands as the veil drifted apart in strands. Rose, sneezing and still fearful of rats, continued to hang back but John caught hold of the smaller of the two boats and dragged it partially out of the boathouse into the sunlight. 'This looks all right,' he said heaving it first onto one side and then the other to inspect the keel.

'It doesn't look all right,' said Rose.

'Ah no, it's sound enough,' he said, giving the boat, which had once been green, a hearty kick in its wooden ribs. He looked at Rose. 'It's filthy, though. What about your white frock?'

Rose sneezed. 'That's no problem,' she said. 'I always wear it only once. It's – it's—' she sneezed again, 'washable. Sorry,' she managed, 'it's the dust.'

'You stand well back and I'll launch her.' He went into the boathouse and found a pair of oars and rowlocks, throwing them into the boat before pushing it down the slipway into the water. He jumped in and Rose went to follow him but he stopped her. 'Hold your horses.' From under one of the seats, he pulled out an old Ovaltine tin obviously meant to be used for bailing. Leaning over the side of the boat, he rinsed it in the lake and then sluiced water several times over one of the wooden plank seats. 'It'll dry out in the sun,' he called. 'Hang on there for a while. I'll just test the machinery while it dries.' He fitted the rowlocks and the oars and began to row in little circles.

With absolute certainty, Rose knew she would remember this precise moment for the rest of her life. It was as if her mind

45

became a camera, snapping all sensations around her in a series of sharp clear pictures: the plashing of the oars in the still water, the flood of song from a skylark high above their heads, the distant barking of a dog, the smells – of dust from the boathouse and of clay from the disturbed undergrowth – the way the sun struck diamonds on the ridges of the circles around the oar blades, the straightness of John Flynn's shoulders as he rowed and as he turned, the way he lowered one of them to look back at her. She realised he had spoken to her. 'Sorry?' she called.

'I said, it's nearly dry now,' he answered. 'I'm coming for you. Will you put the rod and the bag in?'

He manoeuvred the boat to the end of the slipway and took the rod and bag from her, then, shipping the oars, helped her step in. With a shock, she realised it was the first time they had touched. She dropped his hand and hoped he would not notice how abruptly she had done so.

Miss Rose and himself . . . John could not believe what was happening.

While physically he focused on the task as though he were navigating an ocean, as he rowed out into the centre of the lake he was mentally almost in shock. She was sitting straight as a sapling on her seat, hands folded on her lap, looking sideways along the water. In his limited experience of girls, she was the most beautiful creature he had ever laid eyes on. Although she was not tanned, the white dress seemed by contrast to make her skin golden and her long dark hair, caught back from her face in the same band as the previous day, shone like copper in the bright sunshine.

When she had been so close, back there on the rock while he was tying the fly, he had smelled a scent from her like honey and when he had helped her into the boat, her hand in his own, already sweaty from exertion, felt cool and fragile. She raised a hand to shade her eyes from the glare and he noticed that a bracelet of bluish stones glittered on her wrist. He risked a look at her eyes to see if the stones matched them but, in the brightness and with her head turned away, he could not tell.

To steady himself, he concentrated on the oars in his hands. The wood was worn and warm to the touch; he had always found rowing easy, as he did everything to do with physical rhythm: his

46

dancing teacher in the national school had once told him he would make a great drummer. He loved dancing – to the extent that he could ignore gibes that he was a cissy – and had won medals in various categories for Irish stepdancing; at wakes and weddings he was in demand for old-time waltzes. He tried to imagine what it would be like to dance with Rose, to hold her in his arms; she would probably, he fancied, be as light as a lark. He stole another glance at her. She was leaning slightly sideways, trailing a hand in the water; her hair curved forward over her cheek like a curtain. 'I didn't wish you a happy birthday,' he said, to make conversation, any conversation.

'Well, go ahead. Wish me a happy birthday.'

'Happy birthday!'

'Thanks. And now are you going to teach me to fish?'

Something in the way she said it shot electricity through him and, to distract himself, he shipped the oars and picked up the rod. 'I think here is as good a place as any,' he said, 'although I warn you, I'm not too hopeful.' Under her gaze, his fingers shook a little as he tied the fly and he had to take an unusually long time over it.

'What's that one called?' she asked. She was sitting on her hands.

'A Gosling.' He finished the operation.

'Poor little thing,' she said and smiled. He smiled back. The whole scene, the sunshine, the flat, clear water, felt dreamy and unreal. The only certainty became the fishing rod, the hiss and whine of the line as it spun out over the water, the V it made on the surface as he reeled it in.

They spent a half-hour trying for a fish and, as she grew in confidence, he relaxed a little. She seemed to find it easier to handle the rod out here on the water and made one or two very good casts, right where she had aimed. He took the rod from her at one stage and showed her how to dap, flicking his wrist, making the fly skitter across the surface of the water as though it were alive. 'Oh, that's brilliant!' she said. 'I'd never be able to do that.'

'Try it,' he said, handing over the rod, being careful not to touch any part of her. But dapping proved too difficult and after a little while, she said she was tired so he suggested trying somewhere else.

They had drifted slowly with the current and were quite a

47

distance south of the boathouse and closer now to the far shore of the lake. Looking across, he noticed a clump of willow growing out over the water, casting a shadow. 'We might try over there at those trees,' he said, pointing to them, 'it's not so bright.'

'All right,' she agreed. He reeled in the line and set off. Just to the left of the willows, a heron – the same one as yesterday? – was drowsing on one leg in the reeds. As the boat approached, it stretched its neck and wings, rose a few feet above the surface of the water and flapped lazily away from them, resuming its pose in the shallows about twenty yards away. Other than the heron, they were the only moving things on the lake; normally, there might have been swans or a few coots or mallard on the water but the heat was obviously keeping all sensible creatures in the shade.

John again shipped the oars and let the boat drift into the reeds until the bow crunched softly to a halt on the gravel bed. He was about to cast into the shadow of the willows when she spoke. 'John?'

'Yes?'

'It's very hot. Let's just be quiet for a moment.'

'Right-oh.' He felt awkward.

Left to its own devices, the boat lifted off the gravel and drifted southwards once again, swinging gently around so that it was moving stern first. Soon the shadow of the trees was on them, cool relief.

'Could we shelter in there?' She was pointing into where the sweep of the willow had created a sort of cave between the foliage and the grassy bank.

'Sure.' Using the trailing branches as ropes, he manipulated the boat through the leaves and into the shade. The sunlight filtered through the canopy over their heads, creating patterns of light and shadow on themselves and on the boat and he noticed that parts of her hair shone softly and parts were as black as the wing of a young crow. Now what? He was at a complete loss.

'This could be a completely secret place,' she said, plucking a narrow leaf from a branch which trailed into the boat and tracing the central vein with one finger.

'Yes,' he said uncertainly. He had the feeling he was an actor in a play but he did not know what his next line should be.

'No one would ever see us here.'

It was clearly his turn. 'That's true.'

She looked up at him with her head cocked to one side and an odd look on her face. Not trusting himself, he leaned out of the boat and pretended to watch the activity of the water beetles and tiny minnows which darted about at the edge of the water where the clay of the bank crumbled into it. The silence under the leaves was so profound that he could actually hear the tiny disturbances in the water as the insects went about their business. The tension increased as the seconds ticked by until they were startled by the sudden whirring of a bird in the branches above their heads and simultaneously looked up.

Almost without knowing what he was doing, John half stood, leaned forward and kissed her upraised face. He missed her mouth and touched her somewhere on the chin. The action took only a millisecond and he jumped away from her as though scalded. 'Sorry, I'm very sorry.'

'Why are you sorry?' she said softly. 'I liked it.'

He leaned forward again, the timbers of the boat creaking loudly under the movement. He kissed her again, mouth to mouth this time but without touching any other part of her. Her lips responded. They felt warm and full and the scent of her body again reminded him of honey.

Rose wanted the kiss to go on for ever but when he seemed to be about to stop, she drew back from him. She did not want him to think she was too forward. They both looked away from one another into the water.

She used her long hair, letting it fall over her face so that he would not see her expression but she could see him through it. His head was turned sideways and, above the edge of the collarless shirt, she could see a vein jumping in his neck, pulsing so fast that the top button of the shirt was trembling. Her own pulse was bouncing just as hard and she felt confused, ecstatic and fearful all at the same time. The kiss had been wonderful, far, far better than the fleeting, spin-the-bottle experience at the mixed party so long ago. His mouth had felt just as she had imagined. No, better.

She wanted very badly to be kissed again, but, of course,

49

it was not done for girls to take the initiative. She would just have to wait and see what happened. He was picking up the oars. He was going to take them out again on the open lake . . .

Before he could do so, she threw caution to the winds. 'John?'

'Yes?' One of the oars had slipped from its rowlock and he was carefully fitting it back in.

'Are we going now?'

'What do you want to do?'

'I'd like you to kiss me again.' She heard herself giggle nervously. 'Sorry . . . '

He looked at her for a second and then, moving carefully so as not to upset the boat, he came to sit beside her and took her face in both his hands, holding her just under the jaw; his fingers felt cool under her ears and at the nape of her neck as, gently, he fastened his mouth on hers again.

Rose closed her eyes. She felt as though she was swimming and drowning, swimming and drowning. After a while, his lips opened her mouth and she felt the tip of his tongue. She got a fright then and broke the kiss. This was French kissing. A sin.

But he did not let her head go from between his hands, just waited a second and then joined his lips to hers again. She opened her mouth and let him in. It was a strange, scary sensation at first but then her whole body seemed to take on a life of its own, dictating that she put her arms around his neck and push against him. But the boat rocked dangerously. Instinctively, she put out her hands to save herself.

He laughed and she did too. Then they stopped. Rose was finding it hard to breathe. At such close quarters the pulse in his neck looked to her like a little hammer under the skin. 'I think we'd better go,' he said.

'All right.' She put her finger on the spot where the pulse jumped.

He put his hand over the finger and trapped it against his neck. 'You're lovely, Rose,' he said. 'Happy birthday.' Then he kissed her again, so fast she did not have time to respond. In an instant, he had moved away from her and picked up the oars.

After the coolness under the willows, the heat out on the lake beat on Rose's bare head as soon as they moved out. And the dazzle of the sun on the water half blinded her. Out here, she felt exposed, as though she was wearing a big sign which proclaimed what had happened between them under the trees. And soon, all the doubts began to flood in: she shouldn't have done it, she had 'led him on' and now he would not respect her. Her mother would find out – Rose had no doubt at all what her mother would think if she did.

Worst of all, she had committed a mortal sin and would have to tell it in confession. French kissing was a mortal sin.

She looked at John's serious face and wished she, and not he, was rowing. She wanted some way to use all the physical energy that was rocketing around inside her body. What was he thinking? Did boys feel the same sense of shame when things like this happened? But it was she who had asked him to kiss her, wasn't it? He certainly hadn't forced himself on her. On the other hand, he was the first one to touch her. It was all very confusing.

Taking a rest, he let the boat drift when they were half-way back to the boathouse. Rose fought panic; he was taking her back and that would be the end of it. He wouldn't want to see her again. She realised that, more than anything, *she* wanted to see *him* again. The hell with her mother and the nuns and confession – she wanted very, very badly to be kissed again. And again and again.

The boat drifted almost to complete standstill and she took a deep breath: it was now or never. Deliberately, she leaned over and put her hand on John's thigh. It felt surprisingly hard under the fabric of his trousers.

He had been looking over his shoulder and at her touch snapped his head around. She swallowed, but kept her hand in place. 'What are you thinking about?'

'Nothing. What are *you* thinking about?' He was looking at her from under his eyebrows and his eyes seemed more slanted than ever. Summoning all her courage, she told him the truth. 'I'm thinking about you kissing me.' It sounded so bald, her voice shook.

He bent his head and muttered something she could not catch.

'Sorry, John?'

'I am too,' he said, louder.

'I see.'

'So,' he said. He looked away.

'So,' she repeated. She looked for the heron but he seemed to have abandoned his post. She took another deep breath. Might as well say it. Nothing to lose. 'Are we going to see each other?'

'You mean go together?'

She tried to make her voice sound calm. 'Do you want to?'

'What do you think?' He was looking at the floor of the boat.

'If you want to go together, I want to.'

'Yes, I do,' he said it quietly, 'very much.'

If it were possible for a physical body to turn inside out with joy, Rose's did at that moment but she tried to match his low, sober tone. 'All right, so,' she said, as though they were discussing arrangements for a funeral.

He smiled that wide wolfish smile. 'It's not the kind of thing that'd make them dance and sing up there in the Big House – if they knew, like—'

'No,' said Rose. Then she smiled back at him. She was smiling so much today, she thought her face might crack; she thought she might smile for the rest of her life. 'Who's to know?' she said. 'I'm not going to send it to the *Irish Times* or even the *Argus* or the *Democrat* – are you?' Right now, she felt happier than any girl deserved to be on her sixteenth birthday. She had been properly kissed and she had a boyfriend.

'We'd better be careful.' He pulled at the open neckband of his shirt and Rose thought it the sexiest gesture she had ever seen.

'Of course I'll be careful,' she said. She would think about the difficulties later. Maybe tomorrow.

Dropping the oars, he wiped his palms on his trousers and formally extended his hand. Puzzled, Rose took it. 'We haven't been introduced,' he said. 'Good afternoon, Miss O'Beirne Moffat, I'm John Flynn, one of your tenants.'

She laughed a little uncertainly. 'Good afternoon to you, Mr Flynn. Nice to meet you. Live in the gate lodge, do you?'

'Indeed I do, miss.'

'And what, pray, do you do for us O'Beirne Moffats?'

'Completely at your service, miss, in *every* way . . . '

52

He raised her hand to his lips and kissed it, then he turned it over slowly and kissed the palm of it, pressing it hard to his lips so she felt his teeth. Glancing around to check they were unobserved, he went on his knees on the floor of the boat between them and pulled her head towards him. He kissed both her eyes, her neck and, finally, her mouth. She opened it eagerly but he closed it with two fingers on her lips and kissed her again. 'That's for luck, Rose,' he whispered.

As he rowed them back to the boathouse, Rose felt she was floating six inches above her seat. The heat buzzed around her head and she scooped water onto her face so liberally that some of the brackish drops ran into her mouth. 'This is the best birthday I've ever had,' she said, water dripping off her chin. 'When's your birthday, John?'

His birthday, it turned out, was at the end of August, on the 25th. 'I'll know by then whether I'm going away or not,' he said.

'Going away?' She was dismayed. 'Where're you going?'

'Emigrating,' he said. 'Maybe. I don't know yet.'

'Emigrating?' Rose knew emigration was part of life in Ireland but it was something other people did, something written in her history and geography books. 'Where to?'

'Probably Canada, a place called Prince Edward Island.'

'Never heard of it.' She couldn't show him how she felt. 'It sounds romantic,' she said, determined to be positive. 'Is it full of snow and Eskimos and things?'

'To tell you the truth, I don't know much about it. We have second cousins there.'

'Oh, John,' she said quickly, 'couldn't you look for a job around here? And anyway, what about your Leaving Cert?'

'There's not much chance of a job around here,' he said shortly. 'I – we, Derek and me – we may have no choice but to go. And we've left school.'

The penny dropped with Rose. She could have kicked herself for her lack of tact. Obviously Mrs Flynn could no longer afford the fees. 'I see,' she said, desperately casting around for something suitable to say. 'It's getting hotter by the minute,' she said at last, conscious of how feeble it sounded. 'I'm parched.'

'We'll soon be in,' he answered.

Rose trailed her hand in the water again. Some of the light seemed to have gone out of the day. Why did every silver lining have to have a cloud? she thought.

For the present, she refused to think about the possibility of him going away. He was here now, she was here now, the summer was just starting. They had all summer. She might *hate* him at the end of the summer, anyway. He might hate *her*, for God's sake! She stole a look at him. Under the sun his hair glinted like ripe wheat. Oh, God, she thought, half thrilled, half despairing, he's so gorgeous . . .

He pulled the boat up on the slipway and helped her out of it. Taking his hand, she was overcome with a wave of shyness but he kept hold of it while he made sure the boat was secure and then, still on the slipway, took her in his arms and started to kiss her again.

From the boathouse, Rose heard a noise and, thinking it was a rat, she gave a little scream. Both she and John looked towards where the sound had come from.

'Hello,' said Derek, stepping into the sunlight.

'You followed me,' said John, dropping his arms from around Rose and taking a few steps towards his brother.

Derek's face was bland. 'No, I didn't,' he said, 'I was out taking a walk. Just like you. Looking for a quiet place to read.' Rose saw that he had a book in his hand. He held it up and smiled. 'I came as far as the boathouse and saw the doors were open so I went in for a look around.'

'You've never been one for taking long walks.'

'How would you know what I do?'

John clenched his fists. 'You must have been watching us out on the water—'

'Watching you? Of course not,' said Derek. 'Was there something to see?' Then, looking past his brother, 'Aren't you going to introduce me?'

'You were hiding in here and deliberately spying.'

'Nothing much to spy on. I asked you to introduce me.' Not waiting for John, Derek took a few steps forward and held out his hand. 'Hello, Miss Moffat. I'm Derek. The twin.'

Rose took his hand. She felt dreadfully embarrassed that someone else had seen her kissing John Flynn. 'How do you do?' she said.

'Very pleased to meet you, I'm sure,' said John's brother, his tone increasing her discomfort. He was very like John, she saw, the eyes and mouth and even the teeth were the same but seeing the two of them together, Rose noticed Derek's dropped shoulder and that he was slightly smaller than his twin. He was staring at her and she saw herself through his eyes, her cheeks red from the sun and embarrassment, her hair all over the place, her white dress crumpled.

'John was teaching me to fish,' she said. 'It's my birthday, you see.'

'Oh, I see,' he said.

Rose started to gabble. 'It's my *birthday*. Why don't you wish me a happy birthday?'

'Happy birthday, Miss Moffat.' His emphasis made Rose hate her name. *Little Miss Muffet sat on a tuffet . . .*

'You can help me put this boat away,' said John, turning to the rowboat and catching hold of one side of it. 'That's, of course, if you're not feeling weak today?'

'I'm fine, absolutely fine,' replied Derek blithely, ignoring his twin's sarcasm. He crossed to the far side of the boat and caught hold of it. The two of them dragged the craft up the slip and into the boathouse. 'Cheerful little place,' said Derek, brushing aside some of the broken cobwebs which trailed against him as they got the boat inside.

Rose felt as though she were fastened to the concrete slip with six-inch nails. The joy of the day had been diminished. Apart from her chagrin at having been observed, she hated that she had been in some way part of this unpleasantness between the two brothers. She wondered unhappily if she should simply walk off and leave them to it, whatever it was that was bothering them.

John came out of the boathouse and closed one of the double doors. 'Excuse me,' he said to his twin, who was lounging against the jamb of the other one. Derek gave an exaggerated leap out of the way and John closed the second door. 'Should we lock them, Rose?' he asked.

Rose saw he was deliberately cutting out his brother. She glanced at the rusted old padlock a few feet away in the grass. 'I doubt if that thing works,' she said, 'and anyway, I haven't a clue where the key might be.'

'All right,' said John, 'shall we go, so?'

'Can I come too?' asked Derek, smiling.

'Come where?' asked John. 'We're not going anywhere, I'm just walking Rose home.'

'Right up to the door of the Big House?'

'Shut up, Derek!' said John and Rose saw that his face was turning a deep red.

'Certainly,' said Derek again – he exaggerated the local accent, *sairt*'ndly. He turned to Rose: 'Sorry, Miss Moffat.'

John snatched up his fishing rod and bag and set off down the lakeshore at a furious pace. After a second's hesitation, Rose followed him, having to break into a trot to catch up. She heard Derek fall in behind her.

The three of them progressed single file along the edge of the water until they came to the promontory where Rose had first met John. He stopped and turned to face behind him. 'Derek,' he said, addressing his brother over Rose's shoulder, 'I'll see you back at the house.'

Derek threw up his hands in mock surrender. 'All right. See you back at the house.' He turned to Rose and gave a mock bow. 'Cheerio, Miss Moffat.'

'Call me Rose, please,' said Rose, distressed.

'Cheerio, Rose.' He put his hands in his pockets and walked away from them up towards the trees. They watched him go. As he got to the edge of the wood, he reached up and broke a little piece off a horse-chestnut, using the leaves to fan his face.

'I'm sorry about all that,' said John, when he had disappeared from view.

'What's the matter with him? Are the two of you having a row?'

'I don't know, to tell you the truth,' he said. 'Derek's got some sort of a chip on his shoulder these days.'

'But I thought twins were supposed to be so close.'

'They are – we are. That is, we were for a long time, we still are in some ways.'

'And if he gets a pain, do you get a pain?'

'No,' said John quickly, then hesitated. 'Well, yes, actually,' he amended. 'I just automatically say "no" because I'm fed up with everyone asking me that. I do feel his pain – not all the time, but certainly sometimes. And I always know if he's unhappy.'

'How about him?'

'I don't know.' She heard from his tone that the subject was closed. He took her hand. 'I'm really sorry you saw all that,' he repeated.

'That's all right, John.'

He continued to hold her hand. For a minute she thought he was going to kiss her again and her heart banged against her ribcage but he stepped back. 'I'd best be going home now.'

'All right.'

They made arrangements to meet again on the following day. 'For another fishing lesson?' he asked. His mood had lifted, she saw, his slanted eyes were laughing at her.

'More fishing,' she said.

He kissed her on the cheek and walked quickly away from her. As he got to the trees he turned to wave goodbye, brandishing the fishing rod.

Rose managed to get through the kitchen, passageway, hall and up the stairs into her room without running into anyone. She closed the door behind her, took off the dress and threw it on top of the heap in the middle of the floor. Then she bounced onto the bed on her back, gazing up at the chipped, faded plasterwork of the ceiling, tracing the curlicues all around the edges. It was a habit she had developed as a child and she always found it soothing. The turmoil in her mind needed soothing. Already there were problems in her romance with John Flynn. He was going away . . .

But she was so excited, nothing could have dampened her spirits for long. She threw herself on her stomach and closed her eyes to re-create the physical sensations of John Flynn's kisses. Then she became aware that someone was knocking at her door. 'Yes?' she called, her heart sinking.

'May I come in, Rose?' It was Daphne's light voice.

'Just a minute, Mother,' called Rose, getting off the bed and picking up her dressing-gown from a chair. She belted it on and made her way to the door, gathering up an armful of clothes from the floor and pitching them into a corner of the room before opening it.

Her mother, immaculate as always, was holding a package.

Rose saw it was soft. That meant for sure it was something home-made. 'Come in, Mother,' she said, holding the door open.

Daphne O'Beirne Moffat stepped inside and Rose braced herself for a lecture about tidiness, but for once her mother held her tongue. She offered the parcel. 'Happy birthday, darling.'

'Thank you, Mother.' Rose took the present and kissed her mother on the cheek. She injected some enthusiasm into her voice, not difficult to do in her present state of euphoria. 'Can I open it now?'

Her mother looked pleased. 'Of course.'

Rose tore off the wrapping. It was soft as snowflakes, an angora sweater in a beautiful shade of palest blue, worked in a lacy open stitch. Rose, who knew a little about knitting, recognised that the work had been done on very fine needles and must have taken her mother weeks, perhaps months. She held it up against her. 'Oh, Mother,' she cried with genuine delight, 'it's the most beautiful thing I've ever seen. Thanks ever so much!' Before Daphne could stop her, she had thrown her arms around her mother's neck and hugged her.

'Rose, please,' Daphne protested but she was laughing and Rose hugged again. It was a rare moment of communication between them and, unexpectedly, Rose felt her eyes filling with tears. She knew, however, that her mother would hate a scene and blinked them away.

'Thanks again,' she muttered, and broke off the hug to lay the filmy sweater on the bed. 'I'll wear it this evening for dinner.'

'Well, I'm glad you like it, Rose,' said Daphne. 'Where on earth were you all afternoon? I searched everywhere for you.'

'I – I was out with Muffin and Charlie,' lied Rose. 'I took them for a long walk down by the lake.' But Daphne was already looking around the room. 'Rose, you really will have to do some-thing with this room. It's a disgrace. I know it's your birthday and I don't want to nag today of all days but, really, I'm surprised that you haven't developed better habits from the convent. Surely they don't tolerate this kind of thing at school?'

Rose thought of her four-foot by six-foot cubicle in the dormitory. 'We don't have that much space, Mother. But don't worry, I'll clear it up before dinner. I promise.'

'And what are you doing in your dressing-gown in the middle of the day? Were you asleep?'

'No, Mother, I was just changing my clothes when you knocked.'

Daphne cleared her throat. 'Well, happy birthday again and I'm glad you like the jumper.'

'I love it.'

'See you at dinner, then? I think Mrs McKenna has done something special.'

'Good, see you then.' Rose held the door for her mother and, after she had passed through, closed it with relief. She already felt guilty. Here she was, day one, already telling lies about John Flynn.

Derek was nowhere to be seen when John got back to the gate lodge. Their mother had placed one of the kitchen chairs outside the back door and was sitting in it, shredding cabbage into a tin basin at her feet. 'Hello, John,' she said. 'Catch anything?'

'No, I'm afraid not, Mammy,' he answered. 'Seen Derek lately?'

She shook her head. 'I think he said he was going over Carrickasedge way to see Jer Hennessy.' Jer Hennessy was a school friend.

'Well, he didn't,' said John, 'he followed me up by the lake. I met him up there.'

Mary Flynn picked up another cabbage leaf and slid the sharp knife down the backbone. 'There's something eating that boy,' she said.

'I know, Mammy. But I wish he wouldn't take it out on me. I've done nothing on him.' His mother wiped perspiration off her forehead with the back of the hand which held the knife and he saw the weariness in her eyes. 'Don't worry, Mammy,' he said quickly. 'I'll sort him out.'

CHAPTER THREE

There was nothing, thought Rose, quite as miserable as a dripping monkey-puzzle tree. The summer had wheeled past at a speed which terrified her; sitting in the embrasure of her bedroom window, she watched listlessly as the dull grey rain poured incessantly through the gutters and down the walls of Sundarbans, flattening the weeds in the gravel and creating puddles in the hollows of the uneven lawn. The rain had even sucked colour out of the chintzes on the chairs and threadbare Indian rugs on the floor of her room and she shivered as she leafed through the diary, faithfully attended every day since she had met John Flynn.

There were less than twelve hours left in the month of August. And 1 September was the day John was emigrating to Prince Edward Island.

He might as well have been going to another planet. Rose's own family connections were in exotic colonies and former colonies or in England itself, and several of her friends in boarding school had relatives in America. But she had learned from John that 'ordinary' people in Monaghan emigrated not to Boston, the Bronx or Chicago, but to this tiny Canadian province, a practice which had apparently started in the middle of the last century before the famine, when a local priest had moved there, later inviting some of his flock to join him.

When she had looked up the place in her schoolbooks all she could find was a single mention: the Confederation of Canada had apparently been signed in the island's capital, a town called Charlottetown. And when, tentatively, she had mentioned the place to her grandmother, who had correspondents and friends all over the world, all her grandmother was able to tell her was that she thought the children's book *Anne of Green Gables* was set on PEI.

Rose had searched through the huge glass-fronted bookcases in the library of Sundarbans but there was no copy of *Anne of Green Gables* to be found. She did discover the island in an atlas, however. PEI floated in the sea off the coast of Nova Scotia, curved and skinny like a half-sucked jelly-baby.

She leaned her cheek against the coldness of the window-pane. It was typical of God, she thought, to make her last day with John a wet one. They might not even be able to go riding which was the activity they enjoyed most. Her eyes filled with tears. John had taken to horseback as though he had been born to it and the two of them had spent most of the summer, by far the happiest of Rose's life, seeing the Monaghan countryside from the perspective of their saddles.

John and Derek had tried for jobs in local shops and garages, in Carrickmacross and Clones and Monaghan, even in Butlersbridge and Enniskillen across the border. But Northern Ireland was as economically depressed as the Republic and none of the big farmers were hiring. There was nothing for it, John had told her, but to go. He was worried about leaving their mother alone but he and Derek would send money home and at least she would be comfortable. 'And maybe, Rose,' he had said, 'it's all for the best. Maybe I'll become a millionaire in a few years and then I can come back.'

Rose knew that the possibility of him becoming a millionaire while working on a potato farm in Canada was remote. 'I'll never see you again,' she had sobbed on his chest.

He had tried to comfort her, 'I'll be home for holidays, Rose,' but that had only made her weep harder. She knew that, even if it were true, it would be years before it would happen. He might meet someone else, he would change. Things would never be the same again and, in her opinion, her whole life would be over as soon as John left Drumboola.

She loved him so much, it was like a pain right down through the middle of her. Even during their happiest times, *particularly* during their happiest times, the tears would catch her out unexpectedly. The worst was the day he had cried too, holding his head low on his chest. 'I don't want to go, Rose,' he had whispered. She had taken him in her arms and tried to comfort him, but it was useless because her own tears had flowed.

Now here it was, right on them, the day they had both

dreaded. She looked at her watch. It was half past twelve. He had promised to meet her as early as he could, which he thought would be about two o'clock.

Rose set her mouth, stood up and closed the diary with a snap. She would not sit around weeping like a baby, she would make herself useful; she would go to the stables and make sure the horses were ready. If she and John were not destined to go riding today, it would not be her fault.

She blew her nose and went down the stairs and had almost escaped from the house when she heard her name called from the small sitting room. She turned around and went back. Her grandmother was sitting by the writing table at the window, one Pekinese in her lap, one at her feet.

'You called me, Nanna?' asked Rose.

'Yes, darling. I'm really sorry to bother you but I wonder if you'd get me the bottle of Quink out of my room? I've run out, you see.' Rose nodded. She adored her grandmother and was always happy to perform any small service, including the chore of walking the Pekineses around the overgrown pleasure gardens twice a day. Gus's mother was small and neat, always immaculately dressed, with a rope of pearls around her throat. She kept mostly to her room and carried on a voluminous correspondence with old friends around the world. To Gus and Daphne, Nancy O'Beirne Moffat's presence in the house was like a wisp of mist, visible but insubstantial. To her granddaughter, she was a warm and loving confidante.

Up to this summer, when Rose had met John Flynn.

She could not bring herself to tell anyone, not even her lovely grandmother, about John Flynn.

She ran up the stairs and into Nancy's room, which always smelled faintly of 4711 cologne. The dark blue bottle of ink, almost empty, was on the rosewood bureau, which was, other than the huge wooden bed, the largest piece of furniture in the room. Rose had always loved that bureau, brought all the way from South Africa by Nancy's own grandmother more than a century before. She snatched the Quink and ran back down the stairs with it. 'Thank you, darling,' said her grandmother as Rose gave it to her. The Pekinese on her lap sniffed at the bottle and subsided again in a heap of fur. His mistress placed the bottle on the table and stroked him. 'It's a miserable day,' she said to Rose. 'Would you like a game of canasta later?'

Rose heard the loneliness which seeped through the dainty voice and immediately felt guilty about this summer's neglect of her grandmother. But John Flynn had become her whole life and nothing could divert her today of all days. 'Tomorrow, definitely, Nanna,' she said, backing towards the door. 'I – I've a lot to do today. I have to exercise the horses.'

'In this weather?'

'Oh, it'll clear up. It said it would on the weather forecast.' Rose had not heard the weather forecast. 'And, anyway, the horses won't mind.'

Her grandmother continued to stroke the dog. 'All right, dear, I'll look forward to tomorrow, then.'

The rain streamed dark grey off Rose's mackintosh as she made her way to the stableyard. She had not bothered to put on a hat or to take an umbrella and within minutes her hair was plastered to her head and face in long wet strings. What do I care? she thought. It would make no difference what she looked like today.

Perversely wishing to make herself feel even worse than she did already, as she trudged around the side of the house towards the stables she looked up at the sagging outline of the roof. This summer, Sundarbans had been shorn of most of its tall chimneys; their weight had threatened the weakened roof and therefore the house itself. Sundarbans, she thought, wallowing in misery, was coming apart at the seams like an old worn ballgown which no one wanted any more.

Because of the lie of the land, the rear of the house was a great deal taller than the front; the buildings – house, storerooms and a disused dairy – extended on three sides around a cobbled courtyard which was enclosed on the fourth by a high stone wall. The effect was of a prison yard, today more than ever, in contrast to the glorious summer day when the work of taking down the chimneys had begun and when she had been full of her new love. She had found Gus standing in the centre of this yard, his pink face drooping as he watched the group of workmen on the roof.

Rose had been due to meet John for the third time and this was all that mattered; nevertheless, she knew that it was an awful time for her father. 'Daddy?' she had said at last, trying to keep her voice from betraying excitement. 'You know you're always saying Thumper's too fat and needs more exercise?'

'Yes.' Gus's eyes had been fixed firmly on the roof.

'Well, how would it be if I could organise that he gets a bit of hacking?'

'You've enough to do with Tartan.' Tartan was Rose's Connemara pony.

'No, not me. I mean, I *would* be exercising Tartan. It's just that I met John Flynn the other day, you know, from the gate lodge, and he seems keen to learn to ride. I thought, if you didn't mind, that we could kill two birds with the one stone. I haven't much to do around the place and I'd like to teach him, if it's all right with you, Daddy.'

The ringing of a hammer on metal scaffolding was amplified by the acoustic in the yard so she was having to raise her voice to make herself heard. 'So do you think it would be all right?' she repeated when he did not answer.

Gus had looked at her briefly and then back at the roof. 'Money, money, money,' he had said, rubbing the back of his neck.

'Is it all right, Daddy? Can we use Thumper?' She tugged at his sleeve.

Her father had continued to rub the back of his neck but had looked at her around the crook of his elbow. 'I suppose so. Be careful. And all the tack has to be put back properly each time.'

'Thanks, Daddy. I will.'

As Rose had begun to back away, Gus looked after her. 'Don't tell your mother, will you?'

She had started the lessons with John that afternoon.

Remembering Gus's admonition brought a grim smile to her face as she reached the stableyard. It had not been too difficult to manage her romance, even under Daphne's eagle eye. If she did her chores, helped her grandmother, was indoors in the evenings at a respectable hour and was polite and pleasant around the house, her mother seemed to accept that she spent most of her holidays riding her pony or walking the dogs. Muffin and Charlie, she thought, had never had it so good . . .

64

Even in the best of weather, the stableyard was a forlorn place full of ghosts but today the water ran in torrents through the broken gutters and splashed onto the cobbles, making them slick, so that Rose, the soles of whose boots were worn, had to pick her steps carefully in case she might slip. She noticed that the shore in the centre of the yard was clogged; not caring about dirtying her hands, she waded into the miniature pond around it and cleared it, pulling out leaves and clumps of wet hay which she threw aside. She waited until the last of the flood had gurgled away down the drain and looked around. There was no sign of Clicker, the pony they used for the trap but, ears pricked, Thumper and Tartan were watching her across the half-doors of their stalls.

Gus was always talking about the days when six, seven, eight or even ten hunters were permanently stabled here, in the care of staff grooms who had rooms above them. Now, apart from Rose and Gus, the only person to take care of the three remaining horses was Fergie McKenna, the housekeeper's son, who came in for an hour or so every day to muck them out and do the heavy work.

She walked across to the hunter, who was clearly enjoying his new lease of life with all the exercise he was getting. He snickered at her and she stroked his muzzle, loving the soft warm feel of it. 'Oh, Thumper,' she said, 'what are we going to do?'

The horse nudged against her, begging for sugar.

Democratically, Rose caressed Tartan's nose too and then went into Clicker's stable. He was dozing on three legs, backside to the door but opened his eyes and looked around as Rose walked to his head. 'You too, Clicker,' she said, patting his neck, 'you'll miss him too.' She took a handful of hay from the net and held it out. Fastidiously, extending his lips, the pony took a few wisps.

Rose leaned on his warm back; the pony shifted his weight and, inhaling the horsy, pungent smells, she shifted with him. She felt insulated and a little soothed by the sound of the rain, the old pony's calm solidity and the rhythmic grinding as Clicker chewed the hay.

A figure loomed in the door opening. 'Wet enough for you?'

Rose jumped with fright. 'Oh!'

Then, 'Oh, John, it's you—' holding out her arms. But then

65

she noticed the unmistakable droop of one of the shoulders. It was not John, but Derek. The error was understandable as, backlit from outside, his face was in shadow. 'Hello, Derek,' she said, crestfallen.

'Sorry,' he said. 'Sorry it's me.' Even the sound of the rain did not mask the bitterness and irony in his voice.

'Don't apologise, Derek, please,' said Rose unhappily. His fair hair was black with rain and his clothes were saturated.

'You're soaked,' she said, unlatching the half-door. 'Come in out of the rain.'

'Thanks.' He stepped a few inches into the gloom of the stable. Clicker, his handfeeding interrupted, blew hard through his nostrils and turned away from the two of them to snatch a mouthful of hay for himself.

'Are you looking for John?' asked Rose. 'He's not here yet but he should be any minute. He said he'd come as early as possible.'

'That's what I'm here about,' said Derek. 'I've a message for you. He can't come this afternoon. He's gone into the town with Mammy to see the priest.'

'What?'

'John can't come this afternoon, he's—'

Rose interrupted him. 'I heard you the first time. Does this mean he's not coming at all?'

'That's the message. He can't come this afternoon,' Derek repeated.

'Yes, but will he come later, when he's finished with the priest? What's he seeing the priest about?'

'I don't know.'

'For God's sake, you must have some idea—' Rose was frantic.

'I'm telling you all I know. I'm just the messenger.'

'Yes, but you must have some idea what he's seeing the priest about.'

'Mammy wanted the two of us to go but I made a deal with John. I said that I'd give you the message if he helped me persuade her that I didn't need to see the priest – because I was at confession and communion last weekend.'

'And was he not at confession and communion himself?'

'He hasn't been to Mass for weeks.'

His voice was heavy with meaning and she looked hard at him. 'He never told me that,' she said slowly. 'Thanks for the message,' she added. The subject of Mass had never come up between herself and John. Did he think he was in a state of mortal sin because of what they did to one another?

'And Mammy's afraid we'll be messing around with Protestants over there,' said Derek. 'Protestant *girls*,' he added.

She knew he was goading her but would not be drawn. 'Thanks, Derek,' she repeated.

'You're welcome.' He did not move. 'I suppose he'll come over later,' he said. 'When he's back from the town. He's gone an hour back.'

She was unnerved by his immobility. 'Er, how've you been? How's your chest?' she asked.

'Fine. The doctor says there's nothing more to worry about, only to keep my strength up and not to catch cold.'

'That's great, Derek,' she said. Then, when he still did not move, she racked her brains for something else to say. 'Would you like to see around the stables?' was what came out. She knew it was a ridiculous suggestion in weather like this, but felt she had to get out of this dark enclosure and into the light.

'That'd be nice.'

Her brain racing, she led him into the yard. She had never been alone with him before. What was she to do with him? He seemed in no hurry to leave. 'Well,' she said, feeling foolish, 'this is the stableyard, as you can see.' She waved her arm around in a vague circle.

'Yes.' He was very still. The rain continued to drum on the cobbles; it was pouring off his head into his eyes and mouth making him look like a seal but it did not seem to bother him. Unlike her, he was not wearing a raincoat, just a jacket, black with rain. Now that they were out in the open, Rose's unease about being alone with him had abated. She had been selfish, she told herself, so concerned about John and herself that she had overlooked Derek's misery. He was just a boy, after all. Rose tried to picture herself in Derek's position: going away to the other side of the world, no one to miss him except a mother, no money, no prospects.

'Would you like to see the sidecars and traps?' she asked. 'Daddy has a great collection, they're very old. Antiques, as a matter of fact.' He nodded and she dragged open one of the heavy doors. 'Oh, Derek,' she blurted impulsively, 'it's terrible you and John have to go away.'

His face seemed to shatter into a thousand fragments. Then he buried it in his hands and sobbed like a baby.

Appalled, the door still in her hands, she stood riveted for a few seconds until his tears tapped her own misery and she began to cry with him. 'Come inside at least,' she managed to gasp. 'This is stupid, standing out here like this – the two of us, like – like—' She took his arm and led him, unresisting, inside. Then, although she knew it was futile, she patted his arm. 'Derek, Derek, please stop . . . Please, Derek, please stop. I can't bear it.'

He wrenched his arm away from her and, with both hands, grasped the iron-shod wheel of the nearest sidecar, shaking it so hard that the whole vehicle bounced and rattled, filling the stone storeroom with noise. Rose stood behind him, helpless, so near she could smell the wet wool of his jacket. As, bit by bit, he quietened, her instinct was to reach out to hug him but she was afraid. 'Oh, Derek,' she said miserably, 'I wish—'

'What?' He turned to face her but she did not know what she wished or what else to say so she just shrugged apologetically.

Suddenly he lunged towards her and grabbed her by the shoulders, knocking her off balance so she had to save herself by clutching at him. He kissed her then, fierce and hard, trying to force open her mouth with his tongue.

She half screamed and as quickly as he had begun to kiss her he stopped. His eyes wide as a hare's, he backed away from her, through the door of the storeroom, out into the rain. He looked so young and frightened she took a step towards him but he turned away and ran across the yard and out through the wicket gate. He was gone before she could call to him.

Rose's knees felt weak. She sat down on the raised stone platform beside one of the traps and leaned her head against the bodywork which smelt of old varnish; after a minute or so, she realised that, strangely, although her mouth still stung with the pressure of the forced kiss and her heart still thumped, she was less upset than she had a right to be. Derek's face, so like John's

68

but so white and forlorn, had sunk such a well of pity that she could not feel badly towards him.

After a little while she stood up and left the storeroom. Across the yard, the two riding horses watched her movements with interest, but instead of going to them she went back into Clicker's stable. Sometimes she wished she was an animal. An animal was born, ate, worked, slept, ate, worked, slept and died. Life was so simple for an animal.

She noticed a dandy-brush lying half concealed under the straw in a corner of the stable. She picked it up and began to groom Clicker, running the brush along his back and flanks, separating the tangled hair of his mane. 'What am I going to do? What am I going to do?' She repeated the phrase over and over again as she worked in long, sweeping curves.

Clicker shuddered with pleasure, his skin rippling in waves from his shoulder to his wide rump.

As the minutes of his last day ticked away, John seethed with frustration. For his mother's sake, however, he did his best not to let it show.

As it turned out, the visit to the priest had been short and relatively painless; just a blessing and a few unctuous words of advice about 'Catholic chasteness' and 'keeping the faith'. But then they embarked on a round of the Carrick shops, slow crucifixion as each shopkeeper made a point of saying goodbye and donated a small present. It was almost more than John could bear to see the suffering on his mother's face, and at the same time he was desperate to get back to Drumboola and to Rose.

McCann's, the drapers where they bought two white shirts, was their last call. The proprietor, pot-bellied and florid, had insisted on serving them himself and would not hear of any payment. 'No, *no*, Mrs Flynn, sure haven't ye been the best of customers for years and years and, God love us, but it's only yesterday since this gaffer here was making his first communion and now he's away on us! Away on us, hah? Away across the sea to the New World!'

Expertly, he wrapped the shirts in brown paper and twine and then insisted on coming outside the counter to show John and his mother to the door. There were several other customers in the shop and John was scarlet with embarrassment at the stir he was causing. He knew the draper was good-hearted and meant well but could not wait to escape as, pumping his hand, the man continued with his flowery exhortations. 'Be good now, hah? Make your fortune and make your mother here and all of us in Carrick proud of you.' Still shaking John's hand, he turned to Mary Flynn. 'Millions, he'll make, for sure, Mrs Flynn, millions the both of 'em'll make and then we'll all be jealous, hah? Sure, what can you do, don't they have to go? Young men must flower while old men wither?'

At last, they managed to get back to Ned Sherling's car and, as they were driven home, John's flat despair grew. He did not want to go away from here, from this quiet, wet landscape, from his mother, most of all from Rose. He glanced behind at Mary, stiff and suffering in the back seat. For her sake alone, he must not give in to his misery.

The last few days had been the most difficult of his life. Apart from leaving Rose, emigration to the other side of the Atlantic was traumatic within the community, almost the equivalent of pre-planned dying. Air travel was prohibitively expensive for ordinary people and once the emigrant left, there was no guarantee that anyone would ever see him again. Communication from then on was only by letter and he came home only for funerals and then only if he could afford it.

John's sadness at his impending departure from his mother was compounded by guilt about his preoccupation with Rose. At least they were young and for them anything was possible.

But he knew tomorrow could be the last time he and Derek would ever see their mother alive.

'Let me off here, please, Ned,' he said to the neighbour as the car, which for some minutes had been travelling along the perimeter wall of the Sundarbans estate, approached one of the abandoned gate lodges. The gate beside it was locked, but John knew how to get in around it, through a break in the ivy-covered wall a few feet away from it. 'Do you mind, Mammy?' he asked. He and his mother had never spoken about his relationship with the daughter of the Big House, but he knew there was no way she did not know. And, with time running out, today was no day for subtlety.

She shook her head. Her hands were clasped around the handles of her handbag and the folded-over tops of the paper bags containing the goods they had brought from the town. 'Are you sure it's all right?' His guilt stung him. 'I'll stay with you if you like . . . ' But again she shook her head. Relieved – and guilty about his relief – he got out of the car, said goodbye to the neighbour and slipped in through the break in the wall.

The rain had finally stopped but the pathway towards the house, which had not been maintained or repaired for many years, was treacherous with mud and undergrowth and within minutes John's boots were covered in glutinous muck. This was his least favourite part of the estate, largely deforested as the O'Beirne Moffats tried to make ends meet by selling off the hardwoods. At least, he saw, nature had begun the process of repair as little saplings, wild offspring of dead parents, were showing their heads; and although the area was still ravaged and open to the grey sky, a carpet of ivies, fern and bramble was slowly creeping over the brown acres of burnt stubble and stumps. He wondered how long it would be before this wasteland was properly forested again and then realised that it would not matter to him as he would probably never see it.

As he had expected, he found Rose in the stables. She was sitting on a heap of straw in a corner of her own pony's box. The Connemara was saddled but unbridled. She leaped to her feet as he unlatched the half-door. 'I was afraid you wouldn't come . . . '

'Did Derek not give you my message? I had to go into Carrick with Mammy—'

'Well, you're here now,' she said and he saw she was about to burst into tears.

'Don't, Rose,' he said, afraid of his own emotions. 'Please don't. There isn't much time.'

'I know,' she wailed. 'I can't stand it, John.'

'Are we going to go riding?' he asked.

The question only made her worse. She flopped back into the heap of straw. 'What's the point, now?'

'It's still early enough – and the rain has stopped.'

'I know, but there's no point in *anything*, is there?'

'Please, Rose,' he said again. He took Tartan's bridle from

71

where it was hanging on a hook in the wall and fitted the bit into the pony's mouth. 'Is Thumper ready?'

Looking around, he saw her nod although she continued to sob. 'Come on,' he said, leading the pony out into the yard. 'Look – the sun's coming out.' He felt absurdly as though he were humouring a toddler.

She pulled herself to her feet and emerged from the stable. Handing Tartan's reins to her, he went into Thumper's stable to bring him out.

They mounted and walked the horses out of the yard, through the gate and into a large five-acre field, which was a good place to give the animals their heads. After all the rain, there was a surprising amount of heat in the watery sun and as they cantered across the sloping land John, leading Rose, surrendered to the horse's motion. They were riding west and when he turned his head slightly to the left the sun warmed his face. He would miss this, he thought, this warmth and motion, the feeling of exhilaration as with his hands and feet he controlled the power of a running horse. He kicked Thumper on, he must not think about tomorrow or what remained of his time with Rose would be ruined.

They slowed the horses to a quiet walk as they entered the woods at the far side of the field. The path through the trees was narrow and they had to negotiate it single file, Rose leading on Tartan. This part of the demesne was densely wooded with evergreens and although the birds were busy after the rain, racketing about in the branches above their heads, the horses' hoofs were virtually soundless on a thick carpet of needles. John watched Rose's straight back, her long hair drying on her shoulders in separate strands. For the umpteenth time, he had to swallow the obstruction in his throat: what was he going to do without her?

They came to the little clearing which they had come to regard as theirs and dismounted. Having tethered the horses to a hazel bush, they stood facing one another, the momentous nature of the occasion heavy between them.

In a way, thought John, he felt as though they had already left one another. He took Rose in his arms and although at first she was as stiff and heavy as lead, she yielded within seconds and they sank together to the forest floor.

*

That night, Rose knocked softly on her grandmother's door, pushing it open without waiting for a response.

Nancy was propped up in her massive bed, a bedjacket around her thin shoulders. Her face lit up. 'Rose!' she exclaimed. 'This is a nice surprise.' Rose flew to the bed. Sinking to her knees and pillowing her head on the eiderdown she let the tears come unchecked.

The two Pekineses, who had been curled up beside their mistress, jumped off the bed and stalked to their baskets. 'Darling, Rose, darling – what is it? My dear, what is it? What's happened?' Nancy's small face wrinkled with concern and she leaned over to stroke Rose's head. 'What is it, my darling? You can tell me . . . '

Rose continued to sob into the eiderdown, 'Oh, Nanna, it's all over, it's over.'

'What's over, darling? Please, dear, what's over?'

But Rose could manage only to repeat, 'It's over, Nanna, it's over . . . '

'There, there,' soothed Nancy, 'whatever it is, darling, it can't be that bad, you can tell me, I'll help. There, there . . . Poor dear Rose, poor darling . . . Come on, dear, get up off your knees and sit in beside me.'

Rose finally calmed down sufficiently to get under the eiderdown. She laid her head on her grandmother's shoulder. 'I'm really sorry for this, Nanna, it's just . . . '

Her composure threatened to slip once again and Nancy intervened. 'Now, Rose, you must be brave. At least be brave enough to tell me . . . '

Rose swallowed. 'I *love* him, Nanna, and – and he's going away and I'll never see him again.'

'You love who, darling?'

'John. John Flynn.'

'John Flynn? I'm sorry, dear, I don't know him. Have I ever met him?'

'You *must* have, Nanna. You know – the Flynns from the gate lodge, he has a twin, Derek.'

If Nancy was surprised or upset at this revelation, she did not show it. 'Of course, dear. How stupid of me. Of course I know the Flynns. It's just that I haven't seen them for quite a while.' She stroked her granddaughter's dark head. 'You say he's going away?'

'To – to Canada, Nanna. It's the other side of the world.' Rose began to weep again. 'I'll – I'll never see him again!'

'There there, my dear. These things always seem worse at the time. Of course you'll see him again. The world is shrinking. This is nineteen fifty-three, it's not like it's the Middle Ages. There are airliners now and I believe an airliner can reach New York in less than thirteen hours.'

'But he won't have any money and I have no money to go and see him.'

'Rose darling, let money be the least of your worries. Money's nothing, only bits of paper and tin. If you really love him and he really loves you, love will find a way. You're very, very young, my dear—'

Rose pulled away. 'Oh, I *knew* you'd say that. I *knew* everyone would say that we're too young to be in love. But we're *not*. We're really and truly in love, Nanna.'

'I didn't say you were too young, dear. I just said you were young. And in case you think I believe young people can't fall in love, *Romeo and Juliet* was always my favourite Shakespeare play and I saw nothing whatsoever absurd about them falling in love.'

As she listened to her grandmother's gentle voice, Rose calmed a little. 'What am I going to do, Nanna?' she asked. 'He's going tomorrow morning. I was really stupid. I couldn't even say goodbye properly. I got too upset.'

'Did you see him today?'

'Yes, we – we went riding together in the woods.'

'And what happened, darling?'

'I can't tell you, it's just too bad, Nanna . . . ' Rose buried her face in the pillow.

'Maybe telling me will make it feel a little better.'

With her finger, Rose traced an embroidered forget-me-not on the pillowcase. 'There's nothing to tell, really, Nanna,' she said. 'I mean there's no words that could tell you how stupid I was.'

'Try, darling.'

'Well, we were just riding in the woods, like I told you, we did that a lot, I taught him to ride, d'you see – and – and – I knew this would be the last time. Anyway, there's this little glade,' she shot her grandmother a half-apologetic look, 'well, *we* call it

74

a glade. Anyway, we – we got off the horses today as usual and then – oh, Nanna.' She could not continue.

'There, there, darling. Hush.' Rose's grandmother moved away for a second and extracted a handkerchief from a little drawer in her bedside table. She gave it to Rose.

'Well, to make a long story short, Nanna,' Rose said, blowing her nose, 'after a bit, you know – I mean we kissed each other and all – but then I just jumped up on Tartan again and galloped off and left. I didn't even look back.'

Nancy cleared her throat. 'I see,' she said.

Even through her distress, Rose heard a new note in her voice and looked up half suspiciously. 'What do you see, Nanna?'

'Nothing, darling. It's only that I thought – I was afraid—'

'*What*, Nanna?'

'Hush, darling.' Nancy put a finger on her granddaughter's lips. She took a hairbrush from her bedside table and began gently to brush Rose's hair. 'Maybe it was all for the best, my dear . . . '

Lifting her head, Rose surrendered to the soothing rhythm. 'How *could* it be? I just *left* him there. I didn't say *goodbye*! Apart from anything else, it was so *selfish* of me!'

Rose's grandmother considered. 'It's only eight o'clock. Can't you see him again this evening or would it be too upsetting for you?'

'That's partly it,' admitted Rose, 'but the main reason is there's one of those American wakes for him in his house tonight.'

'Couldn't you go to it, see him there?' asked Nancy, who had had no occasion to attend an American wake, so called because on the night before an emigrant left for America it was customary that family, friends and neighbours would gather in his house for a send-off party similar to the send-off given to a corpse before burial.

'No, Nanna,' said Rose, 'I couldn't go there. Even if I could bear it, which I couldn't, I don't think John would be comfortable with me there.' She covered her face with her hands. 'It's just over, that's all, it's just that it's so hard to bear.'

Her grandmother continued with the brushing. 'Poor Rose. Growing up so soon, so fast . . . Where did you say he was going?'

'To Prince Edward Island in Canada.'

'I see. Well, try to look on the bright side, darling, if you can. At least it's not as far as Australia. Now if he was going to Australia, I'd say we'd have real cause for worry. But Canada? Sure, Canada is only a hop, step and a jump away on an airliner.' Nancy gathered up her granddaughter's hair in a thick tail and began to plait it.

'Oh, Nanna, I'm so sorry I didn't talk the whole thing over with you before now. I should have known you'd understand. It's been so awful worrying about this all by myself. I was dreading tonight and now here it is.' Fresh tears poured down her face.

'There there, my dear. You cry all you want to. I'm here. But it's not as bad as you think, it really isn't.'

'Mother wouldn't understand.'

'She might surprise you, dear, but that's up to you. One of the more doubtful privileges of growing up is you have to make your own decisions about whom to trust.'

'I trust you, Nanna, I really do. Sorry about the scene. I just can't help myself crying. I don't think I've cried so much, ever, in all my life.'

'Tears are good for the soul, dear. Animals don't cry, only humans, did you know that? Humans need to cry occasionally.'

Rose managed a wan smile. 'Yeah, well, maybe you're right and maybe you're wrong. I'm *sure* I've seen horses cry.' She was quiet while her grandmother finished plaiting her hair leaving the ends loose. One of the Pekineses, apparently satisfied that some semblance of order had returned to his life, jumped back on the bed and snuggled down beside his mistress. A few moments later, the other followed.

The four of them lay there peacefully in the island of light created by her grandmother's bedside lamp. One of the dogs snored lightly and Rose reached across to stroke its soft furry head.

The gate lodge was transformed for the night. Through a fug of smoke from cigarettes and clay pipes, the talk rode high on a river of music and drink, and the Flynns' poor furniture had been augmented by chairs and trestles borrowed from neighbours.

Although the parlour, never used in ordinary circum-

76

stances, gleamed with polishing and a fire glowed in the grate, everyone had crowded into the kitchen which was now packed so tightly that scarcely a square inch of floor could be seen. Neighbours who saw each other daily, or certainly once a week at Mass, chatted as animatedly to each other as though they had not met for years.

John could not remember feeling more weary. Having handed round platefuls of fruitcake, seedy cake and the sandwiches he had helped his mother prepare, everyone had a drink in hand, and he was having a brief respite from his duties. Looking around, he wondered sadly how much all this was costing his mother but knew that, although she might be paying for it for months or even years, she would never have dreamed of scrimping.

Even though the fire in the stove had been allowed to burn low and the back door was open to the night he found the room stifling and was beginning to get a headache. He wondered if he could slip out for a while into the fresh air and looked around to assess his chances of doing so unnoticed. He saw that his twin, caught like a scrap between two crows, was sitting between a lemon-whiskered old man and the man's toothless sister. John decided to rescue him. 'Will you help me outside, Derek?' he called over the hubbub and was rewarded with his twin's look of relief. 'Another mineral?' John yelled at the two old people, whom he knew were teetotallers. He took their glasses and followed Derek out to where the crates of bottles were stashed in the coolness just outside the back door.

'Jesus, this is desperate,' hissed Derek. 'Do you want a fag?'

'Only a few hours of it to go,' whispered John back. 'No, I don't want any fag. Don't let Mammy see you smoking those things.'

They moved a little away from the doorway and leaned against the wall of the house. John could see their mother at the kitchen table which had been pushed to the wall at the far side of the room. She was buttering bread and in the light from the paraffin lamps, looked unnaturally flushed. 'I'm worried about Mam,' he said then to Derek. 'Do you think she'll be all right?'

'Do you want to end up like them?' Derek jerked his thumb over his shoulder, indicating the old people he had just left. He took a deep drag from the half cigarette he held carefully cupped in the palm of his hand. 'To tell you the truth I can't wait to get away from this shaggin' place.'

'Last night you said you didn't want to go.'

'That was last night.'

'What's happened to change your mind?'

'Nothing.'

'Something must have happened.'

'Nothing. Now will you shut it!'

John looked at him closely but Derek's face was in shadow. He leaned back against the wall of the house and looked up at the moon and stars. The music from the kitchen sounded gay and thoughtless, as though this were a celebration and not a wake. 'It's awfully hard on Mammy, though,' he said after a pause.

'I know,' said Derek. 'But that's not our fault, is it?'

'I don't know whose fault it is,' said John quietly. 'But it's certainly not hers and I certainly don't want to go.' The longing for Rose knifed into him.

They stood for a while, shoulders almost touching. Derek pulled on the cigarette again and the tip of it glowed red in the darkness. 'What's it going to be like, d'you think?' he asked as he exhaled.

'I don't know, any more than you.'

One of the guests came out and saluted them as he made his way to the privy behind the hedge. 'Are you going to write to her?' Derek kicked at a weed and John knew his brother was not referring to their mother.

'We said we would.'

'The great writers! The great corr-es-pond-ents!' He dragged out the word to get maximum value from the venom.

'Stop it, Derek!' The last thing they needed now was a row. 'I'm going back inside. Will you bring the lemonade to those two?'

'I will in me arse!'

John Flynn had lost his temper perhaps four times in his life. He felt he was in danger of it now. He plucked a bottle of red lemonade from one of the crates and opened the twist-cap. He did it too violently and it hissed its fizzy contents all over his hands. He jumped backwards so the lemonade would not catch his trousers but was only partially successful and some of the overflow ran onto his shoes.

He shook off the surface liquid, went back into the kitchen and poured the lemonade into the two glasses. As he brought them across to the two old people, he was conscious of his mother's eyes following his every movement, boring into his back. The volume of talk inside the kitchen had risen as the drink further loosened tongues and as people shouted above the music. Festivity was the last thing John felt like tonight. Derek's words outside were ringing in his head: *It's not our fault.*

It had to be somebody's fault.

The ball of temper inside him swelled and rose like red bile. He had to get away from the suffocating kitchen, away from his mother's sadness. He forced himself to smile as he handed over the lemonade, and backed away immediately in case the old people insisted he sit down. Out of the corner of his eye, he noticed that Derek had come inside again and was busy handing around more sandwiches. Now was his chance.

The tune the fiddlers had been playing came to a skirling finish and one of the men around them called for hush for a slow air. As the talk died down and the thin sweet tune began, John walked purposefully to the back door as though he were going outside for more supplies.

Before he went out, he made the fatal mistake of looking back over his shoulder, catching his mother's eye. Even from that distance, her suffering scalded him and added further heat to his rage. Outside, he tried to tamp himself down by taking deep draughts of fresh air but the adrenalin was pumping harder and harder and he wanted only to flail, to slash at an enemy, any enemy, even one he could not see.

He broke into a run to get away as fast and as far as he could. He tore into the fields behind the house, heedless, pounding along the soggy ground, not caring that his good shoes and new trousers would get ruined, hoping that they would. Panting hard, he ran for five minutes over the open ground, barrelling the air with his chest, splattering through puddles left by the morning rain.

When he came to the end of the fields and as far as the wood he did not bother to find a pathway but, like a stag in flight, plunged straight into the trees, crashing through thickets and undergrowth. His jacket caught on a thorn bush and he vented his rage on it, wrenching it free, ripping the pocket. He tore a rotting branch off an ash tree then and laid about him, assaulting other trees, battering his weapon against their trunks and overhanging leaves until the wood in his hand disintegrated and was only a twig. Using all his diminished strength, he threw it away. Not caring that his hands and cheek were being stung by the needles he leaned against the bole of a spruce for a few moments, trying to regain control of the breath which shuddered and rasped in his chest. After a few minutes the fury ebbed completely away leaving an emptiness he felt would never be filled again.

It was only then he noticed that he had travelled quite a distance, almost as far as the lakeshore; the water, luminous with shades of silver and grey, gleamed only a few yards away under a full heavy moon.

Now he felt stupid – and guilty that he had run away from his own party. He was only making things worse for his mother, who would, no doubt, have missed him by now. But then he thought of the heat, the packed kitchen, the frenetic, false sense of gaiety. He could not go back. Not yet. He moved away from the tree and walked slowly towards the water. When he emerged into the open, he saw he was at a part of the lake which was inaccessible except by boat because the shoreline was swampy and fringed densely with reeds. He could proceed no farther unless he wanted to wade.

The water had eroded the treeline so the roots were exposed in hard tangled skeins. Keeping clear of the reeds, John sat down. He took a deep breath and concentrated on the small night sounds all around him: the quiet whispers in the trees and rustlings in the reeds and the barely audible sound of the water as it lapped against them only inches away from his feet. A fish plopped nearby, so unexpectedly that he was startled. Under the calm moon, the countryside was alive with small things, creatures who would live out their lives and reproduce many generations of themselves before he would see this place again, if ever. The thought covered him like a cold black blanket.

And Rose?

John had no adult in whom to confide his deep love and

passion for Rose but, even if he had, he knew he would have received no consolation or encouragement; no adult would ever believe that a seventeen-year-old could fall so irrevocably and eternally in love. Yet he knew that was exactly what he was. Irrevocably and eternally in love.

And in less than twelve hours he was going away from her. They had not been able to say goodbye to one another.

An owl cried softly. He looked around carefully to see if he could spot it but everything remained still. Then, a little way to his left, he caught some movement out of the corner of his eye. Moving his head slowly and smoothly, he saw what had attracted his attention: a large bird, ghostly grey and silent, raised its head on a long slender neck and shook it briskly from side to side as if to dislodge a dream. It was a goose, an early arrival at this staging post for winter migrants. As his vision cleared, John saw the bird was one of a flock, tucked snugly into the reeds less than sixty feet away. They must have arrived within the past twenty-four hours, he thought, as he had not heard or seen them before.

The moon was high now, painting an oval of white on the surface of the lake near the far shore. After the energy and rage he had expended, John felt flat and cold, as one-dimensional as the moon's image. It seemed appropriate somehow that he and Rose were ending where they had started, on the shores of the lake.

He stood up. It was no use, he simply had to see her again.

He could hardly knock on the front door at this time of night, he thought, but he had to see her. At least to say goodbye properly. Having no idea what he was going to do when he got there, he ran through the trees in the direction of Sundarbans.

Rose, fully dressed, lay stiffly on her bed, 'if-onlys' thick as bristles in the air around her head. If only she had not been so stupid this afternoon. If only he was not going away. If only they were a bit older and she could go with him. If only he was not the poor son of a poor widow. If only she had not met him, she would not be suffering like this now . . .

She should write her diary: at least she had something serious to write about. Grown-up things. But if this was what grown-ups went through, she wanted to remain a child. She picked up the diary and then flung it away into a corner of the room.

Not now. Not when he was still in Ireland, still less than a mile away from her on the same little bit of land.

She tried to picture him at the American wake. He would probably be wearing his good new clothes, the serviceable jacket and wide-bottomed trousers in brown tweed that she had told him were lovely when, proudly, he had brought them, still in their shop bag, to show off to her.

Maybe she could sell her jewels and go to see him: she sprang off the bed and went to her dressing-table on which the red velvet case took pride of place. Sitting on her stool, she took the necklace from its mount, caressing the shimmering stones; then she fastened the bracelet on her wrist, holding her arm this way and that to see the amethysts catch the light.

There was a sudden noise at one of the windows. When it came a second time, she realised someone was throwing gravel at the glass. Heart thumping, she walked across to the window and pulled back the curtains, spilling an oblong of light on a dark figure with an upraised arm.

It was him. John.

She tugged at the window sash to raise it but this particular window had not been opened for years and was tightly stuck. Incredulous with joy, she motioned frantically to him to wait where he was and ran across the room. She flew down the staircase, not caring who heard her and then along the passage towards the kitchen. Giving Roger a hasty thump as she passed, she undid the big bolt on the back door and let herself out.

Never had the house seemed so big as she ran across the back yard, out through the wicket gate and around the side until she came to the terrace in front. She was terrified he might have gone away.

But he was there all right. Standing with his back to the balustrade, still looking up at her window as if expecting her to come through it.

'John!' she cried, running towards him.

He turned around and put his finger to his lips. But she did not care about being quiet and ran straight at him, cannoning

82

into his chest, flinging her arms around his neck. 'Oh, John!' She buried her face against him. He smelled of smoke.

She pulled back, scandalised. 'John! Have you been smoking?'

'No, it's from the party. Come on,' he whispered, 'let's get away from here.'

'Where are we going?'

'Anywhere away from the front of your house.'

He took her hand and they ran together down the steps, across the gravel crescent and then over the grass into the trees. John turned to her then. 'One rule,' he said, still whispering although they were safely out of earshot of anyone who could have heard them.

'What, John?' Reflexively, she was whispering too.

'No tears for either of us. We've only a little time. Let's not waste it.'

'I can't guarantee that.'

'Neither can I, but let's try, all right?'

'All right.'

She put her arms around his neck again and would have kissed him but he said, 'No, not yet. I want us to go to the lake.'

'The lake?'

'I can't explain it. It's just something I want us to do.'

'All right.' She would have gone with him now to Timbuktu.

Hand in hand, knowing every step of the way, they walked through the woods. Although she had been raised in the heart of the country, Rose had never been too keen on some of its creatures, particularly those who were active at night like rats, for instance, or frogs or bats. But with her hand in John's she walked surefootedly and confidently. She was so happy at the stay of execution, she was tempted to pray.

They came out on the shoreline and walked along it until they reached the promontory where first they had met. John turned and took her in his arms. 'Now,' he said.

Gladly she returned his kiss and kissed him and kissed him, his face and neck and ears and his mouth again. He held her away from him. 'Rose, can I see your breasts?'

Recently, although she knew it was a sin, Rose had allowed him to fondle her breasts, but only under her blouse or jumper.

83

She hesitated a moment and then remembered she might never see him again.

He could see her whole body if he wanted.

Slowly, keeping her eyes on his face, which she could see quite well because of the bright moon, she reached for the buttons on the neck of her blouse. Of all days to choose *this* garment! she thought. The blouse, of white cotton with a peter pan collar and leg-o'-mutton sleeves, was fastened from throat to waist with twenty tiny pearl buttons which always took an age to undo.

One by one she unfastened them but a thread from the buttonhole had caught around one and although she pulled and pulled at it, it would not give.

John reached forward to help her and as he worked on the thread, she felt his hands shaking; she also realised he was making efforts to use only the tips of his fingers, so as not to touch the flesh under the blouse. She was reminded of the time she first watched those fingers tying a fly.

At last, the final button was undone. Rose, now shaking too, kept her head high and held the blouse wide while, arching his body like a bow so as not to touch her, he fumbled around her back with the catch of her bra. Eventually he managed to unclasp the hooks and reverently, as though he were unveiling a pair of fragile porcelain shells, he pushed the lace cups upwards until her breasts were fully exposed. He stood back then.

Trembling harder than ever, she kept her blouse wide, offering him the sight. Slowly, he reached forward and placed one hand gently under each breast. Then, as if he were participating in a formal ceremony, he bent and kissed them one after the other, just one kiss on each. When he had finished, Rose expected him to remove his hands but he kept them where they were. Loving the warm, living feel of John's hands, she kept her shoulders back and the blouse as wide open as it would go.

Now he kissed the breasts again, more than one kiss on each one this time, spending longer, moving carefully from one to the other so as not to disturb her balance on the rock. Drowning in the sensation, she closed her eyes and swayed a little. He obviously misinterpreted her movement because he stepped back and dropped his hands. 'Oh, please, don't stop,' she could not help herself, 'please don't stop.'

'Are you sure?'

She nodded. This time, he caught her round the waist and kissed her mouth. She let the leaves of the blouse fall and wound herself around him, feeling the rasp of the tweed jacket against her bare skin. As the kiss went on and on, she wanted to ask him to kiss her breasts again but did not have the courage.

Then he did it anyway. Different kisses, urgent, sucking kisses, using his tongue and his teeth. He pushed her shoulders back so he could hold her round the waist with one hand and take a breast with the other, using it with mouth and hand like a cup. She knew she should tell him to stop now but couldn't. He was going away tomorrow... He was going away tomorrow... Her brain beat the refrain. He moved to the other breast and she moved to accommodate him, pushing it at him. She loved him so much...

'We shouldn't, John,' she murmured, 'we shouldn't...' But he knew she didn't mean it.

'I know, I know,' he said. 'Oh, Rose!'

She used her hands to cup her breasts, to help him; offering them like peaches, she kissed the back of his neck and realised he was saying something against her skin. She could not make out what it was. She pulled at his head. 'What, John? What are you saying?'

'I want to take you into the lake.'

'*What?* Now? Right now in the middle of the night?'

'Yes, why not?'

'But we've no togs!'

The absurdity of the statement hit the two of them. The tension broke and they pealed with laughter. 'Well, if you don't want to be romantic. If you don't want to come skinny-dipping in the moonlight, that's all right with me!'

'Won't it be freezing?'

'Maybe that's what we need. Mortification of the flesh! Anyway, it's still August – summer.'

They laughed again and Rose felt unusually reckless. 'Suppose we're caught?' she asked, although her mind was already made up. Skinny-dipping. Only the most forward people ever did that. She wanted to skinny-dip with John more than anything in the world. But when it came to it, she could not just throw off her clothes, just like that, not in front of him. 'You go first,' she said.

He threw off his jacket and unbuttoned his shirt, undid his laces and kicked off his shoes. He turned his back then and, almost before Rose knew he had done it, had removed his trousers, underpants and socks and was racing into the water. She had no time to appraise what a man's nakedness might be like because it was too dark and all she saw was a brief flash of his bottom before he had immersed it in the water.

'God almighty,' he shouted, 'it *is* freezing!'

Rose hesitated, half glad of the escape route he seemed to offer but fascinated at the sight of him, dark in the silvery water. She made up her mind to follow. 'Don't look,' she said primly.

'Me, look?' he asked innocently. '*Me?*'

'Go on, turn your back!'

He obeyed, turning his head. 'How deep is it?' called Rose, loosening her suspender belt and rolling off her stockings.

'About four or five feet,' he called back, 'not too deep at all. Are you nearly ready? I'm getting a crick in my neck.'

'Nearly,' she shouted, slipping out of her skirt and pants. 'But you're not to look until I'm *in* the water. Up to my neck,' she added.

'Certainly, ma'am,' he said.

Unlike him, Rose did not dash in but picked her way across the stones and little rocks until she came to the water's edge. She put a toe in. 'My God,' she said involuntarily. 'It's awful!'

He turned towards her and she gave a little scream, trying ineffectually to cover her nakedness with her hands. 'I *told* you not to look.'

'Sorry,' he said. 'But how was I to know you weren't in it up to your neck?'

'I'll tell you when.'

'All right, but for God's sake, hurry.'

Gingerly, step by icy step, she inserted her body into the water. The floor of the lake shelved steeply and she was able to swim within seconds. 'I'm in,' she said.

'Thank God for that.'

Self-consciously, she swam around in little circles, getting used to the strange sensation of the water flowing all over her

86

skin. Now that she was in, it was not so cold after all. He swam around too, a little way away from her, in his own little circle. She was conscious that, like her, he didn't know what to do next.

They were not out of their depth and keeping her knees slightly bent so the water would still reach to her neck, she put her feet on the bottom. It was soft and squidgy but for once she did not worry that she was stepping on anything unsavoury or slimy. The water was very clear and, as he continued swimming, she was able to see his body shimmering just under the surface like an ethereal, elongated white fish. 'John,' she said.

'Yes?'

'I love you.' She had never said it. They had never said it.

'I love you, Rose.'

'What are we going to do?'

'No tears.'

'I know. But what are we going to do?'

'This.' He, too, lowered his feet to the bottom and stood so the water was just half-way up his chest. He leaned towards her and crooked his hands under her armpits, raising her so her breasts rose and were floating just on the surface. He kissed them, then clasped her full-length to him and kissed her on the mouth. His lips tasted peaty, like the water.

She felt his hardness rise against her belly and gasped. 'It's all right, Rose, it's all right,' he said. 'We're not going to do anything you don't want to.'

His voice was rough but it excited her. Fleetingly, she thought of the certain damnation she now faced. In the whole world, this was the most sinful thing she could possibly do but deep down it felt right and good and safe. She would have plenty of time tomorrow and in the years to come to reflect on the sinfulness of her actions and to repent. He would be gone tomorrow.

She kissed him back and shimmied against him. His body felt cool and hard, yet at the same time she could feel the heat below the surface of his skin. He raised one knee and she straddled it, half floating. That *thing* pressed between them. She did not dare look down.

'Oh, Rose, you're so beautiful,' he whispered. 'Lie back, I want to see you all.' She surrendered to him and allowed herself to float on her back. 'Can I take this off?' he asked, pulling at the ribbon which still tied her hair.

'Yes.' She pulled it off for him and let it drift away.

He placed one hand under the small of her back, supporting her on the surface, keeping her body steady. With the other he unravelled the plait made by her grandmother and spread her hair upwards from the nape of her neck so it floated around her head. Again and again he did it, separating the strands. She closed her eyes and abandoned herself to the freedom of the water and his hands.

'You are the most beautiful, most lovely creature,' he said, shifting, moving his supporting hand to her upper back, leaving the other free to stroke her.

She knew it was his first time too but when he entered her it was easy. In her convent, Rose had been party to dark secret mutterings about pain, blood, agony and shame but this was nothing like that. It was quiet and gentle, just a tug. It felt utterly natural. Perhaps the buoyancy of the water helped, she thought as, gladly, she clung to him and kissed his wet neck.

CHAPTER FOUR

It was still dark when John woke. The first sensation was of the pressure of Rose's sleeping head in the crook of his arm; the second was of intense cold.

Teeth chattering when they came out of the lake, they had curled themselves together under a lime tree in a bed of leaves and other forest debris, trying to get warm under the inadequate covering of John's jacket. After a few minutes, he had started to stroke her long smooth back. He had kissed her and she had responded and within seconds their desire for each other flared.

The sensations of this second lovemaking were less surprising and far deeper emotionally for John than the first: overwhelmed with love and imminent loss, he had wept when he came, burying his head in Rose's neck, his heart and soul emptying into her as completely as his body. She had wept too as she clung to him. 'John, John, my darling, darling John . . . '

He had no idea what time it was now but guessed it was just before dawn; he saw through the branches that the moon had not yet set but, other than a barely audible whisper in the leaves above their heads, the forest around them was still. He hated disturbing Rose, but getting home was now a matter of urgency. From his limited perspective, he gazed at Rose's face, committing it to memory. She looked so tranquil, the curve of her cheek glimmering like bone china in the faint light, that to wake her would seem like an act of destruction. But he had to. His mother would be distracted.

They had dressed after making love but then had lain down again under his jacket; he saw it had slipped off her shoulder and, very carefully, to give them just a few more minutes together, he moved to replace it but the movement woke her. He lay immobile then and even in the darkness, could discern the succession of expressions as she opened her eyes: puzzlement, followed rapidly

89

by recognition, fright and then despair. 'Oh, John,' she said, throwing her arms around his neck.

He had to be the strong one. 'Rose,' he said into her hair, 'we've got to go now. My mother—'

'Oh, I know, I know . . . '

'Remember we promised each other – no tears . . . '

'I can't help it.'

'Rose, we'll think of some way, *I'll* think of some way, I really will.'

She pulled back from him and he saw she desperately wanted to believe him. 'Do you promise, John? I'll *die* without you.'

'Rose, we're very young. Anything is possible for young people. How often have we been told that?'

'Yes, but—'

'Do you trust me?'

'Of course. Now more than ever. After – you know—' She looked him bravely in the eye.

They lay still for another few moments; he kissed her softly but the urgency to get home now superseded even his need for Rose. She sensed his panic because she put her hand on his shoulder to restrain him from getting up. 'There's one more thing, John.'

'Yes?' Although there was no need for it, he realised they were both whispering.

'Do you know the story about Queen Elizabeth and Lord Essex?'

'No!' He was astonished.

'Well, they were lovers – ' she was rushing, words spilling at twice her normal speed ' – it might have been Sir Walter Raleigh, but anyway, it was one of them – and—'

'What about them?'

'Well, Queen Elizabeth had one of them, whichever one it was, locked up in the Tower of London for months and months, or maybe years – for treason, I think it was – but before she did that – when they were still lovers, I mean – she gave him a ring and said to him that any time, any time at all, no matter how bad things were between them, if he sent her that ring, she would honour his request, *whatever* it was.' John was barely listening to the tumbling words: his mother's white face floated in front of his eyes. But he did not want to hurt Rose. Gently, he disengaged his arm from under her head. 'Yes?'

'Lord Essex was going to be executed,' she continued in a hoarse urgent whisper, 'and Queen Elizabeth waited and waited for the ring, but it never came and the night before it was to happen – the execution – she sent him a note saying "Where's the ring?"; "Send me the ring" or something like that but he didn't and he was executed.'

John sat up and pulled her into a sitting position beside him. 'So, Rose?' he asked, taking her shoulders in his hands and speaking as gently as he could. 'What's that to do with us?' For answer, she unclasped the amethyst bracelet and held it out to him. 'What's that?' he asked.

'This can be our ring.'

'Rose! I can't take that – that's your gift from your father. And it's very valuable.'

'Exactly,' she whispered. 'I know. I just feel it can help us some way. Please, please take it, John.'

'You mean send it to you?'

'Or anything you like. Anything that will help us.'

'You mean sell it or pawn it, don't you?'

'Not necessarily. But, yes, if that is what it takes. Anything to help us. *Anything*.'

'Please, Rose, you know I couldn't take it.'

'Why not? It's *my* jewellery and I can do anything I like with it. Go on, John, please, *please* take it. I'll *die* if you don't. I have to have some hope.'

'All right.' Still reluctant, he took the bracelet which felt warm from her skin. 'Thank you,' he said, 'I'll think of some way to use it for us. Now, Rose, I'll really have to go.' He stood and helped her up. Putting on his jacket, he slipped the bracelet into the pocket.

He took her in his arms and kissed her swiftly. 'No tears. Do you want me to walk you back to the house?'

She shook her head. 'No. Go on. I'll be fine.'

'You'll write?' John struggled to keep his voice steady. Now that the moment was really on them, his insides felt as though a saw was being worked slowly through them from end to end. She nodded and moved back a step. In the darkness, he could not distinguish her eyes but her face was wet when he touched it. 'I love you,' he said.

'I love you too . . . ' He barely heard the words, walking fast, not really seeing where he was going. His body, impervious to the cold and the soft muddy places underfoot, felt as though it did not belong to him and he did not bother to shield his face from the leaves which brushed it.

He had his emotions under iron control by the time he came within sight of the gate lodge but stopped dead, heart thumping with guilt and remorse. The windows glowed with light.

What had he expected? he asked himself. That his mother would accept his absence and go happily to sleep? He took a deep breath and attempted to tidy himself a little, rubbing at his muddy shoes with tufts of grass, wetting the palms of his hands and slicking them through his hair. Then he walked to the house, around the side and in the back door.

Only one lamp, low on paraffin, burned on the mantelpiece, its dwindling light golden on the wall behind it. His mother and Derek were sitting in the shadows, side by side on the settle beside the fire and Ned Sherling, their neighbour, was sitting on a chair on the other side. The kitchen had been tidied: no food to be seen, the kitchen table in its place and all the borrowed chairs racked along one wall. John moved to his mother. 'Sorry, Mammy. I'm really sorry.'

Her face was swollen and red. 'Where were you?' He saw her take in the state of him, the muck on his shoes, the ruined jacket.

'I was above at Swan's Lake.'

'Until this hour?'

'Yes.'

They looked at one another for fully five seconds. 'I see,' she said quietly. She turned to Derek. 'Stoke up the fire, Derek, will you? And put on the kettle.' Derek made no move and, although John did not look at his twin, he knew only too well what Derek's face would show. 'Derek!' His mother's voice cracked.

'I'll have to get logs.' Derek's tone was surly. As he went outside, their mother turned to the neighbour. 'Thank you for watching, Ned. You'll have a cup of tea before you go?'

'I won't, thanks, Mary. I'll have to be going. Might as well do the milking on me way home.'

Their mother rose with him. 'I'm really sorry, Ned, and I'm really grateful.'

'Don't be too hard on the lad. The nights will be long without him.'

'I know,' she said and John's heart nearly broke.

'Mammy,' he started tentatively when she came back from seeing the neighbour out, but she held up her hand to stop him.

'Don't, John. I don't want to know. There's nothing I can do about anything now. I did the best I could.'

Desolate, he leaned against the wall of the kitchen and looked out through the window. The stars were beginning to fade. Only a few more hours in Ireland.

Reaching up to the mantelpiece, his mother busied herself by inspecting the level of paraffin in the lamp and then Derek stamped in at the door carrying an armful of logs, dumping them in the chimney-corner beside the stove. John watched as his twin pulled open the door of the stove, riddled it savagely and threw in three logs, one after the other as though he would batter open the back of the stove with them.

'I think ye'd better go to bed for a bit of sleep.' Mary Flynn had stopped fiddling with the lamp. 'It'll be light soon. Ned said he'd be back with the car at eleven. Ye'll have only a couple of hours.'

'Goodnight, Mammy.' Derek closed the door of the stove and reached out to his mother. He gave her a perfunctory hug and turned away fast, going into the bedroom at almost a run.

'You too, John, go on.'

He had to say something, anything, to try to make it up to her. 'Mammy—'

'Go *on*, John!'

He was by her side immediately. 'Mammy, don't cry. Please don't cry.'

'I'm sorry. I'm sorry.' But she continued to weep as he stood helplessly beside her. Eventually he reached out and touched her arm. She put her hand over his and patted it. 'Give me that jacket, it's ruined. I'll try to see what I can do with it.'

He took it off and handed it to her. She put her hand inside the torn pocket, assessing the damage. 'What's this?'

In his distress, he had forgotten about the bracelet. 'It's – it's a bracelet.'

'I can see that. What are you doing with such a thing?'

'Mammy, please give it to me. It was, it's a – it's sort of a present.'

'A girl's bracelet?'

'Yes.'

'From Miss Rose?'

He gasped to hear the name on his mother's lips. 'Yes, Mammy,' he said when he had recovered. 'Rose gave it to me.'

She wiped her wet cheeks with the back of her hand. 'It's a very valuable thing. It's real gold.'

'I know,' he said quietly. 'And they're real jewels.'

She handed him the bracelet, turned her back on him and held up the jacket to the dwindling light from the lamp, examining the torn pocket. 'Go to bed now, John. Everything's ready. Leave your trousers and your shoes, I'll try to clean them up too. I'll call you at ten for your breakfast.'

He saw her thin back was stooped with tiredness and wanted desperately to make it young again. To tell her he loved her very much. To confide in her about Rose. He bent to take off his shoes and trousers. 'Mammy?'

'Yes?' She half turned towards him.

'Nothing,' he said. 'It's all right. Goodnight.'

'Goodnight, John.'

He placed the trousers carefully over the back of a chair and padded into the bedroom. Derek was hunched into a ball under the bedclothes and the bed shook with his suppressed sobbing. Not bothering to take off his shirt, John slid in beside him. Derek recoiled, moving as far as possible to the edge. 'Bastard!' he hissed. 'Why'd you do it? Bastard!'

John turned on his side, facing the window. He knew he had no chance of falling asleep; he did not even close his eyes but lay watching the light creep up outside the window until he could clearly delineate the mass of the hedge against the paler sky. The blackbird, which had been singing in that hedge all summer, began to tune up as though it were just any old day. John half felt he would wake up and everything would be normal. He would not be going to the other side of the world. He would not have to endure the permanent vision of his mother's anguish. He would be able to see Rose again, just a mile away, to make love to her

94

again, to make love to her for ever, every day, every night.

To his own astonishment, he felt no sense of guilt or shame about what had happened between himself and Rose. It had felt right and natural. That first time, in the lake, he had laughed aloud with joy. She had had her eyes closed but they flew open as he laughed and she had laughed along with him, clinging on to him like a limpet, the water lapping at her chin. 'Is that it, John?'

'I think so!' he had said and still inside her, had swung her round so they made a whirlpool together.

She had slipped apart from him. 'I'm freezing.' He had put his arm around her shoulder and kissed her and had supported her as they stumbled out of the water.

Then, that second time under the lime, it had been so different, intense to an almost unbearable degree. He should probably be ashamed of his babyish weeping; instead, still staring at the gradually pinkening sky outside the window, he concentrated on the memory of Rose's sleeping face.

As he left Rose, the urgency to get home – and the physical repleteness of the adventure – had sustained him and made him strong. Now, physical fatigue and his emotion were combining to make him feel nauseous. Maybe a cup of tea or a drink of water might help. He ensured that Derek was asleep and then, moving quietly so he would not wake him, slipped out of the bed and went into the kitchen.

His mother was working with a needle and thread on the torn pocket and looked up as she heard the bedroom door open. 'John?' He could hear the soft roaring of the fire in the stove. She had refilled the lamp and placed it by her on the kitchen table.

'I couldn't sleep, Mammy.'

'You'll catch your death of cold in your bare feet. Here.' She went to the hook by the back door and took down an old tweed coat which had belonged to his father and which she still used for heavy winter work around the garden. 'Put this on.'

He put on the coat which smelled of many wettings and also of the party the night before. She resumed her seat at the table. 'Nearly finished this now. It'll be as good as new.'

He was supremely conscious of the tinny ticking of the clock on the mantelpiece. Time was running out for him and his mother, tick by tick. Why could he not tell her he loved her? The words trembled in his mouth but would not come out. 'Do you think Dan'll meet us off the boat, Mammy?' he asked.

'I'm sure he will. He wrote he would.'

Tick, tick tick.

None of them had ever met Dan, who was the twins' second cousin on their father's side. He had been born on Prince Edward Island and had never set foot in Ireland. Desperately, John tried again to find the courage to push the loving words out of his mouth, to tell her not only how much he loved her but how much he would miss her. How much he needed now to put his arms around her. 'Would you like a cup of tea?' he asked.

'I wouldn't mind,' she answered, biting off the thread and winding it around her needle.

He got up and went to the stove. 'Mammy?'

'Yes?'

'I – we – it's not as if we want to go, you know.'

'I know, son.'

'It's not too late. We could change our minds.'

'John, do you think I want you to go?' He heard the scrape of her chair on the flags as she pushed it back from the table. 'You can't hang around this place with nothing to do all your life, be a corner-boy. You're too good for that. Both of you are. Whatever chance you have, you won't have it here – and . . . ' she paused and looked away from him, 'it's probably just as well you're going.'

'Wha—'

She held up her hand. 'You don't have to tell me what's been going on this summer,' she said softly. 'I know about you and Rose O'Beirne Moffat.'

Tick tick.

'That's not for our likes, John.'

Tick tick tick.

Outside, the blackbird had found his voice. For something to do, John moved the few steps to the table and blew out the lamp, whitening the room. 'Mammy, I love her.'

'I know you do.' She came round the table and put her hands on his shoulders. 'But you know there's no future in it. You know that.' She raised her face to his and he saw she really did understand what he was going through.

96

Behind him, he heard the kettle begin to sing on the hob. 'The tea,' he said.

She walked to the window and as she pushed open the sash, the blackbird's song flooded the kitchen. 'It's going to be a fine day, thank God,' she said.

All the worn familiar objects in the room became unbearably precious to John: the ancient alarm clock, the battered tin tea-caddy with the faded picture of a Chinese garden, the oilcloth which covered the high mantelpiece, its edges serrated with a pinking shears. He concentrated on spooning the tea into the pot. 'I'll do my best over there, Mammy, to make you proud of me. We'll both do our best. I'll look after Derek.'

'All right.'

'And – and thanks for everything.' The words, said in a rush, weren't much but they were better than none.

'You're welcome, John. You're very welcome,' she said softly. He could no longer see what he was doing and some of the tea leaves spilled on the hob.

His mother's prediction about the weather had been right. That morning, the sun was blazing as Ned Sherling's wheezing car pulled in through the gates. Mary Flynn was not coming to Dublin with them. They were being driven to Carrickmacross in time to catch the twelve o'clock bus; this would have them in Dublin in plenty of time for the eight o'clock sailing to Liverpool. All three of them had deliberately left some tasks until the last minute, packages to be squeezed into suitcases, objects left under beds or in corners, so that when they heard the sound of the car, the departure could be busy.

As the car ticked over noisily in front of the open door and Ned stood uncomfortably over by the hedge, the three of them made fussy trips between the house and the car. When he could find no more to do, John went out into the kitchen where his mother was standing in the doorway to the yard. She turned to look at him as he emerged. 'I'll just say goodbye to Biddygoat,' he said, stalling for more time.

As soon as the goat saw him, she ran towards him as far as her tether would allow. He went to the vegetable patch, pulled a head of lettuce and a carrot and fed them to her. 'Good girl, Biddy, good girl . . . ' Struggling for control so he would not make a show of himself, he stayed with the goat, rubbing her head and pulling her ears until she had finished. Then he gave her one last pat and turned away as, looking for more, she butted him.

Back in the yard, he saw Derek was weeping like a young child, clinging to their mother. His own turn came and it was over in seconds. He hugged his mother's bony shoulders tightly and kissed her cheek. Then, somehow, he found the strength to speak clearly. 'Don't worry, Mammy. Please don't worry about us. We'll be good. We'll be a credit to you, I promise. I'll write often and I'll send you money. Maybe I'll make enough money so you can come out and visit us, maybe even as soon as next year. And we'll come home to see you as soon as possible.'

Mary nodded and attempted to smile. 'God bless you.'

John let her go and turned to his brother who was sobbing helplessly, his head against the metalwork of the car. He grabbed Derek's arm and manhandled him into the back of the vehicle. 'We'd better get a move on, Ned.' He let himself into the front passenger seat and nodded at Ned. The neighbour tipped his cap to their mother. She went inside immediately and it was over.

They were in plenty of time for the bus. As it meandered to Dublin, stopping on demand on the road, calling at every village and town *en route*, John made up his mind that he was going to be as positive as possible. He and Derek were on their way now and there was no going back. And he knew his mother was right about his own world and Rose's but not in the way she thought. Money was the key. His only real chance with Rose lay far away from Drumboola. He should take every advantage of the opportunity.

Just outside Ardee, he held his hand out to his brother. 'Truce?'

Derek looked at him over the curl of smoke which rose from the cigarette between his fingers. 'What truce?'

'You know what I mean.' John kept his hand extended. 'We're going to need each other, Derek.'

Derek looked away from him out through the window. Then, taking his time, he dropped the half-smoked cigarette on the floor of the bus and ground it under the heel of his new shoe. 'All right.'

They were quiet until the bus was labouring up the long straight hill out of Collon. 'Imagine, Derek,' said John then, 'a real white Christmas.' Their cousin had mentioned in one of his letters that they always had snow in winter. The snow they knew in Monaghan was a poor thin effort which within hours turned wet and slushy.

Derek, who was lighting another cigarette, grunted unintelligibly and then, honouring the truce, brightened. 'I wonder will they have sleighs?'

'I suppose so,' said John. 'Otherwise, how would they get around?'

'Horses?' suggested Derek. 'Of course, *you*'d be all right there, wouldn't you? Horses, yes. Just up your street.' It was the only barb of the journey and John let it pass. By the time the bus pulled in under the frilled stone canopy of the bus station in Dublin, he was feeling calm and even optimistic. They had been to the capital only twice before, both times to shop with their mother in Clery's, the big department store in the city centre, but they were armed with written instructions as to how to get from the bus station to the British and Irish Steampacket Company terminal at the North Wall.

It was early evening and office workers were streaming out of the Custom House, the girls in bright cotton dresses and strapped sandals, the men in shirtsleeves, jackets slung over their shoulders. With all his heart, John envied those workers. They were light-hearted and happy. Going home. Maybe going out for the evening. A good education, a steady job. Maybe a girlfriend or a boyfriend waiting somewhere. No problems with money or class – or an uncertain future.

To John, the pungent evening smell of the city was not unpleasant, warm fumes and tar, rubber, dung and dust and a unique sweetish smell from the river water which shone under the September sun like liquid crazy paving.

Derek pointed: 'That must be our boat there,' he said, indicating a high green vessel moored on their own side of the quays.

'Can you see the name of it?' John asked.

'The *Munster*.'

The B and I passenger terminal was little more than a

shed. Although there were more than ninety minutes to go before sailing, a line of taxicabs was discharging passengers at the entrance and inside quite a sizeable crowd already milled around. Seeing all the strange faces, John was seized with loneliness, so acute that he felt almost dizzy from it.

It was Derek who brought up the subject of Rose.

By half-past eight, they had sailed out past the Kish light-house. The evening was calm and, with other passengers, they stood in the stern, watching the wake stream backwards towards the coastline which was slipping away from them. Neither had ever been on or near the sea before and, despite his grief at leaving home, John was impressed at its darkening immensity as the sun dropped lower over the undulating line of violet mountains to the south of Dublin Bay.

Later, when they were seated in one of the dingy and crowded passenger lounges, each of them drinking orange and eating one of the ham sandwiches their mother had packed for them, they were distracted by the sight of a blonde girl of about their age or slightly older. Dressed in a brown tweed costume with straight skirt and buttoned, waisted jacket, she walked past them to order at the bar; from the back, her legs were good, with shapely calves and neat ankles. 'Not bad,' said Derek.

'No,' agreed John, who did not agree at all. 'Not bad.' John now compared all girls to Rose.

'Not a patch on Miss O'Beirne Moffat, though, is she?' Innocently, Derek took a bite from his sandwich and a slug from his bottle of orange.

'No, she's not.' John took a bite from his own sandwich.

'Do you love her or what?' asked Derek.

John was not fooled by the casual tone but decided to be honest. 'Yes, I do,' he said.

'Does she love you?'

'She says she does.'

'Did the two of you actually tell each other you loved each other?'

'Yes.'

The girl at the bar counter turned round and carried two bottles of orange back to her place beside another, older, girl who resembled her and was obviously her sister. The two boys followed her progress across the floor of the lounge. 'I wouldn't mind a bit of that,' said Derek when she had seated herself.

'Know what you mean,' replied John automatically.

'The two of you did it, didn't you?'

The question was more of a statement and John played for time. 'Why do you think that?'

'I don't think it, I know it.'

'How do you know? Have you been spying on us again?'

'Aha, so you *did* do it!'

'I didn't say that.' John was flustered and felt horribly disloyal to Rose.

'Nothing to do with me what you do,' said Derek. 'It's a free country.'

It was almost a relief to get it out in the open. 'All right.'

'What was it like?'

'I'm not discussing it.'

'Please yourself. I'm getting another bottle of orange. Want one?'

'We can't afford it.'

John collected his thoughts while Derek was at the bar. He loved Derek, he was sure he did, but even a saint would find it difficult to deal with Derek's sudden mood swings and switches. On the other hand, they would have only one another to rely on for the next few months and they would have to make the most of it. Which meant, of course, he thought grimly, that the success of their relationship was up to him.

Discussing Rose with him was another matter entirely. But if he could not talk to his twin brother about the most important thing in his life, who could he talk to? The boat was moving from side to side now and he was conscious that his stomach was lurching with it. He hoped he was not going to be sick.

Derek came back with the two bottles of orange and sat down again. 'I hope, by the way, you didn't make a baby . . . '

John, at first thunderstruck by the baldness of the words, recovered enough to stammer, 'You – you can't make a baby the first time.' It was something he had not considered and, from the scraps of rumour and innuendo which constituted his education in sexual matters, was confident that he was right. 'No,' he repeated more positively, 'you can't make a baby the first time.'

'Who told you that?'

'Everyone knows that.'

'Well, I hope everyone is right.'

John was really beginning to feel sick now, too sick to argue. 'I need to lie down,' he said.

The tiered bunks in the men's quarters were arranged dormitory style in three parallel rows and most of them were already occupied when he and Derek went below. They put down their suitcases in the doorway and took in the scene. There were several card games going on, and in a far corner two men and a boy who looked to be about thirteen were having a sing-song – or at least the men were singing and the boy was sitting wide-eyed and silent as empties rolled to and fro at his feet with the motion of the boat.

John's nostrils were struck by a heavy stench, which, after a second or two, he separated into its individual components of drink and stale sweat, the strong smell of Jeyes Fluid and something else, which he saw to his horror emanated from a pool of vomit flowing across the aisle in front of them from under the bed of a man spreadeagled on a bunk near the door. The man was snoring loudly and so relaxed that as the vessel rocked from side to side his head rocked with it. John's already distressed stomach heaved. Averting his head, he stepped across the pool, straining to lift his suitcase high above contamination.

They found two empty bunks about eight rows away from the snoring drunk and stowed the luggage under the bottom one into which John climbed. It was hard and unyielding and smelt strange. Pulling up its rough covering, he saw the reason for the smell: the bunk, which was made of wooden slats, was covered with rubber sheeting.

He put his carry-all behind his head and blocked out the light with an elbow flung over his eyes. Trying to ignore the smells, the singing, the snoring, the rough talk and laughter from the card players, he began to sort out his thoughts and impressions of the last twenty-four hours. Despite his stomach, uppermost was the beautiful, darling face of Rose. He thought about the amethysts, safely tucked into his new toilet bag. Should he tell Derek about them? What was the point? On the other hand, the stones might prove to be the escape for both of them if their new life on the island proved intolerable or pointless.

But suppose he did use them to come home? What then? He would come home as penniless and hopeless as he had left. What use would he be to Rose? His mother's words about himself and Rose rang in his head: *That's not for our likes* . . . Even he could see the futility of inviting Rose O'Beirne Moffat to join him in a life on the scrounge. Oh, Rose! he thought, his eyes filling under the tweed of the jacket sleeve.

Daphne O'Beirne Moffat pursed her lips. 'All right, miss, you'll stay here until you see sense.'

Rose did not acknowledge, not even by a twitch of a single muscle, that her mother had spoken. She was lying on her bed, her face buried in her pillow.

'Did you hear me, Rose?' Daphne's voice rose querulously, 'Rose! Answer me!' When this elicited no response she turned to her husband. 'You talk to her, Gus. You're her father.'

Gus, standing behind Daphne and jingling coins in the pocket of his trousers, wore a look of misery: he hated raised voices, rows, scenes of any sort. But there was no ignoring Daphne's command as she stepped back beside him and indicated with a sweep of her hand that the field of battle was now his. 'Rose?' he said tentatively, taking the few steps which brought him to the side of the bed. 'Rose?' Then, when Rose made no sign that she had heard him, 'Rose, listen, you have to eat, you have to come down some time. You've been here since morning and it's now . . . ' he checked his watch, 'ten o'clock at night. Aren't you hungry, Rose?'

'That's not the issue!' snapped Daphne from behind him. 'What we need to know is where she was last night – *all* night. I have a fairly good idea but I need to hear it from her own mouth!'

'I thought you said I was her father!' The ferocity of Gus's response as he rounded on his wife surprised Rose so much that she turned and raised herself on an elbow. She saw that Gus, his jaw half open, had astonished even himself. Then, before her mother could recover, he pressed home his advantage. 'It's all right, Daphne, I'll deal with the situation. I think it would be a good idea if you did leave it to me. I'll call you if I need you.'

Rose's mother made a small huffing sound but turned on her heel and stalked out of the bedroom. Gus waited until the door had clicked shut behind her then turned back to the bed. He touched Rose gently on the shoulder. 'Now, poppet, what's all this about? You can tell me.'

Rose was up in a flash and in his arms. 'Oh, Daddy! I can't tell you, I just can't, it's too terrible—'

'Why not, Rose?'

'Because you couldn't possibly understand.'

Gus cleared his throat. 'I – er – I might, actually. You might be surprised . . . ' Rose played with her handkerchief. 'This wouldn't have – I mean, this isn't anything to do with that chap from the gate lodge – you know, the one you were teaching to ride on Thumper?'

The look on Rose's face obviously revealed more than she had intended because the colour in her father's pink face heightened. 'I – I see,' he said. 'I knew the two of you were, er – friendly but I suppose I was too caught up in my own affairs to see what was going on. I'm sorry, Rose, but you know, the estate, the bank and everything . . . ' He shrugged his shoulders.

Rose pressed the handkerchief to her mouth. She did not want to be causing such trouble but if her father did not leave now, she was afraid she would say too much. 'I love him with all my heart, Daddy,' she said, her voice muffled. 'And now he's gone for ever . . . ' Fresh tears poured down her face.

'I—' Gus cleared his throat noisily, 'I suppose this is where you were last night? Visiting with him, I mean?'

Rose nodded almost imperceptibly. Gus seemed to be having great difficulty in clearing his throat a second time. 'Poppet, you don't have to answer this if you don't want to, of course, but I am your father and I – that is we – your mother and I, we do care for you and all that. You were just visiting with the chap, weren't you?' The appeal in his voice was unmistakable.

'Of course, Daddy. Of course we were just visiting. It was his last night. He came to the house last night after dark. We'd already said goodbye but not really goodbye if you know what I mean. Anyway, we went – we went for a long walk in the woods.'

'All night, Rose?'

'We couldn't bear to say goodbye to each other. We fell asleep for a little bit . . . '

Gus stood up and walked to the window. 'There's just one thing, Rose – but don't worry, I'm sure there's a perfectly innocent explanation. Your mother says that when she met you coming in through the kitchen early this morning your clothes were very crumpled – very crumpled indeed.'

'I told you that I lay down and fell asleep for a bit.'

'Yes, but she says that they were *very* crumpled. I don't know anything about these things, of course, but she says you were wearing a cotton blouse and it was really a mess. As though it had been wet or something . . . '

'Well, I can assure you – and you can assure her, Daddy, that it certainly was not wet!' Rose spoke with the exaggerated outrage of someone unjustly accused.

Gus turned around. 'Well, that's cleared that up, then. I can tell your mother. I'm sure she'll be relieved.'

'Daddy, she hates John Flynn.'

'How do you know that? Your mother's a good woman, Rose.' There was a note of warning in Gus's voice and Rose picked it up.

'Yes. Yes, I know that, Daddy. Of course, Mother is very good – and I really appreciate all she does for me – and I know she loves me – but, Daddy, be honest! Do you really think she'd approve of me being in love with the son of the gamekeeper? Poor John hasn't a penny—' Rose began to cry all over again.

'Rose, Canada is not the end of the world. He'll be back some time, and in time, you'll meet other nice boys—'

'Oh, Daddy, I knew that's what everyone would say. I *knew* no one would understand. There'll never be anyone like John, never never never!' She jumped off the bed. 'Excuse me, Daddy, I have to go to the bathroom.' Gus took a few steps forward as though to intercept her but she was too fast for him and had crossed the room and vanished through the door before he could reach her.

Gus stood looking for a moment at the door. Then, careful not to make a fuss by closing the door too loudly, he went out of the room.

'Hey, Mom! It's three o'clock in the afternoon. How come you're not at the bridge table yet?' In her cabin on the steamship *White Empress*, moored in Liverpool, Karen Lindstrom tested the springs of the bed in her cabin by bouncing on them. 'I love ships!' she roared happily, watching as the chintz curtains at the porthole fluttered in the draught she was creating. Karen, who was blonde like her father, had inherited her mother's robust physique and the bedsprings groaned.

'For goodness' sake, Karen,' her mother called through the open connecting door, 'calm down. You'll drive me crazy.' She came to the door holding a crystal bowl filled with flowers. 'We've ages to go before we cast off. Read a book or a magazine or something.'

'Can't,' replied Karen, jumping off the bed and doing an impatient jig in the middle of the cabin. 'Boring! Oh, I wish Dad was with us this time. The old *Empress* is his favourite ship.' She picked up two oranges from the fruit basket on the coffee table and began to juggle them.

Her mother sighed. 'Really, Karen! Act your age. The two of us are going to have to live together in close quarters for a whole five and a half days. Give us a chance?' Karen's mother was originally from Glasgow and the burr of her accent was still in evidence. She and her daughter were returning from a visit to the squads of relatives who still lived there.

Karen caught both oranges and flipped them back into the basket. 'Mom, for God's sake, we won't be living in each other's pockets. You'll find cronies as you always do and be at bridge all day every day and I'll be – well.' She grinned, changing tack: 'Would you prefer me to be all doom and gloom like you Celts?'

'Thanks a lot!' Her mother grinned back. 'Of course I don't want you to be gloomy. I'm glad you're happy – but just for the moment, d'you think you could let your joy be just a little less unconfined?'

'Sure, Mom.' Karen grabbed her ski-jacket and moved towards the door of the cabin. 'You get your wish – instant peace! I'm going for a walk, OK?'

'Be careful,' called her mother automatically but Karen was out of earshot before the last syllable was uttered. Once outside the cabin, she pulled on the jacket and set off on a tour of inspection although, since this was her fourth passage on the *White Empress*, she knew the vessel inside out. She was going to make the most of this one because it might well be her last vacation by ship. The pressures of her father's business no longer allowed him the luxury of six travel days tacked on to each end of a trip and he had dictated that next time they came to Europe they would fly.

Karen was genuinely sorry. She was embarking on her twelfth transatlantic crossing and adored the immediate sense of intimacy with strangers; each time they left port she had a sense of being set free in a playground of possibilities. Although the ships of the Canadian Atlantic Line carried large numbers of immigrants in tourist class and therefore a far less obviously glamorous passenger list than the Cunarders or their American and French sisters, first class was a different matter. In Karen's mind, the people in the suite next door could turn out to be American film stars or oil barons, society queens, English dukes, French or other European royalty, tragic widows or – and this was the nub – potential boyfriends. Seventeen and ferociously healthy, Karen viewed all men under the age of twenty-two as potential boyfriends.

Except those in Charlottetown, of course. Charlottetown, PEI, where her father owned the biggest and poshest department store on the island was, in Karen's view, poor territory for romance. None of the local boys measured up to what she required, or thought she required, in a lover.

The air which hit her cheeks as she emerged onto the promenade deck was cold and she pulled her jacket tighter around her. She had selected it from the men's department in her father's store.

Karen did not mind being so big; on the other hand, when she was being honest with herself, she had to concede that perhaps her size and personality could be working against her with the boys in Charlottetown. Most of the ones she knew seemed a little afraid of her. She did not care. Charlottetown was Nowheresville as far as she was concerned and she was impatient to be free of it. Although her loving but very protective parents did not know it yet, Karen, who was entering her last year of high school, had no intention whatsoever of staying there. In fact, she planned not to stay in Canada at all. Her grades were good and she wanted to go to college in some dazzling European capital like Paris, Rome or London – or if she could not gain entrance there, at least to some progressive institution in California or New England.

She left the promenade deck and climbed the wide stairs to the sports deck, which was the second highest on the ship and equipped with a full-sized tennis court. Although her jacket was quilted with down and the court sheltered behind a high bulkhead, she shivered in the keen Mersey wind as she climbed into the gallery seats on the port side. Liverpool pierhead is right in the heart of the commercial district and the Liver Building was dead ahead, but Karen, who had been here so often she could name all the landmarks on the skyline, did not bother to look out over the city but leaned over the rail which ran behind the seats to examine the teeming dockside forty feet below.

The *White Empress* was tied up, stem to stern, behind another, larger liner flying a German flag, and the two groups of passengers, augmented by well-wishers, porters and stevedores, were busily and noisily sorting themselves into queues and boarding parties on the quay, only thirty feet wide and lined with warehouses.

Karen hummed along to the thin, cymballed hymn being played in the midst of the chaos by a Salvation Army band; she could not think of anywhere in the world she would rather be than here as, through the smooth cool steel of the rails under her hands, she felt the quickening of the ship's generators. She craned her head backwards to gaze up and behind her: on her mast, the *White Empress* flew a blue pennant, indicating that she had received her sailing orders; a thin stream of smoke already poured from one of the funnels into the crowd of dingy-feathered gulls which wheeled in the windy sky.

Again she examined the people in the waiting lines. Although the first-class entrance was not doing much business, a queue of people snaked up the gangway at the front of the ship into the tourist section. Immediately, Karen's attention was taken by a couple with a small baby and a toddler.

A few feet away from the foot of the boarding ramp, the baby was being fractious. Fully occupied in calming it, the parents did not see that their toddler was facing the other way and had wandered a few dangerous steps towards the edge of the quay. Karen was about to call out a warning when, from farther back in the queue, a young man darted out, took the surprised toddler

108

by the hand and led it back to its parents. There was a short conversation between the young man and the couple and then the young man went back to his place, joining another.

In her eyrie, Karen sprang to attention. *Two* young men, seeming to be travelling alone and relatively presentable from what she could see. The only problem was that they were queueing for tourist class. Well, she thought, that wasn't insurmountable. Although the sergeant at arms prevented any traffic from tourist class into first, there was not much he could do if a first-class passenger wanted to go the other way and visit tourist. She watched the young men as, patiently, they waited their turn to board. They had not engaged porters, but were dragging their own luggage; she judged they might be about her own age or even a little older and, although they were wearing collars and ties, their clothes were dark and crumpled. Definitely not American or Canadian, she thought, more likely East Europeans.

Refugees, perhaps? Karen's romantic heart beat faster. Two cousins or brothers, orphaned early in a bitter war, now seeking a better life in the New World . . .

She surveyed the rest of the tourist queue. With the exception of two other families with older children, the passengers were mostly in pairs and she found little to interest her. She returned her attention to the two boys, watching them until they had boarded and vanished out of her line of sight.

John gasped when he saw the interior of what was to be their home for five nights and six days. They were travelling as cheaply as possible and had booked an inside cabin with no window or 'private facilities' but he saw it was far more comfortable than he had expected or imagined. His first seagoing experience on the Liverpool boat the night before had been so sordid and uncomfortable that his hopes had not been high. In contrast to third class on the B and I ship, this accommodation was palatial. Its pale green walls decorated with sepia pictures of sailing ships, the cabin boasted a mirrored dressing-table and a carpet on the floor; it had two built-in wardrobes and even its own little washbasin in a corner behind the door. But John's eye was drawn immediately to the real bedclothes and snowy pillows on the bunks, four of them. He wondered briefly who else would be travelling with them but was too tired to care.

He heard a low whistle of appreciation from Derek, who stood behind him. 'God,' said his twin, 'this is terrific!'

'I'm going to lie down.' John stowed his bags in one of the wardrobes and kicked off his shoes. As he was about to climb into one of the lower bunks, he noticed, tucked under a corner of the blankets, a small, folded card, its cover crudely printed, in pink and lime green, with drawings of straw hats and champagne glasses. There was also a welcoming note and a request that passports be brought along to the purser's office. He opened the printed card. It was an outline of facilities on board and included a timetable of activities for the following day. 'There's housie-housie,' he exclaimed, 'and whist and even a cinema – and a library!'

Derek picked up an identical card from the top bunk and opened it. 'And a dance,' he said in excitement. 'Jays, John, look, there's a swimming pool. We're allowed to use the swimming pool! And there's a bar . . . '

'We're not going to drink, we promised Mammy.'

'Speak for yourself.'

'Derek!'

'Well, I'm going for a walk, I'm starving.' Derek man-handled his suitcase into an upright position against the wall of the cabin. Unlike John, he had proved to be a good sailor and had even slept in his bunk the night before. Consequently, he was not nearly as tired as his twin. 'See you later,' he called as he pulled the door of the cabin shut behind him.

John crawled, rather than climbed, onto his bunk. He felt too tired even to lift the blankets but lay on top of them. Grate-fully, he fitted his head into the soft, clean pillow and noticed that the whole cabin shook and hummed from the action of machinery in the bowels of the ship. The vibrations were not unpleasant; on the contrary, he found them soporific and within seconds, the thumps and bangs as other passengers passed up and down the corridor and settled into their own quarters became remote and oddly reassuring as he drifted into velvety dreamless sleep.

Derek strolled along the deck, watching the last passengers boarding, enjoying the sense of bustle as the ship prepared for departure.

A large crowd of passengers, some in tears, waved and called over the rail to various groups of family and seers-off congregated on the quayside. Derek remembered the scalding tears when he left his mother the day before – was it only the day before? – and felt them start again behind his eyes. But he swallowed hard and blinked them away. As of today, Derek Flynn was no longer a blubbering boy.

The boarding ramps were still in place so there was obviously some time still to go before they were on their way. He had not exaggerated when he had said to John he was hungry; his stomach was actually growling and he decided to go in search of a snack bar. The travel agent in Carrick had explained to them that they would be able to change their Irish money on the ship. But where was the bank?

He looked up and down the deck and spotted a boy in uniform, his own age or certainly not much older, emerge from behind a small steel door. 'Excuse me?' Derek called.

The boy, whose cap perched on a head of very distinctive carroty curls, stopped and turned round. 'Yes, sir?' Then, seeing Derek's age, he relaxed visibly. 'What's up, mate?'

'I wonder, could you tell me where the ship's bank is? I want to change some money.' Derek kept his voice formal, as he imagined a passenger should when addressing a crew member.

'Money?' the boy responded, his face bland. 'We don't have an actual bank, sir. But as soon as we set sail, the purser's office will be open and you can change your money there.' He paused and his eyes crinkled. 'Irish money, is it, sir? I was born in Liverpool meself,' he went on, 'but me mam and dad are from Arklow, in County Wicklow. Spent a lot of holidays there. Me mam and dad still do with the little ones.'

'I see. What's your job?' Derek was genuinely curious.

'I'm an apprentice,' said the boy proudly. He looked around as though afraid he might be spotted. 'Shouldn't really be talking to passengers at all – but seeing as how you spoke first and you're a Paddy like myself . . . '

He smiled and Derek smiled back. 'Thanks. Purser's office, you say?'

'That's right. Should be open about half an hour after we sail.'

'Jays, I don't know whether I can last that long. I'm starving.'

'Here—' The boy reached into the pocket of his uniform. 'Have a bit of choccy,' he said, pulling out a squashed bar of Cadbury's Fruit and Nut and thrusting it into Derek's hand. Through the wrapper, Derek could feel it was melting. 'Thanks a million,' he said. 'I'll pay you back when I change my money.'

'No, that's all right. I'm eating too much choccy, anyway. Me name's Andy, by the way.'

'Derek Flynn.'

'Andy Farrell.' They shook hands.

'Better be off. See you around, right?' The young crewman walked away and Derek faced away from the cold wind, tore the paper off the chocolate and stuffed half of the bar into his mouth.

He leaned his elbows on the rail: the activity below seemed to be tapering off. When he finished the first half of the chocolate, he unwrapped the rest and was popping it into his mouth when he heard a female voice. 'Any for me?' He looked around but could see no one.

'Up here!' said the voice.

He looked up and between the two boats, saw the head and shoulders of a blonde girl hanging over a rail on the deck above his. 'Hi there,' she said, the wind blowing her hair about her face.

Derek, embarrassed at his greed being seen, called back a sheepish, 'Hello!'

'Looks like good candy,' said the girl, pushing some of the hair back from her face. 'You got any more?'

Derek shrugged and spread the palms of his hands to show they were empty. 'Sorry.'

'I saw you boarding, you and your friend,' called the girl.

'I see,' said Derek. 'You're travelling too, are you?' He could have kicked himself. Of course she was. She was on the boat, wasn't she?

But the girl did not appear to be put out. 'Where're you guys from?'

'Ireland,' Derek called back, 'and he's not a friend, by the way, he's my brother.'

'Your brother can be your friend too,' retorted the girl.

'Yeah, sure,' answered Derek daringly. 'Depends on the brother.'

112

'Like that, is it?' The girl grinned and, even at that distance, Derek could see she had two rows of perfect white teeth. 'Irish! Do you speak Gaelic?' She pronounced it 'gallic'.

'A bit,' admitted Derek, making a mental note to brush up on his meagre store of school Irish.

'Some of my mother's family speaks Gaelic, they're Scottish.'

Derek hesitated. 'Are you American yourself, or what?'

'Canadian. But half of me is Scottish on my mother's side as I told you. The other half is Swedish.'

'You sound a bit American to me.' Derek had never met a Canadian but each July and August, the Yanks, like summering birds, returned in waves to Drumboola and he recognised a transatlantic intonation when he heard it.

'I wouldn't say that too loudly if I were you,' the girl advised. 'Canadians *hate* being taken for Americans.'

'Sorry, I'll remember. So what part of Canada are you from?'

'Oh, a little place you never heard of,' she said dismissively. 'Charlottetown, Prince Edward Island, but don't—'

'I don't believe it!' cried Derek. 'That's where we're going. At least we're not actually going to Charlottetown but to Kelly's Cross — have you heard of that place?'

'Sure I have,' said the girl. 'What do you know! We'll be neighbours.'

'Is it near Charlottetown?'

'About forty minutes.'

'Well, isn't that amazing!' Derek was genuinely shocked at the coincidence.

'Yeah, amazing. But don't get too excited about PEI,' drawled the girl. 'Hey, you must be getting a crick in your neck. Why don't I come down there?'

'Sure.' Derek could not believe his luck.

'Stay right where you are.' The head was withdrawn and then appeared again. 'What's your name, by the way?'

'Derek. Derek Flynn.'

'OK, Derek, my name's Karen Lindstrom. Pleased to meet you!' The blonde head vanished a second time. Afraid it bore traces of chocolate, Derek wiped his mouth fiercely with the back of his hand. What was he going to say to her when she arrived?

A blonde girl. Good-looking, from what he had seen. He began to panic.

When she appeared beside him, shyness assaulted him. The girl was even better-looking than she had at first appeared. She was as tall as himself but her bigness was not only a matter of height; she had big teeth and a big mouth and big eyes and something else which caused him to swallow hard. Karen Lindstrom had very big breasts.

He forced himself to hold out his hand. 'Hello,' he said.

She seized it and her grasp was so strong he felt the bones of his fingers grinding together. 'Hi!' she said. 'Well, isn't this a coincidence? But I suppose when you think about it, it's not all that coincidental – we're on a Canadian boat going to Canada. It'd be more surprising if you told me you were going to Honolulu.' She dropped his hand and giggled, a surprising, fluting giggle, which did not seem to match her appearance.

Derek smiled back and willed himself not to flinch from her frank gaze. 'What's the weather like in Prince Edward Island?' As soon as the words were out of his mouth, he despised himself. Here I am, he thought, with a beautiful girl, and all I can talk about is the weather. To his relief she did not seem to share his view.

'Not bad,' she answered. 'It's a bit like Scotland – except it's a lot colder in the winter. Speaking of weather, are you a good sailor?'

'You mean, do I get sick? Don't know, really, since I've never crossed the Atlantic before. I was grand last night coming over from Ireland.'

'Well, it can be rough, but this time of the year is usually not too bad. Come on,' she added cheerfully, 'it's freezing standing here. Why don't we take a walk and I'll tell you all you need to know about PEI – which, by the way, could probably be written on the back of a postage stamp.' She led him in and out of doors and along various corridors until they reached an open deck which was crowded with passengers. The wind gusted at them and, despite himself, Derek shivered. Karen noticed. 'Hope you got something warmer than that jacket for the trip. It gets pretty cold out there on the north Atlantic.'

'I have a coat, all right.'

'Good. Where's your brother?'

'He's in our cabin, probably asleep. He didn't get much sleep last night.'

'What's his name, your brother?'

'John.'

'John and Derek. Not exactly Irish names, I would have thought. There's a bunch of Irish in Charlottetown but they all have names like Seán and Michael and Patrick . . . '

'Well, my mother has relatives in the north of Ireland – that's quite near where we live – and in Scotland too. A lot of people in our area have relatives in Scotland and we're named after two of our uncles over there.'

'Well, what do you know, another thing we have in common! What part of Scotland?'

'Haven't a clue. Somewhere up near the Highlands, I think.'

'I see!' She smiled at him and looked up at the sky. He stole a glance at her. She was leaning back slightly, a posture which lifted her magnificent breasts and caused the palms of his hands to tingle. What would he do next? What was he to say? He had never felt more conversationally inadequate in his life. She saved him. 'Come on,' she said, walking briskly ahead of him back the way they had come.

The crowd lining the rail numbered hundreds and when Karen found a space, he squeezed in beside her to see what was going on. Down below, two men were working on the ropes tethering the *White Empress* to the bollards. Desperately, Derek tried to think of something witty to say. He noticed that the gangway was being winched up. 'Looks like we'll be going soon,' he said but at that moment, the ship's siren blasted and he jumped in alarm.

Karen took his arm. 'It's OK, Derek, it's normal. Stand by – there'll be another one soon.' Sure enough, the siren sounded a second time. Squashed in beside her as he was, he hoped she could not feel or hear the thumping of his heart.

'Are your mother and father travelling with you?' he asked.

'Only my mother,' she answered. 'My dad couldn't come this time. Business.'

'What kind of business?' He found if he didn't look at her he could talk better. The bow-rope was now free of the bollard and was being held by three men as the engines roared.

'We've a store in Charlottetown,' Karen answered.

Through the wood of the deck timbers under his feet, Derek could feel the ship straining against her tethers. 'Is it a big one? What do you sell?'

'A department store. Everything.' She too was watching the activity on the quay. The *White Empress*'s siren blew another blast. 'Oh, I love this. I just love it!' Karen threw back her head and laughed. Her hair blew against Derek's face and into his mouth; the taste of it reminded him of bread. 'Sorry.' She laughed again and retrieved the strands, tucking them inside the collar of her jacket and zipping it tight around her throat. The wellwishers ashore began to wave as, slowly, inch by inch, the gap between the bow of the ship and the quay wall widened. Derek leaned over the rail as the screws began to bite, watching the detritus, paper, wrappers, small slivers of wood and plastic bobbing about in the filthy rainbow-slicked water. Now there was no going back and for a split second he was distracted from the overwhelming presence of Karen Lindstrom.

But when he looked again at Karen's lovely face, Derek realised that although there was no going back, the good part was that, in going forward, anything was possible. He just had to handle it correctly.

They stayed at the rail as the liner pulled slowly out into the Mersey and steamed past the cranes and wharves, the lines of cargo ships on North Gladstone Dock. Liverpool glided past them and then, as they headed out into the mouth of the river, coagulated behind them into a grey, smoky haze. Derek, in his inadequate sports jacket, was shivering hard but he tried desperately to control it. Eventually, she took pity on him. 'Come on,' she said.

They walked back the way they had come until eventually they came to the deck where they had met, and stopped in front of the door through which Karen had first emerged. Derek saw it was marked *First Class Passengers Only Beyond This Point*. 'Well, this is as far as I go,' he said awkwardly.

'For the moment,' she said mysteriously. 'But I really have to go now, Mom will think I've fallen overboard.'

116

'Sure.' He wanted desperately to ask her when he would see her again.

'OK,' she said, 'see you around.'

'I hope so,' he said fervently.

'Count on it,' she said, 'now I know where to find you.' She opened the door and stepped across the sill. Holding the door ajar she cocked her head to one side. 'You're cute,' she said and pulled the door shut, timing its closing click to serve as punctuation.

John was panicking in a dense fog. He could not see where he was going. Adding to his fright was the noise; the battering and hammering on his ears and in his head. He opened his eyes. He had no idea where he was. The noise was louder and everything was moving. Then he recognised his brother: Derek was shaking him by the shoulder. 'Come on, John, wake up, wake *up*! It's time for dinner.'

He struggled up on one elbow. 'Where's Mam?' He looked around in alarm. 'Where's thi—' Then he remembered. They were on a ship, bound for Canada. Despair settled loosely around him like a wet grey shawl. 'Leave me alone, Derek,' he said, 'I'm going back to sleep.'

'You'll be sorry if you miss dinner.' Derek continued to shake him. 'This is a fabulous ship, it's really great, John, come on. You have to have your dinner. You can have *steak* if you like. *Steak*.'

The thought of meat of any kind caused John's stomach to flip over. 'Don't mention the word steak. I couldn't manage an egg. Please, Derek, leave me alone.'

'There's eggs too, if you want. You can have practically anything. *Anything!*'

John groaned. He knew he could not stay in bed for the entire voyage and that probably he should attempt to eat something. 'Where's the others?' he asked, pulling himself slowly upright.

'What others?'

'The others that are supposed to be in the other two beds in this cabin.'

'I dunno,' said Derek. 'Maybe they didn't show up, or maybe the ship isn't full.'

117

John felt as though he had been hit on the head. He had no energy at all. 'My clothes are in an awful state,' he said, looking down at his crumpled trousers.

'Well, change them, then.' Derek was in an agony of impatience.

The dining room was panelled in wood and shone with highly polished brass. John's queasy stomach prompted him to notice that the tables, most of which were taken, were fitted with raised lips so that spillages would not leak on to the carpeted floor. He and Derek hesitated at the door and were taken in hand by a steward who showed them to two vacant seats at a corner table.

The meal passed somehow. The adults at their table made efforts to include them in the general conversation but they were so ill at ease that the talk sputtered and died and most of the time they ate in silence. John noticed that Derek was going through the menu, polishing off everything on his plate, steak, chips, mushrooms, tomatoes, all followed by a liberal slice of chocolate cake.

After the meal, they walked along a corridor and then pushed open a heavy steel door, finding themselves out on an open deck, fresh with streams of wind which flowed through a series of rectangular openings. John went over to one of these openings and put his head through, allowing the breeze to cool his cheeks. 'I think I'm a bad sailor,' he said to Derek. 'I'm probably going to be sick.'

'Not now!' Derek was horrified.

'No, I don't think so. But I think if the weather gets bad, I've had it.'

'Well, it won't be too bad. I met a girl and she told me that this time of the year it'll probably be all right.'

'What girl?'

'A girl called Karen Lindstrom. And guess what? She's from Prince Edward Island, where we're going.'

'Really? How did you meet her?'

'You weren't too newsy about Rose O'Beirne Moffat,' Derek retorted.

'Forget it.' John leaned out to look at the water, which creamed away from the side of the ship with a continuous swish, slopping and slapping against the incoming whitecaps. It had been an overcast day but within the past hour or so, the clouds had begun to break up. They puffed along the sky on an opposite course to their own, grey on top, underbellies touched with gold and pink as the sun began to sink.

'Sorry.' Derek's apology was uncharacteristic.

'It's all right. So tell us—'

'I think she likes me, John, really likes me. She's blonde and very big. I mean really big. Fantastic!' With both hands, Derek drew a balloon on the air in front of his chest.

'I see.' John smiled. 'Anything else about her of any interest?'

His twin grinned back. 'Isn't that enough? Actually, she's very nice. I didn't have to do anything, John, she made all the running.'

'Good for you.' John held his face up to the wind. He was beginning to feel better. 'Was she in at the dinner?'

'Well, that could be a bit of a problem.' Derek knitted his eyebrows. 'She's in first class, you see, travelling with her mother.'

'She won't want anything to do with the likes of us.' The moment he said them, John regretted the words. *That's not for our likes, John.* He forestalled Derek's outrage by putting a hand on his arm. 'Sorry, Derek. I really didn't mean that. I'm sure she's lovely and everything will turn out grand.' Derek wrenched his arm away.

'Did you make arrangements to meet?' John ignored the sulking and looked away towards the horizon. He had been told that this is what you were supposed to do when you felt seasick. Concentrate on the farthest physical point.

The *White Empress* boasted stabilisers but when Derek woke, some time in the middle of the night, he found himself pitching in his bunk. Drowsy and comfortable, he became aware that in the corner of the cabin John was vomiting repeatedly. 'You all right?' he called when the retching stopped.

'I'm fine.' The reply was weak and gasping. 'Go back to sleep, I'm better now.'

Derek turned over and snuggled into the sheets. In this windowless, comfortable cocoon, his bed swinging like an uneven

119

hammock, Ireland now seemed as far away as if it were on another planet. He drifted off again and was asleep within seconds.

Conditions had not improved when the steward tapped on the door to call them for breakfast. John, still sick, refused the man's offer of a cup of tea and Derek went alone to breakfast where he scoffed apple juice, which he had never tasted before, bacon, eggs and pancakes with maple syrup, another first. As he mopped up the syrup with the last of his pancake he felt alive and free – and giddy with anticipation. He would meet Karen Lindstrom again today, he was sure of it.

Having changed his money, he found his way to the promenade deck, paid seventy-five cents to the deck steward and was given a deck chair and a plaid rug. He dragged the chair to a part of the deck which was sheltered a little from the wind by the *White Empress*'s superstructure, wrapped himself in the rug and settled down to enjoy the view. Watching out for Karen, adrenalin pumping, he had rarely felt so well. After his last bout of sickness at the beginning of the summer, the doctor had assured him that if he were sensible, his health could be as good for the rest of his life as anyone else's. Well, he thought, it looked as though the doctor could be right.

He looked up and down the deck. A few hardy souls were taking constitutionals, moving carefully along the rails but, except for them, the *Empress* might have been as exclusive to Derek as his own private yacht. The rain was spitting on the wind and he wrapped himself tighter in his rug, putting some of it over his head so it shawled him like a tinker. He felt warm and snug and privileged and lost himself in a fantasy where he and Karen Lindstrom were making love.

'Hi!'

'Hello.' He leaped to his feet, forgetting to unshawl the rug.

'You'd make a great old lady!' Karen laughed heartily and, covered in confusion, Derek whipped the rug from off his head. 'Sit down, sit down, old lady.' She put a hand on his arm and again he noticed how strong she was. 'I'll sit beside you.'

She plopped onto the floor of the deck and, like a magnet, his eyes swivelled to the action of her breasts as they bounced. 'Are – are you sure you don't want the chair?' he stammered.

'Nope. I'm fine here. Lots of green faces around this morn-

120

ing up there.' She jerked a contemptuous thumb over her head. 'How about you? You don't find this weather a bit sick-making?'

'Uh-huh! My brother's not taking it too well, though.'

'Poor kid.'

For the next ten minutes or so, while Derek laughed in appreciation, Karen amused herself by giving nicknames to the few people who were about. 'The Honeymooners,' she hissed as a middle-aged couple marched past them, man in front, woman two paces behind.

'I don't get that one,' said Derek, looking after the pair.

'The Honeymooners, you know, Jackie Gleason.'

'Who's he?'

'Don't you have television in Ireland?'

'No. Well, there is, from the north,' he corrected himself, 'but we've no television station ourselves. And, anyway, very few people have it. Only the rich.'

Karen reached up and put a hand on his arm. 'Don't feel bad. I wouldn't know about Jackie Gleason 'cept I've been on vacation in New England. PEI has no television either. I warn you, I don't know what you're expecting but the island has nothing. A lot of lobsters. A few foxes, a lot of fish, a lot of churches. A lot of potatoes. I hope you like potatoes?'

'So do I. I'll be seeing a lot of them on the farm.'

'Poor you,' said Karen with sympathy. 'So what are we going to do today, Derek Flynn?'

'What do you want to do?' An unfamiliar, bubbly feeling rose in Derek.

'I dunno.'

'I've got an idea,' he said. 'I have a friend in the crew.' Calling Andy Farrell a friend was, he knew, stretching it, but he could work on that later. 'I could get him to show us around.'

'I *know* my way around—'

'But this would be going where you've never been before.' Karen looked doubtful and he pressed on. 'I mean into the engine room, up to the bridge, all that kind of thing.'

'OK,' she said. 'In the meantime, want to visit first class?'

He gasped. 'How can I? There's all the notices. I'm not allowed.'

'Trust me, Derek. We go visit first class.' She performed

an atrocious version of an English public-school accent. 'I feel like a spot of golf!'

Derek giggled. He was beginning to relax and decided that this was the best time he had ever had in his life. 'You mean there's a golf course up there?'

'Yep. And . . . ' added Karen mysteriously, 'you won't have to worry about clubs.' She looked him critically up and down. 'What have you got on under that coat?'

He pulled back the lapel of his tweed coat. 'A jacket and shirt.'

'Mm,' she said. 'No offence, Derek, but we gotta get you something that says "first class"!' She jumped up. 'Wait here.'

He looked after her as, sure-footedly, she negotiated the swaying deck and vanished through a door. Should he go and check on his brother? He shrugged away the thought. John could take care of himself.

Karen was back within five minutes, a navy blazer over her arm. She held it out to him. 'Here, try this on. I bought it in Glasgow for my dad, but it should fit you.'

He took off his coat and jacket and slipped his arms into the sleeves of the blazer. It felt light but warm and, unlike any jacket he had ever worn before, did not constrict the back of his neck. 'It's lovely,' he said. 'What material is it?'

'Cashmere,' she said lightly. 'Turn around, let me see the back.' Obediently, he turned his back to her. 'Stand up straight,' she ordered, 'straighten your shoulders. It's not hanging properly.'

He was mortified, then angry. 'I can't!' He turned round to face her. 'I can't straighten my shoulders. I'm a cripple.' He knew by her reaction that he had spoken more aggressively than the situation warranted. 'I'm sorry, Karen,' he said immediately. 'I'm sorry. Of course I'm not a cripple. But I've had a lung removed and that's why one shoulder is lower than the other.'

'Oh, Derek, you poor thing!' Before he knew it, she had thrown her arms around his neck and was hugging him.

Slowly, he raised his arms and hugged her back. She was warm and scented and hugging her was like putting his arms around a large firm mattress with a pillow at his chest. He loved it. He wanted urgently to bury his head between those breasts. 'Karen?' he whispered, but she dropped her arms and he could

122

not fathom the expression in her eyes as she put her finger on his lips.

Only inches apart, they faced one another, rocking on their feet with the motion of the boat, which seemed to have changed a little, slowing down. 'We must be coming up to Greenock,' said Derek. His pulse was hammering and he was finding it difficult to breathe normally.

'We must be.' She was leaning forward slightly. If he lowered his face just a little, he thought, it would come to rest on those breasts. 'Shall we?' she whispered, just audibly over the engines and the wind.

Derek almost suffocated. 'Why not?' he managed.

Instead of moving she leaned forward another two inches. Her jacket was open and its edges touched his chest. Involuntarily, he leaned towards her, grabbed her shoulders and would have kissed her, but she extricated herself, moving like an eel. 'Derek Flynn, control yourself!'

Maddened, he tried to grab her again but she stepped back another few paces. 'Patience, patience!' she admonished, wagging a finger at him. 'We've plenty of time – and it looks like we have the entire *Empress* to ourselves.' She smiled and walked away from him towards the door. 'You coming?'

He picked up his coat and jacket and followed her. Just before they came to the first-class door she turned. 'Now, the thing to do is to look as though you've been here all your life. Walk as if you know *exactly* where you're going. If we meet a steward or crew member, say "Good morning" and pass on without stopping. You gotta look confident.'

Derek felt far from confident. 'What'll happen if I'm caught?'

'Oh, the brig,' said Karen carelessly.

'The what?'

'The brig – the gaol.'

'You're joking!'

'I am, I am! Derek Flynn, where's your sense of humour? Or your sense of adventure? Think *positive*. You might be a millionaire some day. Might as well get used to what's in store for you.' She closed one china-blue eye in a huge wink.

'All right, so.'

'Atta boy. Now, are you ready?'

He nodded and followed her through the door, trying to look as though this were his proper domain.

As soon as the door closed behind him, he saw that first class was wider, softer and more plush by a mile than tourist. And he need not have worried. There were very few people about and no one paid them any attention. 'Where are we going?' he whispered to Karen as they mounted yet another wide, carpeted staircase.

'I told you, to play golf.'

'But this is a cabin,' he said in surprise when at last she stopped in front of a numbered door. 'Suite,' she corrected, opening it. 'Mom's room is next door.'

He shrank back. 'Your mother.'

'The real golf course is up on top, too windy for today. And relax, Derek, Mom's playing bridge. She's a fanatic. She won't be seen until lunchtime.' She pulled him into the cabin by the arm. 'Sit down,' she said once they were inside. 'Care for a drink?' She removed her jacket and threw it on the bed. Underneath, he saw she was wearing a straight skirt, open cardigan and blouse.

'What kind of drink?' He sat in a little cushioned armchair, one of a pair on each side of the table in the middle of the floor, and looked round the cabin, about six times the size of the one he shared with John. There was a wide basket full of fruit on the table and an ornate dressing-table against one wall. The bed, not a bunk but a real bed with brass head and foot, was covered with a flowered counterpane which matched the curtains at the two portholes. Through an open door, he saw another bedroom, even larger, decorated with different colours. Between them was a bathroom. 'What kind of drink would you like?' repeated Karen, crossing to the connecting door. 'The refrigerator is in Mom's room. She drinks martinis. Do you drink?'

'Sure,' he lied. 'Not martinis, though.'

'So what, then?' asked Karen, waiting. 'A beer?'

'Sure.' He hoped he would not gag.

Before Karen went into the other room, she crossed to the door and shot home the small brass bolt. 'There! Now we'll be nice and cosy.' Derek's heart jumped. He watched her through the open door as she bent low to open the small fridge. The action exposed some of her stockinged thighs, as sturdy as young trees, and stretched the fabric of her straight skirt across the twin rounds of her buttocks. His fingers itched to grab them.

She straightened and closed the fridge door with her foot, then she crossed out of his sight for a moment and he heard another bolt. She stood then for a second in the connecting door. 'All secure!'

Derek started to shake. To cover his confusion, he jumped up and crossed to one of the portholes. 'Do you think the weather will improve?'

'Who cares? Here's your beer. Do you mind drinking it by the neck? It's a bit rough for glasses.'

He shook his head and crossed back to her, taking the beer with a hand he could barely control.

'*Skal!*' She inclined her head and raised the beer bottle in salute.

'What?'

'*Skal* . . . it's what Swedish people say when they raise their drinks in a toast.'

'Oh. *Sláinte.*' He raised his own beer. 'That's what the Irish say.'

'So do the Scots.'

'There you are.'

'I beg your pardon?'

'I said, there you are.' He could not explain the phrase, it was just something everyone said all the time in Drumboola, so he raised the bottle to his lips, trickling a little beer into his mouth. It tasted bitter but he forced himself to swallow it. All the time, he watched Karen covertly. She had no such problem apparently, throwing back her head and taking a long swig.

'Sit down, Derek,' she invited.

He sat again in the chair he had recently vacated and she sat opposite him. He felt he was following instructions as a participant in a new and very exciting game. His hand was shaking as he put the beer on the table in front of him. The action of the ship immediately overturned it.

'Tsk tsk! Naughty boy!' But Karen did not seem over-perturbed about the accident. 'Let's get it cleaned up.'

She finished her own beer – in one long swallow – got up

from her chair and went into the bathroom, emerging again with a large towel. She mopped up the spillage from both the table and the floor around it and pitched the towel into a corner. Then, her hand moving as slowly and deliberately as a snake, she reached into the fruit basket and took out a small tangerine. Delicately, she held it between finger and thumb. 'A little golf, perhaps?'

He held his tongue. He felt like one of the rabbits he and John used to freeze into immobility in the glare of a strong torch before shooting them.

Never for a second taking her eyes off him, Karen slid the fruit basket to one side so that the polished surface of the table between them was clear. 'You take this.' She handed him the tangerine and leaned forward, positioning her body in the chair so that the pillow of her breasts rested on the table in front of her. She opened two buttons of her blouse, just where the material was stretched tightest and as the gap opened, Derek was afforded the sight of bulging, creamy flesh and a deep cleft. He stared, mesmerised, so concentrated that he could see the breasts moving within themselves as the table swayed with the ship.

Karen smiled. She inserted her two index fingers into the cleft and pulled the flesh a little apart. 'Now,' she said, 'here's the hole . . . '

CHAPTER FIVE

It was quiet and unusually tense on the bridge. The *White Empress* had been due to pass Belle Isle more than an hour ago and was now nearly three hours behind schedule. From Belle Isle to Father Point, where they were to take a pilot on board for the final leg of the journey up the St Lawrence, was normally a two-and-a-half-hour run; at this pace it would take seven and the captain was resigned to the fact that they would not dock until mid-afternoon tomorrow at the very earliest.

This voyage had been dogged by bad luck; on the first morning out, the puffer from Greenock, coming to meet them with the transatlantic mail, was lifted by a large swell and thrown against the *Empress*'s hull. There had been no structural damage at all to the liner – only the green line of boot-topping along her side showed there had been any incident at all – but for the next three and a half days, when they had been tossed about by a force eight, the collision had seemed like an omen.

Now here they were, visibility down to about twenty yards, the sea as flat as a disc. The fog which had been forecast by the meteorological service had rolled in right on cue and the captain, under strict orders always to put safety before speed, had slowed his vessel to a crawl of four knots, the equivalent of a doggy paddle. The engines were on standby, two extra lookouts had been posted aloft and the watertight doors between all the bulkheads were closed.

The liner blasted her horn, a long lonely note which reached out and went nowhere in the mist. In the ensuing silence, Andy Farrell strained his ears, listening hard alongside the rest of the crew. Being so junior, Andy would not normally be on watch in such illustrious company but under these conditions everyone lent a hand.

No one on the bridge fully trusted the new-fangled radar

and what they were listening for was an answering horn. Collisions were rare enough, but more common than most of the passengers, snug in their cabins or well-lit public rooms, might have imagined. Most seamen could recite the roll-call of vessels which had foundered in these dangerous waters. Apart from the *Titanic*, there were the *Atlantic*, the *Elbe*, the *La Bourgogne*, the White Star Line's *Republic*; even the great *Queen Mary* had run down one of her escorting cruisers when she was acting as a troop carrier during the war. And that had been in good weather, not in conditions anything like this where another vessel could be fifty yards away with them knowing it.

Listen as he might, Andy could hear nothing untoward. Even the wind which usually rattled and caterwauled in the wires and masts above the superstructure was hushed to a continuous soughing as the *Empress* glided serenely along the silent sea. He visualised her floating not on the water but above it like a wraith.

He glanced at the clock again. It would be night soon, making things worse.

In Derek Flynn's opinion, the fog was a blessing. There had been an announcement over the public address system that they would be delayed in docking, which meant that he would have more time with Karen.

Derek had been searching for Andy Farrell for an hour. Tonight was his last chance to fulfil his pledge to Karen to bring her up on the bridge. He had hoped she might forget his rash promise – which he now bitterly regretted – but for some reason she had brought it up several times and in such a way that it was now a matter of honour that he should deliver what he said he could deliver. He had seen Andy only once since their first meeting, a fleeting glimpse of the boy's red head disappearing round a corner of a corridor ahead of him and Derek had been too far away to attract his attention.

From one of the crew, he had ascertained that Andy was on the bridge and would be coming off watch shortly. So, his back turned to the water and his collar up against the cold thick fog, he hung around where he had been told he could probably intercept the young seaman. He was due to meet Karen after dinner, and his sitting was just half an hour away.

128

John had been seasick for the three days it took for the storm to blow itself out but then he had got out of bed, pounds lighter and ravenously hungry. For the first few hours, Derek had not minded having John around. In his novel condition of permanent euphoria, he had been considerate and even gay, showing off the attractions of the ship. He even promised that 'this girl, I've met, Karen', would be able to get John, too, into first class. But Derek's magnanimity had dimmed somewhat when he introduced his brother to Karen and suspected that perhaps loyalty and fidelity were not Karen's most prominent virtues.

They had met outside the cinema and it was not what she said but what she did: 'Well, hi, John,' tossing her hair back with one hand, an action which, thought Derek, could not but help draw John's attention to her spectacular bosom; whether the gesture was deliberate or not he could not tell. He had watched as Karen took John's hand and pumped it innocently enough but, to Derek's jealous eyes, the handshake had seemed unnecessarily long.

He was becoming seriously worried that he had missed Andy when, to his relief, he spotted the red head coming towards him. 'Andy. Andy!' he called.

The apprentice stopped in astonishment. 'Yes? Oh – it's you, mate.'

'Listen, Andy,' Derek hesitated, 'I've a favour to ask of you. I've met this girl, you see, and she'd really like to see over the ship and I sort of promised, well, I didn't actually promise, but I said I knew someone from the crew—' He stopped, fumbling the words. He was making a mess of this. He took a deep breath. 'So you see, it would be a great favour really, if you could let us see – I mean bring us on a sort of tour.'

'You mean the parts of the ship that passengers don't normally see?'

'Yeah, something like that. The bridge?' ventured Derek.

'Absolutely out of the question,' said Andy. 'I might be able to get you into some of the machinery areas, workshops, you know – but I'll have to ask permission.'

'Thanks. I really appreciate it.' They made arrangements to meet after dinner.

*

John, who had taken seconds of every course, folded his napkin. 'I suppose you're seeing Karen?'

'Yeah.'

John hesitated. 'Derek? Look, maybe it's none of my business but will you be all right?'

'What do you mean?'

'I mean after the trip. I don't want you to be hurt.'

'That's my business.'

'Yes, I know it is, but I'd hate to think—'

'You just look after your own love life, all right?' He pushed back his chair and walked away from the table.

John followed. 'Derek, I'm sorry. I said it was none of my business.'

But Derek barged ahead, ignoring him. Outside, on deck, he continued to walk ahead of his brother, both sets of footsteps echoing on the long lines of smooth wooden planking.

Derek resented mightily how John always probed to the core of his own fears. Of course she would drop him when she got back to her own rich friends. After tomorrow he would have no status in Karen Lindstrom's eyes; even the greatest optimist in the world, he thought, would see no future in a relationship between a rich society girl and a hick Mick potato picker from the sticks. And, of course, his know-all brother was the one who had to *say* it, making it worse . . .

John caught up with him as they went through a door and up the stairs towards the cinema where he was meeting Karen. The evening sounds – a distant laugh, the muffled thump of a door closing below – were pointed by the stillness outside and the unusual smoothness of the ship's passage.

He was not beaten yet, Derek thought grimly. He had one more night and, thanks to the fog, maybe even a bit longer. Now that he had found her, he could not contemplate losing Karen, that big curvy body and all that wonderful, overflowing flesh. She could – and did – drive him into a sexual frenzy within thirty seconds and, whether he was in love or not, he was besotted with the experience. Karen's sexual generosity and sensuality had been a revelation. Although they had not gone the whole way, Derek had learned more about women in the three and a half days he had known Karen than he had ever believed possible. Just the

130

thought of her and what they had done gave him pins and needles.

He shivered. The clammy fingers of the fog had penetrated even the deserted corridors and enclosed decks, empty because most people were warm in their cabins, preparing for the final parties. 'You'll have the pictures to yourself,' he called over his shoulder to John as they approached the cinema, which was tucked away on a corner of E deck. The thaw in his attitude was partially to ensure that John would go inside and not hang around.

The entrance to the cinema was gilded and pillared. On each side sat a grinning plaster figure with a naked bulging belly which Karen had assured him were Eastern gods. 'Here's Karen,' said John, looking over Derek's shoulder.

'Hi.' She bounced up to them. 'Isn't this fog something? And isn't everything so *quiet*?'

Derek's treacherous pulse began to beat as he saw that under her jacket she had cinched a red dress at the waist with a waspie, dividing her body into a pair of luscious hemispheres. 'Hi!' he said. 'John here is just going into the pictures. You smell nice.'

'Thanks,' she said carelessly.

Then, coming towards them, Derek spied Andy's red head. 'Oh, here's Andy Farrell.'

'Who?' Both Karen and John spun round.

'Andy Farrell, the friend of mine in the crew I told you about. This is Karen Lindstrom,' he said, when Andy reached them, 'and this is my brother, John.'

Andy held his hand out first to the girl, just as the *White Empress*'s horn blew, temporarily cutting off conversation. He waited until the reverberations died down. 'I haven't been able to see anyone yet to ask permission to show you around. Is it the three of you?' He looked doubtfully at John.

John looked from him to his brother and then back again. 'No, it's all right,' he said. 'You can count me out.'

'Tell me again what you're interested in seeing.' Derek was grateful to see the young crewman was playing along with his desire to impress Karen. 'Anything, anything at all,' he said enthusiastically, 'we're not fussy, are we, Karen?'

Andy hesitated. 'I'll see if I can get you into the engine room or one of the workshops, all right? I'll go below and see.'

131

'That'd be great.' Derek took Karen's hand.

'Well, I'm going inside,' said John. 'See you later. Enjoy the tour,' he said to Derek and Karen. 'Nice meeting you, Andy.' He passed between the gods into the cinema.

'Right,' said Andy, 'hang on here a minute.'

Ten miles away to the north, the new cook on the coaster *Dorothy Lamont* was boiling up coffee for the crew. He sat on a tiny stool in the low galley, watching as the liquid foamed and bubbled in the blackened coffee-pot – this captain liked his coffee strong enough to strip paint.

The *Dorothy Lamont*, bound for Halifax from Goose Bay via St John's, was old and creaky but sturdy enough. Their freshwater tank had become contaminated with sea water and, to take on fresh supplies, they had put into Battle Harbour where they had been caught by the fog. The captain, to whom time was money and who knew these waters like the back of his hand, had decided to put to sea anyway and they were now steaming along slowly in open water.

The vessel carried a cargo of lumber and smoked fish, and the cook, who had been with her for only two days, already detested the stink, which permeated every nook and cranny and was impossible to escape. Eventually satisfied with the readiness of the coffee, he poured some of it, thick and viscous, into two tin mugs, their insides stained as black as the beverage itself. Carrying the mugs carefully, he mounted the steps to the open deck, ducking through the half-sized door so he would not hit his head.

The captain and first mate were in the wheelhouse. 'Filthy tonight, eh?' said the first mate, accepting his mug. He took a sip and, at the same time, pulled a cord which hung over his head from the ceiling of the wheelhouse, causing the *Dorothy Lamont* to emit a sound half-way between a horn and a whistle but sounding more like a duck's quack. 'Sump'n jammed up that tube,' he said, showing no sign that he intended to do anything about it. 'Prob'ly a bird.'

'Get the boy to see to it,' replied the captain.

'OK if I finish this?' The first mate held up his mug.

'Sure.' The captain took his own coffee. Strictly speaking he should have been served first, but the first mate was nearer the door of the wheelhouse and the cook had already learned that the crew of the *Dorothy Lamont* rarely stood on ceremony. 'It's not ships I'm worried about anyway,' the captain went on, 'we'll hear them before they hear us, I reckon. It's not ships, it's bergs. Saw the first growler not two days ago.'

'Want me to do something about the horn, skipper?' asked the cook, having handed over the coffee. Being new, he was anxious to appear helpful in all matters, even those which did not concern him.

'Nope,' said the captain. 'But keep your eyes peeled. That goes for everyone on board.'

The cook left the wheelhouse and instead of going back down to the steamy galley, went for'ard for a breather. But it was cold and damp at the bow and the fog so muffled the sound of the diesels that the cook fancied he might have been on an aeroplane drifting through the clouds.

Andy was in a dreadful quandary. He knew he was risking disciplinary action and probably his job if he was caught sneaking passengers into the operational areas. On the other hand, he had not found a friendly face to ask; the only person he had encountered so far on his reconnaissance mission had been the assistant chief, a surly individual who spoke little enough to anyone and not at all to juniors, unless it was to give orders. What on earth had possessed him to agree to this?

He had just left the main engine control room and had passed into the stifling air of the room which housed the *White Empress*'s eight oil-fed boilers. Andy always felt claustrophobic in here; there was barely a spare inch of unused space on the grey steel walls all around him and the passageways were wide enough for only one man. He loitered just inside the entrance, watching the white sheets of flame dancing behind the hardened glass window of the nearest burner while he tried to make up his mind what to do next.

Reluctantly, he decided he would just have to face it – he must go back and tell Derek Flynn and the girl that he had been refused permission. It was that simple. His loyalty was to his ship – and what were these people to him, after all? He would probably never see them again after tomorrow. He sighed; it was just that it was not in his nature to promise something and then not deliver.

On leaden feet, he climbed one of the escapes which led into the corridor where he had left the couple. As he opened the door, he saw that Derek Flynn was standing beside the window looking out and the girl – he had forgotten her name – was pacing up and down in front of the cinema entrance. She looked up as he approached. 'I couldn't get back any sooner,' he said. 'I'm really sorry, but I can't oblige. There's no one to ask and I just couldn't bring you down there on my own authority.' He saw the desperate disappointment in Derek's face. 'Sorry, mate,' he said, 'it's just that it's a very bad night. If you'd asked me earlier . . . '

'That's all right,' said Derek. 'It's not your fault.'

'It would have been difficult anyway,' added Andy apologetically, 'even if I had got permission, because at the moment all the watertight doors between the compartments are closed and we'd have to be going up and down ladders over them all the time.'

'Sorry about that,' said Derek to Karen when Andy had sped off.

'Not to worry,' said Karen cheerfully. 'Let's not waste any more time. What'll we do now?'

Derek thought fast; he could think of all kinds of things he wanted to do to Karen, but the need to impress her was still strong. 'Look,' he said, 'do you feel like an adventure? How about trying to get down into the workings of the ship ourselves?'

'Do you think we could?'

'In like Flynn!' said Derek, delighted that she was interested. 'I saw where Andy came out. We could get in that way.' He went to the alcove, about twenty feet away from the cinema entrance, from which he had seen Andy emerge.

There was an immediate hitch; the door had no handle.

He tried to pull it, inserting his fingers as far as they would go into the crack along which the door opened, but failed to budge it. 'Well, that's that, then,' said Karen from behind him.

'What do you mean, "that's that"? I'm not going to let a little thing like a door beat me. There has *got* to be a way . . . '

'Oh, come on, Derek, this isn't going to work.'

'Just give me a minute.' He was leading her down the

corridor when they heard a noise behind them. He spun around. A man in overalls was coming out through the door which swung shut behind him. The man walked in the opposite direction but Derek seized Karen's arm. 'That's it!' he said.

'What?'

'Remember Andy Farrell told us about these ladders that they're all using tonight because of the watertight things. Well, obviously, there'll be more people coming in and out of that door. We'll just wait for the next one.'

'And then what?'

'Well, we'll have to be very quick. It'll take the two of us. Let me see what's in your bag.' Karen handed over her purse and he rummaged around in it. 'Good, good, these'll do,' he said, taking out a small leather change purse and a steel tail comb and explaining what he intended to do.

They loitered near the door for the next five minutes, pretending to be completely absorbed in each other. Derek felt fully alert, energised, that he could achieve anything, climb any height. He was further intoxicated by Karen's proximity and risked kissing her, something he had not done before in a public place. She accepted the kiss but, having caught the spirit of the adventure, pushed him away to continue her watch on the door.

They were rewarded when it opened suddenly and a man's head appeared, followed by his torso. He was holding it ajar with one hand while he climbed out. 'Allow me.' Karen darted over and grabbed the door.

'Thank you,' said the man, surprised and, Derek saw with glee, entirely distracted by Karen's physique, as, widening her eyes, she peeped around the man as he climbed out.

'What's in there, sir?' she asked in a high sweet voice.

The man turned round to look below him. 'Oh, that's a crew area, miss,' he said. 'No passengers allowed.'

Derek moved forward, ostensibly to look down too. 'May I see?' but before the man could turn around to face him, he had dropped the change purse and had moved it forward with his toe, positioning it about two inches from the apex of the door's closing arc and in its path.

'Excuse me, sir,' but the man could not take his eyes off Karen, 'good evening, miss,' he called as, giving a little wave, she

135

skipped towards the entrance to the cinema. When she had vanished between the two entrance gods, he let the door go and walked away.

'Is he gone?' Karen came out.

'Yeah,' said Derek, looking down at his feet and seeing that an inch of the leather purse projected from the opening of the door. 'Great,' he said, glancing around to make sure they were alone.

He inserted the tail of the comb into the opening beside the purse, catching the purse between the fingers of his other hand and working both comb and purse upwards. When he had the purse about eighteen inches off the floor, the door moved slightly and Karen grabbed its edge. 'Good,' whispered Derek, 'hold it tight with both hands.' He continued to work the comb with his right hand and also took hold of the door with the left. Together, their finger knuckles straining, they managed to lever it open a couple of inches, allowing Derek to jam his foot in the opening.

'Suppose there's someone coming up right now?' whispered Karen.

'That's just a risk we'll have to take. Come on, it's only for a minute. We'll just go straight down and straight up again. It'll be something to tell our grandchildren.'

Cautiously, they opened the door wider and, their faces assaulted by a blast of warm air, looked inside. There was no floor inside the door, just a deep square hole, three decks deep. The ladder, fastened to their side of the hole, was made of steel.

'Come on,' whispered Derek, 'there's no one about.'

John, unable to sustain interest in *The African Queen*, fidgeted in his cinema seat. He had missed the beginning of the film and, being so busy with his own thoughts, did not have the mental energy or interest to try to pick up the threads of the story. He was the only person in his row of seats so he did not have to disturb anyone by leaving. Once outside on deck, he did not know what to do next; he was not in the least interested in any of the last-night parties.

The ship was still creeping; the only feeling of movement was the faint vibration under his feet. He crossed to the window and saw the fog was as impenetrable as ever, more so, in fact, because it seemed to be getting dark.

He wondered how Derek and Karen and their new sailor friend were getting on in the engine room. Perhaps he could meet them. John was fed up with being alone. Rose's face, her gentle voice and soft white body filled his every waking thought. He had written her five letters, long, garbled outpourings of pain and loss and love but he knew he would send none of them. If he went back again to his cabin, he would start writing these useless letters again.

He knew that Derek did not want him around, but perhaps the three of them could go into one of the lounges for a drink or something before his brother and Karen disappeared together for the rest of the evening.

Any company, even reluctant company, he thought, would be better than this blackness and there was nothing to lose by trying. He set off down the stairs, hoping to find a spot where he would intercept Derek and Karen on their return from the engine room.

Derek had helped Karen onto the ladder before stepping on the top rung of it himself but once inside what was in reality a square chimney, his head began to spin. Karen, however, was moving steadily downwards one rung at a time and he had to forget his fear. Holding his breath and bracing himself for a fall, he followed, leaning backwards a few inches and feeling his back touching the wall opposite the ladder.

Rung by rung, he abseiled downwards; the farther down he went the more pungent became the smell of oil and diesel mixed with the sweetish odour of heated metal. When at last he was at the end of the first ladder, there was a door to his right but another, shorter, chimney to his left. Looking down, he saw that Karen was already at its foot, looking up at him with an expectant face.

At least this second chimney was wider than the first. But when he stepped off its bottom rung onto the floor, which was made of metal mesh, he almost skidded. 'Careful,' whispered Karen. 'I nearly fell too. It's very slippery.'

He looked around. They were standing in a four-sided well, one side of which was open and led into an area filled with massive, complicated-looking machinery. There was a door to their left.

He opened it a few inches and looked cautiously round it. 'Come on,' he said and, followed closely by Karen, went into the room.

Once inside, they stopped, awestruck. Derek felt a little like one of the Lilliputians in *Gulliver's Travels*. The room, about twenty feet high, was crammed with loudly humming machines, metal behemoths as big as garden sheds; it was lined with rows and rows of pipes, festooned with dials and stopcocks, some of them covered in what looked to Derek like heavy silver paper. All surfaces, floor, walls, ceiling, were grey or greyish, with the exception of some of the pipes, which had been painted bright red and yellow. The hot, fume-laden air was filled with such a volume of high-pitched whining, swishing and rhythmic thumping that there was certainly no necessity to keep their voices down.

'God,' said Karen. 'It's fantastic.'

'Yeah,' said Derek. Now that he was here, such an awesome and incomprehensible display of power almost frightened him. He did not want to show any weakness in front of Karen, however, and slipped an arm around her waist.

The cook, standing on the bow of the *Dorothy Lamont*, inhaled a deep freezing breath. His hair lay cold and wet on the back of his neck but, after the smelly confines of the galley, he welcomed the freshness. A man might almost feel spiritual up here, he thought, pulling up the collar of his jacket and leaning over the bow rail just as the ship let go with another quack, startling him. Smiling at his own foolishness, he watched the swishing water below. The mist hung just feet above the surface, curling and puffing away from both sides of the vessel's snub nose as she cut smoothly through it.

Abruptly, a foghorn sounded, so loud and near that he almost lost his balance. His shock was such that he had no idea from which direction the sound had come. 'Captain! Captain!' he shouted, running back towards the wheelhouse.

Other crew members were coming up through the hatches and from down below he heard the peal of the bell, which gave instructions to the ship's engineer to move the *Dorothy Lamont*'s engines to Dead Slow. The cook had reached the wheelhouse just as the captain barked at the first mate to 'Get that whistle unplugged!' and the note of the diesels changed to a low, intermittent throbbing.

The procedure for ships which have sighted one another before entering fog is to keep to their courses, indicating this to each other by long single whistle blasts. Course changes are also indicated by a whistle. Not having radar and with no clear idea where the other ship was or how close, the captain of the *Dorothy Lamont* was now relying on his considerable experience, judgement and instinct. He made a decision. 'I think it's starboard,' he said, pulling on the wheel so that if, as he guessed, the other ship was ahead of him, his own vessel would turn forty-five degrees towards the open sea and would thereby pass the unknown vessel with plenty of leeway. Strictly speaking, this was against the rules as ships at sea should pass port to port.

The cook's initial panic was dying down and he thought he had better make himself useful by adding his ears to the general listening stations. He backed quietly out and went back on deck.

The wheelhouse was set well aft. The cook picked his way back towards the bow alongside some of the cargo of lumber, secured by chains, which was piled neatly alongside the ship's rails. When he had walked almost as far as the bow, he leaned against a heap of the wood to catch his breath and light a cigarette, the little flame from his Zippo casting a halo in the darkening mist.

The other ship's horn sounded again, so near as to be almost on top of them and as its reverberations died, the cook, straining his ears with all his might, fancied he heard engines. This was almost more than his nerves could bear. His hands started to shake with tension.

Then the whistle of the *Dorothy Lamont*, cleared at last of obstruction, sounded three long urgent blasts. After a few seconds, there was a long blast from the other vessel.

The cook relaxed. Both ships were now aware of one another. Things were under control.

In the crow's nest of the *White Empress*, the young lookout was hawing warm breath through the two layers of wool on his hands, mittens over gloves, which nevertheless had not saved the tips of his fingers from becoming numb. Then, shattering the stillness and perilously close, he heard three whistle blasts. Immediately, he banged his bell three times, moved the lever on the dial in front of him to where his judgement told him the sound had come from and lifted the telephone. 'We heard it,' said the calm voice from the bridge on the other end of the line. 'Can you see anything?'

The lookout strained his eyes through his binoculars in the direction from which the sound had come. He could see nothing except the impenetrable grey of the rapidly darkening fog. 'No, sir. I'm afraid not, sir.'

'You think it's starboard, nor'-nor'-west?' asked the first officer.

'Yes, sir.' The lookout held the telephone until the piercing sound of the *White Empress*'s own whistle had died away, then spoke again. 'I'm sure of it, sir.'

'Keep your eyes peeled, we're slowing down and altering course to port.'

'Yessir.'

He kept his binoculars to his eyes but it was as though the lenses were covered with grey paper.

The cook on the *Dorothy Lamont* and the lookout on the *White Empress* saw one another's vessels at precisely the same moment. The cook screamed as, through the mist, he saw the wall of lights, as high as a three-storey building, sliding past his eyes only twenty-five feet from the bow of the coaster; on the *Empress*, the lookout banged his bell repeatedly and at the same time shouted down the telephone. Reflexively, both captains spun their wheels and ordered their engines to stop but it was too late. Shearing rivets, screeching through steel plate, the *Dorothy Lamont* sliced into the side of the liner.

There was a jolt and a thump, quite moderate in the din of the engine room but it was unusual and the engineer on duty looked over his shoulder towards the source of the sound just as the bow of the *Dorothy Lamont* appeared through the wall and pushed directly towards him. Time slowed down in the engineer's horrified brain and the next second passed like an eternity. First he saw the snout, ugly and black and riding on a huge green waterfall. The snout widened and kept coming. It was coming right towards him, more and more of it, bigger and wider and fatter. He turned to run but his feet slipped on the walkway.

Still the *Dorothy Lamont* advanced. The engineer wriggled desperately along on his stomach, trying to get out of the way but the keel of the coaster crumpled the walkway like a piece of Meccano and caught him, rolling him before it until he came to rest against a steel strut. The strut buckled but a cross-strut snapped. He barely felt the pain as he died, his lungs and heart punctured by his crushed ribs.

Karen clutched Derek's arm. 'My God! What's happening?' The whole room was roaring and shaking around them. They heard a man scream and then through the soles of their shoes they could feel the floor vibrate as though the ship were being hauled over a bed of sharp rocks.

In front of them, about ten feet away, a bracket holding one of the pipes came loose and the pipe, stretched beyond endurance, fractured with a cracking sound, loud as an explosion. Karen screamed as a thin spray of oil shot out like a projectile and hissed onto the flat top of one of the big generators, near where they were standing. The oil ignited immediately and, like an electrically charged tablecloth, spread a thin sheet of white and blue flame all across the top of the machine. Their nostrils were assaulted by an acrid, bitter smell as black smoke began immediately to belch above the flame.

'Derek! Derek!' Still screaming, Karen backed away from the machine but Derek's eye was caught by a small wave of water, about a foot high, which was rippling through the door of the engine room towards them.

John had reached a dead end. He was standing outside a door marked 'Private, Crew Only' when he felt a strange shuddering sensation which seemed to travel right through the ship. There was a sound of stillness, then he heard bells ringing and raised voices.

The door burst open and a steward ran out, racing past him without acknowledging his presence. Almost before he knew he had done it, John had caught the closing door and slipped through it. Two large linen baskets on wheels, each more than four feet tall, stood to one side of him and he crouched between them to get his bearings.

He had obviously stumbled into the crew quarters. The corridor on which he found himself was alive with the sound of bells and the opening and closing of the many doors which lined it. He crouched lower as members of the crew rushed past him, many of them still pulling on jackets. His heart thumped steadily. He waited until the corridor was temporarily clear and then sprinted towards the far end, following the direction taken by the crew. As he began to run, he had no clear idea what he was going to do and, as he neared the end of the corridor, he smelled smoke. Fire! The ship was on fire.

What's more, he felt as though he was smothering. There was no reason for it – there was plenty of air – but he was finding it almost impossible to breathe.

It was Derek! Derek was in trouble.

He found himself at the end of a cul-de-sac, his way blocked by a door. It had no handle. The smell of smoke was stronger down here. Desperately, he tried to open the door by inserting his nails along the jamb but it was absolutely flush. John panicked. He shouted and battered on the door, adding the shouts and battering to the general cacophony around him.

When the cook of the *Dorothy Lamont* saw the collision coming, he had turned to run aft but, as the bow of the coaster travelled into the belly of the *White Empress*, the lumber on both sides of her bow were sheared off their neat heaps by the crumpling plates of the liner and had tumbled into the centre, piling on top of him, pinning him underneath. The pain seared through his ribs and chest and he was sure he was going to suffocate but worse than the pain was the noise, the grinding, tearing, roaring noise that deafened him and that he feared might go on and on for ever.

On the bridge of the liner, the crew had swung smoothly into emergency mode. 'Muster the passengers, sir?' asked the first officer.

'Not yet,' said the captain. 'Damage report?'

'In the process, sir.' Then the first officer smelled smoke.

He turned to the pipe-box. The *White Empress* had an old-fashioned fire-warning system, which sat in a wooden housing on the bridge like several sets of Panpipes, which were, in fact, the open ends of hollow tubes that ran from each of the watertight compartments. Wisps of smoke were curling from the pipe which led into the auxiliary engine room.

'Fire in the auxiliary engine room, sir,' said the first officer crisply to the captain, who was already on the telephone to the chief engineer.

'Thank you,' said the captain. 'The chief already knows. Muster the crews.'

While the first officer lifted his own telephone, the captain operated levers to close all possible air inlets to the engine-room area. The first officer put down the telephone. 'The other vessel is amidships, sir,' he said.

'I see,' said the captain. 'Perhaps if we can assist her to back off, the sea can deal with the fire. Damage report?'

'Number three and four compartments gone, sir. Others holding so far.'

'I see,' said the captain again.

'Shall I have the passengers mustered now, sir?' The first officer picked up the telephone and held it in mid-air.

'Yes, that might be a good idea. Just as a precaution. No alarms. Tell the shack to call general PAN.'

'Yessir.' Even if the collison had buckled one of the watertight doors, the *White Empress* was built to float if two of her watertight compartments were flooded; and, depending on where the gash in her hull occurred, she could survive with several more compartments completely full of water. She was a strong, safe ship.

But, thought the first officer as, calmly, he gave the orders to the bo'sun and the radio officer, so was the *Titanic* . . .

The lights in the room flickered and went out. Through the clouds of thick oily smoke, Derek and Karen, coughing, could see small yellow and blue tongues of flame dancing on the machinery all around them.

'Stairs . . . stairs,' Derek gasped, catching Karen's arm and attempting to lead her towards where he remembered the ladder had been. But she did not respond and her arm dragged downwards, a dead weight on his hand, so heavy that he let her go. His own knees buckled. Every gulp for air caused a paroxysm and within seconds he had slumped to the floor on top of Karen's unconscious body.

Two decks above, John continued to hammer on the door. Then another, a few yards away, burst open. Two men, preceded by billows of smoke, climbed out. To his horror, John saw that they were manhandling between them something big, limp and unwieldy; even from that distance, he recognised the dangling head of a human being. He could not even scream. He raced towards the group of men who, by the time he got there, had clustered around the engineer's broken body.

The door behind them was still open. John dashed through it and had one foot on the ladder behind it when a member of the crew grabbed his arm and pulled him off. 'You can't go down there, son. No passengers here.' John did not protest. Swiftly backing away, he saw, out of the corner of his eye, farther down the corridor, another door opening, more clouds of smoke. He sprinted away from the little group and got to this other door just as the second of two men climbed off the ladder inside. Before anyone could stop him, he had picked up a filthy towel dropped on the floor by the man, had taken a deep breath and holding the damp towel to his mouth and nose, had started to descend the ladder.

On the bridge, the captain had heard about the fatality. He had reports that his firefighting crews were having difficulty reaching the blaze. On one side, it was blocked off by one of the watertight doors, on the other by the bow of the other ship. And it was difficult for them to descend the escape ladders wearing the unwieldy breathing apparatus.

He weighed up his options. He could evacuate the area and flood it with carbon monoxide gas, which would probably prove ineffective because of the leakage that would occur around the gash made by the wedged coaster. Or he could ask the coaster's captain, with whom he was now in telephone contact, to reverse off, thereby flooding the entire compartment. This would have to take place sooner or later – but in case the bulkheads did not

144

hold and the entire ship flooded he should probably wait until rescue vessels were standing by.

But he could not continue to let the fire burn. He made the decision. He would have to trust the sturdiness of his ship. He asked his first officer to issue the order withdrawing all crew from compartments nine and ten. Then he spoke to the captain of the *Dorothy Lamont* asking him to stand by to reverse his engines.

It took John less than twenty seconds to scramble down the ladder and reach solid ground. Someone was shouting at him from above but he ignored it. He felt water slopping around his ankles. He put out his hands, feeling a solid wall to his right, but to his left, through the murk, he saw flames. It was the only way forward. He hesitated for a split second and then, keeping his head low and the damp towel jammed against his mouth, groped towards the opening to his left. His eyes felt as though red hot pokers were searing through them and, although he still had plenty of reserves of breath, his chest hurt as though it was being squeezed by a vice. He tripped on something large, soft yet solid which, half to his horror, half to his relief, he recognised by feel as the bodies of his brother and Karen. He knew immediately he would not be able to get them up the ladder by himself.

Feeling his way, he retraced his steps to the ladder, moving as fast as he could. In the blackness, he stumbled and fell hard against something. Pain scalded along his cheek and ear but he disregarded it, picked himself up and, a few seconds later, found the ladder. He scrambled up to the top, but just before he got there collided with the feet of a man who was obviously coming down to get him. He almost lost his grip on the ladder but made a last, superhuman effort and held on. His chest was nearly bursting and he knew he could not hold his breath for much longer. Then he felt himself being lifted under the armpits and dragged upwards and out into clear air. He collapsed prone on the deck, coughing, gulping in great draughts of air; the deck underneath his burned cheek felt as though it were made of live coals. As soon as he could, he cried out that his brother and a girl were down below. He had no idea what happened next because he passed out.

*

The cook heard the engines roaring beneath him and felt the *Dorothy Lamont* shift slightly. Even through his pain, he recognised that the captain must be pulling her off the other ship. He feared that the lumber trapping him would shift again and he would be a goner. The pain in his ribs and chest flamed to an excruciating level as, summoning all his dwindling strength, he took as deep a breath as his injuries allowed, making one last effort to be heard. 'He-ee-lp!' he screamed but even to his own ears it sounded feeble and too weak to be heard in the confusion and roaring all around him. He gave up and waited for oblivion. At least there would be relief from the pain.

But a miracle happened. The *Dorothy Lamont*'s deck boy who was clinging, white-faced, to the rail of the coaster, thought he heard something – a voice – from under the debris at the bow and hollered the information to a deck hand who relayed it back to the wheelhouse. The captain of the *Dorothy Lamont* immediately stopped his engines and informed the captain of the liner that he was halting the reversal operation.

Almost at the same time, just as the water began to flow faster into the *White Empress* through the already widened gap around the bow of the coaster, the liner's bo'sun sent a runner to telephone the captain that a rescue attempt was under way in the auxiliary engine room. Four of his men, wearing breathing apparatus, had managed to squeeze their way down the escape ladder to search for two young people. While the bo'sun waited for them to come up again, he tried to calculate how long it had been since the collision and reckoned it was perhaps three and a half minutes. He wondered what the chances of survival were for the two young people in the fire and smoke below. He didn't hold out much hope.

The windowless corridor from which he was directing operations was now thick with smoke. The bo'sun, who had propped open the escape door, listened hard but could hear nothing from below. He directed that the dead man's body be covered from view. One of his men ran off to fetch a sheet. Others moved John's prone body to one side until the doctor should come.

After what seemed an age but was in reality less than a minute, the head of the first crewman appeared with a boy over his shoulder. The bo'sun helped his men on the deck take the boy off his rescuer's shoulder and lay him gently on his back. The boy's hair and clothing was soot black but the ship's doctor, who had just arrived on the scene, panting, placed an ear on his chest and nodded affirmation at the bo'sun that the boy was still alive.

As the boy and his brother were carried off to the hospital, the girl was brought up. Her clothing and hair was wet but her face, although streaked black too was largely dry. She had obviously been lying in water but, fortunately, face up. The doctor put his hand on the pulse point in her neck and nodded: she, too, was alive.

It took a while to ease the cook, still conscious but almost delirious with pain, from under his lumber prison. Although one of the crew was trained in first aid, there was no doctor or nurse on board the *Dorothy Lamont* and her captain asked that the medical facilities of the *White Empress* be made available, a request which was readily granted. The liner towered over the coaster, but under the eyes of crowds of fascinated passengers, who now lined the rails, a stretcher and sling were improvised and the cook, strapped on to it, was raised carefully, inch by inch, and taken on board D deck through one of the glassless apertures along the promenade. He, too, was taken to the ship's hospital.

Twenty minutes after the *Dorothy Lamont* sliced into the liner, she began to back off, crumpling sheets of steel as though they were made of tissue paper. As she ground free, the seawater rushed in around her retreating bow, sweeping everything movable before it. Within minutes, the whole engine-room area of the *White Empress* was full to the ceiling.

CHAPTER SIX

My dearest Rose,

I'm very sorry I haven't written to you before now. I did write to you when I was on the ship on the way here, it's just that when I read the letters back, they were so miserable that I tore them up.

I miss you so much, Rose. I hope you think about me even half as much as I'm thinking about you. I think about you all the time. *All* the time. You're the first thing that comes into my mind when I wake up. I try to dream about you at night but it doesn't always work.

I've a bit of news. Maybe you saw it in the newspapers, although I don't know if the *Argus* or the *Democrat* would have news that fast! I'm actually writing this from hospital in Halifax, in Nova Scotia. By now, of course, I should be in McGuigan's, already digging spuds (and I bet that's where you think of me as being!) but things did not turn out that way.

You see, on the last night we were at sea, another ship crashed into us. It was very frightening, Rose, but especially frightening for us. It would take me a year to write it to you (I really, really wish I could see you!) but to make a long story short, Derek and a girl he met on the ship called Karen Lindstrom (very nice – she was going to Prince Edward Island too) were missing when the ships crashed into each other.

As it happened, I was looking for them at the time. I knew they were down in the engine room, Derek had arranged it through a fellow he got friendly with who was on the crew. The next thing, I saw a man being carried out through a door. Rose, he was dead.

I knew it was up to me now and the next thing I

knew I was in the middle of the smoke and the flames. It was the most frightening thing I ever experienced. But thank God I found the two of them. I couldn't lift them so I managed to make it back up the ladder to get help.

They're fine now, both of them. The reason I'm still in hospital is when I was down there, I fell and burned my cheek and my ear. I'm having plastic surgery on it and the doctors here say that after a year no one will hardly know I'd been in an accident at all.

I'm nervous about the operation, of course, but they really are nice here. In fact, everyone's being very nice. Karen's mother and father, the Lindstroms, are paying for the whole thing. After the accident, the ship couldn't go to Quebec, of course, so it was towed by tugs into a place called St John's in New Brunswick. The Lindstroms were there to meet us and they took Derek and Karen with them in a plane straight to Charlottetown but they made arrangements for me to go in a plane to Halifax and there was a car there to meeet me to take me to this hospital.

Must close now. I've very lonely for you, Rose. Lying here I've made up my mind that *nothing* is going to stop me from getting home to see you as soon as possible. I hope you still feel the same.

I love you, darling Rose. I wish I could be with you always. And I will, please God. I *promise* I will.

I hope everything is going well for you. By now, of course, you're back at school in Dublin. I'll send this letter there.

Good luck with the Leaving Cert.

Again, I'm sorry I haven't written before now, but I hope you understand. Please write back as soon as possible. You can write to the address I gave you on Prince Edward Island because by the time you get this and write back, I should be there.

Please write soon.

All my love, always,
John

P.S. The present you gave me is safe and sound. I look at it every day.

Rose kept her spine stiff and her head high as she read the letter in the full, unblinking glare of the head nun's gaze. On the verge of tears, she was determined not to let the nun see it.

She should have warned John. All mail was pre-read, both incoming and outgoing, but this was the first time Rose had ever had reason seriously to suffer from the system. When she had finished reading, the nun took the letter back. 'Do your parents know about this boy?'

Rose concentrated on the sounds she heard, the creaking of the reflector panel in the electric fire which glowed red in a corner of the headmistress's study, the faraway tooting of a car horn in the traffic outside the convent walls. 'Yes, sister,' she said.

'Do they approve of your friendship with him?'

'I don't know, sister.'

'Well, what did they say to you? Did they invite him into your house?'

'No, sister.'

'Why not, do you think?'

'I don't know, sister. It just didn't happen. My father gave us one of his horses so I could teach him to ride,' she added desperately.

'I see,' said the nun, slowly. 'Well, it's your letter.' She folded it back in its envelope and handed it over. 'When are your parents coming to visit you next?'

'Next weekend, sister.'

'Right,' said the nun. 'Tell them I'd like a word, will you?'

'Yes, sister,' said Rose, already planning to fenegle it so that Gus would come on his own. She did not have much faith in how her mother would react to such an interview about John Flynn.

'Where's your beret?' the nun asked. Since the girls had to wear their berets in chapel, it was one of the inflexible rules that berets must be carried at all times folded over the belts of their uniforms. If you forgot your beret, you were fined. 'I – I think it's in the dormitory, sister,' said Rose, glad of the diversion.

'Fined one shilling,' said the nun, turning away and, as she did so, taking a small black notebook and pencil from the pocket of her habit to note the fine.

Rose let herself quietly out of the office. Despite the fine and the worry about the nun having read the letter, its contents were singing in her brain and she could not wait to read it again. She had been called out of class and wondered if she dared not return immediately. Looking at her wristwatch, she saw there were only fifteen minutes to go before the end of the present class period; chances were she could get away with it.

She walked towards the chapel, trying not to hurry, to minimise the squelching made by her crêpe-soled shoes on the polished boards of the floors. But, as she passed the line of class-room doors, behind which all the mundane, underprivileged people pored over dull grey exercise books and muttered grey answers to greyer questions, she had to discipline herself not to run, to skip, to throw her arms in the air. The sun was streaming through the tall windows on the lake side of the school, gilding the panelled walls of the corridor, and she basked in the wide shafts of light as she passed through them. She felt unique, absolutely special. John Flynn had said he loved her, had committed it to paper.

The chapel, unusually, was empty which was just as well for her, she realised belatedly, as she had not fetched her beret. She hesitated, one of the swing doors in her hand, but the longing to reread the letter was so acute she decided that God would have to overlook a bare head for this one time.

The chapel was a new addition to the convent and still smelled of varnish. Through the stained-glass windows on its sunny side, a series of rainbows slid to the floor, painting the blond wood of the pews and splashing colour on the parquet flooring. Choosing a darkish pew on the other side, Rose noticed a bouquet of white roses and freesias which lay in gay ribbons on the shallow steps of the sanctuary; it was not unusual for a past pupil to send her wedding flowers to the chapel. Rose's wedding bouquet, she thought happily, would contain a riot of flowers, roses and freesias, yes, but also daffodils and tulips, violets, stock, dahlias, Michaelmas daisies, even hollyhocks and wallflowers – every single flower in bloom in Ireland on that day.

She took John's letter out of the envelope. Although she had promised to write to him, the momentousness of what had happened between them on that last night had somehow inhibited her and she had been unable to think of anything adequate to say to him. So she had waited for him to write first and when the days and weeks stretched into more than a month, had begun to despair.

Now everything was all right. Everything was more than all right. He loved her.

She loved him too – more than anything in the whole world. Since she had returned to school, Rose had lived in a fantasy. She could not wait to get to bed each evening. While the others had whispered and giggled to each other, Rose had closed her eyes tightly and covered her ears with the sheets, slipping into her minute-by-minute reconstruction of that last night, starting with the sound of the stones on her window. She could feel his skin, the coldness and slippery smoothness of it between her thighs in the water, the strength of his arms, the warmth and passion afterwards under the trees.

She found it almost impossible to concentrate on her study. The margins of her *Aeneid* and trigonometry books were covered with drawings of the curving width of John Flynn's lips and the upward slant of his eyes.

She had confided in no one. Up to this term, she and her best friend, Dolores O'Brien, knew everything there was to know about one another. Both were lazy correspondents and never wrote to one another during the holidays so the first few days of each new term were always spent in a welter of gossip and catching up. But somehow, this time, Rose could not bring herself to tell Dolores about John – although her friend, who was no daw, had guessed something was up and there was a certain coolness between them as a result.

Rose was not quite sure why she had not divulged her secret to her friend. In one way, she felt as though to talk about John and what had happened between them would ruin and maybe cheapen it and, in another way, she felt as though she had taken a leap beyond anything Dolores would or could understand. And for the first few weeks, her own vivid sense memories were enough for her.

Rose hated deception, however, and, more especially, hated anyone's displeasure, so lately she had been wavering; it had become simply a matter of a suitable opening and here it was, the perfect opportunity. She could show Dolores the letter.

He loved her. *He loved her!* Again she had to restrain herself, this time from throwing the pages of the letter in the air.

The silence in the chapel was broken by the loud electric racket of the class bell, followed after a few seconds by the opening of distant doors and the din in the corridor as the girls changed rooms. Rose shot out of her seat and left the chapel, refolding the letter and stuffing it into the pocket of her uniform as she half ran towards her final class of the day.

Her seat was near the front and Dolores' was two rows behind so there was no opportunity to talk. When the nun was writing on the blackboard and had her back to the class, Rose scribbled her friend a note: GOT TO TALK. MEET ME 1.15 USUAL, R, screwed it up and passed it back along the aisle. Fifteen minutes later, the reply came back: OK. D.

Their private meeting place was in the linen closet, its shelves packed tightly with sheets, pillowcases, counterpanes, gym knickers and vests. It being a Saturday afternoon, there was little chance of them being discovered. Saturday was a half day, classes in the morning, mending, letter-writing, dormitory cleaning and shoe-polishing in the afternoon, with few of the nuns around.

She and Dolores, small, mousy-haired and freckled, were now squeezed into a little alcove beside the closet's window. Rose, watching her friend reading John's letter, hugged herself with delight at Dolores' expression. Secrets told in here, in the clean fresh-air smell and natural sound insulation created by the linen, really felt like secrets, she thought to herself as Dolores turned a page. She looked out of the window. The day was still fine and many of the girls were strolling about the forecourt in front of the school in pairs or larger groups. 'Finished,' said Dolores, handing back the letter. 'Well, well, well!'

'Is that all you can say?' asked Rose. But she could see Dolores was mightily impressed.

'What do you expect me to say? It's fantastic,' said Dolores. 'You're some dark horse. All this time and you never told me.'

'I was afraid,' admitted Rose.

'Afraid of what?'

'That's the first letter I've got. I was afraid that he might have forgotten me.'

'Well, clearly he hasn't. To tell you the truth, I was a bit miffed this term. You didn't seem to want to know me.'

'Oh, Dolores, that's not true. Of *course* I wanted to know you.'

'It doesn't matter,' said Dolores. 'The main thing is you told me now. You lucky thing! A hero as well.'

'The only thing is, I don't know if I'll ever see him again.'

'Didn't he say in the letter that he'd move mountains to see you?'

Rose frowned, trying to remember, and Dolores took the letter again. 'Yes, here it is,' pointing, ' "Lying here I've made up my mind that *nothing* is going to stop me from getting home to see you as soon as possible." Oh, Rose!' She threw her arms around her friend. 'God,' she breathed, 'it's fan*tas*tic. It's real love.' She let Rose go. 'Now, tell me all about it.'

They settled on the window seat and Rose told her about the summer with John Flynn, omitting the crucial detail about making love. Maybe she'd tell Dolores that too, in time, but purity was the major virtue stressed in the convent and she was unsure of her friend's reaction to the revelation that she was no longer a virgin. 'Rose, I think he sounds absolutely lovely,' said Dolores when she was finished. 'You're really lucky.'

'There are problems, you know,' said Rose, picking with her fingernail at a piece of putty where the glass in the window met the sash. 'It's hard to explain but John is – he's . . . ' She hesitated, not knowing how to express the four hundred years of class difference between herself and her father's tenants. She glanced at Dolores' expectant face. 'It's, you know, parents and things,' she finished, knowing it sounded lame.

'Rubbish,' said Dolores. 'When you're twenty-one, none of that will count.'

'But I'm only sixteen now. That's *years* away.' Rose turned away from the window and put her head in her hands.

'Rose,' said Dolores patiently, touching her shoulder, 'first things first. The Leaving Cert first. Then you worry about everything else.'

'I suppose you're right. But I'm not interested in the bloody Leaving Cert any more,' said Rose into her hands.

'You're here, aren't you? So you've no choice, really, have you? At least at the moment.'

'But I love him.'

'Then it'll last until you do your Leaving Cert.'

Rose knew in her heart that her friend was right. She fiddled with her beret, back in its rightful place at her belt. 'There's another thing,' she said hesitantly.

'What?'

'Sister Eucharia read the letter and is going to tell my parents.'

'We'll cross that bridge when we come to it.'

'Thanks, Dolores, you're brilliant.'

Dolores smiled beatifically. 'I know.'

They left the closet and went for a walk in the orchard. Now Rose had started talking about John Flynn she could not stop. Five minutes or so into her monologue, Dolores interrupted her. 'You actually did it?' Her eyes were round.

'I didn't say that!'

'Well, you as good as said it.'

'Dolores! I didn't—'

'Well, whatever,' said Dolores peaceably, 'it's your own business.'

'It is.' Rose was half glad it was out in the open.

They had reached a broken pathway, mossy and treacherous in wet weather but picturesque today with high ripe grasses and late wild flowers; the air was unusually mild for this time of September and except for the distant roar of traffic, it was quiet enough to be a country summer Sunday. 'You must come to Sundarbans,' said Rose suddenly.

Dolores was pleased. 'I'd love to.' Each thought the other's house would be heaven. Dolores, daughter of a bank manager, was the eldest of a large, loud family of seven who sprawled all over a modern house in Galway city and thought the notion of being an only child of the gentry would be quite the thing; while Rose had always longed for brothers and sisters, a local cinema, a fish-and-chipper and a manageable, snug house in which the curtains didn't blow in the wind while the windows were closed.

The pathway climbed gently with the rise of the nuns' land

and ended against a broken granite wall; when they got to it, the two of them leaned against the warmed stone, crisscrossed with lichens and whorled fossils but today Rose would not have noticed if it had been inlaid with gold.

Three weeks late, John finally arrived on Prince Edward Island. He was picked up from the hospital in Halifax in Mr Lindstrom's motor car. Sven Lindstrom was red-faced and corpulent with fair eyebrows and lashes over very pale eyes but not a rib of hair on his head. John had liked him on sight but was embarrassed by the man's generosity and kindness. He squirmed uncomfortably as Mr Lindstrom tucked a rug around his knees in the passenger seat of the huge American car, a Lincoln. Except for the local hearse at home, John had never set eyes on such length and opulence in a vehicle. 'Thank you very much, sir,' he said faintly.

'Oh, now,' Mr Lindstrom chuckled, 'we don't stand on ceremony on the Island. "Sir" just makes me feel like a schoolteacher – and I certainly ain't a schoolteacher! And by the way,' he added, 'after a bit you'll notice that nobody around these parts calls the Island anything except that – the Island.' Along the route, Mr Lindstrom gave John a potted history of various Nova Scotia landmarks. The terminal at Caribou was a simple, homely affair and, besides themselves, there were only about twenty vehicles waiting for the ferry.

Although the Northumberland Strait was running moderately, they were only ten minutes out when John felt a familiar wave of nausea and was horribly embarrassed.

Sven Lindstrom, however, was understanding, even amused. 'Don't worry, plenty of folk get sick, a lot older than you, too.' He brought John a sick bag, one of a plentiful supply stashed in containers all over the passenger lounge of the boat.

Once on dry land at Wood Islands, John recovered quickly but Mr Lindstrom insisted, before bringing him out to Kelly's Cross, that he should come to the Charlottetown house and have a rest and a cup of tea. 'Hear you drink a lot of tea in the Emerald Isle.' As John thanked him yet again, he wondered uncomfortably how he could ever repay such hospitality.

Mr Lindstrom was a careful driver but, even so, the trip to Charlottetown took less than forty minutes. John kept his eyes glued to the landscape, reeling in impressions. The island was flatter than he had expected, and with fewer trees; a gently rolling pastureland, it was dotted with brightly painted wooden houses and huge red barns which towered over them. Somehow, because this was Canada, he had expected a carpet of trees. There were trees all right, but in patches rather than sweeps; some were faded but many still wore autumn dress of orange and gold and a few flamed crimson in a shade John had never seen in a tree before. 'Excuse me, Mr Lindstrom,' he asked, 'but those really red trees, what are they called?'

'They're maples, son,' said Mr Lindstrom. 'It's the national tree of Canada.'

There were very few motor vehicles on the road but they had to slow down frequently for horse-drawn traffic. John, comparing everything he saw with what was familiar to him at home, felt there could be little comparison. The roads were wider and straighter, the horses better groomed, the fields gentler and more open; nothing compared with the crabbed rushy farmland he was used to. Nearly every turn on a Monaghan road faced on to another hillock; here, he thought, you could see for miles.

But with the thought came a rush of homesickness, so strong he had to blink back the tears. And Rose? Would there be a letter from her waiting for him at Kelly's Cross? He touched the healing skin on his cheek which was shiny and red and stretched like the skin on a drum; his ear, which had not been grafted but had been left to heal on its own, looked even worse, in his opinion. He had been assured by the surgeon that the scars would fade in time and would be barely noticeable but right now he thought he looked like a freak and was almost glad he was far away from Rose.

He saw they were driving across a long bridge over a stretch of water alive with a species of bird he did not recognise. Hundreds of them, large and black or dark grey, were gliding about on wide lazy wings or diving like arrows into the water. The traffic was heavier now and on the far side of the bridge he could see a cluster of buildings stretching ahead and spreading to right and left along the shoreline. This must be Charlottetown, he thought and sat up eagerly.

He had expected Charlottetown to be rather like Dublin

but again, he thought as they motored into it, he had been mistaken. Dublin was made of stone and was big and noisy with traffic and people. But although there were some stone buildings in Charlottetown, the city, like the farmhouses he had seen on the way in, seemed mostly constructed of wood. There were cars in the streets but well spaced; people chatted to one another on the sidewalks and leaned against parked horse-carts; even the shops were much smaller and in no way as fancy as they were in Dublin. He noticed they were travelling along a thoroughfare named Grafton Street. 'There's a Grafton Street in Dublin!' he exclaimed.

'What do you know!' Sven Lindstrom smiled. 'You see? In no time, the Island will be a home from home.'

White pillars supported a portico outside the front door of the Lindstroms' house, built of reddish stone; the Canadian flag fluttered from a high flagpole in the middle of the wide lawn. Seeing John crane his neck at the flag, Mr Lindstrom explained that tomorrow was Thanksgiving. 'Your folks in Kelly's Cross will probably have Thanksgiving dinner for you,' he added, 'but you and your brother will have to come in and join us here for a meal next weekend.'

'Oh, we couldn't, Mr Lindstrom,' said John. 'You've already done too much. You're too good—'

'Nonsense,' said Sven, pulling the car into a little concrete bay beside the house in which two other, smaller, cars were already parked. 'We're the ones who are grateful and we've got a lot to celebrate this Thanksgiving. Mrs Lindstrom and I can't thank you enough – if you hadn't gone down there into that fire that night, Karen . . . ' He harrumphed to clear his throat and turned off the engine. He got out of the car then, releasing John from the necessity to reply.

John got out and followed his host round the back of the house and in through a door. He found himself in a large square kitchen with appliances, sinks and cupboards all around the walls and a vast table with a thick wooden top taking up the centre. It was a mild day outside but the kitchen was very warm and a middle-aged woman, a huge turkey trussed in a roasting pan beside her, was peeling a mound of potatoes on the table. 'This is Mrs Anderson, our housekeeper,' Mr Lindstrom introduced John to the woman, 'and this is our hero, John Flynn.'

John's injured cheek stung as the heat flamed into his face. But the woman put down her paring knife, wiped her hands on her apron and took his hand, pumping it enthusiastically. 'My!' she said. 'I'm sure glad to meet you, John Flynn, I've heard so much about you. We're all very grateful to you.'

Sven crossed the kitchen and opened the door into another room. 'We're home, Mother,' he called, then turned back to the housekeeper. 'How about a cup of tea, Mabel? We'll have it in the parlour, I think,' he added. 'Come this way, John.'

John followed him out into a hallway, hushed with carpet thicker than he had ever seen, and then into a large wood-floored room, bright with windows on three sides. 'Sit down, son, make yourself at home,' said Mr Lindstrom. 'I think I'll have a highball.'

John looked around uneasily: many of the chairs had spindly, curved legs and looked too fragile to take his weight. He moved to a little couch which had only one arm and as his host mixed himself a drink from a set of bottles on a silver tray, sat carefully on its very edge.

While Mr Lindstrom's back was turned, he looked around. A corner of the room was taken up by a grand piano, the light from outside burnishing its satiny brown wood; dark pictures hung on the walls and china figurines and silver pieces were scattered on little tables. Between two of the windows on one wall was a huge stone fireplace, its grate laid with thick logs. This room, thought John with awe, was bigger than the whole of the gate lodge back in Drumboola and probably had more valuable things in it than were contained in the whole of Carrickmacross. Then the thought struck him that perhaps this was how Rose lived. After all, he had never been inside any of the Big Houses in his own area. Surreptitiously, he checked the inside pocket of his tweed jacket, reassuring himself that the little packet containing Rose's amethysts was still there.

Mr Lindstrom was stirring his drink and walking towards a big armchair beside the fireplace when there was a rush of footsteps and Karen burst into the room. 'John!' she cried. 'You're home!'

She skidded to a halt in front of her father. 'Hi, Dad,' she said, kissing him on the cheek, then turned to John again. 'I hope you're feeling better? How is your face? Oh, my God, it looks really *sore* – is it?' She was wearing a tartan kilt and a white blouse under a pink sweater and John, whose romantic loyalty was utterly committed to Rose, had to admit nevertheless that she looked wonderful.

He rose from his seat to answer her. 'No, I'm fine, it's not sore at all, really grand.'

'Sit down, sit down! I'm sorry I didn't get a chance to thank you for what you did that night. You saved my life, you know.'

'Ah, no,' said John uncomfortably still balanced on the edge of his seat.

'Rubbish,' said Karen. 'Now I have to be your slave for the rest of my life! That's what the Indians say, you know. You now own my soul.'

John had no idea what to say or how to react. He had met Karen only in the company of Derek, who had monopolised her. 'Are you feeling a bit better yourself?' he asked, trying to divert attention from his own health.

'Oh, I'm fine,' she said. 'I still have a bit of a cough and my chest still hurts a bit sometimes but the doctor says I'm nearly as good as new.'

To John's relief, Karen's mother and the housekeeper came together into the room, the latter carrying a large tea-tray. John remained standing while Mrs Lindstrom, whom he had met in hospital in the days following the accident, shook his hand and exclaimed at how well he was looking.

Karen bounded across to Mrs Anderson to help her with the tray. 'Oh, good,' she said when she saw it held a cake stand. 'Company food. You're quite honoured, John – we don't bring this stuff out for just anybody.'

Having served them, the housekeeper left. John sipped his tea and nibbled at a piece of fruitcake, barely tasting it. He felt gawky and out of place in this opulent room and the raw skin on his cheek was throbbing as he mumbled answers to the kind questions put to him by Mr and Mrs Lindstrom.

Karen had seated herself beside him, and bubbled on, chatting and laughing and teasing him, even flirting a little. He wanted to ask if she had heard from Derek but did not have the courage to do so in front of her parents.

160

He was glad when Mr Lindstrom put down his cup and stood up from his chair. 'Well, we'd better get out to Kelly's Cross before dark. Are you going to come out for the ride, Karen?'

With warm invitations to return with Derek, he was seen off from the front door by Mrs Lindstrom. 'And, of course, we'll see you when you go back to Halifax,' she added. John had to travel back to the hospital for a check-up with the surgeon who had performed the operation.

Karen sat between John and her father on the bench seat of the Lincoln. The road to Kelly's Cross led west and soon the tarmacadam gave way to a type of surface John had never seen on a road, soft and brick red in colour. 'It's the iron in the sandstone that gives the dirt that colour,' Karen explained, leaning forward to see over the long hood of the car. 'We'll have to take you up to Kildare Capes – won't we, Dad?'

'What's that?' John asked. Although there was plenty of space, he had to fight his consciousness of her thigh brushing against his own. He could not make up his mind whether she was doing it deliberately or not and surreptitiously squeezed his own legs together to minimise the contact.

'It's up near Tignish on the North Shore,' Karen answered, 'it's where you'll see the sandstone being eroded. Everyone on the Island always talks about erosion. It's been happening for aeons. Soon there'll be none of us left.'

The car trailed a thick fluke of dust as it rolled along the red road, which undulated gently westwards through the well-tended land. Now and then they passed through small forests of evergreens and sparser sprinklings of deciduous trees, brilliant in their autumn finery. John, who had been told repeatedly both in the McGuigans' letters and by acquaintances in the hospital, that PEI was very like Ireland, was finding it difficult to recognise the similarities. To him, the crossroads villages, red- and green-painted Dutch barns, neat shingled houses and immaculate white churches which dotted the land bore no resemblance at all to the higgledy-piggledy grey stone with which he was familiar at home. The only sameness he saw was the soft green of the grass.

Another difference niggled at him until finally he realised what it was. Hedges. There was an absence of high hedges. All the roads in Monaghan bored through open tunnels of high thick

161

greenery – brown in winter – and the traveller glimpsed the fields and vistas only through the intermittent gaps and gateways.

They had been silent a long time by Karen's standards and John wondered if it was his turn to talk. 'Maples?' he asked her, pointing to a particularly vivid group of trees which stood like tongues of fire on top of a hill to their right.

'Yeah, they're great, aren't they?' she said. 'Useful too. You like maple syrup?'

'Yes, it's delicious. I had it on pancakes on the ship.'

'Me too. Yum!' Karen let out a gusty sigh of appreciation and smiled brilliantly at him.

'Do you know how Derek is?' John asked, uncomfortable under her gaze. 'I haven't heard from him at all.'

It was Mr Lindstrom who answered: 'The McGuigans don't have a telephone,' he said, 'but we called a neighbour who enquired for us. He's doing fine.' He gave Karen's knee an affectionate pat. 'If he's doing half as good as Karen here, he's OK!'

Derek, watched by the McGuigans' two dogs and three of their multitudinous cats, was splitting logs in the yard behind the farmhouse. One of the dogs turned her head, pricked her ears, then both animals rushed, barking, around the side of the house towards the front gate. Derek rested his axe and listened. The house was nestled into the side of a hill and sure enough, floating up from the valley, he heard the distinct note of a car engine.

Immediately, he picked up his shirt – his best one usually reserved for Sundays – and put it on; they had received a telephone message via a neighbour that John was coming today and he was hoping against hope that Karen might come with him.

He had not seen her for nearly four weeks. For the first twenty-four hours after the accident on the liner, they had both been very ill, taking oxygen in the ship's hospital. And when the crippled ship had docked in St John's in the middle of the second day, he and Karen had been separated and taken to different hospitals.

At Karen's request, her parents had come to see him. They had been kind but it had been a stilted, uncomfortable meeting. Mr and Mrs Lindstrom, although thankful that their daughter

162

had come through her ordeal, seemed a little bewildered as to what she was doing down in the engine room in the first place. They made it clear to Derek that they attached no blame to him but Derek, miserable and guilty, had been tongue-tied in their presence.

When a representative from the shipping line came to see him to organise payment of his hospital bill and details of his complicated trip from St John's to Charlottetown, he had asked her to telephone the other hospital, but Karen had already been discharged. And although Derek had made a very good recovery, the discovery that he had only one lung had made the medics cautious and delayed his own release.

His stomach started to turn as the note of the car engine became louder. What would he say to her? What did she think of him now – if she thought of him at all? As he regained his strength, he had thought of little else but his longing for Karen. He would be devastated if she did not want anything more to do with him; on the other hand, she had given him no reason to hope.

He buttoned his shirt, spat on his hands and smoothed down his hair. Then, walking as casually as the flotilla of butter-flies in his stomach allowed, he went to the front of the house to wait for the car.

Dan and Peggy McGuigan were ahead of him, leaning on the gateposts, one on each side. Derek joined them just as the automobile became visible in its attendant cloud of red dust. 'There you are, Derek,' said Dan, giving his young cousin a playful shove, 'all dressed up like a spare bedroom.' The McGuigans had reared three sons, all gone to be Yanks in Boston, with Yank wives and Massachusetts number plates on their cars. Dan and Peggy, left to farm three hundred acres without help, would have had to sell up. Neither of them had ever set foot in Ireland but they planned to go there 'some day' and were as loyal to the 'old country' as though they had left it yesterday. In particular, Peggy, whose maiden name was Coady, longed to see the Mon-aghan churchyard where her grandparents were buried. They were frugal, easy-going people whose lives revolved around their home and their local church and Derek, although he missed his mother greatly, already felt at ease with them.

The car came into view around a corner and his heart gave a sickening lurch. There were three people in the front seat and the middle one was definitely Karen. Now that the moment was actually here, he hung back.

As the three got out, he was horrified at the sight of his brother's cheek, covered from ear to nose with a great crescent of livid red skin, stretched so tightly that it shone in the weak sunlight. As he shook hands with John, he could not take his eyes off the disfigurement. All the time, out of the corner of his eye, he watched Karen. Too nervous to approach her in front of the others, he waited until the general introductions had been made and then, as they all trooped inside the house, fell in step beside her. 'How are you, Karen?'

'I'm fine, Derek. How are you?'

Trying to detect her attitude to him, he stared hard at her, but her smile was as friendly and open as he remembered. He had to leave things like that because Peggy directed them to go into the parlour with the others. The room, although shining with polish, had a damp, unused smell. The dark table in the centre was laden with homemade biscuits, fruitcake, butter and small bowls of strawberry preserves. Derek was in an agony of impatience as Peggy brought in coffee and handed it around. If he did not manage to get Karen on her own now, he thought, who knew when he would ever get the chance again? So under the guise of handing around biscuits, he whispered an invitation to Karen to go to see a set of just-hatched ducklings in the barn.

To his relief and delight, she agreed, 'Oh, *sure*,' and excused herself immediately. 'Dad, I'm just going out for a minute or two. Derek's going to show me some ducklings.'

'Don't be long,' warned her father. 'I promised your mother we wouldn't be late for supper. If we're able to eat any,' he added, chuckling, munching on a slice of fruitcake.

Derek led Karen out of the house and round the side. The barn was about fifty yards away, on the other side of a railed yard. Karen padded just behind him, seeming unaware of his seething and panic-stricken lust for her. Now that the moment was here he was desperate. Short of grabbing her, right there in the open, he could think of no way to reintroduce the intimacy they had enjoyed on the ship.

The ducklings, fourteen of them, cheeped and trotted lop-sidedly behind their mother who made a beeline for her nesting box when they came into the cool, dimly lit barn. 'Oh, they're *adorable*!' cried Karen. 'Can you catch one for me? I'd love to hold one.'

Derek braved the hissing of the mother and managed to extract one of the ducklings from behind her, handing its trembling little body gently into Karen's cupped hands.

As she held it against her cheek, stroking its down, Derek decided it was now or never. 'Karen,' he said, trying to be casual but knowing his voice sounded queer.

'Mm?' She was still intent on the duckling.

'Karen, I love you.'

Her eyes flew wide and then to his chagrin, filled with mirth. 'Oh, Derek.' She giggled, then, when she saw his expression, tried to soften the blow. 'I mean, come on now, you hardly know me.'

'I do, Karen, I do. I love you with all my heart.' He tried to grab her but she evaded his grasp to save the duckling from being squashed.

'Derek! Behave! Mind the poor little thing.' She put the duckling on the ground whereupon it scuttled back to its mother.

Derek, who felt his self-control slipping but didn't care, grabbed for her again and tried to force his mouth on hers. She wrestled her mouth away. 'What are you *doing*? Leave me alone – *Derek*!'

He knew he was ruining it, ruining the whole thing, but could not help himself. 'Karen, please, Karen, remember what it was like on the ship – I love you, I love you!' He tried to kiss her again but again she fought him off while the ducklings, alarmed, ran hither and thither around their feet.

Some madness prompted Derek to believe that if he could only kiss her successfully, they could reignite the passion he had been sure was mutual. He would not let her fight him off and managed to back her up as far as a stand of baled barley straw which, under the pressure of their combined weight, collapsed, causing them to tumble on top of its separating components. As they flailed around in a welter of straw and dust, her struggles to throw him off excited him further; she felt so good under him, soft yet firm. Keeping her pinned down with his full weight, he reached for her breasts with one hand and fumbled between her thighs with the other. Suddenly, he felt a sharp pain deep in his shoulder. She was biting him!

The shock made him recoil and she took advantage of it, scrambling out from under him. 'You stupid, stupid, stupid—' she yelled, further words failing her. Wrenching blades of straw from her hair, her eyes were huge and furious as she struggled for invective. 'You're – you're – you're not a *quarter* of the man your brother is!' she yelled finally and stormed out of the barn leaving Derek slowly to pick himself up.

He looked stupidly after her, at the empty door, the paddock outside. The pain of loss was excruciating but the humiliation was even worse. She had not only rejected him, she had told him straight out she preferred his brother.

Six weeks after Dolores read Rose's letter, she was holding her friend's head as Rose retched and heaved over a toilet bowl in the bathroom off the main dormitory. 'Easy, Rose, easy,' she said, well practised with the little ones in her own family, 'easy now, you'll be OK . . . '

The spasm passed and Rose felt able to lift her head. 'I don't know what's wrong with me,' she gasped. 'I've never had a bug like this before, it comes and goes so fast.'

'This is the fourth time this week. Why don't you go to the infirmary again?' suggested Dolores gently. 'Maybe you need a doctor.'

Rose, who was rapidly feeling better, blew her nose on a piece of lavatory paper. 'What do you think it is? Do you think it's the flu – or maybe the food?'

'Could be.' Something in Dolores' tone did not sound right but her expression was unreadable as she handed Rose another square. 'You should go to Matron again,' she advised. 'I'm sure she'll be able to fix you up some way.'

'I'm not going near Matron again.' Rose snorted. 'Salts! That's all that woman thinks about. Salts,' she repeated with disgust. 'I've had enough salts in the last three days to last me a lifetime.'

166

'But you've got to do something!'

'I'm grand now, much better.' She was genuinely feeling almost normal and was even able to smile. 'I'll be fine in a few minutes, honestly. Thanks for staying with me.'

'No problem,' said Dolores, who had been granted permission by the dormitory prefect to miss Mass and to stay with her friend. 'If you're feeling better,' she suggested, 'we'd better get a move on. Mass is well over and the bleddy porridge'll be cold.'

'Coming,' said Rose. She splashed cold water on her face and dried it with the sleeve of her school jumper. 'There,' she said. 'All better.'

The Saturday of that week was cold, wet and blustery and, being November, the afternoon was already dark when the two of them were together in the boot-room, polishing their outdoor shoes. Rose dabbed listlessly at her brogues. 'What time is it?' she asked.

Dolores consulted her watch. 'Nearly half-four,' she said. 'Listen,' she said then, the words coming out in such a rush that Rose looked up sharply, 'this is none of my business, I know, but I'm your friend and I have to say this. I think you should go to a doctor.'

Alarm stabbed at Rose. 'Why? Do you think there's something seriously wrong with me?'

'I don't want to say what's on my mind. Please don't ask me any more, just go and see a doctor.' The two of them were sitting on one of the forms which ran the length of the boot-room. Dolores stood up quickly and placed her shoes in the numbered cubbyhole assigned to her then walked rapidly away.

Rose, taken aback, got up too and put away her half-polished shoes. She caught up with her friend in the senior classroom where Dolores was furiously rooting through her sewing basket. 'Dolores,' she appealed, 'can we please talk?'

Dolores hesitated for a second. 'All right then,' she said, closing the padded lid of the basket. She glanced at the other girls in the room and stood up. 'Come on out into the corridor.'

Rose followed her out and when she was sure they could not be overheard, said, 'Please, Dolores, what's all this about? Why should I see a doctor?'

'Rose,' said Dolores, staring straight ahead at a large picture of St Martin de Porres, 'has it ever occurred to you that you might be pregnant?'

'I can't be!' Rose was genuinely thunderstruck. The words seemed to have no meaning.

'Why not?' Dolores kept her eyes fixed on the halo around the black head of the saint. 'When was your last period?'

Rose's heart started to hammer. 'But my periods are irregular, you know that. Dr Markey says—'

'Have you had one since you came back after the summer?'

'N-no, but—'

'Isn't that a bit long, even for you?'

'Dolores, don't say that. I *can't* be.'

Dolores at last looked at her and Rose saw her eyes were filled with deep pity. 'I'm not saying you are,' she said softly, 'all I'm saying is that I think you should have it checked out.'

'I told you, I can't be pregnant!' Rose's voice had risen and she looked fearfully over her shoulder but there was no one near enough to have heard. 'I can't be,' she repeated in a lower voice. She felt as though the ground under her feet was moving.

'All right,' said Dolores tonelessly. 'Forget it.' She moved back towards the door of the classroom.

Rose, panic-stricken now, grabbed her arm. 'Don't go, please don't go.' She turned away to a glass-fronted bookcase against the wall of the corridor. The titles on the spines of the books were blurred. 'What'll I do?' she whispered. 'How will I do it? I can't tell anyone in the *school* . . . '

She felt Dolores beside her. 'I'll help you, we'll think of something.'

Rose got through the rest of the day somehow. And somehow, as the waves of horror came and went, she had managed to discuss with Dolores how they would get her to a strange doctor without the nuns' knowing. It was Dolores who had come up with the suggestion that the next day, a Sunday, Rose should complain about a severe toothache. A visit to the dentist was just about the only reason the girls were allowed outside the convent walls without a nun in attendance and if Rose's toothache was severe enough, it should get her out on the Monday.

'But we don't know any doctors in Dublin except Dr Flana-

168

gan,' Rose had cried. Dr Flanagan was the ancient medic who attended the school.

'We'll find one,' said Dolores, her small chin wrinkled with determination. 'I'll ask to go with you, I'm sure they'll let me.'

In bed that night, Rose lay awake and terrified. She felt as though she were struggling through a strangling forest, the trees and branches were closing in around her, suffocating her, depriving her of light and air. Suppose Dolores was right? The reality was too horrible to contemplate. A baby. Her whole life ruined. She placed both hands on her stomach: it was as flat and firm as ever. How could there be a baby in there? How would she tell her parents?

The head nun had been true to her word about talking to Rose's father about that first letter from John. Rose had managed to dissemble when her parents arrived for the visit, bearing her mother off to the orchard on the pretext of having to talk to her privately, while informing Gus that the head nun wanted to see him for a minute.

'What about?' Gus's round face had wrinkled with instant worry. He hated anything unexpected. It was usually to do with money.

'I don't know, Daddy.' Rose had shrugged. She was gambling that Gus, hating unpleasantness as he did, would not broach the subject of his talk with the head nun to her mother. She had been right and that episode, at least, had been smoothed over. But how was she going to face this one?

And should she tell John? Suppose it did turn out to be true, how could she tell him in black and white in a letter? Her correspondence with John was now carried out illicitly, via an obliging day girl who was thrilled at being part of a real romance. The day girl had brought a letter from him only the day before yesterday.

How could she phrase something like this in a letter? *Dear John, I'm having our baby . . .*

She had never felt more lonely in her life.

The top sheet on her bed was twisted like a skein of her mother's embroidery thread. Rose threw it off, got out of bed and, tiptoeing quietly so as not to wake the nun or any of the other girls, went out to the bathroom at the top of the stairs. She ran water into the washbasin and sluiced it on her face. Funny. She didn't feel at all nauseous; if it hadn't been for the sick feeling engendered by her fear, she felt quite well, even energetic. She splashed the water on her cheeks until they stung and the sensation helped calm her: there was an even chance it was all a false alarm, she reassured herself. She dried her face on the hem of her nightie and went into the toilet to check if her period had arrived. It hadn't. So she crept back to bed.

She managed to drop off to sleep and spent the rest of the night alternately dozing and starting awake. When the bell rang in the morning it cut across her sleep so violently that she was out of bed before she had properly woken. To her joy, she realised immediately she did not feel sick. She rushed out to the bathroom and checked again for her period. No sign. Still, she thought, Dolores could be just fussing. Funny how things always looked better in daylight.

But the small upsurge of optimism faded during Mass and she was attacked again by severe panic during the morning study period.

The dentist patronised by the convent had offices in Fitzwilliam Square but the two of them walked purposefully past his door. Dolores, who had relatives in Dublin and who had spent many summer holidays with them, knew the city better than Rose and led the way to Baggot Street, where she thought there might be a telephone kiosk.

She was right, but when they reached it, there was no telephone directory. Rose, who was feeling very jittery, started to cry. 'Stop it, Rose,' said Dolores, 'that's not going to help at all. We'll go to the Shelbourne, there's sure to be a directory there. And if we can't find one, we'll ask.'

Rose made an effort to control herself. She knew the Shelbourne Hotel, having been taken there for tea on several occasions during the annual visits she and Gus made to the Horse Show.

'Now the other thing is,' said Dolores briskly as they walked along Merrion Row, weaving in and out of the crowds, 'we'll have to come up with some reason why you didn't actually go to the dentist, in case the nuns check, or the receptionist checks. In fact, depending on the time we have, we might be better off going to his office and pretending we got the time wrong. All right?'

Rose nodded. She thought the two of them must be very conspicuous in their gaberdines and school crests, and even fancied people were looking peculiarly at her stomach. 'Have you got that clear, Rose?' asked Dolores a second time.

'Yes,' said Rose, perversely beginning to resent her friend's bossiness.

When they got to the hotel, Dolores sailed up the steps to the lobby, pushing the circular doors as though she came here every day of her life. It was still morning and inside there was none of the buzz Rose remembered from her Horse Show days, just a few tourists checking in and two porters standing by the desk, chatting quietly. Dolores walked up to them. 'Excuse me?' She asked for a telephone directory, was pointed in the direction of the telephones and led Rose across the lobby.

The two of them opened the directory between them. They had decided to start with the O'Sullivans, because of Dolores' conviction that since there were so many of that name in Dublin, statistically, there were bound to be one or two doctors included.

But right before the first O'Sullivan was a listing for a woman doctor, a Margaret Osuma, with an address in Blackrock. 'That's miles away,' objected Rose, 'and anyway that's not an Irish name.'

'Nonsense,' said Dolores. 'Margaret's an Irish name, isn't it? She's probably married to a foreigner. And we can get a bus in Merrion Square. Be there in no time.'

'How do we know she'll see us?'

'We don't until we ring her, do we?'

Dolores asked for the number through the hotel's reception desk and was directed to a little booth. Straining her ears, Rose could hear Dolores' side of the conversation and gathered that there was an appointment available at 2.15. 'That's hours away,' she mouthed frantically but Dolores ignored her and spelled out her name.

'O'Beirne Moffat,' she said slowly and paused. 'No, it's her first visit.' She listened again. 'Thank you.' She replaced the receiver. 'Listen,' she said when she got back to where Rose was sitting, 'beggars can't be choosers.'

'But how are we going to stay out that long?'

'We just will, that's all.'

By the time they had visited the dentist and been through the charade of making the mistake about the appointment, telephoned the convent and caught the bus to Blackrock, it was well after noon. 'See?' asked Dolores triumphantly as they bowled along the Booterstown Road. 'I told you we wouldn't have all that much time to kill.'

It was a fine cold day and Rose was half diverted by the novelty of her first outing on the top of a double-decker bus. The route to Blackrock ran along the sea; the Dublin suburbs spread gently towards the hills in front of them; to their left, keeping pace with the bus, a train moved along its track at the edge of the water, its locomotive puffing dirty smoke into the bright air like a series of fat commas. 'Wouldn't you love to be on that train?' said Rose with longing. 'I wonder where it's going?'

It was Rose's first internal examination and although the doctor, who turned out not to be foreign at all but Irish and quite young, was kind, she found the experience unbearably embarrassing and shameful. 'Get dressed, Rose,' said the doctor, when she was finished. 'Is there anyone with you?'

Her eyes blurred with tears, Rose could only nod.

'Who is it?' asked the doctor gently, taking her hand.

'My – my friend from school,' whispered Rose.

'Ask her to come in, will you?' said the doctor. She gave Rose's hand an encouraging squeeze and went back to her desk, leaving Rose to put on her clothes in privacy behind a set of screens which separated the examination couch from the rest of the surgery.

Rose asked Dolores to come in and, after introductions, the two of them sat together on one side of the doctor's cluttered desk as she gave them the news that, in her opinion, Rose was definitely pregnant. The room began to spin around Rose's head and she heard the doctor's words as though they were coming from the bottom of the ocean. Dolores took her hand and held it tightly in her own small paw as the doctor continued. 'I won't know with absolute certainty until I get the results of the test back from the laboratory, but I think there's no doubt . . . '

I think there's no doubt. Rose grappled with the words, turning

172

them round and round in her head. They made no sense. She realised the woman was looking at her, as though waiting for an answer to a question. 'I beg your pardon?' she said and felt Dolores increase the strength of the grip on her hand.

'What will you do, my dear?' the doctor repeated.

Rose could think of nothing except the words *I think there's no doubt*.

'Is your mother alive?'

Rose nodded. This experience, the doctor's office, the soft words – the whole thing was completely unreal. Right in front of her in a leather box on the desk, she noticed two little bones side by side. One of them had a rounded end, the other a socket; they were obviously designed to fit snugly into each other. A joint of some sort. She would love to know what sort of bones they were, what joint it was that was so superbly engineered . . . She realised the doctor was still speaking to her. 'The sooner your mother knows the better but, of course, as I said, we won't know for sure until we get the test result.'

Still Rose could only stare blankly so the doctor turned to Dolores. 'Will you be in a position to help her? She's going to need a friend.' Beside her, Rose felt Dolores' vigorous nods of assent.

'Will you telephone me on Thursday?' the doctor asked, still addressing Dolores. She pulled a prescription pad across the desk and scribbled on it. 'This is my home number, I should have the results some time on Thursday afternoon.'

'Thank you, doctor,' said Dolores, taking the piece of paper. 'Thank you very much.' She hesitated. 'There's still some hope, is there?'

'As I said, we won't know for sure until Thursday – but I wouldn't build my hopes. The neck of the cervix is closed. I'm fairly sure she's pregnant.' As they continued to discuss her as though she were not there, Rose, absurdly, transfigured the bones in front of her to the picture of the Wexford train, the row of green carriages glinting in the sun as the locomotive pulled them along. This was a dream. She would wake up and none of this would have happened. She would wake up and be in her dormitory, or safe in her feather bed at Sundarbans.

'Stay in touch,' the doctor was saying now, at least that's

what Rose thought she was saying. She tried hard to concentrate and was glad that Dolores was with her to take care of this amazing conversation.

She heard Dolores' voice thank the doctor: 'Thank you very much, doctor,' it said.

She turned away to the door but then had to wait because Dolores seemed to have more things to say. Her voice was coming and going in waves like the sound on the wireless in the kitchen of Sundarbans. Rose tuned in when she was saying 'We'll talk it over and decide what's best.' Then she felt her arm being taken and heard Dolores again, 'Come on, Rose.'

Even her name sounded odd. Her arm was given a jerk and she allowed herself to be propelled out of the surgery.

CHAPTER SEVEN

Rose chose the small drawing room for the confrontation with her parents.

After the visit to the doctor, she and Dolores had talked about her simply running away to have her baby anonymously in London. But they abandoned the idea as being impractical. Even if Rose were to sell her amethysts, they reckoned they could not muster enough money between them to support her for six months.

The decision to stay was taken during a meeting in the linen closet on a bitter stormy Saturday in early December. 'I could work?' Rose had suggested, but without much enthusiasm.

'At what?' Dolores raised her eyebrows.

'Maybe I could be a waitress in a café.'

'Be sensible, Rose. With no experience? When you're big and heavy? Where would you live?'

'Other people do it.'

'I know, Rose. But you're not other people. Have you ever washed a dish in your life?'

Rose had hung her head. Physically exhausted from lack of sleep — to the extent that the nuns were commenting on her lack of concentration in class — her existence seemed now to have become horribly simplified, concentrated on the point in her stomach where she imagined a baby was growing. Her emotions were teetering wildly all the time between the two extremes of blinding panic and a featureless dejection where she felt like a piece of grey cardboard. The only relief came when occasionally she managed to sleep.

'Look,' Dolores had said at last, folding her arms with an air of finality, 'you know what you have to do. The only thing is to go home and make a clean breast of the whole thing. It mightn't be too bad . . . ' she had added, but without much hope. Both she and Rose knew that pregnancy out of wedlock was still the most heinous crime a girl in rural Ireland could commit.

'I can't face it,' Rose had whispered.

'If you think it'd help,' Dolores offered, 'I'll come with you to tell them.'

'To Sundarbans?' Rose had been astonished and touched that her friend would go this far. Then she had thought it only fair to warn Dolores about just how bad it might be. 'You've met my mother, haven't you?'

'Yes. But you might be surprised. You are her only child, after all.'

'There's another thing,' said Rose. 'It's very, very boring at Christmas at Sundarbans.'

'Listen, Rose,' Dolores said, 'I don't know what you think I'm used to but it's fighting and squabbling and a whole lot of noise I could do without. It'll be a great rest. You'll be doing me a *favour*, for God's sake.'

Rose had known otherwise and was truly grateful. She had even been able to smile. 'Dolores, you're a brilliant friend.'

'Nonsense! You'd do the same for me.'

But now the evil moment was here and the two of them were sitting at a rosewood table in the bay window of the small drawing room at Sundarbans. Outside, the wind sang in the eaves and scurried round among the leaves and debris of winter. It was cosy in the room, the firelight playing cheerfully across the patch of golden fur on the back of one of the Pekineses which snored in its basket.

The girls were pretending to play Twenty-fives but listening out for Rose's mother and father. 'Are you cold?' Rose asked her friend, half standing to refuel the grate. Seeing the house through her friend's eyes, she was very conscious of how shabby everything looked. At least, she thought, there was always plenty of firewood.

'I'm fine,' said Dolores. 'Sit down, Rose, stop fussing. It'll soon be over and we'll know the worst.' Rose picked up her cards again but her hands were trembling. She had suggested waiting to tell her parents until after Christmas Day but Dolores had advised against it. 'They'll know there's something wrong, Rose, in any account. Look at the way you're moping around. They're already asking you what's wrong. You might as well just get it over with.'

They heard two sets of footsteps, one heavy, one light. Rose began to sweat.

'There you are, girls,' said Gus, pushing open the door. 'Mrs McKenna says supper's nearly ready. Hope you like liver, Dolores. Plenty of time for turkey and so on in the next few days.'

'I love liver, Mr O'Beirne Moffat.'

'Good, good. Think I'll have a drink – how about you, my dear?' He turned to address his wife. 'Care for something?'

Rose's mother shook her head. She crossed to a little couch from which she picked up her embroidery frame. She drank hardly at all, sherry on Christmas morning, champagne at celebrations but it was a family joke that Gus habitually offered Daphne a drink when he was taking one himself. He turned to Rose and Dolores. 'How about you two girls? Would you like a lemonade?'

'No, thank you,' they said together, but only Dolores was audible.

'Right, so,' said Gus, turning away and pouring himself a generous measure of whiskey. 'Here's the first today.' He held the whiskey up to the light to admire its colour and settled himself in a wing chair beside the fire. The Pekinese stood, yawned and stretched like a cat, made two full turns and flopped again on its cushion.

Although Rose avoided Dolores' eye she could feel it boring into her, urging her on. Then she could hear her own voice making the announcement, dropping it like a bomb to shatter the peace in the room. She closed her eyes. She had heard herself so loudly that when she opened her eyes again she was almost astonished that no one had moved.

She tightened every muscle in her body. 'Daddy? Mummy?' She had not called her mother by that diminutive since she was three years old.

'Mmm?' answered Gus, who was gazing into the fire.

Her mother looked up from her embroidery and Rose squeezed her eyes shut again. 'I've something to tell you both.'

'What is it?' It was her mother who spoke but through her closed eyelids Rose could sense that Gus had turned towards her from his contemplation of the fire.

'I'm afraid it's bad news. *Very* bad news . . . '

'What, Rose? Come on, don't shilly-shally.' Daphne's voice was sharp with alarm.

Rose opened her eyes and looked bravely at her, straight into the small pale face with its perfectly coiffed hair. Her mother was wearing blue today. 'I'm afraid I'm pregnant,' she said. It was out at last and a wave of something, which to her surprise she recognised as relief, washed over her.

'What?' Gus half rose from his seat. He was not looking at Rose but at his wife.

Daphne O'Beirne Moffat sat like a stone, her embroidery needle poised in the air over the frame like a tiny spear. 'I beg your pardon?' she whispered.

'I'm pregnant,' said Rose, flatly. 'I'm going to have a baby.'

'You're pregnant,' repeated Daphne.

'Yes, Mother.' Rose transferred her gaze to Gus. 'I'm sorry, Daddy,' she said.

Gus moved over to sit beside his wife. 'Are you – are you sure, my dear?' he asked.

Rose looked at her friend for help. Dolores' face was bright red. 'We're sure, Mr O'Beirne Moffat,' she said strongly. 'We're absolutely sure. We've been to a doctor.'

'And what business is this of yours, may I ask?' Rose's mother's voice was as hard as an ice-pick.

'It's every business of mine, Mrs O'Beirne Moffat. I'm Rose's best friend.'

'I'd like to talk to my daughter in private, if you please, Dolores.' Rose's mother inserted the embroidery needle into the canvas, wound a piece of thread around it and placed the frame between herself and her husband on the seat of the couch. She folded her hands in her lap and waited.

Dolores stood up from the table. 'Certainly, Mrs O'Beirne Moffat. Of course,' she said. She walked across to the door and opened it. 'I'll be up in our room, Rose,' she said.

'Now, miss,' said Rose's mother when the door had clicked shut, 'how, may I ask, did this happen?' The thin voice cut like steel into Rose who did not dare look up from her examination of the worn carpet.

'Daphne, please,' Gus entreated. Rose glanced gratefully at him. His face was bright red and he was winding and rewinding a tassel on the arm of the couch through the fingers of one hand.

'I want to know how this happened,' Rose's mother insisted. 'Who's the father?'

'What does it matter, now?' asked Rose, raising her chin.

'Don't speak to me like that! *Who is the father?*'

Not for anything would Rose betray John Flynn. She set her lips in a stubborn line.

'Rose! Tell me this instant!' Her mother's body seemed coiled as if she was ready to spring.

'Daphne.' Gus lumbered to his feet. 'I'm sure Rose will tell us. I'm sure she will. Won't you, Rose?' He appealed across the room.

'Daddy, there's no point in making an issue out of it.' Rose hated what she was doing to her father, placing him in the middle like this. But she couldn't betray John. Abruptly, she floated out of the scene, looking down on it as though she were a spectator.

Almost calmly she heard her mother's voice crack. 'You silly little – little—' and saw her pretty face contort into ugly lines. In her detachment, Rose realised that even under extreme provocation, her mother could not bring herself to swear. Daphne, she knew, considered self-control one of the cardinal virtues.

Rose watched the ugly lines around her mother's mouth as she spluttered, 'What have I ever done to you to deserve this? What have any of us ever done? Your father and I, the disgrace—' Then, to Rose's horror, Daphne began openly to cry, making no attempt to stifle her sobs, fat tears cutting lines on her powdered cheeks. Gus attempted to pat her shoulder but she swiped savagely at his hand, brushing it off. 'You're as bad!' she shouted, tears distorting her voice. 'It's all your fault. If you hadn't been so lackadaiscal with her—' Her voice rose to a half-scream as she turned on Gus, raising her fisted hands as though to pummel his chest. 'How many times did I tell you—'

Rose, who had never seen her mother like this, plunged back into participation, shouting to make herself heard above her mother's screaming. 'Mother, Mother, stop this, stop it, both of you!' The Pekinese, alarmed at the din, jumped out of his basket and skittered, barking, across the floor towards the door.

Daphne did stop. She covered her face with her hands and sobbed as though her heart would break. The Pekinese continued to bark at the door. Rose ran across and opened it to let him out; her detachment of a few seconds before had deserted her and she found her mother's emotion more terrifying than her anger. 'Please, Mother,' she whimpered from the door. 'Please. This has nothing – nothing at all – to do with Daddy. Please don't blame him. It's all my doing. I got myself into this mess.'

'Oh, yes?' snarled Daphne. 'Really?' She dabbed at her eyes with the back of her hand but Rose saw with relief that she was regaining some control. She took a few tentative steps back into the room but Daphne's voice rose again. 'How *could* you do this to me – to us? After all I've – we've— *Who's the father?* I *insist* you tell us his name.'

Rose gathered up all her courage. 'Mother, I've told you,' she said quietly, undercutting Daphne's agitation. 'His name is not important.' She swallowed. 'I love him.'

'*Love!*' Daphne almost spat.

'Yes,' said Rose. 'I love him, Mother. I love him with all my heart.'

'*Then tell us who he is!*'

Daphne crossed to a table by the door on which she had placed her handbag. She opened it, took out a handkerchief and blew her nose. When she had finished, she replaced the handkerchief, snapped shut the handbag and crossed back to the couch. 'Don't bother,' she said as she sat down again. 'I think I have a fair idea. It was that last night, wasn't it? The night before you went back to school in September? When you were out all night?'

Rose looked at the small blazing face. She turned to her father, who was still standing. 'Daddy, I think that's all I want to say for the moment. I'm very, very sorry I've brought this on you – on you both.'

'He'll have to marry you.' Daphne shot the words. She flexed her fingers and studied them. 'On the other hand,' she continued, 'I won't allow it. I couldn't possibly live in this house with—'

'You won't have to, Mother,' said Rose. 'Because the question doesn't arise.'

'Well, you needn't think you're staying around here.'

'No,' agreed Rose, 'I didn't think I would be.'

'Please,' interjected Gus, 'please, let's all calm down and discuss this matter sensibly.'

'Sensibly – *sensibly*? If you'd been sensible with her long ago this would not have happened.'

Gus ignored her. 'Do the sisters in the convent know?' he asked Rose.

'No, Daddy, they've no idea.'

'Well, that's something, anyway,' said Gus, his pink forehead creasing, and Rose, through her own suffering, could see the effort he was making to do the best both for her and her mother and her heart went out to him.

'Daddy,' she repeated, 'I can't tell you how sorry I am, I really can't. I'm really, really sorry.' She wanted with all her heart to go to him, to throw herself into his arms and beg for forgiveness. She wanted him to make it all right. But she knew it was too late. No one could make it all right. Her father would do his best but would not go against her mother. And Daphne's reaction had confirmed her worst fears.

At that moment all the worrying and discussions she had had with Dolores converged on one conclusion, clear as crystal in Rose's mind: the next six months were to be gone through alone.

Daphne would never be able to bring herself to be involved with a boy from the estate gate lodge; Dolores would do all she could but, with the best will in the world, she would be going back to school, getting reabsorbed, doing her Leaving Cert; there was no point in worrying her darling John – and, anyway, she asked herself, even if she did tell him, what could he do from the other side of the world? She might tell John about the baby some time, but certainly not now.

Yes, she thought, making up her mind, the next six months were entirely her own responsibility.

None of them ate that night and the remainder of the holiday was tense and unhappy. For some reason she could not fully fathom, Rose, despite her mother's orders and entreaties, had refused point blank to go to confession and Daphne had lapsed into an injured silence so impenetrable and embarrassing that a simple mealtime request to pass the salt was granted with exaggerated alacrity by everyone else.

Although Gus, Dolores and Rose's grandmother had attempted to be cheerful, the shadow of Rose's baby had dominated their group even at Midnight Mass on Christmas Eve and at the dinner table on Christmas Day. The strain was telling on Dolores, and Rose had insisted that she should go home to her own family as soon as possible. Dolores had at first protested

181

loyally but, after a particularly harrowing and silent supper on St Stephen's Day, had acquiesced.

The following afternoon, the two friends found themselves saying goodbye to one another at the Carrickmacross bus.

Rose drove them both into the town in the pony and trap. As they bowled down the hill and around the corner into the main street, they were both in tears. 'You'll write?' asked Dolores as Rose slowed the pony to a walk.

'Every week,' promised Rose. 'I'll let you know where I am as soon as I know myself.' The uncertainty of her future almost overwhelmed her. 'The only thing I know for sure is that they're not going to let me stay around here,' she said. 'Oh, Dolores, I'm so afraid.' She swallowed hard, trying to be grown-up – after all, she was going to be a mother. She and Dolores had been up all night, talking about what it would be like, how it would feel, would it hurt a lot, how it would be when she gave away the baby – would she see it? would she like it? would it be a boy or a girl?

'Don't be afraid,' said Dolores. 'I wish it was me, Rose. I really do. I'd much prefer to go through it myself than have to think about you going through it. I feel so helpless – I hate not being able to do anything. I wish I could come with you at least.'

'Don't be silly. Sure, you'll be writing, won't you? I know you'll be thinking of me.'

'I'll be thinking of you all the time. I really will. And just think, Rose, by the summer, everything will be over. Maybe,' she hesitated, 'maybe you could come for a visit to Galway then.'

'We'll see,' Rose had replied. She knew in her heart that she would not be going to Galway. 'One thing,' she said, 'please, please don't forget about John, sure you won't?' They had made complicated arrangements to enable Rose's continuing contact with John Flynn. She would write to him, using the school address at the top of her letter, and would fold his letters into her weekly correspondence with her friend. Dolores would then send John's letter on to Prince Edward Island. In order to get around the school censorship system, they would use the friendly services of the day girl whom Rose had used during the previous term.

'Of course I won't forget, Rose,' said Dolores. 'You can trust me, you know you can. One more thing,' she hesitated, 'you're absolutely sure you shouldn't tell John?'

Rose's face hardened. 'I've my mind made up.'

'What will you say in the letters?'

'I told you I'm going to be a writer. Trust me!' Rose tried to laugh but her tears turned the laugh into a sort of giggle. Then she heard the revving of the bus, which had been loading up at the side of the road. 'Oh, God!' She threw her arms around her friend and hugged her fiercely. 'What'll I do without you, Dolores?'

'You'll manage perfectly well,' said Dolores, her voice muffled.

'But I might never see you again.'

'Of course you will. And don't forget, I'll be thinking about you. All the time, like I said. Goodbye, Rose.' Dolores kissed her friend's cheek.

'Goodbye, dearest Dolores.' Rose did not attempt to return the kiss. Through blurred eyes, she watched Dolores climb the steps into the bus but she was crying so hard as the vehicle lumbered away from the stop that, although she waved her hand, she saw her friend's face at the window only as a pale, indistinct oval.

On the second last day of December, Rose and her father boarded the same bus for Dublin. Rose's mother did not come to town to see them off. Her grandmother had wanted to but Rose had begged her not to. 'Please, Nanna, I couldn't bear it, getting on the bus and seeing you there waving, leaving you behind. Please don't come. I'll write to you the minute I get there.'

Rose's grandmother had been shocked and hurt to hear about Rose's pregnancy but, after the initial trauma, had been much kinder about it than her mother, which was only as Rose might have expected. Since her son's marriage, Nancy O'Beirne Moffat's place at Sundarbans was a peripheral and dependent one and she never openly challenged her daughter-in-law. In the week before her departure, Rose frequently took sanctuary in her grandmother's bedroom but there was little Nancy could offer except the comfort of her tolerance.

On the evening of the day Dolores left, Daphne had gone to see the parish priest and through him organised a place for Rose in a Magdalen Home in London, a convent near King's Cross which took in unmarried pregnant girls and women. There were several such establishments in Ireland but they were too close to home. 'I'll hate it, Nanna,' Rose had wailed into her grandmother's arms after she had been told about the arrangements. 'London, I'll hate London. And I'll know no one.'

'You'll make friends, darling,' her grandmother had said, hugging her, 'don't worry. And I'm sure there will be other Irish girls there. Just be a good girl and do what you're told and it'll all be over in no time. It'll only be six months. After that, darling, you'll have your whole long life ahead of you.'

Neither Daphne nor Gus had mentioned John Flynn's name but Rose, who had confided so much to her grandmother on the day John left, wanted desperately to talk about him to someone. She brought up the subject on the night before she was due to travel to London. She had come into Nancy's bedroom to say goodnight and had found her, hands behind her head, lying fully clothed on the bed.

'Sit down, Rose,' her grandmother had invited. 'Would you like a cup of tea?' indicating a Thermos on her bedside table.

'No thank you, Nanna, I just came in to say goodnight.'

'Sit here beside me.' She had patted the bed. 'Do you want to talk?'

'Not especially.' Sitting on the bed, Rose had traced the pattern on the bedspread with her finger. 'There seems nothing much to say any more. It's all been said.'

'You're off tomorrow.'

'Yes. Oh, Nanna, I'm so afraid.'

'I know, darling, I know.'

'I miss him so much . . . ' Rose's voice had dropped to a whisper.

'I'm sure you do, darling. But things will work out, you'll see. It's only six months, remember? You wouldn't have seen him before the end of that anyway, would you?'

'No.' Sliding off the bed, Rose had walked around its foot to the window. She had pulled aside the heavy curtain but there was nothing to see behind it except her own reflection in the dark glass. 'It's different now. Everything is so – so–' but she had not been able to finish the sentence.

Everything was so – what? 'There's something I want to ask you, Nanna. I haven't told John about the baby. Do you

184

think I should?' His name, so sweet, had been difficult to say.

'That depends.'

'On what?' Rose had turned around to face the bed.

'On what *you* want, darling. You're in charge of this situation. It's really up to you. I know you want someone to tell you what to do. But that's for children. Growing up is painful but this is what it really means.'

'I can't make up my mind.'

'You will, Rose – and I'm absolutely sure you'll make the right choice. Take your time. I have great faith in you, darling.'

'Mummy will never forgive me—'

'Oh, she will, don't worry about that. It's hard for her now, she has very high standards, you know, and she's had a shock. But she will get over it. She loves you – we all love you, Rose. The time will fly and then you'll be back with us.'

Rose flew across the floor and into her grandmother's soft arms. 'Oh, Nanna, it's all too much. I won't be able for it.'

'Of course you will, my darling. Of course you will. God always makes the back for the burden.'

'But I've disgraced you all . . . '

'Nonsense, one mistake doesn't make a disgrace.'

Rose had hugged her. 'Will you write to me, Nanna?'

'Write? Me? I'm famous for writing!'

'Thanks. Oh, Nanna, I'm so sorry!'

'Stop saying you're sorry, darling. We all know you're sorry, but it was just one understandable human mistake. Please heed me, Rose, and don't let it ruin the rest of your life.'

'Nanna,' Rose had said fervently, 'I wish everyone was as good as you.'

'Nonsense! No one is good, no one is bad. We're all ragbags. We're all just doing our best.'

Rose tried to hold onto her grandmother's words as the train carrying herself and Gus creaked and squealed into Euston station.

The journey had been a sad, silent one; on the bus ride from Carrickmacross to Dublin, on the mail boat to Holyhead and on the long, endless train tride to London, Gus had spoken only to offer her food or to ask her if she was all right. Despite his silence, Rose, who knew how much this trip was costing her

185

father emotionally, was grateful to him for his tacit support and tried to show him in small ways, smiling at him or touching his arm occasionally when he did say something which needed a response from her.

She already regretted the weakness she had shown her grandmother the night before and was more determined than ever to be strong and to go through what faced her in the next six months with as much dignity as she could muster. So when Gus tried to take all the bags, she would not let him, but insisted on carrying as much as she could handle.

They went out into the weak winter sunshine which was trying to break through the remnants of a fog and the back of Rose's throat was immediately caught by the acrid, smoky air of London. She was so tired that even though she was dreading her first encounter with whoever was in charge at the convent, she was longing to complete the journey and hoped she might soon be allowed to lie down and sleep.

They took a taxi, riding through a series of residential streets lined with modest brick houses and some small shops, none yet open. In the window of an off-licence, Rose saw a sign advertising a New Year's Eve Special Offer of cut-price whisky, gin and champagne and realised with a shock that it was the last day of the year. It was only eleven days since she had come home to Sundarbans from school but it might have been in another century.

The convent was in a quiet street a few hundred yards from King's Cross. Rose's stomach lurched when she looked up at the building which was to be her home for the next six months. Only the roof of the three-storey building was visible behind a high grey stone wall which bore a sign, white lettering on a green background: GOOD SHEPHERD LAUNDRY.

Gus paid off the taxi. They looked along the wall and spotted a heavy door, shining with brasses. Gus pressed the bell but although Rose listened hard, she did not hear it ring. 'What do you think?' asked Gus. 'Do you think it's broken? Will I ring again?'

But Rose was too nervous to answer. All she wanted was to run away from this forbidding place as fast as she possibly could. Now that she was actually here, fear energised her. Her

186

heart thumped in her throat making it difficult to breathe normally. Gus pressed the bell again, but again there was no sound. They were just about to turn away when they heard a noise. A panel in the centre of the door slid back and a nun's head appeared in the opening. 'Yes?'

'O'Beirne Moffat,' said Gus. 'We have an appointment with the Reverend Mother.'

'Oh, yes,' said the nun. The panel was slid back in place and Rose heard bolts being opened. The door was pulled wide and she and her father stepped through, finding themselves in an oblong cobbled yard. 'Good morning,' said the nun, 'we're expecting you. Follow me, please.' She did not extend a hand or wait for a reply but closed the door behind them, bolted it and hurried in front of them towards the building.

Heart still thumping, Rose followed her through another door and into a tiled hall. Here again, everything shone, the floor, the paintwork, the brass rail around a statue of the Blessed Virgin in an alcove, the china jardinière planted with gold- and copper-coloured chrysanthemums in front of it. 'Wait here, please,' said the nun, indicating a bench seat along one wall.

She whispered away out of sight around a corner and Rose sat with her father on the bench. She could see the two of them reflected in the glass of the framed picture of Pope Pius XII, which leaned outwards at an angle from the wall opposite. 'It's nice and bright, anyhow,' said Gus. Somewhere deep in the building, someone laughed, a high, gay sound. 'See?' Gus nudged Rose. 'It really won't be all that bad.'

Before Rose could answer, a different nun swept around the corner and into the hall. She was an imposing figure, tall and thin with immense brown eyes which were creased around the edges with laughter lines. In the crook of her arm, she carried a manila folder. Both Rose and her father stood as she approached, holding out her hand. 'Mr O'Beirne Moffat?'

'Yes,' said Rose's father, shaking the nun's hand.

'And this is Rose.' It was a statement rather than a question. Rose put out her hand. The nun's grip was warm and firm. 'I'm Sister Benvenuto, the Reverend Mother here. You're welcome, Rose.' The brown eyes passed swiftly over her. Rose had the uncomfortable feeling that she was being assessed and that whatever the nun saw now would be immutable. The nun dropped her hand. 'Let's go into the parlour.' She led the way towards one of two doors which led off the hall. 'I've ordered tea. You must be tired after your long journey. Leave your bags there, we can get them later.'

Rose cheered up a little as she followed the nun into a bright carpeted room. This woman seemed entirely unlike the person she had imagined would be in charge of an institution for fallen women.

The parlour was furnished with a piano, a number of easy chairs, a long table of gleaming mahogany and a Victorian what-not which held *cache-pots* filled with greenery. Rose waited to be told where to sit and Gus, always uneasy in the presence of nuns, hovered too. 'Sit down anywhere,' said the nun.

Rose balanced herself on the edge of a club chair. One of the springs in the upholstered cushion stuck uncomfortably into the small of her back but she dared not shift. 'Right,' said Sister Benvenuto who had a trace of an accent Rose could not place but which she guessed was rural English. 'How are you feeling, Rose? You've been well? Any morning sickness?'

'Yes, sister,' whispered Rose. 'But it's gone now.' Shame flooded her face at the matter-of-fact way the nun was talking about her pregnancy in her father's presence. She and Gus had never referred openly to the baby.

Sister Benvenuto noticed her discomfort. 'Don't worry, my dear, this is no holiday camp, of course, but it's not a torture chamber either. My attitude is what's done is done and we have to make the most of things. And don't forget,' she added, smiling, 'you have new life in there. A little miracle of sorts.

'I used to be a nurse, by the way,' she added. She turned her smile on Gus and Rose thought gratefully that she had never seen a wider, more wonderful smile.

There was a knock on the door and a girl, not waiting for an invitation to enter, brought in a tea-tray. Largely pregnant, she had wild thick hair, black as tar; her eyes, under beetling brows, were nearly as black and danced in her head, as with eager curiosity, she looked Rose up and down. 'Thank you,' said Sister Benvenuto. 'Now, Effie,' she added drily as the girl placed the tray on the table, 'as I think you've gathered, this is the new

188

girl, Rose O'Beirne Moffat.' She turned to Rose. 'And this is Effie Brophy. Effie's from Ireland too and I thought you might like to meet her as soon as possible. She obviously can't wait long to see you.'

'How do you do?' said Rose stiffly.

'Howya,' said the girl, smiling, her eyes virtually disappearing in two curved slits of merriment. The effect was irresistible. 'It's Florence, really,' she continued, 'but I hate Florence, I don't think I look like a Florence at all – so everybody calls me Effie.'

Her flat, midlands voice, thought Rose, was like her appearance, rough and merry; this girl's personality was unlike any other she had encountered. 'I see,' she said uncertainly.

Effie was not put out by Rose's hesitancy. 'Do you want me to show her around, sister?' she asked the nun. 'Show her the ropes, like?'

'Let her have her cup of tea first, Effie. Come back in about ten minutes.'

'Right-oh! See you then, Rose.' Not waiting for a response, the girl breezed out of the door.

'Effie's quite a character around here,' said Sister Benvenuto when she had gone. 'We'll miss her when she goes.' She opened the manila file, spreading it on the table. 'Now, Rose, there are a few questions we have to ask, a few things we have to get signed.' Her attitude continued matter-of-fact as she ran down the list of questions, many of them medical – whether Rose suffered from allergies, how many visits she had made to a doctor.

While Gus was signing some documents, Rose looked around the parlour. The walls were decorated with photographs of nuns and pictures of saints, including the Little Flower and one which Rose guessed was St Catherine of Siena. A large and very bright oleograph of Christ, the Good Shepherd, was hung in pride of place over the mantelpiece. Rose, who was familiar with this picture, nevertheless had to stifle a sudden, nervous giggle. The Son of God was looking patiently into the middle distance with a lamb draped around His neck as usual but, to Rose, whose emotions were so finely balanced, this particular lamb looked like an absurd and surprised woolly scarf.

Effie came back, knocking on the door and again entering without waiting for an invitation. 'Are you ready – is she ready, sister?' she addressed Rose and the Reverend Mother all in one breath.

'Yes, I think she's ready,' answered the nun. 'Anything you'd like to ask me, Rose?' she enquired.

'No, sister.' Rose hesitated and looked at Gus. Now that she was going to say goodbye to him, she was swamped with a wave of pure misery.

Sister Benvenuto took charge. She put the cap back on her fountain pen and, snapping shut Rose's file, stood up, addressing both of them together. 'Don't worry, now, Mr O'Beirne Moffat, we'll take good care of her and I think you'll find, Rose, that after the first few days, the time passes very quickly here. As I said earlier, this is not a holiday camp and we believe in the dignity of work. You'll be working in the laundry with the other girls, but they're not a bad bunch, you'll find, and Effie will look after you. Won't you, Effie?'

'Sure, I will, sister. Hope you've got a good strong back, Rose.'

'Now don't frighten her.' The nun smiled.

Rose turned to say goodbye to Gus. She hugged him briefly, burying her face in the lapels of his tweed jacket. Gus smelled strongly of his tobacco, of horses and of Sundarbans and her misery intensified. 'Goodbye, Daddy,' she whispered and then turned towards the door.

Effie was ahead of her, holding it open. 'Yerra, don't worry, Rose,' she murmured, patting Rose's arm. 'You'll be grand . . .' Rose looked back and her father half waved. She saw that his hand was shaking.

Blinded with tears, she turned away and stumbled past Effie through the doorway.

John was bitterly cold when he woke and realised immediately that in his sleep he had thrown off his feather comforter. He pulled it around his shoulders and snuggled down under it, hunching himself into a little ball to get warm.

He always slept with his curtains open. Slipping slowly into the day, his eyes wandered around the furniture and objects in his bedroom, which was one of the pleasures of his new life. He had never before had a room of his own; this one, from which all colour had been bled to shades of palest blue and grey by the snowy quarterlight from outside, was small and simply furnished but, by the standards he had left behind in Monaghan, almost luxurious. The bare boards of the floor were partly covered by a hooked rug; he had a rough wardrobe for his clothes, a washstand and a chest of drawers; if he swivelled his eyes upward he could see the embroidered 'Home Sweet Home' sampler Peggy McGuigan had hung on the wall above his bedhead.

Inside and outside the house, everything was as still as though the planet and everything on it had taken a deep breath. John remembered then that it was New Year's Eve and that tonight, there was to be a *ceili* in a neighbour's house. He would have something interesting to write to Rose in his next letter.

He had not heard from Rose for about three weeks and her last letter had been just a single, rushed page. He supposed that the one which followed was tied up in the delays which always afflicted the post coming up to Christmas. He had not even had a Christmas card from her yet. But in many ways, he thought, he had no need for tangible communication. Rose's presence floated permanently inside him. She was with him when he was working, sleeping, listening to the radio in the farm kitchen in the evenings, or just leaning on a fence looking across the open land of the Island.

His eyes gradually adjusted to the quiet light from the fields outside and in his imagination he superimposed Rose's face on the glass of the window, adjusting the image so that two of the brighter stars in the black sky made eyes. His senses re-created the feel of Rose's cool skin; he closed his eyes and kissed her phantom lips. 'Rose,' he whispered, then, hearing that the whisper was audible, felt foolish. It was time to get up to do his chores. But he wriggled snugly into the bed's warm spot, postponing the leap for a few seconds more.

He had settled in well to the measured life of the farm and the comfortable domesticity of this house. Were it not for missing his mother and his constant longing for Rose, he would have been happier than he could have imagined. The field work was physically tiring, sometimes backbreaking – as when he and Derek had helped their uncle pile mounds of protective barley straw along endless clamps of potatoes – but the compensation was replete physical tiredness at the end of every day and a dreamless sleep until morning.

The work with the potato drills had been just in time because at the end of November, the snow began to fall. Delighted, John had wandered about in this new world of swirling white, tasting it on his tongue, catching delicate, individual flakes on the open palms of his mitts. In the intervals between falls, he had crunched through the sparkling fields, looking over his shoulder to marvel at the line of deep round holes he had left with his boots. Dan McGuigan had recognised his young cousin's pleasure but had warned him that the novelty might well wear off. 'Reckon we've gotten off lightly so far! Wait till we're all holed up in the kitchen and can't get near the barn and them cows's screeching to be milked!' Dan, who was a singer and fiddle player, had taught John a snow song:

> *A sighing wind brings heavy snow*
> *as every good woodcutter knows.*
> *It fills the road, it blocks the door*
> *it lays and stays and waits for more . . .*

It snowed almost every day for nearly two weeks and then, for the remaining two weeks to Christmas, each day dawned clear, blue and brilliant, so bright that neighbours commented on it, hoping that the snow cover might thaw and they would have what they called a green Christmas. But then, on Christmas Day itself, while the two boys were helping Dan to bring extra rations to the animals and fowl, new snow had started to flurry from the sky as though it had been expressly ordered from a celestial Christmas card company. John had been enchanted but Derek, aggrieved at having more rather than less work to do on Christmas Day, had refused to participate in John's wonder at the appropriateness. 'Why do they have to have more food today?' he complained to Dan as John and himself fed armfuls of potatoes into the barrel of the slicer.

Dan, a man of few words, had considered the question as he turned the handle of the machine. 'Dunno, really,' he said at last, having to raise his voice to be heard over the tinny squealing of the worm in the slicer's funnel, 'it's just tradition, I guess.

Reckon it's so the animals'll be so full they'll stay quiet and then us humans can have a good Christmas!' He had laughed then and pushed his ancient, bobbled hat to the back of his head. John, too, had laughed out loud. In the short time he had been here, he had begun to love his shy cousin.

Lying warm in his bed, the thought of Derek now made him frown. His see-saw relationship with his twin was at its lowest ebb in years.

From the first day John had arrived at the farm, Derek had been surly and uncommunicative and every now and then, when working alongside him in the fields or in the farm outbuildings, John had felt his brother's eyes on him. On these occasions when he had turned, he had surprised a look on Derek's face which he could only interpret as hatred. He had tried to find out what was wrong but his brother habitually walked away, or told him to mind his own business.

John was almost sure that Derek's mood had a lot to do with Karen Lindstrom. She had not been in touch, he knew, since that first day when she had driven with himself and her father to Kelly's Cross. She and Derek had gone to the barn to see some ducklings, and it had not been difficult to see from their demeanour when they came back into the house that they had had a row.

So John was inclined to be patient with his twin. He missed Rose so acutely that he knew how Derek must feel; he also understood that every time Derek felt bad he needed to blame someone else.

He might have had an opportunity to say something to Karen had he gone back to Halifax for his check-up with the surgeon as originally planned, but Mr Lindstrom had fractured his wrist a week before the appointment and was unable to drive any great distance. Peggy had called in the doctor from Hunter River who had pronounced that the cheek was healing well and there was no need to see any fancy consultant. Nevertheless, the Lindstroms had insisted on carrying out what they perceived as their duty and a new appointment had been made for after the thaw, when the ferries were running again.

Far away on someone else's farm, a cock crowed. John flung back the comforter and swung his feet onto the rug, leaning over to his night table to light his candle. He dressed quickly and, carrying his boots and the candle, crept down the stairs one riser at a time so as not to wake the rest of the household. As soon as he entered the big kitchen, he was greeted with a frantic scrabbling and rustling in a covered box by the stove. Dan was known locally for his success at hand-rearing animals; a neighbour's sow had farrowed out of season and the runt was the latest resident in the box.

John ignored it. He crossed to the big table which ran down the centre of the room and, putting down his candle, lit the paraffin lamp with the matches set ready beside it on the oilcloth. Then, while he waited for the flame to settle on the wick, he squeezed a fingerful of molasses from the dispenser on the table and sucked greedily.

Since he had come to the Island, John's taste for sweet things had increased in direct proportion to his consumption of Peggy's baking. As he sucked his finger clean, he felt almost guilty. It did not feel right that while his mother scrimped in Drumboola and made do with half of nothing, he and Derek should be living off the fat of the land. *Like princes*, he had written to Rose in one of his letters. But while he did not stint in his descriptions of his new life when he wrote to Rose, in his letters to his mother he held back instinctively on some of the detail of the life he lived in this house of plenty. He knew that she would be happy for her sons, but to point up the contrast between their daily lives and hers seemed to him utterly heartless.

So far, John had been unable to send home any money. The McGuigans, like most of the farm neighbours, were largely self-sufficient and lived well off their land. The only shortages in winter were of green vegetables and fresh fruit; apples were so rare they were eaten entire – core, pips, stem and all; a single orange was so prized it was deemed fit to give as a Christmas present. But Dan and Peggy had their own eggs and fowl and, for variety, two pickle barrels stuffed to the brim with pork and herring. The woodshed was stacked roof-high with fuel, mounds of potatoes and turnips jostled for space in the cellar under the house, and the big pantry off the kitchen, lined with shelf-loads of preserves, jams and bottled fruit, also contained enough cereal and flour to feed two families until next harvest. But, as elsewhere in the farming community, cash was in short supply and the boys worked for their keep, not for wages.

John placed the globe on the lamp and turned the wick up full. The scrabbling in the box by the stove was now punctuated with a high, frantic squeaking. He hardened his heart and crossed to the big black Yarmouth which was at the heart of the kitchen and which in winter-time was never allowed fully to go out.

Having riddled the grate and opened the fire door, he took two handfuls of wood shavings from a box beside the stove and fed them into the stove's open belly, manipulating the dampers and bellows until they curled and flamed bright yellow and orange. Then he threw in some kindling and, one by one, an armful of small logs from a neat stack under the copper water tank attached to one side of the stove. He waited until he was sure the fire was catching before closing the stove door.

The piglet was insistent now and its squeaking was getting on his nerves. 'All right, all right,' he said, lifting the lid off the box and reaching in. The tiny creature, warm and smooth, wriggled in his hands, rooting around blindly for its breakfast. He opened the warming oven to find the bottle of milk nestling among the woollen socks, mitts and hats and fitted the teat into the side of the piglet's mouth. The baby snuffled and gagged but then latched on, sucking noisily, dribbling quantities of the milk over itself and John's sweater.

The fire began to roar behind the doors and he interrupted the piglet's meal to close the dampers a little. Looking at the bottle, he saw there was only an inch of milk left, so he put the piglet back in its box, where it promptly fell asleep.

The kitchen ran the full width of the house, with two windows at each end. John looked to the east; over the graceful wings of snow piled against the glass, he saw that the sky was still dark. The McGuigans always took the clock with them to bed but he guessed it was about six o'clock – about ten in Ireland. Rose was probably not long out of bed. He pictured her, well muffled up, cantering across the iron-hard paddocks and fields of Sundarbans on Tartan, the pony's breath puffing two plumes ahead of him into the frosty air.

John traced the scar on his cheek, much reduced and faded until it now resembled a small pale scimitar. Despite his confidence in their mutual love, he was occasionally prey to doubt. Her letters were wonderful, full of love and longing; but he could not help but notice that, long or short, they were always rushed.

He tried to reassure himself that this was just a symptom of Rose's vigorous personality but could not help wondering sometimes if she recognised the depth and seriousness of his own love for her – and if she returned it with the same profundity.

He dug his fingers into the scar hard until it hurt; he would make the love between himself and Rose work out. If there was nothing else in life for him, he would make that, at least, work out.

He stood up, took a large metal spoon and, lifting the lid from the pot on the stove's hotplate, stirred the breakfast porridge which was warm but not yet bubbling. Replacing the lid, he fed the stove with another log.

Karen's alarm clock shrilled. Taking a second or two to surface into full consciousness, she turned it off. Little by little, she became aware of the sounds around her, the slow creak of the cast-iron radiator in her bedroom, the muffled jingle of sleigh harness from the snow outside.

She realised that it was New Year's Eve and she had a million things to do.

She jumped out of bed and pulled on a pair of slacks and a sloppy wool sweater, but before she left the room she stopped in front of her closet. Opening the closet door she touched The Dress. Hanging in soft folds from its padded hanger, it was Karen's first formal, specially imported from Boston by her father and altered to her exact fit by a local dressmaker. She removed the protective tissue paper and took the garment off the hanger, holding it against her body to see for the millionth time in the closet mirror how it would look on her.

She threw off the sweater and slacks she had just put on and slipped the cool folds over her head, closed the zipper and stood back to stare again at her reflection. Made of aquamarine satin, with sweetheart neckline and tight-fitting sleeves, the dress was deceptively simple; its moulded bodice flowed like a smooth skin across her breasts and waist into a full skirt. Karen piled her tangled hair on top of her head and pirouetted, loving the soft feel of the satin against her bare thighs where it brushed them. She imagined how she would look at the party, with make-up on and her hair done properly. How boys would look at her, how

196

she would dance and sway and dazzle. Downstairs, she heard a door close. As promised, Mabel Anderson had arrived early to start work on the food.

Careful not to crease it, Karen took off the dress, hung it back on its hanger and put on her original clothes again. She flew downstairs, pushing open the swing door to the big kitchen so hard it crashed against the wall. 'Morning, Mabel!'

The housekeeper put her hand over her heart. 'You gave me a fright!' Then she looked fondly at Karen. 'Well now,' she said, 'who's as happy as a clam this morning?'

'Me,' said Karen blithely, taking a packet of cornflakes out of a cupboard and poured a generous helping into a dish, adding milk from the refrigerator and topping off the lot with her own idiosyncratic flavouring, two spoonfuls of maple syrup.

'Heard anything about the MacDonalds?' asked Mrs Anderson, turning back to the coffee. All three of the younger Mac-Donalds, ranging in age from nineteen down to fifteen, had been invited to the party.

'No,' said Karen, her mouth full of cornflakes, 'I haven't. Why?'

'Well,' said Mrs Anderson, shaking her head dubiously, 'I don't want to alarm you, but I think you should be prepared for a call. I heard they'd flu.'

'Oh no!' said Karen, dismayed. 'That's *three* boys short. Where am I going to find *three* boys? Thank you, thank you, God!' She thumped the draining board with her clenched fist.

Turning, she crashed back out through the swing door and taking the stairs two at a time, tore up to her parents' bedroom. She flung back the door. 'Mom, there's a crisis!' she announced from the threshold.

Alarmed, her mother raised herself on one elbow. 'What is it, Karen?'

'It's just awful. The three MacDonald boys, they have the flu – so Mabel says . . . '

'All right, all right, don't panic. Don't you know some other boys you can ask?'

'What other boys? I've asked everyone presentable in Charlottetown.'

'How about asking the Flynns?' Karen's father joined the

discussion, leaning over to squint at the clock on his bedside table. 'Wait a second,' he said then in an exasperated tone. 'Do you know it's only six forty-five?'

'I know, Daddy, sorry, but it's a crisis, it really is.' To her disgust, Karen heard her voice wobble.

'All right.' Sven Lindstrom sighed and pulled a pillow behind his head to prop himself up. 'Well, what about asking those Flynn boys, then? They're nice enough, aren't they? That would be two at least – and then you would only have to find one more.'

'There's the answer, Karen,' said Karen's mother.

Karen thought fast. Since the awful episode in the barn, she had relegated the memory of Derek Flynn to a corner of her brain she reserved for items she would prefer not to think about. But she did have to admit that Derek and his brother were presentable.

She made up her mind. 'All right!' Karen had no desire to have her mother delve, particularly in front of her father. 'Will you telephone, Daddy,' she asked, 'and arrange things?'

'Have I ever let you down?'

'You're a darling.' Karen jumped up, went to her father's side of the bed and gave him a hug.

'I'll be glad when this night is over.' Her mother settled down again on her pillows. 'And for goodness' sake, Karen, wait until a decent hour of the day to start calling people.'

Karen left the room and clattered down the stairs again and into the kitchen. There should be no problem with Derek Flynn, she reassured herself as she poured herself a cup of the bubbling coffee. But as she sipped it, she was aware of a lingering doubt. She hoped that by the end of this night she wouldn't regret the invitation.

Of course she wouldn't, she decided firmly. What on earth was wrong with her? After all, it was going to be a big party and, anyway, Derek's brother would be there with him all the time.

There were fresh fox tracks in the snow in the yard. Carrying the mash, John ran to the henhouse and saw that at the door, the fox had attempted to defeat the chickenwire defences by tunnelling under them. But when he pulled the door open, he saw to his relief that the fowl, fluttering and squawking at his appearance, were all safe. He scattered the mash on the earthen floor and when they were busily pecking, collected the eggs and brought them back to the house.

Dan was still eating his breakfast at the table in the kitchen as John transferred the eggs to a pottery bowl on the kitchen dresser. 'Fox is about,' he said. When speaking to his cousin he had adopted a sort of verbal shorthand, adapting his own speech to Dan's patterns.

Derek, one of whose morning chores was to water the cows in the barn, was nowhere to be seen.

Dan ladled a spoonful of blackberry preserves onto a muffin and took a big bite. 'Me and that old Reynard know each other well,' he said while munching. 'We've a competition, him and me! If I'm lax enough that I can't protect my livestock, then who am I to have them?'

John, who had been brought up with the Monaghan notion that, to a farmer, foxes were merely vermin to be exterminated, was slowly growing used to his cousin's view that on the Island there was plenty for all. 'I've done my chores,' he said. 'I'd like to see where that fox's coming from. Should be easy in the snow.'

'You do that, son.' Dan took a mouthful of thick black coffee. 'Reckon he's near'n King's County by now.'

John, wearing an old pair of snowshoes he now claimed as his own, set off to track the fox cross-country. It was about nine o'clock, just after daybreak, and the sun's disc was low in the sky on a glittering morning of pink and blue and blinding white. The sharp air caught in the back of his throat as he creaked along in the showshoes, his footprints stretching behind him as a line of compacted ovals.

He stopped on the crest of a little hill; John knew that under these snowy fields the red earth was ploughed into long straight ridges, but their covering was now uniformly smooth and even, glittering in the hard winter sunshine. A row of birches had been planted as a shelter belt on the boundary to his left, their branches feathery with snow over pearly trunks; other species dotted the landscape on the hills around, wild cherry and stands of fir, still and straight as arrows on this beautiful white morning. Although he could hear the faint harsh cry of a crow in the distance, nothing moved in the expanse. His exhilaration grew. At that moment, John felt as tall as the clean sky.

He blew through the heavy wool of his mitts to warm his palms. From his vantage point, he could see that the fox had moved in a straight line down to the v of a small valley and was just about to follow when, from behind, he heard a shout and on looking back, saw Dan's distinctive red bobbled hat. His cousin's arms were waving – he was being called back to the farmhouse. When he got into the kitchen, Peggy, already engaged in brushing their good jackets with a bristle brush, was in a state of high excitement. The Lindstroms had invited him and Derek to a New Year's Eve party in the house in Charlottetown and because it was to go on late, they were to stay the night.

The copper steamed on the stove so they could have a bath and their Sunday shoes were lined up for polishing on newspapers on the oilcloth. 'But what about the *ceili* tonight?' asked John. Sensing Derek's immediate agitation, he was none too sure how he felt about going to a party in Karen Lindstrom's house. 'Are we both invited, Peggy?' he continued. 'Are you sure it's both of us?'

'Your name John?' countered Peggy. 'That's what the message said. John and Derek are invited to a party, eight o'clock, Karen Lindstrom's house, Charlottetown. And there's directions too,' she picked up a piece of paper from the table, holding it out to him, 'in case you can't find the house.'

'How'll we get there?' Derek's eyes blazed with excitement. 'Who's going to take us?'

'Reckon that's my job,' said Dan. 'Gotta grease the runners on that sleigh.'

'But you're playing at the *ceili*,' protested John.

'Plenty of time. Party's at eight, isn't it?'

'But it'll take hours to get to Charlottetown and then to get back . . . ' John was still raising any objection he could think of.

'Nope. Not if we take the ice road.'

'What ice road?' asked Derek eagerly.

'Public ice road. Department has it bushed already. I seen it yesterday.' Dan went on to explain that in winter, the Island's Department of Public Works tested the depth and firmness of the ice on the main rivers, then sank holes along the parallel edges of a passage they considered safe for sleigh travel, freezing young spruce trees into the holes as guide posts. 'Journey that'd take us three hours by road'll take less'n two.'

'Why are you making all these objections?' Derek took a step towards John. 'Even if you don't want to go, I certainly do.'

John held up his hands. 'All right, all right. I just don't want to put people to bother.'

'No bother!' Dan and Peggy spoke simultaneously.

All but essential work was abandoned for the rest of the day. Peggy ironed the boys' best white shirts and filled a tin bath with hot water in front of the stove, screening it from the rest of the kitchen with sheets draped along the backs of a row of kitchen chairs. Derek took his bath first. When it was John's turn, he slopped blissfully around in the sudsy water, basking in the delicious warmth. If Rose could see me now, he thought, then frowned, realising that one of the niggles he had about going to Karen Lindstrom's party was a feeling of disloyalty to Rose. Karen was a strange girl, he thought, remembering how forward he had thought her.

They were ready to go at five-thirty, their shirts starched so strongly they almost crackled, good shoes packed in their overnight valise. Dan, muffled and greatcoated, the earflaps of a beaver hat tied firmly under his chin, drove the sleigh round to the front door of the farmhouse and they climbed in. 'Wrap that buffalo round you!' he said. "S gonna be a frizzer out on that ice!'

Safely inside the storm door of the porch, Peggy waved vigorously, 'Goodbye! Goodbye! Have a great time, see you tomorrow!'

Dan clucked at the animal, a bay filly he was training to be a trotter, then, shirring smoothly along the crisp surface of the snow, they set off through the gates and down the road into the valley. The brothers had ridden in the sleigh before, but never at night. Enjoying the ride and the motion of the high-stepping horse whose harness jingled with tiny bells, John snuggled down under the fur rug. It was already dark and the first stars were appearing in the sky, so bright that the snowfields all around them shone faintly like satin. Somewhere in the little hills to their right, a dog barked; another one answered and then a third, deep in the valley in front of them, joined in the conversation. The oil lamps glowed yellow in the windows of their neighbours' houses along the road but nothing moved in the snow except themselves.

John wished with all his heart he was a painter or a writer, so he could somehow capture this scene and these sensations for ever. As they glided along, he tried to conjure up the words which, in his next letter to Rose, could do justice to all this beauty.

Adding to his joy was his unexpected closeness to Derek. The buffalo was not a big one and for it adequately to cover them both, they had to huddle close together, like they used to in bed in Drumboola when they were very small. John could feel Derek's excitement in his own pores and, although he could not repress entirely his worry about the outcome of their visit to Karen, he rejoiced for his twin. He dared not say anything, however, in case he should spoil the peace.

They joined the frozen river below Brookvale and once on the ice, the going was slick and fast and the filly began to enjoy herself. She had been given a feed of oats before they set off and was in high spirits, clipping along as though she were between the shafts of a sulky. They passed another sleigh and met several going in the opposite direction, their lamps almost redundant on such a bright night. John, content and warm against his twin, lay back on the cushions and surrendered to the rhythm of the journey.

They reached the Lindstroms' house just after eight. It was wired for electricity and every window was lit so the whole house glowed like a beacon. The snow had been cleared from the front and Dan had to park the sleigh a little way down the road. 'Off with you now,' he said. 'Enjoy yourselves! Pick you up tomorrow noon.' The arrangement with the Lindstroms was that they would take the boys as far as Kingston, which was approximately half-way to Kelly's Cross.

'All right,' said John, 'thanks.'

He and Derek did not go straight up to the door but loitered just outside the oblong of light which spilled from the house. John's heart was fluttering. He felt exposed and countrified and peculiarly protective of Derek. 'Well, we might as well go in,' he said at last, but made no move.

'We'll wait here a second,' said Derek. 'Maybe someone else'll come along and we can go in with them.'

They pulled up the collars of their coats and stood together in the shadows, each pretending to the other that he was listening to the muffled beat of the music from inside. For several minutes, no one else approached the house and then a car pulled up at the driveway, snowchains crunching. It was Derek who moved. 'Come on,' he said. 'It's now or never.'

To his relief, he saw it was not Karen who opened the door but her father. Sven Lindstrom, having greeted the three on the doorstep, spotted the twins who, by that time, were moving up the driveway. 'Well, hello there – you made it. Lovely to see you – how's the war wound, John?'

'Fine, thank you, sir,' said John, touching the scar on his cheek with his mittened hand. 'Nearly better.'

'I can see that,' said Karen's father as he drew them inside and closed the door. 'You know where to go?' he asked the other three.

'Sure, Mr Lindstrom,' said the girl, who was petite with dark curly hair, but she was not looking at her host. To John's chagrin, she was staring at his scar. He felt horribly embarrassed but willed himself not to touch it a second time.

Mr Lindstrom took his arm. 'Let me show you where to put your things. Then I'll tell Karen you're here – she'll be delighted.'

They followed him up the stairs and into a wide, low-ceilinged bedroom. 'This all right for you?' Mr Lindstrom waved his hand in the air.

'It's – it's wonderful, Mr Lindstrom,' said John. He meant it. The lamps were lit on several side-tables ranged around the walls, giving the room, despite its size, a cosy, inviting feel. The furniture, large and heavy, bore the sheen of much polishing and all the fabric in the room, the heavy swagged curtains, the canopies over each of the beds, the covering on the little *chaise* in the centre of the room, was of matching chintz in the colours of autumn, green and gold and a soft velvety brown.

'Yes, it's really great, thanks a lot.' Derek nodded vigorously in agreement.

Mr Lindstrom took the valise out of John's hand and placed

it on a blanket chest at the end of one of the beds. 'Let's take a look at you,' he said, standing back from them. 'I'd swear you've both grown half a foot since I saw you last!'

John had almost forgotten what a nice person Karen's father was. He laughed. 'Oh, I don't think so. We've got a bit fatter, I think – all that maple syrup.'

'Well, you certainly look well. I'd better get back down to my post,' continued Mr Lindstrom cheerfully, moving towards the door. 'I'm doorman tonight. If there's anything you need, just holler.' He left the room, closing the door gently behind him.

The two boys looked at one another. Derek's face was alight with excitement. 'This is the way to live – hah?' He went across to one of the beds and bounced on it. 'Four-posters.'

'They're not,' objected John. 'There are only two posts.'

'Two posts'll do me.' Derek bounced again, looking upwards at the way the frilled canopy shivered with the movement. Then his voice dropped to a low, urgent whisper. 'Oh, God, John, I love her so much!' His eyes burned into John, who was shocked by the suddenness of the admission. And he knew his brother was now waiting for him to say something specific and significant. He could not think of anything and racked his brain as silence grew between them like a fungus.

'I – I know you do – love her, I mean,' he stammered, too late.

Derek stood up and walked towards the bathroom. 'Yes, well, I'm going to wash my hands.' When he emerged a few minutes later, he was outwardly calm, but there was tension in every line of his body.

John washed quickly and combed his hair. When he was ready, the two of them went down the stairs to the party which, by the sound wafting upwards, was clearly in full swing.

A girl at the end of the stairs saw them coming down. 'Hi,' she said, then called through the open door of the room John remembered as the drawing room, 'Karen! More guests!'

Karen came into the hall just as they reached it. 'Oh,' she said, when she saw them, then, holding out her hand, 'Hello there! You're very welcome.'

From slightly behind him, John heard Derek's intake of breath. Loyal though he was to Rose, he had to admit that Karen looked spectacular. Seeming far older than her seventeen years, her blonde hair was piled loosely on her head and caught at the crown in a diamanté buckle; she wore a dress which fitted her like a shining blue skin, the neckline was cut in two curves, above which swelled the creamy tops of her wonderful breasts. 'Hello,' he said, holding out his hand. Karen's handshake, as he had remembered, was strong and warm.

She smiled. 'How've you been, you two?' she asked but he saw she addressed only himself.

Derek's presence behind him felt like iron pressing into the small of his back so he stood back a little to bring Derek into line with him, to allow the greetings to spread. But when Derek merely continued to stare, tongue-tied, John answered for both of them. 'We've been fine, just fine, haven't we, Derek?' He willed Derek to join in, to say anything at all, but his twin might as well have been struck by lightning.

Karen reached up and touched the scar on his cheek. 'Your wound's great.' She laughed. 'Sorry, I didn't mean it to come out that way but you know what I mean. Looks like you won't need to go to Halifax again after all.'

The touch, with the tips of her gloved fingers, had felt like feathers. 'No,' John agreed. 'Your father's been more than good.' Feeling Derek's pain, he wished with all his heart that she had not touched him.

'You look beautiful, Karen.' Derek's voice, sharp and hard, at last cut in.

'Thanks, Derek,' she said, addressing a point somewhere below Derek's Adam's apple, and immediately turned away. 'Come on inside. I want to introduce you to the troops. Everyone's dying to meet you.' She walked in front of them into the reception room, swaying along on very high heels which gave a seductive, rolling pitch to her hips and bottom. As he followed with his brother, John again willed Derek to calm down, to take things easy.

He felt overwhelmed when he actually entered the drawing room. The noise was considerable. The scatter-rugs had been rolled up and more than a dozen couples gyrated in the middle of the floor to loud music issuing from a radiogram. It was very warm and so bright that the winking lights on the Christmas tree in one corner were barely visible in the communal blaze of the other lights all over the room, the chandelier in the centre of the ceiling, the wall-lights above the blazing fireplace, all the standard and table lamps.

Karen led them directly to a long table which was set against one wall. It was laden with food, sandwiches, filled rolls, cookies, pies and cakes. A small group of boys who were making inroads into the stocks gave way to her as she spooned some raspberry-coloured liquid from a punch bowl into two little glasses. 'Have some cordial.'

'These are the Irish boys from Kelly's Cross,' she said, addressing the group in general. The boys appraised the two new arrivals as she handed them their glasses. 'This one's John, that one's Derek,' she continued. 'They're twins. John saved my life. That's how the scar happened. He was the one who rescued me from the fire when Mother and I were coming back from Europe this fall.'

'Good to meet you, John, Derek,' said one of the boys, shaking hands with each of the twins in turn. He was tall and athletic and had a large J embroidered on his jacket. 'This is Dave, Sam, Jimmy, Patrick and Ezrah,' he indicated the other boys, 'and I'm Billy deFresne.'

The other boys chorused their 'hi's and 'hello's and then turned back to the food. John heard a mutter from one of them. 'Wish I'd rescued her!'

'Well, I'll leave you guys to get acquainted,' said Karen. She swayed off to the other side of the room.

All the boys followed her progress. 'Chee-ee . . . ' said the one who had expressed the wish to have rescued her. He repeated the expletive, elongating the vowels on a long, appreciative exhalation. 'Chee-ee . . . Daddy, buy me that!'

'Somebody already did,' muttered one of the others and Billy spun round.

'Who said that?' All of them lowered their eyes. Billy refilled his glass from the punch bowl. 'Go take a shower, Ezrah,' he said coldly. He turned back to the twins. 'We're all in love with our Karen,' he said, more easily, then laughed. 'But unfortunately she's not in love with any of us.'

On Derek's behalf, John tried desperately to think of some

other topic of conversation. 'If your name is Billy why have you a J on your jacket?' he asked.

'Oh, it's nothing,' said the boy, 'it just an athletics letter.'

'Yeah, nothing,' said Ezrah. 'Only top jock.'

'I see,' said John. He took a sip from his glass. 'Lovely punch,' he said.

'Stick around,' said one of the boys with a giggle. 'It'll get better.'

Two girls joined them. One was plain and heavy, with large pale eyes; the other was the petite dark-haired girl who had come to the party at the same time as the twins.

'Karen says everyone's here now and we're going to have a Paul Jones,' said the small one.

'Oh, goody!' said Ezrah. 'Bet I end up with Mary-Lou Popplewell.'

'Don't be nasty, Ezrah,' said the small girl. She turned to the twins. 'Nice to meet you,' she said, holding out her hand. 'I'm Sarah Richards and this is my friend, Amy.'

'John Flynn – and this is my brother, Derek.'

The four of them shook hands and then Sarah led the whole group to the cleared dance floor. John was nervous. He had no idea what a Paul Jones was and his unease increased when he saw that it looked complicated. The guests were forming two concentric rings by holding hands, boys on the outside facing inwards, girls on the inside facing the boys. He found himself between his brother and Ezrah, facing Sarah and Amy. Karen, who was directing operations, broke into the circle on the opposite side, facing away from the twins.

Karen's father started the music on the radiogram and, to John's relief, the dance proved to be totally uncomplicated. The circles merely started to move in opposite directions at a walking pace.

Then, abruptly, the music stopped and the circles stopped with it. He found himself facing a girl wearing glasses, dressed in stiff yellow taffeta, the skirt ballooning around her fat legs. As the circles dropped hands and moved towards each other, he realised he was expected to ask this girl to dance. 'Hello,' he said awkwardly, as the music started again and the couples began to whirl away, 'my name's John.' The girl hung her head and said something he did not catch. He stooped to hear her. 'I beg your pardon?'

'I know,' she said bravely, raising her glasses. 'I know you're John Flynn. My name's Mary-Lou Popplewell.'

'Nice to meet you. Shall we dance?'

'I'm no good at dancing.'

'That makes two of us!'

They were the last to move off. Although John had lied when he said he was not a good dancer, Mary-Lou's prowess on the floor made it appear as if he had been telling nothing but the truth. The dance was a quickstep and she held his outstretched left hand as though she were fending off a weapon, keeping her head so low that all he could see of her was the back of her head. With his right hand he could feel the taffeta on her back grow hot and greasy as she wrestled with the music and lost.

But as the dance progressed and they struggled around the floor, she was so miserable that John gritted his teeth and did his best to ignore the rhythm altogether, trying to move to Mary-Lou's mysterious inner beat. He managed to propel her into a safe corner, moving around a tiny circle of their own, where they would not be a hindrance to other couples. In a way, he thought briefly, Mary-Lou was doing him a favour. In his efforts to suit her, he had forgotten entirely all his own inhibitions.

'Sorry,' she said for the umpteenth time when despite his best efforts, he trod once again on her foot.

'Don't worry about it,' he replied, 'it's my fault as much as yours.'

She finally looked up at him, and he smiled encouragingly. Her answering expression reminded him of the runt piglet he had held in his arms that morning. Before he knew what he was doing, he had bent his head and kissed her, a swift, consoling kiss on the lips.

Immediately, he regretted the action. She stopped dead as though she had been stung. Then she blushed, the colour rising from her upper chest to the roots of her mousy hair. But her eyes were shining with a radiance which frightened him and for an awful moment, he thought she was going to kiss him back. He braced himself but to his relief, she just smiled – she had a sweet smile, he saw – and started again on her awkward, clodhopping dance.

208

John spotted Derek a few times. His brother, who was also a good dancer, seemed to be doing quite well with a girl who looked far younger than the rest of the group and whose face was wrinkled with determination as she followed the dance.

'Hi, John – I see you've met my best friend.' Karen drifted by in Billy's arms. 'Hi, Mary-Lou,' she continued, dancing away. 'Take care of him now – he's special!'

'I know,' breathed Mary-Lou, gazing up at her partner, glasses glistening under the blazing lights.

'So you're Karen's best friend?' said John, attempting to deflect her alarming attention. He was not surprised that these two were friends. He had noticed before, even in Monaghan, that very good-looking girls frequently teamed up with ugly ones.

'Yeah,' said Mary-Lou. 'We've been friends since kindergarten. Sorry,' she added as John stepped once again on the toe of her yellow taffeta pump.

The music came to a halt and the couples separated. 'Thank you,' said John politely.

'Thank *you*!' said Mary-Lou. She seemed about to say something else but lowered her head. John hesitated and looked around. He saw that everyone was forming circles again. He spotted Derek at the far side of the room, standing a little apart from everyone else. Derek's eyes were on Karen who was talking to her father beside the radiogram.

Mary-Lou was making no move to join the circle. 'Thanks again,' said John awkwardly. 'I think I'd better go see if my brother is all right. He knows no one here, you know.'

'Sure,' said Mary-Lou. 'Maybe we'll get each other again.' She blurted out the words.

'Sure, I hope so.'

Before John could get to Derek, Karen clapped her hands for attention. John saw that her father had vanished and she had now placed herself in charge of the music. 'All right, everyone,' she called. 'This next dance is a ladies' choice.' Her announcement raised an uproar. The girls giggled and started to tease one another; some of the boys groaned theatrically. To emphasise the pretence that they did not care whether they were asked to dance or not, a few of them made a dash for the refreshments table and started to stuff food into their mouths.

While Karen was selecting a record, John walked over to

join Derek who was standing alone, leaning against a wall. 'How's it going? Are you having a good time?'

'What do you think?'

'Well, I saw you dancing with that young one, she looked nice.'

'I wish we'd never come here.'

'To the party?'

'To this shagging country.'

John saw that Derek was looking at Karen again. 'Maybe she'll ask you to dance in the ladies' choice.'

'Me arse!'

'She might, Derek.' Although he was not particularly religious, John murmured a mental aspiration, *Sacred Heart of Jesus in Thee I trust*, that Karen Lindstrom would come over to ask his brother to dance.

The music began. John recognised the song as soon as the lush strings filled the room, Frank Sinatra's moody version of 'My Funny Valentine'. For a breathless moment, he thought his prayer was about to be answered as Karen turned away from the radiogram and walked straight over to where he and Derek were standing.

And then the worst thing that could have happened actually did. She smiled, dropped a pretend curtsy in front of him and held up her arms. 'May I have this dance, John?'

There was nothing he could do. He did not dare look at Derek as he moved away with her in his arms.

To make things worse, for what seemed like an age, they were the only couple on the floor. Derek's suffering pulled at John like a taut rope;. he could feel his twin's eyes boring into his back, making it impossible for him to behave naturally with Karen. He held himself rigidly away from any physical contact with her, a difficult feat during such a slow dance. She felt his standoffishness. 'Are you enjoying yourself?'

'Oh, yes.' He did not want to be rude but, conscious of Derek still watching him, was afraid to look eager.

'You don't seem to be, certainly not at the moment.'

'Well, I wish someone else would come out to dance. I feel a bit of a show.'

Karen leaned backwards in his arms. 'Hey, you guys,' she

called over her shoulder at a large group of girls clustered around the radiogram. 'What's the matter with you all? For goodness' sake, get up and dance!'

The words had the desired effect and within seconds there were ten or twelve other couples on the floor. To John's relief, he saw that the dancers included his brother and relaxed a little. 'You look beautiful tonight,' he said to Karen and meant it.

'Thank you.' She laughed. 'All wasted on this lot, of course.'

'Oh, I wouldn't say that. Some of those boys might be killed in the rush for you.'

'How about you?'

'Sorry?' Alarmed, he played for time.

'How about you?' she repeated softly. 'Would you be killed in the rush, John?'

She was only teasing him, he told himself. Her eyes were full of mischief, or so he hoped. Any other prospect was too ghastly to contemplate. 'Me?' he said, hoping he sounded gallant yet humorous. 'Oh, I wouldn't be killed, I'd get there first! After Derek, of course,' he added carefully. Then: 'Do you think you could ask Derek to dance at the next ladies' choice, Karen?'

She shifted her weight subtly so she was deeper in his arms. 'Mmm,' she said, so ambivalently that he did not know whether it was a 'yes' or a 'no.' He decided to keep his mouth shut for the moment.

The music was warm and sweet. Karen moved against him, forcing physical intimacy, her breasts caressing his chest. John looked guiltily around, hoping Derek could not see what was happening. Luckily, his brother had his back turned for the moment, locked with his partner, like most of the other couples, cheek to cheek. It was obvious from the way she was moving that Karen wanted him to dance the same way with her but he held himself away from her as much as possible. The taller he stood, however, the more she snuggled in after him, pressing her firm body along the length of his own. Her scent in his nostrils became very strong.

John began to sweat and it had little to do with the heat in the room. Despite his loyalties to Rose and to his brother, he

211

felt his body begin to stir in response to Karen's open sensuality and he wished now with all his heart the song was over. He knew Frank Sinatra's version of 'My Funny Valentine' but had never before realised it went on so long.

Karen felt his agitation and no doubt, he thought desperately, his growing erection. She looked up at him with eyes half-closed. '*Now* are you enjoying yourself, Mr Flynn?' The innuendo was unmistakable.

'Please, Karen,' he said. 'Derek—'

'What about Derek?'

'Please,' he repeated uselessly, his treacherous body acting on its own as though he had no control over it.

'Stay there.' Karen left his arms and went over to the radiogram where she moved the needle back to the beginning of the record. Marooned in the centre of the floor, John looked around desperately, sure all eyes were on him and his physical dilemma. He had to use all his remaining shreds of self-control to restrain himself from covering his crotch with both hands like a football player. But to his relief, not only was no one looking at him, no one else even seemed to notice that the record was starting again.

Karen came back and he was forced to take her in his arms again. He felt as if he was drowning. This time he could not resist when she reached up and pulled his head down to her level so they could dance cheek to cheek like all the others. She closed her eyes and her soft hair tingled against his face.

His blood was racing through his veins and his emotions vacillated wildly between wild sexual excitement and something akin to horror. As they slowly circled the room, he saw Mary-Lou Popplewell staring at him from a chair in one corner. She was eating a sandwich. As he caught her eye, she gave a tremulous little smile and raised the sandwich in a half-wave. He could not see Derek anywhere. Seemingly of their own volition, John's arms tightened themselves around Karen.

From the hallway, Derek watched his twin dancing with Karen. He could see only part of the room but each time the two of them came into view, oblivious to anyone except themselves, he felt their betrayal of him like a physical blow.

212

Someone touched him on the shoulder and he jumped violently. 'Well, now, Derek,' Mr Lindstrom said. 'Sorry if I startled you. Are you enjoying the party?'

'V-very well, thank you, Mr Lindstrom,' stuttered Derek, blushing to the roots of his hair. 'I'm – I'm just taking a breather.'

'Sure, sure,' replied Mr Lindstrom. 'Don't be a stranger though – all those lovely girls in there just waiting for a chance to dance with you.'

Derek attempted a smile and escaped back into the drawing room. About half the guests were still smooching around the floor, including, of course, his brother and Karen. He kept his eyes resolutely averted from them and caught a gleam of yellow against the far wall. Imbued with a perverse desire to make the situation as ghastly as possible for himself, to make the grudge against John and Karen even more valid, Derek marched across the room and asked Mary-Lou to dance.

The flesh of her back bulged above and below the straps of her bra, the stiff material of her dress made touching her unpleasant and she danced like a three-legged donkey, he thought scornfully as he pushed her around the floor. Again and again she apologised to him and, for manners' sake, he assured her there was no problem; all the time, however, her hopping, staccato progress served nicely to build up his inner rage.

When she stumbled and almost tripped him too, his patience ran out. 'Look,' he said shortly, 'would you like a glass of punch?' As she hesitated, he saw Karen look across the room at himself and Mary-Lou. He bent his head and kissed Mary-Lou hard.

'You Irish!' gasped Mary-Lou when he had finished kissing her. 'You're something else, you know?'

Derek did not know what she meant and did not care. 'Excuse me,' he said.

He managed to walk out of the room at a normal pace but raced up the stairs to the bedroom where he locked himself into the bathroom and let the tears come.

John stiffened against Karen.

'What is it?' her eyes were half lidded, like a cat's.

'It's nothing,' he said.

213

'Come on, it's something. I can feel it.'

'It's nothing, really,' he mumbled and bent his cheek again to hers. But although he was still as physically excited, inside, he felt as though his heart was breaking.

214

CHAPTER EIGHT

The room spun as John fought sleep, groping for information to fill gaps in his memory of the party.

Never before drunk, he hated the sensation of not being in control. The alcohol had been a silent thief and he had had several refills from the punch bowl by the time he figured out that the bright red liquid was not as innocent as it seemed. He had just finished a quickstep with Karen and was reaching for the dipper to fill his glass when he had felt a rushing, dizzy sensation in his head and had to hold onto the table to steady himself. Two of the other boys at the table, Ezrah and another whose name he could not remember, giggled as they watched his weakness: it was only when Ezrah had raised his own drink in mocking salute that John realised the cordial had been spiked.

His memory continued to blink in and out and the spinning sensation continued even when he closed his eyes and buried his head in the pillow; he hoped he was not going to be sick and was disgusted with himself for his bravado in having more of the punch, spurred by the knowing grins of the other boys at the table.

In the other bed, Derek's heavy snores ceased abruptly. For a few agonising seconds, John, who was not so drunk that he did not dread the almost certain confrontation with his brother about Karen, waited tensely. He relaxed only when Derek snorted, turned over on his side and started again to snore.

John tried to hold onto his wheeling brain as intermittent pictures of the party flashed through like a slide show. He remembered the way some of Karen's piled-up hair had escaped from its fastenings and trailed in soft fronds on the bare skin of her shoulders, cream on cream . . . Horrified that he would even contemplate being attracted to a girl other than Rose, John now felt miserably guilty that he had spent most of the evening dancing with the girl he had always thought of as Derek's. He tossed himself onto his stomach as his memory threw up more scraps of looks, feelings, conversations. 'I shouldn't be dancing with you all the time like this, you know!'

'Why not?'

'What about Derek? Isn't there something between you?'

'Was.'

Even in his present befuddled state he could recall the definite emphasis.

Then he had done something even worse than trespassing on Derek's territory, he had betrayed Rose. 'That's not the only thing you're worried about, is it?' Karen had asked. 'About Derek, I mean.'

And his Judas-tongue had answered, 'Yes, it is, honestly.'

He knew he loved Rose. He loved her with all his heart. But his brain had been giddy, Karen's waist was sinuous under his hand, her hip was swelling out from her waist in a smooth, unbroken curve and even as he was saying the awful words, his body had surged with excitement.

He turned over again as the slide show continued: Derek kissing Mary-Lou, Karen's father and mother leading the countdown to midnight, Karen and himself kissing 'Happy New Year', the circle of hands for 'Auld Lang Syne', Mrs Anderson dispensing a cauldron of hot soup, Karen feeding him soup from her own spoon, Derek kissing another girl, a redhead, Karen with her arms around Mary-Lou, Mary-Lou in tears, Derek wrapped round the redhead.

And one memory above all: Karen pulling him into the large kitchen and backing up against a wall until she could back no farther and the astonishing feel of her breasts under his hands.

The images whirled until they merged and then, gradually, receded into darkness as John descended towards sleep.

He had a vivid dream. He was walking up a mountain but the mountain kept getting higher and higher and no matter how he strove, he could not reach the top, which was smooth, rounded and white and emitted rays of light, like the sky above Drumboola after a storm. The tips of the rays reached him as he climbed but always retreated before him. He wanted more than anything to go fully into that light. He knew that if he could reach the summit

216

he could bathe in it; he felt in his bones it was what he was born to do. So, reaching out his hands, he climbed and climbed until the light was finally in his grasp, warm and smooth like he had known it was going to be.

Then it was solid. He was not on a mountain. He was with Rose and it was her he was holding. She was putting her lips over his. Gladly, he opened his mouth and tasted her tongue. The world was spinning but Rose would help him, the only reality was Rose; she was the way to the light, he rolled over her and realised joyously as he bathed in her that Rose *was* the light. He made love to Rose and cried out because he was happy, happier than he had been in a long time.

Derek woke. For a few seconds, he groped for consciousness and then realised what had woken him; John was in the bed opposite and was making a noise. He was about to shout at him, to shut him up when he realised John was not alone in the bed. All shreds of sleep vanished as, mesmerised, he saw that Karen was with him.

Derek's instinct was to scream; he opened his mouth but nothing came out.

He saw the bedclothes had come partially off John's bed and he could see both of their bodies – Karen was wearing a flimsy nightdress which was ruched up around her waist; her long white thighs were clamped around his brother's back and her head was thrown back on her arched neck.

Derek felt paralysed. Pain and shock were subsumed in a sort of horrified fascination. Although he and Karen had played explicit sexual games, he had never seen anyone fully make love before.

He watched as his brother pumped himself into Karen; watched the two of them become quiet and – through half-closed eyes in case she would notice him – watched her slip out of the bed and pad out of the door. The light from the hallway outside flared briefly over the tumbled bed and then was extinguished.

All the rage and pain came to a head. Derek leaped out of the bed and fell on his brother.

John felt the light ebbing peacefully away, leaving him quiet and dark. Then a pain pierced every part of him, a pain so bad and

217

hard that he could not bear it. Then he saw Derek was standing over him. Derek was in pain. He felt Derek's pain. He wanted to help Derek, to tell Derek he would make the pain go away but he was weak and woozy and Derek's pain was a large black crow beating its wings in his own body.

Then he felt Derek's hands on his neck. He could not breathe. Derek's hands were squeezing, tightening on his throat. With horrified certainty, John realised that his twin was trying silently to strangle him.

He managed to turn on his side, facing away from Derek, straining so Derek had to extend his arms; hunching his shoulders with all his strength, he pulled Derek onto the big bed, but could not dislodge the noose of Derek's throttling hands. His eye muscles stung as they laboured to keep his eyes in their sockets; his tongue seemed to swell in his throat.

All the time he felt the huge wings of Derek's pain pulsing at both of them.

Summoning all his strength, he crossed his hands under his chin and, right hand to Derek's left wrist, left to right, wrenched as hard as he could. For a few moments, they wrestled silently, the bedclothes churning around them, but within seconds, John's superior strength told and he was able to pin his twin's wrists to the bed at either side of his head.

Still Derek did not give up, arching and kicking as grimly and silently as ever and John felt his pain so acutely it was stronger than anything physical he himself was feeling. But now he was simply waiting until his twin should cease to struggle.

Abruptly, the fight went out of Derek and he gave up.

John managed to make the bathroom barely in time to void the contents of his stomach in a violent red torrent.

For the umpteenth time that long night, Rose lifted her head from her pillow. She stretched her left arm high above her head, angling her wristwatch this way and that, trying to catch the faint light which permeated her own cubicle from the nightlight at the end of the dormitory. The gold spots at each of the numerals glittered faintly but it was very difficult to see the hands. Eventually, she figured out that it was either half past four or twenty past six in the morning.

She had made up her mind that day that the way to survive the next six months was to be positive. If she had to be a laundry-maid, she was going to be the best laundrymaid the convent had ever seen. If she was sick, she was not going to moan, if she was lonely, she was going to keep it to herself.

But as the night wore on, her resolve had faltered; at the height of her misery, she had even wavered in her decision not to tell John about the baby. Then, mentally, she had given herself a thorough shake, repeating her conviction that there was nothing to be gained from such a self-centred act.

She placed her hands on her stomach. Was she imagining it or was it beginning to curve a little? 'Oh, God,' she whispered. 'Please help me!' But then, hearing herself, she took them away again. The plea was rhetorical. Rose knew she could rely on no one except herself. And, for now, she was not going to think about the baby. She would think about the baby when it was unavoidable.

She turned her face so it was buried in the smell of Sundar-bans. She had been required to supply her own bedlinen and the sheets and pillowcase smelled of fresh air and soapsuds, the dear and familiar scents of her feather bed at home.

Apart from the glow from the nightlight, which was negli-gible, it was pitch dark in the dormitory. The big room was divided by wooden partitions into small sub-rooms, each with its own flimsy door; as well as a bed, each cubicle was sparsely furnished with just a narrow wardrobe, a wooden chair and a bedside locker.

Having expected that the convent would be a cross between boarding school and a prison, Rose had been encouraged a little by the relatively free and easy atmosphere of the place. The girls were expected to conform to certain rules of discipline and to work hard, but within those constraints, Rose had already con-cluded that they were treated as human beings by the nuns and staff. And on a positive note, as this was England, the nuns and staff here did not seem to think she was damned for all eternity for being pregnant. And it was a relief not to have to worry who would find out, who would say what, who would snigger.

Altogether, the convent housed a complement of twenty-four and although most of the inmates were young, there was a wide range of ages. Her new friend, Effie Brophy, who was nineteen, had introduced them all, including the youngest, a small brown-faced girl, with a pinched, sensitive face, who had apparently just passed her thirteenth birthday.

Effie had also introduced her to two women who were, she said, in their late thirties, perhaps early forties. Both were, according to Effie, mildly mentally handicapped. One or two of the other girls despised them – 'twopence-ha'penny looking down on twopence,' Effie had snorted – but by and large the two were treated gently, almost as pets, by the other girls. They were always given the easiest of jobs in the house and laundry and were protected in all sorts of ways. On being introduced one of them had thrown her arms around Rose, almost crushing the life out of her with a bear-hug.

Would this night never end? It was stuffy in the dormitory and she threw off the bedclothes as the dreary litany of thoughts and fears chased their tails in her tired brain. She looked at her watch again but still could not discern the time. Things always seemed better in daylight, she assured herself. And she would write to John this evening. It might be a bit of an adventure anyhow, she thought. Now was her chance to test her writing talent.

And at least she already had a friend. Effie Brophy had taken Rose proprietorially under her wing, explaining the nuances of the convent life, whom to please, whom to avoid. Rose was slightly overwhelmed by Effie's gusty personality but was nevertheless grateful. Picturing Effie and her merry monkey face, Rose realised that, to her shame, her new friend was the kind of girl to whom she would have barely nodded in school. Up to now, she had been fastidious in her friendships, instinctively avoiding the obvious losers and the uglier of the girls. How could she have been such a snob?

Maybe this was a good thing, she thought doggedly. Maybe this was the best thing that ever happened to her. Maybe God had wanted to teach her a lesson, to pull her down a peg.

For whatever reason Effie had been sent into her life, she was very welcome. Rose recognised how badly she now needed Effie's kindness and exuberance, her uncomplicated offer of companionship. When Effie creased her face to laugh, Rose could not help but laugh too. A friendship with Effie would be a relaxing affair in which she could take a back seat; Effie would do the talking, would always take the lead.

Rose heard someone leaving the dormitory and then, after a few seconds, the distant sound of the lavatory flushing. She wondered how soon she, too, would be running to the bathroom. Effie, who was six months gone, had warned her that this was one of the awful trials of late pregnancy.

Whoever it was was coming back. Rose heard the footsteps move to the far end of the dormitory, hesitate, then come back in her own direction. The footsteps stopped outside her door. A long sliver of faint light appeared. Someone was opening her door, very slowly and quietly. Alarmed, Rose raised herself on one elbow. She wanted to cry out but did not dare. The sliver of light widened and a figure appeared in it. With relief, Rose saw the outline of Effie's wild head.

'Is that you, Effie?' she whispered.

'Ssh,' the figure whispered back. Carefully closing the door, she tiptoed stealthily across the few feet of linoleum to the side of Rose's bed and leaned forward to whisper, 'I was just out in the toilet and I was wondering how you were or were you awake.'

'I've been awake all night,' Rose whispered back.

'Move over.'

'What?'

'Move over! I'm gettin' in.'

'Is this allowed?'

'Of course not,' hissed Effie. 'Move over, for God's sake.'

Rose squeezed herself against the plywood wall of her cubicle and turned half on her side to make room in the single bed for Effie, whose pregnancy was showing large. The bedsprings groaned as she got in.

'God, these bleddy beds,' she complained.

There was no escaping physical contact with Effie's warm bulk as, with a satisfied sigh, she settled the covers around her. Rose had never before been at such close quarters with another girl and at first felt acutely uncomfortable. She forced herself to relax.

'How'd you find the work yesterday?' whispered Effie after a minute or so.

Rose hesitated, aware of her resolution to be positive. 'It'll be all right when I get used to it,' she whispered back, 'but I found it tough going.' After she had unpacked and had her lunch, she had been put to work, taking a stint in the laundry, which was a long, narrow room with high barred windows, opaque with steam.

'It's tough all right,' agreed Effie, still whispering, 'but don't worry, you'll knock a bit of crack out of it after a while. We all have our problems here but we all like a bit of crack. Them English ones sound as if they don't at first, but you'll get used to them. Just don't let them bother you. And if any of them gives you any trouble, you just tell me, right?'

Rose smiled. 'I won't, Effie, I mean I will,' she whispered. 'Thanks.'

'I'm real glad you came, Rose,' whispered Effie. 'Them English is all right, but they're just not the same as us, are they? They don't know how to enjoy themselves, like. Hard to imagine how some of them got themselves up the pole at all.' She gave a subdued snort of laughter and then gave Rose's arm a little squeeze for emphasis. Rose had to smile.

It was a very quiet morning outside, no traffic, no wind, and no one else seemed to be awake. The only sounds were the occasional creaks as the occupants of other beds moved in their sleep. Rose had to resist the temptation to lay her head for comfort on Effie's shoulder. She was feeling drowsy now and wondered sleepily how long Effie would stay.

'Ahh, shi – sugaring hell!' whispered Effie suddenly and explosively. 'The fecker kicked me.'

'What?'

'The baby, he kicked me.'

'Really?' Rose was alarmed. 'Mine doesn't kick – at least I don't think it does.'

'Ah, it wouldn't yet,' advised Effie.

'When will it start?' Effie seemed to know everything.

'Soon now, for you. At my stage, it happens a lot. They quieten down, though, towards the end.'

'How do you know all this so well?'

'It's me second time.'

Rose recoiled as far as the narrow bed would allow. '*What?*'

'Ssh, they'll hear us!'

'Sorry.'

Effie moved to take advantage of the inch of space created by Rose's tiny withdrawal. 'Are you shocked?'

'No,' said Rose, although she was.

'That's the way of the world,' said Effie, closing the subject.

But Rose could not let it drop. 'Where's the baby – I mean, the first baby?'

'Adopted.'

'Did you mind?'

'Yep.'

A sudden rigidity in Effie's body warned Rose not to continue any further with this line of questioning. She was genuinely upset at the revelation that this was Effie's second baby. Was Effie careless with her favours or did both babies have the same father? On the other hand, she thought honestly, what difference did it make? And she was hardly in a position to cast any stones. 'What time is it, d'you think, Effie?' she whispered.

'Oh, I suppose about seven. I'll have to go soon.' Rose had the disconcerting impression that Effie believed she was a perfectly ordinary visitor who had just happened to drop in, as if for afternoon tea.

'All right, so,' said Rose. 'Be careful. Don't get caught.'

John stayed in the bathroom for the best part of twenty minutes. His pyjamas were a mess, he saw, the trousers stained and damp from the wet dream about Rose. His neck was sore and his head throbbed; Derek's attack on him had jolted him into full consciousness and all vestiges of the earlier dizziness and drunkenness had left him.

Derek had tried to kill him.

His reflection, cast at him from a mirrored wall opposite the padded seat on which he was sitting, mocked him. *Weak! Weak! Weak!* cried his mirror-image. *Are you just going to let him get away with trying to kill you?*

Hands shaking slightly, he touched his bruised neck. He could not seriously believe that Derek would have gone through with it. *Oh, yes, he would*, said the John in the mirror. *Weak! Weak! Weak!*

Derek had been asleep – he had heard him snoring. It was some kind of nightmare he was having. *Oh, really?*

This whole situation was a nightmare and was now completely out of hand. Why had they come to this party? He longed for the clock to roll back twenty-four hours.

He stood up. That was stupid babyish talk. He was a man now, out in the world. He went towards the door but hesitated, trying to hear what sounds there were in the bedroom but could detect nothing. Moving slowly and cautiously, fearing that Derek might again launch an attack, he eased himself out of the bathroom and into the room.

John's twin was sitting hunched on the edge of his own bed, his back to the room. His silhouette was wreathed in smoke from the cigarette he held in his right hand.

John ran to his bed and snapped on the bedside light. The bed, he saw, was in an awful mess, all the pillows were on the floor and, in the struggle, the sheets and blankets had been partially dragged off the mattress. Tensing, he faced Derek.

But Derek did not react in the slightest to his reappearance in the room or to the light going on. He put the cigarette to his lips and, taking a deep drag, blew the smoke out in front of him in an expanding blue cloud. John relaxed a little. The fight was clearly over, for the time being at least. He tried to divine what Derek was feeling but came up blank. 'Derek?' His voice sounded hoarse.

'Fuck off!' Derek took another drag of the cigarette.

A hard ball of anger formed in the pit of John's stomach. 'I won't fuck off. You tried to choke me.'

'Pity about you!'

'But why, Derek?' As soon as he had asked the question he knew how stupid it had been. But his anger was rising and he opened and closed his fists, trying to control it as, slowly and deliberately, Derek got off the bed, opened a window and flicked out his cigarette. Even standing as far away as he was, John shivered in the sudden blast of icy air. His anger drained away as suddenly as it had formed.

It flashed through his mind with certainty that with this night the ties between himself and Derek had been finally and terminally severed. Nevertheless, he tried one more time. 'Would you not talk to me, Derek? Can't we discuss it?'

Derek got into bed, pulled up the covers and turned his back. 'Turn off the light, please. I want to go to sleep.'

John hesitated for a second, looking at his twin's rounded back under the bedcovers, then bent to pull his own bedclothes off the floor. He remade his bed in a rudimentary way. Then he switched off the light and got in. Interminable minutes passed as he lay awake in the darkness, trying to ignore the pain which shot up and down his battered body.

From the absence of sound in the other bed he knew that Derek, too, was awake.

Eventually, exhaustion overtook him and he fell asleep.

Some hours later, he became conscious of an urgent knocking on his door. 'Come in,' he called, struggling to sit up.

Mrs Lindstrom opened the door and came right into the room. Through the fog of residual sleep, John saw immediately she was in some distress. 'John! Derek!' she said. 'Get up quickly, Mr McGuigan is here for you.'

John sat up. He felt groggy and ill. 'What time is it, Mrs Lindstrom?'

'It's a quarter of nine,' said Karen's mother. 'I'm sorry,' she said gently, 'but there's been a bit of bad news from Ireland.'

In the other bed, Derek, still half asleep, stirred and turned over, flinging one arm sideways on the pillow, but John sat up further, wincing with the effort. The light was hurting his eyes and the scar tissue on his cheek was stinging.

He tried to concentrate on what Mrs Lindstrom was saying as she came over to the side of his bed and put a hand on his shoulder. 'Your cousin got a message a few hours ago, John. He has your luggage with him. Apparently your mother has been taken seriously ill. You'll both have to go home to Ireland immediately.'

'But, but, how—'

'Don't worry about the "how", John. There's a flight this

morning from the airport to the mainland and Mr Lindstrom is on the telephone now making connections for you both through Boston. We'll help your cousin organise it this end and there'll be time enough to sort things out when you get back. Now, get dressed quickly.' She glanced across at Derek. 'Your brother seems to be still asleep. Tell him to get dressed quickly,' she repeated. 'You have to be at the airport in less than forty-five minutes. There's only one flight out today.'

She left the room.

John, holding his aching head with one hand, crossed the floor and shook Derek with the other. 'Wake up, Derek! There's an emergency.'

'Wha—?' Derek batted savagely at John's hand. His eyes were still closed. 'Fuck off!'

'Derek, Derek! Mam's been taken sick. We've to go home immediately!'

Derek sat up then. 'What did you say?'

'It's Mam. Dan's here. He got a message. Mam's seriously ill.'

'What's wrong with her?' Derek's eyes widened with fear.

'I don't know,' John replied. 'They're saying she's seriously ill. I don't know.'

Derek got out of bed and went to the bathroom. When he returned he stood still in the middle of the room and lowered his head like a bull about to charge. 'There's something I want to say to you, John,' he said in a low, venomous voice. 'And I'm dead serious. Don't you ever, *ever* address me again. Do you understand me? You're not to speak to me. Not ever, ever again.'

'The next twenty-four hours will be crucial.' The young doctor was dark-skinned, the first coloured person John had ever met.

He and Derek were standing in a corridor outside the ward in the Dublin hospital where their mother lay unconscious. 'I'm sorry to say you need to be prepared for the worst,' the doctor continued in his soft, musical voice, 'but on the positive side, your mother has quite a lot going for her. She is, I believe, not old? Only fifty, is that right?'

John realised that he did not know what age their mother was. 'I – I suppose so,' he stammered. 'I—'

'She'll be fifty next month,' Derek cut in.

'Good,' said the doctor. 'There are other positive aspects too. She did not smoke and she is certainly not overweight. On the contrary, she is far too thin even for her build. But I think she may have a good chance. Yes, the next twenty-four hours is the critical period.'

'Would you like a cup of tea, boys?' The offer was from a middle-aged nurse, round-faced and motherly.

'Yes, please,' said Derek. John was too upset to answer.

'Sit down there on that seat, so,' said the nurse, indicating a wooden bench against one wall. 'I'll be back in a jif.' She bustled off, crêpe-soled shoes squeaking on the tiles.

'I'll come back,' said the doctor, turning to follow her. 'Please make yourselves as comfortable as possible.'

'Can we see her?' asked John. He had not slept for nearly thirty-six hours and his voice was hoarse from strain and fatigue. They had travelled all the previous day and night, had been collected at Shannon this morning by Ned Sherling and been driven immediately to Dublin.

He had no idea how Derek was coping; even in this life-or-death situation, John's twin had been true to his threat and there had not been a direct syllable between them since they left the Lindstroms' spare bedroom in Charlottetown. Not even the novelty of flying across the Atlantic in a Super-Constellation had elicited a comment.

The doctor gave them permission to go into the ward. 'But please be prepared,' he said gently, 'you may get a shock. Your mother is hooked up to oxygen and to several intravenous drips. But this is routine for stroke patients. It is not as bad as it looks.'

The ward was lit only by a nightlight above the door. One cubicle near the end was shrouded; the nurse led them to it, pulling the curtain aside and indicating that they should go inside. 'Don't stay long,' she whispered.

At first, John did not dare to look at his mother's face but studied her hands, each neatly by her side. He became aware of a small hissing sound, alien and sinister. Searching for its source, he realised it was coming from an oxygen bottle at the head of the bed.

He had to force himself to transfer his eyes from the bottle to her face.

In the small amount of light which penetrated the cubicle, Mary Flynn's features – or as much of them as he could see because her nose and mouth were covered with a transparent mask – were pale and waxy and not at all familiar. The doctor had certainly not been exaggerating when he had said she was thin. Her face was skull-like, with hollows at the cheeks and temples; her body made only the slightest of mounds under the bedclothes. There was no sign at all of life, no hint of the mother he had known all his life. This still, wafer-thin effigy did not even look like her. He was torn between the wish to run away and the even stronger desire to pick up the frail doll's body in his arms. 'Mammy,' he cried in his heart, 'please, Mam. Please wake up, just for a minute.'

Derek was standing at her head, his face frozen. John moved around to stand beside him and reached forward to take one of her hands but recoiled at the limp, cold feel of it. 'Please, Mammy,' he begged again soundlessly, 'please . . . '

Derek pushed past him and out of the cubicle altogether. John waited until he heard his brother's footsteps recede into the corridor and then forced himself to pick up his mother's hand. It weighed nothing. He bent his head over it and gathering up every ounce of strength in himself he tried to force life into it: 'I promise, Mammy, that if you get well, I'll stay and look after you. I promise. So you have to wake up, please, Mammy. Please.'

Carefully, as if her hand were a small bird, he laid it back on the coverlet exactly where it had been. Once so capable and busy, it looked fragile and useless and he had to fight back scalding tears. He must not cry. He was not a child any more. He leaned forward and being careful not to disturb the mask or any of the tubes, he whispered into her ear, trying one more time: 'Mammy, I still need you. Derek needs you too, we both do. Please wake up.' He wanted to add more, to tell her he loved her but it was too difficult.

He stood there for another minute or so, then turned and

left the cubicle. The nurse, who was on her way back to her station, stopped and waited until he drew level with her. 'Your tea's ready outside,' she said in a low voice. She put one arm around his waist: 'Try not to worry too much,' she said. 'It's bad all right but I've seen people come round from strokes like this. This is the crisis. If she survives this, you never know. Have faith.'

Outside, Derek was seated on the bench beside Ned Sherling. For as long as John could remember, Ned had always seemed to be with them in any emergency or simply when the Flynns needed a lift in his ancient car. He and Derek were drinking tea out of mugs. 'Here's yours, John,' Ned said, picking up a third mug from a tray beside him on the bench. Then he lowered his voice. 'How is she?'

'Bad,' said John. 'She's very bad, I think—' His voice wobbled and to hide his weakness, he took a gulp of the scalding tea.

'Ah, sure, God is good. You never know, you never know. Please God, now,' said Ned. The tone was more urgent than that of a sympathetic neighbour and John looked sharply at him. But he was too tired and upset to wrestle with anything complex and drank his tea.

The tiled basement corridor, drab green walls shadowy in the dim light from a single bulb at one end, was windowless, a dismal, cheerless place in which even the softest of conversations seemed too loud. The nurse came out of the ward. 'I've made a few phone calls,' she said, 'and there are a couple of spare beds in St Ignatius ward. Only two, I'm afraid. But if one of you doesn't mind being public, he can use one of the theatre trolleys.' She pointed to a narrow bed on wheels, one of a pair which were placed neatly against the corridor wall.

'I'll take the trolley,' said John instantly. He wanted to be by himself; he also wanted to stay as close as possible to his mother.

After Ned and Derek had been borne away, the nurse wheeled the trolley to the farthest end of the corridor and, with expert hands, made it look tolerably like a bed. 'Careful, now, you don't wake up on the operating table tomorrow morning.'

John looked at her with wide eyes, so upset he did not

229

know what she meant. The nurse was instantly contrite. 'Sorry. I shouldn't be joking with you. You poor thing, you're all in. Here, take off your shoes.' He was too tired to protest as she bent to unlace them and then he let her help him out of his coat and jacket. He climbed up on the trolley which was high and hard and a little unstable.

He was too tired even to summon up a prayer and fell asleep within seconds.

'John, John, wake up, wake up!'

Someone was pulling him out of the darkness. He tried to resist but the person would not go away. 'Come on, pet, your mother's woken up. Come quickly.'

He struggled and opened his eyes. 'Who—'

'You're in a hospital, pet, remember? Your mother . . . '

He got off the trolley and put on his shoes, fumbling with the laces. His heart was thumping. She was awake. She wasn't dead.

Carrying his coat and jacket, he followed the nurse towards the ward. She stopped at the door and looked up at him. 'Now, don't hope for too much, John. She's had a stroke, remember? This may or may not be the first step to recovery. And at this stage it's unlikely she'll know who you are.'

'Have you called Derek?' John's automatic concern for his twin had not yet been reattuned to their new situation.

'Yes, he's on the way.'

John had to wait for a bit outside the cubicle as there was some medical activity in progress around the bed. The doctor who had warned him not to have too much hope emerged after a few minutes and touched him briefly on the shoulder. 'Not long now,' he said, 'only a few minutes.' John swallowed hard. He found his hands were sweaty and rubbed them on the side of his trousers before slipping in through the gap in the cubicle curtain.

Mary Flynn's eyes were closed and he thought the doctor and nurse had made a mistake in calling him. He could see no difference. But as his eyes adjusted to the semi-darkness, he saw, or thought he saw, a tiny flutter in her eyelids. He sank to his knees. 'Mammy,' he whispered.

There was no response. He picked up the weightless hand. 'Mammy, it's John.'

This time, his mother's eyes opened. She did not turn her head towards him but seemed to be looking straight up at the ceiling. The oxygen gurgled and he realised she was trying to say something through the mask. He stood and bent right over her, lowering his ear to just above the mask. 'What is it, Mammy?'

He waited for an eternity but then she shifted slightly and he heard her. But it was not her voice; it was a hollow, alien sound distorted through the mask and the oxygen.

'Mammy, I didn't understand, say it again, please.' He was trying to remain calm.

Through her hand, he felt the effort she was making but her words, 'Eggh – egghle,' made no sense.

'Mammy, Mammy,' he whispered urgently, 'what is it? Try again, please. Please try again.' But her eyes had closed.

He waited, still holding her hand, but she seemed to have slipped back into unconsciousness. Various images from his childhood flashed through his mind: his mother mashing soft-boiled eggs into cups for himself and Derek, the time she allowed him to bring a jackdaw with a broken leg into the house; the only time he ever saw her dancing – with one of the local men at a harvest dance – her hair flying.

The time a neighbour had looked after himself and Derek so she could go on a day's visit to a friend in Dublin, bringing back two table-tennis bats and two balls and then helping them construct a makeshift table from two planks of wood and two rain barrels. She had even taken a few turns with them, one of the rare occasions in their lives he ever remembered her playing with them.

Carefully, he put her hand back on the coverlet. He had decided absolutely that if she recovered, even if she were to be a cripple for the rest of her life, it was his turn now to look after her. He patted her hand, putting as much urgency as he could into the gesture without hurting her, hoping she could sense his reassurance. 'Don't worry, Mammy, I'll mind you.'

He heard a sound behind him. Derek had arrived.

John stepped back a little from the side of the bed. 'She

was awake for a while but I think she's gone again. Should I tell the nurse?' Derek did not reply. He moved to John's other side and stood staring down at their mother, his face greenish in the nightlight.

John hesitated and then left the cubicle in search of medical authority. When he was half-way up the ward, he realised what she had been trying to say. She had been trying to form the word 'Derek'.

Later in the morning, the boys were again sitting on the bench in the corridor, as far apart as its length allowed. They had been there for more than two hours. Derek was asleep, his head hanging low over his knees and John did not think he could stay awake much longer either, despite the growing noise level as the hospital came to life. He was also feeling very hungry.

The day-shift came on and he saw the nurse who had been so kind to them huddle in conversation with a new girl. She looked once or twice in their direction as she spoke so he knew she was talking about them.

Then the new nurse came swishing towards them. 'Good morning, John,' then, indicating Derek, 'Out for the count, eh?' Although one of his feet was numb, John dragged himself to his feet and went as though to wake his brother but she stopped him. 'No, let him sleep. I'll get the two of you a bit of breakfast and then we'll get the almoner to have a chat with you, all right?'

John was too shy to ask what an almoner was so he simply nodded.

When the nurse came back, she was carrying two trays, laden with porridge, toast and tea. She shook Derek awake and the two of them ate hungrily.

The almoner arrived before John was finished. Seating herself between them, she opened a file. 'Now, which one of you is the oldest?'

'I am!' They spoke simultaneously. It had always been a matter of standing controversy, which their mother had refused to confirm, telling them that they were exactly equal in all ways.

'We're twins,' said John.

The woman nodded. 'I see. Well, whatever. Your mother's going to be with us for a while, I believe?'

'Is she going to – to—' It was Derek.

'We'll just hope for the best,' said the woman. 'Now,' she continued, 'is either of you working?'

'No, miss,' said John. 'Not yet, anyhow, but I'll be looking for a job when I get home. If Mam gets better, of course.'

The almoner looked keenly at him. 'Do you have any other brothers or sisters? And if and when your mother goes home, who'll be looking after her?'

'I will,' said John flatly.

'I'm working,' said Derek suddenly. 'I work for my cousin in Canada. I'll be going back there as soon as possible. If it's money you're worried about, I'll be able to send some.' John looked at him incredulously. How could he desert their mother? And was it only yesterday or the day before that Derek was regretting going to Canada at all?

The almoner turned to Derek, pen poised. 'What do you do there?'

'I work on a farm.'

'Annual income?'

'Well, nothing at the moment. I work for my keep. But if the harvest is good next year, I've been promised to be paid.'

'I see,' said the almoner. She thought for a little then wrote something in her file. When she spoke again, her voice was gentle. 'What I suggest, boys, is that you go home as soon as possible. There's not much good you can do by hanging around the hospital and, anyway, it would be miserable for you. Your mother is going to come to herself very slowly. For the first few days, she won't even know if you're here or not. Have you a way to get home?'

'There's a neighbour here with us with a car. He'll bring us, we can look after ourselves, miss,' John assured her. 'We'll be fine.'

'He'll be fine,' said Derek. 'I'm going back to Canada.'

The almoner looked sharply at him but said nothing. She closed her file and left them.

'Why did you have to be so rude?' John exploded when she was out of earshot. 'That woman was very nice, she was being very nice to us. And you're very quick off the mark to want to go back. Suppose Mammy needs the both of us?' Derek turned sideways on the bench and faced away up the corridor.

233

'Look,' said John, 'whatever happened in Canada – whatever's wrong with you – can't we forget it for the moment? We have more urgent things on our minds.' Without realising it, he had raised his voice and a pair of old men who were sitting on a bench against the opposite wall a little way up from them suspended their chat and looked over at them. He lowered his voice again. 'For God's sake, Derek, this is ridiculous. Mammy's in there – maybe she's dying – and here we are behaving like a couple of wains. Sorry, here *you* are behaving like a wain.'

Derek crossed one leg over the other and studied his nails. John gave up. 'I'm going to the toilet.'

When he came back, Ned Sherling, freshly washed and shaved, had arrived down from his sojourn in St Ignatius' so John was spared the necessity of any further efforts with Derek.

Before they left they went in again to see their mother. Seeing her in daylight, John fancied that she already looked healthier. She still wore the oxygen mask and was still draped with tubes, but her colour was slightly better and her chest rose and fell regularly as she breathed in peaceful sleep. He also noticed, however, that her face now seemed misshapen, with one side distinctly lower than the other.

Then Mary Flynn opened her eyes. They were opaque and expressionless, and stared straight ahead of her. One eyelid did not fully open but drooped noticeably at the corner. 'Hello, Mammy,' he whispered and then heard Derek say the same.

'Good *girl*,' exclaimed the nurse who was with them. 'Look who's here to see you, Mary, John and Derek!'

Mary's gaze slid past them and upwards. It registered nothing except a faraway look of puzzlement. Her chest heaved and the oxygen made that terrible gurgling noise as she tried to say something. 'Egghle . . . '

'It'll take a while,' said the nurse, 'don't be too upset. This is normal after a bad stroke. She'll get a lot better over the next week or so, won't you, pet?' She turned back to Mary and gently settled a few strands of Mary's thin hair behind one ear.

John could not take any more. 'Goodbye, Mammy,' he blurted, 'try not to worry, we'll be back to see you soon again.'

Mary turned her puzzled eyes on him. 'Egghle . . . '

'Derek's here, Mammy,' he said, 'here's Derek,' pushing at Derek's arm. Violently, Derek threw off his hand but it did not matter because Mary did not react or recognise Derek. 'Egghle?' she said again in a questioning voice although seeming to be looking straight at John's twin.

The nurse took over. Motioning to the twins that they should leave and taking Mary's hand, she said, 'The boys are going now, Mary, but they'll be back to see you soon, real soon, in a couple of days. You rest now, Mary. Have a nice sleep for yourself.' She stroked her patient's forehead.

As John came out of the cubicle, he put his hands to his eyes to dash away the tears but then, from the silence up and down the ward, saw that he was the object of all attention. Ashamed that his weakness had been witnessed, he left at a shambling run, Derek following.

Ned was waiting for them outside. 'How is she?'

'A bit better,' It was Derek who was able to answer. 'They think now she's going to be all right.'

'Well, praise be to God,' said Ned.

'They do not!' said John passionately. 'They do *not*! She's going to be a cripple!'

Derek walked away.

John took several deep breaths of the fresh, icy air as they descended the stone staircase to the street. The brightness of the day soothed him. After the green, overheated gloom in which he had spent the last terrible hours, the January wind which swept up Eccles Street hurt the back of his throat and bit at his ears but with every step he felt a small bit better. Maybe the nurses were right, after all. Maybe their mother was going to recover.

'This is the street where Leopold Bloom lived,' said Ned as they reached the end of Eccles Street and turned into Dorset Street where he had left the car.

'Is that right?' said John, supposing that Leopold Bloom was a writer of some sort. Ned Sherling was known around Drumboola as a great reader. Then, across the street, he noticed a telephone box.

Rose.

He could telephone Rose at the school.

Then he remembered she would still be on her Christmas holidays at Sundarbans. He had been so taken up with concern about his mother he had forgotten the possibility that he would actually be able to see her.

It was the next day before he went up to the Big House. Both he and Derek had gone straight to bed when they let themselves into the gate lodge. Derek had stalked into their mother's room without a word and slammed the door, leaving the room they used to share solely to John, who was too tired to care what his brother did or did not do.

He woke refreshed. Grey daylight filtered into the bedroom through the window and the whole house was thrumming with the sound of heavy rain. He jumped out of bed, still fully dressed in the clothes he had worn for the best part of forty-eight hours. He was also very cold and, once again, ravenously hungry.

Going into the kitchen, he lifted the clock on the mantelpiece to check what time it was, an automatic reflex. The hands pointed to ten minutes past three and at first he was astounded – he could not have slept that long – then, shaking it, he realised it was not ticking. His mother had always wound it last thing at night before she went to bed.

He switched on the wireless in time to hear an announcer say 'and that's the end of the nine o'clock news'. He had slept for more than twenty hours. He glanced across at their mother's bedroom door. It was still firmly shut.

Although it was clean and tidy, the kitchen wore a forlorn look of neglect. He opened the range and riddled out the cold ashes, then battled outside into the storm to get some logs from the shed. There was something missing in the yard: where was the goat? Had someone stolen her in their mother's absence? Or had one of the neighbours taken her in care?

He was soaked when he brought the logs and kindling back into the kitchen and his teeth were chattering as he started the fire in the range. It would be a while before it was hot enough to boil a kettle and, while he was waiting, he foraged in the presses and drawers in search of food. There was very little to be had:

236

half a packet of cream crackers, a little butter, a heel of mouldy bread and a half head of cabbage. Although there was some tea and sugar, there was no milk.

His conscience smote him. No wonder his mother was so thin and had fallen into ill health. While he and Derek were eating their way through the fat of the land in Canada, she had practically starved. The discovery hardened his resolve to stay at home and look after her. He was able-bodied and well able to work. She would never have to go hungry again.

He spread the butter thinly on as many cream crackers as it would cover and started to wolf them where he stood by the slowly warming range, scattering crumbs all over the floor. Thinking of Derek, he hesitated before eating the last two but his stomach, still growling, won the day. 'The hell with it,' he rationalised. 'He certainly wouldn't save any for me.'

Over the drumming of the rain, he heard a knock on the back door and, on opening it, discovered Ned Sherling, a can in one hand, a paper bag in the other. The rain had blackened the shoulders of his buttonless raincoat and even in the short trip from his car to the door, his thinning hair had been plastered to his skull.

'Ned!' exclaimed John. 'Come in.'

Ned stamped his feet on the mat inside the door, shaking off the water like a spaniel. He kept his body turned sideways to John, as though poised for immediate flight. 'I just brought you a few things,' he said almost apologetically, holding out the can and the sodden paper bag. 'It's Sunday, no shops like, and I reckoned there wouldn't be much here, what with Mary . . . '

'You're too good, Ned,' said John gratefully, taking the provisions. 'I've just lit the stove. I'll put on a kettle in a few minutes.'

Ned allowed himself to be helped out of the raincoat. John quickly swept up the crumbs and pulled out a chair for him. As he did so, he thought that this was the first time he had ever played host in the gate lodge. He might as well get used to it. He laid out the food on the table. Ned had brought bread, a half-dozen eggs, a half-pound of butter and four streaky rashers. There was fresh milk in the can, the froth still on it from milking. 'Thank you, Ned,' said John again. 'This'll tide us over until we get organised. You'll have a bit of breakfast yourself?'

'Ah no, no,' said Ned. 'Sure, I had me breakfast after the milking.'

'You'll have a cup of tea and a cut of bread?'

'All right, I will, thank you.'

John looked at him curiously. He had always taken Ned's presence for granted. Since he could remember, Ned had been part of the Flynns' life, like the settle-bed in the corner of the kitchen or the eccentric clock on the mantelpiece. Ned, he knew, had lived with a much older sister who had died more than ten years ago. He wondered now how he managed all on his own up in the hills. Up to yesterday, when he had detected that odd urgency in Ned's voice when he had been talking about Mary, he had never thought of this gauche, introverted man as an individual human being, nor considered that Ned Sherling might have feelings similar to his own. 'I want to thank you, Ned,' he said slowly. 'No neighbour could have done as much as you. And I don't mean just driving me and Derek all over the country.'

'Ah nothing, nothing!' said Ned in a rush. 'For God's sake, nothing.'

Mercifully for Ned, the plate on the stove was moderately hot and John was able to busy himself with the frying pan and the kettle. He put the rashers on and turned away to the table to cut the bread. 'There's something I want to ask you, Ned,' he said. 'I'm ashamed to say I haven't thought about it before, well not enough, anyway. How did Mam survive all these years without any money?'

'Well, she used to sell a few eggs and vegetables in Carrick,' said Ned, 'and she had the milk from the goat. Lots of people liked that milk for their sick childher.'

John was having to strain hard to hear him above the gentle sizzling of the rashers. 'I know that,' he said. 'Sure, didn't I sell them myself for her? But that didn't produce enough to keep a bird.'

'And the Canon always gave her a few shillings for cleaning out the chapel.'

Thunderstruck, John looked at him, the bread knife suspended in mid-air. All his life, he had thought his mother's frequent trips to the chapel were to pray. Now he understood why she never let either of them go with her. This man knew more about Mary Flynn than he did.

'Is there anything else, Ned? Where's the goat – and the hens, by the way?' There had been something odd about the shed, too, when he had gone to fetch the wood. Now it came to him that the roosts were empty.

Ned looked at his boots. 'Well, she didn't want you to know,' he mumbled, 'and I only found out by accident—'

'What? Found out what?'

'Well, she had to get the money for your fare to America and for the wake.'

'I thought the McGuigans sent the money for the fare.'

'They sent most of it.'

'Where'd she get the rest from?'

'From Francey Meagher, in Rockchapel.' Ned looked up bravely. 'Francey agreed to wait until ye were gone to take the goat and the hens.'

'That goat and those hens wouldn't fetch enough to pay for all that! Where'd she get the rest?'

'That's all I know,' said Ned but he was again staring at his boots and the telltale red was creeping up from his collar.

John did not need to ask any more. 'I'll pay you back, Ned,' he said.

Ned looked up, galvanised. 'What? What pay back? What are you talking about? What pay back?'

John turned to the stove. The rashers were ready and the kettle was singing. He broke two of the eggs into the pan. They splattered and spat at him causing him to jump back. He pulled the pan farther off the hotplate until they settled down. 'I'm getting a job, Ned,' he said quietly. 'And it's not going to be any Mickey Mouse job either. I'll pay you back every penny.'

Six hours later, John scanned the dark sky but there was no let-up in the bucketing downpour and none in view. He could wait no longer. The Sunday lunch in the Big House would be well over by now and it would be dark soon.

He had prepared carefully, washing himself thoroughly, laundering his best shirt, drying it in front of the fire and ironing it – the latter with not a great deal of success – and polishing his good shoes. He put on his coat and took an old cap of his father's, jamming it well down over his ears. Then, automatically taking a drop of holy water from the small font beside the door, he blessed himself before opening the door and setting off for Sundarbans.

He was drenched before he had gone a hundred yards and although he tried to keep to the shelter of the trees along the side-rails, some of the ruts and potholes were so extensive they were impossible to circumnavigate. He tried to jump one which resembled a miniature pond but splashed right into the middle of it. The water reached to his ankles, ruining all his efforts with his shoes, and he resigned himself to arriving at the front door of the Big House looking like a drowned rat.

His stomach was churning at the prospect of seeing Rose again, but he had an even more urgent priority. He was going to ask her father for a job on the estate.

He ducked a dripping branch which, almost severed from its parent trunk, hung across the rail, and tried to control his nerves by concentrating on something completely outside the present – or the coming ordeal. Fixing his mind on what he would be doing at this very moment if he was back on the farm in Kelly's Cross, he imagined himself travelling in a toboggan or a sleigh across the snow, maybe mashing mangolds or swedes for the stock.

Maybe eating. He pictured Peggy McGuigan's heaped, steaming plates of food, stews and casseroles, potatoes, vegetables, succulent fruit pies, creamy custard . . . His mouth watered. The food Ned Sherling had brought to the gate lodge that morning had been very welcome but, to be fair to his twin, John had left half of it in the warming oven for Derek and he was hungry again.

He and Derek had still not spoken. Derek had taken the food out of the warming oven without comment and retreated into their mother's room to eat it, once again slamming the door after him. He had considered taking Derek into his confidence about asking for the job on the estate, but, not wanting to risk a row or a further snub, thought better of it. At present he needed all his concentration to hold his nerve.

Icy water was now trickling under the collar of his coat but he saw he was almost at the top of the avenue. But, as he came level with the steps of the house, his courage almost failed him. It seemed almost as if the elements were warning him to stay away; between where he stood and the bottom step, a small lake had been gouged out, not only by the rain which continued to hop all around him, but by the torrents which gushed from the broken gutters and cascaded down the steps like a waterfall.

Maybe he should come back another day, he thought.

But he could have been spotted already through a window. Maybe Rose had seen him. There was no going back. He stepped into the water, which was a good four inches deep, and waded towards the steps.

Never having been inside the house, he had no idea whether or not the doorbell worked. He tried it anyway. There was no reply and after a suitable interval, he lifted the knocker and sounded it as loudly as he dared, trying to steer a middle course between being timid and being cheeky. Still no reply. He knocked again, harder this time. After a few seconds, the door quivered slightly and from inside he heard the sound of someone wrestling with bolts. His heart sank. It had been a dreadful mistake to come to the front door. It had probably not been opened in years. But how was he to know?

The door groaned open, dislodging a shower of debris and he was face to face with Rose's mother. Her eyes widened in shock when she saw him. John was not prepared for this and he could have kicked himself for not having taken her into the equation. 'Excuse me,' he started to say, but was cut off as Daphne heaved the door shut in his face.

For a second, he stood there, stupefied, the rain blinding him, running into his mouth and streaming off his chin. Then he got angry. How dare she? Gentry or not, how dare she? Almost before he knew what he was doing, he found himself thundering at the door again, banging the knocker against its plate until he almost took it off its hinge. He deserved better than this. You wouldn't treat a beggar like this.

He thundered on, knocking at short intervals, getting angrier and angrier until the door was opened again. This time, it was the Colonel who stood there. 'What the devil—' he began, blustering, but it was John's turn to be abrupt. All the pent-up anger and sorrow and humiliation came to a head. He clenched his fists by his side and barely restrained himself from waving them.

Before Rose's father could say any more he cut across him. 'I just wanted a word with you, Colonel, but your wife closed the door in my face.' Even as he spoke, his heart was warning him he was ruining any chance of these people's eventual blessing on his relationship with Rose but he was too angry to heed it. 'She slammed the door!' he repeated, his outrage ballooning.

'Tell him to go away.' Daphne's querulous voice issued somewhere from behind Gus's left shoulder.

'Are you going to let me speak to you or not? Sir,' he added.

Gus hesitated, his chin quivering. For a split second, John almost felt sorry for him but his resolve hardened. The eternal rain battered on his head but he did not even attempt to shield any part of himself from it now. Although he had to keep blinking it out of his eyes, he straightened his shoulders and let it flow where it may.

'Augustine!' commanded Daphne in a louder voice. 'Shut that door!' John locked eyes with Gus, mentally forcing him not to listen to his wife.

The battle was over and won in a moment. Gus opened the door a little wider. 'Come in out of the rain, John,' he mumbled. 'You're drenched.'

John cleaned his wringing shoes on the bootscraper and went in. 'You're letting that – that *person* into my house!' cried Daphne as Gus closed the door behind him and John had never before heard a woman's voice reach such a level of shrillness. At the same time, he saw he was dripping all over the floor of the hallway and tried uselessly to limit the damage, pulling the hem of his coat tightly around his body.

Gus turned to his wife and spread his hands, half apologis-

242

ing, half appealing. 'Daphne, all he wants is a chat. You wouldn't leave a dog out on a day like—'

'Get him out of here!' she screamed, her face turning mauve.

All John's anger evaporated. He had spent its force on the knocker and on getting in. He was not afraid any more – of Rose's mother, of the Colonel, of any of it. Seeing Daphne O'Beirne Moffat in this state, he doubted if he would ever be intimidated by her or by people like her again.

'Please, Daphne,' sputtered Gus, 'all the lad wants—'

'I said, get him out of my house.' Daphne's voice slid down the scale until it was low and deadly. In a strange way, John did not feel at all involved in this row between Rose's parents and, still dripping, waited calmly for its conclusion.

The Colonel did a curious thing. He took his watch out of his pocket. He did not look at it but held it in front of his chest, face out, like a charm. 'Daphne, it's my house,' he said gruffly. 'This is one of my tenants and I will see him.' As he spoke, he snapped open and then closed the cover of the watch. For the second time in a minute, John felt a stab of sympathy.

Rose's mother, her face working, did not reply at first. 'Very well,' she said then. 'I shall be in my room. I'd like to speak to you when you are finished.' She turned and clicked away towards the main staircase. Both John and Gus watched her straight-backed progress up the stairs until she had disappeared from view. Neither of them moved until they heard the sound of a door closing.

Gus half turned to John but would not meet his eyes. 'Sorry,' he mumbled. 'Bit upset, you see . . . ' He seemed about to say something else but then discovered the watch in his hand. He replaced it in its pocket.

'Please, Colonel,' said John, 'I'm very sorry too. I lost my temper and I had no right to speak to you the way I did.'

'Yes, well,' said Gus, 'you say you've something you want to talk to me about. Come into the gunroom. Quiet in there. Use it as a sort of private study for myself.'

John followed him across the hall and then along a short corridor. Gus used a key on his watch-chain to open a plain brown door and went ahead into the room, which was small and

243

panelled, furnished with a library table, a davenport and chair and one small couch which had seen better days. The guns, three shotguns and a rifle, were mounted on a rack in a glass case against one wall. But John's eyes were drawn immediately to the dominant feature of the room. Beside the case was the staring glass-eyed head of a tiger, its black and gold stripes lighting up the Irish gloom of this shabby, damp room like a firefly at dusk. Gus, turning to invite John to sit, saw him staring at the trophy and misinterpreted his expression. 'Yes, ah – a hundred years ago, you understand. Nothing at all to do with the present family.'

'It's beautiful, sir,' said John. He meant it sincerely; he had never seen such a beautiful, such an exotic thing. Such a history, such glory had resided this house. For the first time, John saw tragedy in the slide of Sundarbans and the O'Beirne Moffats; for the first time, he realised that personal indignity was a relative commodity.

But Gus seemed to have no such insight; he was simply pleased at the compliment about his ancestor's trophy. 'Oh, yes, thank you, thank you. Sit down, John. Now, what was it you wanted to speak to me about so urgently?' He seated himself at the davenport.

'I'd prefer to stand, Colonel, if you don't mind,' said John. 'I'm so wet, I'd ruin your couch. What I wanted, sir, was to ask you if you would consider giving me a job? A proper job,' he added quickly. 'I have responsibilities now.'

Gus visibly started. He began to lift himself out of his chair but John, afraid he was going to refuse him, rushed on. 'You see, sir, my mother – well, you probably know that my mother has been taken very ill. She has had a stroke. She's in hospital at the moment in Dublin. If she recovers, she is going to need someone to look after her. Derek, my brother, is going back to Canada and he says he will send some money. In the meantime, I'll be looking for work all over the place. I'm qualified now, sir, to do all sorts of farm work. Even though I was in Canada for only a few months, I learned a great deal, horses, cattle, pigs even. And the land. I can do anything on the land now . . . '

Gus was staring at him, still with that unreadable expression.

John looked again at the beautiful creature fixed, for ever

244

snarling, to this incongruous, unsuitable wall, its basilisk stare symbolising the gulf between himself and the O'Beirne Moffats. He had made a dreadful mistake in coming. There was no help here.

'I thought, I was sure . . . ' said Gus, slowly.

John looked hopelessly back at him. His urgency and anger had sustained him up to this but there was no heating in the room and he was beginning to shiver. He tried to stop his teeth from chattering. 'Yes, sir?' he said politely.

'You're – you were very friendly with – with Rose?'

It was the last thing John had expected to arise in this conversation, that Rose's father would bring up the relationship. Had Rose confided in him? His shivering stopped. 'Yes, sir,' he replied, wary, 'I was. I am. We're writing to each other.'

'Are you?' Gus narrowed his pale eyes slightly.

'Yes, sir. But I haven't heard from her for a few weeks. I've been in Canada until a couple of days ago,' he added unnecessarily.

'And you came home because your mother was ill?'

'Yes, sir.'

'Only because of that?'

John was puzzled by this line of questioning. What was the man implying? Did he think all this was a ploy to see Rose again? 'Yes, Colonel,' he said.

Gus stood up and took his watch out of his waistcoat pocket but again did not look look at it. 'Mary Flynn is a good woman,' he said. 'And I was very fond of your father. I'll see what I can do.'

John could not believe his ears. 'You mean you *will* give me a job?'

'Even if I could afford to hire, which I can't, I don't think it would be appropriate for you to work on this estate, do you, John?' Again, John was puzzled by the implication but he was so overjoyed at the Colonel's generally positive response that he did not stop to consider it. 'You mean you'll organise a job for me somewhere else?' he said eagerly.

'Leave it with me,' said the Colonel in a tone which indicated the interview was over. They left the room and the Colonel relocked the door. Then he led John back to the hall but this time

245

into the kitchen and towards the back door. 'Only use that front door for funerals,' he explained as he showed John out.

'I can't thank you enough, sir,' said John, just before he went back out into the rain. He stepped outside and automatically turned his soaked collar up around his throat. Holding it with both hands, he went for broke. 'Excuse me for asking, Colonel, but is Rose at home this afternoon?'

The effect of the question on Rose's father was electrifying. 'No,' he said, fingers flying for his pocket watch. 'She's not here.' For the second time in half an hour, John found a door closed firmly in his face.

Brain whirling, he looked at the worn, rain-soaked wood. He understood now. Gus and Daphne O'Beirne Moffat had found out about himself and Rose – she must have told him, or they had found his letters – and as expected, they were dead set against the relationship.

He thought deeply about this new development as he trudged home, this time not bothering to avoid the puddled pot-holes but splashing straight through them. He would have to get in contact urgently with Rose to find out how she felt about it. She might have told him in a letter which had got delayed by the Christmas mail and might already be there for him in Kelly's Cross.

But where was she now? Did her father mean she was 'not here' just for today – or 'not here' permanently? That should be easy enough to find out in the neighbourhood. He wished with all his heart he was on better terms with Derek. He could have enlisted his help.

He tried to look on the bright side. At least one of his multiplying problems seemed to have some chance of being resolved. He believed Colonel O'Beirne Moffat to be a man of his word. His prospects of getting a job were good.

When he pushed open the back door of the gate lodge and went into the kitchen, he found Derek seated at the kitchen table, drinking tea and eating the remains of what John had left in the warming oven. As soon as the door opened, Derek immediately stood up and, taking the food and tea with him, went into the parlour and shut the door.

*

Two days passed before John recovered enough of his emotional energy to go in search of up-to-date information about Rose.

He spent most of the intervening period cleaning the gate lodge, a task he performed alone. Finding his twin's one-sided war of nerves a great strain, he was just as glad of Derek's almost permanent absence. His brother had assumed the habit of getting up late and, after making tea, left the house for the rest of the day, coming home late, long after John was in bed. John had no idea where his brother was spending his time but assumed it was with some of their old school friends. He wondered sometimes where he was eating but did not waste his energy worrying about it. On saying goodbye to them at Charlottetown airport, Dan McGuigan had pressed fifty American dollars into the hand of each of them. On the trip home from Dublin, John had asked Ned Sherling to change his in the bank in Carrick and also asked him to use some of it to buy a few basic foodstuffs and supplies. He assumed Derek had changed his too, somehow, because his brother never seemed to be short of cigarettes and the smell of stale smoke constantly lingered in the air of the cottage.

After the torrential rains on Sunday, Monday had dawned grey and blustery but dry. John woke about nine o'clock and decided to get to work straight away. He had noticed a tin of Zebrite in the back of one of the presses and had opened the dampers on the range to let the fire burn itself out overnight. After a breakfast of milk and what was left of Ned's bread and butter, he cleaned the stove thoroughly, both inside and out and then carefully blackleaded its outer surfaces. The pungent odour made him sneeze but he persevered diligently with a small brush and a cloth, working the substance into every hinge and crevice and polishing it until it looked almost as good as new.

Just as he finished, Ned arrived, laden with the supplies. He handed them over with the balance of John's money, but would not stay even for a cup of tea. After he had left, John counted out the money on the table. It came to eight pounds, sixteen shillings and fivepence. He looked at it, spread out before him on the chequered oilcloth, then gathered it up carefully and put it away in an old tea caddy on the mantelpiece, which was where his mother had always kept money for as long as he could remember. He felt sad but very grown-up, as though by this action he was now assuming the running of the household.

He lit the stove and while he was cooking himself a panful of sausages, tried to calculate how long the money would last him. He figured that if he lived frugally, he could stretch it out for three weeks or more.

He looked critically at the number of sausages sizzling in the pan. He might as well start now, he thought, so when they were cooked, he put only half of them on a plate. When he had finished eating, he wrapped the others in greaseproof paper and went outside to stow them in the meatsafe fixed to the wall just beside the door.

From habit, he looked up at the sky, which was light grey and racing with layers of piled-up, ragged clouds, too high to threaten rain. He wondered if he should walk down to the post office to make a telephone call to the hospital to find out about his mother. He also wanted urgently to start making his enquiries about Rose's whereabouts. But both prospects were daunting. After the agitation of the previous few days, he felt he needed to quieten his mind.

He went inside and resumed his cleaning, not resting until there was not a single cup, corner, object or piece of furniture in the room which did not sparkle. At the end, he was very hungry again but too tired to make himself a proper meal, which was a blessing in disguise, he thought, considering his need to economise. So he made himself two raspberry jam sandwiches and a cup of tea, washed up, and crawled into bed.

Next day, he cleaned the parlour, polishing the linoleum, the windows, hanging the hearthrug over the clothes line in the back yard and beating the dust out of it with the sweeping brush. He washed and polished all Mary's china ornaments, leaded the grate, washed and polished the tiled surround of the fireplace and even the frame of the embroidered firescreen, used Brasso on the fire irons; he laid a new fire with kindling, shook out the horsehair cushions of the chair and then, because this had evidently not been done for months, had to sweep the floor all over again.

Half-way through this task, he stopped dead. He was behaving like one possessed. What he needed to do was not cleaning but to find out about his mother – and where Rose was.

He gobbled a cold-sausage sandwich and set off at a trot

for the post office. As he came within sight of it, he saw Francey Meagher was waiting outside for it to open. 'How are you, Francey?' he asked, wondering whether or not he should refer to the goat and the hens Francey had purchased to finance the American wake for himself and Derek.

Francey himself solved that problem. 'Fine, John, fine,' he said. 'How's your mother? I hear she's on the mend. By the way, them hens of hers is great layers.'

'That's good,' said John. 'Yes, I think – I hope she'll get better.'

'A terrible business,' said Francey. 'Now if there's anything I can do . . . '

'I know that, Francey,' said John.

The old man had propped his bicycle against the window-sill of the post office and was leaning his backside on the cross-bar. He moved the bike so both of them had access to the window-sill itself. They sat quietly side by side and, after a bit, Francey took out his pipe, putting it unlit into his mouth. 'Fine day, thank God,' he said, his lips clamped over the stem.

It was indeed, quite mild for January. There was little wind and an intermittent sun splayed weak light on the bare hedges and tufted, spongy fields, brilliantly green after all the rain.

Francey hawked and spat expertly so the spittle landed a good six feet from where they sat. John waited a little, then, again looking up the road as though he had spotted something in the distance, he made his voice sound as casual as he could. 'Nothing much happening around here these days. Things are bad up in the Big House, I hear . . . '

'You're right there, you're right there,' said Francey. 'It'll take a power of money to put that place right.'

'Is he hiring at all?' enquired John.

'Yerra, not at all! There'll be snowballs in hell before that place ever makes a go of it again. Not like the old days—'

Before Francey could start on the path of well-worn reminiscence, John cut in. 'Haven't seen sight nor light of the young one, Rose, these holidays.'

'No,' said Francey slowly. 'She's not around. At school in England, I heard.'

John managed to keep his voice steady. He looked up the

road again. 'Is that right? I thought, now, that she was in school somewhere in Dublin.'

'Well, now, that's all I heard,' said Francey. 'She was here for the Christmas, all right, an' another young one with her, but then I heard she went off to England. The Colonel brought her over – or so they say.'

'Is that so?' said John. His heart was thumping. He was dying to ask if Francey had any more information, if, for instance, he knew where in England Rose was, but felt he had already gone far enough. 'Is that so?' he said again, just as the postmistress pulled open the door beside them.

The post office was also a tobacconist's, newsagent's, stationer's and kept a small supply of basic groceries. John used some of his precious money to buy a little Cellophane packet containing five sheets of notepaper and five envelopes and then purchased a stamp. He hesitated for a second and added a threepenny bar of chocolate. He couldn't afford it, he knew, but could not resist the smooth blue look of it. Then, recklessly, he bought twopence worth of Nice biscuits. 'How's your mother?' asked the postmistress, as she totted up his purchases on the back of a paper bag. She was a nice enough woman who flattened her hair tightly to her head in a hairnet, hail, rain or snow, Christmas Day and every day of the year.

'I'm just going to ring the hospital now to find out,' said John.

'I'm praying for her at Mass,' said the postmistress, who was a daily communicant.

'Thank you, Mrs Doody,' said John. 'How much will it cost to ring Dublin?'

'Let's see what you have there,' said the postmistress, counting the coins in his palm. 'You've plenty there,' she said. 'Wait now till I serve Francey and I'll put you through. Have you got the number?' He passed over a crumpled piece of paper which the almoner had given him.

She sold two ounces of plug tobacco and a box of matches to Francey and then, when he had doffed his cap and left, sat at her plug board and dialled the Dublin number. 'It's the Sacred Heart ward,' said John, when he heard her speaking to the Dublin exchange.

The hospital took a long time to answer and John thought the worst. His mother was dead already. He should have come down to ring yesterday. But eventually the postmistress signalled that he should put one shilling and threepence into the black coin box mounted on the wall outside the grocery counter.

The news was moderately good. His mother was off the oxygen and they were going to start physiotherapy on her the following morning.

It was probably Gus O'Beirne Moffat's finest hour. He stood in the small drawing room facing his quivering wife, holding the letter in his hand. 'No, Daphne,' he said firmly. 'This is addressed to Rose and she shall have it.'

For the second time in a week, Daphne, unused to such a phenomenon, was forced to accept defeat. 'Very well,' she said stiffly. 'But I think you are making a big mistake. I thought we agreed. The less Rose has to do with that boy the better.'

The letter had come with the morning post. On cheap blue notepaper, it bore a Carrickmacross postmark and Rose's name and address were printed carefully in large block capitals. Gus looked at it again. 'We don't know that this letter is from him. We don't even know that he is actually the father—' Gus started, but Daphne snorted.

'Oh, don't we?' she said bitterly. 'Who else would it be?'

'You don't condemn a man without a trial,' insisted Gus.

'I don't need a trial. I know. I'm the girl's mother.'

Gus felt for his watch and then stopped himself. 'And I'm her father,' he said quietly. 'I'm sending on this letter.' Sunday's interview with the half-drowned and shivering John Flynn had been preying on his mind. The boy had a lot of courage, he had to admit that. Although he was as appalled as his wife about Rose's predicament, and agreed that on no account should a relationship with John Flynn be entertained, he felt instinctively that the boy was a good sort. After all, he supposed, neither of them had actually planned this horrible situation.

Daphne gave up and stalked out of the room. Gus watched her go and sighed. At the same time, he felt a small thrill of victory. The telephone stood on its own little table in the window.

251

He had done nothing about his promise to try for a job for the lad. Might as well do it now.

He made three telephone calls. The first two were to hunting acquaintances, farmers with good-sized farms a few miles away across the border, one in Armagh, the other in Tyrone. He knew while he was speaking that the postmistress was probably listening in and was discreet, not mentioning John by name, saying only that he was enquiring about a job for the son of a friend. Both calls were in vain: times were hard all round and neither of the farmers could help.

The third call, on impulse, was to the proprietor of a small country house hotel, only recently converted, on a small byroad off the main road from Carrickmacross to Cootehill. Willow House, a seventeenth-century dower house, and its surrounding six hundred acres were owned by an old friend, George Cranshaw, who, like all the landowners, was finding it impossible to make ends meet simply as a farmer.

George had a good trout lake on his land which was a wintering site for several species of duck so he had added to this attraction by stocking his land with pheasant. It also held some grouse and snipe although the numbers were declining.

The tourist industry in Ireland was in its infancy but the British were beginning to trickle in. With the encouragement of the Irish Tourist Association, George had borrowed far more than he could afford to pay back and had refurbished his home, modernising the plumbing. Willow House had only six guest bedrooms but the hope was that he could attract English and continental shooters and fishermen who tended, if the sport was good, to return to the same place year after year. All the other big-house owners in the district were watching the experiment with interest.

'Hello, George,' said Gus, when he got through.

'Well, Gussie, as I live and die!' said Cranshaw. 'How are you, old chap?'

'Fine, fine,' said Gus. 'How's the project?'

'Come on, Gus, give us a chance – it's only January. We have two Americans who are looking for their roots and an Italian who's blasting away at the robins.'

'Never mind, George,' chuckled Gus. 'His money is as good as the next man's.'

'I wish his aim was – I'm afraid for the horses. What can I do for you, Gus?'

'Well, to tell you the truth, I've a favour to ask. Only if it suits you, George, but a son of a friend of mine, good lad, badly needs work. Genuine case. I'd like to help him if I could. Just back from Canada, as a matter of fact. Knows a fair bit about farm management.'

'Does he know anything about game?'

'Never thought to ask him,' said Gus, truthfully. 'But he should. His father was my gamekeeper – and I know the lad fishes. Knows a bit about horses too.'

'I suppose I could do with some help,' said George Cranshaw slowly. 'Would you think this chap is responsible around guns?'

'Absolutely,' said Gus.

'All right. Send him over some time today or tomorrow and we'll have a chat.'

'Thank you very, very much, Colonel,' said John fervently. He was standing in the kitchen of the gate lodge, so elated that he could have kissed Gus.

As though sensing this alarming development, Gus took a step backwards. 'It's only a trial,' he warned, 'but Cranshaw really does seem to need someone and you'd be getting in on the ground floor, so to speak. I said you'd be willing to do anything about the place.'

'Anything at all,' said John. 'I'll do my absolute best, sir, I promise I won't let you down.'

'Do you know anything about shooting?' asked Gus.

'My father's old twelvebore is still here. I've used it, but not much,' John admitted.

'But at least you know how to handle one?'

'Oh, yes, Colonel. Derek and I both do. We used to shoot rabbits for the pot, and—' He stopped himself in time. He had almost found himself admitting that not only did Derek and himself take the ubiquitous rabbits, but frequently took pheasant and other winged game as well.

'Good, good,' said Gus. 'Well, I'll just pop along. Hope it works out.' He turned to go but stopped in the doorway, fiddling with his watch. 'By the way,' he said, looking at the floor, 'I forwarded your letter to Rose. Cheerio!' He was gone.

John had not written to Rose at the Big House.

Then he figured out that one of his letters had been mistakenly forwarded from the school in Dublin. He got busy preparing for his job interview the next day.

CHAPTER NINE

That night, John could not relax. He brought the old alarm clock into the bedroom with him but, terrified it would not go off, raised it a dozen times to check the time. Finally, just before six, he got out of bed and went to the window, having to rasp his pyjama sleeve over the pane to clear a thin layer of ice. Outside, the leafless hedge gleamed like filigree silver under a high, haloed moon. Shivering, he lit his candle and dressed quickly in his best clothes, laid out on the chair from the night before.

He carried the candle into the kitchen and placed it on the window-sill beside the bicycle which dominated the room. The hotel was ten miles distant and he had borrowed the bike, an ancient, cast-iron Rudge, from an old school friend. Having splashed his face and hands with cold water, he bolted a piece of bread and butter and washed it down with a cupful of milk. Then he scribbled a note for Derek, who had, as usual, come in late the night before.

John was reluctant to invite another snub from his brother, but, he told himself as he wrote, there were practical consider-ations: for instance, should the hospital send for them, Derek would need to know where he was. But he also had to admit that there was another reason for the note, that, deep down, he clung to the remnants of hope that a relationship with his twin could somehow, some time, be salvaged.

The heavy bike wobbled a bit as he pedalled it out of the yard but, after a few minutes on the road, he got its measure and settled into a steady rhythm, his tyres leaving a thin, corkscrewing wake through the frost, which on the smaller lanes was nearly as thick as powdered snow. He had the country to himself, an unfam-iliar world of frozen ponds and puddles, white-capped houses and glittering hedges. By the time he saw the hotel, an island of yellow light, his thigh and calf muscles were aching and his stomach was

255

growling with renewed hunger. He parked the Rudge against a hedge just inside the entrance gates and studied his new workplace.

Willow House, its grey stone walls veined with stems of ivy, was square and squat, not at all on the grand scale of Sundarbans, but impressive, none the less, and in a much better state of repair. In the overspill of light from its many windows, John could see that the gravel was raked and free of weeds and the paintwork on the doors and windows was fresh and smooth. The front door was lit by a cheerful pair of brass coach lamps.

He was seized with an attack of nerves. Keeping to the shadows and trying to minimise the sound of his footsteps on the gravel, he wheeled the bicycle into the back yard and parked it against the wall by the door. Then, taking a deep breath, he took off his cap and knocked firmly.

'Yes?' The man who opened the door was wiry, with receding curly hair; his bespectacled, harassed face was narrow and angular, with prominent cheekbones.

'Good morning, Mr Cranshaw,' said John. 'I'm John Flynn.'

The man's face cleared. 'Oh, yes, yes,' he said. 'Flynn, yes. Nice of you to come. Come in, won't you?'

The untidy, stone-flagged kitchen was enormous, the biggest John had ever seen. It seemed to run the full length of the house, with windows at both ends. Ten feet off the floor, a sort of gallery ran along one wall, railed with dark wood like the raftered ceiling. The air was acrid with fumes and John's eye was drawn to a large butcher's block in the centre of the room on which, smoking slightly, a frying pan had been discarded amid a clutter of dishes, sieves, pots, knives and other cooking utensils.

George Cranshaw saw John's eyes flick towards the pan. 'Yes,' he said, 'bit of a problem, this morning, I'm afraid. My cook has – has – well, she's just left me, actually. Bit short-staffed at the moment.' He ran his hand through his curls. 'Dorothy – that's my wife, d'you see – she's away . . . '

John nodded, his attack of nerves receding. He already liked this man, who was obviously a gentle sort. Although not resembling him at all physically, George Cranshaw reminded John of Dan McGuigan. 'That's a pity,' he heard himself say.

256

'Don't suppose you know how to cook a breakfast?' asked George, looking at John but without much hope.

'It depends on what kind of a breakfast you want,' John answered slowly. He knew how to cook rashers, sausages and eggs and Peggy McGuigan had taught him how to make pancakes.

'Anything, anything!' said George Cranshaw, relief shining like a beacon on his little face. 'Beggars can't be choosers. It's easy this morning – only three guests. They're in there now.' He waved an arm vaguely in the direction of the kitchen door. 'Could you make a start straight away? Don't worry, just do the best you can.' Opening a door in a little alcove off the kitchen, he showed John the pantry. 'I'll hold the fort inside for ten minutes or so,' he said, moving towards the door of the kitchen proper. 'Pleased to meet you, by the way.' Flashing a smile, he vanished.

John, although flustered, managed creditably, even finding tomatoes and several pieces of kidney, which he cooked alongside the rashers, sausages and eggs.

'Splendid,' enthused George Cranshaw when he returned to fetch the breakfasts. 'Thank you very, very much. Help yourself to anything you want,' he called back as, balancing a heavy silver tray on one shoulder, he vanished again.

But for once, John was too wound up to eat. He cleaned up the kitchen, then collapsed into a chair at the big table and waited for further orders.

It appeared he had already got the job.

Before having a formal chat with him, George Cranshaw gave John a tour of the hotel, the bedrooms, each with distinctively different colour scheme, were cheerful and spacious and the main hallway, with flagged floor and rose-covered wallpaper, doubled as a storage area for fishing rods, gaffs, nets and protective clothing. Then George pushed open one of the doors which led off the hallway. 'Our drawing room.'

Remembering his manners, John restrained himself from gasping at what he saw.

The sun streamed through two sets of french windows at one end of the room, lighting up an Aladdin's cave of treasures. The upholstery of the sagging sofas and chairs was draped with multi-coloured patchwork quilts, tasselled throws or pieces of faded tapestry. The mantelpiece on the magnificent marble fireplace was laden with stuffed birds and mammals in glass cases, china shepherdesses, two mismatched Chinese vases and several silver trophies stuffed with rosettes and gymkhana programmes. A large ceramic elephant stood on a plinth inside the fireplace fender, surrounded by several wooden decoy ducks. Pot plants, thriving in the heat from two steam radiators fixed to the walls on either side of the fireplace, trailed from antique jardinières in every corner of the room, but also from brass and iron buckets, coal scuttles, broken teapots, old china soup tureens, even a chaney.

The walls were almost completely covered with portraits, landscapes and hunting scenes, samplers, prize certificates, a set of military medals, glass cases full of coins, tropical butterflies and along one side, tiered velvet boxes containing dozens of speckled birds' eggs of all hues and sizes. And every horizontal surface in the room supported photographs of fishermen and shooters displaying their prizes, serious long-haired children, horses, dogs and even a prize pig.

'Bit of a mess, eh?' George Cranshaw chuckled. 'Dorothy's a bit of a clutterbug, I'm afraid, and so was everyone in her family – this is her house, you know – but the guests seem to like it and the tourist board chap said to leave everything as it was. It's the devil to dust. Well, if you've seen enough,' he chuckled again, 'come on into my study and we'll have a chat.'

The room was tiny, but perfectly appointed, with a filing cabinet, kneehole desk and two chairs, one obviously for George. He seated himself and motioned to John to take the other chair. 'Now,' he said briskly, 'the Colonel tells me you really need this job.'

'That's right,' John looked bravely into George Cranshaw's face.

'No experience?'

'Only on a farm, sir.'

'How old are you, by the way?'

'Eighteen, sir.' The lie was instantaneous.

'What about exams – school, that sort of thing?'

'Well, I did my Inter, sir. I got seven honours.'

George Cranshaw whistled. 'I am impressed. Sure you won't be taking me over as soon as I have my back turned?'

John was uncertain as to how he should react. But George Cranshaw continued. 'As well as being a whizz at the sums,' he said, 'it also seems you can cook.'

'Well, not actually, Mr Cranshaw,' John felt he had to be honest, 'I wouldn't call rashers and eggs actually cooking.'

'Can you make a stew?'

'I – I think so—'

'Roast a chicken?'

'Well, yes.'

'Then you can cook.'

'But—' John was flabbergasted. Was he to be recruited as a cook? George Cranshaw saw the bewilderment in his face. 'Don't worry, Dorothy does all the cooking. It's just that if I'm to hire you here you'll have to be able to turn your hand to anything. Gillie, beater, cook, housemaid, cleaner, painter, harvest hand, tractor driver even nursemaid – with me so far?'

John nodded. This was unlike any job interview he had imagined.

'Now,' George Cranshaw continued blithely. 'I expect you'll want to know what your wages and conditions will be?'

'Yes, sir.'

'I haven't worked out the hours, but could you be flexible? Could we work on a day-to-day basis?'

John thought of the reason he was looking for this job in the first place. Again he felt he had to be honest. 'Well, sir, I will have to look after my mother quite a lot.'

'If you'll be flexible, I'll be flexible too. I'm sure we can work something out.'

'Thank you, sir.'

'Oh, please call me George, "sir" reminds me of the navy.' He feigned a shudder. 'Now, about your wages. I had a think about that. Would three pounds be acceptable?'

John swallowed. He knew he was not in a position to argue, but three pounds sounded very little on which to support his mother and himself. The words were out before he could control them. 'Five pounds, Mr Cranshaw.' Scandalised at his own temerity, he tried to keep his face from showing it. 'I'm sorry, sir,' he said, 'but I couldn't work for less than five pounds a week.'

George Cranshaw frowned and he drummed his fingers on

his desk. Then he seemed to come to a decision. 'Four?' he said.

John looked him straight in the eyes. 'Four pounds ten,' he said firmly.

'You drive a hard bargain.' George's mouth was wry.

'Well, sir – George – I intend to work hard. You won't be sorry. I won't let you down.'

'Four pounds two and six.'

John knew he should take the money, which was more than fair. But for his mother, he had to take one more chance. 'Four pounds five shillings?'

For a few seconds, he thought he had gone too far but then, slowly, George Cranshaw nodded. 'You'd better earn it,' he said and extended his hand. 'Welcome to the club.'

As John watched his new employer writing something on a notepad, he could barely contain his elation. He had a job, one he knew he would like; he had a wage which was more than decent. He would be able to save a little so that he would have a cushion for when his mother came home.

Now all he had to do was to find Rose.

Rose stared out through the window of the recreation room, not hearing the shrieks and general hullabaloo behind her. It had begun to snow but although the flurries swirled under the street-lamps and patted the window panes, she did not see them. She had no idea how long she had been sitting. Time had stopped dead for her and she felt it might never start again.

The only reality was the letter her father had enclosed with his own; its contents would not stop repeating themselves; they kept on battering against the inside of her head and, although she already knew them by heart, she read them again. Crudely printed on lined blue paper the letter got straight to the point:

WHY DON'T YOU ASK JOHN FLYNN WHAT HE WAS DOING IN A BED WITH ANOTHER GIRL ON NEW YEAR'S EVE

Rose felt she might faint. She half stood out of her chair but the floor felt uneven so she sat down again, heavily.

'Rose, Rose!' Someone was calling her name, tapping her on the shoulder, but she could not answer; her whole body seemed to be breaking up in a peculiar way. She tried to shrug off whoever was calling her but the person would not go away. 'Rose, Rose, what's the matter, Rose?'

She concentrated on keeping her body together and wished whoever it was would just leave her alone. All she could think of was those words: *Why don't you ask John Flynn . . . in a bed . . . another girl . . .*

'Rose!' The voice was insistent. Someone was clutching at her shoulder, hurting her.

Rose thought she might be sick.

She forced herself to turn around. It was Effie. Effie's face was swimming in the air. Effie was standing there, shaking her, calling her. Rose almost laughed. Effie's eyes were so enormous, her hair so wild.

'Leave me alone,' she managed to say but the words sounded strange.

Effie was turning away from her and shouting, 'Sister—' shouting at the top of her voice. 'Sister, sister, there's something wrong with Rose O'Beirne. Quick, quick!'

Then there was a nun, some nun; and the nun and Effie were walking her out of the room between them but all she could think of was John in a bed, in a bed with another girl. She staggered against the nun but the nun and Effie supported her.

Then there was freezing air on her face and something soft and cold getting in her eyes. It was snow. She was outside in the yard and it was snowing and the nun was telling her to put her head down between her knees. Rose thought it was easier to be obedient, so she put her head down as low as she could but when she did she felt her stomach doubling over and felt sure it was doing that because of the baby. John's baby . . .

Rose started to scream. She shook off the nun and threw back her head and screamed as loudly as she could. The nun tried to stop her and Effie ran inside to get more help but Rose would not stop. She ran away from the nun to the other side of the yard and screamed and clawed at the wall, not caring that she was tearing her nails and hands on the rough concrete, not caring that she was making a show of herself. The nun was pulling at her back and slapping at her but she brushed off the beating hands as easily as she would brush off two midges. Screaming,

261

she ran to the other side of the yard and felt the dirty snow going into her open mouth. She didn't care, she let it melt in with her tears and her saliva and the snot that was running out of her nose.

Other nuns and other girls came, including Sister Benvenuto; then she felt her arms being pinned and her head being forced against Sister Benvenuto's crucifix so she couldn't breathe properly or scream any more but, still struggling, she managed to drag the nun round the yard until she had no more strength left.

The hateful words still beat in her head so she could not understand what Sister Benvenuto was saying to her; she was so worn out she gave in and let the nun half pull, half carry her towards the door of the convent, dragging her in through a circle of shocked faces which energised her, starting the scream again. She wanted to lash out at them all, but Sister Benvenuto caught her and now she did not have the energy.

She let herself be guided up the stairs and straight into the sick bay, into one of the beds; she felt like a floppy rag doll now and the bed felt cool and welcoming. She was crying but the crying felt bittersweet; it hurt her somewhere in the middle of her chest but the pain was welcome. She heard herself saying words as she was crying, but the words made no sense; she heard the words come out like an endless litany: 'Oh, please, please, please, please—' Rose's hip was pricked as Sister Benvenuto gave her an injection, a sort of white light grew all around the bed, then everything went dark.

When she woke up it was daylight. She felt groggy and disoriented and also vaguely nauseous. After a minute or two, she recognised the windows of the sick bay and saw her clothes, neatly folded on a locker beside her bed. A few feet away, a nun sat on a chair, reading her breviary. Rose tried to talk. 'Sister?' but the word was thick in her mouth.

'Good morning, Rose,' said the nun, closing the prayer book. 'Welcome to the land of the living. Would you like a little drink?'

Rose nodded. The nun fetched a tumbler of water but when Rose reached for it, she saw her hand was bandaged. Then she remembered – the most crucial part of it, anyhow. She remembered that John Flynn had been in bed with another girl.

When Rose woke again, it was Effie's face she saw, hovering anxiously about six inches above her own. Her creased features more than ever resembled a monkey's. 'Howya, Rose,' she said tentatively as Rose focused her eyes. 'How're you feeling? Are you all right?'

Rose nodded. She still felt groggy and tired, but her brain was clear. 'What time is it?' she asked.

'It's nearly lunchtime.' She hesitated. 'Do you want to talk about it?'

Rose shook her head. The pain in the middle of her chest had started again, but although her whole body was so tired, she had not the energy to acknowledge it.

'Would it have something to do with this?' Effie asked tentatively, pulling out a crumpled piece of blue paper. 'Sorry,' she said quickly. 'You dropped it in the yard last night and I picked it up. I shouldn't have read it – but I did. No, I'm not sorry, actually, I'm *glad* I did.' Rose felt the tears begin to well in her eyes. 'Surely you don't believe this rubbish?' continued Effie. She leaned over the bed and shook the letter in Rose's face, her eyes boring into Rose's, as though she would transfer some of her own contempt. 'It's not even signed, Rose. It's just someone making trouble.'

'I know who wrote it,' said Rose.

'How do you know?'

'Not that it's any of your business, but there's only one person who knows about John and me and who would have seen what went on in Charlottetown.'

'It certainly is my business. Is it a he or a she?'

'A he.'

'Well, ask yourself, what's in it for him? Why would he do this?'

'I don't know, Effie, I just don't know. Why won't you leave me alone?' Rose turned her face away from Effie's insistence.

'I'm your effing friend, that's why. No man, *no* man, Rose, is worth what you went through last night.' She waved the letter again. 'This John Flynn, I suppose you love the shagger?'

Rose nodded miserably.

263

'Well, if you love him, why would you believe this piece of shit?'

'Please leave me alone, will you?'

'I won't leave you alone. And even if it's true, what has he done, really? Sex is just sex, Rose. Five minutes out of a person's life. Ask any cow or duck or – or even fish! Sex has nothing to do with love.'

'It has to me—'

'Maybe, but you're not a man. All men are the same, Rose,' said Effie quietly. 'All shaggers when it comes to sex. There's none of 'em any better than the rest. And you can't blame them for it. It's in their nature.'

'Oh, Effie,' Rose said, 'I'm really sorry I was rude to you. You're right. All men are shaggers.' The word, which she had never used before, felt round and satisfying in her mouth.

'Attagirl,' said Effie. 'Shaggers!'

The more Rose thought about it the more angry she became. Here she was, only sixteen and a half years of age, locked away far from home, having a baby she would never see again after it was born. John Flynn's baby.

While he romped around in Charlottetown.

She was not going to let any shagger get the better of her. 'I feel better, Effie,' she said, raising herself on one elbow. 'I'll go down to lunch, I think.'

'Are you sure?' asked Effie.

'I'm sure. Will you hand me my clothes?'

Effie lumbered to her feet and got the clothes. 'D'you want this back?' she asked, proffering the blue letter and watching for Rose's reaction.

Rose felt brave and defiant and very grown-up. 'Tear it up,' she said. 'I never want to see it again.'

But in the weeks to come, she found it was not that easy.

Two letters, bearing Irish stamps, came from John in quick succession via Dolores, but, assuming he was back at the gate lodge, she returned both of them unopened to that address. When the third one came, curiosity almost overcame her and she was tempted to open it. Why was he back in Ireland so soon? As she held the letter, she had a niggling doubt. Perhaps she was overreacting? Perhaps he deserved a chance to talk for himself?

But then she thought of the extent of his betrayal, of his body wriggling in a bed with another girl's and her resolve hardened. He would never hurt her like that again. She was finished with John Flynn – finished with men. After his baby was born and adopted, she would resume her life as though he had never existed. And she would never again trust any man.

Like the other two, she put the third letter in an envelope and returned it to the gate lodge. She wanted to make sure he got it – that he knew he was being rejected as comprehensively as he had rejected her.

Each day from then on, Rose worked until her ankles swelled and her back and arms ached, until she thought she might sleep standing up. But at night, sleep eluded her for hour after hour.

In the darkness, John Flynn's face, his wolfish smile, tantalised her imagination; her body was tortured by the memory of his cool wet skin against her own in Swan's Lake, by the peaty taste of his wet neck. She tried to distract herself from these imaginings by deliberately invoking pictures of what he might have done to that other girl in Charlottetown. Had he stroked the girl's breasts? Had he sucked on the girl's nipples the way he had fastened his mouth over her own? Had that other girl discovered the mole which marred his otherwise smooth back?

She also worked on hating John Flynn's baby, hating the way it was invading her life, making her fat and unattractive.

In the middle of February, Sister Benvenuto sent for her. 'I've had a letter from your father, asking how you're getting on,' she said. 'What shall I tell him, d'you think?'

'I'm fine,' Rose said.

'I know you're healthy, Rose, but I don't think you're fine, actually, do you? And we never got to the bottom of that business in the recreation hall that night, did we? What happened that night, Rose?'

Rose shifted her weight. She was sitting on the same chair she had occupied during her first interview in this office. 'I'd prefer not to discuss it, sister,' she said. 'I'm afraid it's private. I'll be fine,' she added firmly. 'I was just going through a bad patch.'

'Well,' said Sister Benvenuto, standing up and handing

Rose Gus's letter, 'there's a bit of good news for you at last. He'll probably tell you himself, but your father plans to come and visit you at Easter. That's only six weeks away.'

'Thank you, sister,' said Rose, taking the letter. 'Can I go now?'

The nun looked at her seriously. 'You really have changed, haven't you?'

Rose did not answer and the nun sighed. 'Off you go! But I wish you'd tell someone what's eating you. A blind man could see there's something wrong.'

'I'm pregnant, sister, that's what's wrong,' said Rose, lifting her head.

'Have patience and courage, Rose,' said the nun.

Fat lot of use courage would do her now, thought Rose, looking down at the buttons of her blouse which now strained at their buttonholes across her enlarged breasts. 'Thank you, sister,' she said as politely as she could and let herself out of the study.

One day towards the end of March, she and Effie were having a break from their work in the laundry. The day was mild and the sparrows were busy in the two horse-chestnuts which grew in one corner and were just coming into pale green leaf. They watched one of the birds trying over and over again to lift a piece of twig off the ground. On the surface, Rose seemed to have reverted to the way she had been before her breakdown.

'Listen,' said Effie, puffing on a Craven A, 'are you going to be all right when I leave?' Effie's confinement was getting perilously close and she was enormous.

'What do you mean? Of course I'll be all right. I'm not a baby.'

'No, but I worry about you. Ever since that night—'

'Look, Effie,' said Rose, 'of course I'll be all right. I'm glad it happened. I was being really stupid about John Flynn. I can see that now.'

'I hope I didn't turn you against him?' Effie was being uncharacteristically serious.

'Not at all, Effie, there was no future in it, anyway.'

Effie exhaled smoke in a long thin stream. 'Will you keep in touch with me?'

'Of course!' Rose looked at her friend. For the first time, she saw that Effie was vulnerable. She had been so dependent on Effie for everything, taking all the time, giving very little. 'Of course we'll keep in touch. Where will you be going?'

'I'm not sure,' said Effie. 'I'm certainly not going back to Offaly.'

'But isn't that where your family is?'

Effie looked around. 'Me feckin' back is killing me!'

'Don't you want to talk about them?'

'I want to kill them!' Effie looked away. 'You wouldn't want to know.'

'I do, of course I do, I'm your friend.'

'I've never told anyone this – I was thrown out of confession. Even the priest didn't believe me.' Rose's instinct told her to keep quiet. Effie threw her butt on the ground and trod on it. 'I told you me first child was adopted?' Rose nodded.

'Well, that's not true.' Effie studied her nails. 'He's – he's in a home.' She said it so softly that Rose barely heard her.

'An orphanage?' she asked.

'No. He's a vegetable.'

Rose was shocked. 'That's dreadful, Effie,' she managed to say after a few seconds, 'you must feel awful.'

'This one's going to be a vegetable too.'

'Oh, Effie!' cried Rose. 'How can you possibly know that?'

'Because I know. I told you you wouldn't be able to take this.' Effie's voice was savage.

'Of course I can. Why are you so sure? I mean, that there's going to be something wrong with this baby too?'

'My fucking father's the father!' Effie turned to look at Rose full in the face. 'There, Rose! What do you think of that?' Her face was white, its frizzy halo blowing forwards in a sudden gust of wind. Impatiently, she brushed it out of her eyes. 'Nothing like that in precious Sundarbans, I expect!'

Rose had turned white too but, instinctively, she knew the only correct response was to be honest. 'Effie,' she said, 'I'm absolutely shocked, but I can't tell you how sorry I am. And I'm very, very sorry that I blathered on about my own stupid problems and was so selfish. Compared to you, I have no problems at all.'

Effie's bloated body seemed to collapse internally like a

pricked balloon. 'It's all right, Rose. To tell you the truth, having you to mind helped me a lot. But I'm scared now of what's going to happen.'

'Does Sister Benvenuto not know the truth?'

Effie shook her head.

'But who's paying for you here? This place is not cheap.'

'My family is rich.' It had never occurred to Rose that Effie's family could have money. She had an older brother with whom she did not get along. 'Did your brother not know what was going on?'

'He knew.' And then Effie shattered what remained of Rose's innocence. 'He helped.'

'Effie!' Rose was almost in tears. 'Why didn't you run away?'

'Where to? Who'd have believed me? I told you I tried the priest. My father's a county councillor, you see – and he's big in the Confraternity.'

'How old were you – the first time, I mean? I mean when he—'

'For as long as I can remember.'

'Did your mother not know?'

'My mother died when I was five,' said Effie, 'but it was going on before then.'

'Oh, God,' said Rose helplessly.

'There's nothing else to say,' said Effie. She lit another cigarette. 'You know it all now.'

Anger began to boil inside Rose. 'I'll help you, Effie,' she said fiercely. 'You can't go back there.'

'I wasn't planning to – I decided over the last few months that I am never, ever contacting any of them again. But I've no money and he certainly won't give me any.'

Rose was thinking furiously. 'You've got to promise me something, Effie. After you've had this baby, you're to come and see me, the *very minute* you get out of the hospital, you understand? I'll have worked out something for us.' She had no idea yet what she would do but she would definitely think of something.

She took Effie's arm. Now that she had a project, she felt purposeful and good. 'Just one thing,' she asked curiously as they walked back inside to the laundry, 'how come you're always in good humour?'

'Habit.' Effie smiled wanly. 'When you look like me, you've got to offer something to the world, now don't you?'

'Effie,' said Rose. 'Stop that. To me you look beautiful.'

Her friend snorted, returning a little to her old self. 'Now, don't go too far, Rose!'

Effie was taken to hospital on Good Friday. She was not in labour, but she was two weeks overdue and her ankles had swelled so badly that the doctor feared toxaemia.

Her baby had still not been born when Rose's father arrived at the convent on Easter Tuesday to take her to tea.

Since early morning, Rose had been in a fever of excitement. She washed and brushed her hair until it shone and borrowed one of the nicer maternity dresses which the girls swopped around among themselves; of heavy navy cotton with white petersham ribbons flowing from a wide white sailor collar to the hem, it made her feel feminine and pretty.

'Daddy!' she called joyfully when she saw Gus standing in the hall. Breaking into a run to throw herself in his arms, something in his expression made her falter. Accustomed to being pregnant, she had forgotten how she must look in her father's eyes.

Then she saw that his reticence was born of shyness and flung her arms around his neck. 'Oh, Daddy, I'm so pleased to see you – how do I look?' Confident of his answer, she pirouetted.

'You look beautiful, Rose.' Gus's voice was gruff.

Rose laughed and took his arm. 'Daddy, you'd say that if I had a sack over my head. I'm as big as the side of a house,' she went on cheerfully. 'Are you sure you won't be ashamed of me out in the big bad world?'

He fiddled with his watch, always a sign, Rose thought affectionately, that he was embarrassed. 'Come on,' she said, tugging at him. 'Let's not waste any time. I have a big project I want to discuss with you.'

Although Easter was early, it was a beautiful afternoon outside, as warm as might be expected in late May. Rose kept her arm through her father's as they strolled through the small streets towards an intersection where Gus hoped to secure a taxi. 'Your mother sends her love,' he said while they waited at the kerb.

'That's nice,' said Rose. Then, playfully, 'Looking forward to being a granny, is she?'

'Rose!' But Gus laughed, then thought better of it. 'She does worry about you, you know.'

'Oh, I know, Daddy. Her letters are full of prayers and exhortations.'

'Rose, please—'

'Don't worry, Daddy. I'll be penitent and proper all the rest of my life. But today it's a beautiful day and I intend to enjoy every minute of it. Here's a taxi.'

'Where would you like to go?' asked Gus as they climbed in.

'Harrods!' said Rose immediately. She knew nothing of London but the other girls in the convent had talked of Harrods as a sort of Mecca to which they all aspired.

Gus directed the driver to take them to the Knightsbridge store via the Mall and Buckingham Palace – 'Might as well see it while we're here, eh, poppet?' – and Rose sat back to enjoy the ride. It was her first outside excursion since she had come to London and as she gazed out of the window, at the strollers and shoppers, she realised what freedom she had lost. But she was not downhearted. In fact, she felt more optimistic and determined than she had ever felt in her life. It felt good to be a woman on a mission, she decided and stored up the feeling for further use. Self-analysis and memory retrieval were habits Rose had fallen into during her months in the convent. The monotonous manual labour at the laundry had the beneficial side-effect of leaving the brain free for other pursuits and during the long afternoons Rose had spent amid the steaming, clanking machinery she had revived her half-baked aspirations to become a writer.

When they got to the store, she was briefly diverted by its grandeur but then took her father's arm. 'Tea, Daddy.' She had to be single-minded. 'I'm starving.'

They took the lift. The baby kicked as it came to a halt but Rose hardly noticed; in the weeks since she had received the anonymous letter, she had trained herself to consider the baby merely as an inconvenience, a sort of purgatory she had to go through until, in less than two months, she would be free.

In the tea room, she ordered hot chocolate, buttered toast and muffins and sat back to enjoy the gentle music being bowed by a dress-suited string quartet.

'Now,' said Gus, when the waitress had bustled away, 'what's all this about a project?'

'Right, Daddy.' Rose sat forward in her chair. 'I've a proposition to put to you.' She had rehearsed what she was going to say and as succinctly as she could, omitting the reasons, she outlined the problems facing Effie. 'Now,' she said, 'remember how good she was to me, Daddy? I wrote to you all about her.'

'I remember.'

'Now this is where we come in.'

'We?'

'Yes, Daddy,' said Rose firmly, 'we, you and I. I need a loan!'

Then, although Gus was not about to say anything, she held up her hand as though to forestall argument. 'Before you say anything, Effie doesn't know about this. I haven't told her yet. But here's the plan. I'm going to suggest to her that she takes a flat in Dublin. She'll need a bit of money to get the flat – you see that, Daddy, I'm sure. Also to tide her over until she can get a job. Daddy, she's a great worker, I promise. She'll get a job in no time—' Rose was losing her tone of adult gravitas. She took a deep breath and slowed herself down. 'Now, Daddy, since it's a loan I'm looking for, you may well ask how I intend to pay you back.'

She paused. 'I want you to sell Tartan. He's my pony, you always said that—'

Rose was halted in mid-flow while the waitress placed their order on the table in front of them. She waited until the woman had left and then continued in a quiet urgent voice. 'I've thought about this a lot, Daddy. You should get a good lot of money for Tartan, there'll probably be enough even for interest.' She tried to read the expression on her father's face but he was adding sugar to his tea and stirring it with a spoon.

'How much of a loan did you want?' he asked eventually, his voice faint.

Under the table, Rose crossed her fingers. 'A hundred pounds,' she said and held her breath.

'I see,' said Gus.

Rose let out the breath. At least he hadn't exploded or turned her down flat. She turned to join in the applause for the

271

string ensemble who were taking a bow. Having rehearsed this scene many times in her head, she felt giddy with relief. On the whole, she thought, it had gone rather well.

What she had not told Gus was that after her own baby was born, she was planning to join her friend in the flat in Dublin. Always provided, of course, that this was agreeable to Effie.

Rose clapped the string ensemble so enthusiastically that the leader turned and gave her a special bow all to herself. She was so enchanted that she did not notice the stricken look in Gus's eyes.

Today was John's first day off from the hotel for two and a half weeks.

He was not complaining; although he had to work so hard, he appreciated the variety and catch-all quality of his duties; he had even managed to save a small amount of money. And now that Derek was no longer around with his silences and his simmering resentment, he had found he was beginning to enjoy his independent existence.

John's twin had been true to his word and, at the beginning of February, had gone back to Canada leaving a note, his only direct communication since New Year's Eve, to say that he was travelling via Dublin and would call in at the hospital to visit their mother. When he found the note, John's first reaction had been to check the tea caddy on the mantelpiece but every penny of his own hard-earned money was still intact. In one respect, at least, Derek had been honourable and John concluded that the passage money must have come from the McGuigans.

Now his mother was due home the following day.

John had managed to find a local girl, Mona McConnell, who, for small wages, was willing to come in every day to help look after Mary who would need constant care and supervision for the rest of her life. She was paralysed along the left side of her body, her eyesight had deteriorated and although she could make herself understood, the stroke had affected her speech. She was also frequently confused and could not remember even who or where she was.

If he could just sort out the situation with Rose, thought John, pottering around the kitchen of the gate lodge, his life would be well under control.

Rose's behaviour in sending back his letters unopened, at first mystified and then tortured him. The postmark superimposed on the letters was London, so at least he had narrowed down her whereabouts; and for a time he had even considered going over there to look for her. He had convinced himself that if he could just talk to her, they could sort out whatever it was that was bothering her. But then he realised almost immediately that not only would the size of the city make that task impossible, but he could not disappear so soon from his new job for any length of time. Willow House, although not always full, had a constant turnover of guests.

John decided that he would have to ask the Colonel straight out about Rose. And he would do it today. He reckoned he had nearly five and a half hours to kill before Mona McConnell arrived.

It was not yet nine o'clock – too early to go up to Sundarbans. On the other hand, he reasoned, if he went up now, he might well run into the Colonel in the stables. Since Fergie McKenna's departure, the master of the house surely had to see to the horses himself, always an early-morning task. And remembering the last interview, it would suit John's purpose not to have to knock blatantly at the front door.

Almost as an afterthought he fetched the pouch containing Rose's amethyst bracelet from his bedroom. He had brought it with him as a talisman when going for interview to the hotel and was quite superstitious about it being lucky for him.

The fine weather of the evening before had held and after a few minutes' walking along the avenue, despite his anxiety at the coming meeting with the Colonel, John, as usual, could not but be affected by his surroundings. The voices of the birds carried on the mildest of breezes, a profusion of daffodils and narcissus bloomed under the chestnuts on both sides of the driveway, and about twenty yards away to his right, in a moist ferny place around a birch copse, he spotted a shimmer of bluebells.

When he came out into the open at the end of the driveway, he stopped in disbelief. Perhaps he had been too fraught – and wet – on the last occasion he had seen it to notice, but the house seemed to have disintegrated more than he would have thought possible since last he had examined it with any degree of thoroughness. The bright spring sunshine showed up the bare wood through the paintwork on the front door and windows and the terrace was littered with debris – the sodden pages of a newspaper caught on the bootscraper, a mush of leaves, small stones and twiglets heaped against the walls and risers of the steps. Dandelions, scutch and young nettles spread unchecked across the gravel. On one side, a piece of the balustrade which fronted the terrace had crumbled away so the house seemed to wear a forlorn, gap-toothed smile. 'Poor Rose,' he murmured to himself and then half smiled at the absurdity of the penniless tenant from the gate lodge pitying the only daughter of the squire.

He skirted the house and went round to the stables, where there was another shock in store. The stalls were locked, unlikely at this hour. He went to the nearest one where he would have expected to find Clicker, the trap pony. Evidently, it had not been opened for some time because the bolt was stiff and he had great difficulty with it.

The stall was empty. So were Thumper's and Tartan's. There were no horses at all in the yard. What was happening?

He went into Thumper's stall and examined it carefully, trying to determine how long it had been since the horse had occupied it but it had been thoroughly cleaned. Only the residual horse-smell and a few wisps in the haynet denoted that there had ever been a horse here at all.

'Can I help you?' It was a woman's voice and John spun around in alarm, shading his eyes. The small figure darkening the stable doorway held two leads, at the end of which waddled two fat little dogs which, as soon as their mistress spoke, immediately began to yip. 'I'm – I'm sorry,' he stammered. 'I was just looking for Thumper.'

'Well, as you can see, Thumper's not here any more,' said the woman drily. 'And I might save you some trouble by telling you that neither are Tartan and Clicker.' The voice was calm and gentle and the woman, who he now saw was elderly, seemed not at all put out at finding an intruder in her son's stableyard. Although he had never met her, John knew that this must be Rose's grandmother.

John's recent training in the hotel came to his rescue. 'Please forgive me, Mrs O'Beirne Moffat,' he said, walking towards her, and extending his hand. 'I'm John Flynn. I live in the gate lodge.'

She took the hand. 'So you're John Flynn.' And then she added a curious rider. 'I might have guessed.'

John knew that Rose had not mentioned her connection with him to anyone and was puzzled by her tone. 'Yes, ma'am,' he said, shaking her tiny, brittle hand.

'Well, John,' she said, 'as you can see, times have changed, and not for the better, I'm afraid. The horses have all been sold. They went at the beginning of February. My son simply could not afford to keep them. Anyway, there was no one to ride them any more. Horses are expensive ornaments.'

'I see,' said John. He was bewildered. How could he have missed that bit of news around Drumboola? And Rose adored her pony. Why had she agreed to give it up? The finances at Sundarbans must be even worse than anyone thought.

The dogs were snuffling around his feet and Rose's grandmother was looking at him as though expecting him to say something else. Her legs, thin as sticks, were encased to the calf in galoshes as though she did not for a moment trust the kind blue sky. 'You're a friend of Rose's, aren't you?'

The question caught him off guard. 'Y – yes, I am,' he said. 'I used to ride with her – actually, she taught me to ride, on Thumper. That's why I was here looking for him,' he added lamely.

The blue eyes did not waver and he knew she was not fooled. 'Yes, I had heard. That you used to ride with Rose, I mean.'

'Well,' he said, 'I suppose I'd better lock up again.'

'Yes, that mightn't be a bad idea.' As he moved away, the dogs set up their yipping again and she made no attempt to quieten them.

John felt very self-conscious as he closed and bolted first Clicker's, then Tartan's half-door. Although he did not look around, he felt that Rose's grandmother did not take her eyes off him for a second. 'Excuse me, ma'am,' he said, when he had to walk around her to close the third door. 'There,' he said when this task was accomplished and turned back to her. She had not moved and he had the strangest feeling that he was there to await further orders. But when she did not speak, he felt he had to. 'Beautiful day, thank God.'

'It is indeed,' agreed Nancy O'Beirne Moffat calmly. Then she startled him again. 'Have you heard from Rose?'

He took a deep breath. 'No, Mrs O'Beirne Moffat,' he said. 'I'm afraid I haven't. And if the truth be told, that's really why I came. I was hoping the Colonel would be here.'

'Well, he'd hardly be locked into Thumper's stall,' she pointed out. 'Anyway, I'm afraid he's away for a few days.'

John grinned. He liked this woman. And of course! Why had he not thought of it before? Rose's grandmother would be sure to know where she was. 'Perhaps you can help me instead, ma'am?'

'If I can, I will.'

He was suddenly very nervous and dug his hands into his pockets. As he did so, his right hand touched the pouch containing the amethysts. Almost without willing it, he brought it out. 'I need to get this back to Rose,' he said, wanting to implore but hoping that he sounded matter-of-fact.

'What is it?' She looked at it with interest.

'It's the bracelet from her jewellery set.' For a few moments, he thought he had made a dreadful mistake. Her head came up and she fixed him with a stare which almost shrivelled him. 'What are you doing with Rose's bracelet in your possession?' she asked.

But John had come this far and she was not going to intimidate him now. He brought his own head up. 'She *gave* it to me, ma'am, last summer. She wanted me to have it – but I want to return it to her now.'

'Why can't you return it without involving me?' He could see she was mollified.

'I don't have her address in London,' he said simply.

'I see.' She seemed to be mulling something over in her mind. Then to his relief, she held out her hand. 'Give it to me, dear. I'll send it with my next letter.'

'And would it be all right if you gave me the address some time?' he risked.

'I think, John, if Rose wanted you to have the address, you'd have it.'

'She doesn't know I'm back in Ireland,' he said, trying it on, but she was not fooled.

'I'll tell her,' she repeated, 'and if she wants you to have it, she'll send it to you herself. Goodbye, John.' She turned to go.

'Just one more thing, ma'am,' cried John. 'Please!'

She turned back. 'What is it?'

'Mrs O'Beirne Moffat, please could you tell me why Rose so suddenly changed schools? I thought she was happy at the one in Dublin. And she stopped writing to me from the time she changed. I just don't understand it.'

She took a step towards him. 'John,' she said softly, 'Rose is a big girl now, with her own motives and feelings. I'll write to her and tell her I've met you. That's all I can promise.' She turned away again, leaving him standing. Then, just before she disappeared through the arched entrance to the yard, she stopped and turned to face him again. 'One more thing,' she called in a high clear voice. 'If it helps you to know this, when I write, I'll tell her that I think she should give you her address, all right?' Then, without waiting for a response, she pulled on the dogs' leads. 'Come on, dears . . . '

There was news. One of the other girls in the convent told Rose as soon as she had come in to the refectory for breakfast. Effie had had her baby.

Rose was still high on her plans and on her father's visit. 'How's the baby?' she asked immediately.

'There's summat wrong with it,' said the girl, whom Rose had never liked.

'Who told you that? And what's wrong with it?'

The girl shrugged. 'Keep your 'air on, luv! All right?'

Rose marched out of the refectory and went to Sister Benvenuto's office. She knocked at the door and entered without waiting for an invitation. The nun was bent low over her desk, a ledger open in front of her. She looked up as Rose came in. 'Rose. Is everything all right? Did you have a nice time with your father?'

'Lovely, thank you, sister.' Then Rose came straight to the point. 'I just heard about Effie. They're saying there's something wrong with her baby. Is that right?'

'I'm afraid so, Rose.'

'What's wrong, precisely?'

The nun took off her glasses and put them carefully on the ledger. 'As you know Rose, we respect the girls' privacy here as much as is practicable. I don't think I can give you that information.'

'Sister,' Rose leaned forward and placed both hands on the edge of the desk, 'I respect Effie's privacy too. But I know all about Effie's first baby. She told me.' *She told me everything*, her expression implied. But then she remembered that she had to be careful. Effie had said Sister Benvenuto did not know the full truth.

The nun stood up from her desk and moved to the window, half turned away from Rose. 'Effie's baby lived only twenty minutes,' she said, 'which, although I suppose I shouldn't say this, is a great blessing to her. The baby was a boy. He suffered from hydrocephalus and many, many other complications.'

Rose's hands flew to her mouth. Poor Effie.

'Even if he had lived, he would have been no better than a vegetable.'

'What's going to happen now?' asked Rose.

'Nothing as far as this convent is concerned. Our involvement with Effie is at an end – until the next time,' she added, so quietly that Rose barely caught the words.

'There won't be a next time, sister. I can tell you that!'

'What?'

'I said there won't be a next time. I can promise you. At least I *think* I can.'

'What on earth are you talking about?'

'I have plans for Effie. And for myself.' Rose outlined what she and Effie were going to do. 'We're both strong and healthy,' she said at the end, 'we'll be absolutely fine and there's no point in trying to talk me out of it.'

'How do your parents feel about this?'

'They don't know yet – about me and the flat, I mean,' said Rose honestly. 'Daddy will be all right, it's Mother who will be the problem.' Her chin came up. 'But they can't *force* me to stay in school. The legal age for leaving school in Ireland is fourteen and I'll be seventeen in two months' time.'

'I see,' said the nun. 'All I can do is wish you luck, my dear – and of course I'll pray for you – for you both. Have you thought any more about your baby? What you are going to do after it's born?'

'Sister,' said Rose very definitely, 'there will be no room for a baby in our flat.' Then, suddenly, for the very first time, she had a twinge of doubt. Instinctively, she pressed her hands to her stomach. The baby was awake and moving. But she hardened her heart. 'It'll be the best thing for the baby – won't it?' she appealed to the nun. 'To be adopted, I mean? After all, I have to think of its future. It will be so much better off with two loving parents who really want it. It'll mean a proper start in life.'

Sister Benvenuto nodded slowly. 'Rose, it's your decision. The conventional advice is what you've just said. But I feel very unsure of everything right now.'

Rose was astounded. She had never before heard a grown-up – and one in a position of authority – admit to indecision or of being unsure. The world was being turned upside down. 'I'm not sure of what you mean, sister,' she said uncertainly.

Sister Benvenuto rubbed her eyes and then put her glasses back on. 'Rose, I've broken enough rules for one evening. I think, if there's nothing else, you'd better go back to the others.'

'Yes, sister. Thank you.'

'Would you like to go and visit Effie?'

'Oh, yes, sister, that'd be great, but what about work?'

'I'll sort it out. I'll arrange it for this afternoon,' said Sister Benvenuto, bending again to her figures. 'Now, off you go.'

Rose's baby heaved so strongly as she shut the door of the nun's study that she had to stop to catch her breath. 'Stop it in there!' she said sternly. Then it dawned on her that it was the first time she had ever directly addressed it.

The galoshes were the undoing of Rose's grandmother.

She brought the dogs round the house and let them off the leads so they could run ahead of her across the lawn and towards the pleasure garden. But as she was following them down the front steps, she skidded on a slick patch of rotted leaves and mud and half tumbled, half slid all the way down, crumpling heavily on to the gravel. The pain knifed through her and she knew immediately she was in trouble. But she tried to keep calm. Perhaps John Flynn would pass this way on his way home. Trying to keep from screaming she concentrated on staying conscious and on listening for his footsteps. Puzzled that she had not come after him across the lawn as she usually did, one of the Pekineses returned; he licked her face, then plopped down beside her, his head on his paws.

Nancy prayed a little as she waited and focused the pain

into a small concentrated dot, a trick she had learned in the Far East.

She was concentrating so hard that she did not hear John when, finally, he came. It was only when she heard the dog barking that she knew help was at hand. 'Mrs O'Beirne Moffat,' he shouted, racing towards her. 'What happened? Oh, my God, here – let me help you up!' He went as though to lift her but she held up her hand although the movement increased the pain to a severity she almost could not bear.

'No,' she whispered, keeping words to a minimum. 'Don't move me. Broken hip. Arm as well. Call help.' With that, she fainted.

Frantically, John looked around but no one else was in sight. Then he remembered: the Colonel was away, but he reckoned Mrs McKenna was in the kitchen. He ran round the side of the house and tried to open the back door but it was locked.

Hammering on it as loudly as he could, 'Mrs McKenna!' he called. 'Come quickly!'

She opened the door. 'What on earth—' she said, her face indignant.

John was breathless. 'Mrs McKenna, there's been a dreadful accident. The old lady, Mrs O'Beirne Moffat, she's fallen down the front steps. She thinks she's broken her hip.'

'Oh, God!' Mrs McKenna made the Sign of the Cross. 'And the Colonel away.'

'Please, Mrs McKenna, we've got to get help. She's not to be moved. Will you ring the doctor? I'll go out and stay with her. Have you any whiskey or anything like that in the house?'

'There's a bit of brandy under the sink.' While John hopped with impatience, she ran to fetch the bottle. He grabbed it from her. 'Call the doctor immediately. No, don't—' he changed his mind, 'ring 999. That'll get us an ambulance. She'll have to go to hospital. And hurry!' he added, running again towards the front of the house.

Rose's grandmother, conscious again, was moaning now and John crouched low by her head. 'Mrs O'Beirne Moffat,' he said softly, 'would you take a drop of brandy?'

'Brandy?' she said with a ghastly attempt at humour. 'Things are improving at Sundarbans! No thank you . . . '

John took off his jacket and folded it to make a flat pillow. She stifled a scream as he inserted it under her head. 'Maybe I'll have a drop of that brandy now,' she said weakly.

He poured a small amount of the liquor from the bottle into the cap and dribbled it slowly between her lips. Mrs McKenna arrived with a plaid rug which John and she laid gently over Nancy's tiny body.

The three of them heard the shrieking of the ambulance siren long before the vehicle itself turned up the avenue. The two attendants dealt quickly and efficiently with Rose's grandmother; after a cursory examination, they slid a litter underneath her and transferred her to the ambulance, causing her the minimum of suffering, although she groaned as she was lifted off the ground. 'Who's coming with her?' The driver looked from Mrs McKenna to John as he closed one of the doors and held the other open.

Mrs McKenna turned pale and crossed herself again. John assumed that, like many older people, she was afraid of hospitals, and did a quick calculation: there were still more than four hours to go before he would be needed at the gate lodge. 'I will,' he said. 'Mrs McKenna,' he said, 'do your best to find Mrs O'Beirne Moffat and tell her what's happened. Do you know where she is?'

'She's in Clones,' said the woman. 'That's all she told me, that she was going to Clones for the day. She took the car,' she added, as if this explained everything.

'Well, Clones isn't such a big place,' said John. 'She should be easy to find. Ring the guards or the parish priest there, all right?' He climbed into the ambulance beside Rose's grandmother. His life now seemed fated to be mixed in with hospitals, he thought as the ambulance jolted off down the rutted avenue.

But maybe this one might lead him back to Rose.

The last he saw of Nancy O'Beirne Moffat was a tiny mound under a hospital blanket as she was wheeled out of the casualty department and towards X-ray. He escaped from the hospital and began to walk in the direction of home, his thumb stuck out for a lift. He was lucky. The first car that came along picked him up and carried him all the way to a crossroads only a mile from the gate lodge.

He got home with an hour still to spare. He fuelled up the stove and sat down to reflect on the events of the day so far. Intuitively, he knew he had a friend in Rose's grandmother and he did not doubt that she would keep her word. And Rose had been quite specific about the amethysts and relating it to the story of Elizabeth and her lover and the ring. *'This can be our ring. Anything you like,'* she had said, *'anything that will help us . . .'*

He was calling in that promise.

Rose saw as soon as she sat down beside the bed how exhausted Effie was. Her eyes were closed and her white face, deprived of their liveliness, looked much older than her nineteen years. The black hair was greasy and plastered close to her head and without its halo Effie looked more than ever like a small monkey. Rose's heart went out to her. She sat quietly beside the bed for several minutes, not wanting to disturb her friend's rest.

She was not feeling so wonderful herself. Although she had received detailed and very specific instructions as to how to get to the hospital, Rose had found her first trip on the tube very confusing and traumatic and was dreading the repeat performance on the return journey.

Effie was lying on her back, as still as a statue, impervious to the chatter and hum of visiting time all around her. Rose looked at the mound under the covers where her stomach was, fascinated to see that it did not appear to have diminished much in size. Somehow, she had expected that after you'd had your baby, you'd go flat immediately, like a balloon with the air let out.

Effie stirred a little and moaned. Rose leaned forward expectantly. 'Effie,' she called softly, 'it's Rose . . . ' Effie's eyes opened slowly and looked around without comprehension. 'It's me,' said Rose, reaching out to take Effie's hand where it lay. Effie's lips moved in reply but Rose could not catch what she said. 'What is it, Effie?' she asked, leaning closer. 'What did you say?' This time she did hear the words.

'Shite, Rose. The whole world's shite!'

'Oh, Effie!' said Rose, half laughing, half crying. 'Is that all you can say? I'm really sorry about your baby, Effie, I really am.'

'Good riddance,' said Effie. But her eyes, too, filled with tears and all Rose could do was to hold her hand tighter.

'Did you see him?' she asked, when she could control her own voice.

Effie shook her head. 'They took him away immediately. They sent in a priest to tell me he was dead.'

Rose was at a loss. Death had never touched her, or anyone close to her before. Her aunt Lizzie, whose amethysts Gus had given her, had been the nearest, and she existed only in old fuzzy photographs. 'Maybe it was for the best, Effie,' she said, knowing how inadequate the words were. 'I'm sure they know what they're doing.'

'I don't care what he looked like or how bad he was, Rose, I'm his mother. They took him away immediately. I was in the stirrups and I never even got a glimpse of him.' Her simian face crumpled.

Every word hit Rose like a hammer blow; she could only imagine what they cost Effie.

Her friend was in the corner of an open ward of about twenty beds. Most of the other beds had cradles at the foot; some of the women were cuddling their newborns, showing them off to their husbands and visitors, as proud and pink as themselves. The occupants of the beds nearest Effie were plainly embarrassed at her show of emotion and had turned away. And in normal circumstances Rose, too, might have been embarrassed. But observing the contentment and joy all around them, she thought that Effie had every entitlement to scream and roar as much as she wanted to. She had called it right: life was shite. Who or what had singled Effie out to suffer all her life? As she stroked her friend's hand, Rose's determination hardened. Effie would have a decent chance from now on.

When Effie was quiet at last, she gave her a handkerchief. 'You poor old thing,' she said. 'Listen, Effie, this may not be the time and the place, but visiting time will be over soon and I want to discuss something with you. And I may not be able to get out again to see you. So I have to say it now. I have a plan for both of us.' Briefly, Rose outlined what she proposed.

When she had finished, Effie's expression was subdued. 'Are you sure about this? That you want us to live together?'

'More than anything in the world,' Rose assured her. 'It won't change the past for you, Effie, or bring your baby back – bring either of your babies back. But maybe we can make up for a bit of lost time. We'll have a bit of a crack trying anyhow.'

283

'Yeah! Feck it! We sure will, won't we?' This time Effie's smile crinkled up in its old way. 'Oh, Rose, thank you.'

Rose smiled back. 'Thanks nothing! Now the only thing is to get the money as quickly as possible. Have you anything at all?'

'*He* sent me a cheque but I've no intention of using it!' Effie almost spat. 'I have me wages from the laundry.' The girls were given a nominal wage for their work, to spend or save as they wished.

'How much have you saved?'

'About twenty-six pounds.'

'I've about twenty-two,' said Rose. 'I have it here. I'll need some of it, but here's eighteen to be going on with. Now, with that and your own money, you should have plenty to get over to Dublin and get a flat and to tide you over for a few weeks. By that time, Daddy should have sent me the hundred pounds. I'll send it over the minute I get it.'

'Be careful now, Rose. I might run off to Las Vegas!' Then she looked worried. 'But, Rose, how am I ever going to pay you back?'

'Don't be a goose. That's not important for now. And aren't the two of us going to get jobs and become millionaires? Dublin won't know what hit it!' At that, a nurse came into the ward and rang a little silver bell. 'That must be the end of visiting time,' said Rose urgently. 'Now listen carefully. Sister Benvenuto says that the Sisters of Charity run a hostel in Mountjoy Square. I've written that down here, see?' She pulled a piece of paper out of the pocket of her smock. 'And for the first few nights, you're to go there to rest until you find your feet.'

'Mountjoy Square,' said Effie.

'Right. Then, when you feel up to it, you start looking for a flat. I don't know how you do that – the papers, I suppose.'

'Leave that to me,' said Effie. 'I can do something for meself, you know!'

Rose saw she was almost the last visitor in the ward. She dragged herself to her feet – her back was really aching now – and leaned over to give Effie a hug. 'Try to get some rest.'

'I never even saw him, Rose,' murmured Effie. 'I was going to call him Sylvester. Just for meself, like, before he went away.'

Rose did not know whether to laugh or cry. 'Sylvester?'

'That was the name of a nun I liked in school,' said Effie in a low voice.

'When we talk about him, that's what we'll call him,' said Rose, 'all right?' She gave Effie a hasty kiss on the cheek and pulled herself away in case she should make a show of herself. She turned at the door of the ward and waved. She was too far away to see the expression on her friend's face, but Effie's hand was raised and waving.

Mona McConnell was as good as her word and arrived punctually at two. In her late twenties, she was small and thin with narrow rounded shoulders. And although she was as neatly turned out as a birthday gift, the effect was of uniform dullness. Mona's eyes drooped at the outer corners as did her mouth and, all in all, she presented as a person who expected very little from life. 'Here, let me take your coat,' said John as she came into the kitchen.

'Thank you, John,' she said, her voice as gentle as her appearance.

'Would you like to see the place?' he offered. 'Not that there's much to see, I'm afraid.'

'Thank you,' she said again, 'that'd be nice,' and he had the unnerving thought that if he had offered to show her the Black Hole of Calcutta, she would have reacted in the same way.

After the brief tour, she made tea. As they sipped it, one each side of the singing stove like an old married couple, John reflected on how strangely his life had worked out; here he was, less than a year left school, and not only employed but an employer. Mona was sipping her tea with one finger daintily crooked out; her self-containment and composure made it easy for him to act naturally. In any event, he thought, although he was younger than most employers in the district, he knew Mona's new job was not unusual. Maids came cheaply in this part of the world.

'What do you need to know about Mammy?' he asked, after a bit, finding himself quite reluctant to break the restful silence.

'What time is she due?' she asked, after some thought. He had expected questions about his mother's continence or eating habits – or at the very least what he himself expected of Mona in the line of duty – and was taken aback. 'Within an hour or so, I expect,' he said. 'Is there anything else? Like, would you need to know how to feed her or anything?'

'We'll manage, I'm sure,' said Mona. She smiled reassuringly, then concentrated again on her tea. John found that she was having the most extraordinarily soporific effect on him and that he might at any minute fall into a pleasurable trance.

He roused himself for politeness' sake if for nothing else. 'How's your father doing, Mona?' During harvest four years previously, Packy McConnell had lost a leg in an accident involving a thresher.

'He's fine, John,' she said. 'Doing as well as can be expected.'

'I see,' he said again. Mona seemed to require no further comment and again he examined her curiously.

By any stretch of the imagination, she had not had an easy life. She had come to John's attention almost immediately when he started spreading the word that he was looking for someone to care for his mother. 'Mona McConnell's the girl for you,' he heard over and over again and each person who recommended her had added a little more information about her and her family so that by the time John had met her, he felt there was little he did not know about her.

Mona's mother had died shortly after giving birth to her and her aunt had moved into the cottage to bring her up. Teresa McConnell was excessively fussy and pious and was known to be imbued with 'notions', thinking herself and her adopted family better than anyone else. Mona had always had to come straight home from school; she had never been allowed to mix with other local children nor, when she got older, to attend any of the local dances. And Teresa, who was said to have a tongue which would strip paint off a corrugated roof, put the run on any of the boys who were bold enough to approach her niece who was, her aunt maintained, being brought up to be a lady.

But whatever Teresa's long-term plan for Mona had been, as a result of her aunt's increasingly disabling arthritis and her father's accident, Mona had found herself, when only in her mid-twenties, as housekeeper and carer for both of her relatives. Teresa had died six months previously, releasing Mona at least from that part of her obligation.

Since Packy could no longer work as a farm labourer, the household had very little money and when John's offer of a job was put to her, she accepted his terms with calm fatalism.

The silence ticked away between them, not bothering either. They were on their third cup of tea when they heard Ned Sherling's car turn in at the gate. For the first time, John realised that he had been dreading this moment. He had put off considering the implications of having his changed and completely dependent mother at home and had concentrated instead on the details. Now he could postpone the reality no longer.

Mona joined him at the door while Ned brought the car in as close as possible, manoeuvring it in the confined space of the yard so that the distance between the passenger door and the house would be at a minimum. Before Ned had switched off the engine, John had opened the passenger door to give his mother a hug but was repelled by a sour smell; Mary had wet herself.

Immediately, he was ashamed of his reaction. Propped up in the car seat by wads of blankets and rugs on either side of her, the back of her head showed a pink patch of scalp through wispy white hair and she looked as frail and vulnerable as a newborn baby. He touched her shoulder. 'Hello, Mammy,' he said, far more brightly than he felt.

At the sound of his voice, she slowly turned her head, a blank look in her eyes. He almost wept when he saw the line of drool which had flowed unchecked down her chin from the paralysed side of her mouth. 'Hello, Mammy,' he said again. 'Welcome home.'

She continued to stare at him without the faintest glimmer of comprehension. Ned had come round to stand behind him. 'She'll be grand when she gets inside,' he said now. 'It's a bit hard on her, the journey and all. She was really looking forward to coming home. Chatted away good-oh for the first while,' he added.

John leaned into the car and scooped his mother into his arms. She had never been heavy but since her illness she had lost a lot of weight and he had no difficulty at all in lifting her clear of the car. As he carried her across the threshold, he paused in front of Mona, not knowing quite what to say or how to introduce Mona to her new charge. He was aware of a moment of panic. Suppose Mona decided the task was just too big?

But Mona's expression of gravity and concern did not alter one whit. She picked up his mother's paralysed hand, which was the one nearest to her, and held it gently in her own. 'Good afternoon, Mrs Flynn. You don't know me yet, but I'm Mona and we're going to be great friends.'

Mona helped him lay Mary on her bed and together they covered her with a blanket. 'She'll be all right there,' said John awkwardly. But he knew that his mother needed to be undressed, cleaned up and put into dry clothes. It was a routine he would have to learn but he could not face it just yet. But was it fair to ask Mona to perform this most distasteful task so soon?

Again, Mona saved him. 'There's tea still in the pot,' she said. 'You go out and offer Ned a cup. He's had a long drive. I'll look after things in here.'

As usual, Ned would not stay to have tea. 'I have a parcel for you from the almoner at the hospital,' he said. He handed over a bulky, paper-wrapped package which bulged in odd places. John tore some of the paper, enough to see what was inside. The hospital had sent home with Mary what she had not consumed in the ward: there was a nearly empty tin of baby powder, a jar of Vaseline, almost full, and three items which brought home to him the full import of what faced him – a brown rubber sheet and two smaller cotton sheets, ragged and worn, which, he assumed, were to be put under his mother and changed each time she wet the bed. Ned was watching him closely. 'And here's her tablets and her prescriptions,' he said quietly, handing John a manila envelope. 'This almoner says you should get your local doctor to see your mother as soon as possible – and – and – to tell you that she'll see us all down.' John knew by Ned's expression he was aware that this message contained both good and bad news. But he finished it none the less. 'Her heart's great . . . I'd better be off,' he said then. 'I – I hope ye'll be all right.' Not waiting for a response, he turned and left. John stood in the door while he started the car. Before Ned drove off, he rolled down the window. 'I'll come round and see ye again tomorrow,' he said. 'To see if there's anything ye want.' He roared off in a cloud of blue smoke.

John went inside and examined more fully the supplies sent by the hospital. His heart sank.

But Mary Flynn slept peacefully for nearly two hours, during which Mona washed her soiled clothes and sorted out the belongings which had been sent home with her from the hospital. She was so deft and quiet that, watching her work, John felt enormous and clumsy. He could find nothing useful to do with himself and was afraid that if he hung around the kitchen watching her she might feel he was supervising her, or putting her to some sort of test.

'Would it be all right if I went out for a walk for a while and left you to it, Mona?' he asked.

'Surely, John,' she said. 'You go ahead. We'll be fine here.' He noticed the plural and his heart lifted. So far, Mona McConnell's tenure at the gate lodge could not be working out better.

Daphne O'Beirne Moffat, unusually dishevelled, was talking to the doctor who had admitted her mother-in-law.

She had been shocked and concerned when she first got the news but quite soon, when it was clear that Nancy was not in mortal danger, her shock changed to irritation. 'I don't *want* to be a nursemaid,' she had admitted to herself as she bumped over the rickety roads towards the hospital in Gus's old Humber.

Daphne was annoyed with her husband. This was typical of Gus, bumbling off to London and leaving her to deal with emergencies. Still out with Rose, she thought. At least if Gus was here he might be able to do *something*. This whole dilemma was Rose's fault.

'What?' she asked the doctor, aware that he had stopped talking and was waiting for her to say something.

'I asked when your husband would be home,' the doctor repeated patiently. 'We'll need someone to sign a consent form for the operation.'

'Well, he's not due home until Thursday at the very earliest,' snapped Daphne. 'He has some business in London tomorrow and he's travelling by boat.' Her temper was not improved by admitting this. All her friends and their husbands now travelled by aeroplane to London from the new airport at Collinstown outside Dublin. But Gus could not afford the fare.

'Could you sign the form?' The doctor passed a hand wearily over his forehead.

'Oh, give me the wretched thing,' said Daphne. She scribbled her signature and followed the doctor to the ward where her mother-in-law lay.

'We've given her something for the pain and she's quite sedated,' he said and Daphne admitted to a fleeting feeling of shame; it was relatively easy to do good works in the community, to visit the sick, as she frequently did, to help out with the Altar Society, even to smooth out silver paper for the mission collections. But it was a different matter, she thought, her shame being replaced with renewed indignation, when the charitable obligation was an unending twenty-four-hour one and right under your own roof. It was something she had feared might happen since she had married Gus, but Nancy had always been so healthy and self-sufficient that the fear had receded. Gus, she decided, would jolly well have to take some of the burden.

Her mother-in-law was awake, but her glazed eyes showed the effects of the sedation. Her right arm was in a sling and the bedcovers were mounded over a large cage affair, which kept pressure off her broken hip. 'I'll leave you to it,' said the doctor. He shook hands with Daphne and left the bedside.

She pulled up a chair and sat beside her mother-in-law's head. Nancy tried to speak, but she was unable to form coherent words and Daphne saw that there was no point in trying to carry on any sort of conversation.

'Don't fret, Nancy.' Daphne smiled as she spoke, quite an effort, but somehow the smile drained some of the irritation and anger away.

Gus's mother smiled back faintly. Her lips moved and Daphne leaned forward to catch the words which were faint but unmistakable. 'I'm sorry.'

She patted Nancy's shoulder and tried to inject as much sincerity into her voice as she could. 'Don't worry about it, Nancy. We'll manage.'

Gus's mother closed her eyes and Daphne wondered furiously if they could afford to hire a temporary nurse at Sundarbans. Probably not, she thought grimly. And there was very little left to sell. She was so lost in thought that she did not hear the approach of a nurse until the girl tapped her on the shoulder. 'Excuse me, Mrs O'Beirne Moffat,' she said, 'but I thought you

290

might like to bring home your mother-in-law's clothes. I'll get you her rings and things too. They're in the safe but you might as well bring them home and if she wants them, sure you can bring them to her the next time you're in.'

While she waited for the nurse to return, Daphne looked curiously around the ward, which was a large one, clearly geriatric, containing perhaps two dozen beds. It was clean and neat, with highly polished floors and scrubbed walls, but there was a strong smell of Jeyes Fluid which did not quite mask other, more pungent odours. She looked back at Gus's mother. Sedated like this, Nancy looked no different from any of the other old ladies in the ward. Daphne's furious irritation was now replaced by depression as she wondered sadly if the same thing would happen to her, if she, too, would end up as one of a row of pathetic, white-haired and rheumy-eyed women, most of whom seemed as dazed as her mother-in-law.

The nurse came back with a manila envelope. 'Here we are,' she exclaimed cheerfully. She spilled the envelope's contents onto the top of the locker and ticked off a list she held in her hand as she placed each item back into the envelope one by one. 'One gold watch – yes – three rings – yes – one rosary beads – yes – a miraculous medal and cross on a silver chain – yes – a bracelet in a purse – yes – one handkerchief – yes – three shillings and elevenpence in coins. That's the lot! All present and correct. She had no handbag,' she went on, 'and the money and the bracelet and the beads were in the pockets of her coat. Now,' she handed Daphne a piece of paper, 'if you'll just sign here that you've received it all.'

For the second time, Daphne scribbled her signature. She took the envelope and stood up. 'There's nothing much I can do here,' she said to the nurse. 'I think I'll go home and try to contact my husband. He doesn't know yet about the accident.'

She telephone Gus's London club the moment she got back to the house but Gus had not returned.

Daphne decided she could allow herself a sherry. But, always fastidious, she decided that first she would put away her mother-in-law's clothes. She hung up the raincoat and placed the galoshes with the other outdoor shoes and boots behind the kitchen door. She put the torn blouse and skirt into her workbasket

– she was too tired and fraught to start on them this evening but would mend them first thing tomorrow – and carrying only the cardigan and personal items, went into Nancy's room.

Nancy's jewellery box contained very few pieces but what was in it was beautiful. She had always had good taste, reflected Daphne as she placed the rings carefully in the slots and shook the bracelet out of its pouch. It flashed purple in the late evening sun and she picked it up, amazed. This was part of Rose's set of amethysts. What was her mother-in-law doing with it?

Frowning, she closed the jewellery box and went into Rose's room. The red velvet case was on the dressing-table as usual. Daphne hung the bracelet on the little hooks designed for it and closed the lid.

She brought the case with her when she left the room. Tomorrow, she thought, never mind what Rose had said, she would put the amethysts in a safety deposit box in the bank where they belonged.

CHAPTER TEN

Two weeks before Mary Flynn came home from hospital, Karen Lindstrom and the young Methodist curate who had only recently arrived in Charlottetown were seated opposite one another in her parents' drawing room. The minister was present at her parents' behest to 'have a little chat'. From the minister's point of view, the 'chat' was not going well.

'But, Karen,' he pleaded, leaning forward so the sunlight which streamed through the window glinted on his horn-rimmed spectacles, 'could you not think of what your mother and father are going through?' The minister's upper teeth protruded and his double chin wobbled with earnestness as he spoke. 'They only want the best for you, naturally,' he continued, 'but they have their own positions to consider. I know it's not what you want to hear, Karen, but Charlottetown is a very conservative community and having an unmarried daughter with a baby on the premises will not, I assure you, be good for business.'

'And, of course, that's all they care about,' retorted Karen. 'Business!'

'That's not true, Karen, and you know it. But your mom and dad are church members too and—'

'So what would Jesus have done in this situation?' she interrupted. 'You tell me that.' She glared at the cleric who bit his lip in distress. 'Would He have cared who the father was?' she asked passionately, warming to a theme she had hit upon just that instant. 'I would have thought Jesus would be happy about a new little baby. New life, Reverend! Isn't that the kind of thing we were always taught in Sunday school? And by the way,' she added maliciously, 'I'm sure you're aware that millions and millions of people, Catholics for instance, don't believe that *Jesus*'s parents were married!' She sat back triumphantly.

The cleric sucked on his teeth. He changed to a different

tack, adopting a wheedling tone as he tried one more time to find out what Karen's mother and father had been trying to elicit from their daughter for the previous two weeks. 'Please, Karen? What's the problem? Maybe if you could let us know *why* you won't tell anyone who the father is. After all, the young man, whoever he is, has a responsibility too.'

'That's impossible,' said Karen flatly. 'I don't know why no one will believe me. I am not going to tell anyone and that, Reverend, is that!' He looked so unhappy that she felt almost sorry for him. 'It wouldn't make anything any different if I did tell people, would it, Reverend?' she asked, more kindly. 'After all, the baby's not going to go away, is it? And even if I did tell people, it's hardly as if we would get married.'

'It has been done, you know,' said the clergyman sadly, taking off his glasses and polishing them on his sleeve.

'Yes, in what era?' scoffed Karen. 'This, if I may remind you, Reverend, is nineteen fifty-four. What's Daddy going to do? Get out a shotgun? And anyway, I'm only seventeen, for God's sake. Child brides went out with the Micmacs!' The Micmacs were the local Indians, now much diminished in numbers.

The cleric changed tack again. 'Well, without revealing his identity, can you at least tell me what kind of person this is?'

'I will tell you that although I'm not in love with him or anything like that, he is the kind of man anyone would be proud to marry. But that is all I am prepared to say on the subject.'

The discomfited clergyman clearly had no idea what to say next. Karen sat back comfortably on the sofa and waited. 'I'll be eighteen in a few weeks, you know,' she explained helpfully, contradicting the spirit of her child bride protestations of just a few seconds earlier. 'I know my own mind. I'm not exactly a baby any more.'

'Evidently,' said the minister faintly. 'Karen, please.'

'Yes?' Karen looked at the ceiling.

'Karen, we're getting nowhere here.'

'Well, I'm glad you can see that. I told Mom and Dad that it was a waste of time bringing the Church into it.' She got to her feet. 'Listen, Reverend,' she said pleasantly, 'you really are wasting your time. I'm not going to give away the name of this baby's father and that's that.'

He conceded defeat and stood too. 'Well, have you thought about what you're going to do after the baby is born?'

'It's much too early. I have – several months to go . . . ' Alarmed, she realised she had almost given some of the game away. 'I'll probably give him or her up for adoption,' she said briskly, 'but, as I said, I won't decide that until nearer the time.'

'Your parents had such plans for you, Karen.'

'What's changed? I'll still graduate high school this summer. So I won't start college in the fall, but I'll start second semester. No problem!'

'Well, I suppose there's nothing more to be said, is there?'

'I'm afraid not, Reverend.'

'Goodbye for now, Karen. God bless you.'

'You too, Reverend.' As she showed him out through the hallway towards the front door she felt, through the closed door of the kitchen at the other end of the hallway, the tension of the unseen listeners. Normally Mrs Anderson and her mother played the radio while they worked but the whole house felt as though it was standing on tiptoe.

In bed later that night, Karen was not half as cocky nor as confident as she had seemed to the unfortunate curate. Never before had she experienced so much concentrated interest in her as people gathered in daily huddles to discuss What They Were Going To Do About Karen. And from time to time in the past two weeks, she had even experienced sneaky enjoyment in the sensation of power over everyone, her parents, the family doctor and some trusted relatives in whom her parents had confided.

Now, as she tossed and turned in her bed, she admitted to herself that the novelty was wearing off. For the first time in her life, Karen was openly at odds with her parents and the atmosphere in the house was tense and getting worse by the day. She had no doubt that she was still the adored daughter, but the comfortable liberalism which she had always believed characterised her parents had been stripped off, exposing a core of rock-hard conservatism. Although no voices had been raised in anger, they were as scandalised by her pregnancy as any Victorians. And as the days ran into weeks and they showed no sign of softening their stance, she had begun inwardly to panic.

Karen was nothing if not fair; perhaps, she reflected, if she

295

had thought enough about her parents, she would not have got pregnant in the first place. She had been casual with her virginity, losing it at the beginning of the previous summer almost on the spur of the moment. She and Billy deFresne, one of the few boys Karen rated at all in Charlottetown, had been necking in the back seat of Billy's car after the school hop and things had just got a little out of control. It had been Billy's first time out too and the whole thing was over in a matter of a few minutes. Then, as with John Flynn, Karen had not given the prospect of pregnancy a second thought. If it had not been for the accident, she might even have gone the whole way with John's twin, that time on the ship. The thought made her shudder.

She looked at the luminous dial of her alarm clock. It was after two in the morning and her imagination was running black rings around itself. Suppose she continued to defy her parents and, like Victorians, they did cast her out? Although, knowing them as she did, she thought this unlikely, perhaps she should consider the possibility? Where would she go? How would she manage? Karen knew she had been pampered and cosseted all her life. Almost anything she had ever wanted she had got, easily and without complaint. This was why this new development in her relationship with them was so upsetting.

She thought back over the curate's words. *Have you thought about what you're going to do after the baby is born?* and of her own pat answer: *I'll probably give him or her up for adoption* . . . Easy enough to say. Was that the right thing to do? She would never have admitted it to anyone but she feared strongly that if she gave up her baby for adoption she might live to regret it. But no one she had ever heard of had reared an illegitimate child in Charlottetown. What would she say to people? How could she walk down the street? She blushed at the thought of the looks that would be cast at her. Karen realised that, despite what she might like to believe, more than a smidgen of her parents' conservatism had been bred into her.

She could decide to keep the baby and leave the Island altogether; she could go to Boston or Philadelphia – or even Toronto or Montreal. Montreal, she had heard, was full of Bohemians and no one would give her a second glance. But she had little or no French, a requirement for Montreal.

One of the other three places, then. But again her imagination painted a horrible picture. She saw herself living in a cold-water apartment in some appalling ghetto, barricaded in against the criminals and other rough sorts who lived alongside her; her pitiful larder would contain only half a packet of Saltines which she would have to eke out for three days until her father's next charitable cheque arrived; her baby, too weak to cry, would be lying in a pathetic little cardboard box in a corner.

Some do-gooder would then break down the door. In her mind, Karen even saw the do-gooder's face: it wore glasses and had a wobbly chin like the Reverend. This do-gooder would snatch up her child from its little box. 'This baby's got rickets,' the do-gooder would cry and she would lose the baby for ever because she was an unfit mother . . .

She heard in her mind something else the curate had said: *What harm would it do you?*

She conceded that she was in such trouble already, that to reveal John Flynn's name to her parents might cause her very little more.

But what about John's life? And the heartbreak and shame to those good people, the McGuigans – and to his own mother, who, by all accounts, was very ill. Karen felt that in all fairness, she should take total responsibility for this mess. After she had started to dance with him that night at her party, she had known immediately that she was far more sexually experienced than he was. Sure, John had reacted, certainly he had – despite her agitation, she smiled at the memory of how strongly – but he was hardly conscious and she doubted if he even remembered her getting into his bed. In fact she was surprised to find that when, half squiffed herself, she slid in against him, he already had an erection.

Some day, she thought savagely, she'd get her own back on that Ezrah for spiking the drinks. But, again, in all fairness, she couldn't pass the whole thing off on the booze. It was her own fault, fair and square.

An additional worry niggled away at the inside of her brain demanding attention. The coupling with John that night had been quiet and noiseless – sometimes, when she was re-creating it in her mind, she wondered if he had even fully woken up – but when she was getting out of his bed and creeping back towards the door, she had developed the strongest impression that she was being observed. She had turned quickly to check on Derek in the other bed but, as far as she could tell in the darkness, he had seemed to be asleep.

She had met Derek only once since his return to the Island. She and Mary-Lou had been browsing in Woolworths two weeks ago – on the day before she had found out she was pregnant, as it happened, when he had come in with Dan McGuigan and the four of them had exchanged wary pleasantries. Derek had been stiff and formal but, then, he had every right to be. She had treated him very badly.

But did he or didn't he know?

Karen took the future logically, step by step. If she stayed around Charlottetown, sooner rather than later her pregnancy would show. There was every possibility she would run into Derek again. He would see that she was pregnant and if he had been a witness to her lovemaking with John, he would be in a position to make life very awkward for her.

Would he be so crass? And even if he was, what could he do? She tried to put herself inside Derek's mind. Jilted, resentful, jealous of his brother. Would Derek be able to resist wreaking some sort of revenge?

She ticked off the possibilities. Since she was almost sure John didn't know he had had sex with her, she could deny it, say Derek was lying.

She could make up the name of someone. Ezrah? Could she get her own back on Ezrah this way? It was tempting but the notion of going to bed with Ezrah made her flesh crawl. She could certainly not lie convincingly about that . . .

Back to the beginning. Suppose Derek did spill the beans and John believed him? She felt instinctively that Derek's twin would insist on doing the decent thing. He would claim the child and want to marry her. But he had a sick mother whom he could not leave, so he would try to get her over to Ireland. Her parents, anxious to have her off their hands and to have a 'normal' family setting for the baby, would agree to this.

Again, Karen shuddered. On the ship, Derek had regaled her with accounts of Drumboola and the meagreness in which

298

everyone there passed their lives. Karen had no intention of spending the rest of her existence in that kind of drudgery.

The conclusion was inescapable. Derek Flynn held her future in his hands and she would have to go and confront him. If he knew nothing, she could proceed securely. If he knew it all, she had to find out what he proposed to do about it.

Derek and Karen were alone in the middle of a vast field of snow. He had bundled her in a buffalo and taken her there by sleigh. She had protested, of course, but he had not heeded her bleating. When he got right to the centre of this vast white plain, he had pulled off the rug and ordered her out of the sleigh to stand in front of him. Again she had protested a little and he had to tumble her out; he had to do it a little forcefully, so she landed face down and half buried in the soft, unblemished snow. The white of the jacket was only marginally darker than the snow itself so that her lower half, encased in the red ski-pants, seemed disembodied, the twin cheeks of her bottom rearing upwards towards him through the tight stretch fabric, a pair of ripe red tomatoes on a bed of ice. There was no pantie-line to mar their smooth round perfection.

He contemplated this splayed, delicious sight for a few moments but did not touch her. 'Stand up, Karen!' he commanded.

She hesitated a little but he knew, of course, that she was slightly afraid of him and quite soon she did as he ordered, scrambling to her feet and turning to face him, but with bent head and trembling mouth. He reached forward and pushed back the fur hood of her ski jacket, so her hair cascaded over her face. Then he raised her chin with one hand. 'You know what I want you to ask, Karen.'

Her eyes avoided his as she whispered the words he had taught her to say. 'Please, Derek, I would like you to unzip my jacket.'

Slowly, ever so slowly, he pulled down the zipper, link by link, revealing inch after inch of creamy bare flesh.

Karen, as he had ordered, was naked under her ski jacket.

'That's a good girl, Karen,' he said to her. 'I'm glad you did as you were told. Now, feet spread as I showed you.' Obediently, she moved her legs a few feet apart. She was trembling and he steadied her down by placing a hand firmly on her crotch. Through the tightly stretched fabric of the ski pants, he could feel the heat. He moved his hand a little and the fabric slid satisfactorily on her wetness. 'I'll deal with that later,' he told her and was rewarded when he felt her muscles clench against his fingers in anticipation.

With his free hand, he peeled the jacket slowly off her breasts, one side at a time. Then he pushed it down off her shoulders altogether and toppled her backwards into the snow which mounded around her so that her breasts, twin hillocks of whipped cream, were presented to him, like her bottom before, on a bed of ice. Lining himself up carefully, he placed a foot on either side of her hips, so that his crotch hovered directly over hers. 'That's a good girl,' he said again. 'Raise them up a little!'

Still obedient, she arched her back and he squatted over her, letting his buttocks rest lightly on her groin while he played for a little bit with the breasts, teasing them, batting them a little from side to side, packing the snow around and between them until only the hard nipples showed on top like sucked cherrystones.

Swiftly then, he pulled down her ski pants and she whimpered as he settled on her to feed . . .

That particular fantasy had begun on the night Derek spotted Karen and her ghastly friend in Woolworths. But to his utter frustration, each time he got to that point in the fantasy, another picture intruded – the one of the dark writhing hump in the bed beside his own on New Year's Eve in Karen's house in Charlottetown.

He went back to the beginning of the fantasy many times – he even threw it out altogether and went for a tried-and-tested formula involving Karen in a swimsuit in the Lower Pond – but try as he might, he could not prevent the superimposition of this second picture.

Eventually, he managed to drop off to sleep but before he did so, he vowed that as long as he lived he was not going to let himself be set up again. If he ever got involved with another girl, it would be he who made the running.

In the following weeks, he buried himself in his work and although the night-time fantasies continued to come to him unbidden, he worked on blocking out Karen's face. But he was not fooling himself: when he had met Karen in the Charlottetown Woolworths, his heart had turned over with desire.

Soon, Dan McGuigan noticed the effect of Derek's efforts around the farm and, one night at supper, marvelled aloud at how he had ever managed before Derek came to the Island. Dan was so complimentary that, for the following few days, Derek even allowed himself to nurture secret hopes that, one day, the holding might be his. He doubted if the McGuigans' citified children would be interested in returning to the unrelenting work on the land and he knew that Dan would never let it be sold.

As he bent now to the task of weeding between the rows of newly sown mangolds, he revelled in the feeling of well-being which radiated through his body. It was the first truly spring-like day of the year, attended by blue skies and picture-book cirrus clouds of fluff. Derek was not ordinarily affected by the sights and sounds of nature, but only a blind or deaf man could fail to notice the benign change from winter to spring. Overnight, the sea winds, which had swept the island for months, had been calmed and it seemed all the birds of the Island had decided to congregate within a radius of a few miles of the farm.

The feeling of the sun on his back was a sort of milestone for Derek. It was the first time since his lung had been removed six years ago that he had taken off his shirt outdoors. For years he had been self-conscious about his dropped shoulder and the long thin scar which advertised his disability; but since coming to the Island, he had thrived. More than seven months of Peggy's feeding and the requirements of constant physical work in the bracing sea air had dramatically improved his health and, as a consequence, his appearance. He was fit and muscular and had grown not only in physical stature but in self-confidence; sometimes he wondered what Dr Markey would make of him now.

In fact, on many levels, Derek was happier than he had ever been. The exceptions were continuing guilt about abandoning his mother – and the memory of how he had been betrayed by Karen Lindstrom with the connivance of his twin. The humiliation of that New Year's Eve party and its aftermath burned in his breast like an eternal flame. He doubted if he could ever, as long as he lived, forgive either of them for it. He had thought long and hard about how he could pay John back. Even the anonymous letter he had sent to John's toffee-nosed girlfriend gave him little satisfaction because he had not been around to see its effects. For all he knew she might not even have received it.

He also resented his own powerlessness in the matter of wreaking revenge on Karen. He had thought of sending a second anonymous letter but abandoned the idea. She would have known immediately who sent it.

Attended now by the farm dogs and several brazen seagulls who followed him along the drills of red earth in the hope of feeding themselves the lazy way, Derek hummed tunelessly as he bent to the backbreaking work. He was overdue for a haircut and to his irritation the front of his thatch fell constantly over his eyes, hindering his efficiency. He brushed it away for what seemed like the thousandth time and finally, exasperated, undid the shirt he had tied around his waist and fashioned a makeshift headband from it, rolling it tightly and fastening it around his forehead. The bulk of the shirt trailed over the nape of his neck and half-way down his back but at least he could work in peace.

He measured how much more he had to go before he reached the end of the drill he was on and took his break. About another fifteen minutes should do it, he decided, and resumed weeding. With no audience except the dogs and the birds, he sang louder, driving himself to the end of the drill.

He was so deeply engrossed in achieving his goal, he did not hear the car approach from the valley. And when the dogs behind him barked, he assumed it was because the seagulls had got too close and without looking over his shoulder, barely missing a beat of the song, he yelled at them to shut up.

Karen had taken time over her appearance, putting on and discarding several outfits before deciding on a full-skirted dress in summerweight wool of palest yellow. The dress, which swung when she walked, was cut in gored panels from neckline to hem and skimmed rather than clung to her body. Moving this way and that to check the effect in her closet mirror, she was satisfied that it broadcast the correct combination of messages she wished to convey. She looked, she hoped, serious yet simple. At the same time, the soft yellow enhanced her blondeness and fair complexion so she looked fresh and wholesome, even innocent. 'Certainly not a scarlet woman,' she murmured and almost laughed as her butter and cream reflection smiled back at her. She certainly felt better now that she was actually *doing* something instead of sitting around moping.

Having rehearsed and discarded several versions of what she would say to Derek, she decided eventually to play it by ear. She would have to see how he reacted to seeing her.

All too soon, she had reached Kelly's Cross, a collection of homesteads and farmhouses scattered through the undulating countryside around a crossroads and a Catholic church. The McGuigans' place was about a half-mile further on; within minutes she saw it, tucked into a fold of the low hills.

Although the family car was in the front yard, there seemed to be no one in the house. 'Hello?' she called. 'Anyone home?' Then, some distance to her left, she heard the bark of a dog.

As she came towards the boundary fence, she saw a flash of white and at the far end, a human figure, wearing some sort of headdress, bent double. Two dogs came bounding towards her, wagging their tails and frolicking around her as she made her way upwards; Karen wished, as she tried not to sink up to her ankles in the soft red clay, that she had not been quite so fussy about matching the yellow dress with shoes of a similar colour.

One of the dogs ran ahead and flopped in front of the man, panting happily in her direction as if to point her approach. The man straightened up, shading his eyes against the sun to look in the direction the animal was indicating.

It was Derek Flynn all right, but not Derek as she had remembered him. Barechested and muscular, this Derek with his torn, leather-belted trousers and strange white headgear, stood above her on the incline, looking for all the world like the highly idealised hero from *Sinbad the Sailor*. 'Hello, Derek,' she called. He removed his hand from his forehead but she realised that with the sun in his eyes, he was still not sure who she was. 'It's Karen,' she said, and stopped.

'Karen,' he said slowly but she was still too far away to divine whether or not he was pleased to see her. As he towered above her on the slope, she wished the lie of the land had been to her advantage and not his.

'Yep,' she answered, moving to close the gap between them. 'Surprised to see me?'

He pulled off the headdress – which she saw now was a rolled-up shirt – and bent to hold the collar of the dog at his feet, although the animal showed no sign of going anywhere. 'You're a long way from home, Karen. What can I do for you?'

Was she imagining it or did he place a slight emphasis on the 'I'? 'Is there somewhere we can talk?' she asked.

'How about here?'

'Well, I feel a bit odd standing here in an open field like this.'

'You don't want anyone seeing you talking to me, is that it?' He stared at her, a hard, unflinching stare and, to her horror, she felt the insolent sexuality in the look and, worse, the leap of her own treacherous body in reply. He dropped his eyes from her face and she had to resist the impulse to cross her hands in front of her breasts like a barrier. At the same time, she felt the nipples harden but did not dare to look to see if they showed through the fabric of the dress. She tried desperately to think of something to say but just when she thought she could bear his silent scrutiny no longer, he turned, slowly and deliberately away from her. 'Let me finish this drill.' As if she was not there, he bent double again and continued with his weeding.

Watching him, Karen was sure he was working more slowly than he had been when she had first come up and she forced herself not to feel insulted. But what called for even more self-control was the racing of her own blood. As he had stared at her, she could not but notice the way his shoulders and pectorals had developed since last she had seen them, and how his back muscles moved under his taut white skin; now she was fascinated at the way his buttocks moved independently of one another as he walked away from her. She even had a strong urge to run her nails along the scar which, under the mid-morning sun, shone like a trace of thin silver. Careful, she warned herself under her breath.

She was astounded at Derek's behaviour. None of her projected scenes with him had cast him like this. After the way she had treated him she had imagined he would be icy, covered in confusion, angry, even shouting. Anything but this cool self-possession.

She was the one who was covered in confusion. What was wrong with her? Had she some fatal character flaw, a *hamartia*, which would eventually lead to her downfall like it had led to the downfall of the Greek heroes in her books on ancient history? She sure had a fatal flaw, she reflected wryly, answering her own question. It was called sex.

And here was another shock. She had always believed that pregnancy put a stop to all of that sort of stuff. Evidently not, she thought, as she tried desperately to keep her eyes off him.

He kept her waiting until he had reached the end of the row then turned towards her. 'All right,' he said, 'let's go.' Without waiting for her to reply, or to see if she was following, he picked up his shirt and walked swiftly down the hill towards the house, so fast she had to trot to keep up within yards of him in her flimsy, unsuitable shoes. She also had to take smaller steps than normal in case she twisted her ankle in the turned earth. She should be livid with him, she thought, but she was not. What was going on?

Whoever coined the phrase about revenge being sweet, thought Derek as he strode jubilantly ahead of Karen, was absolutely right. He had no doubt that she had come to ask him about John. Well, what she would learn about John from him would not be worth her trip out. He was the one to make her dangle and dance. She could twist in the wind and he was going to enjoy it.

He thought he had played the scene with her very well, making her wait as he had while he gathered his wits about him. And she might think she was very smart but he had seen the surge of desire in her eyes. Somehow, he was not sure quite how, he would be able to turn that to his advantage. With nothing at all to lose, he felt confident and absolutely sure that he would be able to deal very well with Miss Karen Lindstrom.

'Where are we going?' she called from behind him.

'The barn,' he answered. 'Or is the barn not good enough for you? Don't worry, there isn't a duckling in sight.' He turned to face her and was rewarded with two spots of colour high on her cheekbones. Her hair had tumbled around her face and in that yellow frock, with her breasts visible only as two soft swellings, she looked like a buttercup waiting to be picked. It was all he could do to stop himself from reaching out to peel down the dress as he had done so many times, both in reality last fall and more recently in his fantasies. Immediately he checked himself. 'I'm sure you don't want Dan and Peggy listening in to whatever it is you want to talk about,' he said, in as formal and frosty a tone as he could muster.

He pulled open the barn door and stepped across the high threshold, leaving her to follow him as best she could. It was chilly and dark inside, and with the stocks of feed much depleted after the long winter, the high-roofed building seemed far bigger than it actually was. He did not turn on the light – he wanted to make this as difficult as possible for her. Footsteps echoing on the concrete floor, he crossed to the wall where the remaining hay was stacked, seated himself on one of the bales and busied himself putting on his shirt while he waited to see what she would do.

He was glad to see that she was clearly at a loss, hesitating in the centre of the floor, her bright hair and dress flickering like a butterfly in the gloom. She crossed over to join him, sitting on an adjacent bale but several feet away. 'I – I came to see you, because—' Her voice faltered but he was not going to help her. 'How's your mother?' she asked suddenly, in a different tone.

'She's on the mend,' he said. 'I haven't heard lately, but no news is good news. I saw her in the hospital on my way back here, she was expected home for Easter. She'll always be a cripple,' he added harshly, not being able to resist the temptation to castigate himself. But then he shut up and waited again. Karen Lindstrom had not come here to discuss his mother.

'How've you been yourself?' she asked, looking over her shoulder.

The next step was going to be her asking about John, he would have bet on it. 'I've been fine,' he said. 'Kept busy, you know.'

Then she burst out with something which took him genuinely by surprise. 'You look great,' she said, sounding more like the shipboard Karen he remembered. 'You must have put on a few inches even since—' He knew she had been going to say 'since Christmas' and said it for her. 'Since Christmas, you mean? Or more likely, since New Year's Eve?'

'Something like that. Look, Derek,' she said impulsively, 'I'm very sorry about what happened. I really am.'

'What are you sorry about?' he asked carefully. Some of his supports were proving to be shaky.

'Derek, don't make me grovel like this!'

'I'm just sitting waiting to hear what you want to talk to me about. I didn't ask you to come out here.' He was not going to let her off the hook that easily. 'Suppose you tell me what you're sorry about and then we'll see if we're on the same wavelength. Spell it out, Karen.'

There was a long, peculiar pause during which they stared at one another. In the dense silence, he heard a small scrabbling in the corner of the barn but paid it little attention. Much to his annoyance, he found he could almost smell Karen's skin. He fought his body's arousal. 'Well,' he said, making a small movement as if to get up, 'if that's all . . . '

'I'm sorry that I was cruel to you at the party,' she said softly and he felt he was being caught in a web she was spinning around him. He had to resist that with all his might.

'Oh, is that all?' He tried to inject heavy sarcasm into his voice but it came out more like an adolescent squeak.

'And, you know, the last time we were in the barn and everything . . . '

'Oh, that,' he said. 'Don't give it another thought.' Her proximity after so many months of frustration was maddening him. He took a deep breath and made one last effort to regain the upper hand. 'This cruelty at the party? How were you cruel, Karen?'

'With – with, you know, John and all that.'

All that . . . he thought. *You mean getting into bed with him!* 'You've a perfect right to *dance* with whoever you like at your own party,' he said as softly as she.

They lapsed again into that loaded silence and he watched the struggles on her face. His brain moved swiftly. It was clear she was engaged in a fishing expedition: although she could not be sure, she suspected he had seen her activities in bed and was worried about his knowing. This was the whole point of the visit.

But why was it so important to her? Karen was a girl who clearly went through suitors like children ate Smarties. Why did she care what he thought? Once again, he heard the scrabbling behind him and to break the hold she was exerting on him, half

307

turned away from her as though to check it out. *Might she actually care about him after all?* But he was still furious and hurt, he reminded himself.

When he looked again, he saw that with one hand she was smoothing the front of her dress, over her stomach. Whether it was nervousness or a deliberate gesture, it was having an effect and he could not help but picture what was under that dress.

With great difficulty, Derek sat still on his bale of hay and waited for Karen's next move.

Karen's body pulsed through the silence. In one sense she was exultant at the change in atmosphere between them. She was on surer ground now.

But had he seen her and John in bed? She was still no further on in her quest for that answer. At the same time, she did not want this strange, heavy silence to continue, nor to mess everything up by reading signals in Derek that were not there. Trusting her instinct, she took a risk, leaving her own bale of hay and moving to sit on the one next to him. 'Do you accept my apology, Derek?' she asked softly. 'Can we be friends?' This close, she could smell the clean male sweat.

'I never said we weren't friends.' His voice was husky. He was as turned on as she was, she knew it in her bones. For an infinitesimal moment, she flicked her eyes to his crotch. He was responding all right.

'Well, that's good, Derek, I'm glad . . . I really am . . . ' She shouldn't have looked down. They had never gone all the way but she certainly remembered the size and strength of him. Almost of its own volition, her hand crept out and came to rest lightly on his bare forearm and she experienced a jolt, like an electric shock. She could not let this happen, she thought, she just could not. But only a tractor could have pulled her away from that bale at that moment.

He had a strange, fixed expression on his face, and she did not know whether he was going to hit her or kiss her. But she knew now it was inevitable that this tension between them, trapped like lava in a volcano, had to force its way out.

For several exquisite moments they sat staring at one another, joined together, her fingertips to his arm. She could feel the individual, risen hairs. 'Derek?' she whispered.

308

The volcano erupted then. As he had last October, he pushed her violently backwards on the bale of hay but this time she opened her arms and grasped his descending body, taking it to her own as tightly as she could, wanting his full weight on her. She pressed upwards against him, feeling that great upright ridge against her pelvis, thrusting against it while he ground it into her. The hay prickled the back of her neck, its fragrance mixed with the smell of his sweat and the clean outdoors scent of his skin.

She wound her fingers into his hair as he reached inside the neckline of her dress and extricated one of her breasts, wrenching it upwards and she didn't care that he might tear either her dress or her bra. She pushed against him as he sucked on it like a baby, feeling the electric lines between her breast and her groin coming alive, wanting to give him more, more, more—

He bit her nipple hard and she cried out with pain and surprise. But he did not stop. Instead, he pulled out the other breast and went to work on it in similar fashion. All the time, he ground into her with his pelvis and his cock and she thought she was going to die with pleasure.

He shifted slightly and she felt him fumbling with the hem of her dress and she flattened out her legs for him, making them long and flat so he could pull up her skirt; she helped him with it, helped him with the waistband of her panties, wriggling and moving so he could get them off. His trousers had a buttoned fly and she fumbled with them, tore at them in frustration until at last she released his penis, thick and warm in her hand. He brushed her hand off and thrust it towards her blindly, once, twice; the third time, it slid home to the hilt as easily as a seal sliding into the sea. Immediately and for the first time in her life, Karen came; the sensation was like a Catherine wheel unwinding and spinning in her pelvis and shooting stars of pleasure to every part of her body, even her fingers and her toes. She cried out in surprise and then, as the sensations continued, wailed and sobbed, on a high note she did not recognise as her own voice. Derek, came too, pumping into her in a frenzy, crying too and laughing, an all-together sound which was at once terrifying and wonderful. She clutched him until the two of them had finished and the waves which shook them both had started to drain away, leaving them panting and spent. The whole episode had taken no more than two minutes.

Then Karen saw that Derek was crying for real.

She stroked the back of his thick, curly hair but felt she did not need to say anything or comfort him. She had vowed she was going to play the scene with Derek by ear. What had happened was far outside any of her wildest speculation.

The barn door did not quite fit and sunlight leaked through a space between its top and the jamb, shafting through the air to hit one of the roof supports just in front of where they were lying. Caught in its narrow beam were thousands of minuscule fibres which they must have raised with their activities in the dusty hay. She felt like one of those motes, free and floating in no particular direction, every blood vessel seemed relaxed. She felt warm and peaceful and as if all her problems had shrunk, too, to the size of a dust particle.

Derek felt clear-headed and sure of himself, physically drained but wonderfully calm and happy; sex with a real woman was far, far better than he had ever imagined it could be. He kissed Karen's neck. As the sun rose higher in the sky outside, the beam of light which was coming in through the top of the barn door had slid down the support pole near them and now played over their bodies. In its brightness, Derek saw that around the aureole of her nipple, Karen had a web of fine hair, as delicate in the sunlight as spun gold. 'Karen,' he whispered. 'Karen.'

'Mm?'

'Is this as much of a surprise to you as it is to me?'

'Sure is.' She opened lazy eyes and looked at him humorously. 'I certainly didn't plan it.'

'What was the original plan?'

'Don't go all huffy on me if I tell you.'

'I won't, I promise.'

'Well, to tell you the truth, I wanted to find out if you had seen me in bed with John.'

He saw she was watching him warily but was too calm to be Machiavellian or to think of any advantages that might accrue by playing games. 'Yes, I did,' he said simply.

'I – I'm sorry, Derek. I was drunk.'

'But that's not why you came out, is it – to say you were sorry?'

310

'No it's not,' she admitted. 'I – I'm not sure why I needed to know. I think maybe I thought you might blackmail me!'

'What?' Derek laughed uncertainly. Then all along Karen's body, he felt a sudden tightening. The look in her eye sent alarm right to his heart. 'What is it, Karen?'

'I'm pregnant.'

Derek could not help himself, he ricocheted away from her as though she was on fire. 'What?'

'I'm pregnant,' she repeated steadily, 'with John's baby.'

All Derek's languor lifted away, leaving him bitter and cold. She had hoodwinked him again. Perhaps, he thought, she had even planned to do this all along and was going to try to saddle him with the child. But the worst thing of all was his physical disgust. How could she have let him push himself into her, when her belly was already full?

'You – you *whore*!' he spat, jumping to his feet and fumbling with the buttons of his fly. Still she did not move, nor did she attempt to tidy herself. 'Cover yourself up!' he screamed. 'You – you *whore*! How fucking *dare* you? How *dare* you do this to me?' Pacing around the barn, he worked himself up into a towering rage; he kicked at an empty milk churn, which fell over, parted company with its lid and clattered across the concrete floor.

'I suppose you think this is a great joke, don't you? Coming here and making a fool out of me.' He shot across to her and leaned into her face, making her flinch. 'Well, you've another think coming,' he shouted, so enraged that gobs of spittle flew out of his mouth and landed on her face. 'You might think I'm only a gobshite, a stupid little country Mick that you can play around with but I'll show you! I'll show you, you, and – and—'

All his life, nothing had gone right for him, nothing. He did love Karen, he was sure of it. She led him on, showing him what it could be like – and then – and now—

The rage and self-pity welled up and fused until he could contain them no longer and he burst into tears. He did not care that she saw him. He turned his face to one of the roof supports in the barn and leaned against it, crying like a baby.

Karen pulled her dress up over her breasts, smoothed it down and waited. She felt detached and wondered again if there was

311

something wrong with her personality. This always happened to her; all her life, she had never been able to feel the appropriate response to any situation, she laughed at funerals, cried at happy endings. Now, the more Derek raged and wept, the calmer she got.

When the storm of weeping abated a little, she got to her feet. 'Derek?'

'Fuck off – whore!' He gestured violently with his whole body but, alert as she was, Karen heard the grief rather than the hatred. She moved a step closer and touched his waist.

'I said, fuck off!' he shouted but his gesture this time was not as violent and she left her hand where it was.

'Not until we talk,' she said, firmly, as she imagined a mother would to her son.

'There's nothing to talk about – whore!' he said again. He pulled himself away from her and sat again on the bale he had just vacated, his hands dangling between his open knees. 'Why'd you do this, Karen? Why couldn't you leave me alone?'

'I told you earlier, Derek, I didn't think that this would happen between us.'

'How can I believe that – now?'

'I can't make you believe it. If you think clearly about it, Derek, you'll believe that I need complications like a hole in the head. What have I to gain from making love with you?'

He clenched the fists between his knees. 'A father for John Flynn's bastard!'

Instinct told her not to rush him, to wait. She let the silence develop between them. Then she spoke very quietly. 'I don't want a father for the baby. I'm giving it up for adoption.'

Another silence developed. Then, his voice muffled, Derek asked, 'Does John know?'

'No, Derek. And that's the way I want to keep it.'

'Then what the hell did you tell me for?' Again he was shouting.

'Because you'd know soon enough.' She crossed the floor and sat beside him on her ruined and scattered bale.

Side by side they sat, each looking straight ahead. Karen saw her panties on the ground in front of her. She picked them up and put them on. As he watched her do it, he spoke in a flat, leaden voice. 'What am I supposed to say?'

'Say what you feel,' she said immediately.

He looked away from her towards the barn door. 'I feel like a right fool,' he said. 'I feel you and John will be laughing at me all the rest of your lives. I wish you hadn't told me. I wish I could have been happy – just for one whole day. I wish we could have more sex. I feel that all I want in my life is you. And I love you.' This last was said so quietly that she almost missed it.

'I'm glad you're not mad any more,' she said. 'We can make love again if you like, not now of course,' she added quickly in case he got the wrong idea. 'But I think you're a brilliant lover. And that's the first time in my life I ever came.' She watched the brief struggle on his tear-stained face.

'Do you really think I'm good at it?' he asked shyly. 'I learned most of it from you on the ship.'

'I told you, I'm being honest today. I might never be as honest again – so you might as well make the most of it.' She realised then she had not been flattering him. The memory of her orgasm was fresh and to her surprise, she really did mean what she had said.

The routine in the gate lodge now was that Mona McConnell held the fort while John was at work and, because Mary Flynn was frequently fractious and demanding at night, Ned Sherling stopped by every evening, usually from eight to midnight, to let him get a few hours of unbroken sleep. Nevertheless, John, existing blindly from day to day, was exhausted: whichever way he turned there was another demand on him and the confines of his life had shrunk to the shape of a tunnel – at one end was the gate lodge and his mother, at the other was the hotel. Although there was nothing wrong with Mona's cooking, he frequently had difficulty in finding the strength to chew his evening meal.

At least he now had a decent form of transport to get him between both ends; George Cranshaw had paid half the cost of a good secondhand bicycle and the heavy Rudge had been returned with thanks.

As he cycled to work this May morning, John, by nature so alert to the changing seasons, barely noticed that summer had spread across the countryside, that dozens of lambs dashed about and butted each other in the fresh grass, that birds of all species carrying twigs and wisps of old hay flew busily across his path, that the hedgerows were white with hawthorn. Then he heard, from an unseen pond or lake tucked away somewhere in the hills, the unmistakable honking of geese. He longed with all his heart to get off his bicycle, to go to Swan's Lake with his fishing rod, or even to take a simple walk.

But he set his mouth in a grim line and bent to the pedals. Willow House was full and he had a busy day ahead.

Last night was the first that Ned Sherling had stayed over. It had been daylight when John woke and found Ned sitting at the kitchen table, a book open in front of him. 'Ned!' he had cried. 'Have you been here all night?' Picking up the alarm clock he had found it was twenty past six. 'Oh, my God, Ned, why didn't you wake me?'

Ned had stood and stretched himself. 'I've all day to sleep if I like,' said Ned. 'And you've your job to go to.' Then Ned had forestalled John's embarrassment and thanks. 'The way I look at things, John, the strands of life go in circles. You do me a favour, I do a favour for the next man and so on and so on. It all comes round in the end. And,' he was mumbling so John had to strain to hear him, 'I told you before – it's a pleasure to help Mary McCarthy.' McCarthy was Mary's maiden name.

As John cycled along, it was not Ned he was worrying about but a conversation he had had with Mona. When she arrived that morning, he could see she had something on her mind. 'Is everything all right, Mona?' he had asked as she took off the coat she wore, winter and summer.

Mona had hesitated, then. 'I met Ned Sherling on the road just now, John, and we had a bit of a chat – about how things were going here . . . '

Cold fear, like a douche, ran through John. 'What were you talking about?'

'I'll leave it to Ned to have a chat with you, John,' she had said, her pale eyes fixed on him. 'It's not my place, really.' He had known better than to press her but her words had confirmed his worst fears. Mona was getting fed up with the arrangement. And he could not blame her. It was thankless, cruel drudgery.

He went about his tasks at the hotel that morning with a leaden heart. At about eleven o'clock, he was helping Dorothy Cranshaw to prepare vegetables for the evening meal when, for the third time in as many minutes, he dropped his paring knife on the floor.

'What's the matter this morning, John?' asked Mrs Cranshaw. 'You're miles away – are you feeling all right?'

'Sorry, Mrs Cranshaw,' he answered.

'Here,' she said briskly, 'these can wait.' She indicated the pile of carrots, onions and leeks piled on the butcher's block in the centre of the room. 'Sit down at the table there. It's time for elevenses anyway – and today, I think, we owe ourselves a drop of sherry. And before you say you don't drink, I *know* you don't, you silly boy. But one glass of sherry is not going to kill anyone.' Obediently, he took the triangular glass and sat at the table. He had never tasted sherry before, it was sweet and aromatic on his tongue. 'Now, come on – tell your aunt Dorothy about what's bothering you.'

John had not had a chance to talk to anyone about his problems. He looked at Mrs Cranshaw's freckled, kind face. She was a bosomy, bright-eyed woman of above average height, given to wearing peasant dresses and sandals even in winter. John liked her enormously and, faced with her obvious concern, it all came pouring out, all the fear, the distasteful, grinding work and the dragging tiredness which, these days, dogged every step he took. 'But the big problem now, Mrs Cranshaw,' he said at last, 'is that I think Mona McConnell has had enough.'

'You poor boy,' said Dorothy. 'One thing is clear anyway. You're going to take a couple of days off from this place. George has worked you disgracefully hard. Slave labour, I'd call it.'

'I don't mind, Mrs Cranshaw. I enjoy it, really I do.'

'I know you do, dear,' she patted his hand, 'and in any other circumstances you'd be living in, which would solve half your problems. It's ten miles in each direction on that bicycle of yours, isn't it?' She stood up and smoothed down her apron. 'Would you trust me to see if I can sort something out?' she asked.

John looked up at her in astonishment. The sherry had warmed and loosened him. 'But what could you do?'

'I don't know – yet.' she admitted. 'But it seems to me that something has to be done. You can't carry on like this. I know Mona and this neighbour of yours are doing Trojan work, but even all of that is not enough. You're worn out, John, anyone can see that. I'm only kicking myself I didn't see it sooner. Now,' she said, her voice becoming brisk, 'do you think you can finish here?' She indicated the half-prepared heap of vegetables.

He nodded and she took off her apron. 'Is Mona with your mother?' She patted him on the arm. 'You just leave things to your aunt Dorothy,' and she was gone. A minute later, he heard the engine of her car start up in the yard.

Questions tumbling over themselves in his brain, John scraped the peel off a carrot. What was it about him that made other people want to help him? The Lindstroms, Ned Sherling and now Mrs Cranshaw, who had known him for only a couple of months. The world was full of decent people, he decided. The thought was barely formed when the longing to see Rose knifed into him so sharply that his eyes blurred and once again, he dropped the parer on the floor.

Mrs Cranshaw returned just over an hour later. John was tightening a washer on a leaking tap in the sink when he heard her car pull into the yard. 'You've finished here – oh, good,' she said when she came in. She kicked off her plimsolls and sat at the table. 'Bring me a glass of lemonade, there's a dear.' He fetched the drink and, as he put it in front of her, she pulled him down into another chair beside her. 'Now the first thing,' she said, her face becoming serious, 'is that I believe your mother should be in a hospital. She needs a lot more care than amateurs can give her on a part-time basis.'

John opened his mouth to reply but she caught hold of his arm. 'I said she *should* be. I had a good look at her, John, and she's never going to get any better than she is now. I know this sounds brutal – I'm sorry, my dear, I really am.'

John hung his head. She was articulating what he himself felt but he was determined that, after a lifetime of hardship, his mother was not going to finish up in St Nathy's, the county psychiatric hospital where the insane, the old and the unwanted rotted to death in their beds. Dorothy Cranshaw leaned forward, her voice gentle. 'I know what you're feeling, John, and it's a credit to you, but you have your whole life ahead of you. Your mother could linger on in this state for years and years.'

'I know that, but—'

Abruptly, she changed the subject. 'What do you think about Mona?'

He looked at her, astonished. 'She's – I don't know, in what way? – she's a great worker, great with Mam. Do you mean do I like her?'

'Possibly, although that might not be all that important. She's an – an *odd* girl, in ways.'

John could not discern which way the conversation was going. He waited for what she would say next. She drained the lemonade. 'Mona and I had a nice long chat,' she said carefully, 'about you, about your mother, about Mr Sherling, about the whole thing. Apparently, Mr Sherling is worried about you too. We're all worried about you, John.'

Again, John waited. He had the feeling that something very important was going to happen. It was like balancing on the edge of a razor blade, one move and he would cut himself.

But then Dorothy Cranshaw went off at another oblique angle. 'I understand Mona has a disabled father who needs help, although not to the extent your mother needs it?'

'That's right, Mrs Cranshaw.'

'Well, here's a proposition for you. The basic idea wasn't actually mine, as it happens – apparently it came from Mr Sherling, this morning, when he was talking to Mona.' She fixed him with a look he could not interpret. 'Mona is shuttling back and forth between her own house and yours and she is worn out too.' John's heart was sick. He knew as much.

Mrs Cranshaw's next words were so bizarre they almost did not register. 'How would it be if you *combined* houses?' she said. 'If you all lived together? Apparently, Mr Sherling would still be willing to help out. And Mona's father is not so disabled that he could not help out a little too.

'Now this is where I – we come in,' she continued, as John looked at her, dumbfounded. 'I think I have the perfect solution. Mona thought you and your mother could move into her cottage but that's a bit small. So what came to mind when I was chatting with her is the fishing lodge in the grounds here, up by the lake – do you know it?' John stared at her. 'It hasn't been used for donkey's years,' she went on, 'and it would need a bit of cleaning up. There's even a bit of furniture in it. It would be just right for you, John. It has four bedrooms.'

Before he could say anything, she grabbed his arm. 'Don't answer straight away, just think about it. But I'm sure you'll see

317

it's the perfect answer. Neither Mona nor you will have to travel to work, and her father, she says, is talented with his hands, joinery, woodturning, that sort of thing. I'm sure George could find things for him to do around the place. Can't you see, John, the whole thing is absolutely perfect.' She clapped her hands with the brilliance of it all. 'And you'd even be doing us a favour. That house will fall down if someone doesn't start taking care of it and we just don't have either the time or the inclination.'

'Couldn't you use it as extra rooms for the hotel?' John's voice was faint.

'I'm not saying but that some time in the future we could use it as some sort of self-catering operation, but that's *very* far away. Decades! Look, I know this is highly unusual – unprecedented, I'd say.' She grinned, her freckled face lighting up with mischief. 'But that's not to say it's not the right idea or that it wouldn't work. You can't go on the way you are. You'll be an old man by the time you're twenty.'

'But even if we did this, how could I ever thank you?' John asked. He felt dizzy.

'Oh, that's easy, old chap! All you have to do is work your fingers to the bone and grow old in the service of the Cranshaws!' She laughed out loud and stood up from the table. 'I always did fancy myself as a Scarlett O'Hara type with slaves clanking away on the plantation!' Still barefoot, she padded across to the sink and rinsed out her empty lemonade glass. But when she turned back to face him, her expression was serious. 'Don't hang about making the decision, John. Let us know tomorrow?'

'Come in, Derek!' Sven Lindstrom's ruddy face was serious and he would not meet Derek's eyes. He turned and led the way into the drawing room, seating himself by the empty fireplace. Although it was still bright outside, the drapes in the room had been drawn and the lamps lit.

All day, Derek had been preparing himself for this meeting. Karen had tried to help him but had succeeded only in making him more nervous than he was already. His knees felt now as though they had no bones in them and he was glad to sit. As he waited for Mr Lindstrom to make the first move, he noticed irrelevant things, like the way the light from the sconce above Mr

318

Lindstrom's head reflected off its baldness; and the fact that the other man, although quite fat by Derek's standards, had particularly dainty feet. He himself had dressed very carefully, in a new sports jacket and slacks, well-starched white shirt and a navy tie Karen had bought him as a present. And that morning, he had spent nearly half an hour polishing his shoes to a brilliant shine.

'This is as difficult for me as it obviously is for you, Derek,' said Mr Lindstrom. 'You know we have – had – great plans for Karen, she's our only daughter.'

'I appreciate that, Mr Lindstrom,' said Derek. His voice was croaky and broken and he had to clear his throat.

'I don't know what to say to you,' continued Mr Lindstrom. 'My wife and I are naturally very disappointed and upset. We brought Karen up – at least we thought we did – to be responsible.'

'She is responsible, she's a wonderful girl,' Derek broke in.

'We thought so – still think so,' amended Mr Lindstrom. 'But the question now is, where do we all go from here?' He looked closely at Derek. 'She tells us you're taking responsibility for the baby.'

This was the tricky bit. Over the past three weeks, the discussion had raged between Derek and Karen. She was adamant that she did not want the true parentage of the baby revealed and Derek's emotions vacillated wildly. After the momentous day in the barn, the two of them had spent every possible minute together. Karen was back at school but her grades had always been good and she was expecting to graduate without much difficulty; so each evening, she drove out to Kelly's Cross and they roamed the countryside, making passionate love everywhere, in her car, in the small stands of trees, in the sand dunes and on one memorable occasion, in the forked trunk of an old oak tree.

Sometimes Derek was able to forget about the baby; other times he raged about it and against it; Karen, however, was always able to calm him down. She was so physically and sensuously attractive that he was helpless in her hands. It had been his own idea to prevaricate, to claim the baby without actually acknowledging it as his own. Karen had wanted him to go the whole way but he had balked at saving his brother's skin. In any event, he had warned her that it would probably backfire; that he was so upset about his brother's treachery that he would not be convincing enough if he had to tell a blatant lie.

He leaned forward in his chair now but his breath seemed to have deserted him. 'Yes, Mr Lindstrom,' he said hoarsely. 'I am. I'm taking full responsibility for the baby.'

'I see,' said Sven Lindstrom slowly, knitting his fair eyebrows and staring straight into Derek's eyes. Derek forced himself not to drop his own. It was a minor battle of wills and they broke it simultaneously.

'What do you intend to do?' This was Sven.

'I will of course abide by your wishes.' This was Derek.

There was a pause, with both of them sitting tensely in their identical chairs. 'You're far too young to get married,' said Sven.

'I know that, sir, practically speaking, that is,' said Derek. 'Karen and I have discussed it, of course, and if she wanted to, well – I would, with your permission, of course, sir, you and Mrs Lindstrom. But she doesn't. At least, not at present. We said we would discuss it again after the baby is born.'

Sven Lindstrom shrugged, a hopeless gesture. 'Yes,' he repeated slowly, 'after the baby is born.'

The hard rim of the chair seat was cutting into the flesh at the top of Derek's thighs. 'I know how disappointing this is for you, Mr Lindstrom, I really do. But if it's any help to you and Mrs Lindstrom, I want you to know that I love Karen with all my heart. What's happened has happened and nobody can undo it, but I want to take care of your daughter for the rest of my life. Oh, I know you might think I just picked that up from the movies, but I tried and tried to think of a better way to put it but I can't. It's the best way I can think of to say it. I can't tell you how much I mean it, sir. More than I've ever meant anything.

'And if you're worried about Karen going below her station, so to speak, sir – I know I've no money or anything like that, well, not at present – but I do have prospects, sir. I'm not going to be a farm labourer all my life. And I'm a *good* farm labourer, as it happens. There are a lot of acres out there in Kelly's Cross and my cousin says that without me he couldn't manage. He says it all the time. I don't know what's going to happen in the future, with the land, I mean, but I know my cousin won't see me stuck. I'm proud of what I do now, sir, and I *know* it's going to lead to better things. For me. And if you agree, sir – and if she agrees – for Karen. And, of course, for the baby.'

It was the longest speech Derek had ever made and by the time it was concluded, he was scarlet with embarrassment and effort. But he kept his chin high and his eyes fixed on Karen's father. He was rewarded with a half smile. 'That was quite a speech, son. How long did it take you to prepare?'

Derek saw there was no malice intended. 'I meant every word of it, sir.'

'I could see that,' said Karen's father. 'But the question still remains, what are we going to do? What arrangements are we going to make? I'm not going to have our daughter's name dragged through the mud of Charlottetown. Although to be fair,' he added, 'Karen seems perfectly prepared to face the music head-on. You know she's determined to graduate from high school?'

'Yes, Mr Lindstrom. And I'm fully behind her there.'

'I'm glad to hear it,' said Sven wryly. 'But do you have any suggestions as to how we can prevent people ridiculing her – and us – and blowing this up into a scandal?'

'No, I don't, sir,' admitted Derek. 'But I can't believe that Karen is the first girl in Charlottetown this has happened to.'

'She's not. But she's the first Lindstrom. And that's all that matters to Mrs Lindstrom and me. We've a business to run, you know.'

This was one problem Derek had anticipated would come up in this conversation. He had an answer ready. 'Mr Lindstrom,' he said, 'if you lose any business as a result of a baby coming into the world, it's business you were always better off without.'

Sven's lips twitched. 'You think so? Well, I must say, you've covered all the angles.'

'Karen and I discussed it fully before we decided that I should come and talk to you—'

'I'll bet you did!'

'—and we agreed that this will be what we call in Ireland a nine days' wonder. This doesn't mean we're taking it lightly, Mr Lindstrom,' he added hastily, 'but, when you think about it, sir, it really is not the end of the world. I do love Karen, I love her very much. And – and I believe, I *think*, that she loves me.'

'Karen is a very . . . ' Sven searched for the right word, 'a very *active* sort of girl.'

Derek hesitated; Karen's father had hit on his major area of self-doubt. Would he be able to handle Karen in the future? He had no way of knowing. 'I think – I know – that I do know a great deal about Karen, sir,' he said as fervently as he could. 'That's the best I can say. But I can't say enough that I love her. And that's as much as anyone can say.'

There was another long pause, then Karen's father stood up and Derek, springing out of his own chair, had the distinct impression that he may have passed some kind of test. To his surprise, he found he was a head taller than Sven Lindstrom. 'I think we've taken this discussion as far as we can for the present,' said Karen's father. 'Come out to the kitchen and have a cup of coffee. I have no doubt that Karen and her mother are there waiting for us.' He smiled then and shook Derek's hand. 'I won't pretend I'm happy, son, because I'm not. But I want you to know that although I'm quite angry at you – what father wouldn't be? – at least I admire your guts. Do the McGuigans know about this mess?'

'Not yet, sir.'

'And please stop calling me "sir",' said Sven, passing a hand wearily over his eyes. 'It makes me feel very old and I hadn't thought of myself as old until all this happened. If we're going to be seeing a lot of one another – as it seems we will – you might as well start calling me Sven.'

On his last evening at the gate lodge, John walked up to the Big House. The rhododendrons along the broken avenue were just coming into bloom but the horse-chestnuts which arched overhead were blazing in full white-candled glory. The weather over the past few days had been humid, occasionally drizzling, and there was no relief in sight; the leaves above his head hung still and calm, the only sounds being the occasional creaking of the wood, the hidden scrabblings in the overgrown verges and the slapping of his own hand at the midges which attacked his neck, face and scalp. He kept an ear open, however, having no wish to encounter anyone from the house.

322

He leaned against a railing post to look for the last time at it, looming huge and grey against the low grey sky. The blank, shuttered windows seemed to have turned inwards on themselves in contemplation of hidden misery and, like a dinosaur which had given up hope of survival, the building squatted among the encroaching weeds as though simply waiting to be overgrown and extinguished. Indeed, the process seemed well begun: a rash of bright green algae, slick in the drizzle, had spread down the walls around the broken downspouts, along the terrace and down the front steps like a sort of skin cancer.

The sight of the deterioration was profoundly depressing and John, who had not really known why he had wanted to come here in the first place, now regretted it. Sundarbans had always been at the edge of his consciousness, the reality in his life. His own and his family's life had centred on the building, the estate and the people who owned it and worked it. He would prefer to have remembered the house as it seemed to have been when he was very young; he had mental photographs of an enormous place, alive with the comings and goings of the gentry, with hunt meets on the lawn, with parties and horses and dogs, with the tree-lined avenue always busy with traffic.

Briefly he considered walking down to the lake, where he had passed so much of his boyhood – and where he had met and fallen in love with Rose – but then decided that there was no point, that he would probably get upset. He thought of all the unopened, returned letters: Rose did not want to know him any more. He must stop being so sentimental.

Then, taking a last look at the sad, sagging façade before turning away, the beginnings of an idea glimmered in his head, an idea so wild and fantastic that he almost laughed out loud.

How would Rose feel about him, he wondered, if, some time in the future, he could revitalise Sundarbans for her and turn it into a vibrant, paying proposition? Running a hotel did not seem all that difficult; he had watched the operations at Willow House with great attention and it seemed largely a matter of common sense, hard work and staying one step ahead of the guests' needs.

The idea was preposterous, he told himself, but his fizzing brain retaliated with the suggestion that all projects started from one idea. And from one person who was absolutely determined to put the idea into practice.

For the next half-hour, staying alert in case anyone came out of the house, John circumnavigated the old building. He counted the windows, the shortened chimneys, the doorways, arches and yards. He went into the shuttered stableyard and, in his mind's eye, saw it populated again with horses, nothing fancy, hacks and ponies for the guests' use. He converted the leaking dairy to a billiard room, furnishing it like the ones he had seen in copies of the thick English magazines on the tables in Willow House. Last summer, Rose had shown him the coal gas plant, long disused and now covered in creeper. He pulled away some of this and looked thoughtfully at its iron frame; he knew nothing about making gas, but Rose had said that there was nothing intrinsically wrong with the plant, it was just that her father could not afford the amount of coal it would take to make enough gas to heat the house.

John became so excited about the whole imaginary project that he forgot the original, nostalgic purpose for his visit to the house and when he had seen enough, dashed back down the avenue, eager to commit his impressions to paper. He had never been particularly good at drawing, but had a good eye for proportion and line and wanted to get everything down before he forgot a single detail.

Mona smiled as he arrived in and took her coat from behind the door. 'Not long more now, John?' she said, as though the two of them were waiting for a bus.

'Thanks a million for everything, Mona,' said John perfunctorily. 'I'll see you tomorrow.' Everything was arranged. The move was being organised with the help of the Cranshaws, with another neighbour, who would lend a horse and dray and, of course, Ned, who had promised to be at the gate lodge by seven at the latest.

When Mona had left, John seized a piece of brown wrapping paper and, working fast, made crude drawings of the Big House, front and back, placing the correct number of windows, doors and chimneys in the right places. In the margins, he made separate sketches of the stables and other yards and, turning the paper over, drew from memory an overall plan of the estate, marking the lake, forests, house and outhouses in what he hoped were approximately the right places.

He was not quite finished when he heard a thump from his mother's room and, breaking off from his work, ran to investigate. 'Oh, Mammy!' he said, his throat constricting with fear. Mary lay, a small, fragile heap of skin and bone, in the middle of the floor. Her back was turned to him and she was not moving.

'Mammy?' he cried again, running to her side. She looked up at him with opaque, bulging eyes and, in despair, he knew that, once again, she did not know who he was. Gently, one by one, he moved each arm and leg to test that they were not broken. All through the operation, she neither resisted nor assisted nor made a single sound. It was as if she were an inanimate plaything. 'Come on,' he said, lifting her, 'let's get you back into bed.'

Her legs and arms dangled free as he picked her up – as easily as if she were a baby animal – and laid her back in the bed. Before covering her up he checked to see that she was dry but Mona had done her job well before leaving. 'What are we going to do with you, Mammy?' he whispered, pulling the bedclothes up to her chin and tucking the quilt around her shoulders. 'I wish you'd come back, just for one day.' She merely continued to look at him with eyes like marbled glass.

He went back out into the kitchen, his previous excitement dead and forgotten. The brown-paper drawing mocked him from the kitchen table. He picked it up and screwed it into a little ball, then opened the stove and threw it inside.

A second later, just before it caught fire, he put his hand into the heart of the fire, risking a bad burn, and retrieved it. Half ashamed at his childishness, he went into his bedroom and put it, still crumpled, into a corner of the suitcase he was taking with him next morning to the fishing lodge at Willow House.

Rose could not believe it when, in the middle of the night, the pain woke her. She had more than six weeks to go; the doctor had assured her that everything was fine and that she had nothing to worry about. And at first it seemed she did have nothing to worry about because the pain ebbed away fast. It was just something she ate . . . But then another pain grabbed the end of her spine and twisted it and, although she tried not to, she cried out loud with fright and surprise. It felt as if her bones were caught in a vice or a corkscrew and being slowly squeezed.

The girl in the next cubicle heard her and woke. 'Rose,' she whispered. 'Rose, are you all right?'

'No,' groaned Rose. 'I don't think so. You'd better call someone.' She felt cheated, almost outraged. It should not be starting now, she was not ready. And she had been told that labour would start slowly; that nature had designed it so there would be long, pain-free intervals, at least at the beginning. But this pain was coming all the time, barely giving her time to catch her breath. And it was far worse than she could possibly have imagined. It filled up her whole body, consuming every nerve, leaving no space even to scream.

She heard her neighbour get up and hurry out of the dormitory and within a short while there was a small crowd of people around her bed. She didn't care who they were or what they were going to do. Through a haze, she felt herself being lifted out of bed; someone was throwing a blanket around her shoulders and then she was being half walked, half carried, down the long flights of stone stairs. Rose could not help her helpers. The pain was too strong, it was her enemy; it swelled and writhed inside her like a monster, trying to pull her spine apart.

The next thing she knew, she was in the nuns' eight-seater van, lying on her side with her knees drawn up on one of the bench seats.

A few minutes more and there was dazzling light, bright white light and white uniforms and the sensation of being carried and then wheeled along, she did not care where. The pain was all she cared about, this long, strong winding-sheet of agony which folded her inside itself so that she was as helpless as a rag doll.

She was lifted again, higher this time, spread out on her back on a hard bed. There was a funny smell, sharp, antiseptic; people were talking loudly to her; she felt her clothes being removed and heard her own voice as though it was something from another part of this bright room. It wasn't her voice, this thin, high screaming, but her throat hurt with the sound so it had to be.

People were shouting at her now, telling her to do things she didn't want to do. They were taking her legs and pulling them apart and taking up her heels, forcing them into some sort of bowls. She tried to pull them down but couldn't: to her horror, they were strapped in. She convulsed against the contractions but they had strapped down her arms too and she found she couldn't move at all. But at least they put some kind of sheet over her, so she had a kind of tent over her knees. And now she couldn't see any of the people because they were all huddled below the tent; all she could see was the ceiling, which was also white and very high. The pain waved and crashed through her and she tried to fight it; she wanted to curl up but, trussed as she was, she couldn't move; they were shouting at her all the time, she heard them shouting at her, telling her to push. She pushed and pushed, she bent her neck on to her chest as far as she was able, straining so hard she felt as though someone were trying to prise her eyeballs off their separate stalks.

They were shouting something different now; she could not make out what they were saying, but there was a new note, a more urgent note. Something was happening. She felt a sharp tearing sensation in her vagina and without being told, pushed again, as hard as she was able, one more push, which took everything she had. Then she heard them shout something unintelligible but there was praise somewhere in the shouting now – she had achieved something; and all she cared about was that the hurting had lessened just a little bit. Then she heard distinct words in what they were saying. 'Once more,' they were crying, 'once more. Come on, Rose, one more—'

Summoning up everything she had left, she bent her neck and pushed again and, this time, something wet and slithery came out of her and the agony drained after it as though it were a bathplug. Rose put her head back on the hard bed and cried.

Someone came close to her, a nurse dressed in green. 'It's a little girl!' she said, beaming. Rose felt she should say something but could not think of anything. She was still sobbing with relief that it was over.

'Good girl,' said the nurse at her head, when, without waiting to be shouted at, Rose pushed out the afterbirth. 'It's all over now,' the nurse said, then, 'Just a little stitch and it's all over.' Rose felt a tightening and pricking in her vagina but after the mountain she had just scaled it was nothing.

327

They undid the straps restraining her wrists and shortly after that let her heels down too and again she was lifted bodily onto a wheeled trolley. A warm blanket was tucked around her and, now sleepily aware of what was happening, she was wheeled out of the room, down a corridor, and into another room where, in a curtained cubicle, she was transferred by expert hands into a real bed. She was sinking into feathery sleep when the curtain around the bed was pulled aside and Sister Benvenuto appeared.

'Well, Rose,' she said, 'you gave us a fright. How are you feeling?'

'Tired, sister,' whispered Rose. 'I'm very tired. I'm sorry I gave you such trouble.'

'All in a day's work,' said the nun. 'It's a girl?'

Rose nodded. She did not really care what the baby was. There was no pain and that was all that mattered. She did not want to be impolite, but she was finding it very difficult to keep her eyes open. The nun pulled a little silver watch from underneath a fold of her habit. 'Ten past five in the morning,' she said. 'You certainly pick your times, my dear!' She pushed a stray piece of hair off her forehead. 'I'll come back in the morning,' she said, but Rose was already asleep.

When next she woke, Rose found herself in yet another bed. She was reluctant to abandon the strands of delicious sleep which clung to her like candyfloss but someone was standing beside her, rattling crockery. 'Breakfast, dear,' said a loud cheerful voice. 'Come on now, wakey-wakey!'

Rose struggled into a sitting position, accepting the tray of tea and toast from the nurse. She looked around and saw that she was in a ward of about twenty beds, identical to the one in which she had visited Effie – when was that, yesterday? The day before? Her brain was working at half speed. She noticed that all of the other women, chatting and laughing together, were out of bed and having breakfast at a long table in the centre of the room.

Still fighting sleep, she looked down at her tray and realised she was ravenously hungry. She lay back on the pillow and with her eyes closed, put one of the limp, cold pieces of toast to her mouth. In this manner she ate everything on the tray and then drank the tea.

She was drifting off to sleep again when someone spoke. 'Howya, Rose!'

Rose's eyes flew open. 'Effie!' she exclaimed joyously. 'I thought you'd be gone.'

'I'm going later on,' said Effie, 'but I rang the convent and Sister Benvenuto told me you were in. God, Rose, you're miles early! How'd you do it? Typical gentry – not staying the course.' She smiled and Rose was glad to see that she was back to her old form. 'How are you feeling?' Effie plonked herself on the bed, almost dislocating Rose's knee.

'I'm fine,' Rose admitted, 'a bit tired.'

'Have you seen the baby?' Effie's tone became a bit guarded. 'I believe it's a little girl.'

'No.' Rose shook her head. 'I haven't seen her.'

'She's perfect, Rose,' said Effie. 'Sister Benvenuto says that although she's in an incubator, because she's so tiny, like, she'll be fine.'

'Tiny?' said Rose with feeling. 'I'd hate to have an overdue one! No one warned me.'

'They never do,' said Effie slowly. 'But she's perfect, Rose, that's the main thing.'

Rose felt instantly contrite for complaining. How must Effie be feeling? 'Will we go and see her?' she asked impulsively, then could have kicked herself all over again for her lack of tact. 'I'm sorry, Effie,' she said humbly.

'For what?' Rose could see that Effie was genuinely astonished. 'I'd love to see her.'

Rose climbed carefully out of bed, tying on the hospital dressing gown. 'Ugh!' she said as she tied its frayed cotton belt. 'I must look a fright!'

'You couldn't look a fright if you put on a flour sack,' retorted Effie.

As they left the ward Rose, her stitches pulling, found it painful to walk. 'When do you start feeling human, Effie?' she asked. 'I feel like I've been through one of the laundry mangles.'

'Me too. You'll be right as rain in a couple of weeks. It's amazing.' Effie knew the way to the nursery and Rose was following her without question when suddenly she stopped dead in her tracks. Effie turned. 'What's the matter?'

'I'm afraid,' whispered Rose.

'What of? What are you afraid of?'

'I'm afraid to see the baby.' Rose found herself gabbling,

as she always did when she was nervous. 'It'd be a mistake to see her. I might get attached, you see—'

'That's not the reason.' There was a trace of contempt in Effie's voice and Rose stared at her.

'No,' she said quietly at last. 'You're right, that's not the reason. I'm just afraid.'

When they came to the glass wall of the nursery, they saw that there were three incubators, all of them occupied. But even from a distance of six feet, Rose instantly identified her daughter. The baby was lying on her stomach, curved arms outstretched as though she was swimming, legs curled up under her, exposing her tiny wrinkled soles. Her screwed-up face was turned towards the window and Rose saw, in miniature, the line of John Flynn's eyebrows and wide-apart, slanted eyes. 'That's her!' Her hands flew to her mouth. 'Oh, Effie, that's her!'

Effie leaned on the glass. 'She's the most beautiful baby I've ever seen,' she said. 'She really is.' There were tears in Effie's eyes and Rose put her arms around her and then found she was crying too.

One of the nurses inside saw the two of them and popped her head round the door. 'Are you all right, ladies?'

Rose saw the two of them from the nurse's perspective, twin waterfalls propping each other up; she giggled through her own tears. 'We're fine,' she said, 'we're just looking at my baby.'

'Which one, love?' The nurse, who was middle-aged, had a cockney accent, like many of the girls Rose had met in the convent. 'And don't say the beautiful one,' she added jovially. 'They all say that!'

'The little girl in the incubator.' Rose pointed.

Immediately, the nurse's face closed over. 'I see,' she said. 'Yes, she's lovely all right, dear. She's doing fine.' She withdrew her head and closed the door.

Rose looked at Effie. 'What did I say?'

'She knows your baby is to be adopted,' said Effie.

Rose leaned against the glass beside Effie and for a long time the two of them gazed at Rose's baby. Once, the baby shuddered and stirred, opening the hand nearest the window like a flower, balling it immediately back again into a minuscule fist. She grimaced as if she was having a bad dream and, for a second,

Rose caught a glimpse of her tongue. Her neck was folded and creased as if there was too much skin for the bones and even at this distance, Rose could see a dark pink mark spreading over the folds. 'What's that mark on her neck?' she whispered to Effie.

'That's nothing,' advised Effie. 'It's only a strawberry mark. Plenty of babies have them. When she gets bigger and her hair grows, it won't show at all, don't worry.'

At that moment, unexpectedly, Rose fell in love with her baby. She felt a pull of feeling deep somewhere, in a place that she had not known existed. The pull was pure and perfect, utterly separate from herself. In the same instant she experienced a profound sense of loss. It would not be she but some other woman who would worry, who would check that the strawberry mark would mean nothing, would not mar her daughter's beauty.

There seemed nothing to say so she turned away from the glass. They walked back towards the ward in silence and she sat on the side of the bed, while Effie sat on the chair beside her, fiddling with the edge of a blanket. The ward was a hive of chat and activity. Several of the other women, washbags in their hands, were queuing up for the bathrooms. One was putting curlers in the hair of another. One was complaining loudly to anyone who would listen that she had not got a wink of sleep. One had decided not to wait for her bed to be made officially and was doing it herself. It was all so normal and healthy that Rose felt she could not have been more isolated and different if she had landed there from another planet.

'You don't have to give her up, you know,' said Effie suddenly, still fidgeting with the blanket.

'What do you mean?'

'What do you think I mean?'

'How do you know? I have to give her up. My parents—'

'There's new laws. You don't have to,' repeated Effie stubbornly. Rose let this information sink in. It was too outlandish – she couldn't. In front of her eyes floated the picture of the baby: the fluff of black hair, the little fists, the strawberry mark. That baby was hers. She could give it – her – a name and they could be together for ever. She could be the one to worry about that strawberry mark. 'I don't know anything about babies,' she said.

'I do!' said Effie. 'I babysat,' she added, to cut off questions but Rose hardly noticed. Her thoughts tumbled wildly about. Herself and Effie in a flat with a baby. The idea was bizarre but at the same time joyful. The baby, her baby, could have two parents, two mothers . . . She could work; she and Effie could both work – the two of them could work at different times of the day, being waitresses or something like that. Effie *needed* a baby. She, Rose, was being selfish in giving up a baby when Effie so clearly wanted one.

And she could not shake off the picture of her baby, so pretty, with those beautiful slanted eyebrows.

But what would her mother say? Rose knew that if she kept the baby, she would never be able to go back to Sundarbans.

'Do you think we could do it?' she asked Effie.

'Of course we can – piece of cake!' said Effie, looking carefully up at Rose from under the frizz of black hair. 'Have you signed anything yet?'

Rose frowned, trying to remember. 'I don't think so,' she said. 'Nothing final, as far as I know.'

'Right,' said Effie. 'That's it, then. We're a family, the three of us. *Little Women* minus two that's us!' Rose knew that *Little Women* was the only novel her friend had ever finished. She had always thought it strange but now that she knew a little about Effie's background, understood why Louisa May Alcott's portrayal of contented poverty and sisterly companionship had been so attractive. She stood up from the bed.

'Let's go back and see her again,' she said. 'We'll have to think of a name for her,' she added as she led Effie out of the ward.

'And have her baptised,' supplemented Effie. 'Will we have it done here – in London, I mean? Or will we wait till we get to Dublin?'

'I'd like Sister Benvenuto to be here,' said Rose. 'She's been very good to me.'

'Yeah,' said Effie. 'All right. That's what we'll do, then.' Already, thought Rose, they were behaving as though they were a couple.

When they got to the nursery for the second time, Effie knocked on the glass, attracting the attention of the nurse who had come out to them before. She came again to the door. 'Yes, ladies?'

'We'd like to go in to the baby, if we could,' said Effie.

'We're not going to have her adopted,' said Rose.

PART TWO

CHAPTER ELEVEN

'Rose! Rose O'Beirne Moffat!' In the back-to-school rush, the stationery department of Eason's in O'Connell Street was crammed and at first Rose could not see who was calling her. Her arms laden with copy-books, refill pads and folders, she scanned the crowd but could see no one she knew. Then, from behind, she felt her sleeve being pulled. 'Rose!'

Turning, she saw a dumpy, frizz-haired woman, aged, like herself, in her early thirties. Wreathed in smiles, the woman seemed not in the least put out at the blank expression on Rose's face. 'Don't you know who I am?' she cried. 'Have I changed that much? You haven't changed a bit,' she added.

It was the woman's voice which gave the lead. 'Dolores!' exclaimed Rose.

'Yeah,' said Dolores. 'Bingo! I've wondered for years what had happened to you, Rose – and now I know that whatever it was, it was all good. You look absolutely bloody marvellous,' she said. 'Like a model. I nearly didn't know you with your hair up – but, then, I'd know those bones anywhere. You're not a model, by any chance? I meant it when I said you hadn't changed, you don't look a day older.'

Just in time, Rose stopped herself from returning the pleasantry. Her school friend had changed almost out of all recognition: her hair had been permed and bleached so much it looked like hay, puffy ankles overflowed the sides of her court shoes, the buttons of her black dress strained at their holes and with each word she uttered, plump dewlaps wobbled against the pearls she wore around her neck. Rose tried to conceal her shock. 'I'm sorry I didn't recognise you immediately,' she said again. 'I'm distracted with all this.' She indicated the pile of school supplies in her arms. 'I hate the beginning of September.'

'Me, too,' said Dolores, whose arms were even more fully

laden than Rose's own. 'But isn't it just typical that we have to do it all! Children are lazy buggers – but what can you do? They have to have the stuff and that's that.' She shifted the load. 'Have you time for a coffee or something?'

'Sure,' said Rose, her voice sounding too hearty in her own ears. 'Just let me pay for these.'

As they queued to pay for their purchases, Rose tried to think of something to say. She and Dolores had once been so close but it had been so long since their last traumatic meeting that day after Dolores' visit to Sundarbans. At first, they had kept in touch by letter, but the gap between Rose's life in the Magdalen Home and Dolores' schoolgirl concerns had proved too wide. Rose's last letter had been a few weeks before her daughter was born. 'I'm really sorry I never answered your last letter,' she said now. 'It's just—'

'Say no more! For God's sake, that was years ago! Anyway, it's as much my fault as yours – I should have persisted.'

'It was just that – you know – with the baby coming . . . '

'I said, don't give it another thought. Anyway, here we are now.' Standing close behind Rose in the queue for the cash register, Dolores chatted away, about the disgraceful price of school-books, about the political news of the day – Ireland was convulsed at the time by allegations that some of its leaders could be involved in illicit gun-running – about the rash of plane hijackings, about how Dublin was falling apart at the seams these days with road works and developers, so that all Rose had to do was to agree or not as she saw fit.

'Where are you living now, Dolores?' she asked as, having paid for her own purchases, she waited for the assistant to parcel her friend's.

'Monkstown.'

'That must be lovely. Are you near the sea?'

'Just across the road from it,' answered Dolores. 'Longford Terrace. Do you know it?' Rose did. The row of tall, elegant houses was among the most beautiful in the city. Her friend, she thought, must have done well for herself.

They emerged into the bustle of O'Connell Street. 'We could go to Bewley's,' suggested Rose but without much enthusi-asm. It was a windy day and the thought of exposing herself to

336

the gales on O'Connell Bridge, weighed down as she was with shopping, was not attractive.

'Not at all,' said Dolores, nodding with her head to indicate an ice-cream parlour on the other side of the wide street. 'Sure, all we want is a cup of coffee – Cafolla's'll be fine!' Without waiting for Rose, she stepped out into the middle of the traffic and threaded her way through it like a small but determined bulldog.

The café was only half full and they got a table without any trouble. 'Phew!' Dolores struggled to stack her parcels in some sort of order under the table. 'I hate shopping.' She attracted the attention of a waitress and, without asking Rose what she wanted, ordered two coffees. 'And a plateful of pastries! Might as well enjoy ourselves!' she chuckled gleefully. 'It's not every day you run into your best friend from school – how long ago was it now, sixteen, seventeen years?'

'Nearly seventeen, I think,' said Rose. She hated herself for her reaction to this meeting – she was already calculating how soon she could get away without seeming to be rude. What was wrong with her? Dolores had been such a good friend.

'God,' said Dolores. 'Time flies, doesn't it? Now,' she crossed both arms under her fat breasts. 'Tell us *all*!' she said, widening her eyes. 'What are you doing with your life, Rose O'Beirne Moffat?'

'Well, for a start,' Rose was determined to be friendly and pleasant, 'I've dropped the Moffat bit. I got tired explaining it. I'm just plain old Rose O'Beirne now.'

'Pity,' said Dolores. 'I kind of liked having a double-barrelled friend. Anyway, what *have* you been doing? Whatever it is it suits you. Are you sure you're not a model?'

'No.' Rose laughed. 'I'm an air hostess, actually – have been for years. What are you doing yourself, Dolores?'

'An air hostess – I am impressed. I knew it had to be something glamorous and exotic,' said Dolores. She waved one ringed hand in the air. 'I'm doing nothing much. Married, the usual – kids, you know—'

'How many?'

'Seven!' said Dolores.

'Seven!' exclaimed Rose, trying to inject admiration into

337

her voice. 'You must have got married straight from school!'

'Uh-huh!' said Dolores. 'I went to university – qualified, too, as a radiographer – but Murty was in some of my science classes and that was that.'

'What does, er, Murty do?'

'He's a dentist,' said Dolores proudly. 'I had to work for the first couple of years to help him qualify but then little Denis came along and, well, you know how it is.'

'Is it boys or girls you have?'

'One boy, six girls.' Dolores laughed. 'But you know men, Murty won't stop until he has a few more heirs!'

'So you're going to have more?'

'Murty says he'd like the even dozen!'

'But, Dolores, what do you want?' Rose could not help herself. 'Do *you* want twelve children? You look a bit – well, tired . . . '

'Do I?' Dolores frowned. 'Maybe – but sure, they rear themselves after a certain age. Denis is nearly thirteen already and Mags – that's the eldest girl – she's brilliant with the younger ones. I can even get out now for a bit of golf.'

'Golf?'

'Yeah, it's great relaxation. Bit of crack, you know! Murty's a member of Elm Park. They're a good bunch.'

Their coffee and plateful of cream pastries came then and Dolores took one of the cakes, biting hard into it so that a large dollop of cream plopped onto the shelf of her bosom. 'Oops!' she said, scrubbing at it. 'Ah, sure, it doesn't matter. This old thing has had its day, anyway. Now,' she said, through a second mouthful, 'that's enough about me. What about you? How's your family?'

'They're fine,' said Rose. Again she felt that strange, unreasonable reluctance to elaborate. 'Mother and Daddy are fine,' she amended. 'But you met my grandmother, too, didn't you, that Christmas?'

'Yes?'

'Well, she died, I'm afraid, only a few months after that. She broke her hip and shoulder in a fall and was doing fine in hospital when somehow or other she developed pneumonia. I don't really know what happened. But, anyway, she died. Now,

338

tell me,' she forced herself to smile, 'what have you been up to – in your own life, I mean, what do you do?'

'You finish first. You work for Aer Lingus? And by the way, whatever happened to your ambition to become a writer?'

'I'd never be good enough to get published,' Rose laughed, 'but I still do the odd scribbling, just for my own benefit, you understand. Maybe some day I'll submit something to some magazine or other, but to tell you the truth, I don't have all that much time for self-indulgence. Hostessing suits me fine. With the way the schedule operates, particularly in the winter, there's a fair bit of time off and I can be at home more with Darina.'

'Darina?'

'My daughter,' said Rose, quietly.

'The same—?' Dolores held the remnants of her cream bun suspended in mid-air.

'Yes, the same one,' said Rose. 'She was born in London and everything was going according to plan – I think I may have written to you that I was going to have her adopted – but when I saw her, I couldn't give her up.'

'I know what you mean,' said Dolores. 'They're gorgeous when they're little, aren't they?' She licked her fingers. 'Must have caused a bit of fluttering in the dovecote at home, though?'

'It did a bit – but Darina was, still is, the most important thing in my life. Much more important than what Mother or Daddy thought. Daddy came round almost immediately. He loves Darina, comes up regularly to visit us. The strange thing is, you just asked me about my writing ambitions, would you believe Darina's talking about the same thing?'

'No! Do you think she's serious?'

'It's too early to tell, of course, I was deadly serious at about that age and look at me! But I think she has talent. Now I'm biased, of course, but her English teacher said it to me the last time I met her.'

'That's amazing. How genes will out, I mean. What about your mother? How does she get on with Darina?'

'She and I don't see eye to eye, I'm afraid,' said Rose shortly.

'But surely when she saw the baby—'

'She's never seen her.'

Dolores gasped. 'You mean to say you've never brought her to – what about the christening?'

'In London. I speak to her on the phone, but I haven't actually seen Mother since Darina was born.'

Dolores let out a slow whistle. 'Not even for your grand-mother's funeral?'

'Well, I might have braved that, I've regretted it since – that I didn't go, I mean – but Darina was very tiny when Nanna died and I was all caught up in the move from London to Dublin.'

'And has she, I mean Darina, has she never seen – crikey, I've forgotten the name of that beautiful house.'

'Sundarbans,' Rose supplied.

'Yeah, Sundarbans. You mean to say your Darina has never seen her ancestral home?'

'Not yet. She's beginning to put on a bit of pressure – you know what teenagers are! I think she believes it's a castle or something.' She toyed with her pastry. 'But Mother still has not forgiven me. Never will now. Oh, in the last couple of years, she's taken to sending Christmas presents. And if I was really honest about it, I could go home on my own – and I probably should. Daddy says that Mother's headaches have got worse over the years and I know if I was a proper daughter I'd go to see her. But I'm not going to disown Darina, go home and swan around Carrickmacross as though she's doesn't exist.'

'Oh, Rose, I'm sure your mother will want to see her only grandchild eventually. I'm sure she will.'

Here were echoes of the old Dolores and Rose responded. 'Maybe some day,' she said. 'We'll wait and see. But you don't know Mother the way I do, Dolores. She would die if I arrived in her precious parish with a grown-up illegitimate daughter. I've no intention of putting Darina through that sort of tension. She has enough to contend with, having no father. Anyway, the whole thing will have to come to a head soon. I can't keep putting her off indefinitely. And she loves Daddy. Maybe this Christmas . . . ' She took a sip of the frothy, pale-coloured liquid in her cup.

'Sure, you could do it some day when your mother is not home. All you have to do is get the bus down there – or drive. Your mother need never know you were in town,' suggested Dolores, ever-practical.

'You've got to be joking. The missing daughter from the local big house blows back into town? She'd hear in less than an hour.'

'You never got married, then?' asked Dolores after a pause.

'No.' Rose shook her head. 'The opportunity never arose. First of all, I was too busy – just keeping our heads above water took up most of my time and energy. When we first came to Dublin I had to do all sorts, waitressing, secretarial work – I was the worst secretary in the world – I was sacked after a week.' She smiled at the recollection. 'And because everything revolved around getting Darina minded, I even took work as an office cleaner for a while. The work was at night, you see.'

'Can't – I just *can't* imagine Rose O'Beirne Moffat in curlers and overalls.'

'Well, it happened,' said Rose quietly. 'Not the curlers, but yes to the overalls. For a whole eight months. That was probably the worst time in my life, even worse, I think, than that time in the convent in London. Then I got a job in a lounge – at least the tips were quite good – and then the ad appeared in the papers for the jobs in Aer Lingus and, thank goodness, I got one of them. Luckily it never even occurred to them to ask what my domestic situation was. It was one of the few times the posh name and address worked to my advantage. It's not only Monaghan that's closed to Darina – to this day, as far as I know, no one in the airline is aware of her existence.' She laughed wryly. 'I couldn't have managed without Effie. She's a friend of mine we've lived with since the beginning and, luckily, she's so good at her job that her supervisor lets her work a lot at home. We manage. And, of course, it's getting easier now that Darina's independent. So with one thing and another,' she added, 'there was just very little time or energy left for social life. I won't say there haven't been men in my life, there've been plenty, but I've never met one who was all that keen to take on the two of us as a package deal.'

'That's ridiculous, Rose. You're *gorgeous*.'

'Oh, plenty of them seemed keen enough, but somehow there was always some problem at the last fence. To be perfectly honest, Dolores, I'm much happier as I am. The three of us have got along famously all these years. In one way, Darina was lucky – she grew up with two mothers.'

Dolores took another of the gooey cakes. 'And how about

– Tom?' she asked, not meeting Rose's eyes. 'Wasn't that his name?'

'John,' corrected Rose. 'John Flynn.'

'Have you seen him since – does Darina know?'

'No,' replied Rose slowly. 'And I have no wish to see him. I suppose Darina will want to meet him some day but I'll deal with that when it happens.'

'Have you told her about him?'

Rose hesitated. 'I decided early on I wouldn't lie to her and I've answered all her questions as they came up. She knows, for instance, that he emigrated to Canada. Funny enough,' Rose looked at her nails, 'I've heard only recently that he's back around home. It's odd I should run into you today, Dolores, after all this time.' She looked up again. 'You know how that sometimes happens? How you haven't heard a thing about someone or something for ages and then somebody brings up the subject and all of a sudden it's all over the place? It was Daddy, of all people, who mentioned his name the other day. Apparently John came home from Canada years ago and is now some sort of hotelier and – would you believe this? – he and a few other people are in a kind of syndicate together and are trying to persuade Daddy to turn Sundarbans into a hotel.'

'And how do you feel about that?'

'I don't know,' said Rose honestly. 'The place is falling down and Daddy hasn't a hope in the wide world of getting enough money to put it right. So maybe a hotel is the answer. I'd hate to see it go altogether, or us having to sell it for a few pounds to some Americans who'll put a swimming pool in the pleasure garden.'

'But with John Flynn involved in running it? What would your mother say to that?'

'To tell you the truth, Dolores,' Rose grinned, 'that would be the most attractive thing about it. It would be good enough for her. I'd love to see her face, having to eat humble pie from the hands of the serf from the gate lodge, knowing that without him she'd be homeless.' She drained her cup. 'Not that any of us, Daddy or Mother or I, have ever, *ever* discussed who Darina's father is. The other day, when Daddy talked about the hotel was, I think, the first time I had ever heard the name John Flynn uttered by either of my parents.'

'But what I meant was, how do you feel about meeting him again?'

'And I meant it when I said I don't know. There was a time when I hated him, really hated him, Dolores, but it all seems very far away now, very long ago and all a bit irrelevant.'

Rose was not being honest. Many, many times in the past years, she had longed to meet John Flynn again. She still dreamed about him occasionally; more frequently – whenever she met any man called John – she remembered that day on the lake when he had sluiced out the old boat and then rowed round in little circles, waiting for the seats to dry so she would not spoil her white dress.

Dolores fingered her pearls. 'What did he do to you that made you hate him?'

Now Rose regretted having said so much. 'Nothing,' she said curtly in a tone which warned Dolores not to pry. She put down her coffee cup. 'Anyway,' she said more gently, 'John Flynn's probably married and settled down with seven kids, just like you.'

'Did you not ask your father? If he's married, I mean?'

'Why would I?' countered Rose. 'I told you – we've never discussed John and I'm not going to start now. And I have not been home, as I told you. Anyway, Dublin is my home now. Drumboola and its citizens are a million miles away from here. I meet a lot of people in connection with my work and socially, and I don't think I've ever run into anyone from County Monaghan, let alone from Drumboola. I'm not interested in whether or not John Flynn is married. It could never be the same again. Even if I was,' she added, 'I've changed so much. And I'm sure he's changed even more. We probably don't have a single thing in common now.'

The longer she spoke, the more Rose realised how unconvincing she sounded. Meeting Dolores had stirred up a lot she had thought was, if not resolved, at least buried so far under the surface that it could not bother her. She had to get away before she got in deeper and uncovered more.

She looked at her wristwatch. 'My goodness, is that the time? I told Effie and Darina I'd be home by six.' She wondered how she could get away from Dolores without making another appointment. Lost intimacy could rarely be regained and she had no wish to try.

343

Then Dolores made her feel like a worm. 'It's all right, Rose,' she said quietly, 'don't worry.' She used the middle finger of her right hand to sweep the crumbs from around her plate, forming them into a little pile. 'I'm not going to barge into your life again, being nosy and all that. I know that we can't take up where we left off. Just like you and your boyfriend, we're different people now. Miles different. You would think my lifestyle is bourgeois, messy and even ridiculous. It's all right,' she said again, as Rose tried to protest, 'don't worry, Rose, it was just nice to see you again, after all these years.'

She chuckled and reached over to pat her hand. 'Now stop looking like that – like a wounded fawn! I don't mind, really. It was a pleasure to be your friend at the time and to do as much as I could for you. Beautiful well-bred girls like you have that effect on people. Accept it and enjoy it, it's like a gift. I would if I looked like you – accept it, I mean. And I'm really glad you're happy, I really am.'

'Are you, Dolores? Happy, I mean?'

'I – I think so,' said Dolores slowly. 'God knows, Murty tells me often enough how lucky I am . . . '

'Well, you are – seven healthy children, all that.'

'I wouldn't give one of them up, of course, Rose, not for a minute. I love every rib of hair on every one of their heads. But I'd make a pact with the devil if I thought he could make me look like you.'

'Oh, Dolores, please don't—'

'Fact of life, m'dear!' Dolores started to gather up her parcels. 'You used to ask me for my advice. Well, my advice to you is to milk those looks for everything you can. I know you're not aware of them – really beautiful women like you rarely are – but they won't last for ever.' She looked directly at Rose. 'And I know your whole life is wrapped up in Darina at the moment, but think about how it'll be after she's gone. She will go, you know, Rose, and in not too many years. Look at your own mother, hasn't seen her only daughter for over sixteen years.' She looked away. 'And I know this next bit is none of my business and I might be way off the wall but I'm going to say it anyway,' she chuckled, 'never could resist meddling. The older I get, Rose, the more I read between the lines of what people are saying, the tone of their voices, the look in their eyes, all that kind of thing. And in my humble opinion, Rose O'Beirne, despite what you say, you are still in love with John Flynn.' She looked back at Rose. 'End of lecture. Sorry!'

They paid the bill and went out into the street. 'There's a taxi,' said Dolores. 'Cheerio now, Rose, it was nice seeing you, it really was – good luck with everything.' Without looking back she walked across the pavement, crowded now with home-going office workers.

Rose, already tired from shopping, could not get a seat on the bus and by the time she let herself into the flat half an hour later, she was irritable. Her mood was not improved by the sight of Darina's school gaberdine, crumpled on the floor of the hallway. 'Darina!' she called.

'Yes, Mammy?' Darina was upstairs in her room.

'Come down this minute and pick this up!' Rose shouted, more sharply than she would normally have done; in addition to her physical discomfort, the meeting with Dolores had rattled her more than she cared to admit.

The door at the top of the stairs opened. 'Pick what up?'

'Your school coat. At once!'

'All right.' Darina clattered down the stairs. 'What's eating you this evening?' She picked up the coat and hung it on the hallstand. 'Got out of bed the wrong way this morning, did we?'

'Don't be cheeky.' But Rose's irritability waned at the sight of her daughter's open, shining face. 'Sorry,' she apologised. 'I didn't mean to sound cranky. I'm just tired.'

'That my stuff?' Darina eyed the Eason's bags in her mother's hands.

'Yeah. In return, will you get me a cup of tea?' Rose piled the school supplies on a chair and went into the living room, where she flopped onto a couch.

A few minutes later, Darina, carefully balancing a cup and saucer on a tray, came into the room. 'Thanks a million,' said Rose, taking it. 'How was school?'

'Oh, the usual,' said Darina. 'Boring. I keep telling you that the Irish educational system is not suitable for someone like me, Mammy. There isn't a single subject that I like or that I'm interested in. Shakespeare and Milton by rote, for God's sake! I know more about real things, things that *matter* in life than any of my teachers.'

Rose sighed. 'Not that old chestnut? The system may or may not suit you, Darina, but I keep telling you it's the only one available. And, like it or not, your interest in philosophy or Zen or whatever it is these days won't put bread in your mouth. You'll just have to knuckle down. It's only for a short time now – you're nearly through the bad bits. I keep telling you, you're cutting off choices if you don't get a good Leaving Cert.' Sipping her tea, Rose knew she sounded like a stuck gramophone record and attempted to lighten the mood. 'Think of it. If you don't play the game you might end up an air hostess like me.'

'What's wrong with that?' Darina picked at her nails. 'It's a job, isn't it? You did all right.'

'Come off it, you know that's not what you want out of your life. To use your favourite word, all that *boring* chitchat with passengers? What about your plans for university? You're sure to find *something* that will coincide with your exalted interests and theories.'

'Don't be sarcastic, Mammy, it doesn't suit you.' But Darina smiled, touching her mother on the cheek. 'I've told you over and over I'm going to be something special. You just wait.'

'Well, let me know when you decide what that might be,' said Rose comfortably. She looked obliquely at her daughter. From time to time, when she caught Darina off guard, she did feel there was something unusual about her. Looking up now at the girl's determined expression, at the way her eyes glowed, she told herself firmly that all mothers thought their offspring were special. 'You won't be anything at all,' she said, 'unless you get up those stairs and do your homework.'

'Homework, homework,' huffed Darina, stalking out of the room, 'that's all grown-ups and teachers ever think about.'

The meeting with Dolores haunted Rose all evening. At about nine o'clock, she got up from the dining-room table where, with Effie, she had been going over the guest list and seating plan for Effie's wedding, to take place in three weeks' time. 'Sorry, Effie,' she said, 'I just can't concentrate. Would you like a cup of tea or coffee – or how about a drink?'

346

'Right,' said Effie, piling sheets of paper into an untidy heap in front of her. 'I'll have a gin and tonic.'

Like all airline cabin staff, Rose had a well-stocked bar. She mixed a gin and tonic for Effie and splashed some soda into a measure of Campari for herself. Over the years they had lived together, Rose's and Effie's musical tastes had come to coincide and the velvety tones of Nat King Cole issued from the record player on top of the drinks cabinet. Darina was in her own room doing homework – Rose hoped – and the living room was quiet and cosy.

She brought the drinks over to the couch which was placed between the two bay windows. Bright and airy, the three-bedroomed flat was actually the upper part of a house, one of a big, solid row along Drumcondra Road, convenient to the airport and also to Effie's job; even before Rose had met her, Effie, using do-it-yourself manuals, had taught herself bookkeeping and now worked for a cash-and-carry operation.

The three bedrooms were set into the attics and lit with skylights, leaving the whole floor beneath as living space. Rose sat on the couch and looked around with a sigh of satisfaction. The calm, restful feel of the place, the high, plasterworked ceilings and peaches-and-cream colour scheme never ceased to give her pleasure. She had fallen in love with this room the moment she had clapped eyes on it.

'I'm going to miss you, you know,' she said now to her friend as the two of them sipped their drinks. She kicked off her shoes and wriggled her toes, revelling in the lushness of the music and the overall peace. 'We've come a long way together.'

'Yeah, but remember you're not losing a friend, you're gaining a third of a bathroom.' The only tremor which shook the even tenor of their lives together was that all three of them accused the others of hogging the single bathroom in the flat. 'And I'm not going anywhere as far as our relationship goes. Marriage is not going to change anything there.'

'That's what they all say!' Rose gave Effie an affectionate thump in the arm. Relaxed and mellow, she settled back to enjoy her drink and to listen to Nat King Cole and when the first side of the album finished, she got up to turn it over. As Effie's departure came closer, the two of them, inevitably, had been reminiscing, dredging up the highlights and, more particularly, lowlights of their sixteen years together. 'Will you ever forget that first flat?' Rose guided the stylus onto the record again. Their first home together, the only one they could get because of the baby, had been a dark, two-roomed horror, which they had left after six months. 'I wonder if that landlord ever got his come-uppance?'

'Yeah, the nerve of that shagger, charging us rent at all! Remember the night half the ceiling fell on Darina?'

'Oh, God!' Rose laughed as she returned to her seat. Darina had been about five months old when lumps of plaster had cas-caded into her cot from the damp ceiling of the bedroom the three of them shared. The event ranked as the nadir of that desperate period; Rose, who was between jobs, hated sponging off Effie's small salary and that night, as she snatched up the baby who was more surprised than frightened, all the frustrations and fears of the past few months had climaxed in a crying jag so severe that Effie had called a doctor.

'The crates?' She dug Effie in the ribs.

'You've got to admit they took the bare look off the place,' Effie retorted. Their second flat had been furnished with only the minimum and one Saturday, Effie, taking Darina's pram, had gone down to the Dublin fruit market and staggered home with as many orange boxes as the pram and her hands could accommo-date. She and Rose had spent all that night nailing them together and 'upholstering' them with padded-up newspapers and cotton remnants they had bought cheaply in a sale.

'They were great,' said Rose now, sipping her drink. 'You were great – but I must admit I prefer this.' She snuggled more deeply into the upholstery of the couch. 'And I'm really glad things have worked out so well for both of us. But I'll still miss you, Effie.'

'Me, too.' Effie's face still crinkled up when she smiled but, with maturity, she had lost the dishevelled look. She had also put on a bit of weight which helped soften her wizened features. In the course of her job training, Rose had learned a lot about grooming and, on her advice, Effie had had her wiry hair cut very short, revealing surprisingly pretty ears. Also on Rose's say-so, she now kept the hair permanently Vaselined, so that it lay sleekly on her small head like an astrakhan cap. Looking at her now,

Rose thought fondly that Effie was never going to win any beauty contests but she had certainly made the most of herself and the very least that could be said about her was that her individualist appearance, once seen, could never be mistaken for anyone else's.

'Happy, Effie?' she asked.

'Mmm,' said Effie. 'Wouldn't you be happy? Thirty-five years old, nearly thirty-six and just when you've given up all hope you're being taken off the shelf by the most wonderful fella in the world.'

She had met Willie Brehony, a civil servant from Cork, when shopping in the local supermarket and thereafter he had insinuated himself into the crevices of her life as craftily as an eel. After her experiences in childhood, Effie had been absolutely determined never, ever to have anything to do with any man and had kept him at bay for nearly two years until, somehow, he managed to break her down. In his early forties, he was small and tubby, with a passion for Gaelic games. His other hobby was the tin whistle, which he carried around in the inside pocket of his jacket, transferring it from outfit to outfit as other men did wallets.

Effie got up from the couch and crossed to the record player, lifting the stylus to repeat the last track. 'I still think the wedding's going to be awful lopsided,' she said. 'I wish to God things were different and I could have a normal wedding. Willie's family are so conservative – I don't know what they're going to think.' All along, Effie had been adamant that no member of her own family was to be invited. She had not been in touch with anyone in Offaly for years.

'Look, Effie,' said Rose patiently, 'if you feel you can handle it, it's not too late to invite them. Invite the whole county.'

'I must be getting sentimental in me old age,' said Effie, refilling her drink.

'Reading too many wedding magazines, more likely,' said Rose, stretching her tired limbs. 'Guess who I ran into today?' She went on to tell Effie about her encounter with Dolores and how it had stirred up old memories and longings. 'Isn't it amazing, Effie? After all this time, his name coming up like that twice in the same month – oh, I know I talk to you about him but that's different. Talking to you is like talking to myself.'

'Not John Flynn again!' Effie groaned in mock horror. 'How many times over the years have we decided that once and for all we're going to kick John Flynn out of our lives? And then, in the next minute, we decide that once and for all we're going to *sort something out*! If I said it once, I said it a thousand times,' she added, 'once there's a child between you, you'll never be finished with a man. When the hell are you going to stop moping and *do* something, Rose O'Beirne?'

'Very impressive, I must say. You've certainly done your home-work.' The bank manager, a stringy individual new to the Carrick-macross branch, turned over the thick file in front of him. The wood-panelled office was stuffy and far too small to hold the five men who had crowded into it. John looked the manager straight in the eye. 'Of course, there are no guarantees, there were no guarantees when George here converted Willow House into a hotel. But it's because of the success there that we believe we can make a go of Sundarbans as a hotel and leisure centre.'

'Travelling the roads, County Monaghan does not appear to me to be a good investment for a tourism project.' The manager fixed him with a stare.

'It all depends on how you look at it,' George Cranshaw broke in. 'We're not going to try to compete with the resorts, and obviously, we can't offer weather-related recreation. But it's my view that in the next decade there will be a worldwide boom in leisure and that the affluent businessman will get tired of lazing about on beaches and will look for something more active. We're already seeing it at Willow House. We started with only six bedrooms and now, even with the extra eight, we still can't cater to the demand.'

'Everything we did has paid off,' it was John's turn again, 'the jetty, the boats, the clay-pigeon range, and in our present brochure we mention the golf course we're putting in and even though it won't be ready for another twelve or fourteen months, we've already had enquiries. We're very confident that there is a market.'

'But what would you do with Sundarbans? Wouldn't you, in a sense, just be competing with your existing operation?'

'Willow House will always be small and quaint, intimate,

if you like,' said the third member of the syndicate, an accountant from Enniskillen. 'We think there is the potential in this area for a luxury complex, something like the Gleneagles set-up in Scotland, not on the same scale, of course—'

'With all due respect,' the bank manager interrupted, 'I've never been to Gleneagles, but knowing you were coming in today, I drove out to Sundarbans yesterday evening, just to have a look at it. It's in a dreadful state of repair.'

John felt it was his turn again. 'We don't intend doing up the entire place immediately, just one wing of bedrooms, the public rooms, the grounds and the stables. Here are the draft drawings,' he passed them across the desk and as the manager studied them, continued, 'One of the key aspects of our proposal is that the local population should be attracted to use the facilities. We will be applying for a full bar licence, for instance. And we would also like to revive the hunt, and perhaps, eventually, to run an indoor equestrian facility.'

'How does the Colonel feel about all this?' asked the manager.

'We would not have approached you if we hadn't spoken to him first,' said George Cranshaw. 'To tell you the truth, Gussie – he's an old friend of mine, by the way – is at the end of his tether. He has run out of choices. Even if he sold the place on the open market, he knows full well that he would not get enough for it as it stands to clear his debts and give him and his wife a decent living. He could convert the place himself, but he has no experience in the hotel business. Our plan will allow him to stay at Sundarbans and to share, eventually, in any profits the place generates.'

The manager gathered together all the files and papers in front of him. 'I'll study these,' he said.

John, his voice husky with conviction, made one last pitch. 'I – we are absolutely convinced that we will make a go of this project. You won't be sorry if you invest in us.'

The manager blinked. 'Well, you certainly make a good case, Mr Flynn, I'll say that for you.' He ushered them out of the office.

On the way back to Willow House, John said very little. The encounter with the bank manager had taken more out of him than he cared to admit; his conviction about the viability of the project had not been false but he knew only too well how daunting it would be. And although the initiative had been entirely his, now that the project was taking concrete form on paper a small part of him half hoped it would not see fruition.

The plans called for him to transfer from Willow House and to live there as manager, with a salary and equity performance bonus. John's worry was how he would manage to live under the same roof as Rose's mother and father, although their living space had shrunk to just three rooms. More pertinently, he wondered if he could bear to rearrange the fabric of Rose's home, to tear down walls and corners she knew, to supervise the redecoration of what used to be her bedroom.

His unrequited love for Rose had settled somewhere in the base of his heart; only at night now, and rarely, did it explode into the violent longing of his earlier years. Nevertheless, as the work on the Sundarbans project became more intense, when, for instance, he mapped the lake with the architect, the thick sediment of desire was stirred up all over again.

Other than this unfinished business, his life had calmed over the years. His mother had died just two years after the ill-assorted little group had moved into the fishing lodge. For a time after her death, John wanted to move away, to make a complete break. He even thought of going back to Canada. But he was held back by a combination of loyalties, to the Cranshaws, who had been so good to him, to Mona and her father, who had uprooted themselves for him, but to his surprise, he had found that the strongest attachment was to Drumboola itself and to Sundarbans.

Mona had waited quietly for him to make up his mind; John never ceased to wonder at her calm acceptance of everything life threw at her – illness, death, hard work, good luck, bad luck – she took everything absolutely at face value. Gradually, without discussion, the depleted household had settled into a new routine, with John as the breadwinner and Mona acting as housekeeper. Meanwhile, Packy McConnell had earned his keep with handiwork and cabinetry, filling alcoves, carving stools and tables and, bit by bit, the lodge had taken on a polished, settled air.

John, working so hard at the expanding hotel, had barely

had time to notice all the improvements at home. As it became successful, Willow House increased its tariffs and took on more staff and, five years after he had first asked for a job, John had been promoted to the position of manager, a position which had actually been his for quite a while.

Driving up the laneway to the fishing lodge, he remembered it was Monday; he always took Monday nights off and frequently, when the weather was suitable, he and Mona's father went out in one of the boats after a few trout.

He found Mona at the kitchen table, separating the counter-foils of raffle tickets and dropping them into a box at her feet. 'Where's Packy?' he asked.

'Can't you hear him?' She raised her eyes to the ceiling.

The internal walls of the lodge were made of stone and John had to strain his ears but sure enough, very faintly, like fairy music, he heard the lilting of Packy's fiddle. 'He's been practising for the wedding all day,' she added. 'Do you know yet whether you'll be able to come?'

The following Saturday, a relative of Mona's was getting married and John, now treated as a sort of honorary McConnell, had been invited. 'I'll see, Mona,' he promised. 'I'll really try.'

'Sure, if you can, you can,' she said. She picked up her cardboard box and shook it to distribute her stubs evenly. 'There's a couple of letters for you on the dresser.'

John picked up the two envelopes, one contained a bill, the second, he saw, was addressed in Derek's handwriting. Leaving the bill aside, he slit open Derek's letter and scanned it. 'Damn,' he said.

'Anything wrong?' asked Mona, putting down her box.

'No, sorry, Mona,' he said. 'Derek has to come to Germany on business in the next few weeks and he thinks it might be a good idea if he brought Bruno and stopped off here for a visit.'

'That'll be nice, John,' said Mona. 'We've plenty of room.'

'I know, but I've little enough time as it is to entertain them and now is the worst possible time for them to land in on us. I'll be all wrapped up in the Sundarbans deal.'

'Don't worry about it,' consoled Mona. 'Sure, aren't Da and I here all the time? We'll look after them. Bruno must be huge by now,' she added.

John continued to scan the letter. 'He's already looking for me to do things for him. He wants me to arrange a hire car to meet him in Dublin.'

'Sure, that's easy enough.'

'I'm sorry, Mona,' said John again. 'Of course they're welcome.' But his first reaction had been the honest one. Derek's presence made him uncomfortable.

The twins had never formally patched up their differences but during the obsequies of their mother's funeral, the heat had seemed to go out of the situation and they had lapsed into wary civility. And although John had not attended Derek's and Karen's wedding, claiming to be too busy at the hotel, he had sent them a wedding present and wrote sporadically.

When their child, Bruno, was five, they had brought him to Ireland for the first time and having him around meant all three of the adults were able to use him as a sort of emotional intermediary. John found him an enchanting child. He was very blond, with Karen's wide blue eyes and sturdy physique.

Bruno had come to visit with his parents on two occasions since, once when he was nine, the last time when he was almost fourteen and nearly as tall as his father and his uncle. On each occasion, John had been struck by the boy's even temperament and calm charm. When Bruno was around, the tension between the twins and between them and Karen was definitely eased.

Mona dropped the last of her stubs into the cardboard box, stood up and yawned. 'When are they coming?'

'The end of October.' John looked out the window. 'The light's going. If we're to go on the lake we'd better get a move on.' He went to the foot of the stairs. 'Packy! Packy?'

The violin music died away and upstairs he could hear the sound of a door opening. 'Hang on a tick,' shouted Mona's father, 'till I get me cap . . . '

John changed his shoes for wellington boots but, to save time, did not bother to change his suit, simply dragging on an old waxed jacket. He was standing at the outside door when Packy, using the banisters as a support, came hopping down the stairs. 'Good evening for it, Johnny,' he said, picking up his walking stick.

They did not speak again until they were installed in the

boat and well out on the small, rushy lake. John always found Packy's undemanding company very soothing. The older man was an excellent fly fisherman and usually caught at the rate of three to John's one. The lake was reputed to hold at least one sixteen-pound brownie. Packy had actually hooked this prize a year or so previously when it probably weighed a couple of pounds less, but his tackle had been too flimsy to get it in and after a twenty-minute battle, the tip of his fly-rod had snapped and the trout had escaped to fight another day. Packy never went out now without equipment and line strong enough to reel in a fish of twice the monster's weight. 'I feel lucky tonight, Johnny,' he said, shooting the rod so the line snaked towards Poulachailin, a deep hole, where, legend had it, a young girl had drowned herself for love. 'He's in there, I just know it, I can feel it in me bones!'

John smiled and flicked out his own rod, settling into the peace of the place. It was about nine o'clock and the trees around the lake were beginning to darken against the sky. The wind had died down and dapped only intermittently across the surface of the lake.

While he fished, the meeting with the bank manager replayed in John's mind like a jerky old movie. The plans to develop Sundarbans had ben growing in his imagination for years and years, ever since he had gone up to see it on his last night at the gate lodge. Patiently, he had bided his time until he was sure the Colonel was in such financial difficulties that he would consider any serious option put to him. Even then John had waited, until the time was right, until Willow House was in a very healthy position and until he sensed that George Cranshaw was looking around for a new challenge. Then, one evening, when George and he were driving back from Dublin having seen the golf-course architect, he had summoned up the courage to broach the subject. George had been at first amused, then sceptical but, little by little, as John talked on, he had seen his boss become intrigued. Months of careful manoeuvring had followed, culminating in the day's meeting in the bank.

The fish were in little danger from him this evening, he thought, then looked at Packy's serious, frowning face and smiled. 'How's the bones?' he asked.

'Wha'?'

'That feeling in your bones that tonight you're going to get him, how's it now?'

'Yerra for God's sake, Johnny, will you cop on. He's there, I know he is . . . '

But he was not, at least not on this particular evening. They fished on unsuccessfully until the light was almost entirely gone and a tiny new moon had lifted over the black line of the trees.

Effie went to bed early and, on impulse, Rose picked up the telephone and dialled the Sundarbans number. Please, God, please, she prayed as the line rang at the other end, please don't let Mother pick it up . . .

Her prayers were answered. 'Hello, Daddy,' she sang, 'just thought I'd give you a call. How are things?'

'Rose!' Her father's tone, as always, betrayed pleasure. 'How are you?'

'Fine. Everything all right?'

'Oh, yes, jogging along, you know, the whole place crawling with surveyors and chappies with theodolites. It's getting a bit difficult to find a peaceful corner to sit down these days.'

'Is the deal going ahead, then?'

'Doesn't look as though I have any choice, poppet. Your mother is a bit upset, of course, but she knows it's either this or the poorhouse.'

'Daddy!'

'Only joking. And at least we know the people concerned. Sad, though.'

Rose's heart began to beat faster. 'How's Mr Cranshaw?'

'Oh, fine, fine. Don't see as much of George as we do of – of – the other people.'

Rose knew that the hurdle had been John Flynn's name but did not press him. 'Is it very bad – the house, I mean?'

'I wish you'd come and see for yourself, Rose, before it's changed for ever. Anyway, there are a few things here you might want to salvage before they end up in the tiphead.'

'What about Mother? You know I won't come without Darina.'

'That's something you'll have to work out among yourselves.' Rose could almost hear the jingling of Gus's watch chain.

'Don't fret, Daddy, it'll come in time,' she said. 'Maybe this is the year.'

'I hope so. Anyway, Rose, you know that no matter what – and no matter what happens to Sundarbans – as far as I'm concerned there will always be a place for you here. And maybe now's not the time to mention it, but you know I'll have an interest in the new place? Financially, I mean?'

'You told me already.'

'Well, of course, that will pass to you, and when the deal is done, I'll be drawing up a new will—'

'Daddy, don't!' Rose was distressed at the notion of ever being without her father, 'I don't want to talk about such things.'

'Don't be silly, Rose. We have to be sensible about these matters. What I want to say is that, of course, should you predecease her, everything will go to Darina.'

'Daddy!'

'That's all, poppet. How is Darina?'

'Blooming.' Rose filled in her father on Darina's progress at school, in ballet and elocution, all her activities. When she had finished the recital, Gus asked if she would like to speak to her mother. 'That's all right, Daddy,' said Rose hastily, 'the next time. I've been on this long-distance call long enough and with Darina on to her friends night and day, this phone bill is bad enough already.'

'All right, then, goodnight.'

''Night, Daddy, see you soon.'

On her way to bed a few minutes later, Rose drew a bath. While waiting for it to fill, she stripped off her clothes and stood in front of the full-length mirror on the back of the bathroom door and studied herself critically, trying to see herself as Dolores had intimated others saw her. *Beautiful well-bred girls like you have that effect on people . . .*

Dolores' words had upset her more than she had realised at the time. Perhaps her old friend was right. The implication was that she floated through life, accepting all, giving little in return. Was that true, or was Dolores, poor plain Dolores, just speaking from jealousy? As soon as the thought entered her head she suppressed it. How dare she think of Dolores as anything other than a wonderful, supportive friend? It was not her fault that Rose could find nothing in common with her now.

But was she right? Rose thought of Effie, already in bed, no doubt dreaming happily about her wedding and her future with Willie. Had Effie stepped into the breach left by Dolores? What had Rose done in her entire life for either of those good, loyal women? *But you organised Effie's escape from her past!* murmured a voice in her brain. Yes, thought Rose, but to whose ultimate benefit? Who babysat for Darina so Rose could work? Who was Darina's substitute father? Who helped create a warm loving home everywhere she went?

Could it be that, subconsciously or otherwise, Rose had engineered the situation because she did not want to take hold of the real issue of what to do about her family, about her own life, about John Flynn?

Her milky image stared back at her. Many of the women she worked with sported year-round tans, but Rose, who could not see the point in lying under the sun to fry her skin, remained determinedly pale. Now she saw this in another light: was this just another symptom of her passivity? While other girls had to slave at looking good, did she take her looks so much for granted that she was just lazy?

Dolores, whether she had meant to or not, had perhaps come perilously close to the truth. It was all too possible that Rose had forgotten how to exert herself in anything, because she had no need to. Although she had had boyfriends, even lovers, she went out socially even less frequently than Effie, preferring a nice, sloppy evening with her friend and Darina by the record player at home. The boyfriends and lovers seemed to fade out of her life as effortlessly as she had acquired them in the first place and she always flopped gratefully back into the peaceful female scene.

She pinched a small fold of skin by her waist. Was it her imagination or did it seem less elastic than it used to be? After all, Darina was more than sixteen years old . . .

Recently, Rose had begun to worry a little about her daughter; although Darina continued to hog the telephone, talking for hours to her numerous friends, Rose had noticed new, solitary tendencies. For instance, Darina had taken to locking the door of her room, resenting any intrusion, preferring the company of books to people.

'Right,' she said out loud to the mirror. 'You're thirty-two years old and you're a disgrace. It's about time you took hold of yourself.' She turned on both taps until they ran to their full extent and got into the bathtub immediately, although the water was only an inch deep. She soaped herself savagely all over and was rinsed off and towelling herself dry long before the water had reached the level at which she normally lolled around in it. She was accustomed to spending up to an hour on her nightly ablutions, drifting in and out of pleasant torpor, adding dribs of hot water every few minutes to keep herself pleasantly warm.

No more of that, she decided now, tying on her dressing-gown. It was action from now on. She pulled a brush through her dark hair, still long and glossy. That was the first thing, she would get her hair cut. She looked ridiculous. A grown woman of thirty-two years old wearing her hair the same way she had at sixteen.

Feverishly, she made plans. Starting tomorrow, she would make herself over. She would take night courses in car mechanics, art, Japanese, whatever was available. She would get out and about and meet people and make an effort. This winter would be the time of her life when she would stop being a spoiled child. She remembered all the half-hearted efforts she had made before, fiery enthusiasms which dazzled briefly and then burned out leaving no trace. This would definitely be different.

She should be grateful to Dolores. It had taken this chance meeting to point out to her that she was drifting through life with no purpose, giving nothing, making nothing; when she died, her passage across the planet would leave not a single footprint.

Except for Darina.

Rose turned out the light in the bathroom and crossed the landing. The door to Darina's room was festooned with Beatles' posters, Beatles' stickers, old Beatle album covers, Beatle badges, even a Beatle calendar. But pride of place, right in the centre, was given to a photograph of George Harrison standing alongside the Maharishi. 'Can I come in, Darina?'

'I'm in bed, Mammy.' Her daughter's muffled voice sounded suspiciously lively.

'Just want to say goodnight,' called Rose through the door. 'I won't stay long, honest!'

There was scuffling inside and then the door opened. 'What is it, Mammy? I was just drifting off.' Her blonde hair was tousled; she was wearing only a short-sleeved white T-shirt and, even in the artificial light, her straight, sleekly muscled limbs were golden from a summer spent in the fresh air.

Looking over her shoulder, Rose saw that the bed had been unoccupied but bit her tongue. 'Sorry, I just wanted to say goodnight, that's all.'

'Goodnight.' They hugged but Darina disengaged immediately and went back into the room.

Just before the lock clicked home, Rose saw that, by a trick of the light, for an instant, her daughter was the reincarnation of John Flynn.

Shaken, she went to her own room and got into bed. Was this the onset of a mid-life crisis? For years having believed her life under control, why now, simply having bumped into someone from the past, was she constantly being reminded of it? She had not seen John Flynn for nearly seventeen years. Why, all of a sudden, was his presence intruding so strongly?

And why so physically?

Rose had never thought of herself as being particularly sensual. For the past seventeen years – at least after she had, as she had thought, 'got over' her obsession with John Flynn – she categorised the feelings she had experienced that summer with him as being simply due to youth and experimentation. A 'first-timeness' which could never again be matched in intensity simply because it was the first time for both of them to be in love.

Over the years she had certainly thought about him, about his strength and gentleness, his lupine smile and Pan eyes. But she had convinced herself that her imagination had enhanced the portrait. For some reason – perhaps the chat with Dolores, perhaps seeing Darina's likeness to him – she was driven by a new and absurd desire to see him again.

'Ridiculous!' she muttered aloud. As she had said to Dolores, John was probably married, settled, even corpulent, red-faced and obnoxious. A businessman. Offering to buy Sundarbans. That was it – he would almost certainly be obnoxious and pushy.

360

But then she remembered again the rowing on the lake that second day and the way the fine hairs on his forearms had glinted gold in the sunlight. For the first time in a decade and a half, Rose's body was flooded with intense physical desire.

She turned over restlessly in the bed. This line of thinking was bizarre. She would try to get some sleep and it would be gone from her brain in the morning. She concentrated on her roster – she was flying to Amsterdam in the morning – and on the upcoming date she had with a new man in two days' time. He was an Irish businessman who regularly commuted between Dublin and London, charming and good-looking, and, she was sure, quite rich.

In her heart, however, Rose knew that this liaison, too, would peter out like all the others. With few exceptions, her relationships with men conformed to a pattern. She and the current man would have a few, enjoyable dates; then he would drop hints that he would like to put the relationship on a firmer footing which always scared Rose off.

Refusing to acknowledge the suspicion that there was an emotional lack in her, she threw herself on her back and thought back over her romances. She had enjoyed making love but, she now had to admit, in a sort of detached way; in a sense she had merely donated her body to whichever man she was in bed with, enjoying his passion instead of fully experiencing her own.

John Flynn, John Flynn, the name flew around her pillow and beat insistently on her brain.

These feelings of excitement and passion were so uncharacteristic that she was almost frightened. It was fantasy, nothing more, she insisted to herself, silly, adolescent stupidity, more suited to a girl of Darina's age than her own. She had read about these mid-life questionings and crises, where perfectly well-adjusted men and women succumbed to outrageous and wholly inappropriate longings. Rose castigated herself for falling into such a cliché. She battered herself with the undeniable fact that she knew nothing about John Flynn now. She would probably hate him. After all, was he not engaged at present in destroying her home?

At ten past two in the morning, Rose threw off the bed covers and went downstairs to the kitchen to make herself a cup of cocoa.

*

John woke so suddenly he hit his head on the wooden bedhead. He was conscious of an overwhelming sense of danger and found it difficult to catch his breath. In the quietness of the bedroom, he could actually hear the muffled, sibilant rhythm of his heart as it thudded against his ribcage. He turned on the bedside light and checked his clock – ten past two. He must have been having a nightmare, he decided, although he could not remember anything about it.

He lay back on his pillows and waited for calm. After a few minutes, the feeling of being in danger was superseded by a feeling of inexplicable physical watchfulness; it was as if the air around the bed had stopped moving and had cleared a space in anticipation of some extraordinary arrival. Each nerve in his body tingled as if connected to its own individual transmitter.

John's daily life was so well under control that such an unusual psychic feeling was very unsettling. Was it something to do with Derek? He concentrated on the steady circle of light which leaked onto the ceiling through the top of the bedside lamp and forced himself to marshal his thoughts. What kind of dream or feeling could have forced its way into his conscious thoughts like that?

His brain refused to calm down. Although he had long ago given up praying in any meaningful way, as a mental exercise, John tried to remember the litanies and aspirations his mother had taught him so long ago.

> *Mirror of justice . . .*
> *pray for us*
> *Seat of wisdom . . .*
> *pray for us*
> *Cause of our joy . . .*
> *pray for us*
> *Spiritual Vessel . . .*
> *Vessel of honour . . .*
> *Vessel of singular devotion . . .*
> *Mystical Rose . . .*
> *Tower of David . . .*
> *Tower of ivory*
> *House of gold*

> *Ark of the Covenant*
> *Gate of heaven,*
> *Morning star . . .*

He stopped, not because he could not think of the next phrase, which was *Health of the Sick*, but because he now realised what had woken him up. *Mystical Rose, Tower of ivory . . .*

Rose. He must have been dreaming about Rose. It was she who was in the air all around him, very close, so close that he could almost feel her hair brush his face. It was a sensation he had not felt for many years.

Although he had thought and dreamed about Rose from time to time, gradually, as the years passed, he had lost heart. His last chance, he felt, had died with Rose's grandmother. Full of hope, he had attended Nancy O'Beirne Moffat's funeral, but as the rituals progressed, John gave up. Rose was not coming.

But she was present in this quiet bedroom as surely as if she were physically lying beside him.

The morning rush-hour in the Drumcondra flat was well under way when Rose, groggy and bleary-eyed, came into the kitchen. Effie was polishing her shoes and Darina was standing at the sink, gulping cornflakes from a plastic bowl. 'Please, Darina,' remonstrated Rose automatically, 'I've asked you at least to sit at the table when you're eating.'

'No time,' said Darina blithely. 'Can I have my money?'

Rose felt physically as exhausted as though she had spent the night running a marathon. 'Hand me my purse,' she replied wearily, then, turning to Effie who was Vaselining her hair at a mirror, 'Is the kettle hot?'

'Just boiled,' answered her friend.

Hoping an overdose of caffeine might stab her with some sort of energy, Rose put two heaped teaspoons of instant coffee into a cup and poured water onto it as Darina came and stood expectantly in front of her, holding out her purse. Rose sighed. 'How much this time?'

'Just the usual.' Rose counted out the money but as she handed it over she noticed that under her arm, Darina was holding a plastic bag. 'What's in the bag?'

'Nothing.' Darina's expression was evasive and Rose went on alert.

'Let me see!'

'Mammy, it's just books.'

'What kind of books?'

'Books I got a loan of and am returning.' Adamant, Rose held out her hand and reluctantly, Darina passed her the bag. It contained a number of illustrated pamphlets of the type given out on the main streets of Dublin by the Hare Krishnas and other sects.

Rose was taken aback. She knew Darina was a voracious reader and inquisitive but up to now she had never, to Rose's knowledge, shown any signs of interest in religion. Any religion. It was all Rose could do to get her out of bed on Sundays to go to Mass. 'What are you doing with these?' she asked.

'Nothing. Just reading them.' Darina was on the defensive now. 'There's no harm in reading them, is there?'

'Of course not! But these—'

'What's wrong with them? Have *you* read them?' And when Rose had to admit she had not, Darina snatched the books back. 'Well, then! You can't criticise them.'

'I hope you know what you're doing. I'd be worried—'

'About what?'

'About you being influenced, Darina, you're still very young.'

'Don't worry about me, Mammy, I'm my own person. Remember? Isn't that what you're always saying you want for me?' Darina's mouth set in a determined line.

'See you two later.' Effie, having completed her toilet, waved as she walked past them out through the door.

'By the way,' Darina seized the opportunity to change the subject, 'since we're talking about me and my influences, have you thought any more about bringing me to Monaghan? You can't put it off for ever. Granny will be dead and I won't even have *met* her.'

Rose did not have the energy to argue. 'We'll see. I was talking to Grandfather last night about it.'

'You were?' Darina's face lit up. 'When are we going?'

Rose began to see a certain inevitability setting in about a visit to Sundarbans. 'When's mid-term?' she asked.

'Around Hallowe'en, I think.'

'We'll see,' Rose repeated.

Darina opened her mouth again to press home her advantage but thought better of it. 'Good,' she said. 'I'm off!' Before she left, she peered into her mother's eyes. 'You look terrible, Mammy.'

'Thanks a lot,' said Rose wryly.

After she was gone, Rose reflected that even the awful drabness of Darina's shapeless uniform of brown and beige could do little to dim her aura of health and beauty. For the second time in twenty-four hours, Rose felt the onset of age.

She had an hour before she had to leave for work and sat at the table, sipping the bitter coffee. It looked as though she could no longer avoid bringing Darina to Sundarbans. On the other hand, as she faced this, she was conscious, deep in her tiredness, of a small bubble of exultation. She might – no, she would – see John Flynn again.

Then it came to her how exactly she would do it.

The amethyst bracelet. She had a perfect right to ask John to return it.

Shortly after her grandmother was admitted to hospital after her fall, Rose's mother had written to her informing her that her aunt Lizzie's jewellery was now in safe keeping in the bank where it should have been all along. At the time, Rose had thanked her lucky stars that her mother had not noticed the missing bracelet and had rushed to write a letter of reply, thanking Daphne for the service.

Her brain was starting to function properly at last and she got up from the table and made a second cup of coffee, slightly weaker this time. This time, she sipped it while gazing out of the window at the snarl of traffic on Drumcondra Road.

On a number of fronts, she thought, this would be a momentous trip. Darina was right – it was high time she saw her real home and, indeed, she should see it before Sundarbans was changed into something horrible and cheap.

Rose decided that, to mark the visit, she would pass on the amethysts to Darina, just as Gus had to herself when she was sixteen. And, she thought, the bubble of excitement expanding, since she could hardly pass on an incomplete set, it would be the perfect excuse to approach John Flynn.

The more she thought about it, the more perfect the timing seemed too, just when there would be a lull in their lives after Effie's wedding.

It would be something for herself and Darina to talk about and to plan.

CHAPTER TWELVE

The concourse of the tiny airport at Charlottetown was gearing up for the flight to Boston. Karen, Derek and Bruno stood awkwardly together in front of the departure gate. 'Thanks for driving us,' said Derek, whose face was pale and sweating and who was puffing a little from the exertions of the hurried walk from the car park. In recent years, he had put on a great deal of weight.

'Isn't that what wives are for?' Karen looked off in the opposite direction. Although she had matured, when she walked into a room, all heads still turned.

'Now don't start, Karen, please, not here.'

'Come on, Dad, we're the last.' Bruno, as blond as his mother, pulled at Derek's arm. Karen's face softened and she threw her arms around him. 'Have a good time, darling, call when you get to your uncle John's, all right? Just to let me know you've arrived.'

'Sure, Mom, we really do have to go now.'

'Goodbye, Karen, I'll call you.' Derek's eyes were aimed a millimetre away from his wife's.

'As you wish.' Her icy tone was diametrically opposed to the one she had used with her son. '*Dad!* Come *on!*' Bruno was clearly embarrassed.

'Coming! Goodbye, Karen.' Derek walked towards the gate. ''Bye, Mom!' Bruno gave his mother another brief hug and followed. Karen watched for a few seconds until the two of them disappeared from view. Then she opened her purse and, shaking out some loose change, walked purposefully towards a pay phone.

The flight to Boston was pleasantly short but by the time the connecting Aer Lingus 707 to Shannon and Dublin was beginning its descent into the Irish capital the following morning, Derek felt wretched. The seats in the aircraft were cramped and uncomfortable for a man of his size and he had not been able to sleep at all. He was so tired, he thought, that if someone had offered him the choice of making a deal worth a million dollars or a clean quiet bed, he would have chosen the latter.

He looked over at Bruno, peacefully slumbering in the seat across the aisle from his own. Bruno's two seat mates had disembarked at Shannon and the boy had put up the armrests and had spread himself across all three seats for the remainder of the flight. His head was propped up on three airline pillows and his down-filled ski-jacket.

'Bruno! Bruno!' Derek called, pulling at his foot. 'Wake up! We're coming in to land.'

The hostess, who was moving along the aisle checking seat-belts, stopped at Bruno's seat and leaned over him, shaking him gently by the shoulder. He started awake, his blue eyes bewildered. Yawning, he struggled upright and secured his seatbelt for the landing. Then he smiled across the aisle. 'Morning, Dad. Sleep well?'

'No, I didn't,' said Derek brusquely. 'Some day they'll invent a machine that'll be comfortable enough for people to ride in and not just for the airlines to make money.'

'Grumpy this morning, I see – don't worry, Dad. The grand soft air of the old country will soon fix you up.' Bruno leaned forward to look out of the window.

Looking out of his own side as the jet continued to lower itself along its flight path, Derek saw that although the morning was bright it had obviously been raining very heavily for quite a time; a tractor travelling along a minor road between the hedges trailed twin fins of spray and the shadow of their own passing momentarily darkened shining mini-lakes in the fields. Derek found himself having difficulty in swallowing, a phenomenon which occurred no matter how many times he flew into Ireland. He did not think of himself as a sentimental man but there was something about coming home which always cracked his businessman's shell, carefully acquired and tempered over the past decade.

He never ceased to wonder at this feeling of glad antici-pation because Ireland always disappointed him. Accustomed now to the free and easy manner of Canadians and North

368

Americans, after a few days at home he always found the closed-in, shuttered approach of his countrymen most frustrating.

He looked again at the back of his son's blond, absorbed head. Bruno had no such reservations about the country of his forebears. He loved Ireland and his Irish relatives in an uncomplicated, open-hearted way, never criticising, never being bored, accepting the lifestyle around Drumboola, so vastly less wealthy than his own, as if born to it.

In the years since he had married Bruno's mother, Derek had grown to love the boy to the extent that he now thought of him as his own. At the beginning, he would spend long moments searching Bruno's face, trying to find traces of John. It was fortunate, he thought, that, although they were not identical, he and his brother were so alike, to the extent that Bruno's parentage could never be questioned. And now, except occasionally when Karen and he hurled insults at one another, it did not seem to matter all that much. Certainly, Bruno had never suspected anything; he loved his dad, loved his uncle, loved his mom, his grandparents and all his Canadian and Irish cousins. He was popular in school and, although no genius, was academically and athletically efficient.

No parents could have asked for a better son but a niggling worry about Bruno's character had replaced Derek's fear of exposure: everything came almost too easily to him. People responded to his physical beauty and wanted to be his friend, to offer him things, to smooth his path. As a result, Derek could not help but wonder what would happen to him if any major obstacle was put in his way. Sven Lindstrom had high hopes that his grandson would follow him and Derek into the family business, but it was clear to Derek that the boy was not tough enough.

He had attempted to discuss the problem with Karen but, more and more, Karen and he could discuss nothing. And with regard to her son, Karen would not hear of any doubts. As far as she was concerned, Bruno was perfect.

The jet finally touched down and, after a few minutes, they were at last outside in the bright windy sunshine. The arrivals formalities were swift and uncomplicated and the pre-booked car was waiting for them. Within forty minutes of landing, the two

369

of them were driving along behind the airport in the direction of Slane and the road north to Monaghan.

'Where's the radio?' asked Bruno, looking in astonishment at the blank dashboard. His hand had reached forward automatically to where it should be.

'You're in Ireland now, son. Car radios aren't automatically supplied over here like they are at home – they're regarded as extras.'

'You don't say! Well, I guess we'll have to talk to each other, then, Dad!'

Derek smiled. 'What do you want to talk about?'

'Oh, nothing. If I think of anything, you'll be the first to know – oh, look, the poor thing!' Bruno's hand flew to his mouth at the sight of a small flock of crows at the side of the road, feeding on the entrails of a fox. The creature lay on its side, mask crushed and bloody, belly ripped open by the birds. 'Do you think it was killed by a car?' Bruno's voice betrayed genuine distress.

'Probably. That's the law of nature. Nothing you can do to change it.'

'It's hardly nature when there's a car involved.'

'Bruno, there are hundreds, perhaps thousands more foxes. Don't worry about that one. Its troubles are over.'

Bruno lapsed into sad silence. His skill and tender-heartedness with animals were legendary among his family and peers. The back yard of the Charlottetown house frequently resembled a menagerie, littered with makeshift cages and containers, all of which housed wounded creatures of one species or another.

The car breasted the hill south of Slane village and the Boyne valley spread to the right and left of them. A pearly mist rose from the river far below, muting the colours of late October; the long, graceful bridge over the river was empty of traffic and Slane Castle, built on the crest of a corresponding hill a couple of miles away, seemed to float above its surrounding forest like a fairy palace. The entire landscape could have been painted by the delicate hand of a water-colourist. 'Oh, Dad, isn't it lovely?' Bruno had clearly recovered from the trauma of seeing the dead fox.

'Sure is, Bruno. This kind of thing is what I miss.'

'But the Island is lovely too.'

'Yes, but I guess the place you're born is always the most beautiful to you, all your life. Just look at that place.' Derek enthused about the castle. 'Wouldn't your mom just love it?'

'Yes.' There was a curious flatness to Bruno's normally light tone and Derek glanced sideways. 'What's the matter?'

'Nothing.'

'Come on, son, I know you. What's wrong?'

'Nothing, Dad, just leave it, will you?'

'I know there's something wrong, tell me—'

'I said leave it!' Derek was taken aback by Bruno's unusual vehemence and they did not speak again until they were coming into the main street of Ardee.

Although he hoped against hope that he was wrong, Derek felt he had a fair idea as to what was bothering the boy. 'Hungry?' he asked, scanning each side of the wide roadway.

'Yeah.' Bruno perked up. It had been a safe question; he was always hungry.

'OK, let's see if we can't find a coffee shop here.' Derek pulled the car into the side of the road and the two of them got out. They walked along until they came to a chip shop with a few stools lined up against a counter fixed to one wall which had just opened for business. Derek ordered two large singles and two coffees and as they munched their way through the chips, again broached the subject of what was possibly on Bruno's mind. 'Something I've been meaning to ask you, son.'

'Yes?' Bruno's attention was engaged by the tremendous explosion of sound as the proprietor of the chip shop heeled a fresh supply into the fat.

'Are you worried about Mom and me?'

'What?' Bruno's head snapped round, his eyes wide.

'You heard me – are you worried about your mom and me?'

'In what way?' Bruno was clearly stalling for time. He stuffed rather too many chips into his mouth at once and Derek felt he had his answer. He must tread very carefully, he told himself, forcing his tired mind into alertness. 'You know we both love you?'

Bruno kept his eyes on his bag of chips and Derek searched hard for something other than a platitude. 'Look,' he said, 'there's

371

no need to be worried. Your mom and I are just going through a bad patch at the moment.' As if fascinated by the movements of the shop owner, Bruno looked over his shoulder towards the huge fryer. 'Bruno!' Derek tried again. 'Look at me!'

'I don't want to discuss this. It's none of my business.'

'But it is your business. I don't want you to worry about us. We'll sort out things in time – we really will.' Derek knew the words sounded hollow but he could not leave matters to lie so lamely and plunged on. 'It's just that adults have very complicated problems, you see—'

'Dad!' There was a real note of desperation now in the boy's voice. 'I told you I don't want to discuss this. Please.'

Defeated, Derek finished what was left in the bag and stood off the stool. 'Let's go, I don't want to get too tired.'

He had to fight drowsiness now as he drove and, at one point, took a bend too widely, narrowly missing a collision with a tractor and trailer coming in the opposite direction. 'Whew!' he said, having swerved the car so violently that it almost ended up in a ditch. 'That was a close one!'

Bruno gazed at him. 'A few of my friends' parents are going through it.' And, when Derek did not immediately respond, 'Divorce, I mean.'

At last it was out in the open. Again Derek cast around for the best thing to say. He knew well which couples in Charlottetown were in trouble. Everyone did in that small, close community. 'Yes, Bruno,' he said, slowing down so his voice could remain calm in face of the engine noise, 'but it's not a fashion that everyone follows just because it's the thing to do. And your mom and I have never even considered divorce.'

Bruno was staring straight ahead. 'But you and Mom don't – don't seem to be very, well, *close* to each other. There's a lot of arguing.'

Derek became seriously alarmed. What precisely had Bruno heard when he and Karen were arguing? He could not bring that up now. 'How long have you been worried?' he asked.

'Oh, a couple of years.'

'I don't know what to say to you to reassure you. All married people have their problems, Bruno, there's no fairytale about marriage. You're nearly sixteen now and I suppose you're

372

old enough to have realised that. And you also know that we did not have the most conventional of beginnings, your mom and I.' He and Karen had decided that as soon as Bruno was old enough, they would let him know that he was already six months old when they married on Karen's nineteenth birthday. They did it to arm him against any snide comments he might encounter in later life and, at least as far as they knew, the strategy had worked.

'That's just it, Dad. Maybe – maybe you got married too young and for the wrong reasons. Like me, for instance!'

Derek was deeply ashamed that Bruno should have kept this burden locked up. 'Oh, Bruno! You were the best reason anyone could ever have to get married. And your mom and I did love each other very much.' Too late, he realised that, in using the past tense, he had committed a fatal error. The car was travelling so slowly that he could see the clusters of worm-eaten fruit in the blackberry hedges which swarmed over the verges. Derek knew he could not salvage the situation but tried his best to sound convincing and reassuring. 'I'm not going to tell you a lie, Bruno,' he said. 'There is no point in pretending that your mom and I have the perfect relationship. We don't. But I want you to understand and believe that we have no plans whatsoever – do you hear me?' He injected as much earnestness as he could summon into his voice. 'I've never considered it and although I can't answer for your mom's secret thoughts, as far as I know, she hasn't either. Do you believe me?'

Bruno's hands were balled in his lap. Derek could see his distress but decided to continue. 'We're just grown-ups now, that's all,' he said slowly. 'All grown-ups start out with great shiny ideas. The object of the exercise is to try to hold on to them and not let the years rub the shine off. Do you understand? I think your mom and I are guilty of letting the shine rub off because we didn't pay enough attention to buffing it. But that doesn't mean, Bruno, that if we work hard enough, we can't get it back again.'

'Sure, Dad. Are we nearly there?' Bruno looked obliquely at him, his face partially hidden by the upturned collar of his jacket. Although he knew he shouldn't, Derek continued anyway. 'Do you feel a bit better now?'

'I didn't feel bad.'

373

'Will you remember that I'm never too busy to talk to you? Will you remember that?'

'Yeah!' To Derek's relief, Bruno grinned. 'Next time you're in a meeting in Halifax with the Japanese I'll fly over and insist on my right to talk to you.'

Derek laughed and put more pressure on the accelerator. 'OK, OK, enough already.'

As he negotiated the last portion of the winding, bumpy road between the high hedges, Derek's fatigue began to tell. He shifted uncomfortably in the seat of the car, far smaller than his own on the Island. He really would have to lose some weight, he thought. Good living and a sedentary lifestyle had contributed, but it was when he had finally managed to give up smoking that the pounds had really piled on.

He wondered how John would look. Probably thin and fit as a whippet, just like he always did. It was almost funny, he thought resentfully, while he was away from Ireland he could go from one end of the year to the other without being affected by his twin, but as soon as he came within a few miles of him, all the old feelings of insecurity surfaced again.

He glanced at Bruno whose eyes were closed. Derek did not know how he could handle it if Bruno learned the truth about his father and turned out to prefer John to himself. 'Only a few more miles,' he said and Bruno sat up.

'Where are we meeting Uncle John?'

'At the house,' Derek replied. 'He's very busy at the moment, something to do with some big deal he's putting together, but he'll come home for lunch and we'll see him then.'

'I hope he takes me fishing.'

'I don't know if it's the weather for it, Bruno, but we'll certainly ask him.'

Derek, who was not remotely interested in fishing, felt a stab of jealousy that 'his' son would be alone – and enjoying being alone – with his twin.

'Are you ready, Darina? For goodness sake, what are you *doing* up there?'

'Nothing!' Darina's muffled reply infuriated Rose, who had spent a sleepless night and had been ready for hours.

'What do you mean, "nothing"?' she yelled. 'Are you ready or not? We'll never get there at this rate.' She drummed her fingers on the kitchen counter. She adored Darina but sometimes it was difficult to keep her temper when faced with her daughter's appalling sense of time. Darina's idea of punctuality was that at the minute she was supposed to meet some of her friends in town, she stepped into the shower. Rose's own boarding-school training followed by the discipline imposed by the airline rosters meant that she could not be late even if she tried.

She was doubly edgy this morning, jittery about the reunion with her mother but more particularly about the forthcoming meeting with John Flynn. She was taking a serious risk doing this, she knew. Perhaps she would have been better to let well enough alone, to live with the perfect bubble of what she had had with John, rather than pricking it to see what was inside. But having taken the decision, she was overcome with impatience – and an unusual fatalism. Whatever would be, would be.

'Good morning!' Willie Brehony came into the kitchen, his dimpled, stubbled face smiling widely, his pyjama jacket gaping over what he liked to refer to as his 'corporation', but which Effie more acidly and correctly called his beer belly.

'Good morning, Willie,' Rose answered perfunctorily.

'I thought ye'd be well gone by now.' Willie ran water into the electric kettle.

'So did I, Willie. It seems Darina has other ideas.'

'Ah, sure, don't be hard on her, seeing the old turrets and baronial towers for the first time. Sure, no wonder she's taking her time. It's a bit like Dorothy going to Oz.'

Rose burst out laughing. 'Oh, Willie, what'll we do for entertainment when you and Effie leave?'

'Who says we're leaving?' He beamed. 'I know a good thing when I see it.'

'Seriously, are you going out to the house this afternoon?'

Willie sighed and settled himself comfortably against the edge of the sink. 'What are Saturdays for, Rose, except for traipsing around building sites in the mud? I could kill that builder! He swore blind the house would be ready in time for the wedding. Now look at us. Lodgers!'

'Go 'way out of that, Willie Brehony! You've been a lodger

all your adult life. A few more weeks isn't going to make any difference.'

'Yeah, but I'm getting used to you, like. Instant family. Good food, women in attendance, run of the whole place.'

'Would you ever shut up and button your pyjama jacket! You're a disgrace to the male species.'

'Yeah, ain't it the truth!' Willie's beatific face looked like a round, happy apple. The kettle boiled and he busied himself making tea. 'Want a cup?' He settled the pot on the cooker and took two cups from the kitchen dresser.

'No thanks,' said Rose. 'I've had my breakfast. Is Effie awake?'

'Yeah, she's awake all right.'

'I'm going up to see what's keeping Darina and to have a word with Effie.'

As Rose climbed the attic stairs to the bedrooms, she reflected she had really meant it when she had said she would miss Willie. It was lovely to have such an uncomplicated, undemanding male about the place. Effie was really lucky. Unexpectedly, her stomach turned over. What was in store for herself over the next few days? She knew she was being absolutely ridiculous, letting her imagination run away with her. *He's married!* She had said to herself over and over again but somehow she could not believe he was. 'If you're not out of there in five minutes, Darina,' she called, 'I'm coming in to get you.' In reply, there was a great flurry of door-banging and of drawers being opened and shut. Rose sighed and knocked at Effie's door. 'Can I come in, Effie?'

'Sure, Rose, I'm awake.'

Effie was propped up on the pillows in the rumpled bed. 'I still don't know how the two of you fit into that small bed,' observed Rose once again.

'Like peaches and cream,' sniggered Effie.

'I just came up to say goodbye. Darina's still not ready.'

'Give her a chance, Rose.'

'I know, I know. First time to the ancestral homestead and all that. I've just had that lecture downstairs from Willie. But how do you think *I* feel?'

'Darina can hardly be expected to understand what exactly you feel about this trip, Rose.'

'You're right. Oh, I wish it was over, Effie. I wish I was there. Or that I'd been there and now I was back – and at least I would know what had worked out.'

'Lookit, Rose, you've been like a hen on a hot griddle for weeks about this trip. Try and bear it for another day or so. This time seventy-two hours, it'll all be over.'

'And I'll be dead. Mother will have run me through with one of her knitting needles.'

'Now, Rose, your mother was perfectly polite when I took that call from her the other day. She said she was looking forward to meeting you and Darina.'

'Yeah. She didn't say that to me, though. She told *me* she hoped I wasn't going to be parading all around the town.'

'Make a few allowances, Rose. The woman is old and feeble now.'

'Not that old! She's only in her early sixties.'

'Well, at least feeble, then. Come on. Give a little, play her game. What harm will it do you for a few days? And anyway, you're enjoying what you're feeling now, right at this minute. Go on, admit it! Aren't you enjoying it? Isn't it the French who say that anticipation is the best part of the love affair?'

'For crying out loud, Effie, I'm a bit long in the tooth to get excited about seeing someone I haven't met for seventeen years. I'm just going to meet him, that's all. To get those amethysts ba—'

'In a pig's eye!' retorted Effie. 'Rose O'Beirne, how long have I known you? This is Effie you're trying to cod! You are still in love with John Flynn.'

'But suppose he's changed beyond all recognition?'

'He probably will, have changed, I mean. But hardly beyond all recognition. And if he has, you won't be in love with him any more, so stop worrying. *Enjoy* this, Rose.'

'Suppose he's married.'

Effie threw her eyes up to heaven. 'I'm sick of this. You could have easily found out if he's married but you haven't had the guts. And you and I both know bleddy well you don't *believe* he's married or you wouldn't be going on like this – like you're sixteen again. Now, shut up, Rose, and go to Sundarbans and meet John and have a wonderful time. And make sure Darina has a wonderful time too.'

377

'It's all very dangerous.'

'So is life, my dear! And when it's not dangerous, it's not worth living. Now, here's my Willie with my tea.' Effie shifted to make room on the bed for the tea-tray. 'Give Rose a kiss, Willie, and get rid of her. If she doesn't leave soon, she's going to drive us all up the walls.'

'All right, all right.' Rose offered her cheek to Effie's husband but just as she did so, the door of the bedroom crashed back against the wall.

'*Boo!*' Rose screamed at the sight of a hideous red and black face surmounted by wild green hair which hovered out on the landing.

'Gotcha!' With a triumphant grin, Darina removed the Hallowe'en mask.

Rose was furious at being seen to be so jumpy. 'Darina, don't sneak up on people like that, you could have given me a heart attack!'

'Easy frighten you!' But then Darina was contrite. 'Sorry, Mammy, it was just a joke.'

'Would you ever go on, the two of you, give my husband and myself a bit of peace?' Effie waved her hand. 'This trip is going to drive all of us mad if you don't leave right now!'

''Bye – come on, Mammy, I'm ready.' Darina tossed the mask aside and pulled her mother out of the room.

Before they left, Rose, whose childhood superstitions had not been entirely overcome, surreptitiously rubbed the forehead of a small stuffed donkey, a present from Spain from one of her colleagues, and which she had named Roger.

Five hours later, Rose's own head felt as though it was being squeezed in a vice. If she didn't get some air soon, she thought, she would suffocate. She looked covertly around the silent group at the kitchen table and wondered for the tenth time since they had arrived what had possessed her to want to come home or to subject Darina to such an exercise in futility. If the morning's conversations between herself, Darina, Daphne and Gus had been replayed from a tape recording, no outsider would ever have guessed the dynamics of what was happening. But under the polite talk and forced joy, it was crystal clear that her mother would never, ever bend; Daphne might pay lip service to 'Christian forgiveness' and 'charity' but Rose now knew for certain that, deep in her heart, Daphne had placed herself and Darina in the roles of permanent outcasts.

The discovery that this upset her was like a physical blow. Over the years, she had come to believe that she was immune to her mother's disapproval but now she found she had been deluding herself. 'Have you heard from Mrs McKenna at all?' she asked as jovially as she could manage. The old housekeeper had been retired for nearly eleven years, but her welfare was the only safe topic Rose could think of at present.

'I believe she's still living with that son of hers,' said Daphne. 'Of course your father is very fond of Fergie,' she added, 'but for myself, I always thought he took advantage of Gus's good nature.'

Rose had had enough. She folded her napkin and placed it beside her unfinished meal. 'I've a bit of a headache,' she said. 'Would anyone mind if I went for a walk?'

'Can I come?' Darina asked immediately.

'It was lovely, Mother,' Rose said then, 'it really was.' In this at least, she could be sincere. Daphne had clearly gone to a lot of trouble. 'It's just that I don't seem to have much of an appetite today,' she added.

'Thank you, Rose.' Her mother acknowledged the compliment with a small incline of her head. 'I do try, you know.'

'Well, as I said, it was lovely. You must give me the recipe.' The main course had been duckling in orange sauce. Daphne smiled faintly and, to Rose, the smile was a spike of disapproval on which she felt herself impaled. *You?* the smile implied. *You don't deserve recipes or anything else.*

Without raising her voice, without saying anything at all, her mother managed to reduce her to a state resembling paralysis. She wanted to scream, to overturn the table, to fling the remains of her dinner in Daphne's face, but finding it difficult to summon the courage even to stand up from the table, she sat on in the resumed silence, staring at her plate. Gus had returned his gaze to his plate and there was no help there.

Darina came to her aid, pushing back her chair so that it scraped loudly on the flagstones of the kitchen. 'Are you coming,

379

so, Mammy?' She turned to Daphne. 'I'm really dying to see the stables and all the rest of it, Grandmother,' she said politely. 'Mammy's told me so much about the whole place over the years.'

'Indeed,' said Daphne. 'Try to imagine it as it was, dear, not as it is now.' She shot a glance at Gus's lowered head.

'Come on, Darina,' said Rose heartily, pushing back her own chair. 'At least we can walk off some of this wonderful lunch. Thank you again, Mother. Maybe we'll join you for coffee in the small drawing room when we get back?'

Daphne raised an eyebrow. 'Certainly, Rose. Although we don't call it the small drawing room any more. Since it is the only habitable reception room in the house, we now refer to it simply as the sitting room.'

'Sure.' Rose attempted to laugh. Since they had arrived, her mother had been constantly gibing at Gus; in the matter of the decline of Sundarbans, it seemed to give Daphne a sort of perverse pleasure to humiliate him in front of his daughter. Rose's instinct was to jump to his defence but she knew that this could only be counter-productive. 'The sitting room it is, then, Mother,' she said as lightly as she could and if Daphne noticed anything peculiar in her tone she did not register it.

At last she and Darina were outside in the fresh air and she wanted to jump and run with the freedom of it. 'God!' she exploded when she was sure they were out of earshot. 'I'm sorry I've exposed you to this, Darina, I really am. We'll get out of here as quickly as we can tomorrow.'

Darina seemed not sure how exactly to react. 'What do you mean, Mammy? She's nice enough, I think. I mean, she doesn't know me yet. It's the first time she's ever seen me, after all, and things are bound to be strange for a while. She's sort of . . . ' She hesitated, searching for the right word. 'I don't know, sort of—'

'Bitchy,' supplied Rose, then instantly regretted it. It was not fair to Darina to place the burden of her own failed relationship on her daughter's young shoulders. 'Sorry,' she said, rubbing the back of her neck, digging the fingers in deeply in an effort to ease the tension headache. 'I didn't mean that. It was just something I said. Mother's had a lot to put up with in her life. She had a lot of expectations when she was younger and I suppose, on all counts, we've failed her.'

'How do you mean?'

'Oh, it's too much to think about. We're not going to be here all that long, let's try to enjoy as much of it as we can.' They had left the house by the back door and she set off, leading the way round the corner of the house. 'It's probably all my fault,' she said over her shoulder. 'We could never get on, Mother and I. Chalk and cheese.'

They came to the front of the house; the flight of stone steps looked greasy and treacherous and Rose put a warning hand on Darina's arm. 'I had no idea things were this bad.'

'It's a bit, well, diseased, all right,' said Darina cheerfully. 'But, oh, it's all so *romantic*!' She raised the small camera she had brought with her – a present from Willie Brehony for her last birthday – and crouching low, snapped the façade of the old house. 'All these years you were telling me about it, you undersold it. It's much, much bigger than I imagined. And much more ancient.'

Rose tried to see the crumbling house through Darina's wide eyes, to see beyond the decay and forlornness and to remember the times she herself had sat in the window of her room, arms around her knees, dreaming down the years to come. 'It's not a bad old place for dreams,' she agreed. 'It just makes me sad to see what's happened to it. It wasn't like this when I was young, although I suppose it was beginning to go downhill. It's the last century we should have seen it. But I do remember, when I was very little, that there used always to be people in the house, guests for dinner, even parties. We hosted the local hunt, you know. Every St Stephen's morning, all the horses and hounds would gather out there on that weedy jungle that used to be a lawn. It's probably been enhanced by my imagination, but I seem to remember, on that day, there were hundreds and hundreds of people all milling around. The sounds were magical, Darina. The hounds would be whining and baying – we always had to lock up our own dogs – and the horses would be stamping and huffing and everyone would be laughing and talking to one another, the people on the horses and the followers on foot.'

She walked carefully down the steps and crossed to the edge of the grass which had been so long uncut that it had reverted to its wild meadow state; thick stands of thistle, dock, cow parsley and dark green nettles contrasted with the pale, feathered heads of a dozen species of weed and grass which bent under the stiff October breeze. Rose pulled the collar of her coat tightly around her throat. 'I always thought Daddy – your grandfather – was the handsomest man there. You should have seen him sit a horse, Darina, when he was younger. He always rode a really big hunter, as wide and as strong as a bear. I had a nanny in those days and, before the hunt moved off, she used to lift me up to sit in front of him for a few minutes. The warm feel of the saddle and the smell of the horse's flesh, so close, and the feel of Daddy's arms around me is something I've always remembered, all my life.' She plucked a piece of grass and rubbed it between her fingers. 'Once, he even allowed me to take a sip from the cup of hot wine he and the other people were drinking. We used to keep special cups for that wine, I think they were silver. I haven't seen them for years – probably sold by now, I suppose. I hated it – the wine I mean – but that day I didn't care about any tastes. I loved it so much that my daddy was allowing me to have it and was giving it to me to drink, holding it so carefully so I wouldn't spill it and spoil my new Christmas dress.'

Rose had tears in her eyes and, not wanting Darina to see them, dashed them away. She moved away from the edge of the meadow. 'I'll get Grandfather to bring you into his gunroom,' she said. 'There's a wonderful tiger head in there.'

'That's a magic story.' Darina pursued her, linking one arm through her mother's. 'You should write it down.'

'I have,' admitted Rose.

'Can I see it some day?'

'If I can find it. I've a lot of stuff bundled away in boxes in the attic. Although I know it's awful, for some reason I could never bear to throw any of it out. I wanted to be a writer once, you know.'

'You still could, Mammy. You could be anything you liked,' said Darina. 'How old were you, that day you were talking about, when Grandfather gave you the wine?'

'I suppose about three. I couldn't have been more than four because the nanny left just before my fifth birthday.'

'Was that when we started to get poor?'

'I expect so. But I didn't really notice, Darina. Children

don't, you know. The changes in the family fortunes were gradual. I know I missed my nanny so I suppose I must have been aware that something was going on, but then when I was seven, as you know, I was sent to Dublin to boarding school and from then on, everything changed.'

'I'm really glad you didn't send me to boarding school,' said Darina quietly. 'I would have *hated* it, I'm sure.'

'It wasn't too bad. I got used to it pretty quickly. It was strange all of a sudden having so many children around.'

Darina pushed back her heavy hair and looked around. 'Where's the pleasure garden?'

'Do you see that pillar there?' Rose pointed to a grey, cylindrical column of stone, the broken tip of which barely showed above the waving grasses. 'That, believe it or not, used to be a sundial. That's how I learned to tell the time. Nanny or Daddy used to lift me up to read it and would teach me the Roman numerals. I could read the sundial long before I could read an ordinary clock. There was an inscription on the face of it. I used to know it, but I can't remember now – something to do with telling only the happy hours.'

'Where's the dial bit?'

'Probably in some antique dealer's shop in Dublin or London,' replied Rose grimly as Darina walked towards the broken piece of stone.

She had been devastated earlier in the day when she had brought the hired car into the open at the top of the avenue. She had tried to prepare herself – and Gus had warned her that things were pretty bad – but the moment she actually saw the house, she realised that her own recollections had been sunlit by time and distance. And in any event, no amount of warning or factual information would have prepared her for the impression made by the decrepit pile of stones which Sundarbans had become since last she had seen it.

At first sight, it did not look fit for human habitation. A small part of the roof had caved in and was shored up with sheets of plastic, which flapped in the wind. Most of the upper-storey windows had been boarded up with plywood, no repairs had been effected to the crumbling balustrades and terrace, the untreated algae had blackened with age and covered a great proportion of the façade like the monstrous fingers of an evil spirit which was inexorably crushing the entire building. To add to the impression of malevolence, as she got closer, Rose saw that the solid brass furniture on the front door had been so long covered in verdigris that it was not green any more but infested with a pale, slimy fungus.

Gus had seen that she was shaken. 'It's not really that bad, poppet,' he had said sadly. 'These new people have had a survey, of course, and although we have wet rot, dry rot, every kind of rot you can imagine, the roof trusses are all right and the foundations and walls and at least some of the interior structures are sound enough.'

Leading Darina to the stables now, she wondered again at how the house could have been allowed to get into that state. After all, there were hundreds and hundreds of acres of farm and forest lands. What had her father been doing? How could he have let the whole thing go so badly down the drain?

At the entrance to the stableyard she found that the wicket gate was locked with a twist of old wire. 'Damn,' she said. 'It was never even shut in my day.' She started to work on the wire.

'You're not that old,' said Darina, giving her a friendly push.

'Today I feel it!'

'Well, we'll go into Carrickmacross and paint the town red tonight.'

'We will not!' exclaimed Rose, still working to straighten out the wire. It was rusty and the red grains were coming off on her hands, staining them. She wiped them on the back of her skirt, not caring that she would dirty it. 'That, my dear, is the last thing we will do. Do you want to have the two of us run out of town on the next stagecoach?'

Darina threw her eyes to heaven. 'I was only joking. I'm sure you're just imagining all this hostility. Things have changed since you were a girl.'

'Not that much.' Rose got the gate open at last and, side by side, they stepped into the stableyard. 'Oh, God!'

The yard was a mess. The stonework needed pointing so badly it was in danger of crumbling; the wooden doors of the locked stalls had rotted in places and showed jagged holes; tall weeds flourished between the cobblestones and in the corners and round the doors and drainpipes; this year's unswept leaves blew this way and that over the compost of the past decade. Darina squeezed her arm. 'Poor Mammy. But I can see what it used to be, like Grandmother said. I really can! Which stall was Tartan's?'

Rose led her to where she had spent so many hours with her pony. The door was padlocked, but one good pull and the holding loop came away from the softened wood of the doorframe. She and Darina entered the dark, cold interior. Even after all this time, the concrete stall still smelled of horseflesh. 'I can *feel* it,' breathed Darina. 'Oh, Mammy, this place is wonderful. I can feel you here!'

Through her sadness, Rose laughed and hugged her. 'Darina, you're such a romantic. I hope you never lose it. But you're right, I was exquisitely happy here – for a time.'

'I bet maybe you've left some of that happiness behind you in the air and that's what we can feel now.' Rose did not feel that any words were necessary in reply. She had never felt closer to her daughter.

'Come on,' she said softly, 'I want to show you some other places that mean a lot to me.'

They closed up the stable, rather unsuccessfully because they could not get the screws of the padlock to stay in their rotted holes. Before they left the yard, she gave her daughter a truncated tour, indicating where the other horses had been kept and also the garage-cum-storeroom where the traps used to be. 'Oh, how wonderful,' said Darina. 'Could we look inside? I've never sat in a pony trap, I'd love to have a go.'

'No,' said Rose shortly, too shortly. 'The door is locked and I don't want to go through all that again.' This was not the reason. The memory of Derek Flynn's strange behaviour in that shed – a memory which had not crossed her mind for years – had suddenly become vivid and she had no wish to linger on it.

She could see Darina was surprised at her vehemence and moderated her tone. 'The traps are all gone, years ago, darling,' she said. 'Sold like everything else which would bring in a few pounds.' She walked in front of Darina, leading her towards the wicket gate.

'Where are we going now?'

'If we're to see everything before the light goes, we have to get a move on,' said Rose. 'I want to show you my favourite spot, the lake. And it's quite a walk.'

They pushed their way through the grasses of the 'lawn' and towards the fringe of the woods. 'I used to sit in my window in the early mornings and watch the deer come out to feed,' remarked Rose just as they got to the first line of trees.

At least the forest, she thought, was almost exactly as she had remembered. The wind, which soughed and snapped in the branches above their heads had, at face level, only the power of a summer breeze. Darina's hair flared alternately white and gold as, moving with a fluidity created by years of ballet lessons, she moved in and out of light pools created by the sun which slanted through the tracery of trunks and boughs. Rose, flooded with love and pride, thought that in this setting and dressed differently, her daughter might have been a young Celtic goddess. She was also filled with gratitude that she could have produced so lovely a creature. *That John Flynn and she together could have produced so lovely a creature*. The butterflies began their erratic dance in the pit of her stomach.

They emerged from the trees onto the shoreline. 'God!' said Darina. 'It's huge! Much much bigger than I imagined. Do we own all this?' The sweep of her arm encompassed the entire expanse of the water in front of her and to both sides. 'The whole thing?'

Rose chuckled. 'Not exactly, as far as I know. To tell you the truth, I haven't a clue what the laws are with regard to lakes. I know we own this bit of the shore, everything which runs along the edge of our own land, but how far out into the water is actually ours, I don't know. We certainly own the fishing rights.' As though it were magnetic, Rose's eyes were drawn to the promontory where she had first seen John. Goose-bumps rose along her arm and on the back of her neck because an extraordinary thing happened: she saw John, standing just where she had seen him that first time on that summer's day. The weather was different, the season, the colours were different, even the lake was different – today it was whipped and frothy – but the feeling of *déjà vu* was so strong, she stopped dead.

'Do you believe in ghosts, Mammy?'

The suddenness of the question, so soon after her own

386

thoughts in that direction, shook Rose. Yet all she saw now was the bare rock of the promontory, its tip breaking up the wavelets which foamed over it. 'Why?' she asked, playing for time.

'No why.' Darina shrugged. 'Just – do you believe in them?'

'I'm – I'm not sure. I'm not prepared to say I know everything about our world, or even this part of it.' Rose struggled to sound matter-of-fact. 'Do you?'

'I believe anything is possible, anything.'

Rose, still recovering from her shock, looked hard into Darina's serious face. 'Listen, Darina,' she asked urgently, 'you're not meddling in anything I should know about?'

'What do you mean?' Darina looked off over the broken water.

'You know what I mean. The occult, spirits, that sort of thing.'

'Of course not.'

Rose remembered the books she had seen in Darina's possession. 'How about that Hare Krishna stuff?'

'That's all in the past. I was just reading them – Mammy, stop worrying! I'm not in the least bit interested in the Krishnas.'

'I do worry about you, Darina, you've become very secretive.' Slowly, they started to walk again, crunching along the pebbles of the shoreline.

'That's not fair, Mammy. I'm sixteen now, I'm entitled to my privacy.'

'But I used to know what you were interested in, what you were thinking about. Now I don't even get to know what you're reading. What are you interested in, Darina?'

'Oh, stuff – lots of things, you know!'

At that moment, Rose realised that somehow, almost without her noticing, Darina had grown in ways she could not follow. Perhaps, she thought, one day Darina would invite her to understand. She would just have to be patient. She did not dare take the conversation any further because to do so would invite comparisons with her own adolescence, and it was almost at this exact age in her own life, that she had discovered she was pregnant. Nevertheless, she could not help herself making one more try. Picking up a stone, she pretended to examine it. 'You'd tell me, wouldn't you?' she asked.

'Tell you what?' Darina's answering expression was careful

387

and Rose had to resist the impulse to press harder, to demand information.

'Just if there was anything I needed to know,' she said.

'Sure, Mammy, of course.'

They parted soon afterwards. Darina wanted to see the boathouse. 'Would you mind if I left you here to have a look at it by yourself?' asked Rose. 'It's only about another two hundred yards ahead – just behind that big clump of rhododendrons you can see jutting out into the water.'

'What are you going to do?'

Good question, thought Rose, who, although distracted by the conversation with Darina, was still slightly shaken by the aftershock of 'seeing' John Flynn. 'I might go into the house, wander around a bit, see just how bad things really are – or I might even go for a drive. See my old haunts.'

'You promised we'd do that together.'

'I'll keep my promise. We can go tomorrow. And don't forget, the next day we've to go into Carrickmacross for that surprise I told you about.' Rose had not yet told Darina that she was giving her the amethysts.

'All right, cheerio. See you in a couple of hours back at the house.' They smiled at one another and Rose turned to retrace her steps.

As she came within sight of the house, she decided to do what, despite her conversation with Darina, she had all along known she would do. She would get into the car and go to see John Flynn.

Having acknowledged the decision, she had to fight to contain a rush of excitement, but it was a losing battle and as she walked towards the car she was sixteen again and just as nervous as though she were going to see him on their very first date. *For Christ's sake, stop it!* she admonished herself. *You're a grown woman with a daughter who's nearly an adult. How would Darina react if she knew her mother was behaving like this?* Deliberately, she imagined Effie's sardonic reaction if told about the 'vision' and its effect.

The keys hung from the ignition of the car, so she had no need to go into the house. Rose roared through a three-point turn and headed off down the driveway. Her plan was to drive to the hotel and simply to have a cup of coffee. Hotel managers were always around and, sooner or later, she was bound to see him. She looked at her watch as she turned out through the gates; it was just after half-past four. Dinner at Sundarbans was at seven. She had plenty of time.

Rose gunned the accelerator. Now that she was actually on her way, she wished the road were straighter and faster. She wished she was on a motorbike instead of in a car. She wished she still believed in the concept of a guardian angel.

'Are you sure you're clear on everything?' George Cranshaw looked at his watch. 'You'd better get a move on, old thing. The plane's due in less than three hours.'

'Yes,' said John. 'I still wish it was you doing this instead of me. You're the one who's made the contact—'

'Nonsense,' said George. 'You'll be absolutely fine. We all have the greatest confidence in you.'

'Well, I hope I won't let you down.'

'Get into that car, *now*!'

'*Heil Hitler!*' John gave a stiff-armed salute and sat in his car. 'You won't forget about Derek?' This three-day trip to Dublin was a last-minute one but crucial to their plans for the Sundarbans project. Although he had been able to have lunch with his twin and Bruno, he was feeling guilty about abandoning them so soon after their arrival. George Cranshaw had promised to entertain the two of them to dinner at the hotel that evening.

'I won't, don't worry. It's all sorted out,' George said cheerily. 'I'll explain to your brother that this weekend is the only one Mr Pickford could spare.'

'I've done that already. I think Derek understands – he's in business himself, after all. By the way, don't let him talk you into getting involved. Since he discovered he had a head for business, Derek can't bear to let anything pass him by and even in the space of one short conversation, I got the impression he wouldn't mind coming in on this one.'

The driver's window was open and George leaned on the sill. 'You wouldn't like that, I know. Although, to be fair, his money's probably as good as the next man's—'

'If he's in, I'm not.' John could see his vehemence had surprised George. 'It's just that in business,' he said, more moderately, 'Derek and I would never see eye to eye. It would be a disaster.' Although he felt no need to explain it to the other man, this was only partially true; in latter years, the physical distance between himself and his twin had conferred an equilibrium on their relationship which John had no desire to upset.

'Don't worry,' said George. 'Now go on – and do try to enjoy yourself while you're in Dublin. You don't have to live in this man's pocket, you know. Bring him around, show him a good time, by all means, but take the opportunity to ditch him now and then. Go out, get drunk, let your own hair down for a bit! You deserve it.'

'Be careful, I might never come back.'

'Oh, you'll come back all right!' With one hand George beat a little tattoo on the window sill. 'Good luck, now. And be gentle, dearie! Part him *nicely* from all that lovely money.' He stood back and waved as John started the car and drove it out through the twin pillars of the hotel gateway.

John turned his mind to the meeting ahead. It was the first time he had ever met anyone who owned a private plane. He hoped the man would not be too intimidating.

As the car picked up speed, he found the breeze through the open window a little nippy and, since the knob on the winder which controlled the driver's window was missing, he had to slow down again to concentrate on the difficult task of closing it by means of the remaining stump. Thus engaged, he did not see, in his rear view mirror, the brand new Ford Escort which was turning in at the gateway through which he had just left.

Rose switched off the engine and took a deep breath. She had to be calm not to attract attention. Through the windscreen, she examined the spruce façade of Willow House. It had changed beyond all recognition from what she remembered of her visits here when she was a child when, in her view, it had been a homely, dull little place, insignificant when placed alongside the much grander scale of Sundarbans.

Now the situation was reversed. Willow House had been transmogrified into a small, frilly palace. Its walls blazed with Virginia creeper, at present at the height of its crimson glory; swagged curtains and pelmets hung inside all the windows; the external woodwork gleamed with fresh paint and the brasses on the front door were obviously given daily attention. The tarmacad-amed car park was placed between immaculate twin lawns, their symmetry broken only by crescent-shaped rosebeds and herbaceous borders. Even the new extension was tasteful: built in the same style as the original house, it was attached to its parent via a curvilinear 'Victorian' conservatory and showed its newness only because the stone had not yet aged sufficiently. 'Well done, George,' said Rose to herself.

She had always been fond of George and Dorothy Cranshaw. Mrs Cranshaw was the only grown-up Rose had ever met who went about barefoot or in sandals, even in winter, and who allowed children to dip their fingers into her jars of home-made preserves and jams and who didn't mind if, as a result, you got the furniture sticky.

She took a deep breath. It was time to go in – but before getting out of the car, she remembered she did not have even a comb with her and checked her appearance in the driving mirror. Luckily, the new, short hairstyle she had worn for the past six weeks had been very well cut and although she had been climbing about in the wind through woods and stableyards, her hair had fallen back more or less into place. Well, she thought, running her fingers through it, it would have to do.

As she entered the lobby of the hotel, she felt as wary as a cat – and strung so tightly that if anyone were to touch her, she might actually snap. Suppose John was the first person she met?

But the lobby was deserted. She crossed to the little reception desk and tapped the bell, the tinny note of which rang far too loudly for her super-sensitised ears.

A door opened behind the desk and a girl came through. 'Good afternoon,' she said pleasantly. 'May I help you?'

'Is it possible just – just to have a coffee?'

'Certainly,' said the girl, pulling a small pad towards her. 'Would you like anything with it?'

'No, thank you. Coffee'll be fine.' To her own ears, Rose's voice sounded false and hysterical but the girl did not seem to register anything unusual.

'I'll have it brought to you,' she said. 'Would you like to

have it in the lounge? Or you could use the sitting room or – it's such a lovely bright day – why not the conservatory?'

'The sitting room,' said Rose, but she had to clear her throat. 'Sorry, I'll have it in the sitting room.'

'Do you know where it is?' asked the girl.

'Yes, indeed,' said Rose. 'I haven't been here for a while but I assume it's still through that door over there?'

'That's right,' said the girl. 'Take a seat and it'll be along shortly.'

Rose let herself into the sitting room in which Mrs Cranshaw had let her loose many times as a child. To her astonishment and pleasure, it had not been changed at all. The room was perhaps smaller than she had remembered but it still looked every bit as well stocked as the middle-eastern bazaars pictured on the postcards her airline colleagues regularly sent her. There was more greenery than she remembered; plants hung, trailed and sprouted from every space not taken up with the other treasures but everything else was just as she remembered – the landscapes and portraits on the walls, the china elephant, the samplers, the wooden ducks, bells, thimbles, photographs, stuffed birds, trophies, coins, medals and the egg collection.

Too nervous to sit down, she wandered around, touching this and that, picking up the family photographs, putting them down again without examining them. She was standing in front of one of the butterfly cases when she heard the door opening behind her. 'Good afternoon!' said a male voice.

Rose whirled around but it was not John.

George Cranshaw stood just inside the door, the coffee tray in his hands. There was a moment while he tried to place her than his face lit up in joyous recognition. 'Rose! I hardly knew you! You're so – so *grown-up*!'

Rose laughed. 'Well, George, I am that! Grown-up, I mean, although sometimes I must admit I don't feel it.'

He put the tray down on a little brass table and stood with his hands on his hips. 'Let me look at you. Well,' he said jovially, 'you look wonderful, life certainly seems to be treating you well. Still footloose and fancy free, I suppose? Suits you, Rose. Being a career woman, I mean.'

'Thank you,' said Rose. Still very nervous, she laughed

again. 'You don't look so bad yourself, George. How's Dorothy?'

'Blooming, as usual. Wait here, I'll get her, she'll be absolutely delighted to see you. You're quite a stranger in these parts, Rose. How long has it been? I'll have to have a word with old Gussie. I was talking to him at length only two days ago – I suppose you know what's been going on about the Big House?'

'Daddy's thinking of little else.'

'Maybe that's why the old so-and-so didn't think it worth his while to mention you were coming. How long are you staying? I'm sure Dorothy will want to organise something.'

'It's a flying visit. Only till Monday, I'm afraid.'

'Well, maybe we can still all get together. Hang on and I'll get her.' He bustled off and Rose poured the coffee into the cup. Her hand was shaking. It was not really so strange that Gus had not mentioned her visit, she thought. And it was clear he had certainly not told his old friend about Darina. It was something she had not reckoned on, a reunion with the Cranshaws.

'Rose, my dear! How lovely.' Dorothy Cranshaw's warm, motherly voice cut into her reverie.

'Hello, Dorothy,' she said, the years falling away. Again she was ten years old and coming here for a jam tea.

European-style, Dorothy kissed her on both cheeks. 'You're gorgeous, Rose. You gorgeous, gorgeous girl! I always knew you'd turn out to be a smasher.'

'Please, Dorothy.' Rose laughed. 'You'll turn my head. You look great yourself. You haven't changed a bit.'

'Phooey. I'm old and wrinkled but the great thing is I don't give a fiddler's. That's one thing about growing old, isn't it, George?' She took her husband's hand and squeezed it warmly. 'A pair of old cushions, George and I. We bolster each other up, tell each other we're improving like old wine, all that sort of tosh.'

'But it's true – you both look lovely.'

'Sit down and tell us all your news, Rose.' Dorothy subsided into one of the patchwork-covered armchairs, her peasant skirt billowing around plump brown knees. Her hair was tied up in a scarf like a babushka's around her head and Rose thought fondly that she still resembled an illustration from *National Geographic*.

'I've a few things to do, so I'll leave you girls to have a bit of a natter,' said George. 'Will I bring another cup, Dorothy?'

393

'No, dear, I can't stop. There'll be chaos in the kitchen if I stay away too long. Rose and I will just do some preliminary catching up and we'll have a nice long chat when she comes back. You will come back, to dinner or lunch, some time before you go?'

'See you later, Rose,' said George. 'Sorry, but although this might appear to be a lull, this time of day is only the calm before the storm in the hotel business.'

'I understand, George. Please, I had no intention of interrupting your work.'

'Don't be silly. We would have been furious if you hadn't dropped by. Wouldn't we, Dot?' George smiled and left the room.

'We certainly would,' said Dorothy comfortably. 'Now, my dear, tell us *all*! You're an air hostess? This much, at least, I know. We see a bit of your daddy – but not so much of Daphne in the last few years. Her health's not great, I believe?'

'I – I'm not sure, to tell you the truth. She seems sort of faded, somehow.'

'Poor Daphne,' said Dorothy. 'I blame myself for not going up there often enough but with this place, what with one thing and another . . . Do you like what we've done with it?'

'It seems marvellous, Dorothy. It really does. Is business good?'

'Booming, thank goodness. Must give you the grand tour. It's a pity John's away – we've a terrific young manager, you know, been with us for years, since he was very young. He grew up with the hotel so to speak.' Dorothy drew her knees up under her: 'But of course – I forgot – you probably knew him when you were young. John Flynn? He used to live in your gate lodge.'

Away? He was away? 'Yes,' said Rose faintly, 'I did know him all right. You say he's away?'

'Gone to Dublin – living it up at the Shelbourne, lucky thing – to try and weasel money out of some Isle of Man tycoon and a commercial bank for this project they're all involved in. George says you're only staying until Monday. That's a pity.' Her eyes crinkled mischievously. 'I'd love you to have met him. He's very eligible.'

'Now that you mention it,' Rose tried to keep her elation from showing, 'I suppose he must be the same age as me. So in

394

a place like this with eligible men so thin on the ground, it is amazing he never got married.'

'Yes,' said Dorothy ruminatively. 'I've never understood how he's escaped for so long. He's grown up to be terribly good-looking, you know – tall with that lovely, curly Celtic thing. Are you sure you won't stay the extra day and meet him?' She giggled.

Rose laughed. 'Unfortunately, Dar—' She had been about to say that Darina had to be back in school on the Tuesday morning but stopped herself.

'Yes?' Dorothy was looking at her expectantly.

Rose was embarrassed, elated, triumphant, fearful, excited, all together. 'I do have something I'd like to tell you, Dorothy,' she blurted out.

'Yes, dear?'

'It's a bit difficult – it's been the most well-kept secret in this district for nearly seventeen years . . . '

'Could I guess, perhaps?' Dorothy's joshing tone was replaced by gentleness and her brown face was serious.

'I beg your pardon?' Rose was nonplussed.

'Could it perhaps be to do with why you were taken out of school and went away – or were sent away – to London when you were only sixteen?'

'How did you know?' Rose gasped.

'Darling, the world turns even for old fogeys like George and me. We guessed,' she said simply.

'Do Mother and Daddy know that you know?'

Dorothy shook her head. 'I don't think so – in fact I'm sure that they don't.'

'Does anyone else in the area know?'

'You never came home, Rose and, well, at the time, that caused a bit of gossip – that was only natural – but I don't think anyone really knew for sure. I'd be careful, though, if I were you – that is if it still matters to you that people shouldn't know. Someone like you from somewhere like Sundarbans is always going to be a focus of interest in this district. The gossip could be revived in an instant.'

Rose realised that Dorothy did not know that she had kept Darina. 'I'm very grateful, Dorothy.'

'For what?'

'Oh, I don't know, for not making judgements, for not discussing it with Daddy.' She paused. 'But there is something you should know.' Then she found it difficult to continue, even after all these years, even in such obviously sympathetic company. It was something to do with being on her home territory. The protection of the Big House was very deeply ingrained. 'There is something,' she repeated. She looked Dorothy in the face. 'I didn't give up my baby. My daughter.'

The older woman's eyes widened but Rose saw nothing in them which prevented her from continuing. 'I kept her, Dorothy. Her name is Darina, she's sixteen, she's the most lovely thing in the world – and she's at Sundarbans right now. I brought her home this morning for the first time.'

'Well, I'll be damned!' said Dorothy. 'Sorry,' she added, grinning, 'not exactly the most appropriate of comments. But you've taken the wind out of my sails. I had no idea.' She hugged her knees. 'Well, isn't your daddy a close one! All the times he's been up to see you in Dublin – he must have seen your daughter too?'

'They love each other.'

'And your mother? Never mind,' said Dorothy quickly, 'it's none of my business.' She unwound herself from the colourful chair and crossed the floor to give Rose a hug. 'Congratulations, my dear, if it's not too late to offer them. I'm delighted for you, and I'm proud of you too. It can't have been easy.' She stood back and held Rose at arm's length. 'You don't mind if I tell George?'

'Not at all, Dorothy. I'm through hiding Darina. She's a person in her own right now. But I'm going to have to take it gently. I don't think Mother has forgiven me – nor ever will.'

'Give her time, my dear. I'll help, I'll work on her.' Then, when she saw the look of dismay in Rose's eyes, she chuckled. 'You might be thirty-odd, Rose, but your face is as transparent as a baby's. Don't worry, I'm not going to go blunderbussing in like big Mrs Busybody. Give me a bit of credit for all my years in the hotel business. And I can assure you, working in a kitchen teaches you a few things about tact and diplomacy. Now, that reminds me, the kitchen. I'll have to leave you, my dear. But you will come back to see us before you leave? Maybe you'll all come to dinner – including Darina?'

Rose had a sudden vision of her mother's face at a public dinner table which included her unacknowledged granddaughter. 'Thank you very much for the invitation, Dorothy,' she said, 'but maybe next time. It's all a bit much at the moment, you know . . .'

'I can well understand. Well, definitely the next time, then?'

'Definitely!'

They kissed and hugged and Rose escaped to her car.

On the way back to Sundarbans, she drove recklessly. It was just after six by the clock on the dashboard and the setting sun dazzled her occasionally as she drove around the twisting, uneven roads. But she did not care. It had been wonderful to confide in Dorothy Cranshaw about Darina. And she knew where John Flynn was – right now. Dorothy had given her the perfect entrée, she could lift up the telephone and call him from Sundarbans or from any call box.

As she reached the bottom of the avenue into the house, she glanced at the empty gate lodge, sturdy and picturesque as always, but wearing a forlorn cap of moss on its slate roof. Like a douche, came the reminder of what Dorothy had said about him: *He's grown up to be terribly good-looking, you know – tall with that lovely, curly Celtic thing.*

Just like Darina.

She would have to be very, very careful.

The sun was bright orange, sinking fast towards the line of trees which rimmed the far end of the lake. Derek had left the car parked by the dark, shuttered gate lodge and he and Bruno had walked cautiously up the driveway to Sundarbans. John having filled him in about the development scheme for the old place, Derek was curious to see the state of the house, but he had no wish to meet either the Colonel or his thin, bitter little wife. So, in order to view the house from a safe vantage point, he had led Bruno towards the lake through the woods, by the path he and John used to take when they were boys.

The wind had dropped and it was very peaceful under the tree canopy as they meandered along. Despite the slowness of the pace, Derek was becoming breathless. He really had to do something about his weight, he thought mournfully. He would start a diet, the third so far this year, on the first morning after he got back to Charlottetown. 'You sure you don't want to come with me to Hamburg?' he asked Bruno, who was pacing surefootedly just ahead of him, rhythmically beating at the trailing branches and vegetation which impeded their passage along the track. Even in Derek's boyhood, this path had been barely wide enough to take one person.

'Thanks, Dad,' Bruno called back, 'but I'd prefer to stay here. I find I'm not a city man myself.'

Derek smiled at the grown-up terminology. He himself was not exactly looking forward to the trip. He was hoping to clinch a deal for the supply of upmarket ski-wear, but he was not all that keen on negotiating with foreign suppliers. He had picked up only a smattering of German and, although the people with whom he normally traded in Germany spoke excellent English, he knew he would find the whole operation a strain.

On the other hand, Derek rarely trusted any of the bigger deals to any of his subordinates. After his marriage, he had begun on-the-job managerial training in his father-in-law's store and much to everyone's surprise, including his own, had shown himself adept at business; and in the years he had helped Sven Lindstrom build his Charlottetown store into a small chain throughout the Maritimes, his skill as a broker, unsuspected in his youth, had proven formidable.

He ducked just in time to avoid being hit by a supple branch which had recoiled from Bruno's swinging hand and sudden cramp bit into the muscles between his ribs, so painful that he almost cried out. He forced his seized body in a backward arch and felt the cramp gradually ease. Bruno, who had gone on a few paces, returned, his face concerned. 'Are you all right, Dad?'

'I'm fine, son, I'm fine,' gasped Derek, straightening to a normal posture. 'Just give me a minute, OK?'

'We worry about you, you know. You should get fit, Dad. It's not hard – I'll help you.'

'It's not hard for you, maybe. Pretty hard for me when I sit at a desk all day. And don't forget I've only one lung. What do you expect me to do, get on a ball team?'

'You could walk to the office—'

'In winter?'

'Sure, why not? Plenty of people walk.'

'Stop fussing.' He saw Bruno's crestfallen expression and moderated his tone. 'All right, I'll see what I can do. Project for the winter, eh?'

They set off again and were soon at the edge of the water, right where the overgrown lawn met the trees. 'Oh, Dad! Look at that sky, isn't it beautiful?'

'Yeah – look at the house, though.' Derek whistled, a long low sound of surprise. 'Looks as though nothing on earth could save that lot. I'm going up to have a closer look – OK?'

'Oh, can't we just walk along by the water? It's so quiet and peaceful here.'

'Let's make a deal. I'll go take a closer look at the house, you take your nature walk, OK? We meet back here in twenty minutes.'

'Sure, thanks, Dad.'

Bruno wandered along the shoreline, stopping to pick up a pebble, kicking at a clump of grass and then peering closely to see what emerged from it. He was searching for shells, insects, water creatures in the shallows. He was so absorbed that he did not see he was being observed until he was only a few yards away from the observer and some sixth sense made him look up.

A piece of rock jutted out into the lake and on it stood a tall slim girl, her back to the flaming sky. The girl's face, turned towards him, was in shadow but her long curling hair, lit from behind, was shot through with tongues of gold.

A peculiar sensation spread through Bruno's bloodstream: starting at the pit of his stomach, it moved right through his body until he felt as though he was filled with air. The skin of his arms and on the back of his neck rose in goose-bumps. He walked right up to the girl and put out his hand. 'Hello.'

'Darina!' Rose pushed open the wicket gate of the stableyard. 'Are you here, Darina?' It had been dark for more than an hour and Rose's mother, conserving dinner, was becoming ill-tempered.

'Damn!' Rose closed the gate again. Where was that girl? She could be anywhere, she panicked. 'But she has a watch, dammit, and she knew dinner was at seven!' In her frustration, she uttered the words aloud.

Grimly, she set off for where she had last seen Darina on

the shores of the lake. 'I'll kill her!' she muttered as she ploughed through the tall grasses of the lawn. Then, in front of her, she thought she saw movement at the line of trees. 'Darina!' she called again.

To her relief, there was an answering call. 'Yes.'

Rose waited until Darina had run across the lawn. 'Where were you?' she asked angrily. 'Mother's furious. The dinner is ruined.'

'Sorry, Mammy,' said Darina breathlessly, 'I'm really sorry, I just got interested and time flew. My watch had stopped.' She held it out apologetically but Rose was too cross to look. 'Interested in what? What were you *doing* all this time?'

'Nothing.'

Something about the way she said it made Rose snap to attention. 'Come on,' she muttered. It was too dark to take a good look at her daughter's face but, again, she felt Darina was hiding something. It was more than a suspicion, she was sure of it.

They went into the house by the kitchen door and as soon as she had closed it, Rose turned on her daughter. 'Now, no lies, what were you doing?'

'Nothing, Mammy, honestly.' But Darina's eyes were shining and her whole body emanated a glow which was almost visible. She looked so marvellous that Rose was genuinely taken aback.

'I – I don't believe you,' she said weakly.

'Oh, Mammy, I just love Sundarbans,' cried Darina. 'It's the most wonderful, wonderful place I've ever seen in the whole world.'

CHAPTER THIRTEEN

Sunday at Sundarbans was a trial for Rose.

It started badly when, at the last moment, Daphne could not face going to Mass locally as part of a family which included Darina. Instead of going to Rock Chapel as she and Gus would normally have done, they all drove miles to a small village church in the neighbouring county of Cavan.

Rose was furious with her mother. Her instinct was to have it out with her but, for Darina's sake, she gritted her teeth and tried to behave as though nothing untoward had happened. Luckily Darina, who since yesterday seemed to be living in a dream world, had not been aware of the last-minute change in plans and did not seem to see anything unusual in the distance travelled. Covertly, throughout the Mass, Rose had watched her daughter: Darina was bubbling with secret excitement, which, if she did not know better, Rose might have interpreted as the first flush of romantic love.

'Happy?' she asked now. Having eaten lunch and browsed through the Sunday papers, the two of them were temporarily – and mercifully, as far as Rose was concerned – free of Daphne. After lunch, Rose's mother had confessed to the onset of one of her headaches and had retired to her room to lie down. Gus was poring over figures at his desk in the gunroom.

'Am I happy?' replied Darina, standing up from her chair and stretching like a cat. 'Oh, yes! I'm so pleased to be here at last. I can feel all the history going right into my pores.'

'Don't go overboard.' But Rose was pleased. 'What would you like to do this afternoon?' she asked, crossing the room to look through the sitting-room window. 'It's a gorgeous day, we should get out and about.'

'Oh, I think I'd just like to walk by myself in the grounds again. It's wonderful out there in the woods and by the lake.'

Rose, hearing a note of carefulness, looked around sharply but her daughter's expression, while beatific, seemed innocent enough. What was she up to? Could she have met someone? 'Why so keen on being by yourself all of a sudden?' she asked casually.

'I'm not! It's just – it's just that I can think better when I'm by myself. And I have a lot to think about,' she added as if this explained the entire situation.

Rose knew her daughter well enough to accept that it would be a waste of time interrogating her any further. 'All right,' she said, 'but I'm disappointed – I was looking forward to your company this afternoon.'

The plea was wasted because, immediately, Darina shot to her feet. 'Thanks . . . thanks for understanding.' Swiftly, she crossed the floor and gave Rose a hug. 'Bye!' Almost before Rose could draw breath, she was gone.

Rose sighed and looked around the empty room. What now? She had not been exaggerating when she told Darina she had been looking forward to a drive through the countryside with her. It would not be the same on her own.

She would have to get out, however, anywhere which would take her from under the same roof as her mother. It occurred to her to go back to Willow House, but then she changed her mind. Dorothy and George might get suspicious. And anyway, they had assured her that John would be away until Tuesday.

Perhaps her father would come out with her? Rose went to the gunroom and, receiving no reply to her knock, gently opened the door. 'Daddy?' Gus's head drooped on his chest as he snored gently in his chair.

Glumly, Rose closed the door and went to the car.

Darina returned in plenty of time for dinner. Throughout the meal, her manners were impeccable but, to Rose, she again emanated that strange evanescence she had taken on after her walk of the previous afternoon. It was puzzling. As far as Rose had been able to ascertain from Gus, there were no boys of Darina's age in the locality. Unless one of the townies had been trespassing? She resolved that if Darina asked to go out again that night, she would not allow it.

But the question did not arise. After dinner, Darina, without being asked, went with the rest of them to the sitting room where

402

they all spent a quiet, relatively peaceful evening. Gus had invested in a television set and the four of them drowsed in front of it until bedtime.

At least, Rose, her mother and father drowsed while Darina simmered.

Next morning, Rose woke with a sense of anticipation. Recognising instantly that it had to do with the possibility of a meeting with John Flynn, she jumped out of bed before it could take hold. Her adolescent behaviour of the past few days, she told herself firmly, would simply have to stop. Nevertheless, as she bathed, dressed and breakfasted with Darina, John Flynn, like a background hum, intruded on any unguarded thoughts.

She was relieved to say goodbye to her parents. Although there had been no more rows and, in general, she was pleased at the way the visit had gone – especially from Darina's point of view – she was looking forward to a resumption of normal life. 'How are you feeling this morning?' she asked Darina as they drove towards Carrickmacross.

'Fantastic!' Darina pulled out her hair from under the collar of her jacket and shook it loose. 'I had a wonderful time, Mammy, thanks for bringing me.'

It was on the tip of Rose's tongue again to question her about what had particularly delighted her but she suppressed the urge. If anything unusual had happened, Darina, she hoped, would tell her in her own good time. 'Nearly there,' she said as they approached the outskirts of the town. 'Excited?'

'Yes. What can it be – in a *bank*? Are you a secret millionaire, after all, and going to share your fortune?'

'Not quite.' Rose laughed. 'Just wait and see. But I think you'll be pleased.' In her handbag, Rose had the receipt for one of Gus's safety deposit boxes and also a letter, authorising the bank to give her access to it. 'I'll give you a clue,' she said gaily as she pulled the car into a space in front of the bank. 'Think purple. And there's one more thing,' she added, 'today is not the end of it. What you get today will be half – well, two-thirds.'

'It has to be money, then,' said Darina in high excitement. 'Fifty-pound notes are purple.'

Rose gave Darina the pleasure of opening the jewellery case and, with great satisfaction, watched her daughter's awed expression as, reverently, she drew out the amethyst necklace. 'Oh, Mammy, they're beautiful, are they real?' She held the stones up to the light.

'They're real all right. I'll tell you all about them on the way home. I was given the set for my sixteenth birthday and after you were born, I always planned to pass them on to you. I hope that in turn you'll pass them on to your daughter. There's a bracelet too, by the way. Sorry it's not in the set at the moment but I know where it is and I'll be getting it back for you—'

'But it's here.' Darina pulled it out.

Rose's stomach turned. 'It couldn't be,' she said stupidly, her brain denying the evidence of the dangling stones.

'Is this not it, then?'

Dumbfounded, Rose took the bracelet and stared at it. How had it been replaced? John would never have approached her mother, so the only way for him to have returned it was via Gus. But why had her father not told her? 'Sorry, I must have made a mistake,' she said faintly. 'This is it all right.' All the lightness seemed to have gone out of the day. She did not want to ruin the moment for Darina, however, and as she handed back the bracelet, plastered a smile on her face. 'How could I have forgotten? I must be in my dotage. Do you really like the set?'

'It's the most lovely thing I've ever seen.' Carefully Darina replaced the jewels on their velvet.

Feeling like a marionette, Rose continued to smile as she locked the safety deposit box and returned it to the bank official.

Every so often during the journey back to Dublin, Darina withdrew the jewellery from its case and played it through her fingers.

Seeing the bracelet again, Rose remembered that it was the only item of the set she had worn. A great anger started in her. She should have been told that John had sent it back. She had promised him, after all. Who knew what might have happened?

The first thing she would do after they got home would be to telephone Gus to ascertain when precisely he had received it and – more to the point – why he did not think it worth his while to mention it. By the time they let themselves into the flat, she was in a fever of impatience to get a moment alone to telephone Sundarbans and, somewhat to Darina's surprise, consented immediately to her request that she be allowed to visit one of her friends to show off the amethysts.

The moment the door closed behind her, Rose, who had not yet taken off her coat, picked up the telephone. Gus was surprised to hear her so soon. 'Is something wrong, poppet?'

Rose tried to control her anger. 'Not really, Daddy, I just have something to ask you.'

'Fire ahead.'

'It's about the amethysts.'

'They were there, I hope. Your mother—' A note of alarm had crept into Gus's voice.

'No, nothing like that, Daddy, they were there, all right. But in a way that's just the point. They were all there.' She paused to let the significance of what she had said sink in. Then, after a few seconds when her father had not reacted, she said, 'Did you hear me, Daddy? They were *all* there!'

'I'm sorry, Rose, I'm obviously missing something.'

Gus sounded mystified and Rose's conviction wavered. 'You really don't know?'

'No, please tell me what you're on about.'

Oh, God, thought Rose, he genuinely didn't have anything to do with it. And, after all, it had been her mother who had lodged the jewellery in the bank. 'I'm sorry, Daddy,' she said, 'there's been some misunderstanding. Is Mother there?'

'Hold on, I'll get her.'

The wait for her mother seemed interminable. 'Hello, Mother,' she said when Daphne at last came to the line. 'There's something serious I need to ask you. You know I was giving Aunt Lizzie's amethysts to Darina today? Well, I thought the bracelet was missing – in fact I know it had been, but it was there. With the set, I mean, the set was complete.' She heard herself starting to gabble, making a mess of it.

'So?' Daphne's tone was frosty.

'So how did the bracelet get to be with the rest of the set, Mother? It was you who put the jewellery into the box.'

'I resent your tone of voice, Rose.'

'Sorry, Mother.' Rose clenched her jaw. 'I didn't mean to interrogate you. But it's a mystery I'd just like to clear up. I was absolutely sure that bracelet was, er, missing . . . '

'If you must know, it was I who found it,' said Daphne coldly. 'If you weren't so careless, Rose—'

'But where? Where did you find it?'

'It came back from the hospital with your grandmother's things. She must have picked it up from where you dropped it, or lost it.'

Nancy? Nancy had it? 'I – I see,' stammered Rose, then, making a great effort, 'I'm sorry to have made such a fuss, Mother, it's just that I had no idea—'

'As I was saying, before you so rudely cut me off, Rose . . . '

Rose then had to endure a stiff little lecture about her character defects. All the while her brain wheeled. John may have remembered she was close to her grandmother – because she had told him so – and maybe, since she herself would not accept any of his letters, he had sent the bracelet to Nancy?

She realised there was silence on the line. Daphne had clearly finished her lecture. 'Sorry again, Mother,' she apologised, 'and thanks a lot for looking after it for me. I appreciate it.'

They said goodbye and hung up.

Rose collapsed onto the telephone seat. She stared at the geometrical design of the wallpaper on the wall opposite as the implications of the call sank in. John had called in the pledge she made him with the amethysts.

And how had she responded? Simply by continuing to ignore his letters.

Afraid that the phone might ring and delay her call to the Shelbourne, Rose left the receiver off the hook while she looked up the number. Her finger was shaking as she dialled.

'Shelbourne Hotel, may I help you?' The sing-song tone of the operator answered after just one ring. 'May I – may I speak to Mr John Flynn, please?' The receiver felt warm in Rose's sweaty hand.

'Is he a guest at the hotel, madam?'

'I believe so.'

'One moment please.' The line went dead for a few seconds and the operator came back on. 'Room 204. Ringing for you.'

Rose listened to the single ring sounding over and over again in his room and told herself that, of course, John would not be in his room at one o'clock on a Monday afternoon. Trying to contact him at this time was stupid. 'No reply, I'm sorry,' sang the operator, cutting in abruptly. 'Would you like to have the gentleman paged, madam?'

'Yes please.' The receiver again dead in her ear, Rose spent the next five minutes picturing the bellboy moving through the tea-lounge, lobby and bar of the hotel, calling out John's name. And what if he was actually there? Stomach churning, she tried to predict how he would react to the page. Embarrassment, perhaps – or maybe curiosity? Perhaps he was with some woman and would be annoyed at being interrupted.

She had had no time to rehearse what she might say but hung onto the peg that it was Dorothy Cranshaw who had suggested she call.

'No reply to the page, madam.' The operator cut in again. 'Would you like to leave a message?'

'No, thank you, I'll call back later.'

'Thank you.'

She telephoned three times during the afternoon. Luckily, Effie and Willie were out taking advantage of the public holiday, probably at their unfinished house, planning its furnishing and decoration. By six o'clock, Rose was pacing the empty flat like a caged animal. She called the Shelbourne again but John still had not returned.

Darina dashed into the hall of the flat just as she replaced the receiver. 'Are you finished, Mammy? You're not going to make any more calls, are you? I'm expecting someone to ring any minute.'

'It's my telephone, Darina!' snapped Rose. 'I pay the bill – or my half of it. You are allowed to use it on the understanding that it's a privilege, not a right. I'll make as many calls as I like.'

'What's eating you? All I said was—'

'I heard what you said and what I said stands!' They glared at one another and then Rose realised she was being unreasonable. 'Sorry,' she said. 'I'm a bit tired, that's all.'

'That's OK. Are you going to be using the phone again?'

'No, it's all yours. Who's ringing you that it's so urgent?'

'Just a friend.'

Rose threw up her hands. 'I'm going to make myself a sandwich. Will I make you one?'

'No, thanks. I'm not hungry, Mother.' Darina only called

407

Rose 'Mother' when she was settling into one of her more stubborn moods and Rose knew better than to challenge her.

She was sitting down to eat her sandwich when she heard the telephone ring, only once, before it was snatched up. She could not hear what her daughter was saying but knew by the tone that she was excited and being secretive about it.

Some boy, she thought with a sigh, hoping that whatever phase Darina had now entered would be a short one. Rose knew that as a parent, she had been lucky so far in that although Darina's close friends were girls, she had gone around in a larger group of boys and girls together. She had been delighted that Darina seemed to look on boys not as mysterious, exciting creatures from another planet as Rose had when she was that age, but as flesh and blood companions. There had, she knew, been romances, but nothing that had caused her any worry. By the sound of what was going on on the telephone, all that seemed about to change.

The thought struck her. Could this call have anything to do with whatever had happened over the weekend?

She sighed. Whether it did or it did not she would not find out until Darina was good and ready to tell her. She heard the phone being put down. There was a long pause and then Darina came into the kitchen. 'Hi!' Her face was flushed but she kept it low so her long hair fell over it like a pair of thick curtains.

Rose waited while Darina made herself a cup of tea. She had a fair idea of what was to come and she was not mistaken, for when Darina was pouring the boiling water over the tea-leaves, she spoke casually over her shoulder. 'You don't mind if I go into town this evening?' Rose deliberately took another mouthful of the sandwich so her mouth would be full and she could not answer immediately, thereby forcing Darina to turn around. 'Did you hear me, Mammy? Is it OK if I go into town for a while?'

'Homework up to date?'

'Sure. We didn't get much over the holiday anyway.'

'Then it's all right by me.' She let the silence build again. Then she asked, her tone just as casual as Darina's had been, 'Who're you meeting, by the way?'

'Oh, just the usual, you know.' But Darina's glittering eyes told a different story and Rose knew, without doubt, that this meeting was with someone new and very significant. *Oh, Darina, be careful!* she cried in her heart, but out loud she simply reminded her daughter that she had to come home on the last bus at 11.30.

'Of course I will,' said Darina. Then she did something even more significant. She came across the room and hugged Rose. 'Mammy, I love you.'

Rose felt dangerously close to tears. 'I love you too, darling,' she whispered.

She heard Darina take the attic stairs two at a time, then the sound of her door slamming, followed by a rapid fusillade of bangs and thumps as she went through her room emptying drawersful of clothes onto her bed and rummaging through her extensive collection of boots and shoes. *You won't be late for this one, my darling baby*, thought Rose. She got up from her chair and stared without seeing through the kitchen window. She recognised now that, without a shadow of doubt, Darina was in love. She had seen in her daughter's eyes the mirror image of her own love for John Flynn when she was the same age.

John. He was only down the road, two miles away. Should she make a fool of herself and ring yet again? He was sure to come back sooner or later and then it occurred to her that she was free for the evening – she could even go and sit in the Shelbourne lobby. For a few moments she struggled with that notion and abandoned it as being the action of a deluded neurotic, not the mother of a teenaged girl who was going to need not only careful handling but all the love and support she could get.

And then there was another factor. Suppose John Flynn rejected her, what then? How would she cope with the humiliation? And how would rejection affect Darina, who would sooner rather than later have to be told exactly who her father was?

Rose turned away from the window. 'Oh, well, your timing was always impeccable.' she said aloud.

She went into the sitting room and poured herself a large gin and tonic. Then she sat on the couch and held up the glass so that the light from the window behind reflected in the bluish bubbles. 'Ah, shit!' she said.

*

Darina had given directions to Bruno and he was already waiting in the lobby of the Skylon Hotel when she went in, standing just inside the door and a little to the left, the collar of his ski-jacket tightly zipped around his throat. He lit up when he saw her and came forward immediately. 'Hi! Would you like a Coke or something?'

'No, thanks.' She smiled at him. 'Let's get out of here – it's a bit close to home!' They touched hands, almost shyly.

'Where would you like to go?' he asked then. 'To a movie or something?'

'No, we've so little time and so much to talk about. Would you mind if we just walked for a while?'

'Isn't it too cold for you, Darina?' His soft Canadian accent separated the three syllables of the name, making a caress of each one. She shook her head. 'I'm dressed for it.' She indicated her knee-length boots and the woollen jumper under her duffel coat. 'So are you. We'll be fine.'

As they left the hotel and walked up Drumcondra Road towards the junction with Griffith Avenue, Darina kept an eye on the windows of the flat in case her mother happened to be looking out. 'That's where I live,' she told Bruno, pointing at the three-storey house.

'Very impressive,' he said. 'Do you have all of it?'

'Just the top storey and the attics,' she said. 'My mother's not rich, you know. We rent.'

'Does your mom know about me yet?'

'No. Besides,' Darina shrugged, 'what's to tell? So I'm going for a walk – so what?'

When they were safely past the house and turning east into the wide, tree-lined boulevard of Griffith Avenue, she took his hand. It had been a late autumn and drifts of crisp, multi-coloured leaves still lay on the path, ankle-deep in places. The houses, set back from the road behind railings and neat gardens, glowed with yellow lights, fuzzy and ethereal through the fog. 'I used to skate along here when I was a child,' said Darina. 'I loved it at this time of the year, crunching through the leaves, letting them get all tangled up in the wheels.'

'Fantastic! But you should see the leaves on the Island in the fall.'

410

'Perhaps I will, one day.'

'If I've anything to do with it you will.'

Darina laughed. Bruno's dogged lack of guile and earnestness amused her. For the thousandth time in three days, she reflected that he was having an extraordinary effect on her; every time she looked at him, or even thought about him, she went warm. As a result of her voluminous reading – she had recently begun exploring the works of Jung and the psychic Edgar Cayce – she was now in the habit of continual probing and self-analysis. Darina felt she knew herself well enough to be certain she was in love.

She glanced sideways at Bruno. 'Where were we – in the story of our lives, I mean?' she asked, raising her arm so he could tuck his hand under it. During both the times they had spent together at Sundarbans, they had, after a brief period of hesitancy, talked non-stop. Darina felt she had never been able to talk so freely.

'Can't really remember,' said Bruno honestly, 'there was so much.'

'There's lots more, believe me.' Nevertheless, she felt no compulsion to talk now as, in step, they walked to the end of the avenue, through Marino and Fairview and out onto the seafront at Clontarf; somewhere along the way, she became conscious that the two of them were breathing together, in rhythm with their walking. As they moved along Clontarf Road, through the fog, she heard, rather than saw, a bus bearing down on them. 'Have you ever been on Dollymount Strand?' she asked.

'Where?' Bruno asked, but she did not stop to explain.

'Run! The stop's just up here.' She ran ahead of him, holding out her hand, praying the driver would see her. At the last minute, the bus squealed to a halt and took them on. There was only one other passenger on board and the bus rattled along slowly in low gear, feeling its way through the fog.

They got off a few stops later, crossed the road and stepped onto the ancient wooden bridge which crossed the estuary and connected the roadway to the strand, which was almost a large island. Out here in the open, the fog seemed even more dense, rising directly off the still water, a pale grey cloud swirling around them, and catching at the backs of their throats. The sound of the traffic was muted and distant and the lights of Dublin port

411

and the city beyond it showed only as faint, barely visible pin-points. 'It's really eerie,' said Bruno as they passed warily across the thick planks of the bridge. 'We have sea-fog at home, acres of it, but this is something else!'

'I always love fog, "the yellow fog that rubs its back upon the window panes".' Eliot was currently Darina's favourite poet.

'I used to be terrified crossing this bridge when I was a child,' she confided then, 'even in bright sunshine. Mammy used to have to carry me across. You can't see it now, it's too dark, but the planks don't fit right together and you can see the water through them. No matter what she said, I was always afraid I'd slip through the cracks. Have you got matches or a lighter?' she asked then, out of the blue.

'No,' he answered, astonished. 'I don't smoke.'

'I don't mean for cigarettes,' she said. 'But we could light a bonfire. I've done it before – although not at night,' she added honestly.

'Are you sure you're allowed to light fires?'

'Everyone does it,' she answered airily although she was not at all sure that the lighting of fires in the dunes *was* permitted. 'We'll ask this man here for a match.' A man walking two small dogs had loomed in front of them.

The man rummaged in the pocket of his coat while the dogs pulled and strained at their leashes. 'Here,' he said, 'take the box. There's only one or two in it. It's awful cold out there,' he added, tipping his hat in farewell.

Blowing on her hands to warm them, Darina led Bruno down onto the beach proper and across the sand to the edge of the water. The man with the matches had been right; it was exceptionally cold and damp; the fog had already permeated her thick clothing.

Energetically, she jogged on the spot. 'I'd love you to be able to see the whole thing. On clear days – and nights – you can see practically the whole city from here, all the way from one side of Dublin Bay to the other. And the beach is miles long, *miles*.'

'Do you come here a lot?'

'Yes, often.'

'With other boys?'

'Sometimes,' said Darina. 'Sometimes I come alone. It's so

huge that no matter how many people are here, even at the height of summer, you can always find places to be completely alone, up there in the dunes.' She pointed behind her. 'This and the Phoenix Park are the two places I like to go. Have you seen the Phoenix Park?'

'No – obviously I've a lot to learn. Dublin's so big after Charlottetown.'

'I'd love to see Charlottetown.'

'You will,' Bruno assured her.

'How can you be so definite? We might never see each other again after you go home.'

'You've got to be kidding!' The fervour with which he said it thrilled Darina but unaccountably she suddenly felt shy.

'Dublin airport must be closed,' she said, to cover her confusion.

'How do you know?'

'Well, this place is on the flight path into it, and I haven't heard a single plane. Have you?'

'You're marvellous, Darina,' said Bruno tenderly. 'Are you cold?' He pulled the hood of her coat over her head and held it tightly over her ears.

'Let's go up into the dunes and light that fire,' she whispered. For a few seconds, they stood together, only inches apart, and she thought he might kiss her. Then, to her disappointment, he let her go.

'What'll we use?'

'Oh there's always stuff around, bits of wood, rubbish. People are not brilliant at cleaning up after themselves.'

In the fog, the dunes had been transformed into an alien, mysterious world where the boundary was the summit of the next hillock and the air was thick with the smell of damp sand and pungent odours. 'Even in good weather,' said Darina, instinctively lowering her voice, 'when you're in here you'd never know you were anywhere near a city. Come on,' she added, more matter-of-factly, 'let's get busy – anything at all you think will burn, but it must be fairly dry.'

'Listen,' he protested, 'you're talking to an Islander here. I know how to light fires.'

After ten minutes or so of searching and gathering, they

413

had a respectable pile of combustible material, papers, pieces of driftwood, cardboard, dead vegetation, even the half-charred remains of an orange box which someone else had tried to burn.

'Let's wait until we're *really* cold,' suggested Darina. 'It's a pity to waste it now.'

'All right,' he agreed. He scooped out a little hollow in the sand and flopped into it. She copied him and lay in her own little hollow, using her hood to cushion her head against the stiff grasses which pricked like needles into any exposed skin.

Side by side, they lay quietly. Darina longed for him to kiss her. She would gladly have initiated it but held back, from some obscure feeling that he should be the one to do it, at least for the first time. In her bones, she felt he was working up to it but, while she waited, found the growing physical tension between them difficult to cope with. 'Do you know anything about psychic stuff?' she asked suddenly.

'What do you mean?'

'You know, the paranormal.'

'Can't say I do,' he admitted.

'Do your classmates in Canada ever consult Ouija boards, for instance?'

'What's that?'

'It's a flat piece of wood or hard cardboard. You put an inverted glass on it and sit around it with other people, holding on to it with both hands. And you all concentrate together and you ask questions – they have to have "yes" or "no" answers – about love, and relationships. The glass moves by itself to give the replies. It's all the rage at school but, of course, the nuns have banned it.' She got up on one elbow to look earnestly into his face. 'Honest to God, Bruno, that glass does move.' She took a deep breath. 'It's moved by the power of combined thought.' She hesitated, unsure of his reaction, but then plunged on. 'It's the universal unconscious, you see, some people believe that our individual minds and spirits are all part of one, greater mind.' She searched his face but in the darkness, could not discern his expression. Afraid she might have turned him off, she flopped back into her niche. 'Anyway, I'm only starting to read about it.'

Bruno turned towards her, placing an arm across her and hugging her to him. 'Tell me more.'

414

'Are you sure you're interested?'

'Of course I am.'

'Well, as I said, I'm only a beginner, but a lot of things I'm reading now make a lot of sense to me. I mean, even when I was much younger, I never could accept the Catholic orthodox teachings we were given in school, about the Blessed Trinity and transubstantiation and that you lived once and then died and went to heaven or hell – but when you start looking into the experience of psychics and even the eastern religions, the whole thing starts to make sense. Christianity, even Catholicism, can be fitted into the wider picture.'

'This is all to do with – what did you call them? – Ouija boards?' Tenderly, Bruno brushed a strand of Darina's hair off her face.

'No, it's miles away from Ouija boards. That's only a game – and a dangerous one. I don't blame the nuns for forbidding it. All my friends still do it all the time, asking about boyfriends and who they'll marry and all that – but the only reason I mentioned it is because when that glass moves it is concrete evidence that there's more to life than what we see, feel or hear. Certainly more than what we're told. Lately I've been reading about karma and reincarnation and astrology and all that. Do you know anything about it?'

'I don't want to appear stupid,' said Bruno, 'but do you mean horoscopes? I'm a Libra,' he added.

'Sort of,' said Darina seriously, 'I'm an Aries – but it's much, much deeper than that. I don't understand half of it. Not yet, anyway.' She lapsed into silence which, the longer it lasted, grew and grew until it was exquisitely unbearable. Bruno's arm across her waist seemed to grow heavier. Although she was inches away from him, she sensed the rigidity in his body and knew he, too, was feeling the charge.

'You're very beautiful, Darina.' In one swift movement, he leaned over and put his lips over hers. The kiss was soft and gentle, questing rather than demanding, a wonderfully different experience from being kissed by Irish boys, who, as far as Darina was concerned, seemed always after as much as they could get.

She turned towards him and put her arms around him; his back felt wide and strong through the padding of his jacket. There was no sound at all; even the hollow sound of the sea, which might have reached them in other circumstances, had been blanketed out by the fog. As he kissed her, Darina could have sworn that for a second she became weightless. She felt she should say something significant but could not think of anything which would not sound stupid or pretentious.

They stopped kissing and sat up to face one another, the only two people on the planet. Darina's skin tingled all over and each organ in her body felt as though it pulsed. 'Do you feel it?' she whispered.

'Yes,' he whispered back and as they stared at one another in the monochromatic gloom, the feeling between them enlarged until it became so agonising and at the same time so exquisitely pleasurable that Darina could stand it no longer.

She scrambled to her knees. 'It's time to light the fire.' She struck a match and set it against the pile of debris.

Staying a little apart, they watched as the flames caught the papers first and then crackled up through the slats of the orange box. With the absence of wind, the fire burned steadily and evenly; wood sparks shot upwards like miniature fireworks, making them jump backwards for fear of being scorched.

Darina watched Bruno's absorbed face. The firelight danced across it, highlighting the cheekbones and blond hair and glinting off his large eyes. He looked like a faun or some other metaphysical creature. Then she thought she was getting carried away. 'More fuel, slave!' she cried. 'We need more fuel if we're to keep this thing going.'

They gathered as much as they could find in the darkness and fog and fed the fire for half an hour, talking sporadically and quietly. 'Isn't it strange, the way we met?' Darina asked, settling down on her hunkers to watch the flames. 'I mean, I was only standing on that rock for about three minutes. I was on my way to see the boathouse and if I hadn't stopped there, even for that short time . . . '

'Yeah,' Bruno agreed, 'but people meet like that all the time, in shops, or on trains. It's just chance that the two of them happen to be on that particular train or in that particular shop together. My mom and dad met on a ship, for instance.'

Darina was reluctant fully to accept Bruno's logical approach. 'I suppose so,' she said slowly. 'But you've got to agree that the way we met was so – so . . . ' She wanted to say 'romantic' but felt it would sound too presumptuous. 'It just seemed so inevitable,' she finished. She fed the last piece of wood to the fire. 'Some day, I'll probably write about it.' She had already confided to him that she wanted to be a writer.

'I hope you'll write good things about me.' Bruno squatted beside her.

Darina laughed. 'Better continue to be nice to me.' Together, they watched the last flare of the fire. Then, as the flames died down and subsided onto a glowing red and grey mattress of embers and ash, Darina's tone became more serious. 'It's so easy, talking to you,' she said. 'It's as though I've known you before. I never have to think of what to say – and I don't worry about what you think, I *know* what you're going to think because I think it myself.'

'I know what you mean.'

'Other boys are always pushing you, to see how far you'll go.'

'You mean sex?'

'I suppose so. But there's more to it than that. I don't feel you're trying to dig things out of me, so therefore I'm willing to give you everything. Do you understand?'

'Everything?' he asked in mock eagerness.

She laughed. 'I'm not afraid of *you*! Anyway we have the rest of our lives – and all the other lives to come.' She gave him a teasing thump in the ribs. 'And if you believe that you'd believe anything!' She felt wonderful, light and airy and absolutely safe. She made as if to punch him a second time but he grabbed her arms and pinned them to the sand behind her head and kissed her, a long passionate kiss, far stronger than the first time.

They came apart and stared at one another. 'I do think we should wait,' said Darina.

He kissed her again, more gently. Then he settled himself under her and took her in his arms, holding her diagonally across his body, her head in the crook of his elbow. Darina lay relaxed in his arms. This must have been what it felt like as a new baby, she thought. She gazed at his face, dim now as the light from the fire died away. He traced one of her eyebrows with a finger and then pulled a rib of the grass, tickling her under the chin with it. 'This is called marram grass, do you know that?'

'No, I didn't – I know now.'

417

'We've dunes on the Island too – wonderful dunes. They move with the wind, marching across the roads. It's really spectacular. And if it wasn't for the marram, they'd be dispersed altogether.'

For Darina nothing in the world existed except the present moment and his face above hers. This, she thought, was the nearest she had ever come to the experience of perfect peace.

Gradually the muffled note of a car engine, slowly getting louder, seeped into their cocoon. Bruno released her gently, got up on all fours and looked out over the dunes onto the beach. 'It's a police car,' he said in astonishment.

'What time is it?'

'Just after a quarter of ten.'

'We'll have to be going soon anyway. I promised my mother I'd be home on the last bus at half-eleven. She'll get worried,' she said.

Together they watched as the dark police vehicle continued its slow patrol. 'We're doing nothing wrong,' said Darina, 'we've nothing to worry about. We've a perfect right to be here. It's a public place. But I suppose we'd better put the fire out just to be safe.' Bruno kicked sand onto the embers, extinguishing them completely. They brushed themselves down and climbed over the dunes, back onto the beach. The tail lights of the squad car were visible only as small red dots.

'Do you think they're looking for something in particular?' asked Bruno.

'Probably people like us.' She grinned.

They walked back onto the bridge and towards the main road. 'I forgot to ask you,' said Darina. 'How did your uncle John react when you arrived at the Shelbourne?' The plan they had concocted the previous day was that Bruno would tell Mona that his uncle John had invited him up to Dublin to stay with him for his last night. 'He wasn't there,' he said, 'so I left a message. Won't he be surprised?'

'It's a bit outrageous all right. What did you say in the message?'

'Just that I was in town unexpectedly – that's the sort of thing Dad would say – and could I bunk in with him?'

'Will your dad be annoyed when he tells him?'

'I dunno.' Bruno shrugged. 'Anyway, there's nothing to worry about now. Dad's in Hamburg, blissfully thinking that I'm tucked up in Mona's tender care.'

'What's she like? How come she lives with your uncle John and isn't married to him?'

'They don't live together – not in that sense, I don't think. I mean they have their own bedrooms. I don't know the full story but it's something to do with long ago when Dad and Uncle John's mother was alive and Mona came in to help. She just stayed, I guess.'

'Is she nice?'

'She's lovely. She's the sort of person that thinks the best of everyone and, to tell you the truth, I felt as bold as a pet pig making up a story for her. Although, of course, I didn't really have to tell lies. Not real lies.'

For a moment, Darina debated the ethics of whether he had actually told a lie or not. She had already noticed that Bruno was astonishingly literal about things. 'That's right,' she agreed loyally, 'you weren't really deceiving her. Bcause you *are* going to stay at the Shelbourne, aren't you?'

'I sure hope so.' Holding hands, the two of them wandered slowly along the landscaped strip which fringed the estuary.

'Oh, Bruno,' said Darina, 'I don't want to go home. God knows when we'll see each other again . . . '

'I'm going to do everything I can to get back here for Christmas,' he said, lightly and so confidently that Darina believed he could actually manage it.

'Oh, Bruno, that would be marvellous,' she said. 'How would you persuade your parents to let you come?'

'They'd come too!' he said in surprise, as though there was never any doubt about it. 'They're always saying they must do it some day and if I've anything to do with it, "some day" will be this year. And that's only a couple of months away. Six or seven weeks, really.'

'But that's still an awfully long time.' With the parting imminent, Darina felt the joy draining away from the evening. 'What time is it now?' she asked.

'Twenty to eleven.'

'We've only a few more minutes . . . ' Darina was overwhelmed by this disaster. She saw a telephone box across the road and made a sudden decision. 'I'm going to ask for an extension!' she said.

Rose and Effie were in the sitting room when the telephone rang. Effie got up to answer it. 'It's Darina,' she said when she came back into the room.

'Did she say what she wanted?' To get off the sofa represented a great physical effort and Rose was irritated. She heaved herself upright and went into the hall. 'Hello?'

'Hello, Mammy,' said Darina and Rose went on full alert. Her daughter's voice was artificially cheery, boding no good. 'Listen, I was wondering if I could stay out a bit late tonight?'

Rose's immediate instinct was to say an automatic 'no' but she held herself back. 'How come?' she asked. 'What's so special?'

'I'll tell you all about it when I get home – if you're still awake, that is. I've met a boy, he's a perfectly respectable boy, Mammy – and he says he'll bring me home safely in a taxi. I'll put you on to him if you like, he's right here.'

'That won't be necessary. Who is he and where are you now?'

'His name is Bruno and we're in Clontarf. I'll tell you all about him tonight or first thing in the morning. We've just been for a walk, along the seafront.'

Rose was silent.

'*Please*, Mammy. I've no school tomorrow.'

Rose heard the desperation in her daughter's voice. It was the first time Darina had ever been so honest about why she wanted to stay out and if she was refused this time, when it was obviously so important to her, Rose feared she might go underground. 'All right,' she said slowly, 'but I'm trusting you now, Darina. You be sure you come home in a taxi. Have you enough money?'

'Plenty. Thanks, Mammy.' Rose was about to put a definite time limit on the extension but the line clicked dead in her ear.

She walked back into the sitting room. Effie looked up expectantly. 'Everything all right?'

'Oh, Effie,' said Rose, 'I hope so.'

*

420

John surreptitiously looked at the clock on the girl's bedside table: how soon before he could decently leave?

The girl snuggled into him, her beautiful young body silky and slick with sweat. She was breathing slowly and quietly and John, feeling guilty, hoped against hope that she was falling asleep. He lay rigidly, forcing himself to breathe just as regularly as though he, too, were sleeping. The arm under her was beginning to prickle with pins and needles but he did not dare move it in case he interrupted her slide into sleep.

Was it ever going to be any different? he asked himself. Occasionally he had managed to stretch out his physical attraction to a girl so it became an affair but the relationship never lasted long; inevitably, the girl started dropping hints, arranging dinner parties with other couples, planning dates ahead and John would feel the situation tightening around him like a shrinking cage and would fight with all his might to break free.

While he waited to be sure that the girl was unconscious, he reviewed the day – and the evening which had culminated in this situation. He and Rodney Pickford had hit it off right away. The older man, although sharp where business was concerned, had proven an intelligent, amiable companion when off-duty. Having seen and heard John's presentation, he had agreed to come in on the Sundarbans deal, adding a considerable amount of money to the funds of the syndicate but, more importantly, adding his clout to the negotiations with one of the commercial banks which, George and John hoped, would match the funds being raised through the local bank in Carrickmacross. The two of them had met three of the commercial bank's officials first thing this morning, the meeting had gone well and, largely as a result of Pickford's heavyweight presence, John confidently expected to bring good news home to George and his other partners.

Being honest, John had to admit that, fuelled with the success of the day and plenty of good food and drink, he had not exactly been dragged against his will into his present predicament. He and Pickford had dined early in the Hibernian Hotel, treating themselves to a celebratory meal during which they did not stint on either the food or the wines. John, whose interest in wine was peripheral and confined largely to the cellars of Willow House,

421

noted that Pickford's choices had been so discriminating that he had earned an approving lift of the eyebrow from the *sommelier*.

The two girls had been in the buttery, to which they had repaired for brandy afterwards, and to his surprise, John, who had assumed that his companion, although fit and athletic – and looking younger than his fifty-odd years – was as staid and conservative as most of the businessmen he met, saw another side of him. He knew Pickford was married with three children, but at the sight of the girls giggling together at a corner table, he moved up a gear. Having ordered the brandies, he turned to the girls and, pouring on the charm, blatantly asked them if he and John could join them.

The older man had taken centre stage from then on, entertaining the two girls with an endless stream of witty and sometimes salacious stories about the goings-on in high society in the Isle of Man and the Channel Islands. He even implied – although he did not exactly say so – that he was on intimate terms with certain members of the Royal Family.

The girls both worked in advertising and were as sleek and well groomed as young racehorses. And they were completely taken with Pickford's sophistication and stream of gallant compliments. After a while John, mildly drunk, went along happily enough with what he knew was inevitable. The group broke up just after eleven. Pickford went back to his hotel with his partner, while John got into the other girl's car for the short trip to her flat in Ranelagh, a southside suburb not far from the city centre.

His arm was almost numb; he had to remove it soon. The girl was starting to snore gently, her upper lip trembling with each intake of breath. Inch by inch, holding his breath, John disentangled himself. And then he remembered the first time he had slept with a girl. Rose, too, had fallen asleep in the crook of his arm. As he continued to withdraw his arm, a tide of self-loathing flooded over him. How could he, having had his first experience of sex – and love – with Rose O'Beirne Moffat, have descended to this level of casual bedding? All the thunderings of the Catholic Church, the dire warnings against sins of the flesh from the Brothers and from the hellfire Redemptorists who gave the annual mission in Carrickmacross – even his poor mother's timid innuendoes – had proven to be well founded.

The flesh certainly was weak. John Flynn's flesh in particular.

He felt dirty, the smell of his post-coital body, sour, sweaty and fetid, was loathsome. The girl stank, too, and her breath was laced with odours of stale drink and garlic. He felt a compulsion to wash off this encounter, to scrub himself clean of it until his skin was raw and tingling, to plunge into a freezing sea – or into the cold black waters of Swan's Lake.

He finished the extrication and eased himself off the single bed. Although the girl was fully naked, he had only partially undressed and still wore his singlet and shirt, open down the front. Still watching her, taking care not to make any sudden movements, he dressed, hating to replace his clothes over his unwashed flesh.

When he was ready to leave, he took a last look at the girl. In sleep, she looked much younger than her twenty-three years and very vulnerable. Around her lips was a red smear, whether from the wine they had shared before the sex, or from her lipstick, he could not tell.

Shame was added to his self-loathing. He should at least leave her a note, he thought and looked around the messy bedsitter for a piece of paper. There was a magnetic notepad – a shopping reminder – fixed to the door of the refrigerator in the kitchen alcove. John took the magic marker attached to the pad and scrawled a note:

HAD TO GO – EARLY START! LOVELY TO MEET YOU. PLEASE CONTACT ME IF YOU'RE EVER IN MY NECK OF THE WOODS.

He hesitated. In all decency, he should add his phone number. He wrote the number of Willow House and not the fishing lodge.

More ashamed than ever – he was now a coward as well as a lecher – he tiptoed to the door of the flat and let himself out, closing the door behind him as quietly as he could. Outside, he gulped deep lungfuls of the freezing, foggy air. Having expected only the short walk back to the Shelbourne from the Hibernian, he had no coat with him but as he started to shiver, welcomed the cleansing coldness.

423

Although he was not familiar with Ranelagh, he set off briskly in what he hoped was the right direction, heels ringing on the pavement. The redbrick, residential streets through which he passed were completely deserted and he tried to remember where the main road was, realising that even when he found it, one-thirty on a Tuesday morning in November was not the most auspicious time to hail a passing taxi.

And when he did reach the main thoroughfare, there was not a moving vehicle of any description in sight and he might have been the only person awake in the entire city. He walked on for about twenty minutes, encountering only a few cats and a single car going in the opposite direction. The streetlights were haloed in the fog, and as he passed over the bridge across a canal, he glanced down at the still water and was struck with the feeling that he was an actor in a surreal black and white movie. He had been walking for about twenty minutes now, however, and as he passed rows of shuttered shops, he felt warmer and calmer. He hoped the girl would not wake until morning and would forgive him for his appalling rudeness. She had been nice enough, in a vapid, undemanding way. But there was no future whatsoever in a relationship between himself and someone like her.

Did he have a future with anyone? Thirty-three years old and no one in sight. Would he end his days like poor Ned Sherling, quietly living out the shreds of his dreams?

He felt guilty about Ned; he had been so wrapped up in business that he had not paid a call on the old man for at least ten days. Ned was getting on now and, although still independent and living at home, his eyesight had deteriorated to the point where he could no longer read his beloved books with any degree of comfort. He never complained, however, and John called as often as he could, bringing him books from the library and reading to him for an hour or so.

John was certain now that Ned Sherling had been in love with his mother, Mary Flynn. Was Ned's fate to be his own? Was he, too, to end his days still yearning after his first, lost love? He was becoming maudlin. He looked at his watch, twenty to two. Those who talked of the early-morning – or late-night – blues were right. 'Come on, Flynn,' he said to himself. 'Get a move on. You've business to do in the morning.'

424

When he picked up his key at the hotel's reception desk, there were two messages for him, one from Pickford to say he would meet him at 8.30 a.m. for breakfast, but the other filled him with alarm. It was timed 6.30 p.m. and was from his nephew. Bruno was apparently in Dublin and wanted to be given accommodation for the night.

But where was he? John's guilt and self-loathing were given a new lease of life. While he was messing around with some girl who meant nothing to him his nephew was wandering homeless round the dangerous streets of night-time Dublin. 'Are these the only two messages?' he asked the night porter.

The man ran his hand around the key cubbyhole. 'Yes, sir, those two, that's all.'

What was he to do? And what was Bruno doing in Dublin in the first place? He wondered if he should try to contact Derek in Hamburg but knew immediately that this was ridiculous. Even if he could find Derek, what could he do from that distance?

Should he call the police? Too early. Bruno was sixteen, not exactly a baby.

That last thought calmed him. At Bruno's age, he himself was already out of school, just barely seventeen he was emigrating half-way across the world. He reminded himself it was only in recent times that sixteen-year-olds were not regarded as fully fledged. But it was Bruno's unworldliness which worried him. He could be anywhere, being taken advantage of by God knows what kind of character. 'Anything wrong, sir?'

The night porter cut into his reverie and John found he had been standing at the desk staring into space. 'No,' he said, 'but if my nephew, Bruno Flynn, calls again, no matter at what time, please make sure I get the message right away?'

'Certainly, sir.'

'And would you mind bringing me up a cup of coffee?' There was nothing for it but to go to his room and wait.

When Rose heard Darina's key turn in the lock of the front door, to calm herself she took as much air into her lungs as she possibly could, exhaling it slowly and loudly. It was the only trick she remembered from a yoga class she had taken and abandoned years ago. She had become more and more frantic as the hours

425

had ticked by. But she must not let her daughter see how upset she was. Calmness and control. That's what she must show.

She heard Darina close the front door and climb the stairs towards the flat. At the same time, a car sped away from the kerb. Well, at least this boy, she thought, whoever he was, had been as good as his word and had got her a taxi home.

The door of the flat opened and closed. 'I'm in here, Darina,' she called. There was a hiatus and then Darina appeared at the door. She looked flushed and her eyes were red as though she had been crying. There was also a softness about her which Rose had not seen before. She opened her mouth to remonstrate with her about the lateness of the hour – it was past three o'clock – but Darina held up her hand. 'Please, Mammy, don't give out. I know it's very late. But we were doing nothing wrong, honestly. The Coffee Dock was closed when we got there and we went to another place called the Manhattan for a sandwich and we were talking so much that the time just went by.' Her voice was flat and lifeless.

'Come on in, tell me about him. Who is he?' Rose patted the couch beside her.

But Darina hung just inside the door. 'I'll tell you tomorrow, Mammy. I don't want to talk about it now.'

'Is everything all right? You look as though you've been crying.'

'I was, but I'm not really sad. Well, I am – but I'm sad and very, very happy all at the same time. You know the way it can be sometimes.' She studied her nails. 'You see, I'm not going to be able to see him again until God knows when. Christmas at the earliest.'

'Why Christmas?'

'Because that's the earliest he'll be here again. He's leaving Dublin tomorrow to go home.'

'Where's home?'

'Well, he's on holiday in Monaghan actually, and that's where he's going tomorrow but then he's going back to Canada.'

Canada. Like a trickle of ice shavings, a premonition of danger crept up the back of Rose's neck. 'What part of Canada, darling?'

'Prince Edward Island. Did you ever hear of it?'

426

'Sure I did.' *Oh, Jesus . . .*

Darina looked up with surprise. 'God, that's amazing! I thought it was really obscure. I'd never heard of it before. I was sure I was going to have to explain to you where it was.'

With a supreme effort, Rose managed to keep her voice steady. 'What's this boy's name?'

'Bruno. Bruno Flynn.'

CHAPTER FOURTEEN

John sat on the side of his bed and watched Bruno as he slept. The boy was stretched out on the carpet, his blond head resting on one of John's pillows and the lower part of his body wrapped in his own jacket plus the counterpane from the single bed. He slept peacefully, lips slightly apart and chest barely moving; one arm was flung outward, displaying the soft underarm hair of recent puberty. He looked so vulnerable and young that John was reluctant to wake him.

Nevertheless, he had to. He leaned down and shook him by the shoulder. 'Bruno. Bruno! Wake up! It's time to wake up.'

Bruno stirred and opened blue, puzzled eyes. Then he focused them on John and smiled and John had to steel himself to be firm. 'Bruno, you and I have to have a talk,' he said. 'Do you know how lucky we were last night?'

'Mmm-mm?' The boy's voice was husky with sleep.

'I said, do you realise how lucky we were? Hotels like this do not take kindly to people coming in at three o'clock in the morning to doss on their floors. Are you listening?' he asked sharply. 'If it wasn't for that night porter—' He halted in mid-flow as Bruno continued to regard him with mild, drowsy eyes.

The porter had been dubious at first, naturally concerned at the request that this beautiful young boy be allowed into the single room of an older man. Bruno's own behaviour had not exactly helped. He had stood quietly apart as the discussions at the front desk progressed, seeming totally uninvolved and adding to John's difficulty in convincing the man that the boy was, indeed, his nephew.

As it happened, all the other rooms in the hotel were full that night and John had managed to persuade the porter to relent only after he was inspired to mention that he, too, was in the hotel business and that George Cranshaw was his boss. The

428

porter, it turned out, had relatives in Cavan and knew George by reputation.

'Sorry, Uncle John!' Bruno sloughed off his sleep and sat upright, the quilt rustling off him. His clothes were scattered around his feet. 'It won't happen again, I promise.'

'You bet it won't! Now, you said last night, or more properly this morning, that you'd tell me what got into you. What the hell were you doing in Dublin? And does your dad know what's going on?'

'I didn't think Dad would mind, Uncle John. And don't worry, there's nothing going on that you or Dad or anyone need be alarmed about. I came up to see a friend, that's all.'

'So suddenly, without telling anyone?'

'I told Mona,' Bruno pointed out. 'She seemed to think there'd be no problem.'

'What did you tell her?'

'That you'd invited me—'

'Well, naturally she thought there'd be no problem. That was a lie, Bruno.'

'Well, sort of.' Bruno seemed to consider the accusation. 'It wasn't really a lie, Uncle John,' he said then. 'I knew you would have invited me if I'd asked you to.' Fully alert now, he smiled his dazzling smile.

John looked helplessly at his guileless face. It was very difficult to deal with this trait of Bruno's, this transparency which seemed on the surface to be so straightforward and honest. And yet he knew that, in the most gentle way, Bruno would always do exactly as he wanted, managing to manipulate people and situations so effortlessly that it was difficult to recognise what was going on. It was not the first time he had noticed his nephew's gift in this direction. 'Look,' he said, man-to-man, 'who is she, this friend? I know she must be a girl,' he went on before Bruno could protest. 'I can't imagine any boy your age going to all that trouble and running around the city in the middle of the night just for a jaunt with another boy.'

'She's a girl all right, Uncle John, a very special girl.'

'What's her name?'

'Darina.'

'I see. Nice name. She's a Dublin girl?'

'Yes.' Bruno nodded vigorously. His demeanour was deadly serious now, as though he were willing to expose everything in his heart and soul.

John sighed. The situation was so far beyond his experience that he felt helpless. Added to which was the awful knowledge that, given his own adventures last night – and his shattering experience when he was almost exactly Bruno's age – he was hardly the appropriate person to make accusations or even to proffer advice. 'Want breakfast?' he asked, changing the subject to give himself a breather.

'Sure.' Bruno's face lit up. 'Can we have room service?'

'All right. *You* can have room service. I'm meeting someone downstairs at eight-thirty.' He lifted the telephone. 'What do you want?'

Bruno asked for a full Irish breakfast, porridge, bacon, sausages, eggs, tomatoes – the whole works. 'God bless your appetite anyhow,' said John as he waited for the kitchen to answer. Even the thought of ordering all that food made him feel nauseous. He had woken up, after less than four hours' sleep, sporting a hangover and feeling thoroughly seedy. He was longing for a hot shower.

By comparison, he thought, glancing across at his nephew, Bruno looked as if he had just dropped in after a healthy downhill run on a sunny ski-slope. The skin of his face, shoulders and arms, all that was visible of him, bore that distinctive golden smoothness which spoke of good transatlantic nutrition and bright outdoor summers. Derek, thought his twin, was a lucky man to have such a son.

Or was he? That curious imperviousness of Bruno was frustrating to say the least. John gave the order, left some coins on the dressing-table for a tip and went into the bathroom to take his shower.

When he came out, Bruno, still barechested, was eating his breakfast, his long, jeaned legs and brown feet stretched out comfortably under a little table by the window of the room. He looked as relaxed and at home as though he were in the kitchen of the fishing lodge. 'This is lovely, Uncle John,' he said between mouthfuls. 'Thanks a bunch.'

'You're welcome, I'm sure,' said John. 'Will you be all right

430

for a while?' he asked as he got dressed. 'I have to meet a man downstairs for breakfast, I shouldn't be too long.'

'Oh, don't worry about me!' said Bruno, 'I'll be absolutely fine. I'll just finish this and I'll be on my way. I might have a shower before I go if that's OK?' he added.

'Where are you going?'

'Back home – back to the fishing lodge.'

'How are you going to get there?'

'By bus, I suppose, or if there isn't one that suits, I'll hitch a ride. I hitched up here yesterday, no problem,' he said, biting into a piece of toast and crunching it loudly. 'Got here in only two rides.'

'If you want to wait, I'll be driving down at about five o'clock.'

'Don't bother about me, Uncle John. If I still haven't managed something by then, you'll see me on the road and you can pick me up.' Again he grinned.

'This girl of yours, Darina,' said John casually, looking at his reflection in a cheval mirror while tying his tie. 'When are you seeing her again?'

'Christmas, probably,' said Bruno.

'Is she going over to visit you?'

'No I don't think so, but come to think of it, that's not a bad idea, Uncle John. Her mom's a stewardess and I think she can get free travel, or very cheap anyhow. But I think I'll be coming here. There isn't much to do in Charlottetown around Christmas. It's a bit dead really. I mean, Darina's used to city life.'

'Charlottetown's a city,' said John defensively. Again Bruno seemed to have caught him wrong-footed, to be in charge of this rolling, changing situation. 'And since when did you arrange to come here for Christmas? That's the first I've heard of it.'

'We only decided last night.'

'We? I assume you mean this girl and you?'

'That's right. It'll be all right, Uncle John, won't it? I mean you wouldn't mind if we came? Mom and Dad have been talking about it for years.'

That much was true, John had to admit. For years he had issued invitations, secure in the knowledge that his twin was

431

unlikely to take enough time off to accept. Christmas and January were peak times for his retail business. 'No, of course we wouldn't mind, Bruno,' he said. Having finished dressing, he picked up the scratch pad from beside the bedside telephone and scribbled a couple of numbers on it. 'Now, if you need me during the day, I'll be at one or other of these numbers and the people at them will know where to get me. Only for emergencies, now, you understand? Have you money for the bus?'

'Sure. Plenty.'

'And if you do decide to hitch, be careful.'

'I always am.'

'All right, I have to run. Look,' he hesitated, 'we won't tell your dad about this episode, all right? I'll tell Mona to keep quiet too.'

'But he would understand, I'm sure he would.' Bruno looked genuinely surprised.

'Look, I haven't time now to go into all of this. Just believe me, Bruno. It's nothing to do with not getting you into trouble, it's to save your father.'

'Sure, Uncle John. Whatever you say.' Bruno stood and stretched, then, seeing John was about to leave the room, 'Would you mind if I made one quick phone call before I leave?'

As he walked down the ornate staircase to the hotel lobby, the picture of Bruno floated in front of John's tired brain as vivid in its beauty as a Michelangelo painting. In other circumstances, he thought, he, too, might have had a son like that.

Then he forced himself to stop thinking about his nephew and to concentrate on Rodney Pickford and the intricate details of their financial dealings.

Rose, pale and hollow-eyed, sat at the kitchen table over a cup of cold coffee. She heard someone coming down the stairs and, thinking it was Darina, assumed a bright smile. But when the door opened she saw it was Effie, dressed for work. She let the smile fade. 'Hi.'

'Are you all right?' asked Effie. 'You look terrible, if you don't mind my saying so.'

Rose put her head in her hands. 'No,' she said in a muffled voice, 'I'm anything but all right. Effie, the most awful thing has happened.'

'Oh, my God – what?' Effie threw down her handbag and crossed the floor in three strides. She crouched in front of Rose. 'What's happened? Is Darina OK?'

'She's fine. Well, as of three o'clock this morning, she was fine. She's still in bed.'

'What is it, then?' Effie gave Rose's knees a little shake. 'For Jaysus' sake, Rose, will you tell me what's after happening?'

Rose could not look at her friend. 'The sins of the fathers,' she said into her hands.

'What? What did you say?'

'I said,' Rose looked straight into Effie's worried face, 'the sins of the fathers.'

She half yelled it, all her frustration and fear combining in the desire to shock Effie, somehow to strike back. The retort had had the desired effect because Effie stood up slowly. 'What's that supposed to mean? You're talking in bleddy riddles, Rose.'

'You did the Bible as well as the rest of us, you know what I mean.'

'I know what the Bible means. What do you mean?'

'Well, if you really want to know, Effie, Darina, my daughter, Darina, has fallen in love with the son of John Flynn's twin brother.'

'Hold on a second, now. That's a bit complicated this hour of the morning. Let me get this straight. You say she's fallen in love with—'

'With the son of her uncle!' Rose shouted. 'Are you deaf? With her first cousin! With John Flynn's nephew! *Now* do you get it?'

Effie stood as still as a stone. 'Why are you shouting at me?'

'Wouldn't you shout if it was your daughter?' Rose dashed away the angry tears and the two of them glared at one another. Then Rose took a long, shuddering breath. 'I'm really sorry, Effie, please forgive me. I don't know whether I'm coming or going.'

'Have a cup of coffee with me, I'm making one for myself. How did you find out?' Effie asked, over her shoulder.

'She told me. Effie, she has no idea who he is. All she knows is that she's in love with a boy called Bruno Flynn who lives in Charlottetown.'

Effie turned on the radio, just as the time signal pipped for

433

eight o'clock and the news. Then, illogically, she slowly turned the volume down until the newsreader's voice was unintelligible. When the coffee was ready, she brought the two mugs over to the table. 'Let's look at this,' she said, sitting down. 'She's in love, you say, but she has no idea who this boy really is?'

Rose shook her head miserably, the tears now pouring unchecked down her face.

'Well, then, let's look at it one step at a time. What's the worst thing that can happen?'

Rose looked at her in horror. 'You know damned well what's the worst thing that can happen, Effie. Leaving me and John Flynn out of it altogether, although,' she said bitterly, 'I am – surprise, surprise! – finding that a bit difficult, Darina and this Bruno are first cousins.'

'That's not so bad,' insisted Effie. 'First cousins are not as bad as second cousins. You can get a dispensation to marry your first cousin but not your second cousin.'

'Who's talking about marriage here? I don't know how old this boy is but I presume he's around the same age as she is. They're both only sixteen. *Sixteen*, Effie—'

'You know what I'm talking about,' said Effie, 'and look at the pot calling the kettle black. You're overreacting, Rose, because—'

'I'm not overreacting!' Rose's voice started to rise again.

'Look,' said Effie, unruffled, 'will you drink that coffee, it's going to get cold.'

'The hell with the coffee! You're not taking this seriously.'

'Of course I'm taking it seriously,' said Effie. 'What are you really afraid of, Rose? They are, as you say, only sixteen years old. Sixteen-year-olds fall in and out of love all the time. This is a passing crush, that's all.'

Rose thought of Darina's eyes, of the changed posture. 'No,' she said definitely, 'I've seen Darina with crushes. This is a lot more than a crush. And,' she held up her hands to ward off whatever Effie might say, 'I know it's none of my business, but I can't bear to stand back and let her get into trouble.'

'Who says she's getting into trouble? You're crossing a million bridges here, Rose!'

'Maybe,' Rose admitted, 'but I just have a feeling about

this. And there's no point in talking to her – you know how headstrong she is. All her life, ever since she was old enough to toddle, once Darina made up her mind about something that was it. And she can twist anyone around her little finger,' she added gloomily. 'You know that, Effie.'

'Yes,' said Effie, 'I know, but deep down she's a sensible girl, she's not going to do anything foolish. Trust your daughter, Rose.'

Rose slowly picked up the mug and took a sip of the coffee. Effie, as usual, had hit the nail squarely on the head. Because of her own fall from grace, she did not trust Darina an inch. On the other hand, feeling that Darina's natural sense of celebration should not be repressed, she had encouraged it. Now, that particular chicken was coming home to roost. She looked mournfully at Effie's dear face. 'You're probably right – I don't trust her. But as usual you're right all the way – I should.'

'Stop me now if I'm over the line but I think that while this has a lot to do with Darina and this Bruno – and, of course, as a mother you've a right to be anxious about that – it has a lot more to do with what's going on in your own life at the moment about John Flynn.'

Rose stared at her, uncomprehending. 'What do you mean?'

'Rose, you're not Darina and Darina's not you. You're separate people.' She counted her fingers. 'Number one, don't suppose automatically that she's going to make the same mistakes as you did when you were her age. Number two, it is possible that one of the things you're angry about is that you're not controlling this one, Rose. This is something she's doing by herself. She's spreading her wings and maybe you're not ready for that yet – but even more important—' She stopped and fiddled with a salt cellar on the table.

'Go on.' Rose was wary, it was unlike Effie to be hesitant. 'You've gone this far,' she said, 'you might as well let us in on number three!'

'Well,' Effie went on, 'did it ever occur to you that – please don't take this the wrong way and fly off the handle – that you might be a bit jealous of Darina?'

'*What?*'

'Just think about it, Rose. It's natural, you know, happens

435

all the time between mothers and daughters, between sisters, between any two people. In this case you just might conceivably be upset – I'm not saying you are, mind you, but if you consider it, it might put things in perspective. You're upset that Darina has the chance to fulfil the dreams you've held all these years. Now you told me last night why you didn't go to the Shelbourne, that it was for Darina's sake.' She shrugged and spread both hands wide over the table. 'All very noble. And just when you're filled with all these feelings of self-sacrifice and maternal concern what does she do? She comes floating in on cloud nine, telling you she doesn't need all this from you, thank you very much, she's managing her own life. And what's more, to add appalling insult to the whole thing, it's not just any boy she's fallen for but another John Flynn. *Your* John Flynn. Or as close as she can get. And she has a much better chance of doing something real about it than you ever did!'

Rose was too stunned to say anything immediately. Her first reaction, as Effie's small speech progressed, had been to reject the concept out of hand, to cry that the notion that she could be jealous of her own daughter was absolutely preposterous. But niggling inside her head was a voice which told her to hold on, to consider what Effie was saying before she rejected it. Perhaps Effie's theory was making her feel so uncomfortable because it contained the seeds of unpleasant truth? 'I've never been jealous of anyone,' she whispered.

'Oh no? Are you St Francis of Assisi reincarnated, Rose? Maybe you're Mother Teresa? With the possible exception of those two people, there isn't a human being who isn't jealous from time to time. It's human nature.'

'But jealous of my own daughter? That's terrible.'

'And as I said, perfectly natural.'

'I love Darina with all my heart.'

'Of course you do.'

Rose waited for Effie to elaborate but she said nothing more, forcing her to continue the thought process for herself. She did love her daughter with all her heart, she thought, but in addition, when she looked very deep into herself, she certainly did want what Darina now seemed openly to have.

Effie was watching the struggle on her face and Rose put up her hands again to hide it. But Effie did not let her off the hook. 'That's only part of it, Rose,' she said gently, 'but when you've faced that bit, all the rest is much easier. Of course you're worried that she'll make a mistake. But she's no longer a little girl and she's going to make big adult mistakes in her life. All you can do from now on is help her see the choices. She'll be the one to do the choosing.'

'Very philosophical,' said Rose, then, realising that she sounded bitter, apologised. 'Have you ever been jealous?' she asked.

'My dear,' said Effie, 'have you ever looked at yourself in the mirror? Have you ever looked at me beside you? The world is full of beautiful people, successful people, people who have had normal childhoods and loving parents and families. Of course I've been jealous.'

'But I never knew – about me, I mean – it never showed.' Rose remembered the meeting with Dolores O'Brien and thought that this was the second time in a matter of months that she was having this conversation.

'Just because you feel it doesn't mean you have to do anything about it,' retorted Effie. 'Once you acknowledge that it's there, once you take it out and look it straight in the face, it's not so bad after all. It's just something else to be tackled, like acne or – or piles!'

The imagery was so absurd that Rose burst out laughing.

'Ain't it the truth?' Effie's eyes disappeared in her crinkled-up face.

They drank their coffee while the newsreader murmured incomprehensibly to himself inside the radio, and Rose, still shocked but calmer now, turned her options over and over. She could forbid Darina to see this boy again, which would be futile, she could do nothing, which would be worse – or she could tell her the truth. 'Do you think I should tell Darina the truth?' she asked Effie.

'I think you should do nothing at all while you're in this state. When's she seeing him again?'

'She said something about Christmas.'

'Sure, that's weeks away, months!' cried Effie. 'Why didn't you say so in the first place? The whole thing will look different then, you'll see. She might even have got over him.'

'I doubt it,' said Rose gloomily.

'Look,' said Effie, standing up, 'I have to go. But for Christ's sake,' she leaned over and took Rose by both shoulders, gripping them hard, 'for the last time, would ya ever effin' sort out this thing with John Flynn? Shaggin' love him or leave him once and for all and let us all get on with our effin' lives.'

'I will, I promise.'

'All right,' said Effie, letting her go. 'If this thing with Darina does that for us, it'll have been well worth it. Look on the bright side, Rose.' She grinned and picked up her handbag from where she had discarded it just inside the door. Then, before she left the room, she turned back, her face serious again. 'I don't mean to minimise this, or make little of it, Rose, I really don't. And I know it's tough, but maybe it's just as well everything is coming to a head now. About time too. Just think of all those years you spent not knowing what your real feelings were.'

As soon as Effie had left, Rose stood up from the table and turned off the radio. Her head ached and her legs felt leaden. She decided to go back to bed for a while. Everything might look a little less bleak if she got some sleep. She was half-way up the attic stairs when the telephone rang and she turned back to answer it. 'Hello?'

'Hello? May I speak to Darina, please?' The young voice gave equal value to the three syllables and Rose knew immediately who it was. 'Who's this speaking?' she asked nevertheless, trying to keep her voice from betraying her.

'Bruno Flynn,' said the boy, with that upward inflection at the end of the sentence which was peculiar to North America.

'I see,' said Rose. She took a deep breath. But it was of no avail. All Effie's counselling, all her own better judgement, balled up in her stomach like a black hedgehog as every shred of self-control deserted her. At this moment, even though her head knew it was completely irrational, her heart hated this boy, hated him with all its might. 'Darina is not available at the moment,' she said. 'And please don't call her again.'

As she slammed down the receiver, she heard a sound above her and looked up. Darina, white-faced, was standing at the top of the stairs.

'Darina – I—' she began but Darina ignored her. She raced down the stairs and pulled open the little cabinet where the

438

telephone directory was kept, pulling and tearing at the pages to find a number. 'Darina, please,' said Rose, 'I'm sorry.'

'Go away! Leave me alone!' The look Darina turned on her was so full of pure hatred that it froze Rose's blood.

'You don't understand—' she cried.

'I understand all right. Now *go away*!'

Rose felt she had no option but to comply. She was too shocked even to cry as, trembling, she mounted the stairs and went into her bedroom. She left the door open and stood just inside it, straining to hear what Darina was doing. It had all happened so fast. What had got into her? How could she undo this?

She heard Darina dialling furiously and, after a short while, heard her ask to speak to Bruno Flynn and something else she could not catch.

'Oh, please, let him not be there,' Rose prayed, although she had long ago forsaken God. Then, for Darina's sake, and for her own, she immediately reversed the prayer: *Please let him answer! Please, please make things all right, please let her forgive me.*

There was a long pause and then she heard Darina say something she could not catch, followed by the sound of the telephone being replaced. Rose found she could not move; the wall of her bedroom was cold against her rigid back muscles and the backs of her clenched fists. She heard Darina come thundering back up the stairs, the sound of her door being closed and locked and then, inexplicably, the sound of furniture being moved.

Slowly, with the greatest of efforts, she peeled herself off the wall and forced herself to cross the landing. 'Darina?' she called, knocking softly on the door. 'Darina, darling? Please? Can I come in?'

When there was no answer, she tried the door handle but, as she expected, the door would not open. 'Please, Darina,' she begged, leaning her forehead against the jamb and closing her eyes. In the adrenalin rush, her tiredness had evaporated and she felt as taut and alert as a bobcat. She tried to project her appeal through the wood of the door by honing every atom of concentration and willpower she could summon. 'Darina, could we talk, please? Will you let me explain?'

She listened hard, trying to figure out what her daughter

was doing. Darina was not rushing around the room but was moving purposefully, opening and closing drawers and moving forward and backwards in some sort of pattern.

She was packing.

'Darina!' Rose yelled in a panic now, thundering on the door with her fists. 'Darina! Stop this this minute! I want to talk to you! Come out here this instant!'

But there was still no reply, just that steady inexorable pattern of movement.

'Oh, God!' Rose fell back against the wall of the landing and covering her face with her hands, slid down it until she was crouched at its base.

The door to Effie's and Willie's room opened and Willie Brehony emerged, his round face concerned. 'What's going on, Rose? I don't want to interfere but is there anything I can do to help?'

Rose looked up at him. 'Oh, Willie! Things have just got out of control. I don't know how it happened, I really don't.'

'What's going on in there?' He indicated Darina's room.

'She seems to be packing. I think she might be going to run away.'

'Now calm down, Rose. If she was running away, it would be in the middle of the night and she wouldn't be letting us all know about it. What happened between you?'

Rose became aware that the noise behind Darina's door had been replaced by an ominous silence. But when the creak of a floorboard betrayed to Rose that her daughter was listening to what was transpiring outside between herself and Willie. She indicated as much to Willie and he helped her to her feet. The two of them went down the stairs and into the kitchen.

Rose told him the whole story and, knowing that he was aware of her own history, left nothing out. She finished with Darina's overhearing her response to Bruno Flynn's telephone call.

'Willie, what am I going to do?'

'Where do you think she'll go?'

'Some friend's perhaps. She has loads of them.'

'The best thing to do is not to try to stop her. She's in a frenzy at the moment – try to put yourself in her shoes. You've the right to stop her, of course, but if you do, she'll hate you all the more. If you let her go she'll calm down. Then the two of you can talk. If you think it would help, me and Effie will contact her in a day or so.'

'No, thank you, Willie, it's awfully kind of you but this is my mess. Oh, God, what a mess!' Tears threatened again but she quelled them with a fierce shake of her head: *I'm the adult here* . . . 'I got myself into this, Willie,' she said. 'I'll have to get myself out. But thanks for the offer – and for listening. I suppose you're right. The best thing to do is to let her go.'

'I'm sure of it,' said Willie. 'So long as you know she'll be safe. And in that regard, for your own peace of mind, you have every right to ask her which friend she's going to stay with.'

'You're very good. How come everyone is better at dealing with my daughter than I am?' she asked sadly.

'We're not. Nobody is. You're a wonderful mother, Rose. Wonderful. Me and Effie were just saying that only a while ago. It's just that we're not emotionally involved like you are. Darina can't hurt us the way she can hurt you and vice versa.' Rose loved the way Willie used words and, traumatised as she was, she almost smiled. But further conversation was cut off by the sound of Darina coming down the stairs, bumping alongside her something heavy, obviously luggage. Rose started for the door of the kitchen and Willie put a warning hand on her arm. 'Careful now.'

Rose stood in the hallway, blocking Darina's access to the flat's entrance door. 'Are you going somewhere, Darina?' she asked in as calm a tone as she could muster.

Darina lowered her head so Rose's view of it was just the crown. 'I'm getting out of here,' she said. Clearly expecting opposition, she held her rucksack tightly in both hands.

'I need to know where you're going. I'm entitled to that much,' Rose added as Darina, startled, looked up.

'I'm – I'll stay at Sharon's,' she muttered, shifting her eyes away so that Rose knew she was lying. But, forcing herself to let that hare sit, she called on all her remaining resources. 'How long do you think you'll stay there? Have you got your school uniform with you?'

'No – yes!' Darina corrected herself immediately. 'It's in

441

the rucksack,' she added, looking warily at her mother out of the corners of her eyes. Clearly, she did not quite know how to deal with this unexpected compliance.

Rose's heart felt as though it were being pulled apart. 'And have you money?' she asked.

'Some.'

'Let me give you a float.'

'It's all right,' muttered Darina, but she waited while Rose went to the kitchen to fetch her purse out of her handbag. She accepted the money Rose gave her – everything in the wallet – without comment. Then, holding it as though it were suspect, she asked. 'What's this all about?'

'You'll need it,' said Rose, thinking that if Darina did not leave right now everything would fall apart. She could not keep this up for much longer. 'Keep in touch, Darina,' she said and turned away, walking up the stairs to her room with as much dignity as she could command. All the way she could feel Darina's eyes boring into her back but somehow managed to resist the temptation to look back down the stairs.

Once inside her room, she waited until she heard the front door opening and closing. Then she ran to the dormer window and stood behind the lace curtain where she could see the front gate of the house but could not herself be seen. After a few seconds, she saw her daughter approach the gate. Darina had plaited her hair into one thick rope which hung long and pale over the rucksack on her back. Under a purple jacket, she wore a flowered mini-skirt and black tights. Her feet were thrust into purple sandals which made her long legs look delicate and spindly. She looked very, very young.

Rose pressed the back of her fist into her mouth as she saw her struggle with the catch of the gate. She stepped back slightly as Darina stopped for a moment or two and looked back at the house, upwards, right at the window behind which Rose was standing. After a second, she relatched the gate and walked towards the bus stop which was about thirty yards down the road. Rose watched until her diminishing figure was obscured from sight by the structure of the bus shelter; she watched the shelter until the bus came; she watched the conductor hop down off his platform to help take on the rucksack; until Darina, her bright

442

plait like an exclamation mark down the middle of her purple back, boarded the bus.

She watched until the bus pulled away into the traffic and was gone finally from view.

Then she rolled onto her bed, curled herself up as tightly as a caterpillar and let the scalding tears burst through.

Dorothy Cranshaw came to the desk of the hotel. 'May I help you?' Professionally, she assessed the girl who stood there: not the sort of guest they were used to dealing with. This girl, young, tall and slim, with blonde, plaited hair, wore a rucksack. German?

'I was looking for a boy called Bruno Flynn,' said the girl. 'I believe his uncle works here?'

Dorothy looked more closely at her. There was something desperately familiar about the face and the wide, slanted eyes. 'I'm not sure Bruno's here,' she said, 'and John should be on his way back from Dublin but we're not expecting him for an hour or so.' She picked up the desk phone. 'I'll ring the place where Bruno is staying. Who shall I say is looking for him?'

'Darina O'Beirne.'

Dorothy almost dropped the telephone but managed somehow to dial the number. 'I know your mother,' she said as casually as she could manage. 'But I thought you'd gone back to Dublin?'

'We did,' said the girl. 'But I hitched back.' She seemed to think that was enough of an explanation and Dorothy did not push it. The familiarity of her features was nagging away at the back of her brain. She knew this girl's face almost as well as she knew her own or George's and it wasn't just that the girl was like Rose because she did not resemble her mother all that much. There was something absolutely familiar about the colouring, the eyes – 'Hello, Mona,' she said as the line was answered at the other end. 'How are you?' She listened to Mona's reply without hearing it and then asked if Bruno was around. 'I see,' she said then when Mona said he was not in. 'Would you mind giving him a message? There's a girl here looking for him, her name is Darina.' She realised that for some inexplicable reason she had deliberately omitted the last name. 'She'll be here at the hotel,' she said, glancing at Darina interrogatively and, when Darina nodded, 'For a while anyway. Thanks, Mona,' she said and hung up. 'Bruno rang his uncle's place about an hour ago,' she said to the girl. 'He's apparently hitching back from Dublin too. He had reached Monaghan town so he should be home quite soon.' As she spoke, Dorothy continued to study the girl; it was driving her crazy that she could not place the resemblance. 'You could go up to the fishing lodge,' she said, 'I'll give you directions, but you're welcome to wait here if you'd like.'

'Thank you very much,' said the girl. 'I'll wait here, if you don't mind.'

'Would you like a cup of tea or coffee while you're waiting?' Dorothy offered.

'Thank you, that would be lovely,' replied Darina and Dorothy thought to herself that Rose had certainly done a good job on the girl's manners. Composed too, an unusual trait for someone her age.

'This way,' she said, coming out from behind the desk and leading the way into the sitting room. She always enjoyed the look of astonishment on the face of anyone seeing the room for the first time and Darina's was no exception. 'It's a bit eccentric,' she apologised, 'but it's been this way for years and the guests seem to get a kick out of it. We call it our Ali Baba room.'

'It's absolutely lovely,' said Darina. 'I think it's perfect.'

'Thank you,' said Dorothy. 'Have a look round, make yourself at home, I'll go and fetch your drink. Tea or coffee?'

'Tea, please.'

It was when Dorothy was bustling down the corridor to the kitchen that she realised why the girl's face was so familiar. She got such a shock that she stopped dead, putting her hand against the wall to steady herself.

John!

That beautiful young girl was the spitting image of John Flynn. Why hadn't she guessed before now? John was her father! Hoping that no one had seen her stupid behaviour, she looked around, then carried on into the kitchen; luckily the evening rush hour had not yet started and she had the room to herself.

Her brain working furiously, Dorothy brewed the tea. Who else knew this stunning truth? Clearly not the girl herself, clearly not John. For some reason best known to herself, Rose had concealed the information all these years. And yet she had arrived

444

unannounced at the hotel only yesterday. Could she have wanted to see John? Maybe she felt it was time to tell him.

And what was she, Dorothy, to do with this new knowledge? It was inconceivable that, in seeing the two of them together, George, for instance, would not deduce that John and Darina were related. Would John himself see it?

And the girl was looking for Bruno. She obviously did not know that he was her first cousin. The whole thing was an appalling mess. And now it had been dumped right here in Willow House.

As she laid the tea-tray, Dorothy decided to plump for Rose. In all fairness, this situation could not be precipitated without her knowledge. She would have to telephone Rose in Dublin to tell her she had realised the truth, that Darina was here looking for Bruno and that John was likely to arrive on the scene any minute.

Rose could make the decisions from that point on.

'Here you are, dear,' she said as she went back into the sitting room, hoping her voice did not sound too hearty.

The girl was holding one of the armless china shepherdesses, examining it closely. 'You have the most beautiful things in here,' she said as, with great care, she replaced it on the mantelpiece. 'I can see why you named it after Ali Baba.'

'It's the very devil to dust,' said Dorothy, putting down the tray. 'Now, if you don't mind, dear, I'll leave you. If you need anything else, just ring at the desk, all right?'

'Thank you very much,' said Darina. 'You're very kind.'

'Not at all. Have fun in here. This is what the Americans call a "hands-on" room. Handle anything you like, dear. See you later.'

Outside, Dorothy took a deep breath. She marched to the telephone and dialled the Sundarbans number. *Please, please let it be the Colonel and not Daphne*, she prayed as she waited.

'Hello, Gussie,' she said, so relieved that Gus answered that she actually smiled. 'Dorothy here,' she continued, 'listen, something's come up and I need to get in touch with Rose in Dublin. Could I have her number please?'

'Right, right,' she wrote the number on a scratch pad, 'thanks a million. Everything all right your end?'

She listened for a few seconds. 'Well, never mind, Gussie,' she said then. 'We'll all live to ride another day. See you soon, all right?'

She stared at the number on the pad for a long time, going over in her mind how she would approach Rose. Then she decided that there was only one way to do it and that was the direct way.

'Hello?'

'Rose,' said Dorothy, 'this is Dorothy Cranshaw.'

'Hello, Dorothy.' Rose sounded surprised, as well she might. Her voice also sounded muzzy, as though she had a bad cold.

'Are you all right, my dear?' Dorothy asked. 'You sound a bit flu-ey.'

'I'm fine, Dorothy. Just a bit tired, that's all.'

'Something's happened, Rose. I don't quite know how to say this, so I'll just come right out with it.' She paused a fraction of a second then plunged right in. 'Darina's here, my dear.'

'*What!*'

'She arrived a few minutes ago. And, Rose – she's looking for Bruno Flynn.'

There was silence at the other end of the line. Dorothy squared her shoulders. 'You'll have to forgive me, my dear, maybe you'll think I'm an interfering old busybody, but you see, John – John Flynn, that is – is due home any moment.' She listened hard but still there was nothing on the line except the atmospherics of a long-distance call. 'I thought I should call you and let you know that,' she continued. 'What do you think we should do?'

'I'm – I'm sorry.'

'Rose, darling, don't be sorry. Sorry for what? I'm on your side. It's just that I don't know what to do. She's in the sitting room now, waiting.'

'Who else knows?'

'No one. And I'm not going to tell anyone. But, Rose . . . ' Dorothy took a deep breath; she would have to come straight out with it. 'As soon as John sees that girl,' she continued crisply, 'he'll know. She probably will too. And certainly George will. She's the image of John.'

Again there was a pause during which the atmospherics crackled and when Rose spoke again, her voice sounded weak.

'Dorothy, I don't know what to do. I'm so tired, this has all happened so fast. Yesterday—'

'I know, my dear, I know,' said Dorothy soothingly. 'It's all a terrible muddle now. But you've kept this a secret for so long that you'll find it might be best to let it all out in the open at last. Do your parents know the truth?'

'They've never said, but I know they know.'

'So what do you think I should do with Darina?' Dorothy asked gently. 'I don't want to put pressure on you, but time is ticking away. They'll all be here together. At least Derek is not due home for another two days. That's something.'

'I'm coming down there!'

Dorothy was cheered to hear the sudden decisiveness. 'I think that's wise,' she said, 'I'll be here and so will George and you can count on us. You can all count on us,' she added, thinking of the shocks in store not only for Darina but for her beloved and invaluable general manager.

'I'm sorry that all this has landed in on you, Dorothy.'

'Stop apologising. How soon can you get here?'

'It's probably too late to hire a car but I'll get there as fast as I possibly can.'

'It's a pity John's already on his way,' said Dorothy, unable to resist the grim humour of the situation. 'He could have given you a lift.'

But Rose was too distracted to react. 'I'll get there as quick as I can,' she repeated.

'Now, remember, you're not the first woman who's found herself in this situation and Darina is not the first daughter either. It's not the end of the world.'

'It's the end of my world.'

'No, it's not, and stop thinking like that. It could be the start of a whole new and much more honest world for you. And you've a right to be proud of what you've achieved with that girl, she's great.'

'Dorothy, I'll never be able to repay you for this.'

'Nonsense! Now hang up the phone, put on a bit of war-paint and comb your hair. I'll see you as soon as you get here. In the meantime, I'll think of something to divert Darina so her path won't cross with John's until at least you've had a chance

447

to think out some sort of plan.' A thought occurred to her. 'Is it all right if she goes out with Bruno if he shows up first?'

'You won't be able to stop her. Darina's very single-minded.'

'We'll see how it goes, so. Anyway, for the moment, it would be the lesser of two evils. Now stop panicking, Rose, and get here safely. All right?'

Rose looked across at Willie's faint profile, lit only by the feeble glow from the dashboard instruments. Dear, dependable Willie, she thought. He had volunteered immediately to drive her to Monaghan and would not entertain any protests. Effie finished work later than he did and they had waited until she came home before they left. She had wanted to come too but had decided against it in the end; the cash-and-carry was in the middle of an audit and she had a very early start the next morning.

Rose saw they were just coming into Cootehill. Ten or fifteen minutes more and they would be at Willow House. Her stomach was churning. What was happening at the moment? Was John sitting expecting her? She saw him in her mind's eye, a graceful, long-legged figure seated on one of the jewel-coloured couches in Dorothy's fabulous room of treasures.

Where were Bruno and Darina? What were they doing? What was going to happen in the next hour?

'Nervous?' asked Willie, picking up on her thoughts.

'Yes. Do you think we should ring to say we're nearly there?'

'What for? They're expecting us anyway, aren't they?'

'Well, Dorothy is expecting us anyway, and I suppose George. I don't know who else.'

Her voice shook and Willie patted her knee. 'Take it easy, girl. They're only human beings like the rest of us. No one's going to shoot you.'

'In a way I wish someone would.'

'Yerra, girl, will you cop onto yourself. This is going to be a nine-days' wonder. This time next year you'll ask yourself what all the fuss was about.'

'Willie, how can I ever thank you?'

'You've already thanked me,' he said seriously, stopping at the crossroads at the top of the town. 'Which way?'

448

'Right,' directed Rose. 'What do you mean I've already thanked you?'

'You brought me Effie,' he said simply.

'I had nothing to do with that, Willie.'

'Oh, yes, you did. If you hadn't been so kind to Effie all those years ago, she probably would have gone back to Offaly and I would never have met her. She might even be dead now,' he added, almost to himself, squinting out through the windscreen.

They drove the rest of the way in silence and Rose's tandem emotions of terror and excitement grew, corkscrewing towards overwhelming nausea. 'Just a minute, Willie,' she gasped. 'Pull in here please, quickly.'

He steered the car into the verge and stopped, just in time to let her get the door open. Again and again she retched on the grass until her stomach was empty and the tears of relief were pouring down her face. Then she leaned against the cold car, letting the air bathe her. Willie came and put his arm around her shoulder; being smaller than she, he had to reach upwards. 'Are you all right, girl? You poor thing, are you feeling better?'

Rose nodded. 'Thank you, sorry,' she whispered.

'If you say "sorry" or "thank you" one more time, Rose O'Beirne, I'll belt you,' said Willie. 'Now, should we go and get you a drink of water or something before we face into this?'

'No, I'll be fine, honestly. I feel much better now.'

And, almost to her surprise, Rose did feel much better when she sat back in the car. She felt weak, but her head was clear and she was not so emotionally charged. She used tissues to wipe the sweat off her forehead and sprayed perfume on her neck and behind her ears. And, absurdly, she remembered the phial of Gold Spot, useful on long flights, she always carried in her handbag. She sprayed it in her mouth and smiled across at Willie. 'Ready for anything now, Willie.'

'I'm right behind you, girl.'

She leaned her head against the back of her seat and forced herself into a mode of acceptance. Whatever would be would be. To help, she concentrated on Effie's parting advice: 'Now remember, Rose, just be yourself. You just turn up and be yourself and everything will be taken care of.'

All she could do from now on was her best.

*

449

Dorothy had been behaving very oddly since he had come back, thought John. And come to think of it, so had George. He looked at George's face, bent over the sheaf of documents he had brought back from Dublin. The older man's expression was serious, intent on what he was reading, but John felt that there was a suppressed nervousness about him. 'Is everything all right, George?' he asked quietly.

George looked like a guilty schoolboy. 'Why should there be anything wrong?'

'Never mind,' said John, 'forget I even asked.' They were sitting in the little office behind the reception desk and he stood up and stretched his cramped muscles. There was definitely something wrong, he thought, as he gazed at the top of the other man's head. George's thoughts were normally written on an open book but tonight he was acting furtively, avoiding eye contact. 'Are you sure there's nothing wrong?' he tried one more time.

George stared at him miserably. Then he stood up and capped his pen. 'Better go and talk to Dorothy,' he said. 'She's in the kitchen, I think.'

'Why do we need to talk to Dorothy?' John was becoming alarmed.

'Dorothy,' said George firmly and John had no option but to follow him out of the room.

They were waylaid out in the hall by a pair of Welshmen who wanted an early start in the morning and to talk at length about the equipment they would need for their shooting expedition; then a French couple needed reassurance about taking their car across the border into the north.

When they finally got to the kitchen, Dorothy, oatflakes steeping in a large bowl beside her, was preparing for next day's breakfasts; she had built a little pyramid of oranges right in the centre of the table ready for squeezing and was stoning prunes. 'Hi there,' she said, looking up as they came in. 'Want a cuppa?' Wiping her hands on her apron, she crossed to the kettle hissing on the range which still co-existed in the kitchen alongside the more modern gas and electrical appliances.

'Thanks,' said George. 'Er, Dorothy,' he went on, 'I've brought John in for a chat.'

John looked from one to the other. 'What is going on? I know there's something.'

'Sit down, John,' said Dorothy. 'I think I'd better make you a cup of tea.'

'I don't want to sit down and I don't want tea! Please, Dorothy, just tell me what's the matter.' But when she sat at the table and George did too, he felt obliged to join them. He was beginning to feel a knob of fear forming in his stomach. 'Is Bruno all right?' he asked.

'He's fine, John, fine,' said Dorothy. 'Look, my dear,' she went on, 'you're quite right, there is something going on. And I wasn't going to tell you because it's really none of my business. But there's someone on the way to see you, John. Any minute now.'

'Who? Is this something to do with Bruno?' Again he looked from one to the other but George, studying the palms of his hands, was no help at all. John looked back at Dorothy. 'Please, Dorothy, I can't stand it, this is dreadful. Just tell me!'

'It's Rose,' said Dorothy gently. 'Rose O'Beirne Moffat. She's on her way to see you.'

The name hit John like a pile-driver. He looked stupidly at Dorothy's concerned, kind face. 'Rose? She's coming here? Tonight?'

She nodded. 'As I said, she should be here any minute.'

It was too much to take in. From their sombre expressions, Dorothy and George clearly knew that this would be more than a casual, unexpected visit. How had these people found out about himself and Rose, about things that happened so long ago? He was afraid to ask questions.

But the old flame of excitement kindled again. Rose. Rose was coming here. She wanted to see him. After all these years he and Rose were going to see each other again.

Almost at once, his joy died down in view of the worried expressions on the faces of Dorothy and George. John rarely let his imagination run away with him but it did so now as a new dread occurred to him. There was something wrong with Rose. She was going to die. She probably had cancer and wanted to make amends. That's why she was coming to see him. 'Did she say why she was coming?' At last he had found his voice. 'I mean, why now?'

'I think I'll leave that to her. That's between the two of you,' said Dorothy.

451

Silence fell on the big kitchen, a suspenseful silence, broken only by the hiss from the range and an intermittent dripping from an old brass tap into the scullery sink. John realised Dorothy was looking at him warily, as though she was ready for him if he did something uncharacteristic or surprising. 'How long have you known?' he whispered.

'About what?'

'That Rose and I – that we—'

'Not long,' she said. 'Only since today. I really had no idea until today. But I might as well tell you now that Rose called here. She and—' She seemed to stop herself suddenly then continued in a rush. 'She was visiting Gussie and Daphne in Sundarbans.'

'Did she ask for me?'

'No. But looking back on it now, I have the strong impression that she came here looking for you.'

'Is she still over at Sundarbans?'

'No, she's coming from Dublin. Look, John, I don't want to say any more. I really don't. Will you have a sherry – please? I think we all need one. George?' She went to her little cupboard and took out three glasses.

But she did not even have a chance to pour the first drink. Because just as she uncorked the bottle, the front window of the kitchen was lit brightly by a pair of headlights.

They all listened intently. It could be anyone, after all – a guest returning from an outing to the local pubs, an ordinary friend.

They all jumped slightly when they heard the bell ring at reception.

Rose covered the bell with her hand, muffling its reverberations. It had sounded too loud, too cheeky.

Willie had insisted on coming in with her in case he was needed but he was trying to make himself unobtrusive, hanging back by the door, trying to conceal his tubby little frame in the shadows. Rose would have preferred, now, if he was not there but she did not want to hurt him by asking him to leave.

But then, after she had tapped the bell, everything and everyone, Darina, Bruno, even Willie, drained away from her mind leaving no trace. Time ceased to have any meaning as she

452

waited through what might have been ten seconds or ten hours; psychically she felt as though she were standing on tiptoe.

Then, from a distance, she heard the sound of an opening door.

Footsteps approached.

Slow, male footsteps.

She looked towards the sound and a second later, he was there. Older, broader, but unmistakable.

He stopped dead just as he came into view and every conscious thought in Rose's head fused until there was only one thought, as clear and hard as a diamond.

Here was John Flynn.

John felt as though he had been assaulted.

She was perfect.

Rose O'Beirne Moffat stood in front of him again and she was perfect.

He could not move. He did not even want to touch her or take her in his arms. He just wanted to look at her. The lustrous hair was short now and her clothes were smarter, more adult, but otherwise she was exactly as he had pictured for so many years.

Then he became aware that someone else was present, a round little man who was standing by the door. Was this, perhaps, Rose's boyfriend? Husband, even? The thought unlocked his paralysis and allowed him to move forward, holding out his hand. 'Hello.'

'Hello,' she said. She did not take his hand but continued to stare at him as though she could not believe what she saw. He realised she was looking at his scar, faded now but still clearly visible and, instinctively, his hand flew up to cover it. She started at the sudden movement. 'What happened to your face? Was that—?'

'Yes. On the ship. I think I wrote to you about it.' He forced his hand back down to his side.

The glow from a small green-shaded lamp on the desk beside her cast an unnatural pallor on her face. His imagination might not have been all that far off – she could be sick, he thought despairingly. This close to her, he could smell her spicy perfume, yet the commercial fragrance was interlaid with another familiar

453

scent, the distinctive musk of her body. 'Long time no see,' he said stupidly.

'Yes.'

There was a small cough behind her and the man who had been lurking by the door took a step forward. 'I'll be in the car if you need me, Rose,' he said.

She turned round. 'Oh, Willie, let me introduce you. This is John Flynn,' she said, then, turning back to John, 'This is my friend, Willie Brehony. He drove me down. I don't have a car,' she added.

'How do you do, Mr Brehony?' said John, some of his professional expertise coming to his rescue. 'Please don't feel you have to go out to the car. Let me sort you out with a drink or something.' While he spoke, he was assessing the other man. She had called him a friend and he could detect no proprietorial belligerence in him; on the contrary, the little man seemed apologetic, as if he felt he had no right to be here. 'What would you like?' John continued, trying desperately to keep his eyes from straying back to Rose.

'No, please!' cried the man. 'I'll be absolutely fine out in the car. I'd prefer it, actually. Breath of fresh air, all that—'

'Well, if you're sure,' said John.

'Do, please, have a drink, Willie,' urged Rose, 'it's been a long day for you. I'm sure you could do with one.'

'Yes, please do. You must have a drink,' said John. He realised that as Willie Brehony backed towards the door, step by step, he and Rose were pursuing the poor man. The situation was becoming absurd, as if the two of them were trying to ensnare this friend, postponing for as long as possible the shattering prospect of being alone.

'No thank you, really.' Willie had reached the door. 'I'd prefer to sit out here by myself. Honest!'

'Are you sure you'll be all right?' John tried again. 'It's a cold night.'

'I'll be fine.' Willie managed to get the door open and escape, leaving the two of them high and dry in the softly lit hallway. Tension between them tightened like a piece of wire as they stood staring at the glass of the door through which Willie had disappeared. Finally John, unable to bear it any longer, addressed Rose's reflection, pale as a wraith in the dark glass. 'You wanted to see me?' His voice sounded hoarse.

'Yes,' she whispered. 'Could we go somewhere a bit private?'

'This way.' He turned and led her towards the sitting room.

In the warm red glow of a dying fire, the room now resembled not a bazaar but the storeroom of a magician: its hundreds of objects glowed and glittered in soft pools of many colours cast by the table lamps; its mirrors reflected light and not form.

John noticed none of this. He invited Rose to sit on a couch and himself took a seat on a chair opposite her. When she obeyed, sitting on the very edge of the couch, the multi-layered light highlighted her face in such a way that his breath seemed to catch on something sharp in his chest. He prayed he would not be called upon to say anything immediately because he was sure he would not be able to form a single coherent word.

But she seemed as tongue-tied as he and the silence enlarged dangerously, charging the air between them so potently that he was afraid his body would betray him. Nevertheless, he forced himself to cross his arms in front of his chest and to wait.

Mirroring his action, she crossed her own arms and finally, looking at the ground, spoke in a very small voice. 'I've something difficult to tell you, John.' She glanced upwards at him for a split second, just a flick of her eyes and the sensation felt like the lash of a whip.

'I – I don't know how to say this,' she said, returning her gaze to the floor.

He refused to countenance that she might be going to die. 'Is it to do with why you stopped writing to me all those years ago?' Somehow he managed to get the words out.

'In a way, yes – but it's even more difficult than that.'

'Why did you do it, Rose?' Now he could not help himself as fear and desire fused in anger. 'Why, Rose? What did I ever do to you? Even if you'd told me! I could have accepted it, *maybe* – if you'd told me.' He leaned forward urgently. 'Why, for God's sake? I loved you and you led me to believe you loved me. What stopped that? Didn't you think I even deserved the courtesy of an explanation?'

She stared at him and seemed confused, which further heightened his anger. 'Jesus, Mary and Joseph, all those letters *returned*! How do you think I felt? At least if I'd known—'

'John, let me explain. I got an anony—'

'I thought we loved each other!' he said, cutting her off, passion making his voice shake. 'I wrote and wrote and then – nothing! How could you have done that, Rose? I even humiliated myself with your grandmother, giving her back those amethysts and begging her to send them to you as a sign. Remember the sign, Rose? Elizabeth and Essex? All that high-flown, noble rubbish?'

She came to her own defence. 'I didn't know that until very recently – honestly, John, only in the last few days. You've got to believe me. She's dead now and I'll never know why she didn't tell me—'

'Why should I believe you? What an idiot – I believed you, then, Rose! More fool me!' Unable to control all the confused emotions – anger, terror, love, hatred, bitterness – surging through his veins, he jumped to his feet. She half rose out of her own chair as if to run away and as quickly as his anger had flared, it died. 'I'm sorry, Rose,' he sat down again. 'I'm really sorry. I had no right—'

'Oh, you have every right, John, you have every right,' Rose cried. 'If only you knew what right you have—'

'What are you talking about?'

She reached out on either side of her and took handfuls of the silk tassels which lay beside her on the couch, bracing herself as though she were expecting a physical onslaught. 'You have every right, John, because – because you have a daughter.'

The words were meaningless to him. What had she just said? He stared at her. Words, words . . . 'I beg your pardon?' he asked.

'You – we – have a daughter.'

CHAPTER FIFTEEN

'Only my mother and father knew – and my friend, Effie, in Dublin. That's her husband Willie out there, waiting in the car. He knows, too, of course. And now George and Dorothy,' added Rose honestly. 'They guessed but, as it happens, not until today, when they first saw Darina.'

'Only the whole world, you mean. Everyone except me.' John felt he was holding onto reality by the merest thread. 'How could you, Rose?'

'I told you – at least I tried to tell you earlier, but you cut me off. I got an anonymous letter telling me that you went to bed with another girl. Some girl in Charlottetown.'

'*What?*'

'Some girl in Charlottetown,' repeated Rose. 'I was livid, John. There was I in a convent in London—'

'But I didn't know you were in a convent. You never even told me that. When did you get this letter? And who was I supposed to have gone to bed with? How could you have believed it?' The injustices piled one on top of the other until he was trembling from head to toe. He was standing at the mantelpiece and gripped it for support. 'And you didn't give me a chance to defend myself.'

'Well, *did* you go to bed with someone else?'

'You were the only person I loved, Rose.'

'That's not what I asked.'

'On my sacred word of honour, I did *not* go to bed with anyone in Charlottetown or anywhere else.'

'But the letter was from Derek!' cried Rose.

'I thought you said it was anonymous—' John began and then the enormity of what she had said sank in. He felt the colour draining from his face. 'Derek sent it?' he whispered. 'How do you know?'

'It was postmarked from home but he was home by the time it was sent and he was the only one who knew what you were doing in Charlottetown. It had to be him.'

'Lots of people from around here knew I was in Charlottetown.'

Rose lifted her chin, a gesture he remembered well. 'Yes, but they didn't see you there. I just know that letter was from Derek,' she said. 'I knew it at the time and I still believe it.'

Anger began to gather like a hard ball somewhere in the vicinity of John's diaphragm. He clenched his fists. 'I'll find out the truth about Derek later,' he said, 'but that still does not excuse you from not telling me about my child.'

'I thought it was for the best at the time,' said Rose. 'Please, John, you've got to believe me.' She raised her hands in a helpless arc by her sides. 'It was all so long ago. I'm really, really sorry.'

'Why are you crawling out of the woodwork now? What's so special about now?'

She looked at him and the depths of misery in her eyes went some way towards appeasing his contempt. But John continued to be goaded by his anger with his twin. 'Well?' he demanded. 'Why now, Rose? And am I to know where she is?'

'It appears she's out for a walk,' whispered Rose. As she looked at him, something she had said earlier began to nag at him. 'What's so special about now? Why the timing?' he asked once again but she just covered her face with her hands and slumped into the couch.

He watched her for a few seconds and although he tried hard to hold on to his righteousness, felt it beginning to slip away. She looked so vulnerable; he wanted to forgive her everything, to forget the last sixteen years, to sit beside her and to take her in his arms.

And then he remembered. She had called her daughter by name. That name was Darina. 'Oh, my God!' Abruptly, he sat on a chair beside the fireplace.

The ormolu clock ticked loudly through the long silence in the room. Then, with a whoosh, the floor of coal collapsed in the grate. John automatically reached for the scuttle to replenish it but having picked up the shovel and tongs, replaced them slowly. 'She's out now, with Bruno?' It was a statement, not a question

458

and when Rose nodded, the enormity of the situation hit him. 'What are we going to do?' he asked.

'I don't know,' she said. 'Effie, that's my friend I told you about, she says it's not such a big deal. That they'll grow out of it.'

'We didn't.' To his own ears, his voice sounded tired and remote. 'Well, I can't speak for you, of course, but I didn't.' He didn't care now if he was making a fool of himself.

'Effie also says that even if it isn't just a crush, they're first cousins and that first cousins are all right. Better than second cousins. According to the Church, that is. Although it doesn't arise, of course, at the moment, she says that if they wanted to get married, the Church would give them a dispensation.'

'Is that so? Who is this Effie? Is she a canon lawyer now as well as a psychologist?'

'I don't blame you for being upset, John, but leave Effie out of it. She's been wonderful. She cares about Darina like a second mother.'

'Maybe Darina would have been better off with a father instead of two mothers.'

'Please, John!'

'Well, wouldn't she? I can't believe you did this to me – and to her. Leaving me out of it, hasn't she some rights in this too, by the way? Does she know she has a father? Or does she think she was abandoned by some heartless monster who left her and her mother to fend for themselves?'

'I thought it was for the best. And I was afraid and confused,' she whispered through her hands.

'I asked you a question, Rose. What does my daughter know about me?'

'Only that you're from Monaghan and that you emigrated to Canada.' She started to cry, her shoulders shaking and he was filled with remorse.

'Oh, Rose, I'm sorry!' He jumped up from the chair and was about to run to her but something, a hurt that was too deep for instant salving, stopped him. 'I'm behaving badly, I know,' he said quietly. 'I'm not usually so sarcastic or so bitter.'

'You've every right. I'm the one who's behaved badly, I should have trusted you. I should have asked you about that horrible letter. I should have told you I was pregnant in the first place—'

'But you were only sixteen. Don't blame yourself. I'm sorry I said those things – how could you possibly take decisions of that magnitude all by yourself?'

'I should have known you better. Oh, John, I loved you so much. I can't tell you how devastated I was—'

'And you have no idea the number of nights I sat and lay awake, trying to puzzle out what had gone wrong, what I'd done. I messed around with those amethysts, I even made novenas, Rose, *novenas!*' They were speaking so rapidly, tumbling the sentences together and over each other that they stopped almost simultaneously and stared at one another.

'I'm so sorry, John,' Rose whispered then. 'Do you forgive me?'

'Forgive you?' But before he could say any more, there was a discreet knock at the door and Dorothy's head appeared. 'Sorry to intrude, but they've arrived back and they're in the kitchen. They're having cocoa at the moment but I thought I'd better see what you want me to do next.' She paused briefly to take in the situation. 'You've obviously told him, my dear?' she asked Rose.

Rose nodded. 'Where did you find them, Dorothy?'

'George went out in the car, he met them on the road – they were on the way up to the fishing lodge, actually.'

John's heart had started to bang against his ribcage. His daughter. His daughter was only a few feet away and he was going to meet her. Suppose she hated him? Dorothy was still standing expectantly in the door. 'What do you want me to do?'

John looked at Rose. 'I'd like to meet her alone – I mean with you, of course – but without Bruno.'

'Will I send her in here?' Dorothy took a step back out of the room.

'Yes, please,' said Rose. 'And, Dorothy, what did she say when she heard I was here? We parted this morning on pretty bad terms.'

'She seemed surprised, but that's all. I'll send her in,' said Dorothy. She glanced at John. 'Do you feel ready for this? I can stall some more, if you like.'

'I don't know whether I'm on my head or my heels, Dorothy. I'm sorry you're involved in this situation, it's not really fair on you and George.'

'If one more person tries to say that to me this evening, I'll clobber him or her! And that includes you, Mr Flynn.' She closed the door behind her with a soft click.

John and Rose avoided one another's eyes and stared at the door. John could not remember when last he had been so nervous. A hundred times in as many seconds he imagined what she would look like, what he would say, what she would say.

It was still unreal. A daughter. He repeated it to himself. A *daughter*.

Then the door opened and she was there.

The room receded, even Rose receded and all he saw was his daughter's face. In some ways it was like tearing a veil off the past. Instantly, he saw both himself and Rose in her but far more than that, he saw Darina. And she was utterly beautiful.

She gave him only the most cursory of glances but hovered inside the door, looking uncertainly at her mother. Then she raised her chin in that gesture which he associated so clearly with Rose. 'I hope you haven't come to take me back, Mother?'

'No, Darina, not unless you want me to.'

The catch in Rose's voice caused Darina to peer closely at her. 'Is there something wrong?' she asked. 'Is Effie all right?'

'She's fine,' said Rose. 'Did you not come across Willie in the car park outside? He drove me down.'

'Willie here?' she asked in genuine astonishment. 'No, I – we – we came in the back way.' Holding onto the doorknob, she waited for something to happen.

John felt as though he was bolted to the floor. He could not have moved or said anything at all even if someone had put a shotgun to his back. He stared at Darina, at her lovely face, the purple sandals; at the way the light fell on her hair, carving shadows in its paleness. He felt, rather than saw, Rose rise from her seat and cross to the door. 'Darina,' she said, 'come into the room for a minute. I have something to tell you.'

John saw the girl hesitate, then look across at him. He saw her eyes widen. Had she guessed?

She allowed herself to be steered towards the couch from which Rose had risen. As she sat, Rose sat beside her and took both her hands in her own. But Darina looked only perfunctorily at her mother; her eyes were now fixed on John and he was sure that in her expression he could read the dawn of scared recognition. He tried to keep his own expression as neutral as possible.

'Darina,' said Rose, her voice shaking, 'there's something that maybe I should have told you a very long time ago, but I didn't think you were ready for it. I hope you'll forgive me.'

Darina was still staring at John.

Rose took a deep breath, then said softly, 'Darina, this man is your father. His name is John.'

John saw she had been about to say something else but had stopped herself; intuitively, he recognised that she had held back from using his surname. And as he watched the play of emotions across his daughter's face, he was glad that the shocks were being doled out to Darina one at a time.

After a short silence during which none of the three moved, Darina removed her hands carefully from Rose's and folded them in her own lap. 'I see,' she said tonelessly.

Rose attempted to take the hands again but Darina resisted, holding them up in the air and out of reach. She looked across at John, still riveted to his spot in the middle of the floor. 'How do you do?' she said, so flatly that John found it impossible to decipher her state of mind. He took a couple of steps towards her but she flinched backwards on the couch.

'This is as much of a shock to me as it is to you, Darina,' he said hoarsely. 'I had no idea of your existence until ten minutes ago.'

'I see,' she said again. Then she turned to Rose. 'Can I go now?' she asked politely. 'Bruno's waiting for me in the kitchen.'

Rose looked at her helplessly. 'Don't you want to stay for a few minutes, ask questions – anything?'

'No, thank you,' said Darina, still in that polite way. 'Maybe later, but not at the moment. May I go?'

Rose nodded and Darina got up from the couch and crossed to the door, leaving without a backward glance.

The two of them looked after her. John's mind was reeling; he felt he had handled the situation very badly but it had all happened so fast. Should he run after her, insist on talking to her? He looked at Rose. 'That was terrible,' he said. 'Oh, Rose,

462

she's so beautiful, but I don't know what to say or do, I'm too shocked. What should I have done? Shouldn't we at least have told her exactly who I am?'

'Maybe I should – but I could see the effect you were having on her and I suppose I couldn't inflict any more on her. I'll give her a little time. I'm sure that after a while there'll be a million things she'll want to know. Anyway,' again Rose put her head in her hands, 'I'm sure if she hasn't guessed by now, Bruno will tell her.' She looked up. 'John?' She hesitated. 'Please, please believe me that I'm desperately sorry about all this. And the awful thing is, it didn't have to happen this way. You might not believe it but I came barrelling down here only on Saturday determined to see you. I can't believe it was only Saturday,' she added in a faraway voice, then, pulling herself together, 'For myself,' she said firmly. 'I came for myself. Nothing to do with Darina – but, of course, if things had worked out as I'd hoped, I would have told you about her. Even if they hadn't, I would have told you anyway.'

John's senses sharpened. 'Worked out? How had you hoped things would work out?'

'Between us, John. I had to find out how things stood between us. I know I'm going out on a limb here but I feel I've nothing to lose now. It was really weird, over the last while, all of a sudden, your name seemed to be everywhere. Daddy was talking about you in connection with Sundarbans and I met an old friend in Dublin and she was asking about you and oh—' Her voice wobbled and she paused to bring it under control.

'Anyway,' she continued more strongly, 'that's all been overtaken by recent events. With Darina in the picture now, we'll have to talk about how we proceed from here, even if—'

'Even if what?' John felt that everything in the world, everything in his life, depended on her next answer.

'Even if we find there's nothing left between us.' She looked at him, her eyes enormous. 'It's been a very, very long time, John. We were children. For all I know, you could have—'

'As far as I'm concerned, we're still children.' He took a moment to steady himself. 'I suppose there are a million things I should say and do to protect myself here, Rose. Half an hour ago I didn't even know you were around, much less that I had a daughter. It's far too much to take in at once. But I suppose you're right, we've – I've very little to lose by being honest. I'll tell you one thing for sure. I've never been in love with anyone like I've been in love with you. I mean, I've never been in love like – since I was in love with you – oh, I'm making a mess of this . . .' He stopped and thumped one fist into the other.

'No, you're not!'

'Do you feel the same?' He risked it, letting the words out one by one.

She nodded. 'Oh, yes, John. Why do you think I came here?'

He gazed at her beautiful, tear-stained face. He should probably take her in his arms, kiss her, hug her, make love to her, but what was happening was too momentous for something so ordinary. 'What next?' he whispered.

'I don't know, but I know it has to be one step at a time,' she whispered back.

The tension snapped and, incongruously, he started to laugh. 'Could we consult this Effie person?' He laughed out loud, a hearty, tension-breaking guffaw and in response, Rose started to giggle too. She covered her mouth with her hand. 'I suppose I could phone her.'

'Oh, Rose!' In two strides he was beside her, pulling her to her feet and crushing her against him. She started to cry again and he felt the tears rolling down his own face too. He had not wept for years but he was not in the least ashamed. They wept together, tears of release, joy – and sorrow for the lost time.

In the kitchen, Dorothy was trying to persuade the two young people to stay another little while. 'Do hang on for just a few more minutes,' she wheedled. 'Your mother will be here shortly, I'm sure, Darina. Anyway, it's so cold and dark out there. George will drop you wherever you want to go in a minute, won't you, George?'

She looked at George for confirmation and then immediately back at the girl. 'But you've got to wait, at least until we have you fixed up with somewhere to stay for the night. You can't go gallivanting all over the countryside without Rose knowing where you are, now can you? Anyway, she might want to take you back with her to Dublin.'

'Thank you very much, Mrs Cranshaw,' said Darina politely, 'but that's between her and me. Anyway, she knows I'm with Bruno.'

Dorothy looked hard at her, trying to determine the thoughts behind that bland, determined expression. Darina was very pale and one of her eyelids was twitching a little but other than that she seemed as composed and self-assured as ever. Nevertheless, there had been a detectable change in her. Whereas before she had seemed willing to endure whatever it was that the adults in Willow House had in store for her, now, despite her forced calm, it was clear that she wanted desperately to escape.

'I'll look after her well, Mrs Cranshaw, I promise.' Bruno spoke up.

Dorothy had already noticed that he never took his eyes off Darina's face for longer than a few seconds at a time. She sighed; the pair of them were so beautiful, and so obviously enthralled with one another, they could have been used to illustrate a textbook on romantic love. 'What do you think, George?' she asked. 'Should I go and fetch Rose and John? After all,' she turned to Bruno, 'he's your uncle. He's in charge of you at the moment – he has to have a say in this too.' Out of the corner of her eye, she noticed Darina stiffen in her chair. Poor girl, she thought, the whole situation was a lot to take in.

'I'll go and get Rose and John,' said George. Standing up, he left the kitchen.

'Now don't be afraid,' said Dorothy briskly when his footsteps had receded down the corridor outside. 'Nobody's going to force you to do anything you don't want to do, but you're both under age. Please remember that. I wouldn't have it on my conscience that I let you go without your families' consent. All right? Can you see things from my point of view?'

Neither of them answered. Bruno was watching Darina but she was staring at the surface of the table, tracing an irregularity in the wood with a spoon. Dorothy cast around desperately for something to say or do. She could not offer them any more cocoa and she felt that sherry was out of the question at the moment. But she could not just sit staring at the two of them until George and the others came back.

'Your dad's back tomorrow?' she asked, making conversation with Bruno.

He took his eyes off Darina long enough to nod. 'Yes,' he said. 'I believe his plane's due at about two. He should be here in the late afternoon.'

Silence again wrapped them all in its clammy grip. There was still no sign of the others and Dorothy could not stand the tension any more. She stood up. 'I've a phone call to make,' she said, 'won't be a second.'

The telephone was fixed to the wall just inside the scullery and while she dialled the number of a London friend, she felt a cold draught on her back and looked around.

The door from the kitchen to the backyard was swinging open on its hinges and she was alone.

A dust of frost glittered on the countryside under a high moon as the two of them sped unheeding through the beds of herbs and winter vegetables in the kitchen garden behind the house, crashed through a wicket gate and came out into a field which sloped upwards towards the woods. After a minute or so, Darina, although she had led their flight, had difficulty in keeping pace with Bruno who loped easily along as though the rough, scutchy land was as smooth as a varsity track. 'Slow down a bit,' she gasped, 'you're killing me.'

He altered his gait to an easy trot, taking her hand in his own. 'What happened back there?' he asked, looking into her face. 'Why are we running away like this?'

In the moonlight, his face was waxy and she touched it briefly. 'I'll tell you when we find some place no one can find us,' she answered, saving her breath. The sandals she wore were unsuitable for running – or even walking on anything except a city street – and half-way across the field she stopped and kicked them off, not caring about the discomfort of the freezing ground through the soles of her tights.

The tights were ruined and she was panting hard when they got to the edge of the wood. Bruno suggested that they stop for a while but she urged him onwards. 'In a minute! I don't know this place at all but there's got to be somewhere we can be safe.' They slowed the pace a little, flitting in and out through the latticework of light and shadow cast by the bare branches. A little off the pathway, Darina spotted a stand of dense, evergreen shrubbery and took him right into the centre of it, forcing the

466

branches apart, breaking many of them, their snapping loud in the stillness. They manoeuvred and manipulated the greenery until they had cleared enough space for the two of them and then, by mutual unspoken consent, settled down in one another's arms, letting the foliage and branches rustle back around them. 'We'll be all right here for a while,' said Darina, wriggling to make herself more comfortable. 'Dammit,' she added, 'my feet are really sore.'

'Now, will you tell me what all this is about?' asked Bruno, hugging her tightly.

'You probably won't believe me.'

'Of course I'll believe you.'

'It's about your uncle.'

'Uncle John?' He was astonished. 'What about him?' Bruno sat up in sudden alarm but Darina pulled him down to her again.

'I'll tell you in a minute. Just let's be quiet for a while.' She offered her face for a kiss and when he put his lips on hers, responded with passion, gripping him fiercely with her arms and legs.

His own responses grew more and more heated until he pulled himself back breathlessly and held her at arms' length. 'I thought you said we'd wait, Darina?'

'That doesn't mean we can't kiss each other.'

'If you kiss me like that, I don't think I'm going to be able to wait.'

'Hold me, then.'

He wrapped himself around her as tightly as he could but still it was not tight enough for her. 'Harder, harder!' she demanded. 'Please, Bruno, if you love me, hug me harder!'

'I love you, Darina!' He squeezed even tighter until she could feel the trembling of his arm, calf and thigh muscles against her own legs and back. Eventually, he released her. 'Please tell me, Darina – what's this all about?'

'Would you still love me,' she asked urgently, 'if I told you something about myself you could never have guessed? Something so awful, you'd find it difficult to believe?'

'Nothing you could tell me would be awful.'

'But this is something you could never, ever have dreamed about. Not in your wildest imagination—'

'For crying out loud, Darina, this is torture!'

'Well, here it is, then. Remember, you asked for it!' She sat up and pushed him away, forcing his arms from her and shrinking as far as she could into the prickly foliage at her back. 'You and I,' she said, the portentousness of the statement making her voice shake, 'are first cousins.'

'First cousins?' he repeated.

'That's what I said. Your uncle John is my father. I only found out tonight.'

He stared at her, his breath misting in the air which was as still as silver. 'Are you sure? he said eventually.

'Yes.'

'I'm afraid I don't know what to say.'

'I don't either.'

Again they stared at one another. 'Can I still hold you?' he asked eventually.

'I wish you would, Bruno, oh, how I wish you would!' Darina struggled with a rush of tears. He took her in his arms and she curved in against the warmth of his down-filled jacket. A branch snapped, loud as a gunshot, and she jumped in fright.

'Don't worry,' he said, stroking her face, 'I'm here.'

She settled in against him and they quietened, breathing together as though in sleep.

'To tell you the truth,' said Darina slowly after a few minutes, 'it's an awful shock, but now that I think about it, I'm not all that surprised.'

'How come?'

She sat up. 'If I tell you why, will you listen?'

'Of course I'll listen.'

'I mean, *really* listen – with an open mind. It's a bit, well – unusual.'

'So is this!' said Bruno with wry humour as he, too, sat up fully and brushed leaves from his shoulders.

'All right,' said Darina, 'here goes.' She put her hands on his shoulders and locked eyes with him. 'One thing I felt immediately when I met you was that we were *destined* to meet and love each other. Did you feel anything like that?'

'I got goose bumps,' admitted Bruno. 'But—'

'Exactly!' Darina gripped handfuls of his jacket. 'That's exactly the kind of thing I'm talking about. Do you know what I think?' she said in a low voice, stringing out the words. 'I think you're my Twin Self. Do you know what that is?'

'Try me.'

'Well it's a bit hard to take in at first. I haven't yet been able to track down the origin of the idea – it may be one of the Greeks. I've loads of books at home and I'm sure I'll find it. Have you ever heard of Edgar Cayce?'

'Where you're concerned, I seem to be spending my life saying "Who's he?" or "What's that?"'

In other circumstances, Bruno's mournful tone might have caused Darina to burst out laughing but she was intent on exposition of her theory and gave his cheek a hasty pat of reassurance. 'I'm sure you know loads of things I don't know in different areas.' She carried on, words tumbling, 'Edgar Cayce is a famous psychic. I've three books about him. Never mind,' she changed tack, 'you *must* have heard of the poets Robert Browning and Elizabeth Barrett?'

'I think so, although I'm not much on poetry,' admitted Bruno, 'Walt Whitman's about the size of it.'

'Well, these were two English poets in the last century who fell in love and became famous as much for being lovers as poets. Their relationship is supposed to be one of the best examples of Twin Selves.'

'I see,' said Bruno doubtfully.

Darina let go of his jacket and crossed her arms across her breast. 'It's a concept that's been around for thousands and thousands of years,' she said, unsure now of how he was taking it. 'To accept it, you have to accept the idea of reincarnation.'

She risked a look at his face. As far as she could tell, he did not seem to be rejecting outright what she was saying. Encouraged, she continued in a rush, 'If you do – and I certainly do now – the whole thing about Twin Selves is not too hard to take in. It means that at one time, way, way long ago, two people were completely spiritually united with each other, but then somehow, in one of their lives together, something happened and they became separated, lost each other. As a result they look for each other in all their later lives, right down the centuries.' She paused, and took a deep breath. 'I think that this applies to us. We're Twin Selves, Bruno. We've found each other at last.'

He was silent and for the first time she felt embarrassed. 'I'm sorry if it sounds a bit bizarre.'

'Is this connected with astrology?'

Carefully, she took his hand. 'Yes and no. Astrology is very old and it's a religion too, you know, but this is sort of alongside it. A lot of the Eastern religions believe in it. Don't you see, now that we know we're first cousins, it makes even more sense. That we recognise each other. That this was destiny, or fate or whatever you like to call it.'

'I don't know,' he said doubtfully. 'Could it be genetic? I mean, if we're first cousins . . . '

'Yeah. But we both know there's more than just genes to the way we feel about each other, don't we?' Darina's eyes were blazing. 'It just *feels* right, absolutely right,' she said eagerly. 'I feel I definitely know you – knew you before – almost as well as I know myself. And I can say anything to you, anything at all.'

He kissed her softly on the lips. 'I believe you, Darina,' he said.

They settled down again, holding tightly to one another, as much to keep warm as for any other reason.

'What about Uncle John?' asked Bruno after a while. 'He's the best. He'd be a great father.'

'We're not going to talk about that side of things yet,' said Darina.

From far away, very faintly, they heard the sounds of people calling their names and then, a few minutes later, the sounds of cars being started and driven away.

'What time is it now?' Rose felt as though her eyes were set in hot coals.

Dorothy looked at her watch. 'Just after three o'clock. My dear, why don't you try to get some sleep? I'll fix you up with a bed. You should both try to get some rest.' She looked across to where John was slumped at the kitchen table.

'What about you, Dorothy?' he said. 'Please, please go to bed yourself. You've a kitchen to run. It's only three hours till you have to be up again.'

'Don't worry about me,' said Dorothy, 'strong as an ox.

470

Anyway, George will be fit and raring in the morning. Can't remember when last George missed a night's sleep. It's a good thing he wasn't on the *Titanic*.' She turned back to Rose. 'I hope your friend will be all right where I've put him.'

'Willie's wonderful,' said Rose. 'I suspect he's like George. I don't know what I would have done without him this last while.' She was too tired to elaborate and let her voice die while she toyed with the remains of the tea in her cup, swirling it around.

John got up from his chair and crossed to the window.

'You know young people,' said Dorothy. 'I'm willing to bet they're fast asleep in some nice dry barn, completely oblivious to all the worry they're causing. You'll see! They'll come back in the morning, bright-eyed and bushy-tailed, asking what all the fuss was about.'

Rose held her tongue. She appreciated Dorothy's concern and hoped against hope that she was right. But her own instinct said otherwise. This was her second sleepless night and her fatigue was combining with the headlong events of the past forty-eight hours, making it difficult for her to separate reality from fantasy. In the back of her mind, she felt vaguely that this whole situation was somehow her fault but at present she could not summon up the energy to think it through. When Darina was back safely, then she could sort out something for the future and then also, perhaps, she could indulge in the luxury of self-recrimination.

In the meantime, all her waning energy was concentrated on staying awake and on trying to project herself into Darina's mind. If she herself was sixteen again, in the company of the boy she loved, if she had been shocked like Darina was this evening, how would she have reacted? Where would she have run to?

She tried to wrestle logically with the possibilities. Darina did not know this area, only the immediate environs of Sundarbans – more than ten miles away. Even if she did decide to head for it she would not know the way. She could have asked for directions, of course, but Rose decided that, in the present circumstances, this was highly unlikely.

The hiding place was close by, Rose was sure of it.

But for two hours or more, the five of them, she and John, Dorothy, George and Willie, had searched the outhouses of the hotel, the fishing lodge, even the barns and sheds of their neighbours; they had trekked through the woods and leafless spinneys by the lakeshore; they had even scoured the half-built shell which would eventually be used by the golfers on the new driving range.

Darina and Bruno had simply vanished, leaving no trace.

'Are you sure it's too soon to call the guards?' Rose, coming to stand beside John at the window, saw their reflections in the black glass, opaque with frost.

He shook his head. 'If there's still no sign of them by morning, then we'll get them in.'

'Anyone want more tea – anything?' Dorothy spoke from behind them.

'To tell you the truth, Dorothy,' replied John, rubbing his eyes, 'at this stage, I could do with something stronger. It's been quite a night and I'm all in. And not sherry, if you don't mind.'

Dorothy searched in her cupboard and brought out a half-full whiskey bottle.

All three of them sat again at the table. Rose was unaccustomed to whiskey and, drinking it neat, found it burned her throat and gullet. She was trying to decide whether or not to ask Dorothy for water when, through the window beside the back door, she distinctly saw a pair of eyes staring into the kitchen. 'My God! Dorothy!' she exclaimed. 'There's someone outside!' She jumped up and ran to the door, pulling it open as fast as she could.

The kitchen cat jumped down off the windowsill and, tail high, ran between her legs, scampering as directly as an arrow for the warmth of the range. The anti-climax was too much and Rose almost lost her self-control. 'Sorry,' she apologised. 'I thought—'

'Close the door,' advised Dorothy. But Rose was straining her eyes, searching for any movement in the undulating landscape around the house, willing herself to see something, anything, which would give them some sense of direction and break the feeling of helplessness.

She felt Dorothy's hand on her arm, drawing her back into the kitchen. 'Rose,' she said, closing the door, 'why don't you take my advice and lie down for a while? Really, all three of us needn't be sitting here like this. It's too late for me to go to bed now and, anyway, I have my second wind at this stage. Why don't you head off? I'll fill a hot-water bottle for you. I promise

I'll call you the very minute, the very second, there's any news.'

Rose's legs felt like lead and the whiskey was making her feel muzzy. Despite her anxiety, the thought of a clean warm bed was enticing. Dorothy saw the hesitation and appealed to John. 'Aren't I right, John? Shouldn't she go to bed for a while? You should, too, of course,' she added, 'but there's no point in trying to persuade you, I know.'

'Yes, Rose, go on,' John agreed. 'I'll stay up with Dorothy and I promise we will call you as soon as we know anything, anything at all – or in any event by nine o'clock at the latest. And I'll go out searching again at first light.' He too went across to her. 'Come on now, be a good girl. You're going to need all your wits about you for the next few days. So are we all.'

Rose gave in. Side by side with John, she watched as Dorothy prepared the hot-water bottle and then, while Dorothy's back was still turned, put her arms around John and gave him a quick, fervent hug.

He bent and kissed her swiftly on the lips and, despite everything, all the worry, all the hassle, her body reacted. Fearful, however, that Dorothy might turn around, she pulled away giving him one final touch on his hand with her own.

'Here you are.' Dorothy brought over the hot-water bottle and shepherded her out of the door. 'You know where to go? Second on the left on the landing. Sleep well, or as well as you can. See you in a few hours.'

Once in the room, Rose took off only her shoes, tights and dress; still in her underwear, she slid gratefully between the crisp cold sheets and huddled herself around the comfort of the hot-water bottle. She was too tired to sort out her tumbling thoughts and emotions but as she dropped into sleep, the faces of Darina and John blurred into one another, grafting together onto one magical, beautiful body.

John, feeling marginally better after his shower and two cups of Dorothy's strongest coffee, stood on a slight incline in the field at the back of the house.

It was just after eight o'clock on the kind of morning which normally exhilarated him: to the east, the sun was about to come up over a horizon streaked with salmon and gold; behind him, the

473

smoke from the hotel chimneys rose in straight, narrow columns towards a sky of hard, brilliant blue. But on this occasion, he was oblivious to the beauty of the black hedges, the whitened, stiff grass. He was trying to concentrate, to pick up any signs he might have missed in the searches of the night before.

He greeted a middle-aged Belgian couple who, equipped with walking boots and blackthorns, were setting out for a walk towards the woods at the crown of the hill. He and Willie Brehony had already been through those woods in the early hours of the morning but that had been in darkness and now John wondered if he shouldn't go there again. He waited until the Belgians were about five or six minutes ahead of him and set off after them. After a few minutes, he had himself convinced that he was headed in the right direction, that if the two young people were anywhere in the vicinity, it was most likely to be up there among those trees.

Although he was dressed warmly in sheepskin jacket, cap and gloves, out here, away from the protection of the house, the frost scoured his cheeks and lips, his nose dripped and his eyes watered continuously. To minimise the discomfort he kept them fixed on the ground.

It was fortunate he did because otherwise he might have missed an oddly shaped object, bright with frost and half-hidden in the scutch about six feet to his left. He walked over to it and picked it up; it was one of Darina's sandals. His heart jumped; at least he was on the right track. He searched around for the sandal's mate and found it a few feet farther on, in a small depression, concealed by a stand of thistles.

He looked for the Belgians; they were skirting the woods, walking briskly westwards along a small ridge. He waited until they had crossed it and had gone from view, then, carrying the sandals, he walked towards the trees with renewed energy. About fifty yards inside the perimeter of the wood he stopped to listen intently but he could detect no extraneous sound. Because most of the trees were deciduous, and therefore bare, he was able to see quite well for some distance.

Another fifty yards in front of him and just to the left of the pathway, he spotted a thicket of evergreens and dense shrubs. If they were anywhere in this wood, it was there.

When he came close to the thicket he saw a litter of twiglets and broken branches, too extensive to have been made by any animal. John could have kicked himself for missing these signs last night but, although there had been a moon, under the trees it had been too dark to pick out details.

The question was, were Bruno and Darina still here?

John stopped dead in sudden fear of what he might find. It had been an extremely cold night.

He walked into the thicket and, forcing the branches aside, was confronted by two pairs of newly woken eyes as startled as those of young deer.

A second later, the two of them had uncurled themselves from under the boy's ski-jacket and scrambled to their feet. The density of the bushes meant that John was standing only inches away from both of them. He controlled his initial instinct to roar at them and managed a creditable 'Good morning!' Then, 'I'm glad to see you,' he said, 'you gave us all a fright! These belong to you, I believe?' he continued, holding out the sandals to Darina. 'You'll need them for the walk back.'

Darina took the footwear without a word and the two of them followed him out of the bushes into the more open spaces of the wood. 'I don't want to go back,' she said sullenly.

'Aren't you hungry? You must be by now,' he answered, careful not to sound aggressive.

'I am – I'm ravenous,' admitted Bruno.

'Then what harm if you come up to the hotel for a meal? Nobody's going to court-martial you, I promise. Anyway, you could do with a bit of a warm-up too, I imagine,' he added, noticing that Darina's teeth had begun to chatter.

They glanced at one another, exchanging some message he could not interpret but then, to his relief, she nodded. 'OK, so.'

He waited until the three of them were out in the open field and the house was in sight before speaking again. 'Your mother will be delighted you're safe, Darina,' he remarked conversationally, 'and that's the main thing, of course. But she's been distracted with worry. I'd go a bit easy on her if I were you.'

'What do you mean?'

'I don't think she could handle a big row.'

'She's the one—' Darina snorted and then stopped herself.

475

'She's the one what?'

'Nothing.'

'Look, I don't expect you to be thrilled at what's happened to you—'

'That's big of you!'

John sighed and bit back his own retort. He shaded his eyes against the sun, now huge and orange and fully above the horizon. They were half-way across the field and the house was in sight when he turned his attention urgently to Bruno. 'You and I had better have a bit of a chat before your dad gets here this afternoon.'

'Sure, Uncle John,' said Bruno. 'Look,' he added humbly, 'I'm sorry we caused worry – we both are, aren't we, Darina?'

'Maybe.'

'She is,' insisted Bruno. 'It's just that she's had a bit of a shock.'

'We all have.' The adrenalin which had been pumping through John's body while engaged in the search was draining away, leaving him exhausted. Then, alarmed, he saw Darina quicken her pace, deliberately getting ahead of them and, afraid she would bolt again, hurried to catch up with her.

His heart melted, however, as he watched her skid her way along the frozen grass in the ridiculous sandals. Although, like the purple jacket and the laddered tights, they looked tawdry in the clean morning light, their very unsuitability pointed to how young she was.

As she went through the gate, the jacket snagged on the catch so she had to turn to pull it free. Her plait had become unravelled and the liberated hair streamed over her bent face, her shoulders and her back, catching the sunlight so it shone as bright as flax. John, still a few yards behind, was caught, somewhere at the back of his throat with love so pure and unexpected that he faltered in mid-stride.

Derek held the money over the coin slots of the old-fashioned black telephone while he waited for the operator to connect him with Willow House. Oh, for the clean, new technology of Canada! It never failed to happen, he thought. Two or three days of struggling with the vagaries of the Irish telephone system always cured him of sentimental notions of coming back here to live.

476

The operator came on the line and instructed him to insert his money; but just as he pressed button A to clear the line, there was a tinny, deafening announcement on the airport Tannoy. He drummed his fingers impatiently until it was finished. 'Hello?' he shouted then. 'Dorothy? This is Derek. There's no reply from the fishing lodge. Would you mind passing on a message?'

'Yes, Derek,' said Dorothy Cranshaw at the other end. 'You're at the airport?'

'That's right. I'm just calling to say I managed to get an earlier connection at Heathrow and I should be home in a couple of hours.'

'I'll pass on the message,' said Dorothy.

It was a beautiful, crisp day and although he was tired, Derek's spirits rose as he bowled along through the countryside in his hired car, taking care on the corners because he noticed that there was still some frost lying in the more sheltered parts of the road.

As he was driving along, he mulled over this intriguing deal being promulgated by John and his partners with regard to the Big House. Should he try to get involved in it? Not that John seemed to be tripping over himself with anxiety to allow him into the deal but that, he was sure, was only a minor difficulty and could be overcome. Money had a loud mouth.

On the credit side, the old house was beautiful and once it was tarted up a bit, it was just the kind of place which could attract not only the Europeans but their richer American cousins. Especially as it seemed it was going to have the added attraction of a resident lord and lady of the manor. On the debit side, he did have reservations about the location: how many visitors could they expect to attract to such a Godforsaken out-of-the-way place as Drumboola?

He decided he would have another chat with John about it tonight. Pity he was leaving so early in the morning.

He was feeling ebullient as, finally, he drove up the small winding track which led to the fishing lodge. John had really lucked out, he thought, as he parked the car on the tidy forecourt. All the comforts of home with none of the attendant hassles. Mona was a lovely person. Karen, thought her husband sourly, could have learned a thing or two from Mona's attitudes.

The thought of Karen had dissipated some of his good

humour. He supposed he should call her. He pushed open the front door of the house, which was never locked. 'Hell-oooo!' he called. 'Anyone home?'

Mona came through from the kitchen. 'Derek!' she said. 'Welcome home.'

'Thanks, Mona. OK if I call Karen?'

'Sure,' she said, going back towards the kitchen.

As Derek waited for the operator to put him through to his home, he braced himself to be pleasant. Lately she had been bugging him about going to a marriage counsellor; he had been resisting but, thinking it through while he was on his own in the Hamburg hotel, he had reconsidered the notion. Perhaps he owed it to her – he would mention it to her now.

'Hello?' He heard her voice, light and unusually gay, then, abruptly, the line went dead while the operator asked if she would accept charges. It was good she was in such a mood, he thought gratefully, for once they might have a civilised conversation. But when she came on again her voice had flattened. 'Hi, Derek.'

'Hi,' he said, determined not to respond in kind. 'How are you, Karen?'

'Fine.'

The line was not great but even through the atmospherics, he recognised that she had become wary. 'It's a normal question, Karen, between husband and wife.' The shot had been fired before he could stop it.

She answered in kind. 'Between a normal husband and wife.'

'Look,' Derek kept a rein on his temper, 'I only called to see how you are, how you're getting on. What've you been doing with yourself while we've been gone?'

'Oh, nothing, the usual, you know . . . ' Something about the way she said the innocuous words made him pay attention. Then she made him actually suspicious. 'How's Bruno?' she asked.

'Oh, Bruno's fine,' he said slowly, mulling over the swiftness of the diversion. 'I've just got in, haven't seen him yet. So,' he paused, 'what kind of things have you been doing? Been going out a bit?'

'Sure. You don't expect me to sit in tatting, do you? Waiting

478

for the return of the lord and master.' Although Derek was accustomed to such sparring, she was unusually defensive, even for her.

'Where?' he asked. 'Where've you been going?'

'Am I answerable to you for my movements? You don't seem all that interested when you're here—'

'Karen!' Derek was losing the battle with his anger. 'What the hell are you up to?'

'What do you mean?'

'You heard me. I know you, you're being evasive.'

'You're the one who's evasive. How do I know what you're doing all the time away on these business trips?'

Like a starburst, the truth showered over Derek; his wife was having an affair. He let it sink in.

'Derek? Derek?' Through the crackle and hiss, Karen seemed anxious now.

Slowly and very deliberately Derek replaced the receiver. He heard a sound behind him and looked around. Bruno was standing at the foot of the stairs.

'Dad, you're back,' he said, but his smile was uncertain.

Remembering his uncomfortable conversation with Bruno about himself and Karen, Derek made a huge effort to compose himself. 'Come and give your old dad a hug!' he commanded. Then, when Bruno had complied, 'Brought you a present.'

'Oh, thanks, Dad!'

Derek, still shaken, wondered if Bruno's enthusiasm was just a little over the top. 'Well, do you want to see it now?'

'Of course!'

Derek took the presents – a Swiss Army knife and a pair of waterproof ski-mitts – out of his briefcase and handed them over. 'They're cool!' Bruno took the gifts. 'Thanks a million, Dad. I love them, I really do!'

He was making such a fuss that Derek was now sure he was stalling. There was something wrong. First Karen, now Bruno. Derek, who suffered from mild tachycardia, felt his heart start to bang about a little. 'Everything OK while I was away?' he asked, hoping he was managing to keep his voice casual.

Bruno hedged. 'I beg your pardon?'

'All right,' said Derek swiftly, 'let's come clean here. What's going on?'

The boy shrugged. 'Nothing much. I know it looks bad, staying out all night and all – but nothing happened, really.'

Staying out all night?

'That's not what I hear.' With no knowledge, Derek was operating entirely on instinct.

'Who've you been talking to?' Bruno's careful intonation proved the instinct to be correct.

'That's my business,' said Derek. 'I want your version of what happened last night.'

'It was perfectly innocent.'

'What was perfectly innocent?'

'We did nothing wrong. It was just that Darina heard a bit of, well, *unusual* news and it upset her so I had to be with her, you see. I really had to, Dad. I couldn't leave her out there on her own.'

Derek struggled to keep his voice calm. 'Out where? And, by the way, who's Darina?' As he waited grimly, he could almost hear wheels turning inside the boy's brain. 'Let's go into the sitting room,' he said abruptly. Inside, he confronted Bruno immediately. 'Now, where were you all night? Who's this Darina, and what were you doing with her?'

'All right, Dad,' said the boy calmly, 'I'll tell you the whole story. But remember you and Mom always said I had to tell the truth, no matter what.'

'That's right.' Derek sat on the edge of a chair in front of the fire.

'And that if I told the truth, I wouldn't get into trouble?'

'That's right. I hope we haven't made a mistake!'

Bruno did not react to the sarcasm. 'Dad,' he said simply, 'I love Darina, but there's a problem. She's my first cousin.'

Derek looked at him in stupefaction. He ran quickly through the possibilities: all of Bruno's first cousins, as far as he knew, were safely at school or in their playpens on the other side of the Atlantic. Surely none of them could have followed him over here without his knowing . . .

'Did you hear me, Dad?' Bruno's anxious blue eyes were at last fixed on his face. 'I said she's—'

'I heard you the first time. Who are her mother and father?'

'That's just it. That's the unusual bit about it. She lives

with her mom in Dublin but she only found out last night who her father is and you see, Dad, what made it such a shock is that he didn't know either!'

'For God's sake, answer the question, Bruno! Who are her mother and father?'

'A woman called Rose O'Beirne – I met her this morning, and, Dad, she's lovely – and believe it or not,' Bruno's eyes widened with the importance of what he was going to say next, 'Darina's father is Uncle John!'

Derek's own eyes flew wide in shock. In his chest, his heart increased its fluttering and banging about but, even without this distress, he could not have answered intelligibly had he been threatened with execution. The pictures and memories crashed about in his brain as wildly as his heart in his ribcage: the scene he had witnessed in Karen's guest bed in Charlottetown nearly seventeen years ago, the veiled and not-so-veiled insults and references to it between himself and Karen in the years since.

It all culminated in one horrifying thought. This Darina . . . this girl was not a first cousin as everyone now thought they had discovered. She was Bruno's half-sister.

'Are you OK, Dad?' Bruno was obviously scared.

'Would you mind getting me a drink?' Derek managed not to stutter.

'Sure!' Bruno jumped up. 'What do you want?'

'Ask Mona if she has any brandy.'

'All right. But, Dad,' Bruno turned back in the doorway, 'it's not that bad, really it's not.'

Derek gripped the sides of his chair. He was really feeling unwell now; in addition to the problem of the fast heartbeat, he was assaulted by a strong wave of nausea and feared he might vomit. He lowered his head and concentrated on breathing deeply. *This could not be happening . . .*

Bruno was back within a minute or so. 'Are you all right, Dad? Mona says she's no real brandy but will this do? She says it's Packy's, that he likes it at Christmas.'

Derek forced himself to look up at the boy's anxious face. He was holding out a dusty, half-empty bottle of cherry brandy. 'That'll be fine,' he gasped. 'Would you pour me a glass, please?'

He almost gagged on the sickly sweet liqueur but, although

it did not improve the tachycardia, it had an almost instant effect on his stomach, warming and calming it. Bruno watched, his face still creased with worry. 'Are you sure you're all right?'

'I'll be all right in a minute. I just got a shock, that's all.'

'Try to see things from our point of view.' Bruno sat opposite him. 'This is difficult to say but there's no point in beating about the bush, is there? It doesn't really matter what you and Mom think or Darina's mom or Uncle John or anyone. I might as well tell you, I love her, I really do, and she loves me too. It's not going to be easy, of course, there's the cousins thing and also we live so far apart from each other but guess what?' He grinned. 'Her mom's a stewardess and can get cheap travel so Darina'll be able to come visit. How about that?'

As quickly as it had broken out, the smile vanished, leaving lines of utter seriousness on his young face. 'Anyway,' he said, 'for me, Darina's the real thing and I know she feels the same. Sorry, Dad, but there it is!'

He hesitated, then went on, rushing, 'In a sort of a way, we both feel it was meant to happen. Like it's our destiny, you know? Well,' he corrected himself, 'she certainly feels it and when she explained it to me, I saw what she meant.'

'What did she explain to you?' Derek felt that if he could just hold onto the glass of cherry brandy, he might wake up out of this surreal dream.

Bruno seemed to have no such sense of unreality. 'Have you ever heard about Twin Selves?' he asked, leaning forwards.

'Twin what? I'm a twin – John and I—'

'No, not really, that's not it. It's nothing to do with our physical bodies. It's a bit hard to take in at first, all together, but there are certain people who are two halves of one self, that's why they're called Twin Selves. Darina explained it to me. Certainly,' he said earnestly, pausing to let the significance sink in, 'when I saw her first, Dad, the very first minute, I got goose-bumps.'

Derek looked at him aghast. This was his own fault. He had lived with this boy for sixteen years – had grown to love him – but had been so busy with other concerns, with making money and developing his business interests, he clearly had no real idea of what might have been going on in Bruno's head. And now, because he had been so inattentive, he had no idea how to deal with this crazy situation. 'Where did you meet this girl?' he asked faintly.

'At the lake, that day you brought me up to Sundarbans. She was there on a visit with her mother.'

Derek raised the cherry brandy to his lips, emptied the glass, then refilled it. 'I'm afraid I don't understand,' he said, buying time while he tried to calm his thoughts.

'I don't understand it either, not totally,' said Bruno, 'but Darina says we *recognised* each other.'

'Well, that's not too difficult to understand. If you're – if you're first cousins. Does this girl look like you?'

'I don't know, I never looked at her, not in that way. I suppose she is like me, a bit,' he added doubtfully. 'She's tall and she's blonde, too – do you think that's it? That even before we knew we were cousins, we recognised each other, physically, I mean? In a sort of subconscious way?'

'Sounds logical.'

'Yes, but,' Bruno's voice dropped several tones, 'it was more than that. We both feel very strongly that we know each other from before.'

'From before what?'

Bruno flushed. 'Before – you know. Before. A past life,' he muttered, embarrassed at last.

Utterly appalled, Derek put down his glass. 'A past life? You mean, reincarnation? That kind of rubbish?'

'It's not rubbish!' Bruno looked up defensively. 'Darina says—'

'I don't care what this Darina says! Now you listen to me, young man. Whatever she says or you think you feel or you think you both feel, you listen to me. This has all got out of hand. And by the way,' he was beginning to find his footing on the safer ground of self-righteousness, 'where has all this been taking place? Up at Sundarbans?'

Bruno's expression was wounded. 'You said you'd listen.'

'I've listened. I've certainly listened and all I heard was nonsense. Past lives, goose-bumps! What were the two of you doing last night?'

'Nothing.'

'Do I have to telephone John at Willow House?'

483

'Telephone if you like, Dad. He wasn't with us so he can't tell you what, if anything, *went on* . . . '

Derek was unused to a challenge of this magnitude from Bruno and almost lost his hard-won advantage but he was getting really angry now. He thumped the armrest of his chair. 'Don't talk to me in that tone of voice, young man! What went on last night?'

'I told you – nothing!' But he could see Bruno was shaken and had lost some of his conviction.

'Where were you?' he thundered.

'In the woods.' Bruno capitulated.

'What woods?'

'Up on the hill behind the hotel.'

'And you spent a whole night in the woods with a girl, in the month of November, and you expect me to believe that nothing happened?'

Bruno, he saw, had gone very pale. 'I don't expect you to believe anything, Dad,' he said quietly. 'I've told you the truth.'

There was a tense silence and as it continued, Derek felt his power ebbing away. In a way he could not define, he had lost a battle he did not understand. 'I can see we're not going to get anywhere on this occasion,' he muttered.

'Or on any other occasion, Dad,' said Bruno calmly, 'because I've told you the truth. There's nothing else to say.'

'Yes, there is – there certainly is. What about the future? You can't think we can all sit idly by and see you wreck your future?'

'In what way am I wrecking my future? All I've told you is the truth, which is that Darina and I love each other. How is that wrecking my future?'

'Suppose she gets pregnant?'

Bruno's mouth dropped open in astonishment. When he had recovered he spoke very slowly and deliberately. 'I don't understand why you asked that question,' he said, 'but let me tell you that there is no danger of that.'

'How can you be so fucking cocksure?' Derek was losing more and more ground but now he did not care. Who the hell was this sixteen-year-old to act so calmly in such an emergency? After all he, Derek, had done for him. That Bruno could not possibly have been aware of what he had done for him nagged in

484

what remained of his rational mind but he ignored it and ranted on. 'You're only sixteen,' he shouted. 'Since when did sixteen-year-olds run the world and its morals and its affairs?'

'Since never, Dad; you're overreacting.' Bruno's gaze was as clear and steady as a blue flame. 'If you want to know the real truth, Darina and I have not made love. Not that it's any of your business.'

'It certainly is my business. You are in my care until you are an adult and don't you forget it.'

'I don't forget it.' Bruno turned his attention to the land-scape outside the window and Derek had the impression that, as far as Bruno was concerned, this matter was now over.

In an effort again to break through, he summoned up his last reserves. 'It's just as well we're leaving first thing in the morning,' he said as forcefully as he could. 'We'll talk again about this.'

'I'm sure we will, Dad,' Bruno replied, still looking through the window. His tone of voice was bland, but so distant that it sent shivers through Derek's overwrought spine. 'Can I go now?' he added.

'Where are you going?'

'Out for a walk.'

'It'll be dark soon.'

'So?' Bruno finally turned to look at him, his eyes mild. 'If you like, I'll take a torch.'

'Be back in time for dinner,' Derek muttered and poured himself a third glass of the liqueur.

He spent the next hour in a daze. Taking the remains of the cherry brandy with him, he went up to the room he was sharing with Bruno and lay down on his bed, willing his heart to stop its frenetic, irregular dance. He tried to marshal his thoughts, to be logical, to take his developing problems one at a time. Remembering the conviction which had blazed in Bruno's eyes, he knew that he was not dealing with logic; this situation was clearly the most pressing.

Bruno had obviously discovered something out of the ordinary in this girl – or had been influenced in some way by her to believe that there was something out of the ordinary in this love affair.

Yet what was so dreadful? These two were only sixteen

485

years of age and would surely grow out of whatever obsession they seemed to have with each other at the moment.

Or would they? So far, they had not made love – at least that was something positive. But assuming they were normal, healthy and energetic, for how long would that be the case?

Over all was Derek's frustration in not knowing how to deal with it. He desired action. But what action? The key to it was distance, he decided. If they could be kept separate as much as possible, then perhaps whatever fever had gripped them would die down and eventually reason might prevail.

Wandering off into an uncomfortable half doze, Derek wondered if he should again call Karen to discuss the situation with her but as quickly as he considered the option, he decided against it; at present he did not have the energy to deal with Karen's reaction, easily predictable in the face of any threat to her baby. And, anyway, he could discuss it with her when they got home tomorrow.

And then they could discuss what was going on with her, he thought grimly.

This trip, so lightly planned, was turning into a nightmare.

Remaining aware of the sounds in the house, the empty glass in his hand, he drifted off. His sleep was uneasy, filigreed with short, frightening dreams, red episodes which had no faces nor shapes and which dropped away each time he awoke to confront them, leaving behind only fear.

Eventually, after he had woken with a convulsive jump, he sat up and looked at his watch. He heard the telephone ringing downstairs and being answered. Then he became aware of strong and appetising dinner-smells wafting through the house and remembered he had not eaten since mid-morning.

He took a quick shower and went downstairs to the kitchen, which was where the family ate all their meals. Mona was standing at the cooker. 'Oh, hello, Derek,' she said as he came in. 'Dinner's nearly ready, I was just going to call you. Is Bruno coming down?'

'He went out for a walk, earlier, is he not back yet?'

'Not yet.' Mona stirred the contents of a pot.

Derek felt he was not in any shape to have a civilised conversation. 'I'll go look at the news,' he said, leaving the kitchen.

486

But once in the sitting room, he did not turn on the television set but sat on a couch. Where on earth was Bruno? That girl had clearly bewitched him.

He forced himself to relax in the peaceful, uncluttered room. Mona's taste in furnishings was as understated as herself, and, as even the internal walls of the lodge were three feet thick, once the door was closed, no sound from any other part of the house permeated through to where he sat. The legacy of the row with Bruno and too much cherry brandy was taking its toll now and his head was throbbing. He rested it on the back of the couch and gazed into the fire of logs and turf which hissed softly to itself in the grate.

He closed his eyes and tried to put himself in John's shoes. How would he feel if he suddenly discovered he had a daughter? *And how would he feel if he discovered he had a son as well?*

Derek's headache intensified as he realised he must be very, very careful.

Such was the sound insulation in the room that he was taken by surprise when the door opened without warning and John, trailing the coldness of the evening with him, walked in.

'Did you see Bruno on the road?' Derek asked.

John shook his head and Derek noticed he was avoiding eye-contact. His twin, he saw, was barely repressing huge anger. On immediate alert, he sat upright. 'What's the matter? You have something you want to say?' He knew he had sounded unnecessarily belligerent and tried to retrieve the situation. 'Sit down, John. Sorry the young fella gave you a fright last night.'

'That's not what I want to talk to you about – well, that, too – but there's something much more important, to me at least.'

Alarm bells sounded in Derek's already overstressed brain. 'What are you talking about?' he asked cautiously.

He saw John clench his fist. 'A letter. That's what I'm talking about. An anonymous letter.'

Derek, who had been half expecting a challenge about Bruno's parentage, was so relieved that he let down his guard. 'What letter are you talking about?' he asked although he knew full well what John meant. He had never thought that his half-forgotten and childish transgression would catch up with him – but in the light of recent happenings, surely it was a relatively trivial matter? To show John how unconcerned he was, he flicked away an imaginary piece of fluff from his trouser knee.

But John clearly did not take it so lightly. His face flushed dangerously and he moved a step closer to the couch. 'You know what letter. Don't play games with me, Derek.'

'OK, OK, I'm sorry! But we were all children then. I really am sorry. Please accept my apology. I agree I shouldn't have done it but it was so long ago, John, and—'

'Is that all you have to say, you bastard?' John teetered on the balls of his feet. His fists rose in front of him as if they had a life of their own.

'Steady on!' Derek shrank back in the couch. 'I said I'm sorry, didn't I?'

'Fucking bastard!' The punch splattered high on Derek's cheekbone, exploding the pain already in his head into a million blinding painlets. He struggled to get up, holding the cheek with one hand, swinging wildly with the other, but John had moved away into the centre of the room, a half-puzzled look on his face as if the punch had caught him, too, unawares.

'I'll get you!' Derek lumbered upright at last and moved towards him. 'How dare you hit me! I'll—' But his heart was again hammering painfully and he had to sit down on a chair. 'I'll get you for this,' he repeated, hearing how feeble it sounded.

'Oh, will you?' John recovered his venom. 'Sixteen, nearly seventeen years, Derek. Seventeen years of my life you ruined with that letter. I might have – I might have—' He punched the air in frustration.

'What?' Derek's cheek was hurting badly but he managed to dredge his voice with scorn. 'What might you have? A liaison with the lady of the manor? Hardly likely, dear boy. I doubt if any letter of mine or anyone else's would have made much difference in that quarter, one way or the other.'

'I'll hit you again, Derek, and this time I'll kill you.' John again took a step towards him and for a moment Derek was afraid.

'Stop it, for God's sake,' he shouted. 'What would Mammy have thought if she saw us carrying on like this?' Mention of their mother had the desired effect and after a moment or two, John dropped his fists. He turned away and stared into the fire.

'You hurt me, John,' Derek complained when he was sure

it was safe to say it. 'I'm sure I'm going to have a black eye.'

'You fucking deserve it.'

'Nice language!'

'The sooner you get out of here, the better for us all.'

'For once, we're in agreement, dear brother of mine. That is, of course, if my son and your daughter descend to this planet long enough for me to extricate him and get him onto a plane. Speaking of which,' he added carefully, watching John's rigid back, 'if, I repeat *if* you can abandon your histrionics for a moment or two, that relationship is a matter I think the two of us should discuss.' He saw John's already stiff shoulders stiffen further.

'I'm willing to discuss all matters which concern my daughter.' John turned slowly and sat in a chair opposite Derek's couch. But before we do,' he said softly, 'there's something I'd like to understand, Derek. What did I ever do to you? As long as I can remember you've been doing me down, doing bad turns, hating me for some reason I can't fathom.'

'I don't hate you,' said Derek defensively. He was still holding his cheek.

'I don't believe you. I think you do hate me – and resent me and are jealous of me. Ever since we were very small.'

'I don't hate you. That's ridiculous.'

'Let's examine this. Leaving everything else out of it, all the petty stuff ever since we were kids, if you don't hate me, why did you try – and succeed, I may add – to destroy the most precious thing in my life by sending that letter to Rose? Come on now, be honest. I'd really like to know. I really would.' He was speaking very carefully and softly; his face was in shadow but Derek could see firelight flash in his wide intent eyes and again felt fear curl like a weed in the pit of his stomach. He could not lose Bruno now. Not now . . .

So he brazened it out, staring at John as the silence ticked between them.

Then his twin deliberately placed both hands behind his back. 'I promise I won't hit you again, not now at least. But come on, Derek, please tell me what's eating you about me.'

Derek continued to stare at him. 'When I sent that letter, I didn't know I was, as you put it, *destroying* any precious thing of yours.'

'Oh, yes, you did. That's why you sent it.'

'I didn't know Rose O'Beirne Moffat was pregnant. How could I have known?'

'That's irrelevant and you know it. By the way, neither Rose nor I knew for certain until a few seconds ago that it *was* you who sent it. Thank you for confirming it for us.'

Derek's fear was stronger than his anger at the neatness of the trap and he managed to keep a grip on his temper. 'You're welcome,' he sneered.

For a few seconds they glared at one another, then John continued. 'Apparently,' he said almost conversationally, 'you said in the letter that I had gone to bed with another girl in Charlottetown. Come off it, Derek. How did you think she would react to that – how would any girl react to it, pregnant or not?'

It was on the tip of Derek's tongue to retort that he had written only the truth but his alarm had temporarily overcome his headache and had fuelled his alertness. 'All I can say is that I'm sorry for doing that, for writing that letter. I don't know what came over me. And I don't hate you. It's ridiculous of you to say that I do.'

'Well, let's see now, do you love me, Derek?'

'I – I—' The unexpectedness of the question set off his headache again.

'*Like* me, then? Come on, Derek, come on!' John's voice lashed into him like a riding crop. 'Do you tolerate me? Which is it – love, like, toleration? If it's not hate or dislike, it must be one of those! It must be *something*, Derek, you must feel something for me.'

'This is stupid. I'm not responding to this kind of barracking.'

'All right.' John's voice dropped again to its hushed half whisper. 'I'll put it a different way. You and I were – are – twins. Even if we're not identical, twins are supposed to be extra close, extra loving. What happened between us, Derek? All the time we were growing up, I certainly loved you.'

'I don't know – I just don't know, John!' The words burst unbidden out of Derek's mouth. He realised immediately he had blown his defences.

'Well,' John sat back in his chair, 'that at least is honest. That may be the first honest thing you have said to me in years.'

490

'I didn't mean—'

'Don't insult me, Derek!' John, who up to this had kept his hands behind his back, brought them out and balled them on his lap. He craned his head forward on his neck like a bull, or a ram. 'Don't – fucking – *insult* me!'

Derek sat very still on the couch, his cheek, head and heart banging in painful disrhythm. John maintained the posture of a charging animal for a long, long minute and then, bit by bit, eased up. 'I'm not letting you off the hook, Derek,' he said, 'but for the moment we don't have time for this. We will talk about this again.' The promise – or threat – was implicit.

He stood up and crossed to the fire, keeping his back to Derek. 'In the meantime,' he said, 'we had better discuss Bruno and Darina and how we are going to cope with that situation. Darina and her mother are staying the night at Sundarbans. I'm going up there in an hour's time and I think all three of us adults should be clear as to what we ought to do.'

CHAPTER SIXTEEN

'Ow! For God's sake, John, why don't you get a better car? This thing is a banger.' The springs of John's middle-aged Hillman complained loudly as they were jolted and bumped over the appalling surface of the driveway to Sundarbans. In an effort to maintain his balance, Derek's legs were spreadeagled in front of the passenger seat and his hands were braced on the dashboard. His complaints were the first words spoken between the twins since they had left the fishing lodge a quarter of an hour previously.

'This car's fine.' John, keeping his eyes peeled for the more vicious holes and ruts, swerved recklessly from side to side. His newly rekindled obsession with Rose was competing at the forefront of his mind with fury at his twin and he was savagely delighted at Derek's discomfort. On the other hand, for the sake of everyone involved in this dilemma, he knew he had better display a little self-control. And Derek was right, he thought; he could have easily afforded a new car – it was simply a project he had put on the long finger. 'I'll see about it soon, I promise,' he said.

After he had calmed down a little, he and Derek had discussed the situation as evenly as possible under the circumstances; they had agreed that their best chance lay in presenting a united adult front to Bruno and Darina. Even while agreeing, however, John had entertained serious doubts as to whether he had any right to intervene – or, more practically, whether Darina would accept the interference.

But, in any event, they were both expecting a showdown at Sundarbans, because when Bruno had still not turned up at the fishing lodge by half-past eight, it seemed certain that he had somehow made his way to the Big House in an effort to see Darina yet again. 'We could ring,' Derek had suggested.

'Yes, and warn them into doing a runner again?' John had shaken his head. Now, as they approached the end of the driveway, he continued to be placatory. 'We're nearly there.'

'Good job,' harrumphed Derek and John marvelled, not for the first time, at how little his twin's sojourn in Canada had affected his Monaghan accent.

In an effort to avoid a crater, he almost sideswiped the sagging side rails. 'Now, let's both take things easy.' He glanced at Derek. 'Don't you go blowing it by losing your temper.'

'Me lose my temper? *Me?*' But they had come out into the open space in front of the house and there was no time for a spat. 'What about the Colonel and the old lady?' Derek asked. 'How are they going to feel about all this – and about us two arriving in on them out of the blue?'

'They're in this too,' retorted John, 'whether they like it or not. After all, Darina is their granddaughter.'

'Yeah,' said Derek gloomily.

John parked the car and the two of them mounted the treacherous front steps. 'This frontage is the first job your group will have to tackle,' said Derek while they waited for the door to be answered.

The syndicate and the safety of tourists were the last concerns on John's mind as Rose opened the door. She looked pale but composed and very beautiful and he had to restrain himself from taking her in his arms. 'This is Derek,' he said. 'You remember him?'

'How do you do?' she said stiffly, without looking at his twin. 'Yes, I remember. Come in, won't you?'

When they were standing inside the entrance hall, two vivid pictures flashed almost simultaneously onto the front screen of John's brain: he saw himself, saturated, poverty-stricken and desperate, begging in this very spot for a hearing from the O'Beirne Moffats. And beside the image glowed another, of the tiger's head in Gus's study. Unlike so many other treasures of the house, so far it had not been sold off.

'Is Bruno here?' he asked and when Rose shook her head in surprise, he exchanged glances with Derek. 'It's just that he said he was going out for a walk more than three hours ago and he hasn't come back. We're almost sure he made his way here. Maybe if we asked Darina?'

493

'She's in her room, I'll go and ask her.'

John hesitated. 'Are you sure it's all right – us being here, I mean? Your mother and father . . . '

'They're in the kitchen. Please come this way.' Rose led them into the small, comfortably furnished sitting room, the surviving jewel in the tatty setting of the house. She waited until they were seated in front of the fire and left them.

'This isn't bad, eh?' Derek looked around appreciatively and John realised that this was the first time his brother had been inside Sundarbans.

'This and the kitchen and a couple of bedrooms are the only habitable rooms in the place,' he said shortly. Cutting off any further attempts at conversation, he stretched out his hands to the heat of the fire.

Derek covertly watched his twin. Seeing Rose O'Beirne Moffat and Bruno's real father side by side made him understand how dangerous his own position was: one injudicious word, just one, might lose him Bruno as a son. It was a possibility he had never openly faced; separated from his twin by such physical distance he had become almost complacent. It had taken something like this threat for him to see how precious Bruno had become to him.

Perhaps, he thought, his love of Bruno was the one truly selfless facet of his life. Yet how selfless was it? Didn't Bruno deserve to know who his real father was?

Such painful introspection was unusual for Derek and his treacherous heart responded to the emotional strain, beginning its awful rat-a-tat-tat.

John cleared his throat, moving his head a little, and Derek, still watching him, saw, as if for the first time, the dark circles under his eyes. The tension was telling on him too.

He tried to put himself in John's shoes but could not. Rose O'Beirne Moffat was beautiful, any fool could see that, and it did not take much insight to see how his brother was so deeply affected by her presence. But to Derek she was too cool and remote; a lifetime of differentness could never be bridged as far as he was concerned. He remembered that adolescent kiss he had snatched from her in the stableyard. How could he have been so crass?

The answer was simple and stark. He had simply wanted what had come so effortlessly to John.

Meeting the two of them for the first time, he thought, an outsider would have been hard pushed to accept that he and John were twins. It was not only the differences in their personalities, the physical gap was now very wide. In their early years, they had been quite alike, particularly as Derek had gained strength and condition out at Kelly's Cross, but John had retained his boyhood leanness and although he claimed not to be fit, he certainly seemed so.

Derek looked down with disgust at his own paunch, his pudgy hands. How had he let this happen?

Before he could fall into any more self-analysis, Rose returned. 'She's not in her room.' Two spots of colour burned on her pale cheeks. 'My father met her about two hours ago. She said she was going out for a walk.'

Derek and John looked at one another. 'Bruno!' they said simultaneously.

Rose raised both hands to the sides of her head. 'What are we going to do with them?'

'It's like trying to control a pair of rabbits in an open field.' John smiled grimly. 'But don't forget, Bruno's going home tomorrow. That'll give us all a bit of breathing space.'

Derek could actually feel the bonds between his brother and Rose; he might as well not have been in the room at all as far as they were concerned, he thought, and felt compelled to assert his presence. 'Shouldn't we go after them?' he asked.

'What do you think, John?' Again, she deflected Derek.

'I'm Bruno's father!' he said indignantly. 'Surely it's what I think—'

'Oh, shut up, Derek! It's what we all think – we're all in this together.' John crossed the room and took Rose by the elbows. 'Let's not panic. Let's take things one at a time.'

'Oh, John.' Rose crossed her arms over her breasts, hugging herself. 'It's freezing out there.'

He leaned in very close to her. 'Wherever they are, they'll be fine. They survived the whole night outdoors last night, didn't they? They're young and very healthy. By the way, do they know the full story?'

'I told Darina the bones of it. Not *everything*!' She shot a look at Derek which severely jolted his heart.

'How did she react?' John was watching her very closely.

'Mixed,' said Rose, with a ghost of a smile.

'Look,' said Derek shakily, 'you two can talk all night if you want to but in the meantime we have something very urgent on our plates.' He was determined not to be intimidated by Rose O'Beirne Moffat, no matter who she was or what he had done to her in the past. 'We should be doing something about that right now instead of nattering,' he added, his voice becoming stronger and more confident.

'Stop it, Derek,' said John.

'I will not stop it!' Derek lumbered to his feet. 'I will not stop it,' he repeated, willing himself to find the strength necessary to make the two of them pay attention, more importantly to stake his own claims. 'That's my *son* you're talking about,' he emphasised the words, 'a son who never gave anyone a moment's trouble until he met this girl who has obviously turned his head with weird talk and notions. Do the two of you know, for instance, that she's convinced him there's some sort of predestination in this relationship?'

'What do you mean?' The other two spoke together.

'I mean, folks, that Bruno and Darina now believe, apparently, that they are some form of astral lovers, that they are reincarnated or something. I seem to remember that the phrase used was "Twin Selves".'

'Darina reads a lot,' said Rose, almost apologetically, 'and I know that at the moment she's thinking a lot too. She's very deep.'

'Deep or shallow, may I point out that under your daughter's expert tutelage my son now accepts that he and Darina were meant to meet, that they have met before in some other life and that everything that happens between them is inevitable.' He was embroidering a bit but at least he had their full attention and he hoped he was establishing beyond doubt the closeness and intimacy between himself and Bruno.

'All this happened in the last few days?' Rose was staring at him at last.

'I guess so. I've been abroad.' Derek let the implications sink in.

'It's not the end of the world – all youngsters go through phases.' John took Rose's hand.

'As far as I'm concerned,' said Derek, with as much dignity as he could muster, 'I don't want my son being influenced like that.' To punctuate his statement, he crossed to the window and pulled aside one of the heavy curtains. The sitting room was at the front of the house and the moon was being kind to the neglected landscape which, under its patina of frost, glistened in an unbroken sweep towards the line of dark trees. But Derek gazed at its black and silver beauty without seeing it. Personal survival was all that he had in mind. Even his physical discomfort, the thudding heart and the headache, newly returned, were of little importance now.

He heard people approaching the door and turned round just as Rose's parents came into the room. Derek had not seen them for years and was unprepared for the changes in the Colonel and his wife. In his mind they were still lord and lady of the manor, who distributed largesse to their tenantry each Christmas and who, at all times, wore their God-given privileges and authority like ermine. He tried swiftly to calculate how old they were and, with a shock, worked out they were probably only in their sixties.

To think he had once been in awe, even in fear, of this pair of old-age pensioners. Mrs O'Beirne Moffat was merely a wisp of a woman, thin-haired, with wide watery eyes. Looking closer, he saw that the Colonel, at least, still displayed some vestiges of what he had been; although he used a walking cane he held himself quite erect, but he had lost a considerable amount of weight and his skin hung in yellow folds over his old-fashioned, studded collar.

'I think everyone knows each other?' said Rose uneasily, watching her mother.

Mrs O'Beirne Moffat's expression of fixed indifference did not change a whit and only the Colonel answered audibly, 'Yes. How are you, John? How d'you do, Derek?' Having delivered this little speech, he seemed to search for a watch or something concealed in the pocket of his waistcoat. Then he changed his mind and turned to his wife. 'Sit down, my dear. Is it warm enough for you in here?'

Daphne walked slowly across the room and sat in the chair nearest the fire. Ignoring the company, she took up a piece of embroidery. The Colonel coughed. 'I gather the two young rascals have gone to ground again?'

'History repeating itself.' The words, fired across the Colonel's like a burst of grapeshot, were surprisingly vigorous from the mouth of a woman who looked as though she would break in two if touched by a sparrow's wing.

'Stop it, Mother!' Rose whirled on her in fury. 'There's no percentage in this.'

'I'm only expressing my opinion. This is my house, still, I presume? I'm still entitled to my opinion? That one thing at least?'

'Please, Daphne.' Gus spread his hands in distress.

John intervened. 'I'm sorry you still feel towards me the way you do, Mrs O'Beirne Moffat. But there were certain circumstances, which some day you may learn from Rose – and which may make you feel differently.'

Derek felt his cheeks begin to burn. He had to divert the conversation again. 'If you don't mind, I'd like to go and look for my son.'

'I believe it's already too late.' Mrs O'Beirne Moffat would not be denied her contribution.

'*Stop it, Mother!*' Rose covered her ears with her hands. 'If you're not going to contribute anything useful to the conversation, please don't say anything at all.'

'Too late for what, Mrs O'Beirne Moffat?' The tension, which for so many hours had been stretched to breaking point in Derek, moved closer to snapping.

'Just too late,' repeated Daphne, fixing her eyes on him. 'And you know precisely what I mean, young man. You and your brother have brought nothing but horror to this house.'

There was an appalled silence as the other four took in the baldness of what she had said.

'Please, my dear.' The Colonel flushed the colour of a turkey cock. 'Dreadfully sorry,' he mumbled to the twins. 'She doesn't mean anything by that, heat of the moment and so on. She doesn't mean it.' He turned to her. 'You're just a little overwrought, my dear—'

'I certainly do mean it. That man' – she pointed a shaking finger at John – 'broke up this family in the first place and now it looks as though he's doing it again, and this time with the aid of his brother.'

'That's enough, Daphne!' The Colonel banged his walking cane on the carpet, his yellow jowls quivering. 'I forbid you to say any more!'

Derek was acutely embarrassed at this public row. He looked at John for some assistance but his twin was staring at the Colonel, a look almost of admiration on his face.

'I'm just saying the truth.' Daphne set her mouth. 'There has never been a hint of scandal on my side of the family, Gus.'

'I said, that's enough, my dear.' The Colonel moderated his tone. He walked across to her and, almost tenderly, tucked a rug around her knees. 'I think I'll go out, have a look around the stables. Could do with a breather, anyhow.' Straightening up, he turned back to Derek and John. 'Storm in a teacup, I shouldn't wonder. The youngsters will be back safe and sound. It's my bet they've just lost track of time.'

'Are you coming, Daddy?' Rose visibly straightened her back and Derek saw the family resemblance to her father as she sailed out of the room.

'Be sure and wear something warm!' Daphne called after her in a tone of voice so completely different that it was as if the preceding conversation had never taken place.

'Good evening, Mrs O'Beirne Moffat.' He heard John adopt his professional hotelier's voice. 'I'm sorry we've disturbed you. Are you coming, Derek?'

Derek was still staring at Rose's mother. 'Yes, I'm coming,' he said slowly. If the situation was not so fraught, he thought, it would have been funny. The woman was bats.

As he left with John, he looked back into the room. The Colonel was patting his wife on the shoulder.

Gus had guessed correctly. Darina and Bruno were curled up together in a corner of the storage shed in the stableyard.

There was only one vehicle left, the ancient trap for which the long gone Clicker was the last pony. Upturned in the corner, it was in such an advanced state of decay that even the tinkers had refused to buy it. One shaft was missing, the other pointed upwards like a preacher's finger through a wavering circle of light cast by a torch which Darina had stood on its end.

The two of them were talking their hearts out. At least Darina was talking and Bruno listened intently as she expanded on her individualistic spiritual theories. 'Once you start thinking about it,' she said earnestly, 'it makes a lot of sense. Each soul is an individual, created trillions of years ago. And the goal is perfection – heaven, if you like. But it has to go through loads and loads of lives, tests really, until everything which prevents perfection is worked on and overcome. Each time you are born, you have a set number of tasks, depending on which life you're leading at the time. Do you understand?'

'I think so.' Bruno knitted his forehead in concentration. 'It could be that this is where all the religions have basically the same idea. Like for us Christians, this perfection is after we die and get to see God.'

'Yes, but the difference is that, when you look at it my way, God gives you more than one chance. Do you think He'd be God if, just because you made mistakes in one life, He'd condemn you to hell for ever and ever?'

'Doesn't make sense, when you put it like that,' Bruno agreed slowly.

'I think everyone sort of knows this in their hearts, no matter what we're taught in school or in church,' Darina went on, 'but they shut it out. Adults particularly. My mother, for instance. She's a wonderful person but she sees things now in such an ordinary way. You've got to agree that adults do shut themselves off from magic.'

'I mean,' she sat up to press home the point, 'I used to believe in fairies and I still do in a way – who's to say there aren't fairies? Who can *prove* there aren't?'

'Now come on, Darina! I draw the line at fairies—'

'No,' she insisted. 'Who's to say? I bet on that Island of yours people talk about ghosts and things.'

'Yes, but that's different.'

'Not so different. They do in Ireland too, even in Dublin, even in the middle of a big city. I'll tell you what I think. I think that when we're all young, much younger than us, we can all believe in all these things very easily because we feel them and we believe our feelings. But then adults get involved in adult things, like jobs and making money and being successful and they don't listen to themselves or each other any more.'

She lay back against Bruno's shoulder. 'My mother is a

great person as I said and very intelligent, but she'd probably have a fit if she heard me talking like this. All she wants is for me to get on in life, be happy, be successful. But maybe when she was our age – maybe when your mother and father were our age too – maybe they all knew this and felt as I do now but they forgot how to remember it. Do you understand? I'm not going to forget it. Especially now I *have* met you—'

'What's that?' Bruno clutched her arm.

Darina had heard it too, footsteps approaching the stable. They held their breath.

Whoever it was pushed open the door. Too late, Darina remembered the torch and grabbed it but the person had seen the light and came right round the side of the trap.

'Hello,' said Gus. 'Must be damned uncomfortable on that hard floor.'

'Hello, Grandad!' Darina's voice was small but determined. 'This is Bruno.'

Outside the kitchen, in the hallway of the fishing lodge, the clock chimed midnight. Hopelessly, Derek looked at the boy he knew as his son. Until this night, he had not realised the extent to which Bruno could be so blithely determined and, for the umpteenth time, asked himself how he could have lived with him for so long and not fully seen this side of him. The intransigence was difficult enough but the insuperable obstacle was proving to be Bruno's unshakeable amiability. Derek had tried cajoling, threatening, reasoning, all to no avail; Bruno was as sweetly intractable now as he had been when they started the discussion over an hour ago.

In one sense, he almost admired him for sticking so rigidly to his guns.

Having been allowed fifteen minutes to say a final goodbye to Darina, Bruno had come away from Sundarbans with John and himself willingly enough, but Derek was uneasy all the way home. Although the conversation between the three of them in the car had been amicable, Derek could not shake off the impression that there was another agenda in Bruno's head to which no one, except possibly Darina, was party.

They were seated at the big kitchen table and the boy looked as fresh-faced and energetic, thought Derek, as though it was nine o'clock in the morning. He decided to give it one final try and summoned up his last dribbles of strength. 'You're too young to understand exactly what's going on, Bruno,' he said as gravely as he could manage.

'Dad, that's an insulting thing to say.' Bruno's lightness belied the words.

'I don't mean to insult you,' replied Derek, 'but there are some things that if you were older, you would be able to take into account.'

'Like what, Dad?'

From somewhere in his childhood, some long-forgotten snatch of catechism class, a word came to his aid. 'Do you know what an impediment is, Bruno?'

Bruno frowned. 'I think so – some kind of bar or obstacle?'

'Well, sort of. But I meant in a much more serious sense. In canon law, for instance.'

'I don't get you.'

'Please, Bruno, will you just take my word for it?' Derek leaned forward to give added weight to his words. 'Will you believe me when I tell you that a serious impediment exists which forbids a relationship between you and Darina Flynn?'

'You mean that we're first cousins? We already know that. That's no problem, really it's not—'

'Much more serious than that. *Much* more serious.' Derek rose and came to stand beside Bruno's chair. 'Do you trust me? Have I ever let you down in the past?'

'No.'

For the first time, Derek saw a shadow of uncertainty in the blue eyes. 'Will you trust me on this one?' he asked.

'In what way?'

'Will you believe me if I tell you that I know something that I'm sworn to secrecy about, which means that there are serious ethical reasons why you can't go on with this girl?'

'I don't believe you.' Bruno stood up. 'Sorry, Dad, I didn't mean that to sound aggressive. I do believe, of course, that *you* believe what you're saying. But you're expecting me to take on trust something you won't even explain to me.'

'It happens all the time between friends, between father and son.'

'Yes, but I thought I explained to you that Darina is now the most important thing in my life. No offence, Dad, but there can be no impediment to that, nothing that I – or she – would pay attention to. I know there are problems. I know I'm young and she's young too and to tell you the truth we think that this is what's bothering everyone about us. But she and I are for real. I'm sorry, but there it is. I didn't look for this. It just happened. I'm not deliberately trying to cause hassle to everyone and neither is she. The only way this could be undone is to turn back the clock, to undo time. And we can't do that, at least not in this life. And, believe me, because this is causing such problems to everyone else, I'm tempted to say that I wish I hadn't met her in the first place. But that would be a terrible lie. I don't wish that – I *certainly* don't wish that. I'm glad I met her beside that lake, so glad I can't put proper words on it. It might sound corny but the only way I can explain what it feels like to love Darina is that she fills up every scrap of air inside me and outside me, all around me, all the time.'

'I know how that feels.'

'Again, no offence, Dad, but that's your business. And if you do know, if you know that truly, deep in your heart, you'll also know that there is nothing you can do to stop us. There's nothing anyone can do.'

'Why won't you believe me?'

'There's nothing to believe. But, Dad, I want you to believe me when I say that even if you did tell me, no matter what it is, it will make no difference.'

Derek looked at the boy's beautiful face, animated with a passion he had never seen in it before and, for an agonising moment, teetered on the brink of telling him the truth. He pulled back, however. Even if he could face the personal trauma and loss, he had no right to tell Bruno anything. Whatever his differences with Karen, Derek yielded that right to her.

He caught hold of Bruno's shoulders. The boy's eyes were on a level with his own. 'You're making a terrible mistake, Bruno,' he said. 'I wish I could convince you what an awful mistake you're making.'

In a last-ditch attempt to make him see reason, he stared into Bruno's eyes as hard as he could. 'I wish I could tell you what's on my mind – I sincerely wish I could. But this secret I'm

503

talking about has to do with two other people and I promised years ago that I would never divulge it. I've no right to tell you about it. I would if I could – I'm sure you can appreciate that.'

Bruno returned the gaze, his own eyes never wavering. 'I appreciate that, Dad. But in the matter of honour, you must accept that I have honour too. I've made certain promises to Darina.'

'What promises?' Derek, shocked, let him go.

'We promised each other we would never tell.' Continuing to gaze into Derek's eyes, he let the sentence hang between them and Derek at last conceded defeat. Overriding all other considerations, he now accepted, at least for the moment, that even if he did tell Bruno that Darina Flynn was his half-sister, the knowledge would make not a whit of difference to what the boy perceived at the moment to be the love of his life and his commitment to this girl. There was even the danger that the exotic nature of the truth might even enhance the adventure for both of them.

The only hope they all had was that the relationship might die a natural death.

So he held his tongue and turned away. 'I think it's time we wrapped it up for tonight,' he said, walking towards the door of the kitchen. 'I've made my position clear to you. We'll talk again some time, maybe at home when the situation has calmed down a bit. I don't know about you, but I'm completely exhausted.'

'And she can come visit?' Bruno was relentless.

'That's up to your mother.' Derek's tiredness pressed down on him like a heavy, smothering quilt. He had tried his best. All he wanted now was sleep. 'Come on to bed, Bruno,' he said. 'It's after midnight and we've an early start in the morning.'

'Sure, Dad.'

They mounted the stairs together. Everyone else was in bed and the house was as quiet as the grave. Derek was too tired even to brush his teeth. He threw off his clothes and, putting on only the jacket of his pyjamas, crawled into bed. He was vaguely aware of Bruno putting out the light and getting into the other bed across the room before sleep at last released him.

*

504

Rose, who was sitting on the edge of Darina's bed, took her daughter's hand. 'You'll be frozen. It's a very cold night.' Her daughter, propped up in the bed, was wearing only a T-shirt.

'Not at all, Mammy. It's not cold. You only *think* it's cold because there's frost on the ground outside. It's all in the mind. I'm fine.'

She was right, thought Rose. It was chilly in the room, but not freezing. 'Have you forgiven me?' she asked, squeezing Darina's hand.

'For what?' Darina's hand did not respond to the squeeze; it lay lifeless in her own as her eyes slid away to a corner of the room.

'You know,' replied Rose. 'I've told you already. I feel none of this would have happened if I hadn't slammed down the phone that time—'

'Please, Mother, leave it. There's nothing to forgive.'

'All right. As long as you know I'm sorry. I just reacted instinctively.' She forced herself to sound matter-of-fact. 'Now, what about you and Bruno? Please believe me, I want to understand what's going on.'

'I've told you and told you. Bruno and I love each other. It's very simple.'

'But Derek – Bruno's father – tells me that you're reading something extra special into this relationship. That you and Bruno believe that it's all fate and predestination. Something like that.'

Darina brought her eyes round. 'So? That's our business, surely?'

'You're on dangerous ground, Darina.'

'I know what I feel and what Bruno feels.'

Rose felt as though she were treading on eggshells. One heavy step and everything would break. 'At least take your time with this, darling, you and Bruno are so young yet.'

'Are you afraid I'll get pregnant?'

Rose managed to conceal her shock. 'That too. But I'm more worried about what this might do to you mentally and emotionally.'

'So you don't care if I get pregnant . . . '

'Of course I care. I'd be very disappointed.'

505

'With all due respect, Mother, you're not exactly one to talk, are you?'

Touché, thought Rose with grim humour. She had asked for that one. 'I made mistakes, Darina, yes,' she said, 'but because I did, I hope you can learn from them.'

'Are you sorry you had me, then?' Darina looked away again.

'Of course I'm not.' Rose realised that she was being very cleverly diverted from her own purpose. 'Please, Darina,' she said, 'I want you to be careful with this boy.'

'I've told you we're not sleeping together.'

'I know that and I appreciate that. Sex adds very complicated aspects to relationships at your age. But that's not what—'

'Well, you're the expert on that—'

'Please!' Rose thought she was beginning to sound like a bleating ewe. She dropped Darina's hand and got up to walk about the room. 'Let me tell you a little about myself and your – your father,' she said. 'You deserve that much.' She glanced at the bed and saw that at least she now had Darina's full attention.

'Mother,' she said flatly, 'this is none of my business. It's past history. I don't want to know any of this.'

'Maybe not,' Rose continued her pacing, 'but I want to tell you. I need to tell you. I probably should have told you long ago – I just didn't have the courage. And I want you to forgive me for that too.'

'This is *embarrassing*, Mammy—'

'It's not brilliant for me either. But I want you to hear it. I loved John Flynn very very much. Probably as much as you love Bruno. There were all kinds of complications for us too – not least that he was a penniless tenant here at Sundarbans and my mother would have been dead set against any relationship with him. Not that I ever gave her a chance,' she added honestly. 'I just *assumed* she would do everything in her power to stop me seeing him.' She paused. 'Just like I think you're assuming things about me.'

'I'm not assuming anything. Anyway, you seem to think you know everything there is to know about Bruno and me—'

506

'Not everything, Darina! That's just the point.' Rose came back to the side of the bed. 'Not everything,' she repeated. 'I recognise the feeling you have for this boy – please believe me that I do. But what I don't understand, and what only you can tell me, is this extra dimension that Bruno told his father about. Twin souls—'

'Selves,' corrected Darina. 'Twin Souls is a different thing.'

'I want to understand, to help.' Rose held her breath. Perhaps if she could get Darina to confide in her, they could all come out of this intact.

Darina started to play with some loose fibres in one of the sheets. 'All I can say is that being with Bruno is like looking in a mirror.' As though conscious that by revealing even this morsel of information she had exposed herself too much, she stopped abruptly and slid down between the bedcovers. 'I'm very tired. Could we leave this till the morning?'

'Go on, Darina, go on, please.'

But Darina turned her face to the wall.

Rose could not bear to let the momentum go. 'I promise I won't interrupt.' She touched Darina's shoulder but that proved to be a mistake. Darina recoiled as though she had been burned.

Rose stepped back a little. 'All right, darling, we'll leave it, so. But you will talk to me again, won't you? This concept isn't new to me, you know, it's just that I've never encountered it face to face. I promise I won't badger you about it ! I just want to try to understand what it *feels* like.'

'Yes, I know, Mammy, please don't go on about it.' Darina looked quickly over her shoulder. 'I will tell you soon, honest.' She sighed, a long, stagey sigh, as if she were falling asleep.

Very slowly and gently, Rose bent and kissed the top of her head; Darina's thick hair smelled of the outdoors and Rose remembered the first time she had touched her lips to the sweetness of Darina's baby hair. 'Goodnight, darling,' she said softly. 'Sleep well.'

Then as she climbed into her own bed, she saw a glimmer of humour in her predicament. It was no wonder, she thought wryly, that the Catholic Church promulgated the view that the highest seats in heaven were reserved for mothers.

*

Derek groped for full consciousness. Some external noise in the fishing lodge had woken him out of a deep and dreamless sleep. He wanted to sink back into it again but felt urgently he needed to identify the sound. He strained his ears but could hear nothing. The room was eerily quiet.

That was it! It was too quiet. He sat upright, snapping on his bedside light.

Bruno's bed was empty.

Stupidly, he stared at the rumpled bedclothes, not willing to believe what he saw. Bruno was in the bathroom, that was it. But no matter how hard he listened, he could hear no stir at all; no footsteps, no flushing. He checked his watch: ten past three.

'Oh, my God.' He said the words aloud and then, because they sounded unreal in the unnaturally quiet room, repeated them. 'Oh, my God.'

He struggled out of the bed, wincing at the coldness of the linoleum on the floor and while he dragged on the clothes he had discarded just over three hours ago, railed in his heart against Bruno. This time the boy had gone too far. The hell with being understanding and all this liberalism. Derek had never lifted a finger against Bruno but what that boy needed, he told himself furiously, was a good belting.

He was in such a state as he laced his shoes that he started to pant; his head began to spin and he had to stop for a few seconds to let it clear. The little brat! John had been right. Trying to control these two was more difficult than herding rabbits in an unfenced field.

This time, he repeated the phrase like a mantra, this time, Bruno had gone too far. Too far. This time, when he caught him, he'd fix him good and proper.

Careful not to wake anyone else, he tiptoed down the stairs and took his overcoat from the hook behind the door. His Hamburg luggage, still not unpacked because of all the commotion the day before, stood in the hall, reminding him that in only a few hours he and Bruno would be on their way home. The sooner the better, he thought. This trip had been nothing but a disaster for everyone. He dreaded telling Karen about it.

At the thought of Karen, his heart fluttered, making him feel nauseous. He was going to have to be careful how he broke

508

all this bad news to Karen. Somehow, despite everything, all the shouting and the rows, she still held something for him, a physical attraction that had dissipated but not died. It was what held them together. That, he thought darkly, and the other hold they had over each other – a hold which, in his more lucid moments, he recognised for what it was. He and Karen could use Bruno to blackmail one another emotionally if they were so inclined. Maybe if they had had children of their own, things might have been different – but it had not happened and neither of them worried particularly about it. Bruno had been enough.

And now what? Of course he had no proof that Karen was having an affair but now that he thought about it, she had been behaving oddly lately; and once or twice he had answered the telephone and whoever it was had hung up. How could he have been so dumb?

Physical jealousy smote Derek, surprising him with its acuteness. Goddamnit, he thought, his anger with Bruno fuelling feverish speculation about Karen, he would have it out with her immediately they got home. Where were those car keys? In his fury, he upended an assortment of keys from a dish on the hall-stand and searched through them but the keys to the rented car were not among them.

He checked the pockets of his overcoat, then the floor of the hallway. No sign.

Perhaps he had left them in the ignition; opening the front door, he went out to the driveway and stopped dead.

John's banger was there all right but the rented car was gone.

Now, as well as dealing with his rage, Derek had to deal with sudden fear. Bruno was a competent driver – since there was no public transport on the Island, all the PEI youngsters were – but he had never driven a right-hand drive vehicle on the left side of the road. Of a frosty road. At three o'clock in the morning.

As well as that, it was illegal for him to drive in Ireland, uninsured and at the age of sixteen. 'You'd better not come across the Guards,' Derek muttered to his reflection in the hallstand mirror. 'Brat, brat, *brat*!' The expression of rage helped clear it and he realised that, no matter what, he had to go after the boy.

He picked up John's keys. Rather than wake him and ask

permission, he assumed it and let himself out into the frost. It was clear and bright and, although his breath misted in front of him, not half as cold as it looked from inside.

He started the car and then had to wait for it to warm up sufficiently to clear the windscreen. While he waited, keeping an eye on the house in case John should appear, he rehearsed what he would say to those two young fools when he caught up with them. He had no doubt they were back in their hidey-hole in the stableyard at Sundarbans. Well, he had a thing or two he wanted to get off his chest; they would get an earful.

Oddly, he felt buoyant and clearheaded; the tachycardia had not assaulted him, as yet anyhow, and although he had had only three hours' sleep, the cold, still air energised him.

He switched on the Hillman's wipers to help the process of defrosting. While he waited a thought struck him, making him feel slightly uneasy. He hoped he hadn't gone too far with the impediment business. Bruno was an intelligent lad; he hoped he wouldn't put two and two together . . .

Derek was mistaken in at least one of his suppositions.

Darina and Bruno were not in the stableyard but in the old boathouse by the lake, only two hundred yards from where they had first met. They were there by appointment, fixed when they had been left alone by the adults to say goodbye.

They had cleaned up one corner and had dragged a pile of rotting canvas and other debris into it to improvise a bed and, fully dressed, were lying on it facing one another. Bruno was kissing Darina everywhere his lips could reach and she was similarly kissing him. The dust was affecting him, causing him to sneeze. He sneezed again now, causing her to giggle and he hugged her desperately. 'I love you, Darina.'

'I love you, Bruno.'

'For ever, for eternity . . . '

'Yes.' She said it with absolute certainty.

'I don't want to leave you.'

'I know.' Propping herself up on one elbow, she looked tenderly at him and stroked his face which was fading in and out of deep shadow; the weak concentric circles of light from a torch in which the battery was running low were the only illumination in the boathouse. 'I wish I could have brought you to a palace,' she said.

'This place is fine.'

Again they kissed. 'Tell me how you got on with your dad,' she asked when they had finished. 'Oh, the usual, you know.' Again Bruno sneezed.

'He doesn't want us to be together.' Darina watched the way the beam from the torch, its weakening now accelerated, made flickering lace of the network of cobwebs above their head. 'None of them do.'

'That's obvious, I'm afraid – but it doesn't matter to me, Darina. It doesn't matter what he thinks, or anyone else for that matter.'

'None of them will accept it, you know.'

Something in her tone caused him to hesitate. 'Because we're first cousins?'

'I think so. But I have the feeling it's something more than that. Something to do with themselves.'

'Funny you should say that,' he said reflectively, pulling her head down so it was resting in the crook of his neck. 'My dad was on about some other stuff, stuff he said he couldn't tell me. A secret.'

'A secret?' Darina stiffened. 'Did he give you any clues?'

Bruno hesitated. 'No, not really—'

'Are you sure? Absolutely sure?'

'Sort of. I wasn't interested in anything he had to say, to tell you the truth. But he did say he was sworn to secrecy by two other people – or that he was sworn to secrecy and there were two other people involved, something like that. He also said it was something to do with an impediment, whatever that is.'

Darina sat up. 'Are you sure that's the word he used, "impediment"?'

'Yeah. Is it important?'

'I'm not sure,' said Darina slowly. 'I need to think.'

'What is this impediment stuff?'

'I can't remember exactly but I think it's something to do with marriage. We studied it in *Apologetics* but I've forgotten.'

'What's *Apologetics*?'

'Ah, it's nothing much. It's the name of a book we had to study in religious knowledge class. It gives you all the arguments to prove that Christ is the One True God, and tells you how to argue against the Christian Scientists and Jehovah's Witnesses. That kind of thing.'

'What's that got to do with us?' In the semi-darkness, Bruno's voice was hushed.

'I think an impediment to a marriage means you can't marry your sister-in-law or your mother-in-law, or your near relatives.'

'Well, that's what he meant, I suppose, I mean, that's us. The cousins thing.'

'But, Bruno, we know that even the Catholic Church lets first cousins get married. I think he doesn't mean just that. Let me think,' said Darina slowly. Then, after a short silence, 'He said he was *sworn* to secrecy by two other people?'

'I definitely remember that he said there were two other people involved. Yes, definitely.'

'*Two* other people—' The enormity of it struck them both at the same time. Each could feel it in the other. Darina started to tremble. 'You know what I think?' she asked, her voice shaky and very young.

'Tell me. Tell me what you think,' Bruno whispered as, instinctively, they moved a little apart.

'I think your mother and father are not your real mother and father at all.'

'Why do you think – surely—'

'I think you're my brother, not my cousin.'

'I couldn't be.' Bruno did not sound as if he meant it. 'I'm only five months younger than you,' he added as if he was begging her to tell him this could not be true.

Again they considered the situation individually.

'Have you seen your birth certificate?' asked Darina.

'Of course.'

'And your mother and father are written in?'

'Yes.'

'And you were definitely born in Canada?'

'I have a Canadian birth certificate and a Canadian passport.'

'Well, that's one thing then. My mother couldn't be your mother because she was rearing me in a flat in Dublin at the time you were born. That's one sure thing. We have to look at your dad, then.'

'What about him?' Bruno's voice held real fear. 'Darina, I don't want to talk about this any more.'

'We have to. You want to get at the truth, don't you?'

'I – I'm not sure I do.'

'Your dad and your uncle John are twins. They both emigrated at the same time, didn't they?'

'Yes. Dad often told me about that boat trip and how he met my mom and how Uncle John . . . ' He trailed off and the silence between them grew terrifying. It was so still both in the boathouse and outside, they could actually hear the minute movements of the cobwebs above their heads.

The light from the torch flared briefly and finally died. Darina could hear her own heart thumping. 'It's your uncle John,' she said into the darkness. 'He's not your uncle. He's your father. That's the secret.'

Bruno did not reply.

'Are you all right?' she asked, reaching out a hand and encountering his. He laced his fingers into hers and held on tightly.

'I'm sorry,' she said. She moved close to him and took him in her arms. 'It's just the two of us, Bruno. Just the two of us. I think we both knew it all along.'

'I didn't know it.' His voice was shuddering. 'I really didn't know it, Darina. I loved my dad.'

'You see now why we knew one another.'

'Yes.'

'But it was more than just brother and sister, half-brother and half-sister, whatever. You and I are in this life to help each other for the next one. Into the next one.' Her voice was getting stronger, with a hint of excitement.

'I don't know what you mean.'

'I'm certain we're here together tonight to find this out and now we've fulfilled out purpose. We've worked out our relationship.'

'Is this more about Twin Selves?'

'Sort of. But, Bruno, if we don't work things out in this life, we'll keep meeting and meeting in future lives until we do and until we do work things out, we'll be unhappy.'

'Darina, I don't understand any of this.'

'You don't have to understand it. You just have to feel it.'

'I wasn't unhappy. I certainly wasn't. No way.' He pulled away from her a little.

'Maybe you didn't know what true happiness was. Didn't you always feel you were sort of searching for something and not really knowing what it was?'

'Ye-es. I suppose so. Now that you mention it. But while I didn't know it, I wasn't unhappy.'

'Haven't you been happy since you met me, since we met one another?'

'Oh, yes. Oh, Darina, yes!' He caught her to him. 'How do you know all this so well? Who taught you all this?'

'I don't know it all – far from it. I just know what I've read but much more importantly what I feel. And I'm certain what I feel is the right thing. I'm certain that if we do the right thing now we'll be transfigured.'

'What?'

'Try to look at it logically, Bruno. They are not going to let us be together, are they? Not now. They all know the real story. They kept trying to keep us apart so we wouldn't find out and they would all be in a mess. Their mess. That's the truth, isn't it? If we let them have their way, tonight, this hour, is the last we will spend together on this earth, in this life. All I know is that, if we let that happen, I will be absolutely miserable without you.'

'What choice do we have?' he whispered, his head against her breast.

'We have a choice. What do we own? We own our souls and our bodies each time we are given one and that is all we will ever own.'

'You really believe that we have more than one life?'

'Hundreds of millions of Buddhists and Hindus can't be wrong.' Darina's voice sounded almost gay. 'Sorry, I'm not making light of it. To answer your question, yes, I believe it. It all makes sense now. Think about it, Bruno. Does it make sense to you that we get one chance *and one chance only* to make good – and then depending on what we make of that chance, we're punished or rewarded for *all eternity*? God couldn't be like that, He just couldn't. At least I don't believe He could.'

'I see what you mean, but—'

'And it's not all that complicated, it's very simple. That's just the point.' Darina's excitement was growing. 'They – all of them – do know it like we do, Bruno, but they don't acknowledge it. People like us do because we still listen to our feelings. And also because we weren't satisfied with the answers they gave us when we asked questions.'

'You mean people like you. You're talking about yourself, Darina. I never asked any of those questions.'

'But now you believe me? At least you *feel* I'm right?'

Bruno considered a long time. 'Yes,' he said at last. 'It does makes sense.'

'You see!' She was triumphant now. 'You see? That's why we met and got so close so soon. It isn't only that we recognise each other and are Twin Selves, it's that we were *sent* to each other. I got this book out of the library a few months ago – I couldn't even tell you the name of it now – but there was one thing in it that particularly struck me. I remembered it and understood it the minute I met you. I can't recall the exact words but it went something like "When the pupil is ready the teacher will arrive." We're teachers of each other. It's only since I met you that I've understood all of this. There's a great difference between knowing and understanding. It's to do with acceptance.'

'And you definitely think we've met before?'

'Yes!' In the gloom, she nodded vigorously. 'And what I feel deep down is that God *wants* us – not only us, everyone – to get into heaven, which is perfection. The Catholic Church is right about that bit. But what they *don't* tell us is that if we don't make a go of it in one life, we get another chance and then another and then another until we work everything out. And along the way, we all meet people who will help us or harm us. And it's up to us to recognise them when they come along. We've a *duty* to recognise them and to work out whatever it is we're supposed to work out with them. That's our task.'

515

'And what happens if we don't?'

'We keep meeting them over and over again until we do.'

'Are you saying, then, that if we don't see each other again after tonight, we'll meet again in some other life?'

She hesitated. 'Yes. But I'm also saying that we've recognised each other, Bruno. We love each other, we've helped each other. We both feel it. Our job in this life is done.'

He was considering his answer when she put a hand on his arm. 'Ssh. Do you hear it?'

They both listened and then, simultaneously, heard the distinct note of a faraway car.

'It's coming up the driveway,' whispered Darina.

'How do you know?' he whispered back.

'Because there's no road near here.'

They listened again. The car was coming nearer. 'It's them,' she said. 'They've missed us and they're coming looking for us.'

'What'll we do?' Bruno hissed.

'Ssh, keep still.'

Tensely, they waited until the note of the engine died. 'Oh, Darina!' He clutched her tightly. 'We can't just stay here waiting for them.' His voice was laced with panic.

'Hush,' said Darina. 'Hush, my dearest darling.' She encircled him with her arms and kissed him slowly and gently on the lips. 'Hush, my baby. Don't worry, everything's going to be just fine. Everything's going to be all right. I promise, everything's going to work out. You'll see . . . ' She crooned to him and kissed him over and over again. 'You just trust me and believe in me and everything's going to work out. No one's ever going to pull us apart again. We're going to be together for ever and ever and ever.'

A few seconds later, they slipped out of the boathouse and took refuge in a sheltered spot in the woods less than a hundred yards away.

'Aha!' said Derek to himself as he rounded the last bend of the Sundarbans avenue. The rented car was parked just before the driveway opened into the space in front of the house. He pulled the Hillman round in front of it and let the engine die.

516

He decided then to conduct the search on his own. No point in waking the whole household, he thought. If he needed reinforcements, he could go back for them later.

Pulling up the collar of his coat, he made straight for the stableyard, finding his way with little difficulty because of the brightness of the moon. He felt as though he were the only living creature on a strange, frozen planet. Since he had left the McGuigans' homestead in Kelly's Cross so long ago, Derek rarely ventured into the countryside and never at night, except to travel through it in his comfortable car. But even he had to admit that this was a beautiful night. Cold, too. But a dry cold, not the kind that gets into the bones.

But, he castigated himself for his inattention, he had no time for looking around or for fanciful admiration of the moonlight. His task was to find that young so-and-so, to detach him and to get him safely home to Charlottetown. He pulled the collar tighter around his neck.

Something – a rat? – skittered across the cobbles in front of him as he let himself into the yard through a broken wicket gate. The door of the trap shed was ajar. 'Aha,' he said again, walking quietly towards it and went inside. It was very dark and so still he could hear his own breath rasping in his chest after the exertion of the short walk. But there was no immediate sight or sound of the youngsters. Cursing that he had not thought to bring a lamp or a torch, he felt his way cautiously around the walls, beginning with the upturned trap in one corner.

Nothing.

They were not here.

'Dammit!' he said aloud.

He left the shed and crossed to the stables, pulling open the doors he could move and listening hard at the ones which were still padlocked.

Nothing.

In a corner of the yard, he spotted a stone archway above a narrow staircase which led to the upper-storey living quarters. Derek's nerve failed him. He knew from his desultory discussions with John that these parts of the stables, earmarked for a leisure centre and pool room in the renovation plans, were in a very bad state of repair, that the floors had fallen in. Even two young people in love, he told himself, were unlikely to have risked messing about up there. So he contented himself with poking his head into the stairwell and listening. He even ventured a sudden startling shout: 'Bruno!'

His voice reverberated hollowly and he waited, straining his ears, until the sound died completely.

Still nothing.

In a thoroughly bad temper, he decided they had to be in the woods again. 'I'll babes-in-the-woods you!' he muttered as he strode out of the stableyard and took a short cut towards the trees through the brambled pleasure garden.

All conversation between Darina and Bruno had died away as they lay curled up together in the depths of the wood, a few hundred feet from the boathouse. Bruno was crying soundlessly, tears pouring unchecked down his face. Darina caught them in her fingers and tasted them, then she kissed him on the lips so he tasted her and them together.

Distantly, perhaps still a few minutes away, they heard someone coming; whoever it was was making no effort to be quiet. 'Come on,' she whispered softly, disentangling herself and pulling at his hand, 'we don't have much time.'

Overwhelmed, he caught her to him again and kissed her. 'Oh God, Darina . . . '

'Do you love me?'

'I love you. I love you . . . '

'I love you too. It's going to be all right, my darling. We'll be together for ever – for ever and ever.'

'I don't know whether I can go through with it.'

'It's the only way. You know that.'

The sounds were closer. Bruno pulled away from her, his eyes wide with fright. 'I've just remembered what it was that was wrong with your argument – about us meeting over and over again in different lives.'

'What?' Her voice was calm and tender.

'You said our job was done in this one.'

'Almost,' she whispered.

'But then why do we need to meet again?'

'We don't need to, we will *want* to and we will be *able* to. That's perfection. That's heaven.' She kissed him again, then locking her arms around his neck, she opened her eyes wide and fixed them on him. 'Such magic, Bruno,' she said, pulling him to his feet. 'Come on, my darling one.'

Obediently, tears still pouring, keeping his eyes fixed on her face, he allowed her to lead him as she backed out of their hiding place, facing him all the time, towards the edge of the radiant lake.

Derek came out into the open just beside the boathouse. That had to be where they were. Why hadn't he thought of it before? He was really getting tired of this. His calves ached from the walking and the surge of energy he had experienced an hour earlier had deserted him. He checked his watch. It was after four o'clock. This was getting beyond the beyonds. If they weren't in this bloody boathouse, he thought, he'd give up being so noble and would raise the alarm at the Big House.

He sighed. It was such a long walk back . . .

The door of the boathouse was open and, holding his breath against the dust, he went inside. The moonlight shafted in through the open door reflecting off something bright on the windowsill. It proved to be a torch, still slightly warm. They'd been here all right.

He reckoned they had probably heard him coming. They couldn't be far away.

He stepped outside again, scanning the shoreline in both directions. He was just about to turn away when he saw that the lake, otherwise flat and calm, was rippling towards him; then, about fifty yards out he saw the source of the disturbance, moving slowly away from the shore towards the centre. Swans, perhaps? The creature, or creatures – now he saw there were two of them, close together – were oddly shaped for swans. If he had not known better, he would have taken them for seals. Curiously, Bruno and Darina forgotten for a few seconds, keeping his eyes on the swimming creatures, he walked further along the shore. After a minute or so he stumbled into something soft and stopped to see what it was.

'Jesus!' His heart jolted sickeningly. He recognised the

bright flashes of Bruno's running shoes. They were out there. Those were two heads. It was them. The stupid fools. They'd die of exposure on a night like this. He broke into a run. 'Hey! Hey! he shouted. 'Come back here. Come back here immediately. You stupid brats – Bruno! I demand you come out of there at once!'

The two heads continued to move inexorably and slowly away from him.

Reflexively, still calling, he kicked off his own shoes and dashed into the water. He ignored his racing heart. 'Bruno! Darina! Come back here, come back here at once!'

He was not paying attention to his footing and slipped on a stone, crashing hard into the water. It was not deep at that point – only about two feet – but the shock and the temperature sent a cannonball of pain blasting into his chest. The cannonball exploded, disabling Derek's shoulders and his arms and his head; it blinded him, setting his lungs on fire.

Gasping for air, he gagged on mouthfuls of the freezing water but it was no use. The pain was so enormous, it filled not only his body but the water around him . . . the air above the water . . . the sky . . . the universe . . .

At last, darkness rolled like fog over the pain. The darkness was grey at first, blessedly grey and soft, then it turned for a while to black and when the black lifted, he was filled with an infinitely peaceful white.

CHAPTER SEVENTEEN

John woke with tears streaming down his face. He was surprised to find himself crying because the dream he had been having was so happy, imbued with warmth, brightness and love. He and Derek had been children again. They were playing in the yard of the gate lodge; their mother had fixed up a makeshift table-tennis table for them and was actually playing with them, against them as it happened, she on one side, they on the other. She was laughing, her hair was shining in the sun and he and Derek were laughing too. The three of them were so close in the dream, such close, happy friends.

But seconds after he woke, the horror of the previous day crashed on his happiness, extinguishing the warmth. He turned over on his stomach, burying his face in the pillow.

Events unrolled in his mind like a movie in slow motion.

Knocking on the guest-room door to wake Bruno and his father for an early-morning breakfast and receiving no reply, John had gone into the room and discovered that their beds were empty. Looking through the window, he saw their car was missing.

Still half asleep, and cranky from an accumulation of sleepless nights and all that had happened, John's irritation at his brother increased yet again. If they were going to leave early, they might have had the courtesy to tell him.

He went downstairs to see if they had left a note. When he discovered they had not, his irritation was replaced with real anger. It was just too much, he thought, pounding back up the stairs to wash and shave.

It was only half an hour later, when he went outside to get into his car, that he realised it, too, was missing.

From that moment on, events had succeeded one another in terrifying sequence. A telephone call to Sundarbans to see if, by any chance, Derek and Bruno had gone there, elicited that Darina was also missing. John was really exasperated now. The two youngsters had clearly run off together in the rented car and Derek had followed them in John's. But where were they?

Rose had wanted to bring in the Gardaí immediately but John had insisted they wait at least until the visitors' departure time had come and gone and she had agreed to that.

Fifteen minutes later, she had rung back in panic, crying that both cars were parked outside Sundarbans and both sets of keys were in the ignition.

They had called the Gardaí then.

At about ten o'clock, the shoes of the young people had been found on the foreshore.

Derek's body, face down in the reeds, had been located only a few minutes later.

By noon, a team of sub-aqua divers had retrieved the other two bodies. Darina's hands were still clasped tightly round Bruno's neck in cadaveric spasm and the divers had to bring them in without separating them.

From then on the day had been a succession of telephone calls, sympathisers, tea, sandwiches, ambulances, the post-mortems, statements, forms to be signed, interviews with the undertakers and the Gardaí and tears, tears, tears.

The only one who had not cried was Rose. She seemed more bewildered than grief-stricken and, although his heart broke for her, John seemed unable to say or do anything which got through to her. It was as though she were seeing the world and the multiple tragedy from behind a panel of glass. Her friends, Effie and Willie, who had arrived in mid-afternoon, had taken her in hand but even they were not able to reach her. She had become uncharacteristically passive and all afternoon Effie and Willie had simply sat on on either side of her in the Sundarbans sitting room, each holding one of her hands. From time to time, even Effie had wept copiously but nothing seemed to penetrate Rose's inappropriate and frightening calm.

It had fallen to John to deal with the undertaker and the priest. He threw himself on his back in the bed as once again he went through the awful details of that interview and those with the policemen, who had been sympathetic but professionally firm.

The clergy, for once, had turned up trumps. The parish priest, a new appointment in the district and relatively young, had arrived just after Effie and Willie and had proved a great help, calming down Rose's hysterical mother and, more crucially, volunteering to telephone Charlottetown to break the news to Karen. He had not been overly intrusive in his questions, but he could not help but react a little as John had unfolded the unusual relationships involved. John did not blame the man for his pursed lips; seen from the priest's point of view, the circumstances rightly belonged in a Tennessee Williams play and not in the damp heart of rural Ireland.

His alarm clock shrilled. It was six a.m. He had to go to Dublin Airport to pick up Karen and her parents who, if they had caught the flights and made the connections on time, were due there at ten-thirty. It was a task he dreaded but one he could hardly delegate to a stranger. Mona had said she would come with him and George had offered the use of his Rover.

He forced himself to get out of bed and crossed the landing to the bathroom. But as he stared into the mirror above the wash basin, it was not his own face he saw but the grotesquely entangled bodies of the two young people, his daughter and her lover. It was an image he would never be able to shed as long as he lived.

He and Rose had both been there when they were brought ashore, their blond hair lank and sodden, water streaming out of their sightless eyes, their gaping mouths, their noses and ears. Although her arms were locked around his neck, fingers interlaced behind his head; his dangled free and, as they were lifted out of the inflatable dinghy, their heads lolled independently on their necks like the heads of newborn babies.

Rose had gasped and he had moved protectively towards her but she had raised a hand to keep him away. It was Gus who had rushed forward with a blanket to cover them where they were placed on the wet, grassy foreshore. In the early hours of the morning, the spell of clean, frosty weather had broken.

The rain, driven on a grey, spitting wind, began again as they all stood around the dreadful, blanket-covered mound. To compound the pathos, John saw that the blanket was not big enough to cover them fully and their bare feet protruded from under it; Darina's long, fine and delicate, like the feet of a dancer,

Bruno's broader and more spatulate. The sight of them was so ineffably sad that John began to weep silently and had to turn away.

His daughter. For two days – less – he had had a daughter. He had never even had a conversation with her.

From time to time the previous day, he had caught himself trying to measure exactly his reaction to his daughter's death. On the one hand, he did not feel as though he had lost a person of his flesh and blood; on the other, every time he stopped for a moment being busy, the image of her limp body clinging to the dead boy's, the bluish cast of her skin, haunted him.

Sickened, he walked away from the mirror. He could not face the intricate task of shaving at the moment and decided to leave it until later.

Mona was already in the kitchen, preparing breakfast. 'Are you all right, John?' she asked. 'Did you manage to get any sleep?'

His emotions raw, John seized on the kind words. He wanted nothing but to put his head on her dear, kind breast. For as long as he knew her, Mona had been minding him, asking him if he was all right. 'I don't say it, Mona,' he said fervently, 'but I want you to know how much I appreciate you and—'

She stood as if thunderstruck and then cut him off. 'Ah John, don't,' she said, her face beginning to flush. 'You've been marvellous to Packy and me all these years.' She picked up the hot frying pan and tilted it this way and that, melting lard. 'I don't know what we would have done without you,' she added bravely and John knew what this had cost her. Mona did not like open displays.

He was determined, however, that she should know once and for all how much he valued her. He walked across the kitchen and took the frying pan out of her hand, placing it carefully to one side of the stove. Then he took her shoulders and turned her to face him. 'I mean it, Mona. You say you couldn't have survived without me. That's rubbish. It's me who couldn't have survived without you. I want you to know that.'

Unshed tears stood in Mona's eyes as she stood rigidly under his hands and for a dreadful moment, he thought he had gone too far, perhaps given her the wrong impression. But she swallowed hard and then said, 'Thank you, John. I'm glad.'

He let her go and went to sit at the table, slumping into

the chair and, although he put his head in his hands, he remained aware of Mona's economical, efficient movements around the stove and the refrigerator as she prepared the food. He hoped that, in being so self-indulgent, he had not been cruel.

'They should be out any minute now, John.' It was more than four hours later and he flinched at Mona's tentative touch on his arm. The arrival announcement had been made at least fifteen minutes before and his nerves were stretched to breaking point.

At the best of times, John hated Dublin airport: the ordered chaos, the tinny announcements, the rushing, preoccupied faces. Today, the noise and bustle seemed particularly inappropriate. He felt like shouting at them all to stop, to show proper respect. He knew he was being silly but it was difficult to accept that everyone else in the world was impervious to the awful tragedy in which he and the three people he was about to meet were enmeshed.

He spotted Karen and her parents before they saw him. She and her mother were walking a little behind Sven, who was pushing a baggage trolley. All three were moving very slowly, looking around them as though not quite sure they were in the right airport. Karen, as far as John could tell, had changed very little: wearing unrelieved black and dark glasses, her blonde hair scraped back from her face in a large bun, she was as statuesque and striking as ever, and John could not help but notice she was attracting glances from almost everyone in the concourse. Taking a deep, steadying breath, he walked forward to greet them.

Karen's mother was also wearing black and dark glasses but the funereal garb was the only visible sign of stress: on the surface, all three were composed. 'Hello, Karen, Mr and Mrs Lindstrom,' said John quietly, shaking each of their hands in turn. 'I'm dreadfully sorry for your trouble.'

'And we're sorry for yours too, John. It must have been such a shock—' Sven's voice was strained and husky. 'Terrible business.'

'You know Mona, Karen?' John then introduced Mona to the older Lindstroms. She shook hands, murmuring her own condolences. She was the perfect person to have along on an awful occasion like this and John was newly grateful.

The car trip to Monaghan was a sad, silent affair. Mona

sat in the front of the Rover with John and Karen sat in the back between her parents; from time to time, John heard her and her mother sniffling and blowing their noses but there were no histrionics and he could not help but admire their impeccable dignity.

As they drove into Ardee, out of the corner of his eye John noticed that the proprietor of an antique shop had stacked a heap of old iron bedsteads on the pavement outside his door. They were perfectly ordinary domestic bedsteads of the type common throughout Ireland, painted or enamelled in black or white. Seeing them, however, John was assaulted by a wave of grief so huge that he got a physical pain in his abdomen and bent almost double over the steering wheel. 'Sorry,' he gasped, 'I have to go into a shop to get something.' He swerved the car into the kerb and jumped out.

The picture his memory had thrown at him was one he had not even known he had stored: he and Derek were about five years of age and had been bouncing uproariously on their bed in the gate lodge whereupon one of the bolts holding the frame together had snapped in two, dumping the two of them to the ground in a heap of springs, mattress, bedclothes, arms and legs. The memory of Derek's childish, laughing face was unbearable.

Dodging a car, John ran across the road into a tobacconist's.

Luckily, there were two people ahead of him at the counter and by the time he was served, he had his features and his emotions in check. At random, he picked up a bar of chocolate and paid for it.

Ironically, the first thing he saw as he set foot on the pavement outside was the hearse at the head of a funeral cortège; all other traffic had stopped in the suddenly hushed street as the hearse trundled slowly along at a walking pace, diesel engine throbbing in discordant accompaniment to the slow tolling of the church bell.

John looked away and, with a huge effort of will, directed his concentration on the task of staying in control. By the time the cortège had passed, he was able to cross the road to the car with a semblance of decorum.

The rest of the journey seemed to pass through endless corridors of silence and by the time he pulled into the forecourt of Willow House, John's nerves were again in tatters. He had booked two rooms for the Lindstroms and, as a distraction, welcomed the activity of checking them in, introducing George and Dorothy and sorting out the luggage. He had put Mr and Mrs Lindstrom's one suitcase into their room and was walking along a passageway carrying Karen's, when she put a hand on his arm. 'Do you have a minute, John? Could you come into my room for a second?'

Her expression was unreadable through the heavy sunglasses but John detected a feverish tension in her, unconnected with grief. If he had not known better, he would have said she was fiercely angry with him. 'To tell you the truth, Karen, I have to get back to the Big House immediately. I said I'd be there at one and it's nearly two now.' The swiftness of the lie startled him. Why had he said that?

They were at her door and he opened it, putting the suitcase inside. To ameliorate what he had just done, he put a hand gently on her shoulder. 'George will bring you and your parents up to Sundarbans as soon as you've settled yourselves. You should probably take a little rest, you must be exhausted. Could we talk later? We'll be seeing a lot of one another over the next few days.'

She stood very still inside her door and something about her blank, black gaze sent shivers into him. 'That's all right, John. And I don't need to rest, thank you. I want to see Bruno as soon as possible. But there's something I really want you to know.'

As it happened, John and Karen had no opportunity to be alone until after the funerals.

This was largely of his doing. George and Dorothy would not hear of him having anything to do with the running of Willow House; they had hired temporary local help so he was free to concentrate on the funerals. And as events succeeded each other in nightmarish, surreal sequence, he became convinced that the key to his own survival was to keep busy, to put others' grief before his own.

He found, as the hours stretched out, that there was a horrible logic to the way things happened; sometimes it was as if he were engaged in a ghoulish game of dominos and although everyone officially concerned was deeply kind, this, in a sense, only intensified each successive ordeal.

First, there was the dreadful business of official identification in the hospital mortuary. He had stood at Karen's side while she acknowledged the corpses of her son and her husband and then at Rose's while she identified his daughter.

Then they all had to wait for the release of the bodies after the post-mortems. By unspoken consent, they had based themselves at Sundarbans where several of the neighbours, including, he saw, the old housekeeper, the indefatigable Mrs McKenna, had come in to help with the constant stream of refreshments needed for the dozens, perhaps scores of sympathisers who came in person. The O'Beirne Moffat name was still big enough in the locality that any death in the family would have been major news; the extent and horror of this tragedy attracted people from all over Ulster, Leinster and parts of Connacht. Several old friends travelled from London and not only Willow House and Sundarbans but many of the other hotels and bed and breakfast establishments in the locality were full.

There was the delicate question as to where Derek and his son should be buried. It was left to John to ask Karen and her parents if they might wish to bring the bodies back to Canada but all three had been absolutely sure that Derek would have wanted to be buried at home.

Then Karen had paused and added, 'And Bruno, had he been asked, would have wanted to be buried beside his dad.' John had been slightly taken aback at her vehemence. Even in the middle of her grief, Karen was playing some kind of sub-text he did not understand. Or perhaps, he told himself later, being so overwrought he was now imagining things.

All the time there were questions, questions, questions: *why, why, why?*

Not least from the media. Although individual reporters did their best to be tactful, they seemed to be everywhere John looked, asking for comments and photographs, prying for reactions. Willie and Effie had volunteered to answer the front door and all telephone calls but the press corps, which included representatives from some of the national papers in Dublin and Belfast – and one stringer for a London tabloid – was not deterred by their frosty rebuffs.

And when they got nowhere at the Big House, the reporters started interviewing local people in pubs and on the streets of

Carrickmacross. Every quotable quote was given a headline. The stringer for the London tabloid discovered the retired postmistress who had known both twins and Rose when they were young. It was Mrs Doody's finest hour.

This unwanted attention was putting an additional strain on everyone's already taut nerves. John had asked the parish priest if he could bar reporters from the church precincts during the funeral service but had been told that this was impossible. The priest did, however, promise that in his homily, he would beg them for restraint.

But, overall, John's main concern throughout the thirty-six hours was Rose, who continued to move and talk with that glazed unnatural calm she had adopted as soon as the bodies were discovered. He was so seriously worried about her that on the morning of the funeral Mass, he called in the local doctor, whom she refused to see. 'Please don't worry about me, John. I'm fine. I'll be fine. I have Effie and Willie and you.' Ramrod straight and already fully dressed in the new black dress and coat Effie had bought for her, she was seated on the side of the bed in the room she had shared with Darina.

'The doctor's waiting downstairs, Rose. He just wants to have a word with you – it won't take a minute, honestly.' He attempted to touch her, to put his arms around her but she held up both hands. 'Not now, please, John. No offence.'

He could not change her mind and had to send the doctor away.

Karen's reaction was, in John's opinion, far more natural and understandable. She sobbed and cried and angrily paced the sitting room and yet, from time to time, he caught her looking at him speculatively with that fierce, angry stare which sent shivers through him. Whatever it was she wanted to tell him would not be pleasant, he was sure of it. He had a horrible feeling it was something Derek had done that she wanted to get off her chest.

It was because of this conviction that he kept avoiding her. He did not think that at this time he could bear any additional condemnation of Derek, or even mildly bad news about him. He was not a reader, but somewhere in the past, probably in a doctor's or dentist's waiting room, he had read an article on the psychology of bereavement which had noted that the most

529

profound grief of all awaits those who have had a bad relationship with the deceased. Instinctively, he knew that this was what was in store for him when he stopped being busy long enough to let it affect him.

If he was to continue to cope, he was sure that whatever Karen had to tell him should be put off as long as possible.

They were all waiting uneasily in the sitting room when John, who had been watching out for them, saw the two funeral limousines pull up outside the house. 'They're here,' he said gently. Mr and Mrs Lindstrom stood up immediately and went across to Karen who was slumped in an armchair, staring into the fire. She allowed herself to be helped up and into her coat. Willie and Effie, who were to travel with the Colonel and Daphne in the second car, got up too. Daphne, who had been quiet this morning, looked at John, mute appeal in her eyes. 'Please, Mr Flynn, would you go and fetch Rose? She's in her room, I believe.'

'Certainly, Mrs O'Beirne Moffat,' he said, surprised at her approach.

He was about to leave the room when she stopped him. 'I just want to say, Mr Flynn, that I – we – the Colonel and I, that is, greatly appreciate what you have done for us all over the last few days.'

John looked at her small, frail figure, rendered even smaller and frailer in the unfashionable black coat and, for the first time, saw not the difficult, spiky dowager, only a desperately grieving, frightened old lady. 'For nothing, Mrs O'Beirne Moffat,' he said. 'For nothing.'

'Yes, John, that goes for me too.' The Colonel fiddled with his watch pocket. 'Thank you. Don't know what we'd have done—'

'Please, Colonel, I only did what was necessary.' John was perilously close to breaking down. 'Please – I'll get Rose.'

But when he knocked on the door of her room, there was no reply. He knocked again and then opened the door a crack. She was still sitting where she had been when he had tried to get her to see the doctor and in exactly the same position, upright and as stiff as a window-dresser's model. Although she was wearing her new clothes, he noticed she had not washed her hair; flat and unkempt, it clung to her head as though it was wet, emphasising her pallor. 'It's time, Rose,' he said, standing just inside the door of the room. 'The cars are here, it's time to go.'

She did not move. It was as though she were in a trance.

'Would you like me to call Effie for you?' he asked.

'No,' she whispered and shook her head imperceptibly. 'I don't want to go there, John.'

John acted on instinct. 'My dearest,' he said, going to the bed and sitting beside her, 'you don't have to go if you don't want to. But I'll be beside you every single moment. And I think Darina would have liked us to be there together. Don't you think?'

'Darina can't think anything,' she said in a monotone.

'No, not now, not that we know of. But I believe she will help us get through this, Rose. I believe she is happy now and she wants us to be with her.'

She turned puzzled, dead eyes on him. 'What?'

He took her hand, glad she did not resist. 'I think she is caring for us in a way we'll only understand in a while. She was, is, a very special girl, Rose.'

'She's dead, John.'

'I know, my darling, she's dead. It's dreadful. Darina's dead.'

The dam burst in Rose then and she threw her head back, rocking back and forth, her mouth open to its fullest extent as a tide of grief poured out of it. The sounds she made were almost unearthly, high and ululating, a primitive scream of prolonged pain; John was frightened at first and then he held her as well as he could as she continued to rock to a rhythm only she could hear.

It went on for several minutes and then she began to quieten, her body spasming with sobs which, being more recognisable, were easier for him to handle than her unbending rigidity.

He held her tightly, crooning to her, gentling her as, so long ago, she had taught him to gentle a frightened horse.

The reception after the funerals was held at Willow House, which was too small to handle the crowds. In one sense, however, this was a blessing. The confusion and press of bodies in the smallish dining room where the refreshments were laid out meant that there was a high buzz of chatter and human contact. As the guests unwound after the tension and sadness in the church and graveyard, a contagious relief-filled gaiety took hold and spread like wildfire. Friends who had not seen one another for years backslapped and renewed acquaintance and related anecdotes of other deaths, other funerals since they had last met.

John, who had insisted on working despite the strenuous objections of the Cranshaws, was busy taking orders for the bar. Running a professional eye over the room, he saw that Effie and Willie were taking care of Rose but that the Lindstroms and the O'Beirne Moffats were sitting as a group a little apart from the main body. All four looked bewildered as they watched the party atmosphere develop.

He gave the bar orders to one of the temporary helpers and went across to them. 'Can I get you anything?' he asked gently. 'A drink? Some soup, perhaps? It's a very cold day.'

'Yes, please, John.' Having checked imperceptibly with his wife, Sven Lindstrom answered for both of them. 'We'll have coffee, if that's all right?'

'How about you, Mrs O'Beirne Moffat? Colonel?'

'A single malt if you have it.' Then the Colonel turned to his wife. 'How about you, my dear?'

'This is dreadful!' she burst out. 'This is disgraceful. Darina is not cold in her grave and it looks like we're *celebrating*.'

'It's customary, ma'am,' said John. His busyness had temporarily succeeded in pushing his grief a little below the surface and now he reflected ruefully that Mrs O'Beirne Moffat's humanity towards him earlier in the day must have been an aberration. 'We take funeral bookings all the time,' he went on. 'I think you'll find that nowadays a function like this has replaced the traditional wake.'

'I still think it's unseemly,' retorted Daphne, the papery skin on her cheeks going pink.

'None of this is John's doing, my dear,' protested the Colonel. 'All he wants to know is if you'd like some refreshment.'

'I'll have a dry sherry, please,' she said. Then she looked directly up at John. 'Sorry,' she said challengingly, as though it was an insult.

Wonders would never cease, thought John as he hurried to fill their order. The old bag was definitely making an effort.

He searched for Karen as he waited for the drinks but there was no sign of her. Probably out in the other room, he thought. The dining room was so packed that some of the crowd had spilled over into the conservatory.

Balancing the drinks and the coffee on a tray, he brought them to the forlorn little group sitting by the wall. 'Have you seen Karen?' asked Mrs Lindstrom. She looked so sad and lonely that John's heart went out to her. The situation was tough enough for him and Rose but, for today at least, they had the support of a close-knit circle of friends. Apart altogether from the trauma of why they were here, this was Mr and Mrs Lindstrom's first visit to Ireland and they, like the Colonel's wife, clearly thought that this high-pitched atmosphere was bizarre.

'I haven't seen her lately,' he replied, having to raise his voice to be heard above the general hubbub. 'I have to go into the kitchen for a moment but when I come back out, I'll search for her. Are you sure you wouldn't like something to eat?' He included all four of them in his invitation but they all shook their heads.

As he left them, he wondered if he should not try to break them up as a group. They were ill-matched and had very little in common. Except, he thought, flashing again on the picture of those connected waxen bodies, that their respective grandchildren fell in love and subsequently drowned. He swallowed hard. He must keep busy.

Dorothy was in the kitchen, helping two of the temporary helpers with buttering bread for more sandwiches. She pushed back a strand of hair which had fallen over her face. 'I was sure we had done enough,' she said. 'These will be ready in a jif.'

'We need more soup,' said John, crossing to the Aga and checking that there was still some left in the stock pot.

'Will you look after it, John?' asked Dorothy automatically and then checked herself. 'What am I saying? John, you *shouldn't* be working like this today. Go on. I'm really sorry.' She came over to him and linked an arm through his elbow. 'How're you doing?' she asked softly.

'I'm fine. I really am,' he answered, adding honestly, 'however long it'll last, though, I don't know.'

'You know that George and I will do anything – anything.'

'Yes, you've both been wonderful, Dorothy.'

'I mean it now – anything! And this may not be the time nor the place to discuss it but we've already decided – if you're agreeable that is and don't have any other plans – that we're going to close the hotel for two weeks over Christmas and we're going to bring you away with us.'

John looked uncertainly at her. 'Away? What about the bookings?'

'Nothing we can't cancel. We can cite renovations, floods, anything you like. And we only have one deposit. It will be no problem. Yes, Switzerland, Florida, somewhere completely different.' She stood back and looked keenly at him. 'You don't have any other plans, do you?'

'Well, that depends—' He thought instantly of Rose and realised that, although he had not acknowledged them, he did have plans. But the plans had been formulated before tragedy overtook them all. 'To tell you the truth,' he said, 'I'm taking everything one day at a time.'

He saw that Dorothy knew exactly what was on his mind. 'Of course, of course,' she said gently. 'But when you've decided – when you see which way the land lies – you let us know. And George and I are absolutely in agreement. If you are coming – and we won't take no for an answer about this – it's our treat. You deserve some kind of pampering, after all these years you've looked after us.'

'Dorothy, you're so kind.' John, realising that lately he seemed to be ladling gratitude as though it was syrup, became embarrassed and, rather than say any more, squeezed her plump arm.

He became aware that someone was watching him and Dorothy. Looking round, he saw that Karen was framed in the open doorway. 'Oh, Karen,' he started towards her, 'your mother and father were looking for you. Are you OK?'

'Would now be a good time for us to have that chat?' she said.

'You go ahead, John.' Dorothy bustled towards the Aga. 'I'll take in the soup.'

'Do you want to come to my room?' Karen asked and again that odd belligerence in her voice inspired dread. He felt, however, that he had been left with no option but to talk to her now.

'Why don't we try the sitting room?' he suggested, leading her out of the kitchen and towards the front hall. For some reason he felt distinctly uneasy about being alone with Karen anywhere but on safely neutral territory. 'Here we are,' he said, opening the door into the Ali Baba room. He stood back to let her pass and closed the door. 'How are you surviving?' he asked, after some hesitation, every nerve and sense so alert he was almost tingling.

'How do you think?' She began to pace the room, and her largeness, the starkness of her black dress against her blonde colouring, seemed utterly out of place in the multi-coloured knick-knackery of the room. So much so that John was afraid she might trample on some of the more delicate objects, or, like a black and white dragon, burn everything to a crisp with one sweep of her breath.

'I'm glad we're getting a chance to talk alone,' he ventured, 'Derek—'

'I don't want to talk about Derek,' she said shortly. 'Although yes,' she whirled to face him, 'maybe I do – now that you mention it.'

Handling them as though they were weapons, she took off the sunglasses which, even while indoors, she had worn all day. John saw she was wearing no eye make-up and that crescents of dark purple had spread from under her eyes towards her cheek-bones. He braced himself for what was coming.

'Not that it matters now,' said Karen, her eyes blazing, 'but I was planning to divorce Derek.'

John had had no idea that the situation between his twin and Karen had come to such a bad pass. The information stunned him. Nevertheless, he got the distinct impression that Karen was using it to punish him. 'I'm sorry—' he began.

'Sorry doesn't even *begin* to describe it!' She folded her arms tightly across her breasts and she again started to pound her way around the furniture.

John was dumbstruck – and his dread of what Karen wanted in earnest to tell him grew alarmingly. Although he was unwilling to prompt her and thereby precipitate matters, his curiosity, too, was growing. The news about herself and Derek would have been bad enough. The real news must be worse even than that.

Karen's pacing grew faster until she cracked her shin against a low circular brass table, upending it and its load onto the carpet. 'Goddamnit!' she exploded, rubbing her leg. 'Goddamnit!'

He rushed forward. 'Are you all right, are you bleeding? Do you need an Elastoplast or anything?'

'I don't want any Goddamn Elastoplast!' she stopped ministering to her shin and straightened up, glaring at him so fiercely that he took a few steps backwards, out of her reach.

But she followed him, her chin thrust out like a pugilist. 'I probably shouldn't be talking to you like this, I probably shouldn't be telling you what I'm going to tell you.'

He retreated still farther until he was almost at the door and he was afraid he would have to back right through it into the hallway when she placed both hands over her ears and stopped inches from his face. 'Goddamnit!' She was almost screaming now. 'I'm so fucking pissed off! I can't stand it!'

John did not dare say anything.

'Do – you – *understand*?' she yelled at him. 'I'm fucking *pissed off*!'

'I understand,' he said quietly.

'How can you fucking understand?' she yelled. 'You don't *know* anything.'

'I don't know what you mean, Karen. And I realise how upset you are, but I wish you'd stop shouting like this, you'll bring everyone else in on top of us.'

'*I don't fucking care!*' She teetered on her high heels as though she were going to levitate and then she collapsed suddenly and noisily into a chair. The draught she created upset several delicately balanced photographs on a nearby side table and, with a small clatter, they tumbled to the ground.

John stood transfixed. Strangely, the more angry and upset she got, the cooler he felt. As though he were a painter or a photographer, he registered everything about her, the way she sat, the way her hands were wound tensely together, the beginnings of a double chin.

For a few seconds, she surveyed him. 'All right,' she said then in a completely different tone. 'I'm sorry for shouting. But before I say what I'm going to say, I want you to know that it was all my idea. That Derek had nothing to do with it – I persuaded him and made him promise and I saw to it that he kept his promise.'

John felt very cold.

'Do you remember that party on New Year's Eve in Dad's house in Charlottetown?' she asked, studying her nails.

'Yes,' he said, 'I remember it very well.'

'Well, what you don't remember, probably – although I've never been sure and I could hardly ask you! – is that I got into your bed later that night when you were asleep and I made love to you. If that's what you could call it,' she muttered so softly that John barely caught the words.

'What?' John's brain could not comprehend. 'Made love? Us? I know we were dancing together—'

'Believe me,' she insisted, her voice rising again, 'I fucking got into your bed later that night and—' she laughed so harshly that the sound struck terror into his heart, 'I took advantage of what was there. Not that you cared all that much about who was in your bed,' she added bitterly, 'you called me Rose.'

'You couldn't have,' John whispered. 'That's not possible.' He remembered his drunkenness as he had gone to sleep. Could she be telling the truth? 'Why are you telling me this now?' he croaked, although the freezing fingers at the back of his neck were forecasting precisely why she was choosing this time.

She looked again at her nails. 'Because I thought you'd like to know that Bruno is – sorry, *was* – your son.'

John felt nothing for a few moments. Then there began a crazed, off-centred movement inside his head as though his brain had become strapped to a buckled cartwheel. The ground felt unsteady under this movement and he splayed his hands to keep his balance. 'I don't believe you.'

She looked insolently at him. 'Oh, you can believe me, all right. And if you don't, just ask Derek!'

Then, as he stared at her in horror, she realised what she had said and her face crumpled. 'Oh, God!'

'You bitch!' John rarely swore but he did not care. His voice throbbed as his rage grew. 'You wait until now, until the boy is *dead*, to tell me that he was my son. You *bitch*!' He felt like striking her and was afraid that he might.

He walked to the french window, which, in that room, was

as far as he could get from her. Outside, a heavy, wind-battered drizzle was falling through the dusk of the November evening but all John saw, once again, was that torturing image of the two bodies streaming water.

His children.

Both of them his children.

Up to that moment had been bad enough. His newly discovered daughter and her cousin—

Now it was his daughter and his son.

John wanted to kill someone. His rage was so red he felt he had to kill someone.

He whirled to face Karen and saw that she shrank immediately from him. He hated her for cringing. He hated this room. Everything bad in his life had happened in this room. He thought that if he did not get away from the room, from this house, from people, his head would actually burst open.

'I'm leaving now,' he managed to say in a strangled, unnatural voice. She was genuinely scared of him, he saw that, and at least that gave him some sort of savage satisfaction. He had to pass her to get out of the door and she half stood as he took the first step. 'John, I'm sorry, I didn't think you'd be this upset, I didn't think—'

'*You didn't think I'd be upset?* What did you fucking think I'd be? What kind of a planet do you come from?' He balled his hands into fists and she leaped behind a chair, putting it between him and her. Her face was now ashen, the purple smudges under her eyes standing out like bruises. Her fear percolated through the murk of his rage and after a few juddering seconds, he relaxed his hands. 'How did you think I'd react?'

When she saw he was not going to hit her, she regained some of her equilibrium but she stayed behind the shield of the chair, watching him. 'I suppose I didn't think. If it helps, I won't tell anyone else.'

'Tell the whole world. Tell the whole scum-filled world! What does it matter now? Karen, why in God's name did you have to tell me?'

For a long, long moment, Karen looked at him from under her eyebrows. Then she brought her head up. '*Somebody* had to pay.'

*

It was more than an hour later when Rose found John.

From the time she had wept in his arms that morning, all through the entire, draining day, she had, without knowing it, come to rely on his quiet, sustaining presence although it was Effie who had actually taken her in charge.

When she had descended the stairs to get into the funeral limousine, Effie had taken one look at her, produced a small white pill and insisted she swallow it. As a result, although she had suffered bouts of uncontrollable shivering and had wept a great deal, a lot of the day had passed in soft-focus. It was as though she herself was not really going through these horrible things and had sent along a lookalike to take her place. She could even stand back and watch the lookalike's performance. The lookalike felt, saw, shivered, wept, thanked people for their commiserations, but did not really experience any of it.

The effect of the tablet was beginning to wear off by the time the guests in the overcrowded dining room had started to thin out. Rose had been sitting quietly in a corner with Willie on one side of her, Effie on the other. The emotional numbness was not wearing off evenly. A wave of loneliness and horror would crash in but, before she had time to react to it, recede, and the lookalike would take over again, talking in quiet murmurs with her friends, many of whom worked with her in Aer Lingus and had travelled down from Dublin.

It was during one of the waves of reality that she noticed John was not in the room. She needed him desperately, needed the comfort of his arms. She stood up abruptly, too abruptly, because her head began to swim. 'Are you all right?' Effie asked.

Rose, the real Rose, suddenly knew she was sick to death of people, even Effie, asking her if she was all right. 'I'm fine,' she answered, 'just going to the bathroom.'

But she did not get to the door of the dining room unscathed, having to endure yet more well-meant and kind expressions of sympathy and concern. 'Thank you. Thank you,' she said to everyone, nodding like a marionette, shaking all the outstretched hands and acceding to the heartfelt hugs from people, some of whom she had never met in her life.

Finally she escaped into the front hall and looked around. Probably in the kitchen, she thought.

She walked down the corridor to the kitchen and opened

the door. Two women she did not recognise were sitting at the table, one with her feet up on a chair. 'I'm looking for John Flynn, the manager,' said Rose. 'Have you seen him recently?'

'Not this last hour, ma'am,' said one of the two.

He was not in the Ali Baba room either, although here Rose saw that the room was in a state of disarray as though a troupe of naughty children had been let loose in it.

He was not in the conservatory nor in any of the upstairs bedrooms. At the end of one of the corridors, she spotted Dorothy and George deep in conversation but did not want to ask them where John was; they would want to take her in charge and she wanted, needed, only John.

The longer the search went on, the more frantic Rose became. Although the lookalike was still in control most of the time, the waves of horror and reality were becoming more frequent now and she wondered if she should ask Effie for another of those pills.

If she could just find John, she thought, he would help her. Finding John became an absolute, an imperative. She hung on to the reality of the search. If she could just find John, she would not have to think about anything else . . . For the moment, searching for him was more important even than finding him.

When she was half-way down the back stairs of the hotel, she had to hang onto the banisters because everything around her started to move, the walls were performing a macabre reel, advancing and receding, the next step of the stairs seemed too far away for her foot to reach. She had to find John Flynn. John Flynn was the only reality.

Making a great effort, she managed to negotiate the rest of the stairs and to let herself out of a side door into the car park which was chock-a-block. Several of the cars were moving as mourners departed.

One car, an old one, pouring blue smoke, was manoeuvring around another which was blocking it so completely that it was able to go forwards and backwards only a few inches at a time. With relief, Rose saw that the driver was John.

'John! John!' she cried, running towards him.

He stopped manoeuvring and peered out at her. The glass of the windows was streaked with dirt and she could not see his expression. She was right at the door and opening it before she realised there was something wrong with him.

'John?' she said uncertainly. The car park was brightly floodlit and she could see his face perfectly but it was not the face she longed for.

Swollen and red, wet with tears, this face was too frightening to look at.

Rose felt trapped. Still holding the door, she dithered, wondering what she should do. 'Hello, Rose,' he said and the voice, too, was peculiar, not what she had expected or needed.

Rose's lookalike clicked in in front of her. 'Can I get in?'

'I'm sorry,' he whispered as she sat in to the passenger seat. 'I'm just not up to staying in there any longer. It's been too much, too long. Too much,' he repeated.

Rose – or the lookalike – felt she should take him in her arms, to comfort him the way he had comforted her that morning. But he was sitting away from her, scrunched into the far corner of his own seat. 'I'm sorry,' he said again. 'I'm not much use at the moment.'

She noticed that wet stringlets had stretched themselves between his upper and lower lips; they thickened and thinned as he spoke but did not break. 'That's all right, John,' she said.

He looked at her out of the corner of his eye. 'I love you very much, Rose.'

She was fascinated by those stringlets in his mouth. 'I love you too, John.' The formula sounded flat, old hat. Did she mean it?

Did he?

The car which had been blocking them, a sleek new Mercedes, began to pull away. They both watched it. 'Nice car,' said John. He took a ball of wet tissue out of his sleeve and attempted to unravel it sufficiently to blow his nose.

'Yeah, it's nice all right. Here – have this!' Rose passed over a pristine, unused tissue from the pocket of her black dress.

'Nice to have money.' He half laughed on the words but he seemed to choke and the phrase turned into a sob.

Again she felt she should reach out to him but her hands would not obey her instincts. He blew his nose. 'Are you going to be all right? When are you going back to Dublin?'

'I think I'll go back tonight with Effie and Willie.'

'They can stay here as long as they like. You know that. We've plenty of room.'

'They have jobs.'

'Yes, of course.'

They lapsed into silence. Rose – or was it the lookalike? – felt watchful, as though she should remember every second of what was going to happen next.

Two more cars were driven out of the car park.

John blew his nose again. 'I'm sorry I'm being so emotional. I'm not usually like this, Rose. I'm afraid I'm going to need a little time. You see, a lot has happened.'

Rose tried to figure it out. Did he mean he'd need time with regard to her? But her tongue, or the lookalike's, answered prematurely. 'Me too,' it said.

'We'll keep in touch?'

'You'll come to Dublin?'

'Yes.'

'Yes.'

He snuffled, a long, porcine sound which Rose hated. 'You never know what's in store for you,' he said then.

'No,' she agreed. 'It's just as well.'

She could think of nothing else to say to add anything of value. They watched as several more cars started up and left. The driver of one of them, a woman whom Rose did not know, hesitated when she saw Rose sitting in John's car and half rolled down her window but Rose looked away and the woman drove on.

He turned to her then and his voice had steadied and strengthened. 'Rose, three days ago – or was it two, or four? I don't remember – I wanted nothing more than to hold you, make love to you, marry you. It was my dream come alive. You were everything to me. You still are.' He played with the tissue. 'But there are some things I have to work out, things that have happened since – and I can't be with anyone for the moment, not even you. Do you understand?'

She nodded. She did not understand. All she understood was that John had been there for her and he wasn't any more. His voice was saying these things but she did not take them in.

She felt she needed to go somewhere else now, somewhere where she could be quiet and alone and could think. Or didn't have to think. She didn't know which.

'It's time I was going, I think,' she said.

'Please say you understand, Rose, and that you'll wait for me. It won't be long.'

'Of course I'll wait for you, John. I've waited this long.' This was obviously the right thing to say because he smiled and took her hand. Her own hand felt like cold Plasticine.

'We'll never be able to put this awful day behind us – but—'

Rose didn't know what to say to help him out. So she waited while he struggled for composure.

'I wish I could think of some really profound things to say,' he went on at last, 'something that wasn't so ordinary or clichéd, but I can't. I'm a plain man.'

'I think I'd better go,' Rose repeated. 'Effie will be waiting.'

For a moment she thought he was going to kiss her. She didn't want him to kiss her, not with those stringlet things hanging in his mouth.

But he just touched her cheek. 'Goodbye for now, my darling. I'll telephone you in a few days when I've sorted myself out a bit.'

'You have my number?'

'Yes.'

'Take care.'

'I love you.'

'I love you too.' Again Rose wondered about the formula, why it slipped out so easily and meant nothing at all.

She was half-way home to Dublin and half asleep in the back of Willie's car when the wild longing for John mixed in with her longing for Darina. The horror would not now be denied. She asked Effie for another pill but Effie said she was afraid to give her any more.

Rose became frantic, terrified, the grief was so painful she thought her ribcage would crack open. There were terrible sounds coming out of her mouth.

Willie was stopping the car and Effie was getting into the back seat with her. Rose knew she was making a show of herself but she couldn't help it; the terrible, hard pain in the middle of her demanded service and the only service she could give it was to weep out hard and loud.

Now there were words coming out of her mouth, words that even she did not understand; she could see that poor Effie thought the words were significant but they weren't. Effie was rocking her back and forth like a baby. Over the sounds she was making, she realised Effie was shouting at Willie, trying to make herself heard, 'Do you know what she wants, Willie? She seems to want something.'

Rose tried to tell Effie that she didn't want anything specific. All she wanted was Darina and no one could give her Darina. It's just that she could not control her tongue and the words would not stop even though she wanted them to.

It was Willie who finally understood what she was saying, *One more day, please, one more day.*

The two of them held her then but it didn't matter. Nothing mattered.

Effie finally got the message that nothing mattered because she was giving her another of the blessed pills, placing it on her tongue and holding her mouth tightly closed until she gulped it down in her saliva.

They waited by the side of the dark road. Willie got out of the car but Effie continued to rock Rose until, after a few minutes, gradually, the words died down and died away.

Rose felt the car starting again and, her head pillowed on Effie's shoulder, finally fell into an exhausted sleep.

Rose's sense of unreality persisted during the first few days after she got back to Dublin. Effie and Willie, who were due to move into their new house by the middle of the month, tried to persuade her to move in with them. 'This flat will be too big for you on your own,' said Effie gently. 'And the memories will be awful for you. You'll need company, someone to look after you.'

Rose's instinct, however, was that she needed to confront her trauma and loneliness and, if she didn't do it alone, she would never have a chance of returning to any semblance of normal life. She thanked Effie and Willie but refused their offer.

The airline, too, was solicitous, offering to grant compassionate leave – an offer which she also refused.

She asked for, and was granted, a transfer back onto the Atlantic run. This meant layovers in New York or Boston – and Chicago in the summer – all cities that she liked. The main reason for her request, however, was that she felt she would get on better with the transatlantic crews than with the girls on the European and London runs. Although she liked the latter, the transatlantic hostesses tended to be older and more experienced and Rose felt that they would be more likely to understand and accept her circumstances, even occasional moodiness, than the younger girls whose concerns were usually more social than domestic.

She went back to work less than a week after Darina was buried and was eating dinner with three other hostesses in a hotel near Central Park in New York when John Flynn telephoned her in Dublin.

John clutched the receiver, the sound of the unanswered ring mocking his ears. It was four o'clock in the afternoon and from early morning he had been trying to pluck up the courage to make the call. He could not understand what was wrong with him and why he kept putting it off. He loved Rose, he was absolutely certain of that. So why was he procrastinating and behaving like a teenager?

There was another thing which was very confusing: for nearly seventeen years he had been able to recall at will every detail of her lovely face and body; now, when he tried to summon it up, all he could see of her face was a blank white disc.

He replaced the receiver. She was probably out at work, he thought. He would try again later on.

He had insisted on going back to work on the day after the funerals. Both Dorothy and George had protested strenuously that it was too soon, that he should take a break, but he had not listened to them. The only concession he asked was that they, and not he, should drive the Lindstroms and Karen back to the airport.

As it happened, the hotel was going through a lull and the only guests were four Welsh fishermen who left in the very early morning and were out all day.

John threw himself into maintenance work, organising the redecoration of four of the original bedrooms and personally pulling up the carpets in the corridors which badly needed replacing.

He also attacked the Sundarbans project with such vigour that George, who was pressed into accompanying him on some of his calls to the principals involved, felt it necessary to make a comment. 'Look, old thing, this is all a bit much. Are you sure you're feeling up to it?'

'Of course I am! I wish people would stop babying me!' John realised he had gone too far. 'I'm sorry, George,' he said, 'but I have the feeling that if I don't do this – if I don't work all the hours God sends – then I'll go off my head altogether.'

'You must take care of yourself.' George, who was driving at the time, kept his eyes firmly on the road ahead. 'No good to anyone, you know, if you go under. Don't know what we'd all do.'

By the end of a fortnight, the need to call Rose had come to the surface and would not be denied. And once John had actually summoned up the nerve to do it, he could not stop. Starting at four o'clock on that first day, he telephoned every half-hour until finally, at about nine o'clock, the line was answered.

But it was not Rose. When he heard Effie's breathless 'Hello?' he almost hung up but made himself speak. 'This is John Flynn,' he said, forcing some brightness into his voice.

'Hello, John,' said Effie. 'Sorry, I'm out of breath – I heard the phone ringing all the way down at the front door and I ran up. You just caught me actually. Willie and I got the keys of our house yesterday and I'm just organising a few things. We'll be gone altogether from here in a few days. I suppose you're looking for Rose?'

'Yes, please, if she's there.'

'Sorry, she's in New York, but she's due back tomorrow. She should be home before lunchtime. Want me to leave a message?'

'Yes, please.'

There was a strained pause. John and Effie did not really know one another. 'How are you feeling, are you managing all right?' It was Effie who came to their rescue.

'I think so. Work helps.'

'I think Rose finds that too. It's early days, John, don't be too hard on yourself.'

'I'll try, Effie, thank you.'

'Right. I'll leave the message for Rose – I'll write it down immediately so I won't forget. Do you want her to call you?'

He gave her the numbers of Willow House and the fishing lodge then changed his mind. He could not bear the strain of waiting beside the telephone. 'No, tell her I'll ring her,' he said. 'I'll ring her between two and four tomorrow.'

'Oh, she'll definitely be here during that time,' said Effie. 'I know that because she's coming out to visit us and she told me to ring her around three to make arrangements for Willie to collect her on the way home from work.'

Rose's heart turned over on the following day when she saw the message on the telephone table. Although Effie had written under the numbers that he would telephone her, Rose's first instinct was to lift the receiver and dial Willow House. She actually picked up the instrument but put it down again.

One half of her was screaming out to talk to him, to see him, to be with him; the other half was shying away from any entanglements and it was this half which was uppermost most of the time.

Even Effie's constant concern was beginning to get on her nerves – although she was sensible enough to know she might have collapsed without it.

Sometimes she wanted to run away altogether, to be anonymous in some big city, bigger than Dublin; or failing that, to some island in the middle of a huge ocean. The Galapagos, the Maldives, anywhere she would not have to see sympathy and embarrassment in other people's eyes.

She put Effie's message into her handbag. She was tired after the overnight flight and decided she would have her sleep first and then, depending on how she felt when she woke up, she would call him.

She was half-way up the stairs to her attic bedroom when she hesitated. She turned and went back down to the phone and took the receiver off the hook.

As far as the space allowed, John paced up and down the tiny cubbyhole behind the reception desk which served as his office. He had dialled Rose's number every five minutes or so since two o'clock but it was permanently engaged. Who could she be on to for that length of time? Effie had said she was calling at three.

John looked at his watch, five to three now. He tried the number again and when the high-pitched tone indicated the situation had not changed, decided to ring the operator.

The operator was helpful but confirmed that the line was busy.

'Could you see if it's engaged speaking?' John felt as though he was pressing a needle into an open wound. But he had to know.

The operator clicked off the line and came back. 'No, sir, no one speaking. Could be off the hook. Would you like me to report it out of order?'

'No, thank you, that's all right, operator.'

His hands shaking, he replaced the receiver in its cradle. He trusted Effie to have passed on the message. Rose had to have known he was going to call at this time. She did not want to speak to him.

At least now he knew.

Almost six weeks later, with the 'latest dates for posting' warnings ringing in her ears, Rose sent a Christmas card to John. She chose a plain one, eschewing robins and Christmas trees and anything with 'joy' in the wording and took great care with what she wrote:

I know it will be difficult for both of us but please try to have a peaceful Christmas. Perhaps we'll meet in better circumstances in the New Year? Thinking of you, Love, Rose.

P.S. I'll be with Willie and Effie Brehony for Christmas.

Although Gus, backed up by the Cranshaws, had tried and tried to get her to agree, she had not been able to face going to Sundarbans for the holiday. Apart from any other consideration, she did not think she could cope with the additional trauma of what was happening to the fabric of the house, since, during a telephone conversation, her father had let it slip that the deal with the consortium was done and the scaffolding was already going up. Her inclination was to lock herself away alone in the

Drumcondra flat and it was only reluctantly she had accepted Effie's and Willie's invitation.

When she had sealed the envelope, she reconsidered what she had written on the card to John: the hint – particularly including Willie's last name in case John had forgotten – might be going too far. But before she could change her mind, she dropped the card into the pillar box and left it to fate. Whatever would be would be.

From that day, she watched her own post, searching for an answering card, a note, anything. She knew she had only herself to blame for John's lack of communication with her but continued to hope. In the period since the funerals, she had allowed a gradual resurgence of feeling for John. But it was still too fragile to hold up to scrutiny.

Yet, when the last post on Christmas Eve had been delivered and there was still nothing from him, she was surprised at the extent of her disappointment. Then she rationalised, telling herself that she had posted her card to him too late for him to reciprocate.

Christmas Day, sad despite the best efforts of Willie and Effie, passed at last and she went home in the early evening. She wanted to be alone but, deep in her heart, recognised that part of her also hoped that John had been unable to find Willie Brehony's telephone number – it being so new – and that he was going to call her at home.

She listened to Christmas carols on the radio and then flicked through the televison channels but there was nothing which did not remind her of her own loneliness. She left the door from the living room to the hall ajar so that she could keep an eye on the telephone. The more she watched it the more silent it became.

Finally, she could stand it no longer. She had retained Effie's piece of paper with John's numbers on it and retrieved it from her handbag. She tried the fishing lodge first. The telephone there was answered on the third ring, by a man, obviously Mona's father, whose name she could not remember.

'Sorry to bother you,' she said in response to his 'hello', 'but I wonder if I could speak to John Flynn, please? And a happy Christmas to you – this is Rose O'Beirne.'

'Happy Christmas, happy Christmas,' shouted the old man,

who like many old people to whom the telephone was still a wonder, did not trust the wires to carry a normal tone of voice. 'No,' he yelled. 'John's not here. Hold on and I'll put you on to me daughter.'

The telephone was put down with a crash and after a minute or so, Mona came on. 'Hello, Rose, I hope you're having a happy Christmas? Well, as happy as can be expected.'

'Thank you, Mona. It's a bit sad, all right, but we're doing our best. Your father tells me John's not there?'

'No, Rose,' said Mona in her quiet voice. 'Mr and Mrs Cranshaw took him away with them to Florida for a bit of a holiday. They'll be gone for a fortnight and will be back on New Year's Eve. He was overworking, you know. We were a bit worried about him and we all agreed that a holiday was what he needed. How are you yourself, Rose?'

'So-so,' said Rose truthfully. 'I'm up and down but I'm managing.' As she spoke, disappointment fought in her breast with elation. *At least he was away. He could hardly have telephoned her all the way from Florida . . . He had probably not even seen her card.* 'You say he'll be back on New Year's Eve?'

'That's right.'

'Would you tell him I rang?'

'I will, surely. Take care of yourself, Rose.'

'I will.'

'And, please God, nineteen seventy-one will be a better year for all of us.'

'Please God.' Rose voice wobbled. She had managed well all day, she must not get emotional now. 'Goodbye, Mona,' she said and hung up before the tears could take hold.

But the tears did come, as they frequently did, when she got into bed half an hour later. For the first time since Darina's death, however, they were not black tears of bitterness. These tears were sharp with purest grief and afterwards, calm and cleaned out, she fell into a peaceful sleep.

John, sifting through a pile of mail without opening any of it, saw that one envelope clearly contained a Christmas card. Dully, he wondered briefly who would have sent him a Christmas card when he was in mourning.

He put it aside on top of the unopened bills and other brown envelopes and scanned Mona's handwritten list of telephone messages, most of which were to do with the Sundarbans project, now moving ahead at all speed. Mona was sitting by the range, her fingers dancing on a pair of knitting needles. 'There's one message I didn't put on there,' she said, 'Rose O'Beirne Moffat rang on Christmas Day and I didn't have a piece of paper handy but I knew I'd remember.'

John's blood stilled. 'Thanks.' He pretended to be absorbed in the list of messages.

After a suitable interval, he went out into the hallway and dialled Rose's number, printed indelibly on the front of his brain. Again it rang unanswered but this time, however, he was not upset. He knew with certainty that now it was just a matter of time before they made contact. Perhaps she was away again on an overnight flight. He glanced at the grandmother clock, half past nine – he had not realised it was so late. The day had flown. He had gone straight to Willow House with the Cranshaws after coming in on the flight and had become immediately caught up in hotel business, getting it ready for its reopening after its two-week closure.

He went back into the kitchen and started to sort the mail, separating bills from circulars, placing the letters which concerned the project into their own little heap. One bill stopped him cold. From the local marble works, it requested payment for the adding of Derek's name to his mother's tombstone:

For engraving of inscription in gold lettering on headstone at Drumboola churchyard as follows:

'AND HER SON, DEREK MATTHEW FLYNN, BORN 25/8/1938, DIED 3/11/1970.'

The favour of eleven pounds is requested with thanks.

The finality of it, seeing it written there in black and white, had a peculiar effect on him.

Florida, he supposed, had been good for him, although he had hated the humidity and longed for the freshness of the Irish air, even the coldness of the rain. But the heat had sapped him to the extent that he had been able to move along as though in a sort of sludge, not letting the events of early November linger too unbearably close to the surface of his consciousness.

Now, on his first day back, here was the pain, sharp as a dagger.

He put the bill aside and opened the Christmas card.

Rose was just coming into Collon. The decision to go to see him had been a last-minute one.

All day, on the first of her three days off, she had been pounding the floors of the flat, looking at the telephone, checking the clocks; he was home by now, he must be home by now – he was probably at the hotel – would she – wouldn't she – how would he react – what would he think?

New Year's Day, a bank holiday, stretched out before her like a desert. Even Effie and Willie were away, visiting Willie's relations in Cork.

At about seven o'clock she looked in the mirror. 'Ah, shit!' she said to her reflection.

She telephoned a friend at one of the car-hire desks at Dublin airport and he agreed to deliver a car to her after his duty finished, which was at eight. She then telephoned Sundarbans and announced to her astounded mother that she was coming down on a visit and would be there by eleven or eleven-thirty.

Her fingers were hovering over the dial for the third time when she changed her mind. She would not telephone him. She would just arrive and surprise him. She'd drive to the fishing lodge before she went to the Big House.

And if he was asleep?

The hell with it, she thought. She'd wake him up. And no one should be asleep on New Year's Eve. She was thirty-three years old. An adult. She could wake up another thirty-three-year-old if she liked.

Anyway, she rationalised, he had had no compunction in rousting her out of her bed seventeen years ago.

She threw a few things into an overnight bag and waited in a frenzy of impatience for her friend to arrive with the car.

John was in bed by ten-thirty. He was exhausted and jet-lagged, too exhausted, he thought, because the moment he lay down, sleep shot away from him. Something pulled at the fringes of his mind and he could not figure out what it was. He strained his tired brain to remember it and was eventually rewarded. . . . *And Her Son, Derek Matthew Flynn, Born 25/8/1938, Died 3/11/1970* . . .

The knot of rage which had lately become all too familiar, began to form again in the pit of his stomach. What right did Derek Matthew Flynn have to such a civilised, *ordinary* inscription on his mother's tombstone? The more John told himself he was being irrational, the more the inscription mocked him.

Since the funeral, he had kept Derek at bay; to dwell too much on the betrayals, the years of jealousy and suspicion, the lack of brotherly concern and love, was too painful.

But now the thoughts would not go away. His brain ticked them off: the monstrousness of the anonymous letter which deprived him of Rose and possibly knowledge of his daughter. If Derek had not written that letter he might have had a normal family life, more children . . .

Then, just as bad, *no, worse* – the deceit Derek lived out with Karen.

For more than sixteen years, John Flynn had had both a son and a daughter and had been deprived of them by his twin. And not only that, deprived of the woman he loved.

Derek's actions had even denied him the dignity of his proper place at the funerals of his children.

Round and round they went as he fulminated, hatefulness following rage following hatefulness in an endless circle of torment.

He tried desperately to be fair: Derek hadn't known Rose was pregnant – *or so he had said*.

Karen had insisted that keeping Bruno's parentage a secret had been her idea. *But had it?*

The more he thought about it, the angrier and more agitated John became. He tossed and turned in the bed, churning up the bedclothes until they were as twisted as anchor-cables.

And then the last straw: *If it were not for Derek's treachery – could those two children have lived? If they had been brought up as they should have been, wasn't it highly unlikely they would have fallen in love?*

He knew that was one question he could not answer, but he jumped out of the bed and, only half aware of what he was doing, dragged on his clothes and shoes, put on his sheepskin and ran down the stairs.

Mona and her father were in the sitting room, listening to the radio. She came to the door when she heard him coming down. 'Are we disturbing you, John? I'll turn it down it it's too loud.'

'The radio's fine. Something's come up, I've to go out for a few minutes. I won't be long.' He muttered it, keeping his face averted while pretending to search the hallstand for gloves. 'I'm going up to the graveyard for a few minutes,' he called.

'Oh.' She nodded as though she understood.

John tried to control his temper as he drove hell for leather along the narrow roads. He had no clear idea in his mind what he was going to do.

He was going to do something, though, that was for sure. Derek wasn't going to get away with it scot-free.

Rose had driven the hired car as hard and as fast as she dared. Now she was in the last few miles and she pushed the tinny little vehicle to its limits. Luckily, it was a dry clear night and there was very little traffic on the road, although as she zoomed through the towns and villages, she saw that the car parks around the pubs were packed.

At last she was bumping up the laneway which led to the fishing lodge. All the downstairs lights were still on and she saw by the dashboard clock that it was only eleven-fifteen. Not too uncivilised an hour to knock on someone's door on New Year's Eve.

Mona answered the door. Her hand flew to her throat in surprise. 'Rose!'

Rose's impatience was like a set of spurs at her back and she could not be bothered with the preliminaries. 'Is John here – could I see him?'

'You've missed him by about fifteen minutes,' said Mona. Then, when Rose's face fell, she added, 'I – I don't know whether it's my place to tell you or not, but he said he was going up to the graveyard for a few minutes. New Year's Eve,' she added by way of explanation. She stood back from the door. 'I'm sure he won't be long – would you like to come in and wait for him?'

'No, that's all right. I'll go up. I just have one or two things I want to discuss with him. About Sundarbans,' she added hurriedly, realising that in Mona's eyes, she was probably acting like a maniac. 'I'll probably meet him on the road.'

'All right, so,' said Mona.

She jumped back into the car and gave Mona a hurried wave as she screeched through a three-point turn. The graveyard? What was he doing up there? Yet she thought she understood.

Ten minutes later, she pulled up at the cemetery gates. His car was there all right, but the driver's door was swinging open and the interior light was burning. The boot lid, she saw, was also gaping. For a few moments, Rose hesitated. The thought of Darina, so still and cold in there, so alone, sounded a note of grief as clear and pure as a tuning fork.

Then she got out of the car and scanned the immediate surroundings. Pulling the collar of her coat around her throat and mouth, Rose closed John's car door so the interior light went off and passed through the semi-circular gate, pausing just inside it to get her bearings.

The graveyard, overgrown with blackberry and hawthorn, straggled across the brow of a little hill where a leafless thorn tree etched itself like a deformed hand against the brilliant sky. The Catholic dead of the district had been buried here for centuries; many of the ancient stone slabs and Celtic crosses leaned at crazy angles or had been overrun by a tangled carpet of ivy, nettles and tough, woody undergrowth. Avoiding the section where Darina lay, Rose swept her gaze around. Although a three-quarters moon shone bright and very white, she could detect no movement. All around was that sharp, sweet smell peculiar to cemeteries, a combination of turned earth, rotting vegetation – and something else she did not care to think about. Stiffening her spine, she picked her way upwards, her footsteps making no sound on the grassy pathway.

The section just ahead was neater, cleaner than the one she had just left; its graves were still tended, the marble tombstones gleaming in the moonlight. But just where the old part of the graveyard ended and the new part began, Rose stumbled over a lichen-covered Jesus figure which had fallen backwards off its plinth and now lay on a cushion of brambles, stony, sightless eyes fixed for ever on resurrection. By some trick of the moonlight Rose felt the eyes of the Jesus were alive and staring at her.

Abruptly, everything in the cemetery seemed larger, more sinister. A statue of an angel, wings outspread, seemed to lunge towards her from the head of a grave just to the side of the pathway; at her feet, artificial flowers, bleached of colour by the moon, pushed malevolent tentacles against their plastic domes as though to engulf her and draw her down; the black earth and gravel on the graves seemed too insubstantial to keep the rotting occupants safely beneath.

She couldn't face it. Retracing her steps, Rose decided she would wait outside the gates beside his car. If indeed he was in here, he had to come out sooner or later. Then she heard a sound, a single chink, as though someone had struck a china cup with a spoon.

She forced herself to stay still and listen. There it was again, unmistakable.

And again.

And again and again – a rhythmic, one-note clinking, coming from the other side of the hill.

Cautiously, a pulse in her throat beating like a trip-hammer, she walked up the hill until she was right at the summit beside the thorn tree and could see over the whole cemetery. She saw John immediately, squatting on a grave, his bright hair outlined against the grave's dark headstone. She tried to call out to him but her throat was too dry and no sound came. Hoping he would hear her and look up, she took a few steps towards him.

'John?' she called. 'John?'

He was so absorbed he did not hear her. When she got closer, she saw he was using car tools – a wheelbrace and tyre iron – as hammer and chisel, holding the iron against the tombstone and tapping it with the wheelbrace in small, chipping strokes. Then she realised what he was doing.

John was attempting to remove lettering off the tombstone. Rose stood stock still. There was something really dreadful going on here, she could taste it. 'John!' she called, louder.

He jumped to his feet and whirled round. And as he stared at her without recognition, she saw his face was harsh with lines she had never seen before. 'It's me,' she said, afraid. 'It's me, Rose.'

He seemed slowly to come back from some kind of dream. His face relaxed and his fixed expression was replaced by one of astonishment and then, to her relief, joy.

'Rose!' he said. Then his joy was replaced with wariness. 'What are you doing here?'

'I came to see you. Mona told me you were here.' She gestured at the tyre iron and wheelbrace. 'What are you doing with those?'

He looked down at the tools in his hands as though they did not belong to him. Then, as if he were finished with them and was tidying them away, he aligned them and took both of them in one hand. He looked at her levelly. 'If I told you, you wouldn't believe me.'

She peered at the tombstone. In the brightness, the new gold lettering was clear and easily read. Two dark patches of chipped marble preceded three of the letters, *r . . . e . . . k*.

Aghast, Rose realised what he was doing. 'You're removing Derek's name from the tombstone!' She took a step backwards. 'That's bizarre, John.'

He did not immediately react. Then he too took a step backwards and leaned almost casually against the tombstone, which was in the shape of a Celtic cross. 'Yes, well, I told you you wouldn't believe me.' He shrugged.

'Why?' she pressed. 'Could you try to explain?'

Again he gave her a long, expressionless stare which made her feel very uncomfortable. 'A lot of it has to do with you, Rose,' he said at last.

'Me?' It was the last answer she would have expected.

Poised on the balls of his feet, she felt he was watching her as though she, and not he, were behaving in this peculiar way. 'That anonymous letter,' he said softly. 'We might have been married, have had kids.'

'I see.' But Rose only partially understood. She felt helpless and totally out of her element. What depths of passion could goad a man into chiselling his twin's name off a headstone?

'I'm sorry you saw this.' He still wore that unreadable, careful expression.

'I'm not!' She raised her chin. 'If we're to be together, John Flynn, there are to be no secrets between us.' She trailed off. The boldness seemed ridiculous in such surroundings and in such circumstances.

There was not a single sound in the cemetery. She could even hear his breathing. Then, far away, a car started, revved up and died again. Rose started to shiver although she was not cold.

'And what if there are some secrets that can't ever be told?' he asked softly.

Her shivering stilled. Suddenly she was very afraid. 'Are there?'

He continued gazing at her with that odd, intent expression. He took a step towards her as though to explain something. Then he seemed to relax a little. Dropping the tools into the middle of the mound of rotting flowers, he walked purposefully towards her.

'No,' he said. 'You know everything there is to know.'